Independent order of Odd Fellows, Ontario Grand Lodge

# Proceedings of the Grand Lodge

of the Province of Ontario, Canada

Independent order of Odd Fellows, Ontario Grand Lodge

**Proceedings of the Grand Lodge**
*of the Province of Ontario, Canada*

ISBN/EAN: 9783337223533

Printed in Europe, USA, Canada, Australia, Japan

Cover: Foto ©Andreas Hilbeck / pixelio.de

More available books at **www.hansebooks.com**

Fraternally Yours
J. W. Jolliffe.

# Independent Order of Odd Fellows.

## PROCEEDINGS

OF

# THE GRAND LODGE

OF THE

## *PROVINCE OF ONTARIO,*

## CANADA.

## Thirty-Ninth Annual Session

HELD AT NIAGARA FALLS,

COMMENCING AUGUST 9TH, 1893.

TORONTO:
DOMINION ODD FELLOW PRINT, 5 JORDAN STREET.
1893.

# ADDRESSES OF THE OFFICERS

OF THE

# GRAND LODGE OF ONTARIO, I.O.O.F.

*Year Ending August, 1894.*

Joseph Oliver, Grand Master, - - - Toronto.

W. H. Hoyle, Deputy Grand Master, - - Cannington.

Thos. Woodyatt, Grand Warden, - - Brantford.

J. B. King, Grand Secretary, - - - - Toronto.
42 King St. East.

Wm. Badenach, Grand Treasurer, - - Toronto.
17 Leader Lane.

Hy. Robertson, Grand Representative, - Collingwood.

P. E. Fitz-Patrick, Grand Representative, - Hamilton.

J. McLurg, Grand Marshal, - - - Woodstock.

L. C. Pascoe, Grand Conductor, - - - Belleville.

M. L. Weber, Grand Guardian, - - Elmira.

Andrew Patterson, Grand Herald, - - Waubaushene.

Rev. F. W. Armstrong, Grand Chaplain, - Trenton.

Rev. T. W. Jolliffe, Junior Past Grand Master, Campbellford.

# INDEPENDENT ORDER OF ODD FELLOWS.

### FRIENDSHIP, LOVE AND TRUTH.

---

## THIRTY-NINTH

# ANNUAL COMMUNICATION

#### OF THE

# Grand Lodge of Ontario,

#### HELD AT

## NIAGARA FALLS, ONTARIO.

---

NIAGARA FALLS, August 9th, 1893.

The Grand Lodge convened at the Town Hall, Niagara Falls, at 9.30 a.m.

Prior to the Grand Master calling the Grand Lodge to order, addresses of welcome were read by his Worship Mayor S. K. Binkley, on behalf of the town, and by Bro. S. D. Warren, on behalf of the Order in Niagara Falls, which were replied to by the Grand Master. The addresses and replies were as follows :—

*To the Grand Master, Grand Officers, Members and Representatives to the Grand Lodge of the I.O.O.F. :*

As Noble Grand and Chairman of the Reception Committee of Niagara Falls Lodge, No. 53, it is my pleasing duty to welcome you to our town, and to extend to you the right hand of Fellowship.

Niagara Falls Lodge, No. 53, was instituted on the 29th day of April, 1869, with 7 charter members. Since then the Lodge has kept apace with the times, and during the interval Cataract Lodge, No. 103, branched from us, located at Drummondville now Niagara Falls South. Our present membership is 125. In May last, Esther Lodge, D. of R., was instituted and I am pleased to report are in a prosperous condition, starting out with a membership of 33. We are looking for an increase in membership at the present session of Grand Lodge.

We appreciate the high honor you have conferred upon us by selecting Niagara Falls as the field for your deliberations. Our only regret is that we have been unable to do more to make your visit a pleasant one, but we hope you will overlook our shortcomings in that regard, and will nevertheless have an enjoyable session.

S. D. WARREN,<br>
Noble Grand and Chairman Reception Committee.

The Grand Master replied as follows :—

*To S. D. Warren, Esq., N.G. of Niagara Falls Lodge, No. 53, Chairman of Reception Committee :*

DEAR SIR AND BROTHER,—On behalf of the Grand Lodge of the Jurisdiction of Ontario, I desire to reciprocate the kind and cordial sentiments expressed in the address you have just presented. I am pleased that we are met in a place where Odd Fellowship realizes its mission and is earnest in its work. You have passed beyond the day of small things, the night of your anxiety has gone and the morning has come radiant in its light and full in its promise of success. Your energy and enthusiasm is seen in the extension of the principles of our Order and in grasping the opportunity which presented itself of establishing another lodge in the suburbs, which I trust may with your own go on and prosper. The men who attempt great things and expect them are the men who succeed.

Cherish the missionary spirit in the work of your lodge, and rest not until all the available material out of which good Odd Fellows are made has been exhausted.

I am pleased also to notice that the Rebekah branch of the Order has here a habitation and a name. The world has been all too long in appreciating the work and worth of woman, though she has always been identified with every movement aiming at the uplifting of the race. We welcome the Sisters to a share in the good work we are trying to do, and I trust that the visit of our Grand Lodge to this place may be productive of much good to all.

His Worship S. K. Binkley, Mayor, on behalf of the town, addressed the assembled brethren as follows :—

*To the Grand Master, Officers and Members Grand Lodge of Ontario, I.O.OF.:*

It is with pleasure I extend to you on behalf of our Municipal Corporation a cordial and most hearty welcome to our town Especially is it gratifying to us that to-day for the first time in our history are we favoured with a meeting of the Grand Body representing a Society of such vast magnitude as you possess—extending to almost every land—a Brotherhood banded together for the elevation of man.

Not only as Chief Magistrate, but as a citizen, and in behalf of our people, I welcome you. Last year—1892—I, with Bro. P.G. William McFaul, was honoured from our Lodge Niagara Falls, No. 53, as Representatives to your session held in the city of Windsor, at which a most pleasant and profitable time was spent. On our way there the thought was suggested to invite the Grand Lodge to meet at Niagara Falls next year. With this inspiration, the invitation was extended and heartily accepted by you, and to-day we realize its consummation (convened in this the 39th session of your noble Order) and further do we congratulate ourselves in having you with us to commemorate this, the most prosperous year of our history as a town. The inauguration of a High School, a building being erected on one of the most beautiful spots in Canada ; the Auditorium of Wesley Park, the building and grounds costing $25,000, which, when completed will be a credit to our town and the country at large ; the opening of the Niagara Park and River Electric Railway, giving one of the most pleasant trips, commanding the grandest scenery to be found in the world. I might go on defining the many points of interest, the Maid of Mist steamers below the mighty cataract on which the most wild and vivid view of the mighty torrent may be seen—the trip must be taken to be realized—and other points with which you will become acquainted.

As a brother Odd Fellow, I greet you in Friendship, Love and Truth—" the tenets of our beloved Order." In them let us show not only in the Lodge room but in our intercourse with the world at large, that we are grateful to our Creator, true to our family and country, and fraternal to ou fellow-man ; ever keeping before us that first great teaching that we can be Odd Fellows only while we are like honest men.

I wish to further add, that my desire is, and in this I only voice the wish of our people, that your visit to us may be pleasant and profitable, that you may carry away with you fond recollections that it was good that we met at Niagara Falls. May our Heavenly Father spare you in your Grand Chapter work.

Allow me to extend to you the Freedom of the Town.

S. K. BINKLEY,<br>
Mayor.

The Grand Master acknowledged the address as follows :—

*S. K. Binkley, Esq., Mayor, Niagara Falls :*

MR. MAYOR,—I am persuaded that I voice the sentiments of every member of this Grand Lodge when I say that we appreciate the warmth of your welcome as uttered in your fraternal address to-day.

It is an open secret, sir, that there were those of our number who during the past year seriously doubted, not the willingness, but the ability of the place to provide suitable accommodation for the members of this Grand body. But the mistake was ours ; we were not posted as to the size and capability of the town. Every Brother has found a home, and still you have room for more. The elaborate decorations on your streets, and the enthusiasm of the people, assure us that we made no mistake in deciding to hold the present session in your midst.

Your public buildings, educational and ecclesiastical, are a credit to you, while the railway facilities you enjoy must add largely to the importance of the place. We do not forget that we are on historic ground to-day, and our hearts thrill with gratitude when we remember that this Canada of ours shines as one of the brightest jewels in the crown of our beloved Queen. Odd Fellows have ever been loyal to the land in which they live ; and every man who believes that our Order has a mission in helping to fraternize the race must be pleased to see the Union Jack and the Stars and Stripes waving side by side. The two great Christian nations they represent are to-day honoured and respected by the whole civilized world.

You will be glad to learn that the past year has been one of the most prosperous in our history. The line of twenty thousand has been left behind, and our hopes are bright and our courage strong for the future.

Permit me again, sir, to thank you on behalf of my brethren, for the kindly words you have spoken. On every side we can see the evidence of your efforts made to secure our comfort while we are with you. You are a highly favoured people in this beautiful border town. Your industries are booming, your business men alert, and your ladies hospitable and handsome. It is no small advantage to live so near one of the greatest wonders of the world. Surely the lines have fallen to you in pleasant places and you have a goodly heritage. To see the wonders of Niagara the people come from every part of our own Dominion, from the Republic to the south of us, and from far beyond the sea. By your kindness we shall be permitted to-day to look again upon this, perhaps the mightiest wonder in creation. In the long ages of the past, through the silence of the forest, has the mighty current rolled, and rushed, and roared, and the billows of the boiling rapids are to-day dancing to the music of the Falls as in the years that are gone. Amid such grand surroundings I feel assured that our stay will be pleasant, and I expect and predict that our conduct while among you will be such, that in the coming days the people of this good town may remember with pleasure the visit of the Grand Lodge of 1893.

The Grand Master then called the Grand Lodge to order, and directed the Grand Marshal and Grand Conductor to ascertain if all present were qualified to remain. Their report being favourable and a quorum of Representatives being present, the Grand Master requested the Grand Chaplain to invoke the Divine blessing.

The Rev. Bro. W. J. Sanders, Grand Chaplain, offered prayer :—

### OPENING PRAYER.

Almighty and everlasting God, our Heavenly Father, we thank Thee that we are again permitted, in the multitude of Thy mercies, to meet in the Annual Session of our Grand Lodge. Vouchsafe Thy blessing to the Grand Master, Grand Officers and the members of this Grand Lodge ; and in all our business, even in the heat of debate, help us to remember that Thine all-seeing Eye is ever upon us, and may all things be done to the glory of Thy Name and the glory of our beloved Order. Remember, we pray Thee, in Thy loving kindness, the dear ones in the homes we have left for a time ; may they be safe under Thy Almighty protection, and in due time may we return to them in peace. Regard with Thy favour the widow, the fatherless and the orphan, and while we try to aid them by tender sympathy and active help, do Thou comfort and relieve them according to their several necessities. We now commit ourselves to Thy loving care ; guide and direct us through life's journey, and save us all with an everlasting salvation. And to Thy name be all the praise, as it was in the beginning, is now and ever shall be, world without end. AMEN.

Whereupon the Deputy Grand Master, by direction of the chair, declared the Grand Lodge duly opened for the transaction of business.

The Grand Secretary appointed Representative J. A. Young, of Thamesford Lodge, No. 258, as his assistant for the session.

The Grand Master appointed Representative Bro. A. S. Scott, of Enterprise Lodge, No. 218, as Official Reporter for the session, and Bro. ————, of Niagara Falls, No. 53, as Messenger.

These appointments were approved by the Grand Lodge.

The Grand Master named the following Committees :—

ON CREDENTIALS—

Bro. J. B. King, Grand Sec. ; Reps. J. M. Henry, of Leamington Lodge, No. 140 ; W. A. Miller, of Orion Lodge, No. 109.

ON ELECTION RETURNS—

Reps. Jno. Donogh, P.G.M., Queen City Lodge, No. 56 ; J. B. McIntyre, P.G.M., of Union Lodge, No. 16 ; and R. W. Bell, P.G.M., Otonabee Lodge, No. 13.

Bro. J. B. King, from the Committee on Credentials, made the following report, which was adopted :—

*To the Grand Lodge of Ontario, I.O.O.F. :*

BRETHREN,—Your Committee on Credentials beg to submit the following report :—

We find, on examining the returns of the several Lodges and Credentials submitted, that the following have been duly elected Representatives to the present Session. Your Committee have yet to complain that many Secretaries have failed to comply with the requirements of the Grand Lodge to send a copy of the Credentials of their Representatives-elect two weeks prior to the Session. In a number of cases the Representative herein reported is not the same as entered on the return of the Lodge, but in such cases the resignation of the Representative and certificate of the election of his successor have been received in legal form.

From latest returns and certificates received, the following are the duly accredited Representatives, and entitled as such to a seat in the Grand Lodge :—

| No. | NAME. | LODGE. | No. | LOCATION. |
|---|---|---|---|---|
| 1 | W. J Simpson | Brock | 9 | Brockville. |
| 2 | A. Y. Kendall | | | |
| 3 | F. R. Sargent | Cataraqui | 10 | Kingston. |
| 4 | W. J. Moore | | | |
| 5 | J. S. R McCann | | | |
| 6 | R. W. Bell, P.G.M. | Otonabee | 13 | Peterboro'. |
| 7 | M. Mowry | | | |
| 8 | J. B. McIntyre, P.G.M. | Union | 16 | St. Catharines. |
| 9 | N. A. Lindsay | | | |
| 10 | C. J. Moore | | | |

| No. | Name. | Lodge. | No. | Location. |
| --- | --- | --- | --- | --- |
| 11 | R. McPherson | Phœnix | 22 | Oshawa. |
| 12 | Hy. Y. Pickering | Rose | 28 | Amherstburg. |
| 13 | Jno. B. Kitchen | Chatham | 29 | Chatham. |
| 14 | W. L. G. Snell | | | |
| 15 | Geo. Powell, Jr | Eureka | 30 | London. |
| 16 | Jno. Hunter | | | |
| 17 | Wm. Cross | | | |
| 18 | J. F. Brown | Elgin | 32 | St. Thomas. |
| 19 | W. E. Cox | | | |
| 20 | J. H Hoshal | Erie | 33 | Port Burwell. |
| 21 | Jas. Woodyatt, P.G.M | | | |
| 22 | Thos. Woodyatt | Gore | 34 | Brantford. |
| 23 | M. A. Craig | | | |
| 24 | A. J. Johnston | Samaritan | 35 | Ingersoll. |
| 25 | A. W. Bell | | | |
| 26 | Archie Baird | St. Mary's | 36 | St. Mary's. |
| 27 | Wm. Box | | | |
| 28 | Wm. Maddiford | Forest City | 38 | London. |
| 29 | R. J. C. Dawson | | | |
| 30 | W. H. Stephenson | Rond Eau | 40 | Blenheim. |
| 31 | R. L Gosnell | | | |
| 32 | Hy. Baker | | | |
| 33 | Sam'l Towner | Avon | 41 | Stratford. |
| 34 | Sam'l H. Weir | | | |
| 35 | E. Scultz | Excelsior | 44 | Hamilton. |
| 36 | A. Brunke | | | |
| 37 | F. C. Cassady | | | |
| 38 | W. Bushell | Frontier | 45 | Windsor. |
| 39 | J. R. Thomson | | | |
| 40 | C. Tucker | Mount Zion | 46 | Newbury. |
| 41 | T. B. S. Austin | | | |
| 42 | A. B. Holmes | Unity | 47 | Hamilton. |
| 43 | D. Moore | | | |
| 44 | C. J. Wall | Dominion | 48 | London. |
| 45 | W. F. Howell | | | |
| 46 | F. Smith | | | |
| 47 | W. Menzies | Canada | 49 | Toronto. |
| 48 | A. Coyell | | | |
| 49 | Geo. Geddes | Otter | 50 | Tilsonburg. |
| 50 | W. Sims | | | |
| 51 | Isaac Hord | Bissell | 51 | Mitchell. |
| 52 | J. T. Hornibrook, P.G.M. | Covenant | 52 | Toronto. |
| 53 | H. Gilby | | | |
| 54 | J. R. Peckham | Niagara Falls | 53 | Niagara Falls. |
| 55 | Jno. Blair | | | |
| 56 | A. Chellen | Collingwood | 54 | Collingwood. |
| 57 | A. McFadden | | | |
| 58 | Henry Town | Fidelity | 55 | Seaforth. |
| 59 | Jno. Donogh, P.G.M | Queen City of Ontario | 56 | Toronto. |
| 60 | A. A. Graham | | | |
| 61 | D. B. Brown | Maple Leaf | 57 | Orangeville. |
| 62 | O. L. Berdan | Howard | 58 | Strathroy. |
| 63 | W. E. Todd | | | |
| 64 | John Bullis | | | |
| 65 | G. W. Maxwell | Kingston | 59 | Kingston. |
| 66 | George Lee | | | |

| No. | Name. | Lodge. | No. | Location. |
|---|---|---|---|---|
| 67 | Wm. James | Corinthian | 61 | Oshawa. |
| 68 | A. Jacobi | | | |
| 69 | W. Dickie | | | |
| 70 | Geo. Porter | Huron | 62 | Goderich. |
| 71 | G. H. Nairn | | | |
| 72 | Alex. Brownlee | Barrie | 63 | Barrie. |
| 73 | Geo. Vickers, Sr | | | |
| 74 | G. P. Henderson | Victoria | 64 | Hamilton. |
| 75 | J. J. Mathews | Friendship | 65 | Petrolea. |
| 76 | Alex. Simpson | | | |
| 77 | Julius Roenigk | Florence Nightingale. | 66 | Bowmanville. |
| 78 | Jno. McIntyre | | | |
| 79 | Hy. Lambrook | Exeter | 67 | Exeter. |
| 80 | J. W. Shepperd | North Star | 68 | Stayner. |
| 81 | Wm. Barr | Hope | 69 | Harrietsville. |
| 82 | W. Macdiarmid, P.G.M. | Lucan | 70 | Lucan |
| 83 | E. M. Clapp | The Toronto | 71 | Toronto. |
| 84 | W. Robson | Eastern Star | 72 | Whitby. |
| 85 | J. E. Farewell | | | |
| 86 | J. J. Craig | Fergus | 73 | Fergus. |
| 87 | Geo. L. Taylor | Bothwell | 74 | Bothwell. |
| 88 | Jno. Nott | Warriner | 75 | Port Perry. |
| 89 | Peter Brown | St. Thomas | 76 | St. Thomas. |
| 90 | Jno. Waddell | | | |
| 91 | S. W. Down | | | |
| 92 | J. H. Sinclair | Oxford | 77 | Ingersoll. |
| 93 | E. F. Waterhouse | | | |
| 94 | Hy. White | Durham | 78 | Port Hope. |
| 95 | J. H. Magill | | | |
| 96 | J. H. Bustin | Nipissing | 79 | Uxbridge. |
| 97 | Wm. Jacobs | Amity | 80 | Prescott. |
| 98 | Jas. Wilkins | | | |
| 99 | W. Row | | | |
| 100 | L. C. Pascoe | Belleville | 81 | Belleville. |
| 101 | Allan McFee | | | |
| 102 | J. A. Coon | | | |
| 103 | C. C. Lypps | Beaver | 82 | Ruthven. |
| 104 | S. S. Cooper | Clinton | 83 | Clinton. |
| 105 | Richard Lee | Walkerton | 84 | Walkerton. |
| 106 | Harry Sneath | Constellation | 85 | Burgessville. |
| 107 | G. B. Joy | Napanee | 86 | Napanee. |
| 108 | W. H. Fletcher | Empire | 87 | St. Catharines. |
| 109 | J. W. Grote | | | |
| 110 | H. M. Bauslaugh | Olive Branch | 88 | Woodstock. |
| 111 | Jno. Mitchell | | | |
| 112 | Jno. J. Cormie | Reliance | 89 | Guelph. |
| 113 | Roderick McLeod | | | |
| 114 | Jno. Hamilton | Ivy | 90 | Parkhill. |
| 115 | Jno. Flanagan | Grand River | 91 | Paris. |
| 116 | R. Brockbank | | | |
| 117 | Wm. McKenzie | Milton | 92 | Milton. |
| 118 | A. M. Lafferty | Western City | 93 | Chatham. |
| 119 | J. D. McDermid | Aylmer | 94 | Aylmer. |
| 120 | Wm. Warnock | | | |
| 121 | Alex. Fraser | Nith | 96 | New Hamburg. |
| 122 | Jacob Baltz | Grand Union | 97 | Berlin. |
| 123 | J. L. Binns | Minto | 98 | Harriston. |

| No. | Name. | Lodge. | No. | Location. |
|---|---|---|---|---|
| 124 | Geo. Lytle | Lindsay | 100 | Lindsay. |
| 125 | J. J. Manning | Golden Star | 101 | Brampton. |
| 126 | H. W. Solmes | Deseronto | 102 | Deseronto. |
| 127 | J. K. Henderson | Cataract | 103 | Niagara Falls, S. |
| 128 | W. R. Webb | | | |
| 129 | W. C. Smith | Crescent | 104 | Hamilton. |
| 130 | Jno. Fotheringham | | | |
| 131 | A. Gillespie | Manilla | 105 | Manilla. |
| 132 | C. Saunders | St. Clair | 106 | Pt. Edward. |
| 133 | C. L. McWilliams | Waterloo | 107 | Galt. |
| 134 | W. A. Dennis | | | |
| 135 | Hy. Barron | Royal Oak | 108 | Forest. |
| 136 | W. A. Miller | Orion | 109 | Georgetown. |
| 137 | Chas. Collett | Laurel | 110 | Toronto. |
| 138 | D. H. Moore | | | |
| 139 | W. Hill | Peterboro' | 111 | Peterborough. |
| 140 | A. McIntosh | | | |
| 141 | D. Sheriff | Lucknow | 112 | Lucknow. |
| 142 | A. Ross | | | |
| 143 | Rev. F. W. Armstrong | Trenton | 113 | Trenton. |
| 144 | Jno. Ormiston | | | |
| 145 | T. O. Middleton | Gananoque | 114 | Gananoque |
| 146 | Geo. Toner | | | |
| 147 | Robt. Peirce | Harmony | 115 | Brantford. |
| 148 | S. M. Thomson | | | |
| 149 | W. Robinson | Naomi | 116 | Markham |
| 150 | F. A. Latshaw | Valley City | 117 | Dundas. |
| 151 | W. Mitson | | | |
| 152 | Robt. Allen | Maitland | 119 | Wingham |
| 153 | A. L. Shambleau | Sydenham Valley | 120 | Wallaceburg. |
| 154 | D. Logan | | | |
| 155 | Jno. D. Shipley | Saxon | 121 | Ailsa Craig. |
| 156 | Wm. McKeith | Streetsville | 122 | Streetsville. |
| 157 | W. H. Pollock | Dresden | 124 | Dresden. |
| 158 | Jas. King, Jr. | | | |
| 159 | W. H. Allen | Stella | 125 | Carleton Place. |
| 160 | N. D. McCallum | | | |
| 161 | E. P. Bateley | Sarnia | 126 | Sarnia. |
| 162 | F. M. Clark | Mizpah | 127 | Belleville. |
| 163 | Jno. Cornelius | | | |
| 164 | N. McPhadden | Charity | 129 | Sunderland. |
| 165 | Peter Steep | Livingstone | 130 | Thorold. |
| 166 | A. W. Easton | Marion | 131 | Renfrew. |
| 167 | Robt. Buzzard | Oakville | 132 | Oakville. |
| 168 | Jas. Harris | Glencoe | 133 | Glencoe. |
| 169 | Casper Ramey | Orient | 134 | Welland. |
| 170 | S. H. Glassford | Peaceful Dove | 135 | Cannington. |
| 171 | Wm. Russell | Cobourg | 136 | Cobourg. |
| 172 | Ch. H. Frost | St. Lawrence | 137 | Brockville. |
| 173 | D. Matheson | | | |
| 174 | A. Bradshaw | Ancaster | 138 | Ancaster. |
| 175 | Jno. Corley | Garnet | 139 | Mount Forest. |
| 176 | Jas. Neil | Leamington | 140 | Leamington. |
| 177 | Jos. M. Henry | | | |
| 178 | M. G. Brethour | Concord | 142 | Kingsville. |
| 179 | O. Bigg | Bay of Quinte | 143 | Picton. |
| 180 | W. R. Powers | | | |
| 181 | Ellerton Porter | Ridgetown | 144 | Ridgetown. |
| 182 | F. Eansor | | | |

| No. | Name. | Lodge. | No. | Location. |
|---|---|---|---|---|
| 183 | Jno. S. Moir | Vivian | 146 | Arnprior. |
| 184 | Wm. Hartley | Model | 147 | Wyoming. |
| 185 | C. Collett | Aurora | 148 | Aurora. |
| 186 | Wm. Martin | Western Star | 149 | Brussels. |
| 187 | Eli Detwiler | Sycamore | 151 | Arkona. |
| 188 | J. M. McAllister | Hayden | 152 | Norwich. |
| 189 | Jno. E. Murray | Wildey | 153 | Granton. |
| 190 | Jos. Symington | Alpha | 154 | Almonte. |
| 191 | A. Fumerton | | | |
| 192 | S. Penncock | Brougham | 155 | Whitevale, |
| 193 | E. McCormick | Pyramid | 156 | Newmarket. |
| 194 | J. Davidson | Thamesville | 157 | Thamesville. |
| 195 | R. A. Snider | Progress | 158 | Guelph. |
| 196 | Geo. Brill | | | |
| 197 | W. K. Wlson | Oak Leaf | 159 | Hamilton. |
| 198 | J. E. Terhune | Listowel | 160 | Listowel. |
| 199 | H. Johnston | Simcoe | 161 | Simcoe. |
| 200 | E. Oliver | Oriental | 163 | Cornwall. |
| 201 | Jos. Casson | Romeo | 164 | Stratford. |
| 202 | Peter McNab | | | |
| 203 | T. Wicket | Beethoven | 165 | Brooklin. |
| 204 | Jos. Carmichael | Hillsburg | 167 | Hillsburg. |
| 205 | T. B. Bentley | Sutton | 168 | Sutton. |
| 206 | Wm Laidlaw | Grey | 169 | Durham. |
| 207 | Geo. A. Henry | Denovo | 170 | Port Elgin. |
| 208 | W. S. Ellis | Alliston | 171 | Alliston. |
| 209 | Alex. Kay | Penetangore | 172 | Kincardine. |
| 210 | W. T. Henry | | | |
| 211 | Jno. Steel | Emerald | 173 | Dunnville. |
| 212 | J. G. Watson | Dolman | 174 | Ayr. |
| 213 | J. H. Powell | Dauncey | 176 | Thedford. |
| 214 | A. E. Paulin | Montana | 177 | Wroxeter. |
| 215 | W. H. Peart | Wellington Square | 178 | Burlington. |
| 216 | Jno. R. Orr | Madoc | 179 | Madoc. |
| 217 | Jas. White | | | |
| 218 | G. A. Ross | Owen Sound | 180 | Owen Sound. |
| 219 | Allen McFarlane | Tecumseh | 182 | Otterville. |
| 220 | L. A. Brink | Teeswater | 183 | Teeswater. |
| 221 | Geo. Suggit | Germania | 184 | Waterloo. |
| 222 | H. Frochlich | | | |
| 223 | David Clayton | Dufferin | 186 | Flesherton. |
| 224 | J. Maecker | Cambridge | 188 | Preston. |
| 225 | Jno. Linton | Parry Sound | 189 | Parry Sound. |
| 226 | Geo. Grant | Chorazin | 190 | London East. |
| 227 | Wm. Reid | | | |
| 228 | J. B. McMicken | Jarvis | 191 | Jarvis. |
| 229 | Rich Ross | Howick | 192 | Gorrie. |
| 230 | C. E. Holmes | Albert | 194 | Toronto. |
| 231 | W. A. Smith | | | |
| 232 | Dan McMillan | Cicerone | 195 | Woodville. |
| 233 | Isaac Unsworth | Florence | 196 | Florence. |
| 234 | D. Robertson | Minerva | 197 | Hamilton. |
| 235 | W. J. Cruickshank | Weston | 200 | Weston. |
| 236 | D. W. McKay | Beacon | 201 | Port Colborne. |
| 237 | W. Acheson | Silver Star | 202 | Milverton. |
| 238 | R. H. Row | Pembroke | 203 | Pembroke. |
| 239 | Jas. Duncan | | | |

| No. | Name. | Lodge. | No. | Location. |
|---|---|---|---|---|
| 240 | H. H. Worden | Acton | 204 | Acton. |
| 241 | W. S. Given | Ahiram | 205 | Paisley. |
| 242 | Adam McGill | | | |
| 243 | Hugh H. McLean | Silver City | 206 | Tiverton. |
| 244 | A. H. Blackeby | Egremont | 207 | Kerwood. |
| 245 | Geo. Thompson | Millbank | 209 | Millbank. |
| 246 | Jas. Armstrong | Brucefield | 210 | Brucefield. |
| 247 | F. Chittick | Lilly | 211 | Dorchester St'n. |
| 248 | Homer Miles | Argyll | 212 | Napanee. |
| 249 | Thos. Upton | Clifford | 214 | Clifford. |
| 250 | T. S. Prodhomme | Freestone | 215 | Beamsville. |
| 251 | M. L. Webber | Elmira | 216 | Elmira. |
| 252 | Jas. Weeks | Mount Brydges | 217 | Mount Brydges. |
| 253 | Robert Smith | | | |
| 254 | Thos. Robinson | Enterprise | 218 | Essex Centre. |
| 255 | A. S. Scott | | | |
| 256 | Andrew Patterson | Georgian Bay | 219 | Waubaushene. |
| 257 | J. A. Smith | Woodslee | 220 | S. Woodslee. |
| 258 | W. Halliday | Chesley | 221 | Chesley. |
| 259 | W. Caldwell | Hensall | 223 | Hensall. |
| 260 | J. H. Parnell | Ottawa | 224 | Ottawa. |
| 261 | F. W. May | | | |
| 262 | D. Walker | Merlin | 226 | Merlin. |
| 263 | J. A. McDonald | Sauble | 227 | Tara. |
| 264 | A. B. Hurrell | International | 228 | Interna'l B'dge. |
| 265 | F. Bowen | | | |
| 266 | Alex. McIntosh | Embro Star | 229 | Embro. |
| 267 | Robt. Gray | Prince of Wales | 230 | Toronto |
| 268 | Allan M. Bock | Elora | 231 | Elora. |
| 269 | D. J. Almas | Equity | 232 | Hagersville. |
| 270 | John Telford | Hanover | 233 | Hanover. |
| 271 | Jno. Clark | Ilderton | 234 | Ilderton. |
| 272 | Chas Slaght | Waterford | 235 | Waterford. |
| 273 | Jas. E. Beemer | | | |
| 274 | H. West | Acorn | 236 | Camlachie. |
| 275 | J. L. Gallagher | Farmersville | 237 | Athens. |
| 276 | W. R. Mathers | Stirling | 239 | Stirling. |
| 277 | W. H. Hubble | | | |
| 278 | A. W. Cameron | Carleton | 240 | Ottawa. |
| 279 | T. A. Hood | | | |
| 280 | R. Hawkins | Rideau | 241 | Smith's Falls. |
| 281 | R. Craig | | | |
| 282 | Jno. B. Reid | Wilton | 242 | Toronto |
| 283 | H. B. Dawson | Port Arthur | 243 | Port Arthur. |
| 284 | Jno. H. Dickinson | Thornbury | 244 | Thornbury. |
| 285 | V. Buell | Mallorytown | 245 | Mallorytown. |
| 286 | E. R. Robbins | Orillia | 246 | Orillia. |
| 287 | Jno. Waldon | Gordon | 247 | Palmerston. |
| 288 | J. B. Ferris | Campbellford | 248 | Campbellford. |
| 289 | G. Gillespie | | | |
| 290 | Jas. Birchard | Beaverton | 249 | Beaverton. |
| 291 | J. W. Holme | Ridgley | 250 | Oil Springs. |
| 292 | Moses J. Dickie | Bracebridge | 251 | Bracebridge. |
| 293 | A. E. Middleton | Floral | 252 | Toronto. |
| 294 | R. E. Walker | Caledonia | 253 | Caledonia. |
| 295 | D. H. McIntosh | Alba | 254 | Pakenham. |
| 296 | F. J. Marshall | Grand Valley | 256 | Grand Valley. |

| No. | Name. | Lodge. | No. | Location. |
|---|---|---|---|---|
| 297 | J. S. Milloy | Credit | 257 | Erin. |
| 298 | J. A. Young | Thamesford | 258 | Thamesford. |
| 299 | Joel McLeod, Jr | | | |
| 300 | Thos. Spence (of Gore 34) | Lynden | 259 | Lynden. |
| 301 | S. D. Watt | Meaford | 260 | Meaford. |
| 302 | George Barnes | Gold Hill | 261 | Rat Portage. |
| 303 | A. J. Holmes | | | |
| 304 | E. Gear | Norwood | 262 | Norwood. |
| 305 | F. Nettleton | East Toronto | 263 | East Toronto. |
| 306 | H. H. Neilson | Fraternity | 264 | Perth. |
| 307 | Joel Barlow | Delta | 265 | Delta. |
| 308 | Wm. Jule | Messanabie | 266 | Chapleau. |
| 309 | J. T. Campbell | Algoma | 267 | F. William East |
| 310 | Jas. W. Campbell | Stanley | 268 | Lanark. |
| 311 | Jas. McClurg | Woodstock | 269 | Woodstock. |
| 312 | J. R. Armitage | | | |
| 313 | E. E. Johnstone | Lansdowne | 270 | Lansdowne. |
| 314 | E. W. Ross | North Bay | 271 | North Bay. |
| 315 | Geo R. Cumming | Lakeview | 272 | W. Toronto Junc. |
| 316 | B. F. Doxee | Hastings | 273 | Hastings. |
| 317 | J. Porter | Midland | 274 | Midland. |
| 318 | D. Wilkinson | Fairy | 275 | Huntsville. |
| 319 | A. B. McRae | Sheard | 276 | New Dundee. |
| 320 | Thos. Hayne | Lambton | 277 | Brigden. |
| 321 | J. K. Pearce | Rockliffe | 278 | Ottawa. |
| 322 | G. W. Griffith | Grenville | 279 | Kemptville |
| 323 | F. A. Tallman | Balmoral | 280 | Merrickville. |
| 324 | A. B. Cracknell | Arthur | 281 | Sault Ste. Marie. |
| 325 | A. W. Watson | Sudbury | 282 | Sudbury. |
| 326 | E. V. Pooler | Earnscliffe | 283 | Janeville. |
| 327 | W. Bowen | Lyn | 284 | Lyn. |
| 328 | A. W. Reveler | Morewood | 285 | Morewood. |
| 329 | Jno. Humberstone | Ripley | 287 | Ripley. |
| 330 | J. G. Gillespie | Chesterville | 288 | Chesterville. |
| 331 | S. A. Smith | Glanworth | 289 | Glanworth. |
| 332 | R. S. Richardson | Tweed | 290 | Tweed |
| 333 | A. Humphrey | Rodney | 291 | Rodney. |
| 334 | T. A. Wilson | Minnetonka | 292 | Keewatin. |
| 335 | Wilber Sherry | Thomasburg | 293 | Thomasburg. |
| 336 | G. E. Post | Broadview | 294 | Toronto. |
| 337 | Fred Gallegher | Manotick | 295 | Manotick. |
| 338 | R. J. Stewart | Pontypool | 296 | Pontypool. |
| 339 | A. T. Smith | Mayflower | 297 | Parham. |

Your Committee find that Bro. Dr. Parnell is one of the Representatives of Ottawa Lodge, as shown by the returns of the Lodge, but a letter has been received with a certificate stating that Bro. W. Prenter was elected at a meeting subsequent to the regular night of election. The matter was laid before the Grand Master, who decided that Bro. Dr. Parnell is the legally elected Representative.

Your Committee therefore recommend his recognition as Representative.

The name of Bro. James McNally appears as one of the regularly elected Representatives of Aylmer Lodge, No. 94, but a telegram has been received stating that J. D. McDiarmid takes the place of Bro. McNally, who has resigned.

Your Committee recommend that Bro. McDiarmid be admitted as a Representative of that lodge.

Your Committee submit the following :—

*Resolved,*—That the Representatives herein named be now confirmed, and that those who are now present be admitted and instructed in the Grand Lodge Degree.

*Resolved,*—That the Past Grands named herein who are present be also admitted and instructed in the Grand Lodge Degree.

*Resolved,*—That all Representatives and Past Grands herein named who may not be now present be instructed in the Grand Lodge Degree in the ante-room upon being vouched for by a member of this Committee.

*Resolved,*—That this report be adopted.

Respectfully submitted.

J. B. KING,
J. M. HENRY,
W. A. MILLER.

The roll was now called, when the following Grand Officers and 329 Representatives answered to their names :

OFFICERS :

| | |
|---|---|
| REV. T. W. JOLLIFFE, BOWMANVILLE, - - | Grand Master. |
| JOSEPH OLIVER, TORONTO, - - - - | Deputy Grand Master. |
| W. H. HOYLE, CANNINGTON, - - - | Grand Warden. |
| J. B. KING, TORONTO, - - - - | Grand Secretary. |
| WM. BADENACH, TORONTO, - - - - | Grand Treasurer. |
| W. H. COLE, BROCKVILLE, - - - - | Grand Representative. |
| HY. ROBERTSON, COLLINGWOOD, - - - | Grand Representative. |
| O. E. FLEMING, WINDSOR, - - - - | Grand Marshal. |
| ROBERT MEEK, KINGSTON, - - - - | Grand Conductor. |
| A. MITCHELL, BOWMANVILLE, - - - | Grand Guardian. |
| I. B. AULPH, BRACEBRIDGE, - - - - | Grand Herald. |
| REV. WM. J. SANDERS, MANILLA, - - - | Grand Chaplain. |
| P. E. FITZ-PATRICK, HAMILTON, - - - | Junior Past Grand Master. |

The Grand Master appointed Reps. W. H. Cole, P.G.M., S. H. Glassford, and Samuel Towner, Committee on Distribution of subject matter in the several reports to appropriate Committees.

The Grand Secretary, on request of the chair, rose to read the Minutes of the last session, when on motion the Minutes as printed in the Journal of Proceedings were adopted as so printed.

The Grand Master, Rev. Bro. T. W. Jolliffe, presented and read his annual address, which was on motion referred to the Committee on Distribution.

# GRAND MASTER'S REPORT.



*To the Grand Lodge of Ontario, I.O.O.F.:*

GRAND OFFICERS AND REPRESENTATIVES,—In the order of a well-arranged Providence we are permitted once again to assemble in annual session. Our first thought is one of gratitude to God for the mercies enjoyed and the blessings bestowed during another year. The circumstances by which we are to-day surrounded are favorable. A goodly measure of success has crowned the work of the past year, and we look hopefully into the future. In accordance with the custom and require· ment of our laws I herewith submit for your consideration a report of the Official year, together with some of the many decisions given by me during that time, also some suggestions which I sincerely hope may be of service to us in the noble work in which we are engaged.

### I.—NEW LODGES.

It is only reasonable to expect in a young country like our own where villages are developing into towns, and towns growing into cities, that applications should be sent in from time to time asking new Lodges to be formed in those localities where the banner of Oddfellowship had not yet been unfurled. The following Lodges have been instituted since the last report was presented.

1st. Minnetonka, No. 292, Keewatin. Instituted Sept. 21st, 1892, by J. Giffen Clarke, D.D.G.M. This Lodge starts out with very fair prospects of doing good work for the Order.

2nd. Thomasburg Lodge, No. 293, at Thomasburg. Instituted by the Grand Master, on the 26th of Sep., 1892. A great deal of enthusiasm was shown at the opening of this Lodge. Brethren came from Belleville, Campbellford, Hastings, Norwood, Tweed, Madoc and other points to assist at the Institution and encourage by their presence; thirty-seven were initiated, and the number has been increased by many members since that time.

3rd. Broadview Lodge, No. 294. Instituted by the Grand Master, on the 19th of Dec., 1892. If a good locality, excellent hall, and working members mean anything we may expect to hear of progressive work for the Order here.

2

4th. Manotick, No. 295, Manotick. Instituted March 24th, 1893, by Bro. H. C. Reynolds, D.D.G.M. The report received in reference to this new Lodge was most encouraging in its character, and if they continue as they have begun will soon make a good record.

5th. Pontypool, No. 296. Instituted on the 25th of April, by the Grand Master. This Lodge is located at Pontypool on the C.P.R. The village is not large, but the Lodge has in it many of the best citizens, including two medical men, clergymen and the business men of that place ; the membership is upwards of forty and more to follow.

6th. Mayflower Lodge, No. 297. Instituted by Bro. A. T. Smith, D.D.G.M. Judging from reports received and opinions expressed by those who are familiar with the neighborhood, a fairly good Lodge may be built up at Parham. They have with commendable zeal erected a hall which will soon be ready for dedication.

7th. Comber Lodge, No. 298. Instituted on the 20th July, by Gordon E. Pulford, D D.G.M. The village of Comber is on the M.C.R., some 30 miles east of Windsor; it is a growing place and will furnish material to build up a good Lodge. Great discretion has been shown in reference to admission of members. The present membership is twenty-nine, with more in sight.

I would respectfully suggest that Charters be granted to these Lodges. I have placed them in the following Districts:—

| Minnetonka | Lodge, | No. | 292....Keewatin, | District | No. | 48 |
|---|---|---|---|---|---|---|
| Thomasburg | " | " | 293....Thomasburg, | " | " | 33 |
| Broadview | " | " | 294....Toronto. | " | " | 19 |
| Manotick | " | " | 295....Manotick, | " | " | 39 |
| Pontypool | " | " | 296....Pontypool, | " | " | 33 |
| Mayflower | " | " | 297....Parham, | " | " | 36 |
| Comber | " | " | 298....Comber, | " | " | 1 |

II.—REBEKAH DEGREE LODGES.

I am pleased to say that this branch of the Order also has enjoyed a year of prosperity, as the following list of new Lodges will show :

1st. Flora, No. 21, was instituted at Sault Ste. Marie on the 2nd Nov., 1892, by Bro. A. B. Cracknell, D.D.G.M.

2nd. Lucknow, No. 22. Instituted 9th Dec., 1892, by J. B. King, Grand Secretary.

3rd. Inglewood, No. 23, at Waterford, on the 27th Dec., 1892. Instituted by Bro. John Waddell, P.G., of St. Thomas.

4th. Prudence, No. 24, located at Brantford. Instituted Feb. 24th, 1893, by Bro. R. Brockbank, of Paris.

5th. Alberta, No. 25, Kincardine.   Instituted on the 27th April, 1893, by Grand Secretary King.

6th. Ivey, No. 26, Galt.   Instituted April 28th, 1893, by Sister  Alma Brill, of Guelph.

7th. Esther, No. 27, Niagara Falls.   Instituted May 18th, 1893, by Sister Esther Fraser, of Windsor.

8th. Colfax, No. 28. Sarnia.   Instituted May 29th, by Bro. John Gibson, P.G.M.

9th. At the Well, No. 29, Almonte.   Instituted June the 10th, by Bro. P. McCallum, D.D G.M.

10th. Aberdeen, No. 30, Deseronto.   Instituted July 6th, by Sister E. Lee, D.D.G.M., of Kingston.

Judging from the reports sent me by those who were charged with the duty of instituting these Lodges I anticipate that each one will render a good account of itself.

### III.—COMMITTEES.

The following Committees have been appointed during recess :—

* Committee on Laws of Subordinates :—Bros. W. A. Rawlings, P.G., of St. Catharines ; D. Robertson, P.G., of St. Catharines ; and J. A. Morton, P.G., of Wingham.

Committee on General Purposes (formerly Printing and Supplies) :—Bros. W. F. Mountain, P.G.,of Toronto ; W. Badenach, Grand Treasurer, of Toronto ; J. B. King, Grand Secretary, of Toronto.

Auditor :—Bro. A. C. Stewart, P.G., of London.

On Fraternal Correspondence :— Bro. Henry Robertson, P.G M., of Collingwood.

On Odd Fellows' Relief Association :—Bros. John Donogh, P.G.M., of Toronto ; L. C. Pascoe, P.G., of Belleville ; W. W. Wood, P.G., of Brockville.

On Reduction of Representatives :—Bros. John Donogh, P. G M., of Toronto ; J. B. McIntyre, P.G.M., of St. Catharines ; Jno. Welsh, P.G.P., of Stratford ; Thos. Woodyatt, P.G.P., of Brantford ; T. C. Lazier, P.G., of Belleville.

---

* It will be observed that there are only three on this Committee instead of five as formerly.  It was found that three could do the work as efficiently as five, with less expense to the Grand Lodge.

Committee on Insurance:—Bros. Hy. Robertson, P.G.M., of Collingwood; W. H. Cole, P.G.M., of Brockville; John Donogh, P.G.M., of Toronto; J. B. King, Grand Secretary, of Toronto; Wm. Badenach, Grand Treasurer, of Toronto; Wm. H. Hoyle, Grand Warden, of Cannington; J. McLurg, M.D., P.G., of Woodstock.

Committee on Celebration Semi-Centennial:—Bros. T. W. Jolliffe, Grand Master, of Campbellford; John Donogh, P.G M., of Toronto; J. Oliver, D.G.M., of Toronto; W. H. Hoyle, G.W., of Cannington.

Committee on Souvenir for Members:—Bros. J. B. King, Grand Secretary, of Toronto; A. A. Graham, D.D.G.M., of Toronto; Alf. Coyell, P.G , of Toronto.

### IV.—CERTIFICATES.

During the year the following certificates were granted to members of defunct Lodges:—

1892.

| Sept. | 13. | T. Dorland Smith.. | Port Stanley | Lodge, No. | 95.... | Port Stanley. |
|---|---|---|---|---|---|---|
| " | 13. | David Watt........ | Peabody | " | 99.... | Waterford. |
| " | 22. | Wm. Glover....... | Temple | " | 238.... | Penetang. |
| Nov. | 4. | C. R. Reynolds.... | Lorne | " | 175.... | West Lorne. |
| Dec. | 5. | E. F. Rymal........ | Mystic | " | 128.... | Waterdown. |
| " | 5. | A. H. Robson...... | " | " | " .... | " |
| " | 5. | Ferdinand Slater... | " | " | " .... | " |
| " | 5. | Henry Clark....... | " | " | " .... | " |
| " | 5. | Wm. Clark........ | " | " | " .... | " |
| " | 5. | Chas. Raspberry.... | " | " | " .... | " |
| " | 5. | W. O. Serley....... | " | " | " .... | " |

1893.

| Feb. | 13. | Philip Usher........ | Ark | " | 191.... | Springfield. |
|---|---|---|---|---|---|---|
| Mar. | 16. | Rev. John Veale.... | Palmerston | " | 123.... | Palmerston. |
| May. | 18. | David Heron....... | Mystic | " | 128.... | Waterdown. |

### V.—DISPENSATIONS.

Applications have been made by several Lodges to wear regalia on Anniversary occasions, Decoration ceremonies, &c. In each case the permission was granted.

### VI.—ANNIVERSARY.

I issued at the proper time the usual Anniversary proclamation. Am glad to know that it was so largely and appropriately observed.

### VII.—ODD FELLOWS' RELIEF ASSOCIATION.

This Association under the able Presidency of Bro. Dr. Fife Fowler, P.G.M., and the efficient management of Bro. R. Meek, P.G., the Secretary, has gone forward by leaps and bounds, and

the past year has been the best in its history.    The rapidly
increasing membership and the ever-growing Reserve Fund
speak volumes in favor of the skill with which it is managed.
By a careful selection of its risks the death rate has been low,
while the continual influx of young men has had the effect of
keeping the average age at about the same figure as that of ten
years ago.    I had the opportunity of attending the annual meeting at Kingston.    The report was most encouraging and augurs
well for the future of the Association.    The large attendance at
the meeting, especially of those from a distance, was proof of the
genuine interest that is being taken in the work of the Association.    Every man who lays claim to a reasonable share of
intelligence will admit the desirability of making some provision
for dependent ones in case the bread-winner is taken away.    I
do not know of any similar institution (all things considered)
which is to-day offering insurance with terms as favorable and
rates as low as those which obtain in the Odd Fellows' Relief
Association.    May it go on and prosper in its noble work.

### VIII.—DECORATION DAY.

There are few things better calculated to make a favorable
impression on the minds of those who are not members of the
Order than the annual observance of the custom of decorating
the graves of our departed brothers.    Every year the custom
is becoming more prevalent and in many places the day selected
by the Odd Fellows for decorating the graves of their dead is
set apart as the civic holiday, and the people generally take
advantage of it to deck the graves of their own dead.    It has
been my privilege during the year to be present at Bowmanville
and Peterboro' on Decoration Day.    At the former place there
was a large turnout of the citizens and much interest was manifested.    At the latter place some thousands of people were
present to witness the ceremony.    At each place I delivered an
address suitable to the occasion and believe good results will
follow.    I trust that our brethren everywhere throughout the
jurisdiction will see to it that this beautiful custom shall be
fittingly observed.

### IX.—OFFICIAL VISITS.

I have endeavoured to do what seemed possible along this
line during the year.    Pressure of work in connection with a
heavy pastoral charge at Bowmanville often compelled me to
say no when my heart said yes in response to numerous invitations.    It was a matter of regret to me that I had to refuse

invitations from Ottawa, Hamilton and other centres.   Knowing that I could only make a limited number of visits, I tried to select those places where it appeared to me I could do the greatest amount of good.   Every place I visited I was received courteously and kindly, and to the best of my ability advocated and defended the principles of Oddfellowship.   The many letters I have received from the Lodges in those places to which I have gone have led me to believe that some good has accrued to the Order as the direct result of work done in this way.

September 27th.—Visited Thomasburg for the purpose of instituting new Lodge.   Was hospitably entertained at the comfortable home of Bro. J. R. Orr, at Madoc, who, in company with other brethren, drove me out to · Thomasburg, 16 miles distant.   There I found Grand Secretary King, D.D.G.M.'s Doxsee and Stuart, and a host of others ready to help in the work.   The institution, initiation, election, installation of officers, &c., kept us busy till 3.30 in the morning.   The kindly feeling evinced by brethren from Belleville, Tweed, Madoc, Campbellford, Norwood, and other places, was seen in the large attendance of the brethren.   Indeed so many were crowded into the Lodge room that sixty had to retire before the degrees were conferred.   This was a matter of regret, as many of them had travelled all the way from Belleville to be present at the institution.   This Lodge started right and continues to prosper.

Oct. 4.—Visited Eastern Star Lodge, Whitby ; by arrangement Grand Secretary King was also present.   Trouble had arisen in the Lodge, consequent on the expulsion of a Bro. Thompson.   Bro. A. R. Rowland claimed the expulsion and trial preceding it were irregular and unjustifiable.   After a long and patient investigation, we found that the action of the Lodge was perfectly legal, and the steps taken by them were the only ones that could properly be taken.   However much we may feel disposed to sympathize with a man, yet when a brother is guilty of conduct unbecoming an Odd Fellow, and he persists in his attempts to create discord, he should be made to step down and out.   Bro. King and I addressed the Lodge at some length. The Whitby brethren have had their own share of trouble with some refractory members, but for them we trust the night is passed and the morning of a better day has come.

Oct. 6.—Took the train for Berlin on my way to New Dundee, to lecture in the interests of our Order there.   A minister (who ought to have known better) had come over from Boston and had spent some weeks in the neighborhood holding meetings for the purpose of denouncing secret societies, particularly Oddfellowship.  Bro. Bowden had, previous to my visit, written an excellent letter in defence of our principles.  This appeared in a local paper, and Oddfellowship was being discussed warmly. I found a crowded church ; many of those who were present were by no means friendly to the Order.  For two hours they gave me a careful hearing.  I then proposed that they should question me and I would, if possible, answer them frankly and fully.  Only a couple of questions were asked ; these were satisfactorily answered, and I trust this visit was productive of good. I have written some lengthy replies to Mr. Stoddard's intemperate and vicious attacks on the Order, which have been kindly published by the Waterloo *Chronicle.*

Oct. 18.—I visited Otonabee Lodge, Peterboro'—a live Lodge, well officered and good attendance.  I gave an address on the " Mystery and Mission of Oddfellowship," which was well received.  After adjournment, partook of an excellent oyster supper in an adjoining room, and a very pleasant time was spent.

Nov. 23.—Attended an At Home given in the new hall, Toronto, by the Rebekahs; a good programme was well rendered, after which I gave a twenty-minutes address on the Rebekah work.

Dec. 6.—Went to Manilla, the Lodge in that place having invited me to give an address at a concert to be held in the Methodist Church.  The attendance was good.  Bro. W. H. Hoyle, the Grand Warden, was also present and gave a very practical and eloquent address on " The Benefits Arising from Oddfellowship."  I endeavored to follow up on the same line. The hearty thanks of those present were tendered Bro. Hoyle and myself.  I was driven to and from the station and kindly entertained at the home of the Methodist minister, Rev. Mr. Power.

The next day drove over to Cannington and was made welcome to the comfortable home of Grand Warden Hoyle and his genial wife.  While there, arranged to pay an official visit to Cannington at another time.

Dec. 19.—Instituted Broadview Lodge, in the City of Toronto ; was ably assisted by P.G M. Donogh, D.G.M. Oliver, Grand Secretary King, D.D.G.M. Graham, G.T. Badenach, and many other brethren of the city, whose praise is in all the Lodges, and who are veritable hustlers when there is work to be done.  Practical speeches were given by several of the visitors, followed by a little talk from myself on " How to Build up a Prosperous Lodge."  We retired to rest at an early hour that morning. Broadview has wonderful possibilities within reach and no doubt will make good use of her advantages.

Jan. 12, 1893.—This was a red-letter day in the history of Oddfellowship in Toronto. The occasion being the dedication of the magnificent Temple erected as a home for the Order. After an enjoyable drive through the city the ceremony of dedication followed. This was conducted by our own Dr. Cl. T. Campbell, Grand Sire. It was a pleasant thing that this beautiful building was to be dedicated during his term of office. The Oration was delivered by Bro. the Hon. J. W. Stebbins, Deputy Grand Sire, Rochester, N.Y. It was clear in conception, beautiful in thought and eloquent in language, and will live long in the memory of those who were fortunate enough to be there. The brief address of Grand Sire Campbell was also a gem. May both these honored brethren long live to help on the noble work. In the evening a banquet was given and the whole affair reflected very great credit on those who planned and carried it to such a successful issue. After dinner, addresses were given by Grand Sire Campbell, Deputy Grand Sire Stebbins, P.G.M's. Fitz-Patrick, McIntyre, Robertson, Donogh ; P.C.P. Jno. Welsh, Stratford, the Grand Master, Deputy Grand Master, Grand Warden, Grand Secretary King, Grand Treasurer Badenach. If I have omitted the name of any Brother who took part in the speaking I must here and now ask his pardon, as I cannot at this writing lay my hand on the memorandum.

March 7.—Visited Cannington to take part in a concert and entertainment given by the Odd Fellows in the town hall. The attendance was good ; the programme creditable indeed. I spoke for half an hour on " The Object and Aim of Oddfellow-ship." Such gatherings as these may be made very useful in the interests of the Order. Grand Warden Hoyle, succeeds in keeping Oddfellowship well to the front in Cannington.

March 10.—Went to Galt where I was well entertained by Bro. Blackeby and his good wife. In the evening I met a number of the brethren in the Lodge-room and gave an informal talk on " Our Work."

On Sunday, the 11th, I had the pleasure of preaching to the brethren in the large Methodist Church ; the building was filled and we had an excellent service. A kindly-worded letter sent me soon after my visit leads me to hope that much good to the Lodge may be the outcome of my pleasant visit to Galt.

17.—I visited Oshawa to attend an " At Home " given by the Rebekahs of that town. The meeting was not a large one.

Evidently the brethren of that good town are not very enthusiastic in the work of the Rebekahs.  D.D.G.M. Warren and a few others encourage the Sisters all they can.  Brethren rally to the help of the Rebekahs.  I spoke at some length on the "Worth and Work of Woman," and hope my visit was not in vain.

March 29.—Attended meeting at Cobourg Lodge, 136.  Gave an address to the brethren, who filled the Lodge-room ; later in the evening attended a banquet given by the Lodge.  The *menu* was excellent and all tried to make the occasion a pleasant one.  Fitting addresses were given by three resident ministers, two medical men, and a number of local lights in the Lodge. I gave another address on " Our Work as Odd Fellows."  The D.D.G.M., Bro. Hamly, and a number of others were present from Port Hope, Bowmanville and other places.

April 8.—Visited Campbellford, and on the following day preached to the Odd Fellows in the Methodist Church there. The turn-out was very creditable ; visitors were present from West Toronto Junction, Norwood, Hastings and Sterling. After service, accompanied the brethren to the Lodge-room, where I was cordially thanked for the sermon ; following that, I made a few practical remarks to the brethren.  I am indebted to Bro. J. B. Ferris, P.G., for kindness shown me while in Campbellford.

April 12.—Visited Florence Nightingale Lodge, Bowmanville ; saw the second degree conferred in a very efficient manner.  This is a good Lodge and has in it many zealous wideawake members.  Addressed the Lodge " On the work we are trying to do."

April 25.—Went to Pontypool to institute a new Lodge in that village.  The Grand Secretary was also present and lent us valuable aid in the work.  A large number came down in a special car from Peterboro, bringing with them their paraphernalia, also the goat, which afforded a great deal of amusement to the small boys of the village.  The team from Peterboro' took charge of the Initiatory work and the conferring of the degrees. It would be a difficult matter to get a team together who would be able to take the palm from the Peterboro' boys.  My wish was that brethren from Lodges where the work is done in a loose, slipshod way could have been present and they would have discovered beauties in Oddfellowship they never dreamed of.

April 28.—Accepted invitation, and was present at an " At Home " given by the members of Florence Nightingale Lodge.

A choice programme, musical and literary, was presented Cake, fruit, lemonade, etc., were served, after which I delivered an address on " The Reason why I am an Odd Fellow."

April 30.—In the morning I preached to the brethren of No. 66 in my own church, on the parable of the "Good Samaritan." Tried to emphasize the special teaching therein contained, viz: "Take Care of Him." A good collection was given for a charitable object.

June 8.—Accompanied by the Grand Secretary from Bowmanville, went to Stirling, where I had been invited to lay the foundation stone of a new Presbyterian Church. We were joined at Peterboro by Dr. Bell, P.G.M. A procession was formed from the station at Stirling to the site of the new church. After laying the stone with appropriate ceremonies, I gave an address suitable to the occasion. After dinner a platform meeting was held on the agricultural grounds. Good addresses were given by Rev. Bros. McFarlane and Taylor, Grand Secretary King, Grand Warden Hoyle, and P.G.M. Bell. I also had the opportunity of speaking again. The day was pleasant; everything passed off agreeably and I was informed the total proceeds netted the church about $600, including a purse of eighty dollars given by the Odd Fellows. A neat silver trowel was presented to me, which will be treasured as a reminder of what was to me a very enjoyable day. I have been requested to be present at the opening of the church. I intend (D.V.) to be there. In the evening of the same day we visited the Peterboro Lodge; the attendance was good and the Brothers enthusiastic. Bro. King and I spoke at some length to the brethren, who gave us a right royal welcome.

July 4.—Visited Campbellford Lodge, No. 248. Assisted by D.D.G.M. Doxsee, of Hastings, I installed the officers, and gave a little talk to the brethren. Taking into account the size of the place and the large number of societies in it, I should say this Lodge is doing very well.

July 7.—Visited Peterboro' to take part in the Decoration ceremony. The interest was general; thousands of people were gathered in the cemetery to witness the beautiful and imposing ceremony. After the graves had been decorated, addresses were given by the local clergy and the Grand Master. I felt glad that I belonged to an Order whose ministries cease not with this life, but which continues its watchful care over the resting places of the silent dead.

July 10.—Visited Queen City Lodge, Toronto, and addressed the brethren. Here everything seems to be done decently

and in order.   In company with Bro. A. A. Graham, D.D.G.M.,
I then visited Laurel Lodge.   Two candidates were initiated
in a creditable manner.   This Lodge a few months ago was so
low that its best friends for a while dispaired of its life, but
lately a number of young, active men have been brought into the
Lodge and they are steadily rising to a good position.

July 17.—In company with Bro. Morton, of 248, I visited
No. 273, at Hastings.   The attendance was good.   An Epis-
copalian clergyman had just vacated the principal chair, while
the chair of V.G. was occupied by the  Presbyterian minister
of that village.   When the regular business was over I had an
opportunity of addressing the brethren on " Our work  and the
best way of doing it."

On August 1st I visited  Port Hope to take part in the Decoration  ceremony.   The  arrangements  were  perfect  and  the
enthusiasm intense.   The  procession  was  one  of the finest we
have ever seen on a similar occasion.   About twenty graves
were decorated.   The choir of the Methodist Church supplied
excellent music, and addresses suitable to the occasion were given
by  Grand  Chaplain  Saunders,  of  Lonsdale,  and  myself.   On
returning  to  the  Lodge-room  congratulatory  speeches   were
made ;  votes of thanks were tendered the  visiting brethren and
speakers, and an adjournment was made to the Queen's Hotel,
where  an  excellent  dinner  was  served.   Durham  Lodge  is
doing  well.

August  3rd.—Visited  Lodge  No. 81,  at  Belleville.   Was
cordially welcomed at the Lodge, where I gave an address on
the " Duty of the Hour."  This is a stronghold of Oddfellowship,
and the brethren are earnest and  enthusiastic in their work and
deserve to  succeed.

This concluded my round of visits.   Gladly would I have
responded to invitations from many other places had it been
possible.

X.—WEAK LODGES.

Tottenham.—Having been notified that Tottenham Lodge,
255, was in a languishing condition I engaged the Deputy
Grand Master to visit Tottenham and ascertain the condition
of things there.   Matters were found to be in poor shape when
the  D.G.M. made his visit there in January.   A few brethren
retained a nominal connection with the Order, but none were
good on  the books.

Bro. Oliver's letter to me *re* Tottenham will be found in
the Appendices to this report.

SEAFORTH.—I learned that this Lodge, while financially in good condition, is numerically weak and non-progressive. Bro. A. H. Blackeby, G.C.P., visited the Lodge on the 28th June. The total membership was seventeen. It may be that other societies make competition keen, and yet, in a town like Seaforth, there should be a vigorous Lodge of Odd Fellows. I sincerely trust that the brethren there will put forth every possible effort to lift Oddfellowship to that position it is entitled to in their community.

CLINTON.—There is here a small Lodge of almost discouraged members—practically no funds, and little enthusiasm on the part of the few who remain. Bro. Blackeby also visited this Lodge by request, and tried to stimulate the Brothers to renewed effort. The suggestion made in his report accompanying this is practical, and the strong probability is that things would take on a change for the better if the efficient team of Huron Lodge will go up and show these brethren what can be done in the way of making the work attractive. I have written to the team and have reason to believe they will comply.

### XI.—FIRE.

Almost every year we have had one or more Lodges mourning over lodge-room, furniture and paraphernalia being destroyed by fire. With all the facilities for insurance at reasonable rates, surely no Lodge should fail to insure its property. During the past year Caledonia Lodge has been the sufferer. On January 19th, I was sorry to learn that their hall and contents had been burned. I also learned with regret that on December 28th last, Brougham Lodge No. 155, Whitevale, lost its effects by fire. By my direction the Grand Secretary sent to each Lodge a dispensation to continue at work. I recommend that duplicate charters be given to each of these Lodges.

### XII.—CHANGE OF D.D.G.M.

In the month of January Bro. W. R. Hutchison, of Huntsville, D.D.G.M. of District No. 42, resigned his commission as he was leaving the Province. I appointed to the vacant position Bro. D. Wilkinson, P.G., Huntsville.

### XIII.—INVASION OF TERRITORY.

During the year there has been three complaints that certain Lodges have proposed and initiated persons whose place of residence was nearer to another Lodge than that which they had joined. To avoid any unpleasantness of this kind, boundaries should be clearly defined, and one Lodge should sacredly respect the rights of another. It might be well to ask in this connection, if a uniform rate of initiation could be agreed upon in cities where there are several Lodges, then men would not travel past two or three good Lodges to join some distant Lodge, because the initiation fee was less than in the others.

### XIV.—GRAND INSTRUCTOR.

The need of some one whose duty it shall be to visit each subordinate Lodge in the jurisdiction, to give instruction in the ritual-laws of the Order, the unwritten work, the proper way to keep Lodge accounts, and various other matters pertaining to the good of the work, is one that is pressing itself upon us. Many of our Lodges are in small towns and villages where it is sometimes difficult to find the right man to take a responsible position in the Lodge. With a visit, and timely help of some judicious counsellor, many a disheartened Brother would put forth renewed effort. Many of our D.D.G.M's are noble men, and hard workers, but they find it difficult to visit as often as circumstances seem to require. The Grand Master, unless he should happen to be a gentleman of leisure, cannot possibly respond to a tithe of the calls that comes to him. I have no doubt that many a weak Lodge could be lifted out of its weakness if we had the right man to go at the right time. Whether a properly qualified person can be found willing to take such a position, I know not, but that it would be a benefit to the Order I am fully persuaded.

During the year it has been suggested that the time has come when we should have an agent—call him what you please—whose special duty it shall be to lecture and organize Lodges in those places where we are not represented. I have no sympathy with the tactics employed by some societies to gain a foothold; they are beneath the dignity of an Order like this. At the same time it might be well to consider if something more than we are now doing might not be done with advantage to ourselves. We are grateful for past success, but there remains very much territory that might be pre-empted for Oddfellowship.

### XV.—APPEALS FOR AID.

I have received several applications for leave to canvass the Lodges in this jurisdiction for funds to aid various enterprises. Some of these appeared to me to be worthy, yet in view of the depression existing in business circles, joined to the fact that

many of our Lodges had all they could do to meet local claims.
I did not deem it wise to grant permission.

### XVI.—COLUMBIAN DEMONSTRATION.

I have received from Marshal-General John C. Underwood,
a circular informing me that a monster demonstration of the
Order is desired in Chicago, on September 25th, and asking the
co-operation of this grand body.  As the session of this Grand
Lodge was so near, I did not deem it wise to call the Executive
together, believing that the matter would be dealt with promptly
by the Grand Lodge.

### XVII.—THE GRAND SIRE.

As soon as we were informed of the elevation of our beloved
Brother, Dr. Cl. T. Campbell, P.G.M., to the position of Grand
Sire, a telegram was sent congratulating him on the honor so
worthily bestowed.  Bro. Campbell brings to this office a clear
head, a warm heart, and executive ability of no mean order.  In
honoring P.G.M. Campbell, the Sovereign Grand Lodge has
honored itself.  We trust that his term of office may be pleasant
to himself and one of unprecedented prosperity to the Order.

### XVIII.—VISIT OF THE GRAND SIRE.

During the year the Grand Sire visited Hamilton and
delivered a magnificent address to an audience which filled
Association Hall.  The D.D.G.M. of that District in his report
says, that the large increase of members of that District is due
largely to the influence of that visit.

### XIX.—COMPETITION.

The D.D.G.M. officers and district delegates of District No.
9, presented a silver cup for competition between the Lodges
This cup was not to become the permanent property of any
Lodge till it had been won four times in succession.  The competition consists in the opening and closing of the Lodge, and
the initiatory ceremonies.  The points in the competition were :
accuracy of ritual ; accuracy of secret work ; elocution and
general effect.  Excelsior Lodge, No. 44, won the cup for this
term.  The phenomenal success which has attended this experi-
ment in the Hamilton District suggests that it might be tried
with advantage elsewhere.

### XX.—DOMINION ODD FELLOW.

The weekly visits of this paper have been welcome. It continues to improve, and it should be taken by all who wish to
keep in touch with our work. The post-card notes containing
brief items of the doings of the Lodges throughout the Dominion
are an excellent feature. Some true Brother in each Lodge
would do well to see that items of interest are promptly
forwarded.

### XXI.—INSURANCE AND BONDS.

The renewal receipts for insurance on the Grand Lodge
property, and the guarantee bonds of the Grand Secretary and
the Grand Treasurer have been in my possession during the
year.

### XXII.—THE REBEKAHS.

This branch of the Order is making good progress, as will
be seen by the number of new Lodges formed during the year,
and the efficient work that has been done. The genial President, Mrs. J. B. King, of Toronto, and the indefatigable Secretary, Mrs. J. Waddell, of St. Thomas, have had the welfare of
the Order constantly before them, and their work has been
appreciated. A grand work is being done by many of the sisters
in visiting the sick and the distressed, caring for the poor, and
relieving the wants of the needy. In Toronto alone, 380 such
visits were made. Lately a voluntary committee has gone
systematically to work to relieve all cases that may come under
their notice, of widows or children of deceased Odd Fellows who,
at the time of their death, were either in arrears or suspended.
This committee is supported by voluntary contributions from
members of the Order. Surely work like this will meet its
appropriate reward, and should tend to close the mouth of
adverse criticism forever.

### XXIII.—REPORT OF DISTRICTS.

My relations during the year with the District Deputies have
been cordial in their character; it has been a pleasure to
correspond with them. With one or two exceptions, they have
given evidence of being capable and efficient men, ready at all
times to give me such information as I desired. I regret, however, that two brethren who have occupied the position of D.D.
G.M. have not felt themselves called upon to report to the Grand
Master during the year. This is unfortunate for the Districts
over which they have presided. I am always glad to see faithful

service recognized, and hence I was pleased to see that a number of the most efficient D.D.G.M.'s have been re-elected. Others might have been, but they declined in favor of someone else. I would suggest that all the reports of the D.D G.M.'s for the past year be placed, at the close of this session, in the hands of my successor, so that he can learn from them the points requiring attention, and direct his efforts accordingly.

XXIV.—THE DISTRICT SYSTEM.

Judging from the reports received, this appears to be working well. The meetings are made interesting and instructive by the introduction and discussion of such questions as have an important bearing on our work. Few if any, I imagine, would be willing to go back to the old style of doing things. I give an extract from some of the reports, which may be of interest :—

District No. 2.—" That this District memorialize the Grand Lodge of Ontario, asking them to instruct the Grand Representatives from Ontario to the Sovereign Grand Lodge, to request that body to change the age for admission into the membership of this Order from twenty-one to eighteen years of age."

" That the Grand Lodge be memorialized by this District to leave the matter of mileage and per diem to the delegates of District meetings."

" That we ask the Grand Lodge to change the terms in Subordinate Lodges from an optional semi-annual, or annual, to a compulsory annual term."

" That we memorialize the Grand Lodge to decide that mileage and per diem be not paid to any but legal Representatives of the Subordinate Lodges."

" That in the estimation of this District meeting, it is time that our Grand Lodge was taking steps to prohibit all persons who deal in spirituous liquors from joining our noble Order : therefore we ask the Grand Lodge to take such steps as will prohibit liquor dealers, bartenders, or liquor clerks from joining our Order."

District No. 24.—" Recommends that the Noble Grand, previous to being installed in his office, shall be examined in open Lodge as to his proficiency and ability to deliver the charges of his office."

District No. 19.—" Asks if it would not be possible for some of the larger Districts to be reduced, either by re-distribution or division."

District No. 39.—"That by the adoption of either of the two systems proposed by Special Committee on Representation, and forwarded by them to the several Lodges in Ontario, the Lodges in outlying Districts will not receive equal justice with Lodges in cities and towns, and that this District favors the present system of Representation."

District No. 42.—"That this District take no action on the question of Representation to the Grand Lodge, believing the present system to be the best."

District No. 16.—"That this District approve of the scheme that each Lodge have one Representative, and that the Lodges entitled to more than one Representative have proxy votes."

District No. 19.—"This District decided that they were not in favor of either of the schemes of Representation as laid down in the report."

District No. 41.—"This District decided that the proposed change from Lodge Representation to District Representation at the Grand Lodge, will in the opinion of this District work injury to the Order in this jurisdiction, and will not decrease expense: we therefore recommend that Representation be left as it is."

Many of the Districts have made no reference to the question of Representation at the Grand Lodge; but of those that have done so the majority are in favor of the present system.

XXV.—COMMITTEE ON REPRESENTATION.

This Committee has done its work faithfully and well, as the report laid before this Grand Lodge will indicate. It is clear and comprehensive, and with the information it contains in our hands, the Grand Lodge will be in a position to discuss this important matter, and decide the question of Representation.

XXVI.—ODD FELLOWS' HALL, TORONTO.

The erection of this beautiful building on the corner of Yonge and College Streets, will mark an era in the history of Oddfellowship in Toronto. The structure is beautiful in conception, imposing in appearance, and is well calculated to serve the purpose for which it has been erected. It is sufficiently central to be a meeting-place for a number of the city Lodges. The committee charged with the duty of carrying out the work deserve much credit for their labor. Every want has been so fully met, that little if anything more can be desired.

3

### XXVII.—DECISIONS.

It would be unwise to insert all the questions asked me and the decisions given. I will therefore give only a few that may be of interest. Hundreds of questions are sent to the Grand Master which might be answered by the brethren themselves, if they would only consult the Ontario Digest.

No. 1.—The commission to the D.D.G.M.'s was dated Aug. 29th, for one year. A Brother appointed to the office of D.D.G.M. retains that office until his successor receives his commission.

No. 2.—A Brother dies while in arrears to the Lodge. His wife has no legal claim, but it is always in order to do something for dependent relations in the way of a gratuity.

No 3.—It is not lawful to use the Funds of a Lodge for the purpose of prosecuting a man who has been expelled for conduct unbecoming an Odd Fellow.

No. 4.—It is not lawful to wear any badge in a Subordinate Lodge in place of the Regalia prescribed by law.

No. 5.—It is not necessary to have a two-thirds vote to expel a Brother, a majority vote is sufficient.

No. 6.—It would not be lawful for a team to have their photograph taken in the paraphernalia of the Lodge-room.

No. 7.—It is not lawful for a Subordinate Lodge to publish the odes, the form of ceremony used in decorating the graves of deceased brethren, or the form adopted by the Grand Lodge to be used at funerals.

No. 8.—Benefits should be paid for the benefit of a Brother who is insane as in any other sickness.

No 9.—A Lodge is not legally bound to pay expenses incurred in carriage hire, when attending a funeral, unless authority be given by the Lodge to hire carriages for the purpose.

No. 10.—A Subordinate Lodge decides to purchase a lot for the purpose of erecting a hall thereon. At the following meeting exception was taken to the action on the ground that two weeks' notice (as required by By-laws) was not given that such a motion was to be submitted to the Lodge. The action was illegal, the required notice not having been given.

No. 11.—A notice of motion is not necessary to enable a Lodge to vote a sum of money for the relief of distressed members.

No. 12.—It is competent for a Lodge to remit a portion of the initiation fee to a clergyman, if it desires to do so.

No. 13.—An N.G. has no right to vacate his chair to take part in any debate in the Lodge.

No. 14.—A Contingent Fund should be kept separate from other funds.  It is not lawful to take money from the General Fund for suppers, entertainments, etc.

No. 15.—All matters in connection with degrees, not provided for in the Digest are properly subjects for local legislation.

No. 16.—It is not lawful for a Lodge to initiate as a member a person whose residence is nearer some other Lodge than theirs ; and if they do so the Lodge which is nearer can demand the amount paid as initiation fee.

No. 17.—A Lodge may provide by its By-laws for the reduction of its weekly sick benefits, after any member has received benefits for twelve months of continued sickness, and such By-laws shall apply to any member who may be receiving benefits at the time of its adoption.

No. 18.—The consent of the Grand Master would not make it legal for a Lodge to initiate a person not more than twenty years of age.

No. 19.—A Brother, feeble in health and advanced in years, offers to compromise his claim on the Lodge for a present cash payment.  While the offer may be reasonable it seems contrary to the genius of Oddfellowship.  It would be better to inform the Lodge when he is sick and get such benefits as he is entitled to.

No. 20 —All revenue in the way of rentals for a hall used by a Lodge should be paid into the General Fund.

No. 21.—No money can be diverted from the General Fund to form a Contingent Fund.

No. 22.—The By-laws of a Lodge require dues to be paid quarterly in advance.  A Brother is taken sick a few days after the first meeting night in the quarter, his dues are not paid, hence he is not entitled to benefits.

No. 23.—Any Past Grand in good standing in the District can be a candidate for D.D.G.M., whether he is a Representative at the District meeting or not.

No. 24.—The proper course of procedure in appealing against the decision of the District Committee is the same as appealing against the decision of a Lodge.

### XXVIII.—AYLMER AND RIDGELY LODGES.

During the year I have had a large amount of correspondence on a case in which these two Lodges are interested, and,
as it may come before this Grand Lodge, I give the facts of the
case briefly, and my action in regard to it.  In the month of
November, 1890, Rev. Bro. Ferguson, a member of Aylmer
Lodge, but residing at Oil Springs, was attacked with typhoid
fever.  The sickness was of such a severe character that it was
ordered by the physician to procure a trained nurse from the
hospital at London, at $10.00 per week.  The Secretary of
Aylmer Lodge was telephoned, and he replied that his Lodge
would no doubt uphold them in what they did in the matter.
Some  time afterward Ridgely Lodge was notified that they
would allow only six dollars a week for a nurse.  At the time
this notice was received, Bro. Ferguson was not expected to
live from one day to another.  A competent nurse could not be
obtained for a sum less than $10.00 a week, and the said nurse
had to be retained for ten weeks.  Ridgely Lodge drew on its
Treasurer for $105 to pay the fee of the nurse, and her expenses
from London.  Aylmer Lodge sent to Ridgely Lodge $60, being
pay for the nurse for ten weeks, at $6.00 a week. (Ridgely Lodge
had paid $10.00 a week.)  A draft was made on Aylmer Lodge
for the balance, $45.00.  The draft was returned with $1.40
charges, so that Ridgely Lodge is out of pocket $46. 40.  The
contention of Aylmer Lodge is that they paid all that the By-
laws of their Lodge authorized, and that they are not responsible.  On the other hand, Ridgely Lodge was placed in a very
difficult position.  To have discharged the trained nurse for an
inefficient one meant, in all probability, Bro. Ferguson's death.
They feel that they should not lose the amount they had expended in excess of that which they received.  My opinion was
that Bro. Ferguson should pay the amount in dispute.  I wrote
and advised him to do so.  He replied that he was not responsible.  I wrote again, but to no purpose, and I presume that the
matter is yet unsettled and will come before you.

### XXIX.—FRATERNAL VISITS.

I have been pleased to learn from reports sent in that a
great number of fraternal visits have been made during the year.
These have been productive of much good, and I am persuaded
that very great benefit may be derived by Lodges thus visited.
A stimulus is given to the cause, and an enthusiasm evoked
that prompts the members to greater effort in endeavoring to
spread the principles of Oddfellowship.

### XXX.—APPEALS.

I am aware of only three appeals to come before you :

1st.—That of Bro. Ronan, of Ottawa, against the decision of the Grand Master *re* the election of Degree Master of Victoria Lodge, No. 21.   The case in brief is this : On November 18th the first nomination was held for the office of Degree Master ; Bro. P. G. Prenter was nominated for the office.  No other nomination was then made and no objection was taken, so the nomination was closed for that night.  On the evening of December 16th the regular meeting of the Lodge was held ; there was a second nomination as provided for by by-law.  Bro. Prenter was present. The Secretary read Bro. Prenter's name as nominee for Degree Master and asked if there were any further nominations.  Bro. Ronan was then nominated, and the nominations were declared closed.  The election followed ; but just before proceeding with the election and after the nomi- nation was declared closed, Bro. Prenter wished to decline.  The D.M. refused to allow him to withdraw his name then, as the nominations were closed.  On counting the ballot it was found that twenty-two votes had been cast, of which Bro. Prenter received eighteen and Bro. Ronan four.  Bro. Prenter was declared elected, and was informed that he could resign on the night of installation if he saw fit to do so.  On the night of installation (January 20th) Bro. Ronan raised a point of order, and asked the Degree Master if Bro. Prenter was legally elected, as he had not given his consent to his nomination for the office. The Chair ruled that Bro. Prenter was legally elected.  Bro Ronan appealed from the decision of the Chair to the Lodge. On a vote being taken the decision of the Chair was sustained. P. G. Ronan then appealed from the Lodge to the D.D.G.M., who was present.   The D. D. G. M. stated that he would sustain the decision of the Lodge.   P. G. Ronan then gave notice that he would appeal to the Grand Master for his decision on the case.  I carefully examined the by-laws submitted, and my decision was that as Bro. Prenter was present on the second night of nomination, and did not object to being a candidate for the office until after the nomination was closed (when it was too late to withdraw), that he was legally elected to the position of D.M., and that the decision of the D.D.G.M. in the case should be sustained, against the decision of Bro. Ronan's appeal.

2nd.—The second appeal is that of A. R. Rowland against the action of Eastern Star Lodge in expelling him from the

Order on April 4th, 1893. The D.D.G.M. sustained the action of the Lodge, and the Grand Master sustained the decision of the D.D.G.M. Mr. Rowland appealed to me for an arrest of judgment, which I declined to grant.

3rd.—An appeal from P.G. Fred Gallagher, of Ottawa, from the decision of Bro. Reynolds, D.D.G.M., voiding the election of P.G. J. H. Parnell as a Representative to this Grand Lodge. The N.G. declared the election illegal, as some of the candidates were in arrears, also some of those who voted at the election. P.G. J. H. Parnell, who was in good standing at the time of his election as Representative to the Grand Lodge, June 26th, 1893, refused to be a candidate for the position at the second election of Representatives, claiming that he had been legally elected already. The action of the N.G. in ordering a new election was sustained by the Lodge. The D.D.G.M., who was present, was then appealed to : he sustained the decision of the N. G. and of the Lodge, hence the appeal.

All the papers in each case are ready to place in the hands of the Committee on Appeals.

XXXI.—MORTUARY.

During the year many members of our Order have been called away by the angel of death, and they are sadly missed by their Lodges and families. The rapidly revolving years remind us that our opportunity for work is brief, and will soon be gone, hence the need of doing all we can now to lighten the burdens of others. Two of the officers of this Grand Lodge have been called upon to pass through the waters during the past year. Bro. Meek, Grand Conductor, has lost his respected and honored father, and Grand Representative, Henry Robertson, has had his home darkened by the removel of a gifted and devoted wife. I know I voice the feelings of this Grand Lodge, when I say we sympathize with these Brethren, and pray that they may meet again those who have preceded them to that land where there is no more death. On the 4th of April, 1893, G. P. Dickson, P.G., died in the city of Toronto. Though not taking any active part in the work of the Order for a few years past, on account of the weight of years, yet in the early history of Oddfellowship in this Province, he was a conspicuous figure—earnest and enthusiastic in his endeavors to advance the interests of Oddfellowship, he won and held the respect of his Brethren. On hearing of his death, the Grand Secretary thoughtfully ordered a wreath to add to the floral offerings at the funeral ; his action met with my approval as I am sure it did with yours. The gift was much appreciated by Bro. Dickson's family.

On Oct. 23rd, Bro. Hy. McAfee, Past Grand Master, died at
his home in Detroit. We saw him while at Windsor ; though
in feeble health, it was not thought that the grim reaper would
so soon visit him. Bro. McAfee was one of the pioneer Odd
Fellows of Ontario, and was a faithful and earnest worker in
the cause for many years, until health giving way, he was compelled to retire from active labour, but he never seemed to lose
his love for the Order, which remained warm and strong to the
end.

### XXXII.—DELAYED REPORTS.

As I was about finishing my work on this report I received
some reports in which I find suggestions which perhaps should
have a place here. *District No.* —. " That we strongly recommend the appointment of an Organizer, whose work it shall be
to visit the weak Lodges and to start new ones in the districts
whence comes the call for the banner of Oddfellowship to be
unfurled." One Lodge disapproves of the main proposition : (1)
because there is no certainty in it that any Lodge will be represented by one of its own members ; (2) because the new order
of things might lead to inharmony between the Lodges. The
alternative scheme of electing one Representative in each Lodge
who shall cast the full vote of it, leading of course to the reduction in the Capitation tax, though it is not desired, still is preferred to the other. Cataraqui Lodge also passed a recommendation to the effect that the Capitation tax be kept at a rate that
will allow the payment by the Grand Lodge of a reasonable remuneration to the Grand Master for the inroads upon valuable
time required in the performance of his duties, and of the payment of a suitable salary to an Instructor and Organizer, whose
employment the Lodge considers of prime importance in the
spread of Oddfellowship. This Lodge adds : " The revenue of
the Grand Lodge should be sufficient to enable it to dispense
with any profit upon the sale of supplies to the Subordinate
Lodges, and it is urged that the Grand Lodge furnish such
supplies at actual cost." *District No. 13* recommends the Grand
Lodge to adopt a resolution to initiate at the age of eighteen.

### XXXIII.—ADMONITORY.

Every Lodge in the Jurisdiction should insist on proper
qualification on the part of the Brother who aspires to the office
of N.G. Making all due allowance for the lack of verbal memory
on the part of many, I am of the opinion that any member of
our Order aspiring to office, can by a little application and per-
severance so master his work that he will be independent of the

Ritual when giving the necessary instruction to an initiate in opening and closing the Lodge. The impressions made upon the mind of a candidate at initiation are lasting, and the work should always be performed in such a manner that every intelligent man may carry home with him a lofty conception of the initiatory ceremony. Let every Brother do his work to the very best of his ability, and the result will be seen in the increased interest and attendance at the Lodge meetings.

We should never seek to have quantity at the expense of quality, in our Lodges. An unworthy man, once admitted into the Lodge, is capable of a great deal of mischief, and if he does not succeed eventually in wrecking the Lodge, he will probably succeed in bringing the whole Order into disrepute in his own locality, and thus good men will hesitate to join us. As you value peace, harmony, good-will and success, guard well your ballot-box.

A serious leak in our membership each year is the result of suspension for N.P.D. If it is worth while putting forth an effort to get a man into the Lodge, surely it is worth a greater effort to keep him there. A careful record should be kept of the addresses of the absentee members. Each one should receive quarterly, an epitome of the doings of his Lodge, accompanied, perhaps, by a suggestion that a prompt remittance will keep him good on the books. If this were generally practised, I am persuaded that our membership would show a marked improvement.

### XXXIV.—WELLINGTON SQUARE LODGE.

In compliance with the order of the last Grand Lodge, the funds of this Lodge have been restored. On the 4th of April, 1893, a cheque was sent to the trustees of this Lodge for $2,154.69. Our hope is that prosperity may attend the brethren of this Lodge.

### XXXV.—CORRESPONDENCE.

As usual, this department of the work has taken up a great deal of time, not merely in the work of replying, but in looking up authorities, etc. Many enquiries are sent to the Grand Master, which should go to the D.D.G.M. first. However, I have replied to every Brother that has written to me. Usually, all letters have been answered on the same day that they were received, and I trust there is no ground for complaint here.

### XXXVI.—THANKS.

I desire, before closing my report, to say, that I am largely indebted to the D.D.G.M.'s (whose names are too numerous to mention), who have, by the prompt and efficient discharge of their duties, aided me in my work. My acknowledgments are due to Grand Sire Campbell, Past Grand Masters Robertson, Bell and Fitz-Patrick, for many kindnesses shown me during my term of office.

P. G. Blackeby in visiting Lodges at my request (when unable to do sc myself), deserves grateful mention.

Deputy Grand Master Oliver has placed me under a debt of gratitude, not only by visiting Lodges, but during the time I was attending conference, packing up and removing from Bowmanville to Campbellford and getting settled, he kindly took the work of Grand Master, and performed it with the utmost satisfaction.

And last, though by no means least, I have to thank Grand Secretary King. His services have been rendered cheerfully and promptly, and I have learned to appreciate more and more his ability and zeal in our work. Even when burdened by his own work he has made time to render me the assistance I needed. May a kind Providence long spare our worthy Secretary to discharge his important and manifold duties. In my many visits to the Secretary's office during the year, I have always found him busily engaged. I have also learned that a large amount of work is done by his assistant. Without expressing any opinion as to the salary the Secretary should receive, I am persuaded that the amount, $100.00, voted to the assistant, is not adequate remuneration for the work done, and I would respectfully recommend the Grand Lodge to add something more to the amount given for clerical assistance.


XXXVII.—CONCLUSION.

And now, Brethren, in closing I can only say I hope my year's administration has met with your approval. I have not been able to accomplish all I had hoped to do, but with the care of a large church upon me most of the year, I can say I have done my best to serve your interests. Conscious of the honor you conferred upon me a year ago, in permitting me to fill the office of Grand Master, I have striven as best I could to advance the cause which we have at heart, and to uphold the dignity of the Order. I hope and trust that the Sessions of this Grand Lodge may be marked by intelligent devotion to the great principles we inculcate, and that peace and good-will may prevail. May the coming year be even more successful than the past. I shall ever cherish pleasing recollections of the many acts of kindness I have received from my Brethren. It will be a joy to think of in the coming days. I look into the faces of many Brethren with whom we have worked in harmony in the bygone years.   Some are here for the first time—to learn and to work.   I greet you all in the name of the great Brotherhood to which we belong.

May He who is the source of all wisdom and light, aid us in our deliberations, and may the influence of Oddfellowship continue to extend, until the day dawns and the shadows flee away.                    Fraternally yours,

T. W. JOLLIFFE, *Grand Master.*

# APPENDICES.

### Appendix A.

### OFFICE OF THE GRAND MASTER,

· BOWMANVILLE, AUG. 29, 1892.

DEAR SIR AND BROTHER,—Enclosed with this circular you will find your Commission as District Deputy Grand Master for the year on which we have recently entered.   Will you kindly acquaint yourself with the duties, powers, and responsibilities connected with the office ?

You have been recommended for this position by those who have confidence in your loyalty, ability, and fitness for it.

In the discharge of your duties be true to the vows you have taken and the principles you have espoused.   Deal fearlessly and impartially in all questions and disputes that may be referred to you.

It will be your duty to see that the laws of the Order are pro-perly enforced and observed, and that all things in connection with Lodge management are done decently and in order.

It is of the utmost importance that the unwritten work should be correctly given ; in visiting the various Lodges under your care, let the work be exemplified on each occasion.

I must depend very largely upon you for information regard-ing the work in your District, hence you will see the necessity of rendering to me at the close of each term a full report of the District and of your official acts.

My earnest hope is that peace and harmony may prevail, not only in your District but throughout the entire jurisdiction, and that the year may be one of very great prosperity.

I remain,

Yours fraternally,

T. W. JOLLIFFE, *Grand Master.*

OFFICE OF THE GRAND MASTER,

TORONTO, OCTOBER 10th, 1892.

*To the Subordinate Lodges and all whom it may concern, greeting :—*

The attention of Subordinate Lodges and all members thereof throughout this Jurisdiction is hereby called to the following provisions in the laws of the Sovereign Grand Lodge relating to Insurance organizations which purport to be Odd Fellows' Associations :—

(1) " This Grand Body will not permit any organization, member, or association of members ; individual, or association of individuals, to use the name, initials, title, emblems or mot· toes of the Order in the prosecution of any scheme of insurance among the members of the Order, or otherwise, nor to solicit membership in any Lodge, Encampment, or other organization of our Order, unless such organization or association shall first submit its form of organization and manner of doing business in detail to the Grand Lodge of the State, district or territory in which it is located and in which it purposes to solicit membership, and make an annual report to such Grand Lodge, and obtain its annual permit so to do."—1890 Journal, 12, 251.

(2) " Each Grand Lodge shall annually send notice, either in its published proceedings or otherwise, to each Subordinate Lodge in its Jurisdiction to what organization or organizations it has granted permit, and shall see that no others solicit membership within its territorial limits, or use the name, initials, title, emblems or mottoes of the Order in connection with any Insurance scheme—provided said permit shall not be construed as an endorsement of such associations."—1890 Journal, 12, 251.

(3) " No member of the Order shall, either directly or indirectly use or sanction the use of any of the emblems, the name or any of the titles, or the mottoes or the initials thereof of this Order, in the prosecution of any private business or enterprise.
*   *   *   *   *   Any member of the Order, or officer of a Lodge or Encampment who shall be guilty of the offence defined and set forth as above shall be considered guilty of a fraud upon the Order, and shall be suspended or expelled from membership at the option of his Lodge or Encampment."—1889 Digest, Sec. 381.

(4) " Unless an association has the sanction of a State Grand Body, as provided by law, it is illegal for it to do business as an insurance company under the name of the Order, and the ' Odd Fellows' National Benevolent Association ' is such an illegal association unless authorized as above.  The business transacted by that or any similar association is a ' private business or enterprise ' within last above section.  Any member of the Order engaged in any such business is liable to charges and expulsion."—Digest, 1889, Sec. 382.

The Odd Fellows' Funeral Aid Association of the Counties of Lincoln and Welland and the Mutual Aid Association of London, Ontario, have been granted permission by the Grand Lodge to transact business in accordance with their several applications in their own localities.

You are, however, hereby notified that the only insurance organization which has complied with the foregoing requirements of the Sovereign Grand Lodge, and thus is permitted to use the name, emblems or mottoes of the Order in any way in this Jurisdiction, is the " Odd Fellows' Relief Association of Canada :"  Head office, Kingston.  Any other insurance organization using the name or emblems of the Order in any way does so illegally, and the agents or promoters thereof render themselves liable to the penalties above set forth.

ATTEST :                      Fraternally,

J. B. KING,                         T. W. JOLLIFFE,
*Grand Secretary.*                        *Grand Master.*

---

APPENDIX C.

OFFICE OF THE GRAND MASTER.

*To the Officers and Members of the Subordinate Lodges of the Independent Order of Odd Fellows, Province of Ontario, and to all whom it may concern :*

In accordance with the usual custom and in pursuance of the resolution of the Sovereign Grand Lodge, I, THOMAS WALTON JOLLIFFE, Grand Master, by authority vested in me, do hereby enjoin upon all Subordinate Lodges in this Jurisdiction to take appropriate action for the due commemoration of the 26th day of April, 1893, the Seventy-Fourth Anniversary of our Order, by suitable exercises in observance of the day, and by public thanks-

giving to Almighty God for His manifold mercies to us individ-
ually and collectively.

Done in the town of Bowmanville, Province of Ontario, Canada, this eighth day of March, Anno Domini, eighteen hundred
and ninety-three, and of the Order the seventy-fourth year.

ATTEST :

J. B. KING,                        T. WALTON JOLLIFFE,
    *Grand Secretary.*                         *Grand Master.*

---

APPENDIX D.

TORONTO, JAN. 30th, 1893.

*Rev. T. W. Jolliffe,*

*Grand Master, I.O.O.F.,*

*Bowmanville, Ont.*

DEAR SIR AND BRO.—In accordance with your instructions I
visited Tottenham last Wednesday, and found that the Lodge
there was in a very bad shape, in fact there is no Lodge there.
There are some nine or ten members who still hold a nominal
connection, but have paid no dues for about a year, and are all
in a bad standing. After consulting with them I came to the
conclusion that the best thing they could do would be to dispose
of sufficient of their assets, pay their dues, and pay the debts in
connection with the Lodge, and then try and amalgamate with
Alliston Lodge. I have asked the Grand Secretary, J. B. King,
to write them in regard to the amalgamation and wait their reply to our enquiries.

Trusting that I have done what will meet your approval, believe me to remain, dear sir,

Yours fraternally,

JOSEPH OLIVER,
    *Deputy Grand Master.*

Appendix E.

Clinton, May 22, 1893.

*Rev. T. W. Jolliffe, Grand Master I.O.O.F.*

Dear Sir and Brother,—At the last meeting of our Lodge, a motion was made and carried by members then present, that I write you asking your aid and advice in regard to the position in which we stand as a Lodge of Odd Fellows, and I will put the case plainly before you and hope and trust that you will give us your valuable assistance in the matter. We are very near a defunct Lodge. Our bank account on April 17th last, was $68.49, and our last Members' Return gave 24, on the 31st of December, 1892 ; but I fear by the end of June that 18 will be our number. You may say, take heart yet Brother, but I am afraid it is no use. One of our Brothers is laid up out in Littletin, Col. ; he has been on our hands for the past year, and now I fear he is nearly gone (poor fellow), and by the time we pay his benefits, which are, funeral benefits $30.00, and $70.00 death benefits, we would be done. We have good furniture and an organ. I would ask you, would it be right for us (the Lodge) to sell them to pay the benefits ? Now, as to our chance for cutting down expenses, I don't think there is much room. We pay $50.00 a year rent and we re-let to the I.O.G.T. for $50.00 a year, but we have to find light, fuel and the care-taking, for which we pay about $25.00 a year ; so you see we run it about as cheap as can be. We have not had a new member for over a year, and in fact none of us have heart to take anyone up, the way things are. It is a hard job for us to get a meeting now ; we have only had seven meetings this year ; very often we go up and can only muster four Brothers. Hoping that you will write us advice on the matter,

I remain,

Yours fraternally,

F. C. Alcock,

Clinton Lodge, No. 83, I.O.O.F.         *Recording Secretary.*

---

Appendix F.

Hensall, May 25, 1893.

*T. W. Jolliffe, G.M., I.O.O.F.*

Dear Sir and Brother,—I received yours of May 12th, and visited Fidelity, No. 55, on Saturday, May 20th, as Wednesday, their regular meeting night, was the 24th, and we thought it well not to go then. I investigated the matter as well as possible under the circumstances. As there were no charges and we had no witnesses to fall back on, we had to take their word for it, but as a good many of the members are good responsible men, with whom I have been acquainted for some time, and whose word is reliable, I have no doubt their story is correct ; and I am happy to tell you there is no evidence to support the report. The present membership of the Lodge is seventeen, of these, nine live in Seaforth, or vicinity ; the rest are scattered all over the country. Of the nine in Seaforth, two never attend the Lodge meeting, so that the whole work of carrying on the Lodge devolves on seven members. They deny that they ever refused any candidate that was worth accepting ; in fact, since the membership dwindled down to the present number they have not refused anyone. They have also in the past used every reasonable effort to get new members, as well as to reinstate any old members that may have fallen behind. With regard to the financial standing, the amount of cash in the treasury at end of last term was one hundred and two dollars. Some years ago, when they had a good membership, they bought a piece of ground and built a fine hall, with a store underneath and hall above, but there has been a mortgage on this property all along, which is not paid off yet. All the money they could save after paying running expenses and benefits has been applied to this. Their expenses are large ; the interest and insurance last year was fifty-four dollars, more than half their membership fees. They spent on repairing the roof of the building, etc., four hundred and fifty-one dollars, last year, and have been spending every year a considerable sum on repairs. As you might expect, the most of the members who have stuck to the Lodge are advanced in years and they have to pay a good deal in benefits. They have one old man, now seventy-two years of age, to whom they have been paying three dollars a week, and expect to pay it as long as he lives. So after all, when they take their expenses out of the rent and dues, there is not so very much left for paying off the mortgage. As to the reason why they do not get in more members, they claim that it is due to so many other new societies starting up, giving cheap insurance, and to the widows' benefits being done away with. Their meetings are held weekly. When they can get enough members present to open they do so, but it often happens that there are not enough there. They say that they are determined to hold on as long as they can in hopes that things may take a change and that they may be able to get in more members, and I do not see what more can be done under present circumstances. If there is any other information I can give or other service which can be done, I will be glad to do it.

Yours in F.L T.,

J. MACDIARMID,

*District Deputy Grand Master.*

Office of the Grand Master, Acting.

Toronto, June 15, 1893.

To——————D.D.G.M., District No.——.

My Dear Sir and Brother,—Herewith you will find the P. W. in cipher for the incoming term. Before you install the officers of the Lodges in your District or communicate the term P.W. you will please be assured that the return and Capita Tax have been sent to the Grand Secretary.

The large increase in membership has necessarily increased the work in the Grand Secretary's office, and as the Grand Lodge books must be closed not later than the 20th July, under Grand Lodge By-law 64, you will see the urgent need of each Lodge being prompt, in order that his report may be full and complete. I trust you will impress this upon each Lodge in your District.

I am gratified beyond measure to learn that the prospects indicate that the past term has been a most prosperous one, and no doubt you are justly entitled to a share of the glory that successful work is sure to bring.

You will kindly send to the Grand Master a full report of your official acts during the year past, and with it such suggestions as your interest in the Order and your experience during the year will warrant, looking to the perfecting of our Order in its every part. The Grand Master must depend very largely on his deputies for information as to the necessities and requirements of the Order in their several Districts. He depends on you. Be prompt and full in your report.

Kindly see that the minutes of the District Meeting are promptly sent in so that the new District Deputies may be appointed and assume their duties as early in the fiscal year as possible.

The Grand Secretary has sent blank forms to each Lodge. When you write your Lodges, urge on them to have everything in readiness for you to install their officers on the first meeting night in July. A little sacrifice on your part at this time will demonstrate the wisdom of your selection to so important an office as District Deputy Grand Master.

Hoping to hear from you promptly and fully,

I am,

Fraternally yours,

Joseph Oliver,
*Acting Grand Master*

P.S.—The Grand Master being engaged in his ministerial duties, I am but assisting him until he gets settled in his new field of labour.    You will please send your report, after this month, direct to Rev. T. W. Jolliffe, Grand Master, Campbellford.

## APPENDIX H.

TORONTO, JULY 17, 1893.

*Rev. T. W. Jolliffe, Grand Master I.O.O.F.,*

*Campbellford, Ont.*

DEAR SIR AND BRO.,—I enclose you herewith a report received from Brother Blackeby, who I instructed to go to Seaforth and Clinton.    You can see what he says in regard to these Lodges, and in the meantime I do not see that anything can be done.

Yours fraternally,

JOSEPH OLIVER.

## APPENDIX I.

*Joseph Oliver, Esq., Acting Grand Master I.O.O.F.,*

*Toronto, Ont.*

DEAR SIR AND BRO.,—The mission entrusted to me by you of enquiring into the position and prospects of Seaforth and Clinton Lodges was duly entered upon, and in pursuance thereof I fixed, after some correspondence, the 28th of June as the date of my visit to Seaforth, and the 11th of July to Clinton. Accordingly, on the 28th ult. I visited Fidelity Lodge, Seaforth. Six of their own members were present at the meeting and one visiting Brother from Stratford. · The number of members residing within reaching distance of the Lodge is eight, and the total membership seventeen.    The Lodge is in a good financial position, owning property to the value of about $5,000.    Regarding the stories that have been circulated, to the effect that the members of this Lodge do not desire to admit new members, I found no evidence whatever.    In my opinion the Lodge is slowly dying

4

of sheer inanition. Of the Brothers present at the meeting all belonged to some other society, most of them to two or three, and I regret to say that their activity in society matters seemed to be all utilized in the upbuilding of these other organizations. As a natural consequence Oddfellowship languishes. After acquainting myself with the position of affairs, I addressed the Brothers at some length, pointing out that it was only by well applied efforts on the part of the membership that our Order had acquired its present commanding position ; that no Lodge was ever made to flourish by any series of fortuitous circumstances ; that other Lodges in their own section of country, not so fortunately placed as Fidelity Lodge, were growing and prosper-ous, because their members believed in and worked for Oddfellow-ship ; that no Lodge could expect to flourish which did not contain at least a leaven of members who were Odd Fellows first, last, and all the time ; and in conclusion pointed out to them instances of other Lodges which had been reinvigorated by laying hold of the means ready at their hands for creating a renewed interest in the work of our Order.

Some of the Brothers promised that they would go to Strat-ford to see the dramatized floor work as rendered by the excellent team of Romeo Lodge, and the N. G. also promised to consider the possibility of getting up an " at home " in their Lodge-room, to which invitations should be issued to eligible candidates, and at which an address on the work of the Order should be given by some qualified Brother. I would recommend that Romeo Lodge be communicated with, and if possible their team be secured for a visit to Seaforth. By showing the Brothers there how beautiful and how impressive the work of the Subordinate Lodges can be made it would be, I think, the best way of im-parting a measure of energy and enthusiasm, which they at present so sadly lack, and which the Stratford brethren possess in abundance.

At Clinton, on July 11th, I found six Brothers present. There is here a financial difficulty to face. The Lodge has, practically, no funds and has one member in receipt of continu-ous benefits. There was very serious consideration being given to abandoning the ship. After addressing the Brothers for a short time they agreed to make one more effort to sail their craft into smooth water. I ascertained that there was a fairly good prospect of getting back some of their lapsed members, and on my advice they passed a resolution agreeing to take back lapsed members on payment of one year's dues, provided such members were not over 40 years of age and could pass a satisfactory medical examination. There was also the prospect of getting in one or two new candidates.   All the Clinton brethren seem to need is a little more faith in the Order and in their own ability to work out of their present difficulties.   Here again a good work can be done by a flourishing Lodge in a neighbouring town.   If the team of Huron Lodge will undertake —as I have no doubt they cheerfully will—to go to Clinton and put in one good night's work, they will undoubtedly be the means of putting some much needed animation into the Clinton Lodge.   I feel quite sure that you have but to call the attention of our enthusiastic Brother C. A. Nairn, team-captain of Huron Lodge, to this matter to enlist his hearty sympathy in such a worthy missionary work.

Trusting and believing that some good will be accomplished by my visit to these two Lodges,

I have the honour to be,

Yours fraternally,

A. H. BLACKEBY.

GALT, July 17th, 1893.

APPENDIX J.

REPORT OF GRAND REPRESENTATIVES *re* REBEKAHS.

The following Report has been received from the Grand Representatives :—

*To the Grand Master and the Grand Lodge of Ontario, I.O.O.F.*

Your Grand Representatives beg leave to present the following report:—

In accordance with the instructions of the Grand Lodge as found on page 5331 of the Journal of 1892, your Grand Representatives submitted certain questions to the Grand Sire, Bro. Cl.T.Campbell, and obtained from him the following decisions:—

1. The Provincial Convention of the Rebekah Degree of Ontario has not power to impose a tax on Rebekah Lodges in Ontario for any purpose.

2. The Grand Lodge of Ontario has no power to authorize said Convention to impose such tax.

3. The Grand Lodge of Ontario has power to impose such tax itself and to collect the same and to pay the proceeds over to the Provincial Convention.

The latter decision is based upon the legislation of the Sovereign Grand Lodge in 1890, as found on page 12295 of the Revised Journal of that year, as follows :—

"Resolved,—That the Grand Lodges of the various jurisdictions may, for the purpose of defraying the expenses of Rebekah State Conventions, levy a *per capita* tax upon Subordinate Lodges of the Degree of Rebekah within their respective jurisdictions, and disburse the money received therefrom for the purpose indicated, and in such manner as such Grand Lodge shall determine."

All which is fraternally submitted.

W. H. COLE,

HY. ROBERTSON,

*Grand Representatives.*

The Grand Secretary, Bro. J. B. King, presented the following report and statistics, which were referred to the Committee on Distribution :—

## GRAND SECRETARY'S REPORT.

NIAGARA FALLS, AUG. 9, 1893.

*To the Grand Lodge of Ontario, I.O.O.F.:*

Another year has passed since many of us, with fond good-byes parted at the close of the session of 1892, hoping to meet near old Niagara's cataract a year later. To very many the hope has been gratified, though to some that pleasure has been denied. Some of our brave workers have been summoned home to give an account of their stewardship ; others are by sickness laid aside—temporarily, let us hope ; while doubtless many are wondering why the fickle ballot ignored their fond hopes. To one and all—old and new—a most cordial greeting is given.

The record of the past year has been made, and it is for those of the present to profit by its experience, and so direct our efforts

in the future that continual and lasting prosperity will attend
the Order.

Clause 1.—When our forefathers laid the foundation of Oddfellowship, they little dreamed that it would so soon develop
into the grand proportions it has assumed and become one of
the noblest benefit societies the world has seen, whose benefac-
tions have been the marvel of the age, amounting in the aggregate to millions of dollars; nor that the result of their fore-
thought would be so extensively copied as it has been, until
to-day hardly a new society exists that has not its principal features copied from Oddfellowship. It is our duty and privilege
to extend this influence of the Order, nor be satisfied until in its
ramifications it covers our happy Dominion from shore to shore;
and thus prove ourselves "worthy sons of worthy sires."

In view of this, it appears that the time has now arrived for
this Grand Lodge to provide a substitute for the widows' annuities,
which for so many years were a distinctive feature of the Order
in Ontario, and which was, no doubt wisely, withdrawn; though
the act of the Grand Lodge has not in every case been as loyally
accepted as it should have been, and thus set at rest forever the
vexed question of widows' annuities.

As the ages of Lodges and members increase, the demand for
funeral benefits and benefits for protracted sickness will un-
doubtfully increase. To provide for these, and in the language
of our Ritual "have the strong assist the weak," each Lodge, at
a merely nominal cost per member, may provide for the payment
promptly on the death of a Brother, of one hundred or one hundred and fifty dollars (quite enough for present needs), and also
for the payment of stated benefits to the chronic sick and aged
members, and instead of Lodges promising to pay $250 to
$350 on each death, which at times has seriously crippled some
good Lodges, the payment of the sum named would come out of a
general funeral benefit fund, and would not be felt by any. If at
any time of life a benefit is a necessity it is when a Brother has
been laid aside from earning his daily wage for a year; then,
if possible, the benefit should be increased, not lessened. Most
provident men could easily withstand a few weeks' sickness
without calling for benefits, if it was necessary, but few Odd
Fellows could hold out two or more years without feeling the
great deprivation and entailing severe hardship on wife and loved
ones; or when old age takes away the ability to earn the daily
wage, then Oddfellowship should come in and to a great extent bear, or at least help to bear, the burden—the many helping
the few. This could all be done and the dues of the members
of the Lodges not increased, but a trifle, if any. The amount
hitherto placed to the credit of the Widows' and Orphans' Fund

would be amply sufficient, if funded ; the possibility of the failure of any Lodge to meet the demands upon it for these purposes would be done away with, and the Order in Ontario strengthened almost beyond calculation ; and now that prosperity has been so marked, everything that can add to our efficiency must be looked into. I have received through the kindness of Bro. Jas. B. Nicholson, Grand Secretary of Pennsylvania, copies of the laws recently adopted by that State on this question, which are herewith submitted. By looking well to the financial and beneficial features of the Order, and thus making it an absolutely safe and desirable system of relief and benefits, need not in any sense diminish our present happy social features.

Though money is not the only essential for happiness and success, yet it is a very important feature in both, and added to perfect social society, a perfect and wise benefit system, we strengthen the ties that bind the Order together.

Clause 2.—The several duties devolving upon the Grand Secretary have been performed as promptly as possible. The work of the office has greatly increased with the increase of Lodges and membership, yet every letter has been promptly answered and every order for supplies promptly filled, though to do so assistance to a greater extent than ordered by the Grand Lodge had to be secured. During the months of August, December, January, June and July, it is impossible for one to do all the work of the office, compiling returns, conducting correspondence, preparing tables, etc. As I believe much of our prosperity is due to the prompt issuing of information to the Lodges, I ask that the course I have adopted in sending out circulars and statistical information be approved by the Grand Lodge. The statistical information issued in January is made as complete as possible, as it is really the report of the fiscal year's work as submitted to the Sovereign Grand Lodge.

Clause 3.—The Receipts and Expenditures of the past year have been as follows. The balance of the year's transactions is slightly on the wrong side, but that is accounted for by the very large increase in mileage at Windsor last year, but for which a gain of $2,000 would have been recorded :

RECEIPTS.

| | | |
|---|---:|---:|
| Capita Tax | $10,178 | 53 |
| Charters | 260 | 00 |
| Supplies | 1,793 | 93 |
| Interest, Wellington Square Lodge | 49 | 12 |
| "        Grand Lodge | 96 | 63 |
| Grand Lodge Cards | 3 | 00 |
| Rebekah Tax | 236 | 65 |
| Rubber Stamps | 40 | 55 |
| Odd Fellows' Relief Association | 10 | 00 |
| | $12,668 | 41 |

EXPENDITURE.

| | | |
|---|---:|---:|
| Paid for supplies ......... ..................... | $1,551 | 11 |
| Printing and Stationery................,....... | 1,178 | 50 |
| Salaries .................................... | 1,700 | 00 |
| Office expenses.................................. | 618 | 06 |
| Mileage and per diem, 1892 ..................... | 6,221 | 60 |
| Postage...................................... | 284 | 95 |
| Rebekah Convention Tax ...................... | 240 | 70 |
| General expenses............................. | 427 | 03 |
| Grand Master................................ | 199 | 55 |
| Law Costs......................... ........... | 8 | 00 |
| Insurance and Guarantee Bonds................. | 51 | 55 |
| Sovereign Grand Lodge Tax..................... | 150 | 00 |
| Special Committees.............................. | 71 | 90 |
| Charter Fee refunded Dauncy Lodge............. | 30 | 00 |
| Printing Charters ................................ | 9 | 70 |
| Ontario Government Registration Fee ............. | 50 | 00 |
| | 12,792 | 65 |
| Excess of Cash paid out ........................... | $124 | 24 |

Clause 4.—As directed by the adoption of the report of the
Committee on Finance, one thousand copies of the Journal of
Proceeding of 1892 were printed and distributed as directed.
There have been many letters received expressing satisfaction
at the departure of having the Journal bound in cloth, as they
were last year.  The fact that the Journals are now books, and
likely to be preserved and read, justifies the additional expense
of binding and postage in issuing.

Clause 5.—Early in the year I made up the table of mileage
to Niagara Falls, and notified each Lodge and Grand Officer by
Circular the distance arrived at, which was taken from the latest
and best railroad time tables ; but two Lodges claimed an error,
and these were duly corrected.  I would suggest that in every
case, where a Lodge fails to notify the Grand Secretary to the
contrary, that the mileage made out by him be considered fixed,
and no change made at Grand Lodge.  Much valuable time
would in this way be saved, as the mileage report could be
adopted at an early stage of the session.

Clause 6.—The very satisfactory arrangement of a single
fare for the round trip has again been made with the several
railroads and steamboat companies, and the Lodges duly informed by circular of the same.

Clause 7.—As required by the election laws, the several
forms were duly prepared and sent to the Lodges.  220 Lodges
have sent in their " Election Returns," in proper form,
registered.  27 Lodges have not sent them in at all ; while

some' Lodges, with seeming perfect indifference, have sent them in in the first envelope that came handy, though the properly addressed envelope must have been at their hand.

Clause 8.—The returns of the past two terms have been received with more than ordinary promptness and bear evidence, that for the most part, greater care than usual has been exercised in their preparation. We are making history that will be valuable as it is perfect, therefore too great care cannot be exercised in making out these returns. The past half-year has been one of far more than ordinary activity amongst the Lodges, which simply gives evidence of what a determined effort will produce. The Lodges and members at the beginning of the year set out to accomplish a certain object, viz: to greet our Grand Sire, Dr. Campbell, at this session with a roster of over 20,000 members. That their effort has been successful, and the desired point easily passed, should encourage every member of every Lodge, knowing that he is advancing the interests of the best fraternal organization in existence and advancing the great cause of humanity, to start out this year with the determination to do his utmost to make this year as the past, only much better, and close our Grand Sire's term of office with 23,000. It can be done. The same energy and zeal continued that has made the past year so bright with good works and noble deeds will make future years equally brilliant.

Clause 9.—On April 1st, 1893, a petition was received from Bro. R. Meek, Secretary Odd Fellows' Relief Association, accompanied with ten dollars, asking for a certificate from the Grand Lodge under the eleventh resolution of the Report of the Committee on Insurance (Journal 1892, page 13083); that the Association had complied with all the laws of the Province and of the Order. The laws all having been complied with, the certificate was duly issued.

The Grand Sire having decided that the several county associations, which pay a sum according to membership, on the death of a member, being purely local associations, did not come under the laws respecting Insurance Associations. Those doing business in London and in the counties of Lincoln and Welland have not been required to take out certificates, but have been permitted to continue business as hitherto, making annual reports to the Grand Lodge, which reports are appended hereto.

There is no doubt but that these Insurance Associations, more particularly the Relief Association of Canada, have contributed in no small degree to the prosperity which has attended the Order in Ontario during the past year, and they should be encouraged in every possible way by the Grand

Lodge and be patronized by every Odd Fellow who can secure a certificate in them. The Report of the Odd Fellows' Relief Association hereto attached shows that Association to be one of the best in connection with the Order and worthy the consideration of every Brother who desires insurance. If that Association was patronized by members of the Order, generally, as it should be, the desire so often expressed of making the Order an Insurance Society would be heard no more, as the Brotherhood, as a rule, would be enabled to have all the insurance they could carry, $2,000, and at a rate as low, or lower than if the Association was conducted by the Order.

Clause 10.—On March 31st, 1893, upon receipt of a formal request from the Trustees of Wellington Square, accompanied by a certificate over the seal of the Lodge, that the Trustees were duly elected and authorized to receive the same, the funds of that Lodge. with accumulated interest, amounting in all to $2,154.64, were, by direction of the Grand Master, restored to the Lodge, and the receipt thereof has been duly acknowledged.

Clause 11.—The Register of Past Grands has been completed so far as it could be from the returns received. Many Lodges have neglected to send in their list of Past Grands. An effort will be made during the coming year to have the Register completed.

Clause 12.—In order that the proper provision may be made for the collection of the Rebekah tax, I would recommend that in accordance with the report of the Grand Representatives, referred to by the Grand Master in his report, that Grand Lodge By-law No. 97 be amended by adding to the Clause the words, " Save for the purpose of defraying the expenses of the Rebekah Provincial Convention."

Clause 13.—There is a great desirability for a more easy and less expensive mode of transferring membership from one Lodge to another. If we would retain the many members who from time to time leave their home and mother Lodge to locate in another locality, and who, missing their accustomed Lodge, might soon drift away and are lost to the Order. Many, very many, could be kept as members, if they could more easily join the Lodge where they are called on to reside, either by a dual membership, or by the Lodge which has for years had the benefit of their dues, advice and labour, assisting them to join another Lodge. The subject is worthy of special attention at this time when our desire is so great to extend our usefulness by getting new members and by retaining those we have.

Clause 14.—There is a matter of importance that was inadvertently overlooked at the last two Sessions of the Grand Lodge that should have its full consideration this year. Bro. Jno. Ormiston, of Gananoque Lodge, served a portion of a year as Grand Master. Prior to his resignation of that office he had been to some expense in the ordinary discharge of his duties. At the time I asked him for a statement of expenses incurred, but owing to the destruction of his office and part of its contents by fire the record had been destroyed. Through an inadvertent omission your Grand Secretary neglected to refer to the fact in his report and the matter was entirely overlooked. I would recommend that the Finance Committee be instructed to ascertain the expenses of Bro. Ormiston and report on the same, that they may be paid, and tardy justice done the Brother.

In this connection, it is a well-known fact that Bro. Ormiston has been for years a zealous member of this Grand Lodge, and has also done very much to advance the interests of his own Lodge, and of the Order in general, more particularly in the Eastern Section of the Province. The causes which led to his resignation were evidently such as he had little or no control over ; therefore, I would respectfully recommend that the Representatives of this Grand Lodge in the Sovereign Grand Lodge be directed to request that this Grand Lodge be authorized to recognize his services and that the title of Past Grand Master be given to Bro. Ormiston, no such title having been given for the year in which he served the Grand Lodge.

Clause 15.—During the year past, twelve Veteran Jewels have been issued to the following Lodges, as per certificates fyled :

```
1892.                                                             No.
August  6....Victoria Lodge, No  64.....Jno. Kerner..................36
   "    26....Union Lodge, No. 16.......Adam Purves, P.G.P..........37
   "    26....    "              "      .......J. B. McIntyre, P.G.M.......38
Dec'r. 16....Unity Lodge, No. 47...... Wm. Amor, P.G...............39
   "    23....Brock Lodge, No. 9.......................................40
   "    24....Valley City Lodge, No. 117.George Lees..................41
   "    31....Samaritan Lodge, No 35...S. Schofield .........    ......42
1893.
Jan'y.  13....Excelsior Lodge, No. 44....William King................43
   "    13....     "              "    ....James Perrin................44
   "    13....     "              "    ....R. C. Cooper................45
   "    13.. .     "              "    ....Henry Griffith...............46
   "    13....     "              "    ....J. H. Carmichael ............47
```

Clause 16.—The financial affairs of late Mystic Lodge, No. 128, Waterdown, have been finally wound up by Bro. Geo. Ross, Special Deputy, by the sale of the furniture of the Lodge for

$25.00, which amount has been received and placed to the credit
of the defunct Lodge.   The sum of $50, recommended by Bro.
Ross in his report last  year to be paid to the widow of the late
Bro. Stock, of Waterdown, can now be paid, and I would recommend that it be at once paid to the said widow.

Clause 17.—The following appeals have been received and are
herewith presented :

A. R. Rowland, Whitby, vs. Eastern Star Lodge No. 72.
Ridgely Lodge, No. 250, v. Aylmer Lodge, No. 94.
Garnet Lodge, No. 139, on behalf of the wife and family of
Robert Hassard, vs. Teeswater Lodge, No, 183.
R. Ronan, P.G., Ottawa, vs. the Grand Master and D.D.
G.M.
A. R. Rowland vs. District Committee.

Clause 18.—There is often great difficulty experienced, by
Lodges in getting a proper and safe report, and claim for sick
benefits, by non-resident members.  Bro. Chas. Packert has
prepared a form of application for benefits, which it would be
well for the Lodges in general to adopt.  The form has been
kindly supplied by Bro. Packert, who would no doubt consent
to its general adoption.

Clause 19.—The Rebekah branch here has in the past been
seriously handicapped for want of a Constitution.  In view of this
I have prepared, and herewith submit for the consideration of the
Grand Lodge, a Constitution for Rebekah Lodges, compiled from
the best available laws ; and with the object in view of strengthen-
ing and benefiting this branch of the Order, I would respectfully
recommend that the Constitution as it shall be adopted by the
Grand Lodge be spread upon the Journal of Proceedings of this
year, and that the Committee of General Purposes be instructed
to have it reprinted in suitable size and form, and that each
Rebekah Lodge be supplied free by the Grand Lodge, with a
sufficient number to give to each member a copy, and that new
Rebekah Lodges, when instituted, be given a supply.
I would further respectfully recommend  that all old Lodges,
which have not already adopted a code of by-laws, as well as  all
new Lodges  hereafter instituted, be required to adopt and have
printed within three months, a code of by-laws, rules of order,
etc.
It is necessary that the Grand Lodge should define the duties
of officers of the Rebekah Convention more clearly than they are
at present, so that conflict of authority between the officers of
the Grand Lodge and those of the Convention may be avoided.

In all matters pertaining to the institution of new Rebekah Lodges, returns communicating pass words and instructions *re* installations, and instructions to District Deputies, your Grand Secretary has dealt directly with the Lodges ; the laws of the Order. stating that these Lodges stand in the same relation to the Grand Lodges as Subordinate Lodges do.

Sister Mrs. Maggie Waddell, Secretary of the Provincial Convention, has proved herself to be an enthusiastic and zealous officer, a fact I have much pleasure in bearing testimony of.

During the past year, ten new Rebekah Lodges have been instituted. Books were supplied to each at the same rates as to Subordinate Lodges. There has been unusual activity in this branch of the Order, the result will doubtless be a great and lasting benefit to Oddfellowship.

It would be wise to make provision for the resusitation of those Rebekah Lodges which held charters prior to the legislation now governing the Rebekahs, as doubtless ere long many of these Lodges will desire to resume work.

The work and present standing of the Rebekahs will be seen from the accompanying abstract, from the semi-annual returns of the Lodges, which cannot but be of much interest to our Sisters as to all Brothers who admire their work.

The standing of the Rebekah Lodges on December 31st is shown in the accompanying Report submitted to the Sovereign Grand Lodge. As most of the new Rebekah Lodges instituted this year were instituted subsequent to January 1st they do not appear in that Report.

During the year ten new Lodges have been instituted, each under the most favourable auspices, the membership on June 30 being 1446, an increase since last we met of 450.

ABSTRACT FROM RETURNS OF REBEKAH LODGES FOR YEAR ENDING 31st DECEMBER, 1892.

| Name. | No. | Location. | Admitted. | | Died. | | Ceased. | | Members per last Report. | | | Present Member-ship. | | | Relief. | Expenses. | Receipts. | Assets Last Report. | Present Assets. | Tax Year. |
|---|---|---|---|---|---|---|---|---|---|---|---|---|---|---|---|---|---|---|---|---|
| | | | Bros. | Sisters. | Bros. | Sisters. | Bros. | Sisters. | Bros. | Sisters. | Total. | Bros. | Sisters. | Total. | $ c. | $ c. | $ c. | $ c. | $ c. | $ c. |
| Victoria | 1 | London | 3 | 10 | 2 | | | 1 | | | | 1 | 9 | 10 | 10 00 | 11 58 | 64 80 | | 43 22 | 2 20 |
| Oshawa | 3 | Oshawa | | | | | | 20 | 7 | 41 | 48 | 7 | 21 | 28 | | 60 26 | 37 81 | 224 91 | 202 46 | 6 10 |
| May Queen | 5 | London E. | | 9 | | | 17 | 49 | 24 | 65 | 89 | | 25 | 32 | 18 00 | 22 30 | 47 45 | 99 30 | 106 45 | 8 40 |
| Naomi | 6 | Windsor | 54 | 6 | 1 | | 9 | 15 | 28 | 65 | 93 | 72 | 56 | 128 | 13 00 | 217 83 | 217 53 | 755 70 | 742 40 | 20 40 |
| Louise | 10 | Kingston | 21 | 17 | | | 11 | 11 | 24 | 45 | 69 | 34 | 51 | 85 | | 77 63 | 121 64 | 152 38 | 196 39 | 16 50 |
| Beatrice | 12 | Guelph | 17 | 13 | | | 13 | 7 | 47 | 42 | 89 | 51 | 48 | 99 | | 192 58 | 83 05 | 219 64 | 110 11 | 18 60 |
| Jubilee | 13 | Chatham | 2 | 7 | | | 6 | 7 | 10 | 30 | 40 | 6 | 30 | 36 | | 48 25 | 58 05 | 71 00 | 80 80 | 6 70 |
| Edna | 14 | St. Thomas | 2 | 7 | | | 17 | 8 | 47 | 46 | 93 | 32 | 45 | 77 | 287 00 | 80 00 | 429 07 | 110 72 | 172 79 | 16 30 |
| Harmony | 15 | Gananoque | 12 | 11 | 1 | 1 | 31 | 11 | 101 | 93 | 194 | 81 | 92 | 173 | | 124 56 | 123 18 | 43 46 | 392 03 | 36 60 |
| Olive Branch | 16 | Toronto | 25 | 20 | 1 | 1 | 36 | 15 | 135 | 91 | 226 | 123 | 95 | 218 | | 271 59 | 203 90 | 421 32 | 352 90 | 42 10 |
| Myrtle | 17 | Elora | 3 | 1 | | | | | 11 | 15 | 26 | 14 | 16 | 30 | | | | 19 63 | 14 50 | 6 00 |
| Excelsior | 18 | Internat'al Bridge | 9 | 17 | | | 1 | | 17 | 17 | 29 | 20 | 34 | 54 | | 191 84 | 223 36 | 1 80 | 33 32 | 10 00 |
| Mizpah | 19 | Collingwood | 26 | 16 | | | | | | | | 26 | 16 | 42 | | 42 29 | 72 33 | | 30 04 | 8 00 |
| Donalda | 20 | North Bay | 13 | 9 | | | | | | | | 13 | 9 | 22 | | | | | | 2 20 |
| Flora | 21 | Sault Ste. Marie | 11 | 8 | | | | | | | | 11 | 8 | 19 | | 59 75 | 64 20 | | 4 55 | 1 90 |
| Lucknow | 22 | Lucknow | 35 | 24 | | | | | | | | 35 | 24 | 59 | | 6 30 | 62 75 | | 56 45 | 5 90 |
| Inglewood | 23 | Waterford | 9 | 4 | | | | | | | | 9 | 4 | 13 | | | 13 00 | | 13 00 | 1 30 |
| Totals | | | 242 | 179 | 5 | 2 | 141 | 144 | 446 | 550 | 996 | 542 | 583 | 1125 | 328 00 | 1406 76 | 1822 12 | 2249 59 | 2551 46 | 209 20 |

Clause 20.—On June 16th, 1893, as required by the law, I renewed the Certificate of Registration with the Ontario Government to continue our work under the new Insurance Act, the fee of twenty-five dollars for such renewal being paid.

This Registration includes the Encampment Branch, the Rebekah Branch, the Odd Fellows' Funeral Aid Association of the counties of Lincoln and Welland, and the Odd Fellows' Mutual Aid Association of London, Ont.

Tables showing the work of the Associations named, as well as of the Odd Fellows' Relief Association, which being a purely insurance organization, reports to and receives authority from the Sovereign Grand Lodge, are hereto appended. The totals of the whole showing a grand financial result of work done by the Order in Ontario in the interests of humanity. I had hoped to be able to give the figures from each Province, so that the grand total expended by the Order in the Dominion of Canada might be seen at a glance, but in this I have been so far disappointed, though I expect to have it by another year.

In this connection I beg to say that through the courtesy and kindness of Bro. Will. J. Vale, Deputy Registrar of Friendly Societies for Ontario, I have obtained a list of all Lodges which have been incorporated under the laws of Ontario, principally under Chap. 137, R. S. O., under consent given by this Grand Lodge. The incorporation of these Lodges is legal under the present insurance laws, and I am of opinion that all Lodges not already incorporated should be required to incorporate at once, or within a given time, say by January 1st, 1894. They would then be, as without a doubt every Lodge should be, under the legal control of the Grand Lodge, and having a legal status they would be in a better and more safe position than they can other-wise be. The modus of incorporation (which must be done through this office) is extremely simple and inexpensive, the cost being but one dollar ; the form to be observed is given here-with, and the necessary copies will be sent to Lodges on application.

The following is a list of the Lodges now incorporated, with year of incorporation :—

| Lodge. | No. | Year. | Lodge. | No. | Year. |
|---|---|---|---|---|---|
| Otonabee | 13 | 1884 | Unity | 47 | 1879 |
| Phœnix | 22 | 1879 | Dominion | 48 | 1874 |
| Rose | 28 | 1883 | Otter | 50 | 1875 |
| Eureka | 30 | 1874 | Bessell | 51 | 1875 |
| Elgin | 32 | 1881 | Niagara Falls | 53 | 1882 |
| Samaritan | 35 | 1875 | Fidelity | 55 | 1874 |
| St. Mary's | 36 | 1881 | Queen City of Ontario | 56 | 1875 |
| Forest City | 38 | 1879 | Maple Leaf | 57 | 1888 |
| Mt. Zion | 46 | 1880 | Howard | 58 | 1875 |

| Lodge. | No. | Year. | Lodge. | No. | Year |
|---|---|---|---|---|---|
| Corinthian | 61 | 1879 | Pyramid | 156 | 1881 |
| Victoria | 64 | 1886 | Thamesville | 157 | 1881 |
| Hope | 69 | 1878 | Progress | 158 | 1878 |
| Fergus | 73 | 1880 | Oak Leaf | 159 | 1879 |
| Bothwell | 74 | 1880 | Listowel | 160 | 1877 |
| Warriner | 75 | 1877 | Oriental | 163 | 1881 |
| St. Thomas | 76 | 1876 | Romero | 164 | |
| Nipissing | 79 | 1877 | Beethoven | 165 | 1879 |
| Beaver | 82 | 1883 | Hillsburg | 167 | 1884 |
| Clinton | 83 | 1876 | Sutton | 168 | 1877 |
| Walkerton | 84 | 1880 | Grey | 169 | 1880 |
| Empire | 87 | 1879 | Penetangore | 172 | 1877 |
| Reliance | 89 | 1877 | Dolman | 174 | 1880 |
| Ivy | 90 | 1876 | Lorne * | 175 | 1880 |
| Grand River | 91 | 1875 | Montana | 177 | 1880 |
| Milton | 92 | 1880 | Owen Sound | 180 | 1881 |
| Aylmer | 94 | 1882 | Teeswater | 183 | 1880 |
| Port Stanley * | 95 | 1876 | Germania | 184 | 1880 |
| Nith | 96 | 1879 | Dufferin | 186 | 1881 |
| Grand Union | 97 | 1881 | Cambridge | 188 | 1880 |
| Golden Star | 101 | 1876 | Parry Sound | 189 | 1880 |
| Crescent | 104 | 1876 | Chorazin | 190 | 1879 |
| Waterloo | 107 | 1887 | Howick | 192 | 1880 |
| Royal Oak | 108 | 1879 | Victor * | 193 | 1878 |
| Laurel | 110 | 1876 | Albert | 194 | 1882 |
| Peterboro' | 111 | 1879 | Florence | 196 | 1880 |
| Harmony | 115 | 1875 | Weston | 200 | 1886 |
| Naomi | 116 | 1880 | Silver Star | 202 | 1880 |
| Valley City | 117 | 1875 | Pembroke | 203 | 1886 |
| Maitland | 119 | 1880 | Ahiram | 205 | 1880 |
| Sydenham Valley | 120 | 1877 | Silver City | 206 | 1879 |
| Saxon | 121 | 1877 | Egremont | 207 | 1879 |
| Palmerston * | 123 | 1877 | Argyll | 212 | 1880 |
| Dresden | 124 | 1879 | Clifford | 214 | 1880 |
| Sarnia | 126 | 1877 | Freestone | 215 | 1880 |
| Mystic * | 128 | 1886 | Elmira | 216 | 1888 |
| Livingston | 130 | 1877 | Mt. Brydges | 217 | 1885 |
| Marion | 131 | 1884 | Georgian Bay | 219 | 1882 |
| Oakville | 132 | 1878 | Woodslee | 220 | 1883 |
| Glencoe | 133 | 1880 | Chesley | 221 | 1887 |
| Peaceful Dove | 135 | 1877 | Hensall | 223 | 1886 |
| Ancaster | 138 | 1886 | Ottawa* | 224 | 1882 |
| Concord | 142 | 1880 | Merlin | 226 | 1884 |
| Bay of Quinte | 143 | 1880 | International | 228 | 1885 |
| Ridgetown | 144 | 1875 | Prince of Wales | 230 | 1884 |
| Riverside * | 145 | 1880 | Elora | 231 | 1887 |
| Vivian | 146 | 1883 | Ilderton | 234 | 1885 |
| Model | 147 | 1879 | Temple * | 238 | 1885 |
| Aurora | 148 | 1877 | Carleton | 240 | 1887 |
| Western Star | 149 | 1877 | Milton | 242 | 1886 |
| Sycamore * | 151 | 1875 | Port Arthur | 244 | 1888 |
| Hayden | 152 | 1880 | Ridgely | 250 | 1887 |
| Wildey | 153 | 1882 | Floral | 252 | 1888 |
| Alpha | 154 | 1879 | Gold Hill | 261 | 1891 |
| Brougham | 155 | 1880 | Lakeview | 272 | 1890 |

* Now Defunct.

PROVINCE OF ONTARIO.—INSURANCE CORPORATIONS' ACT, 1892.

## APPLICATION FOR INCORPORATION.

*No*........

TO THE REGISTRAR OF FRIENDLY SOCIETIES FOR ONTARIO,
　　　　　　　　Department of Insurance, Toronto, Canada.

The undersigned Applicant , holding the [office *or* respective offices, *as the case may be*] .....................hereinbelow, specified after [his *or* their, ............names, being to the said office duly [elected *or* appointed, *as the case may be*]..................in the Friendly Society known as the [*name of Society*]................................................ and acting and being authorized to act for and in behalf of the said Society, HEREBY MAKE APPLICATION pursuant to and in terms of the Insurance Corporations' Act, .892, (and amending Act ), FOR THE INCORPORATION of the [said Society, *or as the case may be*]..................... ........................under the name of the [*proposed corporate name*] ................................................................having its [*Head Office, or as the case may be*],.................at..................... in the Province of Ontario.

And the said Applicant , of [his *or* their]..........own knowledge, and having the means of knowing, further declare that *Exhibit A*, hereto annexed, truly sets forth the facts out of which the present Application has arisen ; also that *Exhibit B*, hereto annexed, is a true copy of the rules of the body proposed to be incorporated ; also that *Exhibit C*, hereto annexed, correctly sets out the names of the persons who are to be its first trustees or managing officers, and correctly states the mode in which their successors are to be elected.

| | |
|---|---|
| SWORN before me at the............ | [*Name*].............................. |
| in the County of................. | [*Office*]...................... |
| this........day of.............. | [*Name*]........................... |
| A.D. 189 | [*Office*]...................... |
| ............................... | [*Name*]...... ...................... |
| ............................... | [*Office*]...................... |

Clause 21.—All by-laws received from Lodges for approval have been at once sent to Bro. W. A. Rawlings, and as promptly returned by him. The work of the past year has been very arduous, as very nearly one hundred by-laws of Lodges and amendments have been reported on; yet there are not a few Lodges working under by-laws adopted years ago, now not at all in harmony with the Constitution as recently adopted. Lodges should see that it is for their interests to have their laws always corrected up to date. In this respect I think it would be a move in the right direction if the Constitution was supplied to Lodges by the Grand Lodge at the cost of printing them, Lodges to provide themselves with by-laws only. This would do away with a grievance Lodges so often express of being required to reprint their Constitution by-laws so frequently, and would possibly save many changes being made in the Constitution of Subordinates.

Clause 22.—I have great pleasure in again bearing testimony to the influence of the *Dominion Odd Fellow*, and regret that the Lodges do not more generally take advantage of its columns for their own benefit, by advertising their Lodge and night of meeting. A well-conducted newspaper like the *Dominion Odd Fellow*, if patronized as it should be, is of great advantage to the Order.

Clause 23.—The total expenditure of Ontario in all the various objects of insurance, benefits and relief, since 1856, has aggregated the immense sum of over one million dollars, to ascertain which I compiled the accompanying table from the Journal of the Grand Encampment to add to the other tables submitted :

| | |
|---|---:|
| By Subordinate Lodges in Benefits and Relief.............. | $836.988 34 |
| " Subordinate Encampments.... ..... ................. | 31,327 65 |
| " Odd Fellows'-Relief Association, Death Claims Paid..... | 297.737 00 |
| " Disability Claims Paid............................... | 2,900 00 |
| " Mutual Aid Association of London, Death Claims Paid.. | 558 50 |
| " Odd Fellows' Funeral Aid Association of Lincoln and Welland, Death Claims Paid....................... | 4.445 91 |
| " Rebekahs not tabulated yet .. ..................... | |
| Total.................................... | $1,173,957 40 |

One million one hundred and seventy-three thousand nine hundred and fifty-seven dollars and forty cents.

## RECORD OF BENEFITS AND RELIEF.

GRAND ENCAMPMENT OF ONTARIO—NO BENEFITS REPORTED UNTIL JUNE, 1878.

| YEAR. | Deaths. | Amount paid for Burying the dead | No. Sick. | Weeks Sick. | Amount Paid. | Widows. | Amount Paid. | Special Relief. | Total Benefit and Relief. |
|---|---|---|---|---|---|---|---|---|---|
| Prior to 1878 | 62 | | | | | | | | |
| For year ending June 30th, 1878 | 14 | $85 00 | 127 | 508 | $653 41 | 6 | $50 00 | $10 00 | $798 41 |
| "  "  "  1879 | 12 | 75 co | 119 | 540 | 704 38 | 6 | 43 00 | 35 00 | 857 38 |
| "  "  "  1880 | 15 | 160 00 | 152 | 754 | 875 90 | 6 | 30 00 | 79 60 | 1,145 50 |
| "  "  "  1881 | 11 | 155 00 | 133 | 631 | 796 32 | 7 | 35 00 | 74 50 | 1,060 82 |
| "  "  "  1882 | 16 | 145 00 | 142 | 753 | 1,013 34 | 8 | 40 00 | 46 20 | 1,244 54 |
| "  "  "  1883 | 15 | 176 85 | 247 | 845 | 1,085 03 | 5 | 50 00 | 159 50 | 1,471 48 |
| "  "  "  1884 | 13 | 235 00 | 196 | 1023 | 1,335 33 | 10 | 56 85 | 199 00 | 1,826 18 |
| For six months ending Dec. 1884 | 2 | 10 00 | 84 | 432 | 567 07 | 5 | 150 00 | 56 80 | 783 87 |
| For year ending December 1885 | 20 | 174 00 | 232 | 1339 | 1,852 27 | | | 18 28 | 2,045 05 |
| "  "  "  1886 | 20 | 290 00 | 221 | 1134 | 1,615 34 | | | 7 75 | 1,913 09 |
| "  "  "  1887 | 17 | 220 00 | 215 | 992 | 1,354 20 | | | 144 35 | 1,718 55 |
| "  "  "  1888 | 18 | 236 50 | 295 | 1380 | 2,307 08 | | 25 00 | 59 16 | 2,627 74 |
| "  "  "  1889 | 24 | 185 00 | 309 | 1560 | 2,523 18 | | 10 00 | 80 26 | 2,798 44 |
| "  "  "  1890 | 27 | 251 35 | 355 | 1901 | 3,048 52 | | 35 00 | 60 50 | 3,395 37 |
| "  "  "  1891 | 15 | 205 00 | 283 | 1938 | 3,668 14 | | 10 00 | 46 00 | 3,929 14 |
| "  "  "  1892 | 25 | 215 00 | 407 | 1979 | 3,445 19 | | 10 00 | 41 90 | 3,712 09 |
| Totals | 326 | $2,818 70 | 3517 | 17,709 | $26,844 70 | 53 | $544 85 | $1,119 40 | $31,327 65 |

### FIRST TWENTY-FOUR LODGES, NOS. 9 TO 52.* (CALENDAR YEAR.)

| Year. | Number of Members. | Number Sick. | Ratio. (1 in) | Number of Weeks Sick. | Average duration of sickness, by weeks and days. (w. d.) | Average Sickness per Mem., Weeks. | Amount paid for Sick Benefits. ($ c.) | Average Amount per week. ($ c.) | Average cost per Member. ($ c.) | Number of Deaths. | Ratio of Deaths. (1 in) | Number Initiated. | Ratio of Initiations. (1 in) | Receipts for Dues. ($ c.) | Average per Member. ($ c.) | Total Initiation Fees. ($ c.) | Average per Member. ($ c.) | Actual Cost of $4 per week S.B. ($ c.) |
|---|---|---|---|---|---|---|---|---|---|---|---|---|---|---|---|---|---|---|
| 1882 | 3,456 | 428 | 8.07 | 2,143⅞ | 5..0 | .617 | 6,373 82 | 2 98 | 1 81 | 35 | 99 | 380 | 9.00 | 20,326 04 | 5 88 | 7,790 80 | 2 25 | 2 46 |
| 1883 | 3,502 | 536 | 6.53 | 2,208⅞ | 4..1 | .630 | 6,990 26 | 3 17 | 2 00 | 18 | 194 | 299 | 11.71 | 19,921 87 | 5 68 | 5,538 85 | 1 58 | 2 52 |
| 1884 | 3,509 | 498 | 7.02 | 2,317½ | 4..4½ | .660 | 7,164 69 | 3 09 | 2 04 | 16 | 219 | 278 | 13.08 | 20,160 98 | 6 74 | 4,777 97 | 1 36 | 2 64 |
| 1885 | 3,462 | 494 | 7.00 | 2,714⅞ | 5..3½ | .783 | 8,127 69 | 2 99 | 2 34 | 24 | 144 | 188 | 18.41 | 20,736 97 | 5 99 | 3,098 74 | 89 | 3 13 |
| 1886 | 3,370 | 442 | 7.62 | 2,511⅞ | 5..4¾ | .745 | 7,563 15 | 3 01 | 2 24 | 32 | 105 | 214 | 15.75 | 21,069 75 | 6 25 | 3,554 90 | 1 05 | 2 98 |
| 1887 | 3,348 | 472 | 7.09 | 2,565⅜ | 5..3 | .766 | 7,625 99 | 2 97 | 2 28 | 27 | 124 | 214 | 15.64 | 21,220 91 | 6 01 | 3,477 55 | 1 03 | 3 06 |
| 1888 | 3,386 | 531 | 6.37 | 2,779⅞ | 5..1½ | .821 | 8,641 63 | 3 10 | 2 55 | 27 | 125 | 269 | 12.59 | 22,014 87 | 6 50 | 4,584 24 | 1 35 | 3 28 |
| 1889 | 3,580 | 521 | 6.87 | 2,834⅞ | 5..3 | .792 | 8,561 02 | 3 02 | 2 39 | 21 | 170 | 322 | 11.11 | 22,829 13 | 6 37 | 6,438 00 | 1 80 | 3 16 |
| 1890 | 3,653 | 688 | 5.31 | 3,434⅞ | 5..0 | .940 | 10,666 96 | 3 10 | 2 92 | 42 | 87 | 269 | 13.20 | 22,166 02 | 6 07 | 4,194 00 | 1 15 | 3 76 |
| 1891 | 3,722 | 546 | 6.81 | 3,444⅞ | 6..2 | .925 | 10,300 72 | 2 99 | 2 76 | 36 | 103 | 274 | 13.58 | 22,790 17 | 6 12 | 4,577 32 | 1 23 | 3 69 |
| 1892 | 3,740 | 708 | 5.28 | 4,037⅞ | 5..5 | 1.079 | 13,100 67 | 3 24 | 3 50 | 47 | 79½ | 264 | 14.16 | 22,898 10 | 6 12 | 4,194 97 | 1 12 | 4 32 |

### THE LAST TWENTY-FOUR LODGES, NOS. 209 TO 234.†

| Year. | Number of Members. | Number Sick. | Ratio. (1 in) | Number of Weeks Sick. | Average duration of sickness, by weeks and days. (w. d.) | Average Sickness per Mem., Weeks. | Amount paid for Sick Benefits. ($ c.) | Average Amount per week. ($ c.) | Average cost per Member. ($ c.) | Number of Deaths. | Ratio of Deaths. (1 in) | Number Initiated. | Ratio of Initiations. (1 in) | Receipts for Dues. ($ c.) | Average per Member. ($ c.) | Total Initiation Fees. ($ c.) | Average per Member. ($ c.) | Actual Cost of $4 per week S.B. ($ c.) |
|---|---|---|---|---|---|---|---|---|---|---|---|---|---|---|---|---|---|---|
| 1882 | 991 | 89 | 11.13 | 401⅞ | 4..1 | .404 | 1,004 58 | 2 50 | 1 01 | 4 | 248 | 253 | 3.09 | 4,613 86 | 4 65 | ‡6,157 48 | 6 21 | 1 61 |
| 1883 | 1,089 | 125 | 8.07 | 452 | 3..4¼ | .415 | 1,519 15 | 3 36 | 1 39 | 7 | 155 | 178 | 6.11 | 4,651 10 | 4 27 | 3,100 60 | 2 84 | 1 66 |
| 1884 | 1,105 | 111 | 10.86 | 422⅞ | 3..5¾ | .382 | 1,206 15 | 2 85 | 1 09 | 7 | 157 | 133 | 8.30 | 5,069 30 | 4 58 | 2,157 55 | 1 95 | 1 52 |
| 1885 | 1,117 | 129 | 8.40 | 459⅞ | 3..4 | .411 | 1,431 72 | 3 11 | 1 28 | 5 | 223 | 131 | 8.52 | 5,224 43 | 4 67 | 2,081 17 | 1 86 | 1 64 |
| 1886 | 1,123 | 128 | 8.78 | 461⅞ | 3..4¼ | .411 | 1,317 72 | 2 85 | 1 17 | 10 | 112 | 131 | 8.57 | 5,616 72 | 5 00 | 2,012 25 | 1 79 | 1 64 |
| 1887 | 1,116 | 122 | 9.15 | 489 | 4..0 | .410 | 1,498 72 | 3 06 | 1 34 | 5 | 223 | 121 | 9.14 | 5,410 49 | 4 84 | 1,846 48 | 1 65 | 1 64 |
| 1888 | 1,148 | 127 | 9.00 | 471⅞ | 3..5 | .438 | 1,412 56 | 3 00 | 1 23 | 8 | 143 | 173 | 6.63 | 5,584 19 | 4 86 | 2,459 31 | 2 14 | 1 75 |
| 1889 | 1,226 | 126 | 9.73 | 535½ | 4..1¾ | .436 | 1,557 13 | 2 90 | 1 27 | 2 | 613 | 162 | 7.57 | 5,705 02 | 4 65 | 2,381 48 | 1 94 | 1 74 |
| 1890 | 1,230 | 187 | 6.58 | 594⅞ | 3..1¼ | .483 | 1,817 94 | 3 05 | 1 48 | 6 | 205 | 157 | 7.83 | 6,018 17 | 4 89 | 2,206 20 | 1 79 | 1 93 |
| 1891 | 1,217 | 172 | 7.07 | 578 | 3..2¼ | .475 | 1,775 33 | 3 07 | 1 45 | 14 | 87 | 112 | 10.86 | 6,698 46 | 5 50 | 1,981 98 | 1 62 | 1 90 |
| 1892 | 1,287 | 219 | 5.87 | 728 | 3..2¼ | .565 | 2,366 14 | 3 25 | 1 84 | 11 | 117 | 132 | 9.75 | 6,802 51 | 5 28 | 2,051 74 | 1 60 | 2 26 |

* First 24 Lodges—containing 5 resuscitated Lodges—and the average age of the 24 being 19 years on Dec. 31, 1882.
† Average age of these Lodges, 2½ years on Dec. 31, 1882.          ‡ Five new Lodges in 1882.

Clause 24.—The following report of the Grand Encampment, for year ending 31st December, 1892, submitted as required by the Insurance Act, was duly received and sent in duplicate to the Insurance Department :—

```
Number of members, as per last report.....  ................          3,266
Initiated during the year ending Dec. 31st, 1892  ....  .........   299
Admitted by Card.........................................           15
Reinstated  ..............................................          20—    334
                                                                        ________
                 Total ...................................               3,610
    From which deduct—

Withdrawn by card .......................................           39
Suspended for non-payment of dues .......................          164
Suspended for cause .....................................            1
Expelled .................................................           3
Deceased .................................................          25—    232
                                                                        ________
            In membership, Dec. 31st, 1892 ...............               3,378

Number of Patriarchs relieved.................      407
Number of weeks' sickness for which Benefits
      were paid...............................     1979
Amount paid for the relief of Patriarchs........         $3,445 19
Amount of relief to Widowed Families..........               10 00
Amount of Special Relief......................               41 90
Amount paid for Burying the Dead.............               215 00
                                                            _________
            Total amount of Relief paid.....         $3,712 09
            Invested Funds of Subordinates..........            $20,463 10
Total Amount of Annual Revenue..............                    10,221 61
```

Clause 25.—The unerring law of the increase of sickness and death as the Lodges and their members grow older and by which we must be governed, if those who are now members would have on hand the funds out of which they may draw when their turn comes, are pretty clearly set forth in the accompanying table. It will be seen that the rate in the older Lodges, which have a record from which the facts may be gleaned, have nearly doubled in ten years, and as year follows year the record of the younger Lodges is gradually creeping up. We are a benevolent, benefit-paying, as well as a fraternal society, and we cannot afford to ignore or make little of the necessity of the business part of Odd Fellowship being done on sound business principles. The accompanying tables are submitted in order that every Lodge in Ontario may see itself as it will appear in the not distant future, when its members, now healthy and strong, will be approaching "the sere and yellow leaf" time of life, and its ratio of sickness and death are away up and taken cognizance of for the benefits of others coming on. It may be that in time they will be wisely guided and so conduct their business that when their last old member makes his demand there may be no doubt of the ability of the Lodge to meet it.

Clause 26.—The following table will show the unerring increase in sickness as the age of the membership increases, the rate in 1892 being more than double that of 1875:—

## AVERAGE MEMBERSHIP AND SICKNESS FOR THE PAST EIGHTEEN YEARS.

| Year. | Membership. | Weeks' Sickness. | General Average per Member. | | | |
|---|---|---|---|---|---|---|
| | | | Days. | Hours. | Minutes. | Seconds. |
| 1875 | 10,188 | 3,566 | 2 | 8 | 26 | 51 |
| 1876 | 11,322 | 4,938¼ | 3 | 1 | 16 | 50 |
| 1877 | 12,172 | 4,430⅔ | 2 | 13 | 8 | 53 |
| 1878 | 12,332 | 4,267 | 2 | 10 | 7 | 47 |
| 1879 | 12,442 | 5,024 | 2 | 19 | 50 | 14 |
| 1880 | 12,168 | 5,009⅔ | 2 | 21 | 14 | 45 |
| 1881 | 12,776 | 5,316 | 2 | 21 | 54 | 12 |
| 1882* | 13,755 | 6,623⅔ | 3 | 8 | 53 | 42 |
| 1882† | 13,861½ | 2,755⅔ | 1 | 9 | 24 | 00 |
| 1883 | 14,173 | 6,682¼ | 3 | 7 | 12 | 48 |
| 1884 | 14,330 | 7,202⅔ | 3 | 12 | 26 | 13 |
| 1885 | 14,591 | 7,754 | 3 | 17 | 16 | 42 |
| 1886 | 14,847 | 7,896½ | 3 | 17 | 21 | 10 |
| 1887 | 15,353 | 8,624 | 3 | 21 | 22 | 4 |
| 1888 | 16,060 | 10,231¾ | 4 | 11 | 1 | 5 |
| 1889 | 16,940 | 10,261¼ | 4 | 5 | 45 | 44 |
| 1890 | 17,707 | 12,539¼ | 4 | 22 | 58 | 21 |
| 1891 | 18,390 | 11,842¼ | 4 | 12 | 10 | 57 |
| 1892 | 19,452 | 14,046⅔ | 5 | 1 | 19 | 30 |
| 18½ years. | 272,859 | 139,010⅔ | ........ | ........ | ........ | ........ |
| Grand Average | 14,749 | 7,514 | 3 | 13 | 35 | 20 |

* Year ending June 30, 1882.　　† Six months ending Dec. 31, 1882.

Clause 27.—With the object of indicating as clearly as possible the inevitable results of increasing age in Lodges as in individuals, I submit the following table of the record of sickness and sick benefits and of deaths in Ontario during 1892, and trust that the warning it sounds will not be unheeded.

| Lodges in Groups of 24. | | | Members. | Brothers Sick. | Ratio. | | | Weeks Sickness. |
|---|---|---|---|---|---|---|---|---|
| 9 | to | 51 | 3,556 | 687 | 1 | in | 5.24 | 3,939½ |
| 52 | " | 76 | 2,746 | 452 | 1 | " | 6.07 | 2,290 |
| 77 | " | 102 | 2,123 | 351 | 1 | " | 6.04 | 1,588⅔ |
| 103 | " | 129 | 2,370 | 357 | 1 | " | 6.63 | 1,562 |
| 130 | " | 156 | 1,571 | 240 | 1 | " | 6.54 | 973 |
| 157 | " | 184 | 1,392 | 204 | 1 | " | 6.82 | 965⅔ |
| 185 | " | 215 | 1,341 | 214 | 1 | " | 6.26 | 779½ |
| 216 | " | 242 | 1,634 | 244 | 1 | " | 6.69 | 865 |
| 243 | " | 266 | 1,307 | 157 | 1 | " | 8.31 | 665⅔ |
| 267 | " | 294 | 1,412 | 140 | 1 | " | 10.07 | 417¼ |

| Lodges in Groups of 24. | | | Average sickness per Member. | | Sick Benefits. | Cost per Member. | Died. | Ratio. | | |
|---|---|---|---|---|---|---|---|---|---|---|
| | | | Dys. | Hrs. | | | | | | |
| 9 | to | 51 | 7 | 18 | 12,722 56 | $3 58 | 44 | 1 | in | 81 |
| 52 | " | 76 | 5 | 20 | 6,989 84 | 2 54 | 21 | 1 | " | 130 |
| 77 | " | 102 | 5 | 5 | 4,515 44 | 2 13 | 13 | 1 | " | 163 |
| 103 | " | 129 | 4 | 11 | 5,436 29 | 2 29 | 18 | 1 | " | 132 |
| 130 | " | 156 | 4 | 8 | 2,842 07 | 1 81 | 11 | 1 | " | 143 |
| 157 | " | 184 | 4 | 20 | 2,922 80 | 2 10 | 14 | 1 | " | 99 |
| 185 | " | 215 | 3 | 12 | 2,565 61 | 1 91 | 9 | 1 | " | 149 |
| 216 | " | 242 | 3 | 17 | 2,666 98 | 1 63 | 12 | 1 | " | 136 |
| 243 | " | 266 | 3 | 13 | 2,060 35 | 1 58 | 9 | 1 | " | 145 |
| 267 | " | 294 | 2 | 2 | 1,398 84 | 99 | 6 | 1 | " | 235 |

RECORD OF THE ODD FELLOWS' MUTUAL AID ASSOCIATION
OF LONDON, ONT., FROM ORGANIZATION IN 1880 TO
DECEMBER 31ST, 1892.

| Year. | Age when Admitted. | No. of Members Admitted. | No. of Members Lapsed. | No. of Members entitled to Indemnity. | No. Died. | Average Age at Death. | Receipts. | Death Claims Paid. | Expenses of Management. | Cost per Member for Death Claims Paid. | Cost per Member for Management. |
|---|---|---|---|---|---|---|---|---|---|---|---|
| 1880 | .... | 44 | .... | 44 | .... | .... | $40 50 | ........ | $24 56 | $0 50 | $0 05 |
| 1881 | .... | 19 | 1 | 55 | 1 | .... | 50 94 | $27 50 | 2 12 | .... | .... |
| 1882 | .... | 17 | 2 | 64 | .... | .... | 10 55 | ........ | 5 75 | .... | .... |
| 1883 | .... | 7 | .... | 75 | .... | .... | 40 00 | ........ | 8 41 | .... | .... |
| 1884 | .... | .... | .... | 75 | .... | .... | 1 00 | ........ | 1 50 | .... | .... |
| 1885 | 36 | 5 | .... | 72 | 2 | 39 | 38 00 | 72 00 | 7 10 | .... | .... |
| 1886 | .... | 7 | 10 | 69 | 2 | .... | 76 15 | 64 50 | 8 35 | .... | .... |
| 1887 | .... | 3 | 11 | 69 | .... | .... | 3 55 | ........ | 1 56 | .... | .... |
| 1888 | 60 | 18 | 2 | 80 | 1 | 63 | 61 30 | 40 00 | 11 95 | .... | .... |
| 1889 | 29 | 4 | 2 | 83 | 1 | 34 | 45 25 | 41 50 | 10.18 | .... | .... |
| 1890 | 36 | 15 | 6 | 87 | 3 | 38 | 136 90 | 118 50 | 11 96 | .... | .... |
| 1891 | .... | 11 | 1 | 94 | .... | .... | 22 00 | ........ | 12 60 | .... | .... |
| 1892 | .... | 11 | .... | 96 | 4 | 65½ | 218 65 | 194 50 | 8 08 | .... | .... |
| | | 161 | 35 | | 14 | | $744 79 | $558 50 | $114 12 | | |

Average amount paid on each death, $39.89.

Total receipts, $744.79.

Total expenditure, $672.62.

Balance on hand December 31st, 1892, $63.07.

JOHN HUNTER,
*President.*

ALFRED DAVIS,
*Sec.-Treas.*

RECORD OF THE ODD FELLOWS' FUNERAL AID ASSOCIATION COUNTIES OF LINCOLN AND WELLAND, FROM ORGANIZATION IN 1872.

| YEAR. | Members. | Deaths. | Avr'ge Age. | Mortuary Rate. | Amount Paid Death Claims. | Cost of Management |
|---|---|---|---|---|---|---|
| 1872.... | 93 | ........ | ......... | ............ | ........... | $19 88 |
| 1873.... | 96 | ........ | ......... | ............ | ........... | 16 50 |
| 1874.... | 109 | 2 | 30 | 1 in 54.50 | $109 91 | 1 00 |
| 1875..... | 136 | ........ | ......... | ............ | ........... | 13 63 |
| 1876.... | 136 | 1 | 62 | 1 in 136 | '36 00 | 15 11 |
| 1877.... | 155 | ........ | ......... | ............ | ........... | 11 50 |
| 1878.... | 155 | 1 | 41 | 1 in 155 | 155 00 | 24 74 |
| 1879.... | 152 | 1 | 62 | 1 " 152 | 152 00 | 19 03 |
| 1880.... | 150 | 1 | 62 | 1 " 150 | 150 00 | 11 69 |
| 1881.... | 149 | 1 | 61 | 1 " 149 | 149 00 | 37 89 |
| 1882.... | 147 | 2 | 57.50 | 1 " 73.50 | 293 00 | 18 75 |
| 1883.... | 150 | ........ | ......... | ............ | ........... | 18 84 |
| 1884.... | 161 | 1 | 38 | 1 in 161 | 161 00 | 19 85 |
| 1885.... | 176 | 1 | 40 | 1 " 176 | 176 00 | 13 05 |
| 1886.... | 176 | 4 | 50.75 | 1 " 44 | 695 00 | 29 00 |
| 1887.... | 165 | 3 | 40 | 1 " 55 | 472 00 | 31 42 |
| 1888.... | 156 | 4 | 49.25 | 1 " 39 | 603 00 | 68 48 |
| 1889.... | 137 | 3 | 61.33 | 1 " 45.50 | 450 00 | 22 00 |
| 1890.... | 137 | 2 | 48 | 1 " 63.50 | 267 00 | 34 75 |
| 1891.... | 133 | 4 | 67 | 1 " 33.25 | 477 00 | 35 81 |
| 1892.... | 133 | ........ | ......... | ............ | ........... | 30 50 |

General Average Age, 51.90 years.

Call at each death.............................. $     1 10

Proportion for expenses  ...........................     10

Average amount paid......................  ........   143 41

Total Receipts......................................   5,104 67

  "     Expenditure  ..............................   4,939 32

            Balance, Dec. 31, 1892 ................ .....   $165 35

RECORD OF THE ODD FELLOWS' RELIEF ASSOCIATION OF
CANADA, FROM DATE OF ORGANIZATION, MAY 12, 1874,
UP TO 31st DECEMBER, 1892.

| Year. | Period. | Number of Members. | Deaths. | Average Age. | Mortuary Rate. | Total Revenue. | Death Claims. | Disability Claims. |
|---|---|---|---|---|---|---|---|---|
| 1875... | 12 mos | 364 | ..... | ..... | ..... | $　952 01 | ..... .. | ..... .. |
| 1876... | ..... | 813 | 3 | 41.66 | 3.69 | 3,385 90 | $ 1,400 00 | ..... .. |
| 1877... | ..... | 885 | 7 | 33.43 | 7.91 | 5,388 52 | 3,255 00 | ..... .. |
| 1878... | ..... | 854 | 5 | 41.80 | 5.85 | 7,615 66 | 5,700 00 | ..... . |
| 1879... | ..... | 832 | 4 | 44.75 | 4.81 | 4,874 23 | 4,125 00 | ..... .. |
| 1880... | 18 mos | 984 | 10 | 38.20 | 6.78 | 11,494 11 | 8,075 00 | $400 00 |
| 1881... | 12 mos | 1040 | 6 | 42.16 | 5.77 | 8,214 64 | 6,000 00 | ..... .. |
| 1882... | ..... | 1193 | 11 | 40.72 | 9.22 | 14,921 15 | 11,800 00 | 500 00 |
| 1883... | ..... | 1494 | 7 | 44.28 | 4.68 | 12,454 37 | 7,000 00 | ..... .. |
| 1884... | ..... | 1876 | 7 | 41.85 | 3.73 | 13,850 81 | 10,500 00 | ..... .. |
| 1885... | ..... | 2203 | 16 | 44.18 | 7.26 | 20,718 91 | 14,500 00 | ..... .. |
| 1886... | ..... | 2418 | 10 | 45.30 | 4.14 | 19,220 73 | 15,000 00 | ..... .. |
| 1887... | ..... | 2641 | 18 | 33.94 | 6.82 | 19,644 34 | 15,500 00 | ..... .. |
| 1888... | ..... | 2848 | 19 | 42.21 | 6.67 | 31,972 94 | 29,000 00 | ..... .. |
| 1889... | ..... | 3099 | 25 | 46.40 | 8.07 | 42,523 57 | 26,282 00 | ..... .. |
| 1890... | ..... | 4036 | 27 | 45.33 | 6.69 | 50,359 62 | 42,500 00 | ..... .. |
| 1891... | ..... | 5135 | 33 | 44.48 | 6.43 | 62,421 87 | 40,000 00 | 1,000 00 |
| 1892... | ..... | 5935 | 37 | 43.16 | 6.24 | 81,053 60 | 57,100 00 | 1,000 00 |
| | | | 245 | | | 411,066 98 | 297,737 00 | 2,900 00 |

Death claims................................ $297,737 00
Disability claims........................... 2,900 00
Total ....................................... $300,637 00

## STATEMENT " A."

AMOUNTS DUE BY LODGES, JULY 20, 1893.

| Name of Lodge. | Lodge No. | Amount. |
|---|---|---|
| Otter | 50 | $38 65 |
| Deseronto | 102 | 25 |
| Model | 147 | 50 |
| Western Star | 149 | 5 50 |
| Sycamore | 151 | 8 00 |
| Hayden | 152 | 19 10 |
| Grey | 169 | 07 |
| Tecumseh | 183 | 50 |
| Teeswater | 182 | 16 50 |
| Cambridge | 188 | 50 |
| Acton | 204 | 25 |
| Egremont | 207 | 16 00 |
| Georgian Bay | 219 | 25 |
| Sauble | 227 | 1 55 |
| Equity | 232 | 50 |
| Hanover | 233 | 15 75 |
| Thornbury | 243 | 75 |
| Floral | 252 | 9 75 |
| Tottenham | 255 | 15 75 |
| Lansdowne | 270 | 50 |
| Glanworth | 289 | 11 75 |
| Beatrice, D of R. | 12 | 1 00 |
| Mizpah, " | 19 | 10 |
| Lucknow | 22 | 6 65 |
| Esther | 27 | 15 20 |
| Aberdeen | 30 | 14 25 |
| Total | | $194 57 |

Examined and found correct.

CHAS. PACKERT, }
A. C. STEWART, } *Auditors.*

TORONTO, July 29th, 1893.

AMOUNTS DUE TO LODGES, JULY 20TH, 1892.

| NAME OF LODGE. | LODGE No. | AMOUNT. |
|---|---|---|
| Barrie | 63 | $ 25 |
| Toronto | 71 | 16 25 |
| Beaver | 82 | 15 |
| Peterboro' | 111 | 58 00 |
| Naomi | 116 | 24 37 |
| Mystic | 128 | 75 70 |
| Brougham | 155 | 1 25 |
| Thamesville | 157 | 50 |
| Emerald | 173 | 75 |
| Silver Star | 202 | 25 |
| Acorn | 236 | 50 |
| Campbellford | 248 | 1 15 |
| Bracebridge | 251 | 25 |
| Norwood | 262 | 7 80 |
| North Bay | 271 | 25 |
| Royal | 286 | 9 25 |
| Victoria, D. of R. | 1 | 1 40 |
| Oshawa " | 4 | 80 |
| May Queen " | 5 | 55 |
| Naomi " | 6 | 30 |
| Our Sisters " | 7 | 2 00 |
| Bethuel " | 9 | 3 00 |
| Atthewell " | 29 | 3 30 |
| Wingham " | | 5 00 |
| Total | | $213 02 |

Examined and found correct.

TORONTO, July 29th, 1893.

CHAS. PACKERT, } Auditors.
A. C. STEWART, }

## SUPPLIES ON HAND, JULY 20, 1893

| Qty | Item | Price | Amount |
|---|---|---|---|
| 2 | Subordinate Lodge | $2 40 | $4 80 |
| 9 | Rebekah Funeral Ceremony | 15 | 1 35 |
| 7 | Degree Lodge Installation Books | 2 00 | 14 00 |
| 24 | Grand Lodge Cards for Members Defunct Lgs. | 10 | 2 40 |
| 99 | Dismissal Certificates | 21 | 20 79 |
| 79 | Visiting Cards | 21 | 16 59 |
| 134 | Withdrawal Cards | 21 | 28 14 |
| 1 | Rebekah Visiting Cards | 21 | 21 |
| 6 | Digests, Sovereign Grand Lodge | 3 00 | 18 00 |
| 11 | Anniversary Ceremony | 21 | 2 31 |
| 30 | Funeral Ceremony | 26 | 7 80 |
| 20 | Diplomas | 60 | 12 00 |
| 4 | Odes, Book Form | 50 | 2 00 |
| 204 | Odes, Subordinate Lodge | 4 | 8 16 |
| 125 | Odes, Rebekah | 4 | 5 00 |
| 5 | Rebekah Certificates | 30 | 1 50 |
| 192 | Members' Receipt Books | 85 | 163 20 |
| 79 | Question Books | 50 | 39 50 |
| 91 | Orders, A. T. P. W. | 50 | 45 50 |
| 82 | Orders, Term P. W | 50 | 41 00 |
| 13 | Visitors' Register | 75 | 9 75 |
| 25 | Officers' Roll Call | 42 | 10 50 |
| 47 | Orders on Treasurer | 60 | 33 60 |
| 39 | Return Books | 40 | 15 60 |
| 7702 | Propositions @ 15c. per 100 | | 11 55 |
| 16 | Minute Books | 1 00 | 16 00 |
| 86 | Reports on Character | 65 | 55 90 |
| 89 | Members' Registers | 70 | 62 30 |
| 40 | Receipt Books, Treas. to Secty. | 50 | 20 00 |
| 350 | Treasurers' Bonds | | 2 36 |
| 295 | Trustees' Bonds | | 1 57 |
| 1915 | Decoration Ceremony | 1 | 19 15 |
| 14 | Veteran Jewels | 4 75 | 66 50 |
| 18 | Prayer Cards | 4 | 72 |
| 880 | Degree Certificates | ½ | 4 40 |
| 8605 | Medical Examinations @ 65c. per 100 | | 55 93 |
| 12 | Subordinate Lodge Floor Work | 40 | 4 80 |
| 12 | Rebekah " " " | 40 | 4 80 |
| 15 | Financial Secretary's Books Packert's | 1 35 | 20 35 |
| 16 | Recording " " " | 1 35 | 21 60 |
| 13 | Treasurers' " " | 1 35 | 17 55 |
| 751 | Ontario Digests | 45 | 337 95 |
| 291 | Rebekah Propositions | ½ | 1 46 |
| 3 | Rebekah Rituals | 2 25 | 6 75 |
| | | | $1235 24 |

## STATEMENT OF SUPPLIES ON HAND, JULY 20, 1893.

| SUPPLIES. | On hand July 20, 1892. | Purchased during the year. | Total. | Sold during the year. | On hand July 20, 1893. |
|---|---|---|---|---|---|
| Combined Rituals | 4 | 76 | 80 | 78 | 2 |
| Rebekah Funeral Ceremony | 13 | ...... | 13 | 4 | 9 |
| Grand Lodge Cards | ...... | 24 | 24 | 1 | 23 |
| Dismissal Certificates | 62 | 200 | 262 | 163 | 99 |
| Visiting Cards | 12 | 1900 | 1912 | 1833 | 79 |
| Rebekah Visiting Cards | 60 | ...... | 60 | 59 | 1 |
| Digest Sov. Grand Lodge | 12 | 18 | 30 | 23 | 7 |
| Anniversary Ceremony | 15 | ...... | 15 | 4 | 11 |
| Funeral Ceremony | 50 | 50 | 100 | 70 | 30 |
| Diplomas | 20 | 25 | 45 | 25 | 2 |
| Degree Charts | 5 | ...... | 5 | 5 | ...... |
| Odes, Book form | 5 | 12 | 17 | 13 | 4 |
| Ode Cards, Subordinate Lodge | 556 | ...... | 556 | 352 | 204 |
| Ode Cards, Funeral | 61 | ...... | 61 | 61 | ...... |
| Odes, Rebekah | 3 | 400 | 403 | 278 | 125 |
| Rebekah Certificates | 5 | ...... | 5 | ...... | 5 |
| Book of Forms | 5 | 12 | 17 | 17 | ...... |
| Members' Receipts | 70 | 206 | 276 | 84 | 192 |
| Question Books | ...... | 100 | 100 | 21 | 79 |
| Orders, A. T. P. W | 11 | 100 | 111 | 20 | 91 |
| Orders, Term P. W | ...... | 100 | 100 | 18 | 82 |
| Visitors' Register | 23 | ...... | 23 | 10 | 13 |
| Officers' Roll | 46 | ...... | 46 | 21 | 25 |
| Orders on Treasurer | 3 | 100 | 103 | 47 | 56 |
| Return Books | 46 | ...... | 46 | 7 | 39 |
| Propositions | 4275 | 10000 | 14275 | 6753 | 7702 |
| Minute Books | 19 | 15 | 34 | 18 | 16 |
| Reports on Character | 2 | 100 | 102 | 16 | 86 |
| Members' Register | 5 | 100 | 105 | 16 | 89 |
| Treasurers' Receipts | 70 | ...... | 70 | 30 | 40 |
| Treasurers' Bonds | 526 | ...... | 526 | 176 | 350 |
| Trustees' Bonds | 404 | ...... | 404 | 109 | 295 |
| Decoration Ceremony | 1965 | ...... | 1965 | 50 | 1915 |
| Veteran Jewels | 7 | 20 | 27 | 13 | 14 |
| Prayer Cards | 47 | ...... | 47 | 29 | 18 |
| Degree Certificates | 880 | ...... | 880 | ...... | 880 |
| Medical Certificates | 2105 | 10000 | 12105 | 3500 | 8605 |
| Subordinate Lodge Floor Work | 18 | 30 | 48 | 36 | 12 |
| Rebekah    "    " | 2 | 30 | 32 | 20 | 12 |
| Recording Secretary's Work, Packert's | 22 | ...... | 22 | 6 | 16 |
| Permanent    "    " | 24 | ...... | 24 | 9 | 15 |
| Treasurer's Work, Packert's | 23 | ...... | 23 | 10 | 13 |
| Ontario Digests | 811 | ...... | 811 | 60 | 751 |
| Rebekak Propositions and Reports | 291 | 1000 | 1291 | 1000 | 291 |
| Rebekah Rituals | ...... | 30 | 24 | 21 | 3 |
| Withdrawal Cards | 69 | 4 | 519 | 385 | 134 |

## PROFIT AND LOSS ACCOUNT.

### Detailed Statement of Receipts and Expenditure.

#### RECEIPTS.

| | | |
|---|---|---|
| Capita Tax | $10035 00 | |
| Charter Fees | 220 30 | |
| Supplies | 490 24 | |
| Interest | 96 63 | |
| Miscellaneous | 14 87 | |
| | | $10857 04 |

#### EXPENDITURE.

*General Expenditure as ordered by Grand Lodge—*

| | | | |
|---|---|---|---|
| Mileage and Per Diem | | $6221 60 | |
| Grand Auditors | $52 20 | | |
| H. Robertson, Com. on Correspondence | 50 00 | | |
| J. A. Young, Assistant Grand Secretary | 6 00 | | |
| Janitor at Windsor | 10 00 | | |
| Official Reporter | 15 00 | | |
| Committee on Insurance Law | 23 00 | | |
| W. A. Rawlings, Chairman By-laws | 75 00 | | |
| Grand Master's Expenses, 1892 | 14 88 | | |
| Badges for Grand Lodge | 37 70 | | |
| Government Assessment | 50 00 | | |
| Incidentals | 38 25 | | |
| Sovereign Grand Lodge Tax | 150 00 | | |
| Typewriter | 105 00 | | |
| | | 627 03 | |

*Printing and Stationery—*

| | | | |
|---|---|---|---|
| Journals of Grand Lodge | $719 10 | | |
| Grand Master's Reports | 46 50 | | |
| Grand Secretary's Reports | 63 00 | | |
| Foreign Relations Reports | 51 00 | | |
| Grand Treasurer's Reports | 6 00 | | |
| Circulars, Committee Reports, etc | 292 90 | | |
| | | 1178 50 | |

*Office Expenses—*

| | | | |
|---|---|---|---|
| Rent | $308 00 | | |
| Office Help, per resolution | 100 00 | | |
| Telephone | 45 00 | | |
| Repairs and Furniture | 35 75 | | |
| Cleaning Office, Coal, Incidentals | 129 31 | | |
| | | 618 06 | |

*Salaries—*

| | | | |
|---|---|---|---|
| Grand Secretary | $1500 00 | | |
| Grand Treasurer | 200 00 | | |
| | | 1700 00 | |

*Miscellaneous—*

| | | | |
|---|---|---|---|
| Grand Master | $199 55 | | |
| Guarantee Bonds | 51 55 | | |
| Law Costs | 8 00 | | |
| Postage | 277 33 | | |
| Special Committees | 71 90 | | |
| | | 608 33 | |
| | | | 10953 52 |

Balance............... $ 96 48

Examined and found correct.

CHAS. PACKERT, } *Auditors.*
A. C. STEWART, }

TORONTO, August 1st, 1893.

## BALANCE SHEET—GRAND LODGE OF ONTARIO, I.O.O.F., JULY 20, 1893.

| Ledger Folio. | LEDGER TITLES. | Inventory. $ c. | Ledger Balances. Dr. $ c. | Ledger Balances. Cr. $ c. | Profit and Loss. Dr. $ c. | Profit and Loss. Cr. $ c. | Stock Account. Dr. $ c. | Stock Account. Cr. $ c. | Assets. $ c. | Liabilities. $ c. |
|---|---|---|---|---|---|---|---|---|---|---|
| 311 | Stock | | | 12069 28 | | | | 12069 28 | | |
| 324 | Supplies | 1263 60 | 773 36 | | | 490 24 | | | 1263 60 | |
| 301 | Rebekah Tax | | 3 70 | | | | | | 3 70 | |
| 303 | Printing and Stationery | | 1178 50 | | 1178 05 | | | | | |
| 304 | Office Expenses | | 618 06 | | 618 06 | | | | | |
| 305 | General Expenses | | 627 03 | | 627 03 | | | | | |
| 306 | Salaries | | 1700 00 | | 1700 00 | | | | | |
| 307 | Profit and Loss | | | 14 87 | | 14 87 | | | | |
| 309 | Grand Treasurer | | 10496 51 | | | | | | 10496 51 | |
| 310 | Capita Tax | | | 10035 00 | | 10035 00 | | | | |
| 312 | Furniture and Regalia | 608 87 | 608 87 | | | | | | 608 87 | |
| 313 | Interest | | | 96 63 | | 96 63 | | | | |
| 313 | Special Relief | | | 105 90 | | | | | | 105 90 |
| 315 | Insurance | | 51 55 | | 51 55 | | | | | |
| 316 | Funds of Defunct Lodges | | | 258 30 | | | | | | 258 30 |
| 317 | Charters | | | 220 30 | | 220 30 | | | | |
| 319 | Mileage and Per Diem | | 6221 60 | | 6221 60 | | | | | |
| 320 | Postage | | 277 33 | | 277 33 | | | | | |
| 321 | Special Committees | | 71 90 | | 71 90 | | | | | |
| 323 | Ontario Relief Association | | | 10 00 | | | | | | 10 00 |
| 311 | Grand Master, Expenses | | 199 55 | | 199 55 | | | | | |
| 318 | Law Expenses | | 8 00 | | 8 00 | | | | | |
| 327 | Rubber Stamps | | | 7 23 | | | | | | 7 23 |
| | Statement "A" | | 194 57 | | | | | | 194 57 | |
| | Statement "B" | | | 213 02 | | | | | | 213 02 |
| | | 1872 47 | 23030 53 | 23030 53 | | | | | | |
| | Net Loss.. | | | | | 96 48 | 9648 | | | |
| | | | | | 10953 52 | 10953 52 | | | | |
| | Net Capital... | | | | | | 11972 80 | | | |
| | | | | | | | 12069 28 | 12069 28 | | |
| | Total Assets | | | | | | | | 12567 25 | |
| | Total Liabilities | | | | | | | | | 594 45 |
| | Assets over Liabilities | | | | | | | | | 11972 80 |
| | | | | | | | | | 12567 25 | 12567 25 |

Examined and found correct.

CHAS. PACKERT,  |<br>A. C. STEWART,  | *Auditors*

TORONTO, August 5, 1893.

# REPORT OF AUDITORS.

*To the Grand Lodge of Ontario, I.O.O.F.*

The undersigned beg to report that they have carefully examined the books and accounts of the Grand Secretary and found them correct, and that they have verified the statements submitted herewith.

They have also examined the books and vouchers of the Grand Treasurer, which have been found correct. The amount in the hands of the Grand Treasurer, being $10,496.51 ; of this amount $364.20 are trust funds ; the general fund being $10,132.31.

They find that fines recorded some years ago against Sycamore Lodge ($8 oo), and Egremont Lodge ($16.00), still appear in their accounts as unpaid balances, and Capitation tax for two terms ($5.75) appears against Hanover Lodge, to which they would call the attention of the Finance Committee for their consideration, with a view of having the payment of the amounts either enforced or remitted.

It will be noticed that a slight difference of $28.36 appears between the detailed statement of supplies and the balance sheet. This is occasioned simply from the fact that in transcribing the items from the book to the statement sheet a few items were overlooked, and the books being closed the statements could not conveniently be altered. This, however, does not affect the financial statement, but will rectify itself at next audit.

They are pleased to note that the balances against Subordinate Lodges have been very much reduced ; most of the amounts which do appear are on account of the returns of some Lodges having been received but the cash not being remitted until after the books were closed. The amount appearing as being overpaid by Lodges, on the other hand, being from the fact that some have remitted cash, but returns were not sent in at time of closing books.

All of which is respectfully submitted.

CHAS. PACKERT, } Auditors.<br>A. C. STEWART, }

Toronto, August 2, 1893.

# ANNUAL STATEMENT.

## ABSTRACT FROM THE SEMI-ANNUAL RETURNS, **YEAR** ENDING 31st DECEMBER, 1891.

### LODGES.

| | |
|---|---:|
| No. of Lodges 31st Dec., 1891 | 237 |
| Instituted during the year 1892 | 8 |
| | 245 |
| Defunct—Mystic, No. 128 | 1 |
| Lodges, 31st Dec., 1892 | 244 |

### MEMBERSHIP.

Year ending 31st Dec., 1892.

| | | |
|---|---:|---:|
| Initiated | 2,155 | |
| Reinstated | 144 | |
| Admitted by Card | 168 | |
| | | 2,467 |
| Suspended for Cause | 11 | |
| Suspended N. P. D. | 918 | |
| Withdrawn | 305 | |
| Expelled | 14 | |
| Died | 157 | |
| | | 1,405 |
| Net Increase | | 1,062 |
| Add Membership 31st Dec., 1891 | | 18,390 |
| Membership 31st Dec., 1892 | | 19,452 |

Average Membership per Lodge, 79.61.

### RELIEF FOR YEAR 1892.

| | | |
|---|---:|---:|
| Number of Brothers who received Sick Benefits | 3,037 | |
| "      Widows who received Relief | 186 | |
| "      Orphan Children who received Relief | 86 | |
| Amount paid Sick Benefits | | $44,119 78 |
| "      Surgeons' Fees | | 5,125 21 |
| "      Nursing Sick Brothers | | 2,135 09 |
| "      Relief of Widows | | 13,306 00 |
| "      "      Orphans | | 7,234 46 |
| "      Burying deceased Brothers | | 6,741 56 |
| "      "      Wives of Brothers | | 1,847 50 |
| "      Special Relief and Charity | | 2,835 34 |
| Total | | $77,344 94 |

An average for each day of 1892 of $210.63.

6

Number of Brothers who received Sick Benefits.......    3,037
    Being 1 in each 6.42 of the entire Membership.
Number of Weeks' Sickness.........................    14,046¾
Amount of Sick Benefits..............................    $44,119 78
Average amount paid to each..................    $14 53
Average cost per Member for Sick Benefits...........    2 26
Average duration of sickness..........4 weeks, 4 days, 9 hours.
Average duration of sickness if spread over the entire Member-
    ship ......................5 days, 1 hour, 19 min., 30 sec.
Surgeons' Fees and Nurses............................    7,260 30
Average cost per Member.............................    $0 37½
Number of Widows...................................    186
Amount paid to Widows.............................    13,206 00
Average paid to each...............................    $71 00
Average cost per Member............................    68
Number of Brothers died............................    157
Amount paid for Funeral Benefits.....................    6,701 56
Average for Funeral Benefit.........................    $42 68
Average cost per Member............................    34½
Average Death rate..............................    1 in 124
Number of Wives of Brothers died..................    74
Amount paid for Funeral Benefits.....................    1,847 50
Average paid for each...............................    $24 96
Average cost per Member............................    09½
Number of Orphans in the care of Lodges...........    86
Amount paid to Orphans.............................    1,234 46
Average to each....................................    $14 35
Average cost per Member.. ........................    06⅗
Paid for Special Relief and Charity.........................    2,835 34
Average cost per Member...........................    14¾
Total amount paid for Relief and Charity...................    77,344 97
Total amount paid for Current Expenses...................    60,943 68
Total amount of other Expenditure...........................    19,000 00
 
    Total Disbursements..............................    $157,288 65

Average cost per Member for Relief and Charity........    $3 97
Average cost per Member for Current Expenses.......    3 13
Average cost per Member for other Expenditure.......    98

Total average cost per Member for all purposes......    $8 08
Total average receipts per Member.................    9 33

Excess of Receipts over Expenditure per Member....    $1 25

RECEIPTS OF LODGES.

Initiation, Degrees and Cards..............................    $ 32,734 72
Average per Member..................................    $1 68¼
Dues and Reinstatement.................................    106,122 57
Average per Member.................................    5 45½
All other sources (as interest, rent, etc.).....................    42,652 19
Average per Member...............................    2 19¼

    Total average receipts per Member............$9 33

    Total receipts......................................    $181,509 48

FUNDS AND HOW INVESTED.

Cash in Bank and in Treasurer's hands......................... $175,104 30
Invested in Mortgages and securities...........................  184,220 20
Invested in Buildings, Land, etc...............................  261,451 31
Invested in Furniture, Regalia, etc............................  165,781 60

    Total.................................................. $786,557 41

FUNDS.

General Benefit Fund.......................................... $669,627 15
Widows' and Orphans' Fund.....................................  104,031 79
Contingent Fund...............................................   12,898 47

    Total.................................................. $786,557 41

The very large increase in sickness and death during the year, more particularly noticed in the first half of the year, was no doubt caused by the epidemic, la grippe, which prevailed in the winter of 1891-2—the number sick 3,037, and the deaths 157, being the largest in our history, warns the Lodges to be as careful as possible in the management of their fiscal affairs. for careful as we may be in our selection of members, epidemics will play their part, and our Lodges must be prepared for them.

The following is an abstract from the returns of Lodges, Term ending 30th June. as perfect as it could be made, owing to so many Lodges neglecting to send in returns promptly :—

ABSTRACT FROM RETURNS, FOR SIX MONTHS ENDING<br>JUNE 30, 1893.

Number of Lodges, June 30. 1893...............................      247

MEMBERSHIP.

Membership, December 31, 1892.................................           19,452
Initiated during the Term.............................. 1,367
Admitted by Card.......................................    92
Reinstated.............................................    88
                                                 1,547
Suspended for Cause....................................     2
Suspended, Non-Payment Dues............................   417
Withdrawn..............................................   190
Expelled...............................................     5
Died...................................................    69
                                                 683
    Net Increase.......................................           865

    Present Membership. June 30, 1893...........            20,316

Number of Brothers who received Sick Benefits.......  1,685
    "    weeks' sickness for which benefits were paid.  7,702½
Amount paid for Sick Benefits.................................  $24,383 47
    "    Lodge Surgeons.....  ...........................  2,612 39
    "    Nursing Sick Brothers......................  1,207 98
    "    Special Relief and Charity....................  1,467 67
Number of Widows relieved.........................  180
Amount paid for their relief...............................  6,597 59
Number of Orphans cared for.......................  52
Amount paid to them......................................  402 00
Number of Brothers died........  ...................  69
Amount paid for Funeral Benefits...  ...................  3,285 50
Number of Wives of Brothers died..................  30
Amount paid for Funeral Benefits..........................  555 00

    Total Relief...........................  $40,511 60

Average cost per member for the six months..........  $  1 99
Average amount paid out per day....................  221 37

### RECEIPTS OF LODGES.

Initiations, Degrees, Cards, etc.............................  $20,550 31
Dues and Reinstatements.................................  57,388 24
All other sources.......  ...............................  23,849 42

    Total................................................  $101,787 97

### FUNDS.

General Fund..........................................  $680,469 52
Widows' and Orphans' Fund..............................  102,914 18
Contingent Fund.......................................  9,700 64

    Total................................................  $793,084 34

These figures are subject to a slight change after the few delinquent Lodges shall send in their returns.

COMPARATIVE TABLE, SHOWING THE MEMBERSHIP, SICKNESS, DEATHS, ETC., WITH AVERAGES FOR THE PAST TEN YEARS, TO DECEMBER 31, 1892.

| | 1883 | 1884 | 1885 | 1886 | 1887 | 1888 | 1889 | 1890 | 1891 | 1892 |
|---|---|---|---|---|---|---|---|---|---|---|
| Number of members | 14173 | 14330 | 14501 | 14847 | 15354 | 16060 | 16940 | 17707 | 18390 | 19452 |
| Number of members who received Sick Benefits | 1703 | 1685 | 1708 | 1668 | 1787 | 1952 | 2091 | 2972 | 2407 | 3037 |
| Ratio | 1 in 8.32 | 1 in 8.54 | $8 49 | $8 90 | $8 58 | 1 in 8.23 | 1 in 8.10 | 1 in 5.96 | 1 in 7.64 | 1 in 6 40 |
| Average amount paid each | $14 00 | $12 95 | 16 14 | 14 27 | 17 15 | $15 98 | $15 22 | $13 33 | ....... | $14.53 |
| Total number of weeks' sickness | 668⅞ | 7202¾ | 7754⅞ | 7896½ | 8624 | 10231½ | 10261¼ | 12539⅞ | 11842½ | 14046⅞ |
| Average days' sickness per member | 3.30 | 3.51 | 3.74 | 3.72 | 3.93 | 4.45 | 4.24 | 4.95 | 4.50 | 5.05 |
| Average cost per member for Sick Benefits | $1 68 | $1 52 | $1 90 | $1 60½ | $1 73 | $1 89 | $1 88 | $2 23 | $1 99 | $2 26 |
| Number of deaths | 84 | 86 | 91 | 94 | 99 | 103 | 110 | 134 | 123 | 157 |
| Ratio per 1000 | 5.92 | 6 | 6.27 | 6.33 | 6.44 | 6.41 | 6.49 | 7.56 | 6.68 | 8.07 |
| Average Funeral Benefits paid in each case | $28 26 | $27 66 | $34 29 | $30 14 | $31 20 | $30 85 | $26 78 | $36 22 | $42 20 | $42 15 |
| Average cost per member for Funeral Benefits | 0 16 | 0 16½ | 0 21½ | 0 19 | 0 20 | 0 19¾ | 0 17½ | 0 27 | 0 28 | 0 34½ |
| Average cost per member for Sick and Funeral Benefits | 1 84 | 1 68½ | 2 11½ | 1 79½ | 1 93 | 2 07¾ | 2 05⅜ | 2 50 | 2 27 | 2 60½ |
| Average receipt from each member for Dues | 5 19 | 5 24 | 4 99 | 5 38 | 5 39 | 5 49 | 5 49 | 5 52 | 5 57 | 5 45½ |
| Average receipt per member for Initiations and Degrees | 2 01 | 1 78 | 1 50 | 1 72 | 1 66 | 2 00 | 1 78 | 1 75 | 1 63 | 1 68¼ |
| Average receipt per member from all other sources | 1 92 | 2 03 | 2 25 | 2 09 | 1 93 | 2 48 | 2 33 | 2 13 | 2 07 | 2 19¼ |
| Average total receipt per member | 9 12 | 9 05 | 8 74 | 9 19 | 8 98 | 9 97 | 9 60 | 9 40 | 9 27 | 9 33 |
| Average cost per member for current expenses | 3 04 | 3 28 | 3 85 | 3 59 | 3 64 | 4 36 | 4 37 | 3 96 | 4 14 | 3 13 |
| Average cost per member for Sick and Funeral Benefits and current expenses | 4 88 | 4 96 | 6 18 | 5 38 | 5 57 | 6 43¾ | 6 42⅜ | 6 46 | 6 41 | 5 73½ |

## TABLE SHOWING THE RISE AND PROGRESS OF THE ORDER IN ONTARIO SINCE 1856 TO DECEMBER 31, 1892.

| Year. | No. of Lodges. | Members. | Initiated. | By Card. | Reinstated. | Withdrawn. | Suspended. | Expelled. | Deaths. | Revenue. | | Benefits. | | Average Lodge Membership. |
|---|---|---|---|---|---|---|---|---|---|---|---|---|---|---|
| 1856 | 12 | 605 | 171 | 11 | ... | 21 | 38 | 20 | 2 | * | | $299 | 00 | 50.46 |
| 1857 | 15 | 738 | 200 | 12 | 7 | 22 | 58 | 39 | 2 | * | | 796 | 00 | 49.20 |
| 1858 | 15 | 738 | 167 | 7 | 16 | 17 | 50 | 67 | 4 | * | | 467 | 74 | 49.20 |
| 1859 | 12 | 556 | 196 | 3 | 4 | 23 | 56 | 108 | 6 | * | | 596 | 00 | 46.33 |
| 1860 | 13 | 534 | 96 | 4 | 6 | 19 | 72 | 48 | 6 | * | | 1338 | 00 | 41.07 |
| 1861 | 14 | 544 | 105 | 2 | 13 | 14 | 79 | 43 | 4 | * | | 1242 | 68 | 31.91 |
| 1862 | 15 | 500 | 92 | 7 | 3 | 27 | 63 | 29 | 4 | * | | 803 | 00 | 33.33 |
| 1863 | 15 | 573 | 82 | 5 | 9 | 15 | 64 | 3† | 6 | $3174 | 60 | 858 | 48 | 38.20 |
| 1864 | 16 | 512 | 142 | 10 | 5 | 12 | 62 | .... | 5 | 4104 | 24 | 1040 | 20 | 32.00 |
| 1865 | 14 | 539 | 155 | 7 | 5 | :6 | 65 | 2 | 7 | 4165 | 41 | 826 | 98 | 38.50 |
| 1866 | 15 | 647 | 211 | 11 | 8 | 26 | 36 | 3 | 11 | 6013 | 84 | 1239 | 00 | 43.20 |
| 1867 | 14 | 907 | 287 | 24 | 12 | 80 | 49 | 2 | 1 | 7635 | 13 | 1382 | 00 | 64.80 |
| 1868 | 17 | 1103 | 399 | 29 | 7 | 44 | 35 | .... | 7 | 5948 | 27 | 2145 | 24 | 64.88 |
| 1869 | 20 | 1443 | 484 | 40 | 14 | 67 | 113 | 7 | 7 | 13332 | 59 | 2547 | 70 | 72.15 |
| 1870 | 30 | 2302 | 758 | 91 | 13 | 109 | 147 | 3 | 17 | 18611 | 56 | 3290 | 26 | 76.73 |
| 1871 | 44 | 3495 | 1259 | 141 | 21 | 184 | 177 | 7 | 21 | 28865 | 97 | 4716 | 53 | 79.43 |
| 1872 | 66 | 5079 | 1864 | 206 | 18 | 294 | 334 | 7 | 25 | 42974 | 33 | 6277 | 95 | 76.95 |
| 1873 | 86 | 6774 | 2108 | 223 | 20 | 355 | 412 | 16 | 46 | 58615 | 37 | 10822 | 78 | 78.76 |
| 1874 | 115 | 8578 | 2439 | 226 | 46 | 396 | 436 | 19 | 56 | 42861 | 53 | 12963 | 37 | 74.60 |
| 1875 | 141 | 10188 | 2369 | 351 | 85 | 448 | 617 | 23 | 52 | 8999 | 50 | 16187 | 92 | 72.25 |
| 1876 | 156 | 11322 | 2269 | 266 | 65 | 386 | 980 | 22 | 73 | 98214 | 07 | 19403 | 20 | 73.28 |
| 1877 | 175 | 12172 | 1981 | 296 | 176 | 470 | 885 | 30 | 89 | 107561 | 30 | 22080 | 84 | 69.55 |
| 1878 | 180 | 12332 | 1776 | 190 | 88 | 339 | 3316 | 23 | 77 | 106866 | 19 | 21287 | 92 | 68.51 |
| 1879 | 186 | 12442 | 1400 | 190 | 103 | 337 | 1206 | 51 | 79 | 101723 | 94 | 25141 | 47 | 66.89 |
| 1880 | 188 | 12168 | 1305 | 97 | 150 | 287 | 1558 | 23 | 87 | 102424 | 38 | 26075 | 76 | 64.72 |
| 1881 | 192 | 12776 | 1783 | 151 | 177 | 318 | 1038 | 69 | 74 | 113951 | 81 | 29719 | 47 | 66.54 |
| 1882 ‡ | 200 | 13755 | 2071 | 188 | 191 | 304 | 1048 | 31 | 101 | 138292 | 35 | 34618 | 92 | 68.77 |
| 1882 § | 202 | 13861 | 1984 | 196 | 182 | 370 | 1089 | 26 | 98 | 141474 | 28 | 34488 | 07 | 68.61 |
| 1883 | 204 | 14173 | 1538 | 165 | 139 | 274 | 1169 | 10 | 84 | 129375 | 50 | 38881 | 72 | 69.47 |
| 1884 | 204 | 14330 | 1453 | 132 | 118 | 261 | 1186 | 13 | 86 | 129832 | 74 | 41224 | 56 | 70.24 |
| 1885 | 208 | 14951 | 1305 | 200 | 118 | 234 | 1076 | 8 | 91 | 126787 | 60 | 44072 | 38 | 70.15 |
| 1886 | 211 | 14847 | 1524 | 139 | 140 | 214 | 1130 | 9 | 94 | 136536 | 10 | 47507 | 13 | 70.36 |
| 1887 | 215 | 15353 | 1606 | 140 | 141 | 225 | 1047 | 7 | 99 | 137981 | 19 | 52232 | 68 | 71.41 |
| 1888 | 218 | 16060 | 1799 | 152 | 161 | 264 | 1021 | 10 | 103 | 159975 | 91 | 53878 | 67 | 73.66 |
| 1889 | 224 | 16940 | 1854 | 210 | 159 | 256 | 929 | 8 | 110 | 162758 | 62 | 62522 | 04 | 75.66 |
| 1890 | 232 | 17707 | 1950 | 183 | 209 | 289 | 1136 | 16 | 134 | 166533 | 52 | 71374 | 90 | 76.34 |
| 1891 | 237 | 18390 | 1841 | 162 | 157 | 264 | 1063 | 15 | 123 | 170454 | 09 | 65293 | 84 | 77.59 |
| 1892 | 244 | 19452 | 2155 | 144 | 168 | 305 | 918 | 14 | 157 | 181509 | 48 | 77344 | 94 | 79.71 |

$836,988 34

* Annual Receipts not given on the Returns.

† Expulsions for cause only ; hitherto members were expelled for N.P.D.

‡ This is for the year ending 31st June, 1882.

§ This is for the year ending 31st December, 1882, from which date all statements are afterwards made.

TABLE SHOWING PLACES WHERE THE GRAND LODGE HAS MET DURING THE PAST SEVENTEEN YEARS, WITH RELATIVE COST FOR MILEAGE AND PER DIEM AND OTHER EXPENSES OF THE GRAND LODGE—1876 TO 1892.

| YEAR. | Place of Meeting. | Number of Officers and Representatives. | Miles Travelled. | Average. | Mileage and Per Diem. | | Number of Members. | Cost per Member for Mileage and Per Diem. | All other expenses of Grand Lodge. | | Cost per Member all other expenses of Grand Lodge. |
|---|---|---|---|---|---|---|---|---|---|---|---|
| | | | | | $ | c. | | c. | $ | c. | c. |
| 1876 | St. Catharines | 213 | 51,367 | 269 | 3,678 | 40 | 11,322 | 32½ | 2,256 | 71 | 20 |
| 1877 | Belleville | 231 | 83,295 | 360 | 4,906 | 28 | 12,172 | 40½ | 2,864 | 99 | 23½ |
| 1878 | Toronto | 230 | 50,752 | 221 | 3,414 | 10 | 12,332 | 27½ | 3,201 | 61 | 26 |
| 1879 | Hamilton | 237 | 46,355 | 199 | 3,280 | 06 | 12,442 | 26¼ | 2,767 | 47 | 22 |
| 1880 | Guelph | 232 | 45,895 | 194 | 3,261 | 80 | 12,168 | 26½ | 3,992 | 17 | 32¾ |
| 1881 | Brantford | 239 | 50,353 | 210 | 3,516 | 14 | 12,776 | 28 | 4,001 | 59 | 31¼ |
| 1882 | Toronto | 257 | 52,883 | 206 | 3,657 | 32 | 13,755 | 26¼ | 3,176 | 86 | 23 |
| 1883 | Ottawa | 260 | 173,525 | 667 | 8,505 | 02 | 14,192 | 60 | 3,130 | 57 | 22 |
| 1884 | St. Thomas | 253 | 30,270 | 119 | 3,031 | 51 | 14,453 | 21 | 3,716 | 92 | 25¾ |
| 1885 | Hamilton | 261 | 25,524 | 97 | 2,906 | 40 | 14,408 | 20 | 3,353 | 51 | 23¼ |
| 1886 | London | 267 | 32,983 | 123 | 3,231 | 15 | 14,762 | 22 | 3,339 | 87 | 22½ |
| 1887 | Peterboro' | 273 | 43,974 | 161 | 3,826 | 70 | 15,141 | 25½ | 3,383 | 22 | 22¼ |
| 1888 | Barrie | 292 | 46,726 | 160 | 4,044 | 30 | 15,961 | 25½ | 3,647 | 22 | 23 |
| 1889 | St. Catharines | 296 | 43,020 | 145 | 3,929 | 00 | 16,628 | 23½ | 3,507 | 01 | 21 |
| 1890 | Toronto | 305 | 38,026 | 124 | 3,731 | 30 | 17,415 | 21¼ | 4,394 | 41 | 25¼ |
| 1891 | Stratford | 314 | 42,134 | 134 | 3,985 | 70 | 18,210 | 21¾ | 4,801 | 95 | 26¼ |
| 1892 | Windsor | 339 | 81,666 | 241 | 6,221 | 60 | 19,122 | 32 | 5,029 | 19 | 26¼ |

The Grand Lodge meeting in August, the figures are given for year ending June 30th.
In 1883, Ottawa, only 60 per cent of the cost of mileage was paid.

The accompanying is a complete list of the Deaths for the year ending 31st December, 1892, with ages, etc. :—

| Name. | Age. | Lodge. | No. | Location. | Married or Single. | Children. | Date. |
|---|---|---|---|---|---|---|---|
| Seaton, Wm..... | 62 | Brock .......... | 9 | Brockville .... | M | .. | Sept. 23 |
| Black, W. W.... | 32 | " .......... | 9 | " .... | M | .. | Oct. 13 |
| Henderson, W. H | 36 | Cataraqui ...... | 10 | Kingston ..... | M | 3 | Aug. 13 |
| Potter, Henry... | 31 | " ...... | 10 | " ..... | M | .. | Dec. 5 |
| Rombough, M. J. | 56 | Otonabee ....... | 13 | Peterborough . | .... | .. | Oct. 17 |
| Noble, James.... | 63 | Union.......... | 16 | St. Catharines. | M | 5 | Dec. 30 |
| Wilson, Alex..... | 37 | " .......... | 16 | " | M | 2 | Dec 1 |
| King, Alf. E..... | 31 | Phœnix....... | 22 | Oshawa ...... | M | .. | Ap'il 19 |
| Braidwood, Alex. | 43 | " ...... | 22 | " ...... | M | . | July — |
| McLerie, John... | 67 | Chatham ...... | 29 | Chatham ..... | M | .. | Feb. 12 |
| Brock, Thomas... | 69 | Eureka......... | 30 | London ...... | M | .. | Jan. 7 |
| Baillie, John .... | 65 | " ........ | 30 | " ...... | M | .. | Oct. 28 |
| Pringle, John.... | 72 | " ........ | 30 | " ...... | M | .. | Nov. 1 |
| Reed, Edward... | 54 | " ........ | 30 | " ...... | M | .. | Dec. 26 |
| Shaw, Robert.... | 26 | Elgin.......... | 32 | St. Thomas ... | .... | .. | Feb. — |
| Harrison, Hy.... | 50 | Gore .......... | 34 | Brantford .... | M | .. | Feb. 2 |
| McTaggart, Wm. | 62 | " ........ | 34 | " .... | M | .. | Feb. 12 |
| Castello, Daniel.. | 77 | " ........ | 34 | " .... | M | .. | June 27 |
| Beer, Wm....... | 49 | " ........ | 34 | " .... | .... | .. | Sep. 26 |
| McKinney, Alex.. | 40 | " ........ | 34 | " .... | .... | .. | Nov. 12 |
| Dee, F. O........ | 70 | " ........ | 34 | " .... | .... | .. | July 18 |
| Sudworth, Wright | 66 | Samaritan ...... | 35 | Ingersoll ..... | M | 1 | |
| Allen, A. A...... | 51 | " ...... | 35 | " ..... | M | 2 | |
| Othen, Jas....... | 53 | St. Marys ...... | 36 | St. Marys .... | M | 7 | Jan. 30 |
| Box, Richard.... | 66 | " ...... | 36 | " .... | M | 2 | June 25 |
| Knox, Andrew... | 58 | " ...... | 36 | " .... | M | 6 | Aug. 3 |
| Lowe, Thos J.... | 45 | Forest City..... | 38 | London ...... | M | 3 | May 27 |
| Wood, Thos...... | 30 | Avon........... | 41 | Stratford ..... | .... | .. | Jan. 2 |
| Humphrey, J. W. | 50 | " .......... | 41 | " ..... | M | .. | Oct. 27 |
| Trow, James.... | 66 | " .......... | 41 | " ..... | M | 5 | Sep. 10 |
| Cox, Thomas.... | 44 | Excelsior ...... | 44 | Hamilton..... | M | .. | Feb. 18 |
| McNeil, W...... | 29 | " ...... | 44 | " ..... | S | .. | |
| Armstrong, J..... | 24 | " ...... | 44 | " ..... | M | .. | |
| Wilson, H. A.... | 41 | Frontier ........ | 45 | Windsor ..... | M | . | Ap'il 24 |
| Rose, John....... | 32 | " ........ | 45 | " ..... | S | .. | June 28 |
| Reid, W. E...... | 67 | " ........ | 45 | " ..... | M | .. | Sep. 15 |
| Atherton, Thos... | 73 | " ........ | 45 | " ..... | M | .. | Oct. 14 |
| McAfee, Henry... | 77 | " ........ | 45 | " ..... | M | .. | Oct. 23 |
| Allardyce, Arthur | 30 | " ........ | 45 | " ..... | M | .. | Dec. 23 |
| Acheson, J. L... | 43 | Unity .......... | 47 | Hamilton..... | M | .. | Feb. 3 |
| Kleinsteiber, Hugo | 37 | " .......... | 47 | " ..... | M | .. | Mar. 23 |
| Kellond, George.. | 75 | " .......... | 47 | " ..... | M | .. | April 6 |
| McKenzie, Donald | 55 | " .......... | 47 | " ..... | M | 2 | Oct. 2 |
| Dyas, J. J........ | 54 | Dominion ...... | 48 | London ...... | M | .. | |
| Morrison, Hugh A | 50 | Covenant ....... | 52 | Toronto ...... | M | .. | Mar. 20 |

### LIST OF DEATHS—*Continued.*

| Name. | Age | Lodge. | No. | Location. | Married or Single. | Children. | Date. |
|---|---|---|---|---|---|---|---|
| Wilson, Chas.... | 48 | Covenant........ | 52 | Toronto ...... | M | 1 | June 19 |
| Irwin, James..... | 47 | " ....... | 52 | " ...... | M | 6 | Dec. 4 |
| Sampson, Joseph. | 23 | Collingwood .... | 54 | Collingwood .. | S | .. | Mar. 4 |
| McGee, Wm..... | 62 | " ....... | 54 | " .. | M | 5 | Sep. 27 |
| Gray, James..... | 47 | Queen City ..... | 56 | Toronto ...... | M | 6 | Jan. 2 |
| Alexander, Jos. A. | 42 | Howard ........ | 58 | Strathroy...... | M | .. | Jan. 7 |
| McPherson, A... | 33 | " ....... | 58 | " ...... | M | .. | Oct. 12 |
| Mullens, Geo.... | 50 | Corinthian...... | 61 | Oshawa ...... | M | .. | Mar. 22 |
| Wickens, Jas..... | 42 | Barrie.......... | 63 | Barrie........ | M | 3 | Feb. 10 |
| Anderton, Jas.... | 54 | " | 63 | " ....... | M | 6 | Aug. |
| Moses, Richard.. | 32 | Flo. Nightingale. | 66 | Bowmanville.. | M | 2 | Jan. 10 |
| Southwell, G..... | 52 | Eastern Star.... | 72 | Whitby ...... | M | 12 | Feb. 19 |
| Pringle, J. R..... | 56 | " .... | 72 | " ...... | M | | May 15 |
| Thompson, M. J. | 42 | " .... | 72 | " ...... | M | 2 | |
| Munsy, D........ | 35 | " .... | 72 | " ........ | M | 4 | |
| Clegg, D. W..... | 22 | " .... | 72 | " ...... | S | .. | |
| Catto, W........ | 29 | Bothwell ...... | 74 | Bothwell ..... | M | 3 | Feb. 27 |
| Deyell, Wm...... | 24 | St. Thomas ..... | 76 | St. Thomas ... | S | .. | Feb. 11 |
| Berry, Mark..... | 29 | " ..... | 76 | " ... | M | 1 | May 21 |
| Hopperton, Jos... | 37 | " ..... | 76 | " ... | M | 7 | Oct. 30 |
| Budd, Thos...... | 34 | Oxford ......... | 77 | Ingersoll...... | S | .. | Jan. 28 |
| Trayes, J. B..... | 50 | Durham........ | 78 | Port Hope.... | M | 2 | Oct. 14 |
| Willson, Dr. B. A | 61 | Belleville ...... | 81 | Belleville ..... | M | 3 | Jan. 13 |
| Ridley, Chas. M. | 66 | " ....... | 81 | " ..... | M | 2 | Sep. 12 |
| Montgomery, Thos | 38 | Empire......... | 87 | St. Catharines. | S | .. | June 5 |
| Springer, Wm... | 62 | Olive Branch... | 88 | Woodstock ... | M | .. | Ap'il 9 |
| Currie, John..... | 39 | " ... | 88 | " ... | S | .. | Sept. 7 |
| Emery, R. B..... | 54 | Reliance........ | 89 | Guelph ....... | .... | .. | Mar. 26 |
| Finlayson, Jas... | 40 | Grand River.... | 91 | Paris......... | M | .. | June 10 |
| Flack, H J...... | 62 | Nith........... | 96 | New Hamburg | M | 7 | Ap'il 29 |
| Williams, T. S... | 49 | Lindsay ........ | 100 | Lindsay ...... | M | 5 | May 13 |
| Northmore, R. E. | 30 | Deseronto .... . | 102 | Deseronto .... | M | .. | Feb. 10 |
| Simmons, J...... | 24 | " ...... | 102 | " .... | M | .. | June 3 |
| Phillips, Geo..... | 56 | Crescent........ | 104 | Hamilton...... | M | .. | May — |
| Doughty, Geo.... | 41 | Waterloo ....... | 107 | Galt.......... | M | 3 | May 7 |
| Gammon, Fred. H | 34 | Royal Oak...... | 108 | Forest........ | M | 3 | Aug. 15 |
| Anderson, Joseph. | 48 | " ....... | 108 | " ........ | M | .. | Oct. 16 |
| Corbett, Alex. C. | 26 | Peterboro'....... | 111 | Peterboro' .... | S | .. | Ap'il 14 |
| Stephenson, Thos. | 23 | " ....... | 111 | " .... | S | .. | May 26 |
| Farquharson, J. M | 35 | Lucknow....... | 112 | Lucknow ..... | M | 2 | Mar. 6 |
| McHardy, Geo... | 52 | " ....... | 112 | " ..... | S | .. | July 16 |
| Bateman, Thos. W | 23 | Valley City..... | 117 | Dundas ...... | S | .. | Ap'il 10 |
| Williamson, Jos.. | 48 | Maitland ....... | 119 | Wingham..... | M | .. | Nov. 7 |
| Taylor, W. E.... | 40 | Sydenham Valley | 120 | Wallaceburg .. | M | 2 | Jan. — |
| Anderson, Wm... | 56 | " | 120 | " | M | 4 | Dec. 5 |
| Kennedy, J. F.... | 31 | " | 120 | " | M | .. | July 1 |
| Shepley, John.... | 49 | " | 120 | " | M | .. | Nov. 30 |
| McEwen, F...... | 50 | Stella .......... | 125 | Carleton Place | M | 1 | Jan. 21 |
| Quackenbush, G.A | 33 | " .......... | 125 | " | M | .. | Dec. 23 |

LIST OF DEATHS—*Continued.*

| Name. | Age. | Lodge. | No. | Location. | Married or Single. | Children. | Date. |
|---|---|---|---|---|---|---|---|
| Baker, Abram.... | 38 | Mystic ......... | 128 | Waterdown... | M | 9 | Feb. 9 |
| Fair, J. T. A...... | 46 | Cobourg........ | 136 | Cobourg...... | M | 4 | Oct. 27 |
| Scringer, James.. | 47 | " ........ | 136 | " ...... | M | 5 | Nov. 3 |
| Kelley, J. H...... | 23 | Ancaster ....... | 138 | Ancaster ..... | S | .. | May 21 |
| Black, Wm...... | 52 | Leamington .... | 140 | Leamington... | M | .. | Aug. 10 |
| Atkins, F. F..... | 51 | Bay of Quinte... | 143 | Picton ....... | M | .. | Ap'il.13 |
| Campbell, A. D... | 45 | Vivian ......... | 146 | Arnprior ..... | M | 9 | Feb. 24 |
| Price, Thos...... | 39 | " ......... | 146 | " ..... | M | 5 | Ap'il.14 |
| Milne, H. W..... | 26 | " ......... | 146 | " ..... | M | 1 | May 24 |
| Reid, Geo. R..... | 66 | Model.......... | 147 | Wyoming .... | M | .. | Feb. 27 |
| Idle, Rev. D..... | 47 | Aurora ......... | 148 | Aurora ....... | M | 3 | Ap'il.16 |
| Patterson, W. S.. | 61 | Sycamore ...... | 151 | Arkona....... | M | .. | Mar. 7 |
| Henderson, David | 38 | Thamesville .... | 157 | Thamesville .. | S | .. | Jan. 6 |
| Keating, Dr. T. A. | 54 | Progress........ | 158 | Guelph....... | M | 5 | Mar. 13 |
| Harris, Wm...... | 61 | Listowel........ | 160 | Listowel..... | M | 4 | Jan. 30 |
| Boyle, Peter..... | 55 | " ........ | 160 | " ...... | M | 3 | Feb. 22 |
| Rutherford, Dr. J. A | 35 | DeNovo ........ | 170 | Port Elgin.... | M | .. | Feb. 26 |
| McLardy, Wm. B. | 62 | Penetangore .... | 172 | Kincardine ... | M | .. | Jan. 24 |
| Morgan, Hiram.. | 43 | " .... | 172 | " ... | M | 6 | Mar. 17 |
| Purdy, Wm....... | 46 | " .... | 172 | " ... | M | 2 | Aug. 22 |
| Bautinhimer, P... | 66 | Dolman ........ | 174 | Ayr .......... | M | 2 | Jan. 7 |
| Scott, Jas........ | 37 | " ........ | 174 | " .......... | M | 2 | Feb 14 |
| Waterman, Geo.. | 29 | " ........ | 174 | " .......... | M | 4 | Oct. 30 |
| Chadwick, D. K.. | 37 | Teeswater ...... | 183 | Teeswater .... | M | 2 | Jan. 25 |
| Fraser, Alex..... | 30 | " ...... | 183 | " .... | .... | .. | July 27 |
| Hammitt, W. F.. | 33 | Chorazin ....... | 190 | London ...... | M | 2 | Aug. 13 |
| Hipkins, J. T..... | 23 | Albert.......... | 194 | Toronto ...... | M | .. | June 24 |
| Young, Chas E... | 21 | Florence ....... | 196 | Florence...... | S | .. | Oct. 13 |
| Gray, Frederick.. | 42 | Silver Star ..... | 202 | Milverton .... | M | 4 | |
| Attridge, Samuel. | 42 | " ..... | 202 | " .... | S | .. | |
| Smith, Jacob S... | 42 | " ..... | 201 | " .... | M | 3 | Aug. 28 |
| Beatty, Duncan N | 30 | Pembroke ...... | 203 | Pembroke .... | S | .. | June 26 |
| Anderson, R..... | 34 | Argyll.......... | 212 | Napanee ..... | M | 4 | April 2 |
| Nottle, John...... | 34 | Freestone....... | 215 | Beamsville.... | .... | .. | Dec. 6 |
| Arnold, John..... | 64 | Mount Bridges.. | 217 | Mount Bridges | M | 6 | |
| Sutherland, J. F.. | 44 | " .. | 217 | " | M | 3 | Oct. 23 |
| O'Connell, M..... | 36 | Ottawa ... ..... | 224 | Ottawa ....... | M | 3 | Mar. 30 |
| Samson, L. J..... | 47 | " ........ | 224 | " ....... | M | 4 | Oct. 12 |
| Murray, Jas. C. . | 35 | International ... | 228 | Intern'l Bridge | M | 3 | April 9 |
| Munro, Angus.... | 42 | Embro Star..... | 229 | Embro ....... | M | 4 | July 29 |
| McCutcheon, Jno. | 27 | Prince of Wales. | 230 | Toronto ...... | M | 1 | Ap'il.13 |
| McFall, Wm..... | 25 | " | 230 | " ...... | S | .. | Dec. 9 |
| Worden, Ralph.. | 33 | Waterford...... | 235 | Waterford.... | M | 4 | Ap'il.21 |
| McDonald, Jas.... | 36 | " ...... | 335 | " .... | M | 1 | Dec. 22 |
| Blancher, Sala... | 69 | Farmersville.... | 237 | Athens ....... | M | .. | July 6 |
| Holmes, J. G..... | 27 | Wilton ......... | 242 | Toronto ...... | S | .. | June 17 |
| Mitchell, Robt. C. | 32 | Thornbury ..... | 243 | Thornbury .. | M | 3 | Feb. 21 |
| Doxsee, C. H.... | 46 | Campbellford... | 248 | Campbellford . | M | 7 | June 3 |
| McPherson, John. | 39 | Grand Valley... | 256 | Grand Valley. | S | .. | Nov. 18 |

LIST OF DEATHS—*Concluded.*

| Name. | Age. | Lodge. | No | Location. | Married or Single. | Children. | Date. |
|---|---|---|---|---|---|---|---|
| McNee, John A... | 34 | Thamesford .... | 258 | Thamesford... | S | .. | Mar. 12 |
| Houston, Jos. L. | 34 | Gold Hill....... | 261 | Rat Portage... | S | .. | June 20 |
| Vosburgh, John.. | 50 | Norwood ....... | 262 | Norwood ..... | M | | ... |
| Scott, Archie..... | 33 | " ....... | 262 | " ....... | M | 4 | Dec. 9 |
| Bower, C. A..... | 31 | Fraternity...... | 264 | Perth ........ | S | .. | April 3 |
| Seaman, Sidney.. | 33 | Delta........... | 265 | Delta ......... | S | .. | Oct. 8 |
| Fisher, Elijah.... | 32 | Rockliffe........ | 278 | Ottawa ....... | M | 2 | Aug. 15 |
| Spence, John B... | 32 | " ....... | 278 | " ....... | M | 2 | Dec. 10 |
| Barron, J........ | 35 | Earnscliffe...... | 283 | Janeville...... | M | 2 | Jan. 6 |
| Asher, W. J...... | 42 | " ....... | 283 | " ....... | M | 2 | May 25 |
| Nichols, J........ | 41 | Glanworth..... | 189 | Glanworth.... | .... | .. | Dec. 18 |
| Hardy, Wm...... | 21 | Tweed ......... | 290 | Tweed ....... | S | .. | July 21 |
| Tweedie, Sanford. | 24 | Dresden........ | 124 | Dresden...... | S | .. | Mar. 27 |
| Hamstock, Jas... | 34 | Sutton ......... | 168 | Sutton........ | W | 1 | Mar. — |

It is to be hoped that Lodge Secretaries will learn the benefit of greater promptness in sending in their returns. It is as easy for a Secretary to make out his report in time for the first meeting in January and July as it is to dally along for three or four weeks. The facts required are as well at hand on the last night of the term as ever after, and having the work of the term all before him, it would seem that there is no real reasonable excuse for the delay of even one week. When Secretaries learn that the information asked for in their return is not for the use of any one person, but for the benefit of their Lodge and the general good of the Order, then will they appreciate better the value of greater promptitude in sending them in.

All of which is fraternally submitted,

J. S. King.

Grand Sec'y.

## STATEMENT OF RECEIPTS BY THE GRAND SECRETARY FOR THE YEAR JULY 20TH, 1892, TO JULY 20TH, 1893.

| Date. | LODGE. | No. | Total. | Capita Tax. | Supplies. | Sundries. | Charter Fee. |
|---|---|---|---|---|---|---|---|
| **1892.** | | | | | | | |
| July 21 | Frontier | 45 | $63 25 | $63 25 | | | |
| | Beaver | 82 | 14 00 | 14 00 | | | |
| | Glencoe | 133 | 13 75 | 13 75 | | | |
| | Victoria | 64 | 6 40 | | 6 40 | | |
| | Delta | 265 | 11 25 | 11 25 | | | |
| | Midland | 274 | 12 25 | 12 25 | | | |
| | Wellington Square | 178 | 7 25 | 7 25 | | | |
| | Streetsville | 122 | 12 00 | 12 00 | | | |
| | Maitland | 119 | 14 00 | 14 00 | | | |
| | Waterloo | 107 | 56 | | 56 | | |
| | Durham | 78 | 15 | | 15 | | |
| | Lucan | 70 | 6 00 | 6 00 | | | |
| 22 | St. Thomas | 76 | 86 85 | 86 50 | | 35 | |
| | Niagara Falls | 53 | 30 00 | 30 00 | | | |
| | Thornbury | 243 | 8 25 | 8 25 | | | |
| | Milton | 92 | 6 25 | 6 25 | | | |
| | Erie | 33 | 4 25 | 4 25 | | | |
| | Collingwood | 54 | 1 00 | | 1 00 | | |
| | Thamesford | 258 | 2 03 | | 2 03 | | |
| 23 | Clinton | 83 | 1 68 | | 1 68 | | |
| | St. Clair | 106 | 24 25 | 24 25 | | | |
| | Ridgetown | 144 | 1 25 | | 1 25 | | |
| | Enterprise | 218 | 30 00 | 30 00 | | | |
| | Floral | 252 | 9 50 | 9 50 | | | |
| 26 | Romeo | 164 | 1 68 | | 1 68 | | |
| | Clinton | 83 | 6 00 | 6 00 | | | |
| | Sarnia | 126 | 19 00 | 19 00 | | | |
| | Lindsay | 100 | 85 | | 85 | | |
| | Waterloo | 107 | 2 80 | | 2 80 | | |
| | Algoma | 267 | 14 25 | 14 25 | | | |
| 28 | Lakeview | 272 | 19 00 | 19 00 | | | |
| | Chorazin | 190 | 35 | | | 35 | |
| | North Star | 68 | 12 25 | 12 25 | | | |
| | Balmoral | 280 | 1 68 | | 1 68 | | |
| | Maitland | 119 | 7 00 | 7 00 | | | |
| | Marion | 131 | 1 75 | 1 75 | | | |
| | Canada | 49 | 50 75 | 50 75 | | | |
| 30 | Ahiram | 205 | 25 50 | 25 50 | | | |
| | Leamington | 140 | 33 25 | 33 25 | | | |
| | Hillsburg | 167 | 10 75 | 10 75 | | | |
| | Crescent | 104 | 57 50 | 57 50 | | | |
| | Penetangore | 172 | 3 36 | | 3 36 | | |
| | Sutton | 168 | 9 00 | 9 00 | | | |
| | Alpha | 154 | 75 | | 75 | | |
| | Constellation | 85 | 1 50 | 1 50 | | | |
| | Embro Star | 229 | 12 50 | 12 50 | | | |
| Aug. 1 | Laurel | 110 | 6 75 | 6 75 | | | |
| | Lorne | 175 | 1 68 | | 1 68 | | |
| | Elora | 231 | 4 48 | | 4 48 | | |
| | Orient | 134 | 1 00 | 1 00 | | | |
| 2 | Lethbridge | | 3 52 | | 3 52 | | |
| 3 | Maitland | 119 | 14 75 | 14 75 | | | |
| 4 | Progress | 158 | 3 08 | | 3 08 | | |
| | Minerva | 197 | 1 30 | | 1 30 | | |
| | Mystic | 198 | 48 70 | 4 00 | | 44 70 | |
| 5 | Arthur | 281 | 1 32 | | 1 32 | | |
| | Wilton | 242 | 22 25 | 22 25 | | | |
| 6 | Harmony | 115 | 2 80 | | 2 80 | | |
| | Peterboro' | 111 | 4 12 | | 4 12 | | |
| | Sudbury | 282 | 11 75 | 11 75 | | | |

STATEMENT OF RECEIPTS.—*Continued.*

| Date. | LODGE. | No. | Total. | Capita Tax. | Supplies. | Sundries. | Charter Fee. |
|---|---|---|---|---|---|---|---|
| **1892.** | | | | | | | |
| Aug. 8 | Rond Eau | 40 | 2 53 | | 2 53 | | |
| | Grand Un.on | 07 | 1 68 | | 1 68 | | |
| 17 | Supplies | | 60 | | 60 | | |
| 19 | Otter | 50 | 1 85 | | 1 85 | | |
| | Pembroke | 203 | 3 36 | | 3 36 | | |
| | Sydenham Valley | 120 | 3 36 | | 3 36 | | |
| | Midland | 274 | 1 62 | | 1 37 | 25 | |
| | Carleton | 240 | 3 00 | | 3 00 | | |
| | Gold Hill | 261 | 3 36 | | 3 36 | | |
| | Dauncey | 176 | 55 | | 55 | | |
| | Gananoque | 114 | 3 00 | | 3 00 | | |
| | Niagara Falls | 53 | 1 40 | | 1 40 | | |
| | Elmira | 216 | 1 68 | | 1 68 | | |
| | Egremont | 207 | 50 | | 50 | | |
| | Chesterville | 288 | 3 36 | | 3 36 | | |
| 22 | Gold Hill | 261 | 3 64 | | 3 64 | | |
| 23 | Peaceful Dove | 235 | 2 00 | | 2 00 | | |
| 25 | Bracebridge | 251 | 1 68 | | 1 68 | | |
| | Brock | 9 | 24 | | 24 | | |
| | Madoc | 179 | 3 10 | | 3 10 | | |
| | Forest City | 38 | 1 68 | | 1 68 | | |
| | Campbellford | 248 | 5 10 | | 5 10 | | |
| | Rockliffe | 278 | 3 36 | | 3 36 | | |
| | Chatham | 29 | 3 36 | | 3 36 | | |
| 26 | Frontier | 45 | 1 68 | | 1 68 | | |
| 27 | Hillsburg | 167 | 1 12 | | 1 12 | | |
| | Harmony (Degree of Rebekah) | 15 | 3 36 | | 3 36 | | |
| | Minnetonka | 293 | 30 00 | | | | 30 00 |
| | Thomasburg | 292 | 55 10 | | 25 10 | | 30 00 |
| 29 | North Star | 68 | 2 50 | | 2 50 | | |
| 30 | International | 228 | 1 68 | | 1 68 | | |
| Sept. 1 | Mizpah (Degree of Rebekah) | 19 | 12 55 | | 12 55 | | |
| | Nelton (Manitoba) | | 10 35 | | 10 35 | | |
| | Pyramid | 156 | 1 68 | | 1 68 | | |
| | Jarvis | 191 | 84 | | 84 | | |
| | Earncliffe | 283 | 3 36 | | 3 36 | | |
| 6 | Tecumseh | 162 | 1 68 | | 1 68 | | |
| | Empire | 57 | 3 36 | | 3 36 | | |
| | Argyll | 212 | 60 | | 60 | | |
| | Dresden | 124 | 1 40 | | 1 40 | | |
| | Covenant | 52 | 2 80 | | 2 80 | | |
| | Thamesville | 157 | 11 25 | | 11 25 | | |
| | Grand River | 91 | 1 85 | | 1 85 | | |
| | Hastings | 273 | 3 50 | | 3 50 | | |
| 10 | Supplies | | 60 | | 60 | | |
| 12 | Cataraqui | 10 | 1 25 | | 1 25 | | |
| | Niagara Falls | 53 | 1 68 | | 1 68 | | |
| | Bothwell | 74 | 60 | | 60 | | |
| | Mt. Brydges | 217 | 1 25 | | 1 25 | | |
| | St. Lawrence | 137 | 1 00 | | 1 00 | | |
| 13 | Kingston | 59 | 75 | | 75 | | |
| 14 | Grand Union | 97 | 6 00 | | 6 00 | | |
| | Veteran Jewels | | 10 50 | | −10 50 | | |
| | Supplies | | 60 | | 60 | | |
| 15 | Lakeview | 272 | 6 00 | | 6 00 | | |
| | Brock | 9 | 3 36 | | 3 36 | | |
| | Credit | 257 | 60 | | 60 | | |
| 17 | Ridgetown | 144 | 35 | | 35 | | |
| | Mount Zion | 46 | 50 | | 50 | | |
| | Prince of Wales | 230 | 85 | | 85 | | |
| 19 | Supplies | | 60 | | 60 | | |
| 21 | Reliance | 89 | 1 12 | | 1 12 | | |
| | Louise (Rebekah) | 10 | 50 | | 50 | | |

### STATEMENT OF RECEIPTS.—*Continued.*

| Date. | LODGE. | No. | Total. | Capita Tax. | Supplies. | Sundries. | Charter Fee. |
|---|---|---|---|---|---|---|---|
| **1892.** | | | | | | | |
| Sept. 22 | Meaford | 260 | 50 | | 50 | | |
| | Sutton | 168 | 60 | | 60 | | |
| | Naomia (Rebekah) | 6 | 2 93 | | 2 93 | | |
| | Penetangore | 172 | 30 | | 30 | | |
| 23 | Royal Oak | 108 | 1 68 | | 1 68 | | |
| | Orion | 109 | 1 12 | | 1 12 | | |
| 24 | Constellation | 85 | 50 | | 50 | | |
| 29 | Walkerton | 84 | 1 10 | | 1 10 | | |
| 30 | Waterloo | 107 | 75 | | 75 | | |
| | Supplies | | 60 | | 60 | | |
| | Cataraqui | 10 | 85 | | 85 | | |
| Oct. 1 | Sarnia | 126 | 1 25 | | 1 25 | | |
| | Chesley | 221 | 6 00 | | 6 00 | | |
| | St. Lawrence | 137 | 3 36 | | 3 36 | | |
| 7 | Gore | 34 | 3 36 | | 3 36 | | |
| 10 | Canada | 49 | 3 36 | | 3 36 | | |
| | Ahiram | 205 | 2 80 | | 2 80 | | |
| | Free-stone | 215 | 1 68 | | 1 68 | | |
| | Amity | 80 | 1 25 | | 1 25 | | |
| | Enterprise | 218 | 3 08 | | 3 08 | | |
| | Otonabee | 13 | 3 00 | | 3 00 | | |
| | Flora (Rebekah) | 20 | 20 00 | | 15 00 | | 5 00 |
| 12 | Western City | 93 | 3 36 | | 3 36 | | |
| | St. Thomas | 76 | 4 20 | | 4 20 | | |
| | Thomasburg | 293 | 3 50 | | 3 50 | | |
| | Ridgely | 250 | 2 10 | | 2 10 | | |
| | Otonabee | 13 | 1 00 | | 1 00 | | |
| 13 | East Toronto | 253 | 1 68 | | 1 68 | | |
| 18 | Union | 16 | 3 36 | | 3 36 | | |
| | Grand River | 91 | 60 | | 60 | | |
| | Model | 147 | 1 25 | | 1 25 | | |
| | Reliance | 89 | 50 | | 50 | | |
| | Samaritan | 35 | 85 | | 85 | | |
| | Fairy | 274 | 84 | | 84 | | |
| | Pembroke | 203 | 3 25 | | 3 25 | | |
| 19 | Weston | 200 | 1 25 | | 1 25 | | |
| 20 | Farmersville | 237 | 85 | | 85 | | |
| | Stirling | 239 | 40 | | 40 | | |
| 21 | Corinthian | 61 | 1 12 | | 1 12 | | |
| | Oakville | 132 | 1 78 | | 1 78 | | |
| 22 | North Bay | 271 | 1 68 | | 1 68 | | |
| 24 | Elgin | 32 | 2 08 | | 2 08 | | |
| | Hensall | 223 | 1 25 | | 1 25 | | |
| | Sheard | 276 | 24 | | 24 | | |
| | Huron | 62 | 3 36 | | 3 36 | | |
| 26 | Supplies | | 25 | | 25 | | |
| | Beethoven | 165 | 56 | | 56 | | |
| 27 | Western Star | 149 | 56 | | 56 | | |
| | Walkerton | 84 | 1 68 | | 1 68 | | |
| | Balmoral | 280 | 48 | | 48 | | |
| | Tweed | 290 | 50 | | 50 | | |
| 28 | Lindsay | 100 | 3 40 | | 3 40 | | |
| | Lucknow (Rebekah) | 22 | 5 00 | | | | 5 00 |
| | St. Mary's | 36 | 1 68 | | 1 68 | | |
| | Niagara Falls | 53 | 1 25 | | 1 25 | | |
| | Dufferin | 186 | 1 68 | | 1 68 | | |
| 29 | Trenton | 113 | 3 36 | | 3 36 | | |
| | Carleton | 240 | 3 36 | | 3 36 | | |
| | Lansdowne | 270 | 50 | | 50 | | |
| Nov. 1 | Thamesville | 157 | 9 22 | | 9 22 | | |
| | Lorne | 175 | 1 00 | | | 1 00 | |
| 2 | Valley City | 117 | 1 68 | | 1 68 | | |
| 4 | Florence Nightingale | 66 | 5 39 | | 5 09 | 30 | |

## STATEMENT OF RECEIPTS.—*Continued.*

| Date. | LODGE. | No. | Total. | Capita Tax. | Supplies. | Sundries. | Charter Fee. |
|---|---|---|---|---|---|---|---|
| 1892. | | | | | | | |
| Nov. 4 | Bay of Quinte | 143 | 3 86 | | 3 86 | | |
| 8 | Thornbury | 243 | 1 68 | | 1 68 | | |
|  | Carleton | 240 | 1 50 | | 1 50 | | |
| 9 | Lindsay | 100 | 1 50 | | 1 50 | | |
|  | Inglewood (Rebekah) | 23 | 15 67 | | 15 67 | | |
| 11 | Grand River | 91 | 85 | | 85 | | |
|  | Campbellford | 248 | 4 95 | | 4 95 | | |
| 14 | Germania | 184 | 70 | | 70 | | |
|  | Aurora | 148 | 24 | | 24 | | |
|  | Grand Valley | 256 | 35 | | 35 | | |
|  | Jarvis | 191 | 1 00 | | 1 00 | | |
| 15 | Norwood | 262 | 2 00 | | 2 00 | | |
| 16 | St. Lawrence | 137 | 05 | | 05 | | |
|  | Acorn | 236 | 35 | | | 35 | |
|  | Chatham | 39 | 1 40 | | 1 40 | | |
|  | Constellation | 85 | 1 40 | | 1 40 | | |
| 19 | Cobourg | 136 | 50 | | 50 | | |
|  | Excelsior (Rebekah) | 18 | 45 | | 45 | | |
|  | Alpha | 154 | 6 72 | | 6 72 | | |
|  | Peaceful Dove | 135 | 50 | | 50 | | |
|  | Collingwood | 54 | 4 20 | | 4 20 | | |
| 21 | Aylmer | 94 | 3 36 | | 3 36 | | |
|  | Thamesville | 157 | 3 50 | | 3 50 | | |
| 22 | International | 228 | 1 25 | | 1 25 | | |
|  | Otonabee | 13 | 70 | | 70 | | |
|  | Woodstock | 269 | 1 68 | | 1 68 | | |
| 24 | Thomasburg | 293 | 20 | | 20 | | |
| 26 | Waterford | 235 | 1 68 | | 1 68 | | |
|  | Owen Sound | 180 | 6 00 | | 6 00 | | |
| 28 | Supplies | | 60 | | 60 | | |
| 30 | Model | 147 | 2 09 | | 2 09 | | |
|  | Deseronto | 102 | 1 00 | | 1 00 | | |
| Dec. 1 | Lucknow (Rebekah) | 22 | 13 20 | | 13 20 | | |
|  | Waterloo | 107 | 6 00 | | 6 00 | | |
|  | Jarvis | 191 | 3 50 | | 3 50 | | |
|  | Leamington | 140 | 3 64 | | 3 64 | | |
| 2 | Argyll | 213 | 1 10 | | 75 | 35 | |
|  | Glencoe | 133 | 18 | | 18 | | |
| 5 | Georgian Bay | 219 | 2 68 | | 2 68 | | |
|  | Germania | 184 | 1 68 | | 1 68 | | |
|  | Lynden | 259 | 1 25 | | 1 25 | | |
|  | Huron | 62 | 1 25 | | 1 25 | | |
| 8 | Broadview | 294 | 30 00 | | | | 30 00 |
|  | Oriental | 163 | 4 20 | | 4 20 | | |
|  | Dominion | 48 | 50 | | 50 | | |
|  | Morewood | 285 | 35 | | 35 | | |
|  | Edna (Rebekah) | 14 | 6 00 | | 6 00 | | |
|  | Madoc | 179 | 3 20 | | 3 20 | | |
| 12 | Prince of Wales | 230 | 70 | | 70 | | |
|  | Lucknow | 112 | 4 20 | | 4 20 | | |
|  | Wingham (Rebekah) | | 5 00 | | | | 5 00 |
|  | Amity | 80 | 1 68 | | 1 68 | | |
|  | Rose | 28 | 1 12 | | 1 12 | | |
|  | Lambton | 277 | 1 25 | | 1 25 | | |
|  | Chesterville | 288 | 1 00 | | 1 00 | | |
|  | Millbank | 209 | 75 | | 75 | | |
|  | Constellation | 85 | 85 | | 85 | | |
| 13 | Ridgetown | 144 | 1 00 | | 1 00 | | |
| 14 | Oakville | 132 | 3 78 | | 3 78 | | |
| 15 | Hope | 69 | 50 | | 50 | | |
| 16 | Bay of Quinte | 143 | 1 25 | | 1 25 | | |
|  | Unity | 47 | 5 25 | | 6 25 | | |
|  | Frontier | 45 | 3 36 | | 3 36 | | |

STATEMENT OF RECEIPTS.—*Continued.*

| Date. | | No. | Total. | Capita Tax. | Supplies. | Sundries. | Charter Fee. |
|---|---|---|---|---|---|---|---|
| 1892.<br>Dec. 17 | Naomi (Rebekah) | 6 | 35 | | | 35 | |
| | Donalda (Rebekah) | 20 | 2 75 | | | 2 75 | |
| 19 | Floral | 252 | 75 | | 75 | | |
| 20 | Ilderton | 234 | 2 69 | | 2 69 | | |
| | Supplies | | 1 00 | | 1 00 | | |
| | Gold Hill | 260 | 1 25 | | 1 25 | | |
| | Thomasburg | 293 | 1 40 | | 1 40 | | |
| | Alpha | 154 | 3 00 | | 3 00 | | |
| 22 | Western City | 93 | 1 40 | | 1 40 | | |
| | Madoc | 179 | 6 00 | | 6 00 | | |
| | Gore | 34 | 1 25 | | 1 25 | | |
| 23 | Glanworth | 289 | 23 49 | | 23 49 | | |
| 24 | Valley City | 117 | 5 25 | | 5 25 | | |
| | Enterprise | 218 | 3 36 | | 3 36 | | |
| 27 | Naomi (Rebekah) | 6 | 28 | | | 28 | |
| | Inglewood (Rebekah) | 23 | 5 00 | | | | 5 00 |
| 28 | Prudence (Rebekah) | 24 | 5 00 | | | | 5 00 |
| | Gananoque | 114 | 5 23 | | 5 23 | | |
| 30 | Cobourg | 136 | 90 | | 90 | | |
| | Olive Branch | 88 | 5 31 | | 5 31 | | |
| | Sycamore | 151 | 2 00 | | 2 00 | | |
| 31 | Avon | 41 | 53 50 | 53 50 | | | |
| | Leamington | 140 | 1 00 | | 1 00 | | |
| | Samaritan | 135 | 5 25 | | 5 25 | | |
| | Naomi (Rebekah) | 6 | 11 60 | | | 11 60 | |
| 1893<br>Jan. 3 | Beacon | 201 | 1 68 | | 1 68 | | |
| | Donalda (Rebekah) | 20 | 12 95 | | 12 95 | | |
| | Excelsior | 44 | 60 | | 60 | | |
| 5 | East Toronto | 263 | 14 75 | 14 75 | | | |
| 6 | Grand Union | 97 | 70 | | 70 | | |
| 7 | Nipissing | 79 | 15 75 | 15 75 | | | |
| | Sutton | 168 | 9 00 | 9 00 | | | |
| | Weston | 200 | 7 30 | 7 30 | | | |
| | Cicerone | 195 | 5 50 | 5 50 | | | |
| | Western City | 93 | 17 60 | 17 25 | | 35 | |
| | Alliston | 171 | 9 25 | 8 00 | 1 25 | | |
| | Alpha | 154 | 32 25 | 31 75 | 50 | | |
| | Chatham | 29 | 39 50 | 39 50 | | | |
| | Cataraqui | 10 | 66 61 | 61 25 | 5 36 | | |
| | Olive Branch | 88 | 30 85 | 30 50 | | 35 | |
| | Marion | 131 | 16 75 | 16 75 | | | |
| | Oxford | 77 | 25 75 | 25 75 | | | |
| | Thomasburg | 293 | 3 85 | | 3 85 | | |
| | Acorn | 236 | 5 75 | 5 75 | | | |
| | Oak Leaf | 159 | 1 25 | | 1 25 | | |
| | Fraternity | 265 | 45 | | 45 | | |
| | Pembroke | 203 | 26 75 | 26 75 | | | |
| | Ridgetown | 144 | 26 50 | 26 50 | | | |
| | Otter | 50 | 1 75 | | 1 40 | 35 | |
| | Victoria | 64 | 16 75 | 16 75 | | | |
| | Cobourg | 136 | 1 85 | | 1 50 | 35 | |
| | Mallorytown | 245 | 10 50 | 10 50 | | | |
| | North Bay | 261 | 18 50 | 18 50 | | | |
| | Romeo | 164 | 33 75 | 31 75 | 1 68 | | |
| | Lyn | 284 | 7 00 | 7 00 | | | |
| | Brock | 9 | 28 00 | 28 00 | | | |
| | Ivy | 90 | 16 95 | 16 95 | | | |
| | Flora | 231 | 16 00 | 16 00 | | | |
| | Deseronto | 102 | 21 85 | 21 75 | 10 | | |
| | Port Arthur | 244 | 18 00 | 18 00 | | | |
| | Peterboro' | 111 | 61 00 | 61 00 | | | |
| | Samaritan | 35 | 38 85 | 38 50 | | 35 | |
| | Amity | 80 | 48 25 | 48 25 | | | |

**STATEMENT OF RECEIPTS.—*Continued.***

| Date. | LODGE. | No. | Total. | Capita Tax. | Supplies. | Sundries. | Charter Fee. |
|---|---|---|---|---|---|---|---|
| 1893.<br>Jan. 7 | Peaceful Dove | 135 | 10 00 | 10 00 | | | |
| | Harmony | | 17 30 | | | 17 30 | |
| | International | 228 | 36 50 | 36 50 | | | |
| 9 | Progress | 158 | 27 75 | 27 75 | | | |
| | Clifford | 214 | 1 75 | | 1 75 | | |
| | Excelsior | 44 | 35 00 | 35 00 | | | |
| | Hillsburg | 167 | 10 25 | 10 25 | | | |
| | Alba | 254 | 11 75 | 11 75 | | | |
| | Grand Valley | 256 | 8 75 | 8 75 | | | |
| | Stella | 125 | 30 75 | 30 75 | | | |
| | St. Lawrence | 137 | 25 75 | 25 75 | | | |
| | Gold Hill | 261 | 38 75 | 31 75 | 7 00 | | |
| | Minnetonka | 293 | 12 00 | 12 00 | | | |
| | Manilla | 105 | 6 50 | 6 50 | | | |
| | Mount Brydges | 217 | 28 05 | 25 50 | 2 80 | | |
| | Argyle | 212 | 21 25 | 21 25 | | | |
| | Walkerton | 84 | 15 50 | 15 25 | | 25 | |
| | Saxon | 121 | 85 | | | 85 | |
| | Dominion | 48 | 38 50 | 38 50 | | | |
| 10 | Waterloo | 107 | 1 00 | | 1 00 | | |
| | Missanabie | 266 | 21 25 | 21 25 | | | |
| | Teeswater | 183 | 8 00 | 8 00 | | | |
| | Algoma | 267 | 14 50 | 14 50 | | | |
| | Sydenham Valley | 120 | 38 50 | 38 50 | | | |
| | Beaver | 32 | 13 75 | 13 75 | | | |
| | Merlin | 226 | 8 00 | 8 00 | | | |
| | Ilderton | 234 | 8 25 | 8 25 | | | |
| | Woodstock | 269 | 21 06 | 20 25 | 81 | | |
| | Saxon | 121 | 10 75 | 7 25 | 3 50 | | |
| | Lucknow | 112 | 21 25 | 21 25 | | | |
| | Rodney | 291 | 12 00 | 12 00 | | | |
| 11 | Fraternity | 264 | 15 75 | 15 75 | | | |
| | Reliance | 89 | 38 50 | 38 50 | | | |
| | Fairy | 275 | 10 50 | 10 50 | | | |
| | Oriental | 163 | 10 25 | 10 25 | | | |
| | Silver Star | 202 | 12 35 | 12 25 | 10 | | |
| | Forest City | 38 | 30 50 | 30 50 | | | |
| | Friendship | 65 | 44 60 | 44 25 | | 35 | |
| | Jarvis | 191 | 5 75 | 5 75 | | | |
| | Waterford | 235 | 25 75 | 25 75 | | | |
| | Florence Nightingale | 66 | 35 25 | 35 25 | | | |
| | Alpha | 154 | 85 | | | 85 | |
| 12 | Oxford | 77 | 3 81 | | | 3 81 | |
| | Lansdowne | 270 | 18 00 | 18 00 | | | |
| | Delta | 265 | 10 85 | 10 50 | | 35 | |
| | Phœnix | 22 | 19 00 | 19 00 | | | |
| | Sheard | 276 | 8 00 | 8 00 | | | |
| | Royal Oak | 108 | 21 25 | 21 25 | | | |
| | Beacon | 201 | 8 75 | 8 75 | | | |
| | Ridgely | 250 | 2 46 | | | 2 46 | |
| | Minto | 98 | 10 75 | 10 75 | | | |
| | Eastern Star | 72 | 25 50 | 25 50 | | | |
| | Charity | 129 | 7 20 | 6 75 | 10 | 35 | |
| 13 | Brougham | 155 | 28 14 | 3 75 | | 24 39 | |
| | Broadview | 294 | 27 78 | | | 27 78 | |
| | Stanley | 268 | 8 50 | 8 50 | | | |
| | Lynden | 259 | 6 00 | 6 00 | | | |
| | Sheard | 276 | 84 | | | 84 | |
| | Dresden | 124 | 33 18 | 31 50 | 1 68 | | |
| | Cobourg | 136 | 23 00 | 23 00 | | | |
| | Farmersville | 237 | 11 10 | 10 75 | | 35 | |
| | Concord | 142 | 16 50 | 16 50 | | | |
| | Simcoe | 161 | 2 52 | | | 2 52 | |

STATEMENT OF RECEIPTS—*Continued.*

| Date. | LODGE. | No. | Total. | Capita Tax. | Supplies. | Sundries. | Charter Fee. |
|---|---|---|---|---|---|---|---|
| **1893.** | | | | | | | |
| **Jan.** 13. | Parry Sound | 189 | 13 50 | 13 50 | | | |
| | Grand River | 91 | 27 75 | 27 75 | | | |
| | Deseronto | 102 | 1 68 | | 1 68 | | |
| | Collingwood | 54 | 36 25 | 36 25 | | | |
| | Bay of Quinte | 143 | 24 75 | 24 75 | | | |
| | Alliston | 171 | 1 68 | | 1 68 | | |
| | Mizpah (Rebekah) | 19 | 4 10 | | | 4 10 | |
| | Elgin | 32 | 58 50 | 58 50 | | | |
| | Bothwell | 74 | 11 00 | 11 00 | | | |
| | Exeter | 67 | 11 75 | 11 75 | | | |
| | Excelsior (Rebekah) | 18 | 5 50 | | | 5 50 | |
| | Hensall | 223 | 13 75 | 13 75 | | | |
| | Florence | 196 | 21 00 | 21 00 | | | |
| | Aylmer | 94 | 32 50 | 32 50 | | | |
| | Union | 16 | 54 00 | 54 00 | | | |
| 14 | Beacon | 201 | 8 75 | 8 75 | | | |
| | Lakeview | 272 | 2 03 | | 2 03 | | |
| | Cataract | 103 | 13 50 | 13 50 | | | |
| | Bracebridge | 251 | 16 35 | 16 00 | | 35 | |
| | Glencoe | 133 | 13 50 | 13 50 | | | |
| | Mount Zion | 46 | 5 35 | 5 00 | | 35 | |
| | Thamesville | 157 | 12 50 | 12 50 | | | |
| | Minerva | 197 | 19 10 | 18 75 | | 35 | |
| | Belleville | 81 | 46 75 | 46 75 | | | |
| | Mizpah | 127 | 28 75 | 28 75 | | | |
| | Howard | 58 | 26 75 | 26 75 | | | |
| | Germania | 184 | 25 68 | 24 00 | 1 68 | | |
| | Embro Star | 229 | 12 25 | 12 25 | | | |
| | Dolman | 174 | 12 25 | 12 25 | | | |
| | Elmira | 216 | 10 50 | 10 50 | | | |
| | Fidelity | 55 | 4 25 | 4 25 | | | |
| | Aurora | 148 | 19 85 | 19 50 | | 35 | |
| | Albert | 194 | 40 75 | 40 75 | | | |
| | Prince of Wales | 230 | 11 75 | 11 75 | | | |
| 16 | Grand Union | 97 | 15 | | | 15 | |
| | Garnet | 139 | 17 25 | 16 00 | 1 25 | | |
| | Manilla | 105 | 90 | | | 90 | |
| | Flora (Rebekah) | 21 | 3 65 | | | 3 65 | |
| | Missanabie | 266 | 5 04 | | 5 04 | | |
| | Lilly | 211 | 9 00 | 9 00 | | | |
| | Gore | 34 | 56 25 | 56 25 | | | |
| | Owen Sound | 180 | 15 25 | 15 25 | | | |
| | Dufferin | 186 | 6 50 | 6 50 | | | |
| | Meaford | 260 | 12 00 | 12 00 | | | |
| | Jubilee (Rebekah) | 13 | 3 60 | | | 3 60 | |
| | Woodstock | 269 | 1 00 | | 1 00 | | |
| | Excelsior | 44 | 26 25 | | 26 25 | | |
| | Unity | 47 | 69 25 | 69 25 | | | |
| | Woodslee | 220 | 3 75 | 3 75 | | | |
| | Madoc | 179 | 29 75 | 29 75 | | | |
| | Sterling | 239 | 33 00 | 33 00 | | | |
| | Campbellford | 248 | 25 75 | 25 75 | | | |
| | Hastings | 273 | 9 75 | 9 75 | | | |
| | Thomasburg | 293 | 15 50 | 15 50 | | | |
| | Millbank | 209 | 4 00 | 4 00 | | | |
| | Beethoven | 165 | 9 00 | 9 00 | | | |
| 17 | The Toronto | 71 | 16 75 | 16 75 | | | |
| | Sudbury | 282 | 17 20 | 13 00 | 4 20 | | |
| | Wellington Square | 178 | 8 73 | 8 50 | 23 | | |
| | Oakville | 132 | 13 50 | 13 50 | | | |
| | Georgian Bay | 219 | 19 25 | 19 25 | | | |
| | Ahiram | 205 | 26 10 | 25 75 | | 35 | |
| | Lucknow | 112 | 3 30 | | | 3 30 | |

## STATEMENT OF RECEIPTS — *Continued.*

| Date. | LODGE. | No. | Total. | Capita Tax. | Supplies. | Sundries. | Charter Fee. |
|---|---|---|---|---|---|---|---|
| **1893.** | | | | | | | |
| **Jan.** 17 | Vivian | 146 | 19 28 | 17 25 | 1 68 | 35 | |
| | Harmony | 115 | 39 85 | 39 50 | | 35 | |
| | Nith | 95 | 16 50 | 16 50 | | | |
| | Rondeau | 40 | 25 85 | 25 50 | | 35 | |
| | Penetangore | 172 | 28 25 | 28 25 | | | |
| | Grand Union | 97 | 20 95 | 20 75 | 20 | | |
| | Midland | 279 | 12 25 | 12 25 | | | |
| 18 | Balmoral | 280 | 10 75 | 10 75 | | | |
| | Corinthian | 61 | 50 25 | 50 25 | | | |
| | Bissell | 51 | 1 12 | 56 | 56 | | |
| | Livingstone | 130 | 11 00 | 11 00 | | | |
| | Napanee | 86 | 15 25 | 15 25 | | | |
| | Beaverton | 249 | 12 25 | 12 25 | | | |
| | Dauncey | 176 | 6 50 | 6 50 | | | |
| | Silver City | 206 | 16 50 | 16 15 | | 35 | |
| 19 | Ganaroque | 114 | 48 75 | 48 75 | | | |
| | Fergus | 73 | 19 25 | 19 25 | | | |
| | Huron | 62 | 28 75 | 28 75 | | | |
| | Rose | 28 | 25 00 | 25 00 | | | |
| | Kingston | 50 | 67 90 | 64 00 | 3 90 | | |
| | Lindsay | 100 | 21 75 | 21 75 | | | |
| | Denovo | 170 | 11 75 | 11 75 | | | |
| 20 | Edna (Rebekah) | 14 | 7 70 | | | 7 70 | |
| | Minnetonka | 292 | 1 85 | | 1 50 | 35 | |
| | Walkerton | 84 | 56 | | 56 | | |
| | Freestone | 215 | 8 00 | 8 00 | | | |
| | Inglewood | 23 | 2 50 | | | 2 50 | |
| | Norwood | 262 | 8 75 | 8 75 | | | |
| | Stella | 125 | 1 68 | | 1 68 | | |
| | Durham | 78 | 28 00 | 28 00 | | | |
| | Trenton | 113 | 14 50 | 14 50 | | | |
| | Eureka | 30 | 26 00 | 26 00 | | | |
| | Rideau | 241 | 28 50 | 28 50 | | | |
| | East Toronto | 263 | 85 | | 85 | | |
| | Howick | 192 | 3 00 | 3 00 | | | |
| | Maple Leaf | 57 | 13 25 | 11 75 | 1 50 | | |
| | Chesley | 221 | 7 25 | 7 25 | | | |
| | Streetsville | 122 | 11 75 | 11 75 | | | |
| | Ripley | 287 | 9 75 | 9 75 | | | |
| | Ottawa | 224 | 35 25 | 35 25 | | | |
| | Rockliffe | 278 | 13 50 | 13 50 | | | |
| | Morewood | 285 | 5 00 | 5 00 | | | |
| | Carleton | 240 | 31 35 | 31 00 | | 35 | |
| | Chesterville | 288 | 8 50 | 8 50 | | | |
| | Earnscliffe | 283 | 13 00 | 13 00 | | | |
| | Grenville | 279 | 18 75 | 18 75 | | | |
| 21 | Belleville | 81 | 2 00 | | 2 00 | | |
| | Equity | 232 | 6 50 | 6 50 | | | |
| | Golden Star | 101 | 13 30 | 10 75 | 2 55 | | |
| | Otonabee | 13 | 32 75 | 32 75 | | | |
| | Wildey | 153 | 8 10 | 7 75 | | 35 | |
| | Excelsior | 44 | 3 56 | | 3 56 | | |
| | Rideau | 241 | 1 68 | | 1 68 | | |
| | Sycamore | 151 | 9 50 | 9 50 | | | |
| | Huron | 62 | 1 00 | | 1 00 | | |
| | Thamesford | 258 | 27 75 | 27 75 | | | |
| | Lambton | 277 | 14 60 | 14 50 | 10 | | |
| | North Bay | 261 | 40 | | 40 | | |
| | Lakeview | 272 | 19 25 | 19 25 | | | |
| | Glanworth | 289 | 11 25 | 11 25 | | | |
| | Bothwell | 74 | 1 05 | | 1 05 | | |
| | Orient | 130 | 5 25 | 5 25 | | | |
| 23 | Tweed | 294 | 1 01 | | 06 | 35 | |

STATEMENT OF RECEIPTS—*Continued.*

| Date. | LODGE. | No. | Total. | Capita Tax. | Supplies. | Sundries. | Charter Fee. |
|---|---|---|---|---|---|---|---|
| 1893. | | | | | | | |
| Jan. 23 | Floral | 252 | 1 96 | | 1 96 | | |
| | Crescent | 104 | 59 25 | 59 25 | | | |
| | Royal | 286 | 9 75 | 9 75 | | | |
| 24 | Olive Branch (Rebekah) | 16 | 1 00 | | 1 00 | | |
| | Brucefield | 210 | 6 50 | 6 50 | | | |
| | Egremont | 207 | 3 50 | 3 50 | | | |
| | Niagara Falls | 53 | 30 85 | 30 50 | | 35 | |
| | Chorazin | 190 | 31 25 | 31 25 | | | |
| | Supplies | | 60 | | 60 | | |
| | Sarnia | 126 | 3 36 | | 3 36 | | |
| | Beatrice (Rebekah) | 12 | 9 90 | | | 9 90 | |
| | Warriner | 75 | 17 50 | 17 50 | | | |
| | Beaverton | 249 | 1 68 | | 1 68 | | |
| | Victoria (Rebekah) | 1 | 1 00 | | 1 00 | | |
| | Victoria | 64 | 1 00 | | 1 00 | | |
| | Gordon | 247 | 17 24 | 11 00 | 6 24 | | |
| | Chorazin | 190 | 2 80 | | 2 80 | | |
| 25 | Lindsay | 100 | 1 00 | | 1 00 | | |
| | Floral | 252 | 9 75 | 9 75 | | | |
| | Listowel | 160 | 22 25 | 22 25 | | | |
| | Oshawa (Rebekah) | 3 | 2 80 | | | 2 80 | |
| | Barrie | 63 | 31 00 | 28 25 | 2 75 | | |
| | Hope | 60 | 19 93 | 17 50 | 2 43 | | |
| 26 | Broadview | 294 | 1 00 | | 1 00 | | |
| | Oak Leaf | 159 | 10 50 | 10 50 | | | |
| | Dolman | 174 | 2 00 | | 2 00 | | |
| | Milton | 92 | 8 75 | 8 75 | | | |
| | St. Mary's | 56 | 34 25 | 34 25 | | | |
| | North Star | 68 | 11 00 | 11 00 | | | |
| 27 | Cambridge | 188 | 1 68 | | 1 68 | | |
| 28 | Excelsior | 44 | 1 00 | | 1 00 | | |
| | Louise (Rebekah) | 10 | 5 45 | | | 5 45 | |
| | Grenville | 279 | 2 08 | | 2 08 | | |
| | St. Thomas | 76 | 90 70 | 86 50 | 4 20 | | |
| | Prince of Wales | 230 | 15 | | 15 | | |
| 30 | Model | 147 | 10 00 | 10 00 | | | |
| | Arthur | 281 | 15 50 | 15 50 | | | |
| | Ridgely | 250 | 21 00 | 21 00 | | | |
| | Empire | 87 | 27 00 | 27 00 | | | |
| 31 | Credit | 257 | 9 50 | 9 50 | | | |
| | Broadview | 294 | 10 75 | 10 75 | | | |
| Feby. 1 | Olive Branch (Rebekah) | 16 | 21 80 | | | 21 80 | |
| | Clifford | 214 | 18 50 | 18 50 | | | |
| | Elmira | 216 | 6 00 | 6 00 | | | |
| | Valley City | 117 | 26 25 | 26 25 | | | |
| | Ancaster | 138 | 16 00 | 16 00 | | | |
| | Supplies | | 3 00 | | 3 00 | | |
| | Covenant | 52 | 6 71 | | 6 71 | | |
| | Lilly | 211 | 6 00 | | 6 00 | | |
| | Samaritan | 35 | 6 36 | | 6 36 | | |
| | Wilton | 242 | 2 03 | | 2 03 | | |
| 2 | Tweed | 290 | 13 75 | 13 75 | | | |
| | Crescent | 104 | 1 40 | | 1 40 | | |
| | Eastern Star | 72 | 1 68 | | 1 68 | | |
| | Hastings | 273 | 2 60 | | 2 60 | | |
| | Maitland | 119 | 14 25 | 14 25 | | | |
| | Western Star | 149 | 6 00 | 6 00 | | | |
| 3 | Clinton | 83 | 6 00 | 6 00 | | | |
| | Naomi (Rebekah) | 6 | 1 20 | | | 1 20 | |
| | Frontier | 45 | 62 25 | 62 25 | | | |
| | Supplies | | 75 | | 75 | | |
| | Canada | 49 | 57 75 | 57 75 | | | |
| 4 | Lucknow | 112 | 9 00 | | 9 00 | | |

STATEMENT OF RECEIPTS—*Continued.*

| Date. | LODGE. | No. | Total. | Capita Tax. | Supplies. | Sundries. | Charter Fee |
|---|---|---|---|---|---|---|---|
| 1893.<br>Feby. 4 | Victoria Degree | .... | 3 85 | .......... | 3 85 | .......... | .......... |
| 6 | Leamington | 140 | 33 75 | 33 75 | .......... | .......... | .......... |
|  | Orillia | 246 | 8 50 | 8 50 | .......... | .......... | .......... |
|  | Victoria | 64 | 55 | .......... | 20 | 35 | .......... |
| 7 | Collingwood | 54 | 5 04 | .......... | 5 04 | .......... | .......... |
|  | Emerald | 1'3 | 6 25 | 6 25 | .......... | .......... | .......... |
| 8 | Ottawa | 224 | 1 00 | .......... | 65 | 35 | .......... |
|  | Lindsay | 100 | 75 | .......... | 75 | .......... | .......... |
| 9 | Waterloo | 107 | 75 | .......... | 75 | .......... | .......... |
|  | Vivian | 146 | 70 | .......... | 70 | .......... | .......... |
|  | Sarnia | 126 | 20 50 | 20 50 | .......... | .......... | .......... |
|  | Fairy | 275 | 50 | .......... | 50 | .......... | .......... |
| 10 | Orillia | 246 | 4 70 | .......... | 4 35 | 35 | .......... |
|  | Supplies | .... | 1 68 | .......... | 1 68 | .......... | .......... |
| 11 | Deseronto | 102 | 50 | .......... | 50 | .......... | .......... |
|  | Erie | 33 | 4 50 | 4 50 | .......... | .......... | .......... |
| 13 | Thamesville | 157 | 1 60 | .......... | 1 60 | .......... | .......... |
| 14 | Ark | 181 | 1 00 | .......... | 1 00 | .......... | .......... |
|  | Gold Hill | 261 | 85 | .......... | 85 | .......... | .......... |
|  | Oxford | 77 | 85 | .......... | 85 | .......... | .......... |
|  | Thomasburg | 293 | 1 50 | .......... | 1 50 | .......... | .......... |
| 15 | The Toronto | 71 | 1 96 | .......... | 1 96 | .......... | .......... |
| 16 | Germania | 184 | 6 00 | .......... | 6 00 | .......... | .......... |
| 17 | Royal Oak | 108 | 45 | .......... | 45 | .......... | .......... |
|  | Excelsior (Rebekah) | .... | 84 | .......... | 84 | .......... | .......... |
|  | Nipissing | 79 | 1 70 | .......... | 1 70 | .......... | .......... |
|  | Union | 16 | 3 36 | .......... | 3 36 | .......... | .......... |
|  | Harmony | 115 | 4 61 | .......... | 4 61 | .......... | .......... |
|  | Minerva | 197 | 35 | .......... | .......... | 35 | .......... |
|  | North Bay | 261 | 70 | .......... | 70 | .......... | .......... |
|  | Durham | 78 | 6 00 | .......... | 6 00 | .......... | .......... |
| 20 | Jarvis | 191 | 2 53 | .......... | 2 53 | .......... | .......... |
|  | Manotick | 295 | 30 00 | .......... | .......... | .......... | 30 00 |
|  | Silver Star | 202 | 3 36 | .......... | 3 36 | .......... | .......... |
|  | Pyramid | 156 | 10 00 | 10 00 | .......... | .......... | .......... |
|  | Laurel | 110 | 6 75 | 6 75 | .......... | .......... | .......... |
| 21 | Broadview | 294 | 3 00 | .......... | 3 00 | .......... | .......... |
|  | Maitland | 119 | 1 68 | .......... | 1 68 | .......... | .......... |
| 22 | Otter | 50 | 33 00 | 33 00 | .......... | .......... | .......... |
|  | Constellation | 85 | 12 25 | 12 25 | .......... | .......... | .......... |
|  | Hayden | 152 | 23 75 | 21 50 | 2 25 | .......... | .......... |
|  | Tecumseh | 182 | 15 50 | 15 50 | .......... | .......... | .......... |
|  | The Toronto | 71 | 1 50 | .......... | 1 50 | .......... | .......... |
| 24 | Unity | 47 | 1 26 | .......... | 1 26 | .......... | .......... |
|  | Beatrice (Rebekah) | 12 | 1 25 | .......... | 1 25 | .......... | .......... |
|  | Exeter | 67 | 1 40 | .......... | 1 40 | .......... | .......... |
|  | Gananoque | 114 | 1 19 | .......... | 84 | 35 | .......... |
|  | May Queen (Rebekah) | 5 | 3 20 | .......... | .......... | 3 20 | .......... |
|  | Frontier | 45 | 85 | .......... | 85 | .......... | .......... |
|  | Silver City | 206 | 3 36 | .......... | 3 36 | .......... | .......... |
| 25 | Harmony (Rebekah) | 15 | 40 | .......... | 40 | .......... | .......... |
| 27 | Warriner | 75 | 1 20 | .......... | 85 | 35 | .......... |
|  | Montana | 177 | 5 75 | 5 75 | .......... | .......... | .......... |
|  | Leamington | 140 | 1 25 | .......... | 1 25 | .......... | .......... |
|  | Dresden | 124 | 3 50 | .......... | 3 50 | .......... | .......... |
| March 1 | Algoma | 267 | 13 44 | .......... | 13 44 | .......... | .......... |
|  | Belleville | 81 | 12 00 | .......... | 12 00 | .......... | .......... |
| 2 | Madoc | 79 | 3 50 | .......... | 3 50 | .......... | .......... |
|  | Aurora | 148 | 1 25 | .......... | 1 25 | .......... | .......... |
| 4 | Harmony (Rebekah) | 15 | 60 | .......... | 60 | .......... | .......... |
|  | Caledonia | 253 | 4 00 | 4 00 | .......... | .......... | .......... |
|  | Orient | 134 | 2 03 | .......... | 1 68 | 35 | .......... |
|  | Sauble | 227 | 4 25 | 4 25 | .......... | .......... | .......... |

STATEMENT OF RECEIPTS—*Continued.*

| Date. | LODGE. | No. | Total. | Capita Tax. | Supplies. | Sundries. | Charter Fee. |
|---|---|---|---|---|---|---|---|
| 1893. | | | | | | | |
| March 4 | Pembroke | 203 | 75 | 75 | | | |
| 6 | Elgin | 32 | 4 86 | | 4 86 | | |
| | Fergus | 73 | 1 12 | | 1 12 | | |
| | Tecumseh | 182 | 2 53 | | 2 53 | | |
| | Grand Lodge of Manitoba | .... | 27 95 | | 27 95 | | |
| 8 | Minnetonka | 292 | 4 66 | | 4 66 | | |
| | Brucefield | 210 | 1 68 | | 1 63 | | |
| | Louise (Rebekah) | 10 | 1 20 | | | 1 20 | |
| | St. Clair | 106 | 3 36 | | 3 36 | | |
| 10 | Cicerone | 195 | 3 36 | | 3 36 | | |
| | Pembroke | 203 | 90 | | 90 | | |
| | Dauncey | 176 | 84 | | 84 | | |
| | Cataraqui | 10 | 1 20 | | 1 20 | | |
| | Parry Sound | 18) | 23 | | 2 ) | | |
| 11 | Owen Sound | 180 | 70 | | 70 | | |
| | Freestone | 215 | 3 50 | | 3 50 | | |
| | Forest City | 38 | 56 | | 56 | | |
| 14 | North Star | 68 | 6 12 | | 6 12 | | |
| | Manotick | 295 | 16 40 | | 16 40 | | |
| | Inglewood (Rebekah) | 23 | 1 30 | | | 1 30 | |
| | Amity | 80 | 3 25 | | 3 25 | | |
| 15 | Western City | 93 | 1 00 | | 1 00 | | |
| | Montana | 177 | 84 | | 84 | | |
| | Rondeau | 40 | 2 80 | | 2 80 | | |
| | Oakville | 132 | 75 | | 75 | | |
| | Alberta (Rebekah) | 25 | 5 00 | | | | 5 00 |
| | Canada | 49 | 6 51 | | 6 51 | | |
| 17 | Wildey | 153 | 25 | 25 | | | |
| | Leamington | 140 | 1 35 | 1 00 | | 35 | |
| | Myrtle (Rebekah) | 17 | 3 00 | | | 3 00 | |
| | Lucan | 70 | 6 00 | 6 00 | | | |
| | Acton | 204 | 3 50 | 3 50 | | | |
| | Minnetonka | 292 | 29 95 | | 29 95 | | |
| | North Star | 68 | 1 50 | | 1 50 | | |
| | Meaford | 260 | 1 50 | | 1 50 | | |
| | Hanover | 233 | 3 75 | 3 75 | | | |
| | Arthur | 281 | 4 85 | | 4 85 | | |
| | Flora (Rebekah) | 21 | 1 90 | | | 1 90 | |
| | Grand Lodge of Manitoba | .... | 7 85 | | 7 85 | | |
| | Caledona | 253 | 28 | | 28 | | |
| 21 | Marion | 131 | 50 | | 50 | | |
| | Silver City | 206 | 1 00 | 1 00 | | | |
| | Albert | 194 | 3 36 | | 3 36 | | |
| | Hensall | 243 | 45 | | 45 | | |
| 22 | Otter | 50 | 7 00 | | 7 00 | | |
| | Constellation | 85 | 1 60 | | 1 60 | | |
| | Montana | 177 | 1 68 | | 1 68 | | |
| | Meaford | 260 | 75 | | 75 | | |
| | Leamington | 140 | 1 05 | | 1 05 | | |
| 23 | Cataraqui | 10 | 4 91 | | 4 91 | | |
| | Florence | 196 | 2 49 | | 2 49 | | |
| | Acorn | 236 | 1 34 | | 1 34 | | |
| 24 | Bracebridge | 251 | 40 | | 40 | | |
| | Orient | 131 | 85 | | 85 | | |
| | Chatham | 29 | 2 00 | | 2 00 | | |
| 27 | Odd Fellows' Relief Asso | .... | 10 00 | | | 10 00 | |
| 28 | Woodstock | 209 | 3 36 | | 3 36 | | |
| | Romeo | 164 | 2 08 | | 2 08 | | |
| | Thornbury | 243 | 8 25 | 8 25 | | | |
| | Dresden | 131 | 75 | | 75 | | |
| 29 | Louise (Rebekah) | 10 | 1 12 | | 1 12 | | |
| | Peterboro' | 111 | 3 00 | | 3 00 | | |
| | Pyramid | 156 | 85 | | 85 | | |

STATEMENT OF RECEIPTS—*Continued*.

| Date. | LODGE. | No. | Total. | Capita Tax. | Supplies. | Sundries. | Charter Fee. |
|---|---|---|---|---|---|---|---|
| **1893.** | | | | | | | |
| March 29 | Waterloo | 107 | 3 36 | | 3 36 | | |
| | Erie | 33 | 60 | | 25 | 35 | |
| | Eastern Star | 72 | 60 | | 60 | | |
| 30 | Walkerton | 84 | 1 68 | | 1 68 | | |
| | Cataraqui | 10 | 2 00 | | 2 00 | | |
| 31 | Wellington Square | 178 | 49 12 | | | 49 12 | |
| April 1 | May Flower | 296 | 54 99 | | 24 99 | | 30 00 |
| | Alberta | 25 | 15 25 | | 15 25 | | |
| | Wilton | 242 | 21 00 | 21 00 | | | |
| | St. Clair | 106 | 23 50 | 23 50 | | | |
| | Waterloo | 107 | 33 50 | 33 50 | | | |
| 3 | Minerva | 197 | 15 | | 15 | | |
| | Thamesford | 258 | 3 36 | | 3 36 | | |
| | Owen Sound | 180 | 1 78 | | 1 78 | | |
| | Trenton | 113 | 1 30 | | 95 | 35 | |
| | Lakeview | 272 | 3 36 | | 3 36 | | |
| | Esther (Rebekah) | 26 | 5 00 | | | | 5 00 |
| | Phœnix | 22 | 85 | | 85 | | |
| | Hillsburg | 167 | 2 94 | | 2 94 | | |
| 4 | Olive Branch (Rebekah) | 16 | 56 | | 56 | | |
| | Alpha | 154 | 1 25 | | 1 25 | | |
| 5 | Supplies | | 75 | | 75 | | |
| | Otonabee | 13 | 3 36 | | 3 36 | | |
| 6 | Eastern Star | 72 | 1 00 | | 1 00 | | |
| | Wildey | 253 | 50 | | 50 | | |
| | Florence | 196 | 2 53 | | 2 53 | | |
| | Parry Sound | 189 | 4 00 | | 4 00 | | |
| 7 | Bay of Quinte | 143 | 50 | | 50 | | |
| | St. Lawrence | 137 | 1 40 | | 1 40 | | |
| 8 | Supplies | | 1 20 | | 1 20 | | |
| | Reliance | 89 | 7 00 | | 7 00 | | |
| 10 | Grand Union | 97 | 1 45 | | 1 45 | | |
| | Simcoe | 161 | 21 10 | 18 00 | 3 10 | | |
| | Pontypool | 297 | 53 36 | | 23 36 | | 30 00 |
| | Ivy (Rebekah) | 27 | 17 10 | | 17 10 | | |
| | Floral | 252 | 84 | | 84 | | |
| 12 | Rideau | 241 | 4 20 | | 4 20 | | |
| | Orion | 109 | 12 75 | 12 75 | | | |
| 13 | Beatrice (Rebekah) | 12 | 2 24 | | 2 24 | | |
| | Weston | 200 | 1 68 | | 1 68 | | |
| | International | 228 | 3 33 | | 3 33 | | |
| 17 | Hayden | 152 | 3 50 | | 3 50 | | |
| 19 | Covenant | 52 | 40 | | 40 | | |
| | Madoc | 179 | 2 80 | | 2 80 | | |
| 20 | Valley City | 117 | 2 50 | | 2 50 | | |
| | Durham | 78 | 1 12 | | 1 12 | | |
| 21 | Concord | 142 | 85 | | 85 | | |
| 22 | Cobourg | 136 | 1 00 | | 1 00 | | |
| 24 | Merlin | 226 | 1 20 | | 1 20 | | |
| | Port Arthur | 244 | 60 | | 60 | | |
| 25 | Grand Valley | 256 | 1 12 | | 1 12 | | |
| | Frontier | 45 | 75 | | 75 | | |
| 26 | Jarvis | 191 | 84 | | 84 | | |
| | Mizpah | 127 | 3 20 | | 3 20 | | |
| | Progress | 158 | 3 20 | | 3 20 | | |
| | Concord | 142 | 50 | | 50 | | |
| | Wellington Square | 178 | 3 36 | | 3 36 | | |
| 27 | Norwood | 202 | 1 68 | | 1 68 | | |
| | Minerva | 197 | 1 43 | | 1 43 | | |
| 28 | Corinthian | 61 | 2 24 | | 2 24 | | |
| 29 | Sycamore | 151 | 1 25 | | 1 25 | | |
| May 1 | Cataraqui | 10 | 3 36 | | 3 36 | | |
| | Pembroke | 203 | 4 93 | | 4 93 | | |
| 2 | Covenant | 52 | 46 00 | 46 00 | | | |
| | Argyle | 212 | 3 36 | | 3 36 | | |

## STATEMENT OF RECEIPTS—*Continued.*

| Date. | LODGE. | No. | Total. | Capita Tax. | Supplies. | Sundries. | Charter Fee. |
|---|---|---|---|---|---|---|---|
| **1893.** | | | | | | | |
| May 2 | Owen Sound | 180 | 50 | | 50 | | |
| | Cambridge | 188 | 12 75 | 12 75 | | | |
| 3 | Bracebridge | 251 | 25 | 25 | | | |
| | Enterprise | 218 | 30 00 | 30 00 | | | |
| | Alpha | 154 | 1 69 | | 1 69 | | |
| | Royal Oak | 108 | 1 68 | | 1 68 | | |
| | Supplies | | 84 | | 84 | | |
| 6 | Stirling | 230 | 75 | | 75 | | |
| | Penetangore | 172 | 5 80 | | 5 80 | | |
| 8 | North Bay | 271 | 2 96 | | 2 96 | | |
| | Minnetonka | 292 | 1 68 | | 1 68 | | |
| 9 | Clinton | 83 | 1 24 | | 89 | 35 | |
| | Hensall | 223 | 84 | | 84 | | |
| | Deseronto | 102 | 1 68 | | 1 68 | | |
| | Atthewell (Rebekah) | 29 | 5 00 | | | | 5 00 |
| | Beethoven | 165 | 35 | | | 35 | |
| | Dolman | 174 | 1 25 | | 1 25 | | |
| | Excelsior | 44 | 30 | | 30 | | |
| | Sarnia | 126 | 3 42 | | 3 42 | | |
| 10 | Denovo | 170 | 3 60 | | 3 60 | | |
| | Bracebridge | 251 | 1 68 | | 1 68 | | |
| | Fraternity | 264 | 40 | | 40 | | |
| 11 | Peterboro' | 111 | 1 12 | | 1 12 | | |
| | Madoc | 170 | 1 25 | | 1 25 | | |
| | Lakeview | 275 | 3 00 | | 3 00 | | |
| 13 | Beacon | 201 | 56 | | 56 | | |
| | Olive Branch (Rebekah) | 16 | 1 68 | | 1 68 | | |
| | Sydenham Valley | 120 | 56 | | 56 | | |
| | East Toronto | 263 | 40 | | 40 | | |
| 13 | Fergus | 73 | 85 | | 85 | | |
| | Ilderton | 234 | 3 06 | | 3 06 | | |
| | Colfax (Rebekah) | 28 | 5 00 | | | | 5 00 |
| | Missanabie | 266 | 25 | | 25 | | |
| | May Queen (Rebekah) | 5 | 1 00 | | 1 00 | | |
| 16 | Pontypool | 296 | 3 00 | | 3 00 | | |
| | Thamesford | 258 | 1 00 | | 1 00 | | |
| 18 | Georgian Bay | 219 | 1 35 | | 1 00 | 35 | |
| | Walkerton | 84 | 45 | | 45 | | |
| | Mystic | 128 | 1 00 | | | 1 00 | |
| | Harmony (Rebekah) | 15 | 75 | | 75 | | |
| | Aberdeen (Rebekah) | 30 | 5 00 | | | | 5 00 |
| | Union | 16 | 1 68 | | 1 68 | | |
| | Montana | 177 | 1 25 | | 90 | 35 | |
| 19 | Penetangore | 172 | 2 50 | | 2 50 | | |
| 20 | Peaceful Dove | 135 | 1 68 | | 1 68 | | |
| | Port Arthur | 244 | 1 00 | | 1 00 | | |
| 22 | Grand Union | 97 | 1 00 | | 1 00 | | |
| | Mayflower | 207 | 5 94 | | 5 94 | | |
| 25 | Sutton | 168 | 85 | | 50 | 35 | |
| | Western City | 93 | 75 | | 75 | | |
| 27 | Amity | 80 | 3 36 | | 3 36 | | |
| | Crescent | 104 | 7 12 | | 7 12 | | |
| | Louise (Rebekah) | 10 | 1 25 | | 1 25 | | |
| 27 | Ivy | 90 | 6 00 | | 6 00 | | |
| | Oak Leaf | 159 | 50 | | 50 | | |
| | Lucknow | 112 | 1 68 | | 1 68 | | |
| | Garnet | 139 | 1 00 | | 1 00 | | |
| | Leamington | 140 | 1 05 | | 1 05 | | |
| 29 | Beacon | 201 | 50 | | 50 | | |
| 30 | Earnscliffe | 283 | 1 25 | | 1 25 | | |
| 31 | Elgin | 32 | 85 | | 85 | | |
| | Ridgely | 250 | 1 40 | | 1 40 | | |
| | Fraternity | 264 | 1 68 | | 1 68 | | |
| June 1 | Ancaster | 138 | 4 61 | | 4 61 | | |
| | Ottawa | 225 | 4 10 | | 4 10 | | |

STATEMENT OF RECEIPTS—*Continued.*

| Date | LODGE | No. | Total | Capita Tax | Supplies | Sundries | Charter Fee |
|---|---|---|---|---|---|---|---|
| **1893.**<br>June 2 | Prudence (Rebekah) | 24 | 15 50 | | 15 50 | | |
| | Brougham | 155 | 3 50 | | 3 50 | | |
| | Gore | 34 | 5 60 | | 5 60 | | |
| | Otonabee | 13 | 4 21 | | 4 21 | | |
| | Kingston | 59 | 6 72 | | 6 72 | | |
| | Cataract | 103 | 3 36 | | 3 36 | | |
| | Campbellford | 248 | 2 40 | | 2 05 | 35 | |
| | Sauble | 227 | 1 96 | | 1 96 | | |
| | Teeswater | 183 | 35 | | | 35 | |
| | Harmony | 115 | 2 75 | | 2 75 | | |
| | Owen Sound | 180 | 18 | | 18 | | |
| | Saxon | 121 | 1 50 | | 1 50 | | |
| 5 | Supplies | | 75 | | 75 | | |
| | Florence Nightingale | 66 | 2 53 | | 2 53 | | |
| | Grand River | 91 | 35 | | | 35 | |
| 6 | Canada | 49 | 91 | | 56 | 35 | |
| 7 | Prince of Wales | 230 | 1 68 | | 1 68 | | |
| | Emerald | 173 | 5 39 | | 5 04 | 35 | |
| 8 | St. Mary's | 36 | 25 | | 25 | | |
| | Hillsburg | 167 | 35 | | | 35 | |
| | Milton | 92 | 35 | | | 35 | |
| | Cataraqui | 10 | 75 | | 75 | | |
| | Norwood | 262 | 35 | | | 35 | |
| | Queen City | 56 | 35 | | | 35 | |
| | Sheard | 276 | 10 | | 10 | | |
| | Bothwell | 74 | 35 | | | 35 | |
| 9 | Oxford | 77 | 35 | | | 35 | |
| 10 | Grey | 169 | 21 | | 21 | | |
| | Thomasburg | 293 | 35 | | | 35 | |
| | Millbank | 209 | 1 25 | | 1 25 | | |
| | Sudbury | 282 | 35 | | | 35 | |
| | St. Lawrence | 137 | 85 | | 50 | 35 | |
| | Stanley | 260 | 35 | | | 35 | |
| 12 | Waterford | 235 | 35 | | | 35 | |
| | Lyn | 284 | 35 | | | 35 | |
| | Orillia | 246 | 1 68 | | 1 68 | | |
| | Walkerton | 84 | 35 | | | 35 | |
| | Brucefield | 210 | 35 | | | 35 | |
| | Broadview | 294 | 68 | | 68 | | |
| 13 | Phœnix | 22 | 2 38 | | 2 38 | | |
| | Napanee | 86 | 35 | | | 35 | |
| | Hope | 60 | 35 | | | 35 | |
| | Enterprise | 218 | 35 | | | 35 | |
| | Frontier | 45 | 35 | | | 35 | |
| | Leamington | 140 | 1 68 | | 1 68 | | |
| | Valley City | 117 | 35 | | | 35 | |
| | Huron | 62 | 35 | | | 35 | |
| | International | 228 | 35 | | | 35 | |
| | Broadview | 294 | 3 77 | | 3 77 | | |
| 14 | Waterloo | 107 | 3 00 | | 3 00 | | |
| | Dresden | 124 | 85 | | 85 | | |
| | Caledonia | 253 | 35 | | | 35 | |
| | Acton | 204 | 56 | | 56 | | |
| | Thamesville | 157 | 35 | | | 35 | |
| | Algoma | 267 | 1 35 | | 1 00 | 35 | |
| | Fraternity | 264 | 35 | | | 35 | |
| | Cicerone | 195 | 35 | | | 35 | |
| 15 | Wildey | 153 | 85 | | 85 | | |
| | Germania | 184 | 1 00 | | 1 00 | | |
| | Lucan | 70 | 35 | | | 35 | |
| 16 | Denovo | 170 | 35 | | | 35 | |
| | Elgin | 32 | 35 | | | 35 | |
| | Marion | 131 | 35 | | | 35 | |
| | Lakeview | 272 | 75 | | 75 | | |
| | Manotick | 295 | 7 70 | | 7 70 | | |

STATEMENT OF RECEIPTS—*Continued.*

| Date | LODGE | No. | Total | Capita Tax | Supplies | Sundries | Charter Fee |
|---|---|---|---|---|---|---|---|
| 1893. | | | | | | | |
| June 16 | Olive Branch (Rebekah) | 16 | 35 | | | 35 | |
| 18 | Naomi (Rebekah) | 6 | 1 68 | | 1 68 | | |
| 19 | Dominion | 48 | .2 20 | | 1 85 | 35 | |
| | Cambridge | 188 | 38 | | 03 | 35 | |
| | Amity | 80 | 35 | | | 35 | |
| 20 | Dufferin | 186 | 35 | | | 35 | |
| | Hensall | 223 | 35 | | | 35 | |
| | Parry Sound | 189 | 35 | | | 35 | |
| | Penetangore | 172 | 1 47 | | 1 12 | 35 | |
| 21 | Model | 147 | 35 | | | 35 | |
| | St. Clair | 106 | 35 | | | 35 | |
| 22 | Dolman | 174 | 35 | | | 35 | |
| 24 | Victoria | 64 | 17 00 | 17 00 | | | |
| | Milton | 92 | 86 | | 86 | | |
| | Amity | 80 | 1 68 | | 1 68 | | |
| | Mizpah (Rebekah) | 19 | 75 | | 75 | | |
| | Howard | 58 | 83 | | 48 | 35 | |
| 26 | Thomasburg | 293 | 1 40 | | 1 40 | | |
| 23 | Donalda | 20 | 75 | | 75 | | |
| 30 | Madoc | 179 | 35 | | | 35 | |
| | Alliston | 171 | 1 19 | | 84 | 35 | |
| | Cataract | 103 | 35 | | | 35 | |
| | Romeo | 164 | 35 | | | 35 | |
| | Acton | 204 | 35 | | | 35 | |
| | Ahiram | 205 | 3 20 | | 3 20 | | |
| | Laurel | 110 | 6 00 | | 6 00 | | |
| July 3 | Harmony | 154 | 4 50 | | 4 50 | | |
| | Atthewell (Rebekah) | 29 | 13 00 | | 13 00 | | |
| | Royal | 286 | 6 35 | | 6 00 | 35 | |
| | Unity | 47 | 5 04 | | 5 04 | | |
| | Otter | 50 | 3 50 | | 3 50 | | |
| | Lucknow | 112 | 5 04 | | 5 04 | | |
| | Friendship | 65 | 3 35 | | 3 35 | | |
| | Stanley | 268 | 10 25 | | 10 25 | | |
| | Chatham | 29 | 5 60 | | 5 60 | | |
| | Kingston | 59 | 10 55 | | 10 55 | | |
| | Frontier | 45 | 3 36 | | 3 36 | | |
| | Lynden | 259 | 5 75 | 5 75 | | | |
| | Grenville | 279 | 35 | | | 35 | |
| | Jubilee (Rebekah) | 13 | 3 40 | | | 3 40 | |
| | Avon | 41 | 58 46 | 53 75 | 4 36 | 35 | |
| 4 | Atthewell (Rebekah) | 29 | 75 | | 75 | | |
| | Waterloo | 157 | 39 25 | 39 25 | | | |
| | Bissell | 51 | 6 10 | 5 75 | | 35 | |
| | The Toronto | 71 | 16 00 | 16 00 | | | |
| 5 | Fairy | 275 | 11 00 | 11 25 | | 35 | |
| | Hope | 69 | 18 75 | 18 75 | | | |
| | Wellington Square | 178 | 9 00 | 9 00 | | | |
| | Rodney | 291 | 1 62 | | 1 62 | | |
| | Otonabee | 13 | 1 25 | | 1 25 | | |
| | Walkerton | 84 | 85 | | 85 | | |
| | Lyn | 234 | 7 75 | 7 75 | | | |
| | Colfax (Rebekah) | 28 | 14 50 | | 14 50 | | |
| | Flora (Rebekah) | 21 | 2 60 | | | 2 60 | |
| | Prince of Wales | 230 | 11 50 | 11 50 | | | |
| | Excelsior (Rebekah) | 18 | 5 20 | | | 5 20 | |
| | Ivy (Rebekah) | 26 | 6 30 | | | 6 30 | |
| 6 | Delta | 265 | 11 75 | 11 75 | | | |
| | Lambton | 27 | 14 50 | 14 50 | | | |
| | Union | 16 | 56 18 | 54 50 | 1 68 | | |
| | Romeo | 164 | 34 00 | 34 00 | | | |
| | Listowel | 160 | 21 85 | 21 50 | | 35 | |
| | St. Marys | 36 | 35 00 | 35 00 | | | |
| | Cataraqui | 10 | 65 25 | 65 25 | | | |
| | Myrtle (Rebekah) | 17 | 3 50 | | | 3 50 | |

## STATEMENT OF RECEIPTS—*Continued.*

| Date. | LODGE. | No. | Total. | Capita Tax. | Supplies. | Sundries. | Charter Fee. |
|---|---|---|---|---|---|---|---|
| 1893. | | | | | | | |
| July 6 | Bracebridge | 251 | 16 75 | 16 75 | | | |
| | Dolman | 174 | 13 25 | 13 25 | | | |
| | Phœnix | 22 | 21 25 | 21 25 | | | |
| | Penetangore | 172 | 32 25 | 32 25 | | | |
| | Alberta (Rebekah) | 25 | 4 70 | | | 4 70 | |
| | Sauble | 227 | 4 00 | 3 75 | 25 | | |
| | Orillia | 246 | 1 32 | | 1 32 | | |
| 7 | Norwood | 262 | 8 50 | 8 50 | | | |
| | Reliance | 89 | 40 25 | 40 25 | | | |
| | Parry Sound | 189 | 13 75 | 13 75 | | | |
| | Aurora | 148 | 19 75 | 19 75 | | | |
| | Farmersville | 237 | 5 50 | 5 50 | | | |
| | Maitland | 119 | 35 | | | 35 | |
| | Beacon | 201 | 11 25 | 11 25 | | | |
| | Chatham | 29 | 46 50 | 46 50 | | | |
| | Marion | 131 | 17 75 | 17 75 | | | |
| | Simcoe | 161 | 75 | | 40 | 35 | |
| | Sheard | 276 | 7 75 | 7 75 | | | |
| | Walkerton | 84 | 15 75 | 15 75 | | | |
| | Unity | 47 | 76 25 | 79 50 | 75 | | |
| | Gore | 34 | 45 75 | 45 75 | | | |
| | Beaver | 82 | 13 50 | 13 50 | | | |
| | Comber | 298 | 30 00 | | | | 30 00 |
| | Bothwell | 74 | 10 25 | 10 25 | | | |
| | Exeter | 67 | 12 00 | 12 00 | | | |
| 8 | Lakeview | 272 | 16 25 | 16 25 | | | |
| | Albert | 194 | 1 25 | 1 25 | | | |
| | Alba | 251 | 85 | | 85 | | |
| | Port Arthur | 244 | 23 55 | 19 50 | 4 05 | | |
| | St. Lawrence | 137 | 27 50 | 27 50 | | | |
| | Argyll | 312 | 18 00 | 18 00 | | | |
| | Pembroke | 203 | 29 00 | 29 00 | | | |
| | Wildey | 153 | 12 00 | 12 00 | | | |
| | Bay of Quinte | 143 | 29 00 | 29 00 | | | |
| | Trenton | 113 | 17 50 | 17 50 | | | |
| | Sudbury | 282 | 14 50 | 14 50 | | | |
| | Rose | 28 | 23 50 | 23 50 | | | |
| | Mt. Zion | 46 | 5 50 | 5 50 | | | |
| | Ivy | 90 | 18 25 | 17 00 | 1 25 | | |
| | Collingwood | 54 | 36 50 | 36 50 | | | |
| | Millbank | 209 | 5 50 | 5 50 | | | |
| | Ahiram | 205 | 26 50 | 26 50 | | | |
| | Elora | 241 | 16 25 | 16 25 | | | |
| | Nith | 96 | 15 75 | 15 75 | | | |
| | Brock | 9 | 29 25 | 29 25 | | | |
| | Maple Leaf | 57 | 15 80 | 13 00 | 2 80 | | |
| | Lindsay | 100 | 23 25 | 23 25 | | | |
| | Canada | 49 | 50 25 | 50 25 | | | |
| 10 | Round Eau | 40 | 40 | | 40 | | |
| | Thamesville | 157 | 14 00 | 14 00 | | | |
| | Glencoe | 133 | 13 60 | 13 25 | 35 | | |
| | Albert | 104 | 45 25 | 42 25 | | | |
| | Listowel | 160 | 85 | 85 | | | |
| | Chesterville | 288 | 80 | | 45 | 35 | |
| | Harmony (Rebekah) | 15 | 17 30 | | | 17 30 | |
| | Inglewood (Rebekah) | 23 | 2 70 | | | 2 70 | |
| | Clifford | 214 | 20 10 | 19 75 | | 35 | |
| | Rodney | 219 | 13 75 | 13 75 | | | |
| | Arthur | 281 | 16 00 | 16 00 | | | |
| | Grand River | 91 | 27 50 | 27 50 | | | |
| | Owen Sound | 180 | 15 25 | 15 25 | | | |
| | Chesley | 221 | 6 80 | 6 45 | | 35 | |
| | Thamesville | 157 | 1 25 | | 1 25 | | |
| | Grand Valley | 256 | 1 25 | | 1 25 | | |
| | Samaritan | 35 | 39 25 | 39 25 | | | |

STATEMENT OF RECEIPTS—*Continued.*

| Date. | LODGE. | No. | Total. | Capita Tax. | Supplies. | Sundries. | Charter Fee. |
|---|---|---|---|---|---|---|---|
| 1893. | | | | | | | |
| July 10 | Fidelity | 55 | 4 91 | 4 00 | 56 | 35 | |
| | Silver Star | 202 | 13 50 | 13 50 | | | |
| | Prudence (Rebekah) | 24 | 6 50 | | | 6 50 | |
| | Grand Union, | 97 | 22 25 | 22 25 | | | |
| | Tweed | 290 | 13 05 | 13 05 | | | |
| | Model | 149 | 9 25 | 9 25 | | | |
| | Pontypool | 296 | 9 25 | 9 25 | | | |
| 11 | Beaverton | 249 | 35 | | | 35 | |
| | Peaceful Dove | 135 | 10 25 | 10 25 | | | |
| | Belleville | 81 | 1 00 | | | 1 00 | |
| | Thornbury | 243 | 35 | | | 35 | |
| | Amity | 80 | 50 50 | 50 50 | | | |
| | Woodstock | 209 | 25 25 | 25 50 | | | |
| | Alba | 254 | 11 50 | 11 50 | | | |
| | Dominion | 48 | 39 50 | 39 50 | | | |
| | Elgin | 32 | 58 25 | 58 25 | | | |
| | Floral | 252 | 10 00 | 10 00 | | | |
| 12 | Fraternity | 265 | 19 25 | 19 25 | | | |
| | Florence | 196 | 21 00 | 21 00 | | | |
| | Orillia | 246 | 6 75 | 6 75 | | | |
| | Aylmer | 94 | 3 36 | | 3 36 | | |
| | Broadview | 294 | 18 25 | 18 25 | | | |
| | Clinton | 83 | 4 75 | 4 75 | | | |
| | Amity | 80 | 1 25 | | 1 25 | | |
| | Mizpah | 127 | 28 50 | 28 50 | | | |
| | International | 228 | 37 50 | 37 50 | | | |
| | Barrie | 63 | 26 75 | 26 75 | | | |
| | Denovo | 170 | 11 50 | 11 50 | | | |
| | Royal Oak | 108 | 19 75 | 19 75 | | | |
| | Charity | 129 | 7 25 | 7 25 | | | |
| | Chorazin | 190 | 29 50 | 29 50 | | | |
| | Manilla | 105 | 7 25 | 7 25 | | | |
| | Otonabee | 13 | 34 25 | 34 25 | | | |
| | Missanabie | 266 | 21 25 | 21 25 | | | |
| | Laurel | 110 | 12 00 | 12 00 | | | |
| | Ripley | 287 | 13 25 | 13 25 | | | |
| | Simcoe | 161 | 18 50 | 18 50 | | | |
| | Jarvis | 191 | 5 50 | 5 50 | | | |
| | Equity | 232 | 5 50 | 5 50 | | | |
| | Waterford | 235 | 27 25 | 27 25 | | | |
| | Caledonia | 253 | 4 00 | 4 00 | | | |
| 13 | Pyramid | 156 | 9 75 | 9 75 | | | |
| | Meaford | 260 | 13 75 | 13 75 | | | |
| | Aylmer | 94 | 33 75 | 33 75 | | | |
| | Eureka | 30 | 25 50 | 25 50 | | | |
| | Dresden | 124 | 29 50 | 29 50 | | | |
| | Sycamore | 151 | 11 75 | 11 75 | | | |
| | Dufferin | 186 | 6 25 | 6 25 | | | |
| | Milton | 92 | 7 25 | 7 25 | | | |
| | Supplies | | 60 | | 60 | | |
| | Edna (Rebekah) | 14 | 8 20 | | | 8 20 | |
| | Howick | 192 | 2 50 | 2 50 | | | |
| | Western City | 93 | 18 25 | 18 25 | | | |
| | Crescent | 104 | 67 50 | 67 50 | | | |
| | Ancaster | 138 | 17 00 | 17 00 | | | |
| | North Star | 68 | 12 00 | 12 00 | | | |
| | Cicerone | 195 | 5 00 | 5 00 | | | |
| | Warriner | 75 | 17 00 | 17 00 | | | |
| | Napanee | 86 | 15 25 | 15 25 | | | |
| | Gananoque | 114 | 63 25 | 61 25 | 2 00 | | |
| | Stella | 125 | 30 00 | 30 00 | | | |
| | Freestone | 215 | 8 00 | 8 25 | | 35 | |
| | Enterprise | 218 | 30 25 | 30 25 | | | |
| | Concord | 142 | 14 50 | 14 50 | | | |
| | Queen City of Ontario | 56 | 86 25 | 86 25 | | | |

### STATEMENT OF RECEIPTS—*Continued.*

| Date | LODGE | No. | Total | Capita Tax | Supplies | Sundries | Charter Fee |
|---|---|---|---|---|---|---|---|
| 1893. July 14 | Prince of Wales | 230 | 45 | | | 45 | |
| | Eastern Star | 72 | 26 75 | 26 75 | | | |
| | Sutton | 168 | 1 68 | | 1 68 | | |
| | Balmoral | 280 | 10 50 | 10 50 | | | |
| | Mallorytown | 245 | 11 25 | 11 25 | | | |
| | Algoma | 267 | 16 00 | 16 00 | | | |
| | Louise (Rebekah) | 10 | 10 00 | | | 10 00 | |
| | Mizpah | 10 | 6 40 | | | 6 40 | |
| | Sydenham Valley | 120 | 38 00 | 38 00 | | | |
| | Merlin | 226 | 10 00 | 10 00 | | | |
| | Trenton | 113 | 25 | 25 | | | |
| | Rideau | 241 | 30 50 | 30 50 | | | |
| 15 | Milton | 92 | 84 | | 84 | | |
| | Manilla | 105 | 50 | 50 | | | |
| | Credit | 257 | 10 00 | 10 00 | | | |
| | Thamesford | 258 | 28 25 | 28 25 | | | |
| | Durham | 78 | 29 00 | 29 00 | | | |
| | Erie | 33 | 5 00 | 5 00 | | | |
| | Collingwood | 54 | 1 68 | | 1 68 | | |
| | Fergus | 73 | 19 75 | 19 75 | | | |
| | Oak Leaf | 159 | 13 50 | 13 50 | | | |
| | Minerva | 197 | 18 75 | 18 75 | | | |
| | Lilly | 211 | 11 00 | 11 00 | | | |
| | Brougham | 155 | 4 75 | 4 75 | | | |
| | Belleville | 81 | 54 00 | 52 00 | 2 00 | | |
| | Corinthian | 61 | 50 75 | 50 75 | | | |
| | Deseronto | 102 | 23 75 | 23 75 | | | |
| | Olive Branch | 88 | 31 25 | 31 25 | | | |
| | Stanley | 268 | 8 75 | 8 75 | | | |
| | Madoc | 179 | 30 00 | 30 00 | | | |
| | Campbellford | 248 | 25 75 | 25 75 | | | |
| | Thomasburg | 203 | 17 25 | 17 25 | | | |
| | Hastings | 273 | 9 50 | 9 50 | | | |
| | Stirling | 239 | 33 25 | 33 25 | | | |
| | Frontier | 45 | 60 75 | 60 75 | | | |
| | Leamington | 140 | 35 25 | 35 25 | | | |
| 17 | Germania | 184 | 26 00 | 26 00 | | | |
| | Elmira | 216 | 10 50 | 10 50 | | | |
| | At the Well (Rebekah) | 29 | 3 30 | | | 3 30 | |
| | Colfax (Rebekah) | 28 | 1 40 | | | 1 40 | |
| | Peterboro | 111 | 58 35 | 58 35 | | | |
| | Woodstock | 260 | 1 25 | | 1 25 | | |
| | Howard | 58 | 28 75 | 28 75 | | | |
| | Gold Hill | 261 | 7 70 | | 7 70 | | |
| | Beethoven | 165 | 8 75 | 8 75 | | | |
| | Saxon | 121 | 7 50 | 7 50 | | | |
| | Hillsburg | 167 | 11 25 | 11 25 | | | |
| | Grey | 160 | 6 00 | 6 00 | | | |
| | Ivy (Rebekah) | 26 | 28 | | 28 | | |
| | Thornbury | 243 | 9 00 | 9 00 | | | |
| | Olive Branch (Rebekah) | 16 | 20 70 | | | 20 70 | |
| 18 | Sydenham Valley | 120 | 5 04 | | 5 04 | | |
| | Carleton | 240 | 30 | | 30 | | |
| | Germania | 184 | 1 68 | | 1 68 | | |
| | Earnscliffe | 283 | 35 | | | 35 | |
| | Cobourg | 136 | 23 25 | 23 25 | | | M |
| | Midland | 274 | 12 75 | 12 75 | | | |
| | Egremont | 207 | 4 00 | 4 00 | | | |
| | Huron | 62 | 29 00 | 29 00 | | | |
| | Ridgetown | 144 | 28 00 | 28 00 | | | |
| | Victoria (Rebekah) | 1 | 1 20 | 1 20 | | | |
| | Florence Nightingale | 66 | 37 25 | 37 25 | | | |
| | Progress | 158 | 28 00 | 28 00 | | | |
| | Orion | 109 | 13 00 | 13 00 | | | |
| | Golden Star | 101 | 10 00 | 10 00 | | | |

STATEMENT OF RECEIPTS—*Continued.*

| Date. | LODGE. | No. | Total. | | Capit. Tax. | | Supplies. | | Sundries. | | Charter Fee. | |
|---|---|---|---|---|---|---|---|---|---|---|---|---|
| 1893. | | | | | | | | | | | | |
| July 18 | Empire | 87 | 27 | 35 | 27 | 00 | | | | 35 | | |
| | Valley City | 117 | 25 | 25 | 25 | 25 | | | | | | |
| | Royal | 286 | 9 | 25 | 9 | 25 | | | | | | |
| 19 | Trenton | 113 | 10 | 00 | 10 | 00 | | | | | | |
| | East Toronto | 263 | 15 | 50 | 15 | 50 | | | | | | |
| | Constellation | 85 | 14 | 25 | 13 | 00 | 1 | 25 | | | | |
| | Brucefield | 210 | 7 | 00 | 7 | 00 | | | | | | |
| | Beatrice (Rebekah) | 12 | 8 | 30 | | | | | 8 | 30 | | |
| | Gordon | 246 | 12 | 75 | 12 | 75 | | | | | | |
| | Cambridge | 188 | 12 | 25 | 12 | 25 | | | | | | |
| | St. Thomas | 76 | 87 | 00 | 87 | 00 | | | | | | |
| 20 | Broadview | 294 | 1 | 68 | | | 1 | 68 | | | | |
| | **Romeo** | 164 | 1 | 68 | | | 1 | 68 | | | | |
| | **Otonabee** | 13 | 3 | 00 | | | 3 | 00 | | | | |
| | **Maple Leaf** | 57 | 5 | 00 | | | 5 | 00 | | | | |
| | **Vivian** | 146 | 17 | 50 | 17 | 50 | | | | | | |
| | **Niagara Falls** | 53 | 31 | 00 | 31 | 00 | | | | | | |
| | Ilderton | 234 | 8 | 25 | 8 | 25 | | | | | | |
| | Garnet | 139 | 17 | 90 | 17 | 00 | | 55 | | 35 | | |
| | Gore | 34 | 60 | 25 | 60 | 25 | | | | | | |
| | Howick | 192 | | 35 | | | | | | 35 | | |
| | Alpha | 154 | 31 | 00 | 31 | 00 | | | | | | |
| | Sarnia | 126 | 26 | 53 | 22 | 00 | 4 | 53 | | | | |
| | Naomi (Rebekah) | 6 | 13 | 40 | | | | | 13 | 40 | | |
| | Rondeau | 40 | 28 | 00 | 28 | 00 | | | | | | |
| | Excelsior | 44 | 36 | 25 | 36 | 25 | | | | | | |
| | Cataract | 103 | 13 | 25 | 13 | 25 | | | | | | |
| | Alliston | 171 | 7 | 50 | 7 | 50 | | | | | | |
| | Georgian **Bay** | 219 | 19 | 50 | 19 | 50 | | | | | | |
| | Lucknow | 112 | 26 | 25 | 26 | 25 | | | | | | |
| | Lucknow (Rebekah) | 22 | 6 | 60 | | | | | 6 | 60 | | |
| | Fraternity | 265 | | 35 | | | | | | 35 | | |
| | Maitland | 219 | 15 | 50 | 15 | 50 | | | | | | |
| | Sutton | 168 | 8 | 75 | 8 | 75 | | | | | | |
| | Teeswater | 183 | 8 | 50 | 8 | 50 | | | | | | |
| | Simcoe | 161 | 1 | 68 | | | 1 | 68 | | | | |
| | Olive Branch | 88 | | 40 | | | | 40 | | | | |
| | Lansdowne | 270 | 18 | 75 | 18 | 75 | | | | | | |
| | Livingstone | 130 | 10 | 50 | 10 | 50 | | | | | | |
| | Orient | 134 | 5 | 50 | 5 | 50 | | | | | | |
| | Acorn | 236 | 6 | 25 | 6 | 25 | | | | | | |
| | Chesley | 221 | | 50 | | 50 | | | | | | |
| | Streetsville | 122 | 14 | 10 | 11 | 75 | 2 | 00 | | 35 | | |
| | Oakville | 132 | 14 | 75 | 14 | 75 | | | | | | |
| | Woodslee | 220 | 3 | 25 | 3 | 25 | | | | | | |
| | **Comber** | 298 | 23 | 90 | | | 23 | 90 | | | | |
| | **Hensall** | 223 | 12 | 50 | 12 | 50 | | | | | | |
| | **Covenant** | 52 | 45 | 00 | 45 | 00 | | | | | | |
| | **Carleton** | 240 | 32 | 25 | 32 | 25 | | | | | | |
| | **Milton** | 242 | 21 | 00 | 21 | 00 | | | | | | |
| | Oxford | 77 | 27 | 25 | 27 | 25 | | | | | | |
| | Friendship | 65 | 44 | 00 | 44 | 00 | | | | | | |
| | Oriental | 163 | 14 | 32 | 14 | 32 | | | | | | |
| | Ottawa | 224 | 36 | 25 | 30 | 25 | | | | | | |
| | North Bay | 261 | 21 | 25 | 21 | 25 | | | | | | |
| | Grenville | 279 | 19 | 25 | 19 | 25 | | | | | | |
| | Rockliffe | 278 | 15 | 00 | 15 | 00 | | | | | | |
| | Earnscliffe | 283 | 15 | 75 | 15 | 75 | | | | | | |
| | Morewcod | 285 | 6 | 25 | 6 | 25 | | | | | | |
| | Chesterville | 288 | 9 | 25 | 9 | 25 | | | | | | |
| | Manotick | 295 | 5 | 25 | 5 | 25 | | | | | | |
| | Forest City | 38 | 30 | 00 | 30 | 00 | | | | | | |
| | Interest | | 96 | 63 | | | | | 96 | 63 | | |
| | Totals | | 12077 | 66 | 10187 | 78 | 1793 | 93 | 435 | 95 | 260 | 00 |

Bro. W. Badenach, Grand Treasurer, submitted the following report, which was referred to the Committee on Finance :—

## GRAND TREASURER'S REPORT.

Toronto, August 8, 1893.

*To the Officers and Representatives of the*
*Grand Lodge of Ontario, I.O.O.F.:*

Brethren,—As required by law and custom I present herewith my annual report of Receipts and Disbursements for the year, and balance on hand, July 21, 1893.

### DR.—GRAND TREASURER.

| 1892 | | | | | |
|---|---|---|---|---|---|
| July 20. | To Balance ......................................................... | | | | $12,775 39 |
| " 31. | " Cash from Grand Secretary........... | $657 64 | | | |
| Aug. 31. | " " " | 278 95 | | | |
| Sept. 30. | " " " | 94 26 | | | |
| Oct. 31. | " " " | 112 90 | | | |
| Nov. 30. | " " " | 88 72 | | | |
| Dec. 31. | " " " | 261 11 | | | |
| 1893. | | | | | |
| Jan. 31. | " " " | 4,319 90 | | | |
| Feb. 28. | " " " | 576 50 | | | |
| Mar. 31. | " " " | 326 27 | | | |
| Apr. 30. | " " " | 342 62 | | | |
| May 31. | " " " | 211 88 | | | |
| June 30. | " " " | 153 44 | | | |
| July 21. | " " " | 5,244 22 | | | |
| | | | | | 12,668 41 |
| | | | | | $25,443 80 |

### CR.—GRAND TREASURER.

| 1892. | | | | Order. | |
|---|---|---|---|---|---|
| July 30. By Paid | F. W. Warren, D. D. G. M., Special Services ........................................ | | | 1 | $ 3 45 |
| Aug. 4. " " | Type Writer.......................................... | | | 2 | 105 00 |
| 5. " " | C. Packert, Auditor ............................ | | | 3 | 25 50 |
| " " | A. C. Stewart, Auditor ....................... | | | 4 | 26 70 |
| " " | Sovereign Grand Lodge, supplies ...... | | | 5 | 20 00 |
| " " | C. Blackett Robinson, Printing and Stationery ............................................ | | | 6 | 198 35 |
| 12. " " | Hy. Robertson, P.G.M., preparing report on Fraternal Relations .................... | | | 7 | 50 00 |

|  |  |  |  | Order |  |
|---|---|---|---|---|---|
| 1892. | By | Paid | J. A. Young, assistant to Grand Secretary | 8 | $ 6 00 |
| Aug. 12. | '' | '' | Thos. Hillier, Janitor...... ........... | 9 | 10 00 |
|  | '' | '' | J. A. Auld, Official Reporter .... ...... | 10 | 15 00 |
|  | '' | '' | H. Robertson, P.G.M., special Committee on Insurance.... ..................... | 11 | 8 45 |
|  | '' | '' | Cl. T. Campbell, '' '' | 12 | 5 25 |
|  | '' | '' | W. H. Cole, '' '' | 13 | 2 00 |
|  | '' | '' | H. Robertson, fee for preparing forms for Insurance Committee .... ............ | 14 | 4 00 |
|  | '' | '' | J. Donogh, Special Committee on Finance | 15 | 2 00 |
|  | '' | '' | W. A. Rawlings, gratuity .............. | 16 | 75 00 |
|  | '' | '' | P. E. Fitz-Patrick, balance account, expenses ................ ........... | 17 | 14 88 |
|  | '' | '' | Sovereign Grand Lodge, supplies ...... | 18 | 167 00 |
| 18. | '' | '' | J. B. King salary 2 months ............ | 19 | 250 00 |
|  | '' | '' | Mileage and per diem, Officers and Representatives, Session of 1892, Windsor | 20 | 6,221 60 |
| 24. | '' | '' | Dominion Express Co.... .. ....... | 21 | 7 65 |
| 27. | '' | '' | Mrs. Patterson, caretaker of offices .. .. | 22 | 8 00 |
|  | '' | '' | Wm. Badenach, Grand Treasurer's salary | 23 | 200 00 |
|  | '' | '' | '' Committee on Insurance | 24 | 5 30 |
|  | '' | '' | Brown Brothers, badges for Grand Lodge ............................. | 25 | 37 70 |
|  | '' | '' | Lugsden and Barnett, trunk straps ..... | 26 | 1 25 |
| 31. | '' |  | T. W. Jolliffe, Grand Master, on account expenses ............................. | 27 | 25 00 |
| Sept. 1. | '' | '' | London Guarantee Company, Guarantee Bonds, Grand Secretary and Grand Treasurer ......................... | 28 | 36 25 |
|  | '' | '' | Ontario Government, Registration fee .. | 29 | 25 00 |
|  | '' | '' | Jno. Pringle, coal ...... ........ ..... | 30 | 28 00 |
| Oct. 3. | '' | '' | A. Harris, quarter's rent .... ... ...... | 31 | 77 00 |
| 4. | '' | '' | Mrs. Patterson, caretaker .. .. ...... .... | 32 | 8 00 |
| 21. | '' | '' | Grand Master and Grand Secretary, expenses to Stratford and Thomasburg | 33 | 34 75 |
| 29. | '' | '' | Wm. Briggs, Unabridged Dictionary.... | 34 | 14 00 |
| 31. | '' | '' | Postage Stamps ...................... | 35 | 44 67 |
|  | '' | '' | Incidentals, exchange, telegrams, &c .. | 36 | 26 21 |
| Nov. 5. | '' | '' | Sovereign Grand Lodge, supplies ...... | 37 | 141 00 |
| 14. | '' | '' | Express charges, and duty on supplies.. | 38 | 6 35 |
| 16. | '' | '' | W. H. McGillivray, tucker binders .... | 39 | 5 50 |
| 22. | '' | '' | Grand & Toy, stationery .............. | 40 | 2 45 |
| 30. | '' | '' | E. M. Clapp, stove for office .. .. ...... | 41 | 25 75 |
| Dec. 2. | '' | '' | *Dominion Odd Fellow*, circulars, printing, &c................................ | 42 | 119 70 |
| 3. | '' | '' | Barclay, Clark & Co., printing Charters | 43 | 9 70 |
|  | '' | '' | Fullerton & Co., law costs ......... .... | 44 | 2 00 |
|  | '' | '' | J. A. Gorrie, reglazing windows .. .. .. | 45 | 10 00 |
| 4. | '' | '' | Mrs. Patterson, 2 months' services...... | 46 | 8 00 |
| 13. | '' | '' | W. & E. A. Badenach, Fire Insurance .. | 47 | 15 30 |
| 14. | '' | '' | Express Charges and postage stamps .... | 48 | 35 00 |
| 19. | '' | '' | Grand Master, account of expenses...... | 49 | 50 00 |
|  | '' | '' | Dauncy Lodge, No. 176, Charter fee refunded ........................... | 50 | 30 00 |
| 22. | '' | '' | Grand Secretary, account salary ....... | 51 | 500 00 |
| 29. | '' | '' | Sovereign Grand Lodge, supplies ....... | 52 | 4 50 |

| 1892. | | | | Order. | | |
|---|---|---|---|---|---|---|
| Dec. 31. | By | Paid | Postage Stamps . ..... ...............     | 53 | $ 36 | 85 |
| 1893, | " | " | Incidentals, Express, telegrams, pens, &c | 54 | 20 | 55 |
| Jan. 3. | " | " | Bell Telephone Co., rent of phone 6 months ............................ | 55 | 22 | 50 |
| | " | " | A. Harris, quarter's rent of offices.. ..... | 56 | 77 | 00 |
| 14. | " | " | J. Might, City Directory ............. .. | 57 | 5 | 00 |
| 19. | " | " | Sovereign Grand Lodge, supplies ..... .. | 58 | 299 | 00 |
| | " | " | Grand Secretary, account salary........ | 59 | 125 | 00 |
| Feb. 2. | " | " | Express charges and duty on returned Jewels........ ...................... | 60 | 16 | 45 |
| 6. | " | " | Express charges and duty on supplies ... | 61 | 4 | 50 |
| 8. | " | " | Brown Brothers, supplies as per contract | 62 | 212 | 90 |
| 13 | " | " | Sovereign Grand Lodge, supplies ....... .. | 63 | 36 | 00 |
| 18. | " | " | Dominion Express Co., charges and duty | 64 | 2 | 50 |
| 28. | " | " | Grand Trunk Ry., freight and duty on Journals ............................. | 65 | 13 | 55 |
| Mar. 2. | " | " | *Dominion Odd Fellow*, Journal of Proceedings 1892.......................... | 66 | 719 | 10 |
| 6. | " | " | *Dominion Odd Fellow*, Circulars and Printing .............................. | 67 | 13 | 50 |
| 10. | " | " | Mrs. Patterson, caretaker, 3 months .... | 68 | 12 | 00 |
| 18. | " | " | Jno. Pringle, ton of coal .............. .... | 69 | 6 | 50 |
| 20. | " | " | Dominion Express Co., charges.......... | 70 | 19 | 15 |
| | " | " | Grand Secretary......................... | 71 | 250 | 00 |
| 21. | " | " | Jos. Oliver, D.G.M., expense to Tottenham | 72 | 5 | 00 |
| 31. | " | " | Wellington Square Lodge, No. 178, return of funds held in trust ................ | 73 | 2,154 | 64 |
| | " | " | Rebekah Convention, Cap. tax........... | 74 | 112 | 50 |
| April 3. | " | " | A. Harris, quarter's rent of Offices .. ..... | 75 | 77 | 00 |
| 5. | " | " | W. H. McGillivray, envelopes ...... .... | 76 | 15 | 35 |
| | " | " | Joseph Oliver, D.G.M., expenses to Orillia | 77 | 6 | 50 |
| | " | " | *Dominion Odd Fellow*, supplies.......... | 78 | 31 | 50 |
| 6. | " | " | Special Committee on 50th Anniversary. | 79 | 10 | 15 |
| 12. | " | " | Special Committee to Niagara Falls ..... | 80 | 16 | 30 |
| 15. | " | " | Grand Secretary, account salary......... | 81 | 125 | 00 |
| | " | " | Sovereign Grand Lodge, supplies ........ | 82 | 160 | 00 |
| | " | " | Dominion Express Co., charges and duty. | 83 | 7 | 80 |
| 29. | " | " | Postage Stamps .......................... | 84 | 64 | 97 |
| | " | " | Grand Master, on account of expenses.... | 85 | 50 | 00 |
| May 4. | " | " | Mrs. Patterson, caretaker, 2 months..... | 86 | 8 | 00 |
| 18. | " | " | Grand Secretary, account of salary ...... | 87 | 125 | 00 |
| | " | " | J. Pape, Florist, wreath for the late Bro. G. P. Dickson ........................ | 88 | 6 | 00 |
| 26. | " | " | Canadian Express Co., charges and duty. | 89 | 4 | 00 |
| | " | " | Sovereign Grand Lodge, supplies ........ | 90 | 36 | 00 |
| 29. | " | " | Mail Printing Co., circulars .. ........... | 91 | 4 | 50 |
| 30. | " | " | Brown Brothers, supplies as per contract . | 92 | 222 | 70 |
| | " | " | Incidentals, express charges and duty on supplies................................ | 93 | 29 | 49 |
| June 5. | | " | *Dominion Odd Fellow*, Printing and Stationery............................... | 94 | 50 | 75 |
| 12. | " | " | Fullerton & Co , law costs .............. | 95 | 2 | 00 |
| | " | " | Sovereign Grand Lodge, supplies ........ | 96 | 165 | 00 |
| | " | " | Ontario Government, renewal of Registration................................. | 97 | 25 | 00 |

|  |  |  |  |  | Order. |  |
|---|---|---|---|---|---|---|
| June. 15. | By Paid | Grand Secretary, account salary | | | 98 | $125 00 |
| 22. " | " | Express charges and duty | | | 99 | 2 80 |
| 30. " | " | Mrs. Patterson, 2 months' services | | | 100 | 8 00 |
| " | " | Incidentals, postage stamps, sent in as cash | | | 101 | 41 73 |
| July 3. " | " | A. Harris, quarter's rent | | | 102 | 77 00 |
| 7. " | " | Bell Telephone Company, rent of phone | | | 103 | 22 50 |
| " | " | Brown Brothers, stationery | | | 104 | $ 8 55 |
| " | " | *Dominion Odd Fellow*, circulars, &c | | | 105 | 15 25 |
| 11. " | " | Grand Master, account of expenses | | | 106 | 30 00 |
| 17. " | " | A. H. Blackeby, expenses visiting Seaforth and Clinton | | | 107 | 9 80 |
| 20. " | " | Incidentals, express charges, etc, | | | 108 | 7 60 |
| " | " | Office help | | | 109 | 100 00 |
| " | " | John Donogh, P.G.M., for Special Committee on Reduction of Representation | | | 110 | 29 65 |
| " | " | Brown Bros., supplies, 200 Receipt Books | | | 111 | 164 80 |
| " | " | Postage Stamps received as cash | | | 112 | 15 30 |
| " | " | Rebekah Convention, Cap. tax | | | 113 | 128 20 |

14,947 29

By cash on hand :—

| | | |
|---|---|---|
| Funds of defunct Lodges | 258 | 30 |
| Special Relief | 105 | 90 |
| Grand Lodge available funds | 10,132 | 31 |

10,496 51

$25,443 80

We, the undersigned, have examined the books and vouchers of the Grand Treasurer, and find them correct—the balance in the hands of the Grand Treasurer being ten thousand four hundred and ninty-six dollars and fifty-one cents ($10,496.51).

CHAS. PACKERT, | *Auditors.*
A. C. STEWART, |

TORONTO, July 31st, 1893.

The chair announced the following Standing and Special Committees :—

ON DISTRIBUTION OF SUBJECTS IN THE SEVERAL REPORTS—

Bro. W. H. Cole, P.G.M.; Reps. Samuel Towner, Avon Lodge, No. 41 ; S. H. Glassford, Peaceful Dove Lodge, No. 135.

ON LAWS OF SUBORDINATES (*appointed in the interim*)—

Bros. W. A. Rawlings, Donald Robertson, Union Lodge No. 16, St. Catharines; J. A. Morton, Maitland Lodge No. 119, Wingham.

ON FINANCE—

Reps. A. H. Blackeby, Waterloo Lodge, No. 107; J. B. Ferris, Campbellford Lodge, No 248; N. S. Given, Ahiram Lodge, No. 205; W. A. Dennis, Waterloo Lodge, No. 107; J. B. Reid, Wilton Lodge, No. 242; Weir Acheson, Silver Star Lodge, No. 202; A. T. Smith, Mayflower Lodge, No. 297.

ON PETITIONS AND CORRESPONDENCE—

Reps. R. W. Bell, P.G.M., Otonabee Lodge, No. 13; F. Gallagher, Manotick Lodge, No. 295; G. W. Maxwell, Kingston Lodge, No. 59; Geo. Geddes, Otter Lodge, No. 50; J. K. Pearce, Rockliffe Lodge, No. 278.

ON STATE OF THE ORDER—

Reps. Jno. Donogh, P.G.M., Queen City of Ontario, No. 56; Jno. Ormiston, Gananoque Lodge, No. 114; A. W. Cameron, Carleton Lodge, No. 240; F. A. Latshaw, Valley City Lodge, No. 117; J. J. Craig, Fergus Lodge, No. 73; Rev. F. W. Armstrong, Trenton Lodge, No. 113; A. McFarlane, Tecumseh Lodge, No. 182; P. McCandlish, Unity Lodge, No. 47.

ON LEGISLATION—

Reps. Thos. Woodyatt, Gore Lodge, No 34; A. M. Lafferty, Western City Lodge, No. 93; Allen McFee, Belleville Lodge, No. 81; J. McLurg, Woodstock Lodge, No. 269; J. E. Terhune, Listowell Lodge, No. 160; W. A. Sinclair, Oxford Lodge, No. 77; D. Robertson, Minerva Lodge, No. 197.

ON MILEAGE AND PER DIEM—

Reps. M. L. Weber, Elmira Lodge, No. 216; J. W. Grote, Union Lodge, No. 16; E. F. Waterhouse, Oxford Lodge, No. 77; George Brill, Progress Lodge, No. 158; Joseph Carmichael, Hillsburgh Lodge, No. 167; William Laidlaw, Grey Lodge, No. 169; A. Jacobi, Corinthian Lodge, No. 61.

ON JUDICIARY—

Reps. James Woodyatt, P.G.M., Gore Lodge, No. 34; J. T. Hernibrook, P.G.M., Covenant Lodge, No. 52; D. H. Moore,

Peterboro' Lodge, No. 111 ; Wm. Menzies, Canada Lodge, No. 49 ; Wm. Reid, Chorazin Lodge, No. 190 ; R. Brockbank, Grand River Lodge, No. 91 ; J. S. R. McCann, Cataraqui Lodge, No. 10 ; J. B. McIntyre, P.G.M., Union Lodge, No. 16.

ON APPEALS—

Reps. Wm. Macdiarmid, P.G.M., Lucan Lodge, No. 70 ; Alf. Coyell, Canada Lodge, No. 49 ; O. L. Berdan, Howard Lodge, No. 58 ; J. E. Farewell, Eastern Star Lodge, No. 72 ; J. H. Magill, Durham Lodge, No. 78 ; J. J. Manning, Golden Star Lodge, No. 101 ; Henry White, Durham Lodge, No. 78.

ON GENERAL PURPOSES (*appointed in the interim*)—

Bors. W. F. Mountain, Canada Lodge, No. 49 ; Wm. Badenach, Grand Treasurer ; J. B. King, Grand Secretary.

ON DISTRICTS—

Reps. W. T. Henry, Penetangore Lodge, No. 172 ; W. J. Cruickshank, Weston Lodge, No. 200 ; T. G. Gillespie, Campbell-ford Lodge No. 248 ; J. H. Bustin, Nipissing Lodge, No. 79 ; E. M. Clapp, The Toronto Lodge, No. 71.

ON ELECTION RETURNS—

Reps. John Donogh, P.G.M., Queen City of Ontario Lodge, No. 56 ; H. M. Bauslaugh, Olive Branch Lodge, No 88 ; J. R. Peckham, Niagara Falls Lodge, No. 53.

ON DEGREE OF REBEKAH—

Reps. A. A. Graham, Queen City of Ontario Lodge, No. 56 ; J. H. Waddell, St. Thomas Lodge, No. 76, Robt. Peirce, Harmony Lodge, No. 115 ; A. M. Boch, Elora Lodge, No. 231 ; George Lee, Kingston Lodge, No. 59 ; Harry Gilby, Covenant Lodge, No. 52.

ON FRATERNAL RELATIONS (*appointed in the interim*)—

Bro. Henry Robertson, P.G.M., Grand Representative.

SPECIAL COMMITTEE NO. 1—

Reps. S. M. Thomson, Harmony Lodge, No. 115 ; B. F. Doxee, Hastings Lodge, No. 273 ; G. A. Ross, Owen Sound Lodge, No. 180 ; R. J. C. Dawson, Forest City Lodge, No. 38 ; A. W. Bell, Samaritan Lodge, No. 35.

SPECIAL COMMITTEE NO. 2—

Reps. Thos. Hayne, Lambton Lodge, No. 277; George Suggitt, Germania Lodge, No. 184; I. Unsworth, Florence Lodge, No. 196; George Thompson, Millbank Lodge, No. 209; F. A. Smith, Woodslee Lodge, No. 220.

SPECIAL COMMITTEE NO. 3—

Reps. A. B. Hurrell, International Lodge, No. 228; J. H. Powell, Dauncey Lodge, No. 176; V. H. Peart, Wellington Square Lodge, No. 78; A. Allen, jr., Rideau Lodge, No. 241; George Post, Broadview Lodge, No. 294.

SPECIAL COMMITTEE NO. 4—

Reps. J. H. Parnell, Ottawa Lodge, No. 224; E. W. Ross, North Bay Lodge, No. 261; A. B. McRae, Sheard Lodge, No. 276; S. A. Smith, Glanworth Lodge, No. 289; Wm. Yule, Missanabie Lodge, No. 266; C. J. Wall, Dominion Lodge, No. 48.

SPECIAL COMMITTEE NO. 5—

Reps. George W. Griffith, Grenville Lodge, No. 279; A. Ross, Lucknow Lodge, No. 112; W. H. Pollock, Dresden Lodge, No. 124; F. M. Clark, Mizpah Lodge, No. 127; John Corley, Garnet Lodge, No. 139.

SPECIAL COMMITTEE NO. 6—

Reps. W. H. Allen, Stella Lodge, No. 125; M. G. Brethour, Concord Lodge, No. 142; Ellerton Porter, Ridgetown Lodge, No. 144; G. H. Nairn, Huron Lodge, No. 62; J. W. Sheppard, North Star Lodge, No. 68.

SPECIAL COMMITTEE NO. 7—

Reps. Alex. Brownlee, Barrie Lodge, No. 63; W. Robson, Eastern Lodge, No. 72; Wm. Jacobs, Amity Lodge, No. 80; John Flannagan, Grand River Lodge, No. 91.

SPECIAL COMMITTEE NO. 8—

Reps. G. Gillespie, Manilla Lodge, No. 105; Isaac Hord, Bissell Lodge, No. 51; C. L. Williams, Waterloo Lodge, No. 107; Geo. Toner, Gananoque Lodge, No. 114.

**REPORT No. 1.**—Rep. Jno. Donogh, P.G.M., from the Special Committee on "Reduction of Representation in the Grand Lodge," presented the following report. On the motion of Rep. J. Donogh, P.G.M., seconded by Rep. J. B. McIntyre, P.G.M., the consideration of the report was made a special order, the first business after roll call on Friday morning, 11th inst.

*To the Grand Lodge of Ontario, I.O.O.F.:*

Your Special Committee on " The Reduction of Representation in the Grand Lodge," acting under the instructions contained in the resolutions found on page 5341 Journal Grand Lodge of Ontario, 1892, as follows :

Moved by Rep. J. Donogh, and seconded by Rep. J. Welsh ;

*Resolved.*—That whereas, it is expedient to reduce the number of representatives to this Grand Lodge ; and, whereas

It is advisable to adopt some system of representation by districts as a substitute for the present plan of representation by Lodges ; and whereas

It is not desirable that such radical changes should be effected without receiving full consideration from the entire membership.

*Resolved.*—That a special committee of five be appointed to serve during recess with instructions to consider and prepare a plan for the reduction of representation in this Grand Lodge.

*Resolved.*—That the proposed amendments to the Constitution of this Grand Lodge found on page 5,159, Journal 1891, and entitled " Membership," be referred to the Special Committee on reduction of representation.

That the Special Committee be instructed to have their report prepared and published within four months of the annual session, so as to be considered by the various District Committees as well as the Subordinate Lodges, before its presentation at the next session of the Grand Lodge.

Have given full consideration to the matter and beg leave to present the following report :

In order to ascertain the procedure in other jurisdictions, your committee issued a circular to Grand Secretaries, asking for answers to a series of questions relating to the management of Grand Lodges, and the information obtained, which is tabulated in a schedule attached to this report, will no doubt, be considered of great value, apart from its connection with the question under consideration.

From this schedule it will be seen that a large number of the Jurisdictions give to all Past Grands the full privileges of attending Grand Lodge and voting on all questions. But in such cases the expenses are borne either by the attending members or by the Lodges. It is needless to point out the grave objections that lie against this system, if such a name may be properly applied. The expenses of representation fall most heavily upon the weaker or more distant Lodges, while the Legislation is controlled by the Past Grands, who attend the sessions and a preponderating influence will always be exercised by the district or town in which the Grand Lodge is held.

Some eighteen jurisdictions are reported as having a representative system more or less similar to our own, the expenses being in some instances borne by the Grand Lodge and in others by the subordinate Lodges.

Only three jurisdictions, viz: Ohio, Missouri and Iowa are governed on the District Representation plan but these are three of the strongest and most prosperous on the roll of the Soverign Grand Lodge, and it will be noticed that in these jurisdictions the ratio of expense to membership is very slight indeed.

In our own Grand Lodge the membership has been increasing steadily until the attendance is approaching 350, and when to this is added the members attending the Rebekah Convention the number becomes a serious tax upon the hospitality and the resources of the places to which the Grand Lodge is from year to year invited.

In fact, it is certain now, that the Grand Lodge meetings must be confined to the large cities, so long as the membership remains at its present figure.  Is it not a question worthy of consideration as to whether the order would not be more largely benefitted if the Grand Lodge were reduced to such proportions as to admit of its entertainment in towns and large villages which at present are entirely debarred from tendering invitations.

Would not the business of the Grand Lodge be as efficiently transacted by say 125 representatives as it is at present by 350 and is not the large reduction in taxation which would be possible under the district plan, worthy of consideration by the Subordinate Lodges upon whom the burden falls?  And further would not the District Committees gain in influence and importance when active service in the District becomes an essential qualification for election to the position of representative to Grand Lodge.

Your Committee submit a scheme for representation on the District plan and also a schedule which exhibits the probable appoitionment of representation on the District Plan and the expense for mileage and per diem of a Grand Lodge elected on this basis.  A glance at the figures will show that an annual saving of $2,500 at least can be made by the adoption of the proposed scheme, and this will allow of a reduction of two-fifths in the Per Capita Tax.

The following amendments to the Constitution and By-laws of the Grand Lodge are offered for the purpose of carrying out the proposed scheme and notice is hereby given in accordance with Section 27 Constitution.

## AMENDMENT TO CONSTITUTION.

### Strike out Sec. 5 and substitute therefor—

5. Representation in the Grand Lodge shall be by districts and two hunhred shall be the unit of representation.  The number of representatives to which each District is entitled shall be ascertained by dividing the total membership of the Lodges comprised in the District by two hundred, any remainder being considered as equal to another full number.

The semi-annual returns for the 31st of December next preceding the election shall be the basis of representation.  The election of representatives to the Grand Lodge shall be held in the Lodges on the last regular meeting night in June.  Every candidate must be a Past Grand in good standing in his subordinate Lodge.

### BY-LAWS.

#### NOMINATION AND ELECTION OF REPRESENTATIVES TO GRAND LODGE.

1.  Nominations shall be made at the last regular Lodge meeting in May. Immediately upon nominations being made, the Recording Secretary shall forward by mail a list of the candidates to all other lodges in the District.

2. The election shall be held at the last regular Lodge meeting in June, under the order of business for "election of officers." All members in good standing shall be entitled to vote. When all qualified members who desire to do so shall have voted, the ballot shall be declared closed. The ballots shall be counted in open lodge by the Noble Grand, Vice-Grand and Recording Secretary, the result announced and entered upon the minutes. An abstract of the votes cast shall be drawn up and forwarded without delay to the Deputy Grand Master in the form of certificate herewith appended. [*Form No. 1*]. No ballot shall be counted which contains a larger number of names than the District is entitled to elect.

## Form No. 1.

ELECTION RETURNS—REPRESENTATIVE TO GRAND LODGE.

Hall of .............. Lodge, No. ....

*To .................... Deputy Grand Master:*

*We hereby certify that at an election held on last meeting night in June, 18.., in accordance with the provisions of the Constitution of the Grand Lodge of Ontario, I.O.O.F, the following was the result:*

*District No. ....*

|     | Name | Occupation | P.O. Address | | | | | | |
|-----|------|------------|--------------|---|---|---|---|---|---|
| Bro. .......... | .......... | .......... | .......... P.G., of No. ...., rec'd .... votes. | | | | | | |
| " | " | " | " | " | " | " | " | " | " |
| " | " | " | " | " | " | " | " | " | " |
| " | " | " | " | " | " | " | " | " | " |
| " | " | " | " | " | " | " | " | " | " |

(SEAL)                                           ........ ........, *N.G., V.G.*

                                                 ........ ...... *R. Sec'y.*

Which certificate shall be enclosed in an envelope, marked, " I. O. O. F. Vote of ........ Lodge No...., for Representative of District No...., ...... Ontario," and addressed : " To ......, Deputy Grand Master, ......, Ontario.

3. The Deputy Grand Master shall not later than the fifteenth day of July, call to his assistance two disinterested Past Grands in good standing, residents of the district in which the Deputy Grand Master resides, and shall proceed to open and count by Districts the vote cast for representatives. If any of the returns shall be found to be incomplete informal or irregular, the Deputy Grand Master shall immediately transmit such schemes to the Lodges from which they came and request the correction of the errors.

Should it be necessary to transmit back to the Lodges any incorrect returns, the Board of canvassers (having canvassed all correct returns) shall adjourn for not less than ten days nor more than twelve days, when they shall meet again, complete the canvass and record upon a tally sheet the number of votes received by each candidate. The candidates receiving the highest number of votes in the District shall be declared elected, to the number of representatives allotted to such district.

When a question shall arise as to the choice between two or more candidates who may have received an equal number of votes, the Board of canvassers shall cast lots and the one so chosen shall be declared elected.

4. The Board of canvassers shall prepare and sign a report in duplicate [Form No. 2,] and shall forward one copy of the same immediately to the Grand Master and the other to the Grand Secretary, who shall then forward

to each representative elect a certificate of his election in the form hereto appended [Form No. 3] and a copy of such certificate shall also be sent to each subordinate Lodge.

## Form No. 3.

### REPRESENTATIVE'S CERTIFICATE.

*To the Grand Lodge, I. O. O. F., of Ontario :*

*I hereby certify that P. G————————, of————Lodge, No—, has been elected a Representative to the Grand Lodge of Ontario, from District No——, commencing with the next annual session.*

*(Dated.)*                                                  ————— —————,*Grand Secretary.*

## Form No. 2.

### CERTIFICATE OF ELECTION :

*To the Grand Lodge I. O. O. F., of Ontario :*

————— ————— —————*18* .

*We hereby certify that we have canvassed the Election returns of the various subordinate Lodges submitted to us and find that the following Past Grands have been elected representatives to the Grand Lodge.*

| DISTRICT AND NAME | OCCUPATION. | P. O. ADDRESS | LODGE | NO. OF VOTES REC'D. |
|---|---|---|---|---|
| | | | | |
| | | | | |

5. All resignations of representatives must be directed to the Grand Master and all vacancies occurring in any other way must be at once reported to the Grand Master, who shall fix dates for nomination and election and notify the Grand Secretary to order an election under the forms herein provided.

Should a vacancy occur between the election and the session of the Grand Lodge, the Grand master shall direct the Deputy-Grand Master to summon the Board of Canvassers and certify to the election of the candidate having the highest number of votes next succeeding the lowest number necessary to election.

## Strike out By-Laws 3 and 4.

## Amend By law 54 so as to read :

The Grand Lodge shall be entitled to receive from each Subordinate Lodge the sum of thirty cents per annum for each unsuspended member on its books, as shown by its semi-annual return for December thirty-first. Payment to be made with the December return.

As an alternative scheme your committee submit a proposition to reduce the membership to one representative from each lodge, which will make a difference of over one-fourth in the number while preserving the present status of the lodges as to voting power in the Grand Lodge.

Amend Section 5, constitution of Grand Lodge to read as follows :

Sec. 5.—Every Lodge within the jurisdiction shall, at its last meeting in the month of June, annually elect by ballot from amongst its Past Grands in good standing, a representative or representatives as follows, that is to say : one representative who shall be entitled to receive mileage and per diem and on a call of the yeas and nays shall have power to cast the full vote of his Lodge on the following basis, viz : One vote where the number of members returned in the semi-annual report of the current term shall be 100 or less ; over 100 and under 200, two votes ; 200 or more, three votes. But each Lodge shall have the privilege of electing one or more additional representatives on the same basis as the voting power conferred, who shall be known as " extra representatives " and who if present at Grand Lodge shall have all the privileges of representatives but shall not be entitled to mileage and per diem.

Amend By-Law 54 by striking out the word " fifty " in second line and inserting the word " forty " in lieu thereof.

Fraternally submitted,

JOHN DONOGH, P.G.M.
THOS. WOODYATT, P.G.
JOHN B. McINTYRE, P.G.M.
JOHN WELCH, P.G.
T. C. LAZIER, P.G.

SCHEDULE SHOWING Apportionment of Representation on District plan;
Unit of Representation, 200; Districts as arranged on pages 5436-41,
Journal 1892.   Mileage per diem on the basis of Stratford Session.

| District No. | Membership, Jan. 1, '93 | No. of Representatives. | Central Point for Mileage. | Mileage per diem. | District No. | Membership, Jan. 1, '93. | No. of Representatives. | Central Point for Mileage. | Mileage per diem. |
|---|---|---|---|---|---|---|---|---|---|
| 1 | 744 | 4 | Windsor......... | $52 60 | 26 | 513 | 3 | Collingwood.... | $25 40 |
| 2 | 621 | 4 | Dresden......... | 44 80 | 27 | 161 | 1 | Midland........ | 15 10 |
| 3 | 410 | 3 | Bothwell........ | 29 25 | 28 | 54 | 1 | Parry Sound... | 18 90 |
| 4 | 848 | 5 | St. Thomas ..... | 42 00 | 29 | 124 | 1 | Sutton......... | 13 10 |
| 5 | 335 | 2 | Tilsonburg ..... | 16 70 | 30 | 626 | 4 | Port Perry..... | 51 60 |
| 6 | 240 | 2 | Simcoe ......... | 17 50 | 31 | 253 | 2 | Lindsay ....... | 27 60 |
| 7 | 215 | 2 | International B'e | 23 50 | 32 | 204 | 2 | Cobourg........ | 27 80 |
| 8 | 576 | 3 | Niagara Falls... | 33 45 | 33 | 449 | 3 | Havelock ...... | 46 20 |
| 9 | 1041 | 6 | Hamilton........ | 54 00 | 34 | 396 | 2 | Madoc ......... | 32 70 |
| 10 | 599 | 3 | Brantford....... | 24 00 | 35 | 699 | 4 | Picton......... | 68 20 |
| 11 | 657 | 4 | Ingersol ........ | 30 40 | 36 | 868 | 5 | Lansdowne..... | 59 10 |
| 12 | 759 | 4 | Strathroy....... | 34 60 | 37 | 522 | 3 | Smith's Falls... | 63 60 |
| 13 | 331 | 2 | Forest.......... | 17 70 | 38 | 235 | 2 | Cornwall ...... | 47 40 |
| 14 | 535 | 3 | Sarnia.......... | 30 45 | 39 | 505 | 3 | Ottawa ........ | 70 50 |
| 15 | 284 | 2 | Goderich ....... | 16 50 | 40 | 347 | 2 | Almonte ....... | 44 70 |
| 16 | 632 | 4 | St. Marys ...... | 26 40 | 41 | 290 | 2 | Pembroke...... | 50 80 |
| 17 | 812 | 5 | Fergus.......... | 43 75 | 42 | 108 | 1 | Huntsville ..... | 17 65 |
| 18 | 245 | 2 | Streetsville...... | 17 40 | 43 | | | | |
| 19 | 1156 | 6 | Toronto......... | 62 40 | 44 | 269 | 2 | Sault Ste. Marie | 69 30 |
| 20 | 139 | 1 | Newmarket..... | 12 10 | 45 | | | | |
| 21 | 160 | 1 | Orangeville ..... | 10 75 | 46 | | | | |
| 22 | 344 | 2 | Palmerston ..... | 15 80 | 47 | 130 | 1 | Port Arthur ... | 53 30 |
| 23 | 148 | 1 | Brussels........ | 8 40 | 48 | 127 | 1 | Rat Portage.... | 67 90 |
| 24 | 308 | 2 | Kincardine...... | 20 70 | — | | | | |
| 25 | 276 | 2 | Port Elgin ...... | 21 30 | | 19287 | 120 | | 1577 30 |

Mileage per diem paid at Stratford to 315 Representatives......$3,844 80

Questions submitted to the Grand Secretary of each State
and Provincial Grand Lodge.

1. Are your Grand Lodge Sessions Annual or Semi-Annual ?
2. What number of working Lodges, December 31st, 1892 ?
3. Number of Members, December 31st, 1892 ?
4. Is your Grand Lodge composed of (i) Representatives of Lodges, (ii) Representatives of Districts, or (iii) Past Grands at large ?
5. Have Grand Officers and Past Grands the right to vote in Grand Lodge on matters of legislation ?
6. How many Representatives present at last session ?
7. How many days does session last ?
8. What is the rate of Mileage paid to Representatives of Grand Lodge ?
9. What is the rate Per Diem ?
10. What is the annual Per Capita Tax, and how collected ?
11. Are the expenses of District Deputy Grand Masters paid ?
12. If paid, by whom—Grand Lodge or District ?
13. Total amount of Mileage and Per Diem paid at last session ?

SCHEDULE OF REPLIES sent to the questions submitted to Grand Secretaries.

| | 1 | 2 | 3 | 4 | 5 | 6 |
|---|---|---|---|---|---|---|
| Alabama | Annual | 64 | 3000 | Representatives | Yes { Except on call of votes by Lodges. } | 77 |
| Arizona | " | 13 | 600 | Past Grands | Yes | 18 |
| Arkansas | " | 120 | 3860 | Each Lodge 1 Rep. | No | 82 |
| British Columbia | " | 22 | 1954 | Representatives | { Only Grand Officers Representatives & P. G. M's. } | 30 |
| California | " | 355 | 30350 | Representatives | Grand Officers | 590 |
| Colorado | " | 103 | 7004 | Representatives | Yes { Exc'pt a vote of Lodges is called. } | 104 |
| Connecticut | " | 76 | 14036 | Past Grands | Yes | 350 |
| Delaware | " | 35 | 2966 | Past Grands | Yes | 200 |
| 1890—District of Columbia. | Semi-Annual | 15 | 1871 | Representatives | | 49 |
| Florida | | | | | | |
| Georgia | | | | | | |
| Idaho | Annual | 41 | 1565 | Representatives | Officers vote | 75 |
| Illinois * | " | 760 | 42725 | Representatives | | { 722. 12 offic'rs 32 Com. } |
| Indiana | " | 581 | 33000 | Each Lodge 1 Rep. | | |
| Iowa | " | 548 | 31321 | District | No | 92 |
| Kansas | " | 381 | 20619 | Representatives | Yes | 370 |
| Kentucky | " | 165 | 8000 | Represn's 1 for 25. | No | 300 |
| Louisiana | " | 28 | 1022 | Rep's and P. G's. | No | 26 |
| Lower Provinces, B. N. A. | " | 52 | 3850 | Representatives | Yes | 112 |
| Maine | " | 128 | 20139 | Past Grands | Yes | 300 |
| Manitoba | " | 26 | 1858 | Representatives | Yes, with exceptions | 23 |
| Maryland | " | 106 | 9227 | Past Grands | Yes | 350 |
| Massachusetts | Semi-Annual | 220 | 45275 | Past Grands | Yes | 400 |
| Michigan | Annual | 416 | 25000 | Representatives | No | 430 |
| Minnesota | " | 196 | 13187 | Past Grands | Yes | 300 |
| Mississippi | " | 35 | 1456 | Representatives | Yes | 30 |
| Missouri | " | 460 | 23000 | District | No | 75 |
| Montana | " | 44 | 2463 | Representatives | No | 40 |
| Nebraska | " | 183 | 8500 | Past Grands | Yes | { 173 Rep. 265 P.Gs. } |
| Nevada | " | 24 | 1554 | Representatives | Officers vote | 115 |
| New Hampshire | " | 84 | 12000 | Past Grands | Yes | 200 |
| New Jersey | " | 234 | 23000 | Rep's and P. G's | Yes | 165 |

* Facts taken from Journal, as the report was not received.   April 4th, '93.

The numbers in head line correspond to the questions as numbered.

| 7 | 8 | 9 | 10 | 11 | 12 | 13 |
|---|---|---|---|---|---|---|
| 3 | 6 cts. one way... | $4 00 | $1 00 | No............ | ........... | $1978 36 |
| 3 | 10 cts............. | ........ . | 2 00 | ... | .... | 450 00 |
| 3 | 6 cts............. | 2 00 | 1 00 | No.. | .... | 1632 92 |
| 3 | 10 cts............ | 2 00 | 0 80 | No... | .... | 526 00 |
| 4 to 5 | { Actual Travelling Expenses. } .. | ........... | 35c. to 50c. | No.. | ........... | 4294 00 |
| 2 to 3 | 5 cts. one way... | 3 00 | 7 per cent. | No. | ........... | 3647 35 |
| 1 | ............... | .......... | 0 12 | Yes. | By G. L.... | |
| 1 | ............... | .......... | 5 per cent. | Yes.... | By G. L.... | |
| 2 | None | None.... | 45c. on all not in arrears. | No. | No..... | |
| ..... | ............... | .......... | ............... | ... | ........... | ............... |
| ..... | ............... | .......... | ............... | | | ............... |
| 3 | Actual cost ..... | 2 50 | $2 00 | No... | ........... | 1699 77 |
| 3 | 6 cents ......... | 3 00 | ................ | | ........... | { 5785 08<br>{ 6897 00 |
| ..... | 5 cts. one way... | 2 00 | ................ | | ........... | 4600 00 |
| 3 | 6 cents ......... | 3 00 | 5 per cent. | No.......... | ........... | 3164 86 |
| 2 | 7 cts. one way... | 2 00 | $0 60 | No.......... | ........... | 7551 78 |
| 3 | Actual expenses. | ......... | 7 per cent. | No.......... | ........... | Pd by L'dges |
| 3 | do. | 3 00 | $1 25 | No.......... | ........... | 376 90 |
| 2 | { 3c. to Officers and one Rep-resentative. } | 2 00 | 0 17 | { pd. for att'g Gd. Lodges. } | ........... | 652 89 |
| 1 | ............... | .......... | { 25c. each candi'te<br>5c. each degree.<br>10c. each member } | Yes........... | By G. L... | ............. |
| 2 | Actual cost...... | 2 00 | $0 60 | No.......... | ........... | 2111 50 |
| week | Actual mileage... | .......... | 0 40 | No... ........ | ........... | 239 50 |
| 1 | ............... | .......... | 0 40 | Yes.......... | By G. L.... | ...... |
| 3 | 3 cts. each way.. | 2 00 | 0 50 | No.......... | ........... | 7315 45 |
| 2 | 8 cts. to one Rep. | 2 00 | 0 50 | No....... | ........... | 4385 00 |
| 2 | 6 cts. one way... | 2 00 | 20 per cent. | Yes.......... | By G. L.... | 532 90 |
| 2 | 6 cts. one way... | 3 00 | 5 per cent | Yes.......... | By Lodges | 1412 00 |
| 2 | Actual.......... | 4 00 | $1 50 | No....... | ........... | 1315 40 |
| 3 | 5 cents......... | 2 00 | 10 per cent. | No.......... | ........... | 2581 95 |
| 3 | Actual cost ..... | Expenses. | $1 25 | No....... | ........... | 506 00 |
| 1 | Officers & Com.. | Act. exp's | 0 15 | Yes.......... | By Lodges | 200 00 |
| 2 | 6 cents ......... | .......... | 0 20 | No... ........ | ...... | 594 85 |

Schedule of Replies sent to the questions submitted to Grand Secretaries.

| | 1 | 2 | 3 | 4 | 5 | 6 |
|---|---|---|---|---|---|---|
| New Mexico | Bi-ennial | 16 | 762 | Rep's and P. G's. | All Members are legislative members. | 14 |
| New York | Annual | 656 | 62000 | Representatives | Officer vote | 600 |
| North Carolina | " | 100 | 4100 | Past Grands | Yes | 74 |
| North Dakota | " | 44 | 2116 | 1 Rep. ea. Lodge | Grand Officers | 46 |
| Ohio | " | 704 | 60710 | Districts, 78 | No | 76 |
| Ontario | " | 244 | 19449 | Representatives | No. | 330 |
| Oregon | " | 114 | 5685 | Rep. Lodges | No | 148 |
| Pennsylvania | Semi-Annual | 1042 | 101258 | Rep. Lodges | No | 837 |
| Quebec | Annual | 19 | 1382 | Rep. Lodges | No | 42 |
| Rhode Island | " | 50 | 6373 | Past Grands | Yes | 398 |
| South Carolina | " | 21 | 704 | Past Grands | Yes | 100 |
| South Dakota | " | 83 | 3500 | 1 Rep. each Lodge | Officers & P.G.M's. | 75 |
| Tennessee | " | 140 | 4500 | Representatives | No | 116 |
| Texas | | | | | | |
| Utah | Annual | 17 | 1466 | Rep. of Lodges | Yes | 89 |
| Vermont | | | | | | |
| Virginia | Annual | 88 | 5239 | Rep. of Lodges | No | 80 |
| Washington | " | 129 | 7300 | Rep. of Lodges | Grand Officers and Representatives. | 168 |
| West Virginia | " | 118 | 7580 | Rep. of Lodges | No | 104 |
| Wisconsin | " | 314 | 16761 | Rep. and P. G's. | Yes | 259 |
| Wyoming | " | 17 | 879 | Rep. of Lodges, P. G's. at large— All P.Gs. can vote | Yes | 21 |

The numbers in head line correspond to the questions as numbered.—*Continued.*

| 7 | 8 | 9 | 10 | 11 | 12 | 13 |
|---|---|---|---|---|---|---|
| 3 to 4 | Actual expenses.. | $2 00 | $1 50 | { Abolished as nuisance. } | .......... | $ 650 00 |
| 3 | .............. | ........ | 0 1 | No.... ........ | ........ | ............ |
| 3 | Actual expenses to one Rep.. | | 1 00 | No........ ....... | ........ | 1482 00 |
| 3 | 7 cents ........ | 2 00 | 10 per cent. | No .... ...... | By G. L... | 786 01 |
| 4 | 8 cts. one way... | 4 00 | 5 per cent. | Yes............. | ......... | 2655 12 |
| 3 | 5c. one way...... | 2 00 | $0 50 | Yes.......... | By District | 6121 30 |
| 3 | { Actual expenses one Representative. } | 2 50 | 1 00 | Yes.......... | { By each Lodge. } | 2561 25 |
| 3 | 6 cents ......... | ......... | 0 32 | Yes.......... | By G. L... | 11083 91 |
| 1 | Actual fare...... | 2 00 | 0 60 | Yes.......... | By G. L... | 427 76 |
| 1 | ............. | ......... | 0 40 | Yes.......... | By G. L... | ........... |
| 2 | Officer's paid.... | 3 00 | 10 per cent, | No....... .... | ........ | 40 15 |
| 3 | 10 cents ........ | 2 00 | 10 per cent. | No..... ....... | ........ | 1122 80 |
| 2 | 6 cents ......... | 2 50 | $1 00 | No........... | ........ | 264 546 |
| 2 | 5 cts. one way... | 2 00 | 1 30 | No..... ...... | ........ | 460 20 |
| 3 | Actual expenses.. | .... .... | 0 50 | No....... .... | ........ | 747 28 |
| 3 | " " .. | 2 00 | 1 00 | Yes.......... | ........ | 4144 75 |
| 3 | Actual expenses.. | ......... | 0 40 | No... ......... | ........ | 1723 10 |
| 3 | 6 cts. one way... | ......... | 0 50 | Yes.......... | { By Lodge visited. } | 2548 98 |
| 2 | Actual expenses.. | 3 00 | 10 per cent. | No....... .... | { By L'dgs visited, from $2 to $5. } | 652 35 |

Bro. S. K. Binkley, on behalf of the Order at Niagara Falls, verbally invited the Grand Lodge to a trip on the Electric Railway at 2:30 this afternoon, the trip to extend over the entire line, Queenston to Chippewa and return, which, on the motion of Rep. J. T. Hornibrook, P.G.M., seconded by Rep. W. H. Cole, P.G.M., was accepted.

The following was adopted :—

*Resolved,*—That, when the Grand Lodge adjourns this morning Session, it does so to meet at nine o'clock to morrow—Thursday morning.

The following, moved by Bro. H. Robertson, P.G.M., Grand Rep., seconded by Bro. W. H. Cole, P.G.M., Grand Rep., was adopted :—

*Resolved,*—That the exemplification of the unwritten work be made a special order for 3 o'clock p.m., August 10th.

**REPORT No. 2.**—Bro. W. H. Cole, P.G.M., from the Committee on Distribution, made the following report, which was adopted :—

*To the Grand Lodge of Ontario, I.O.O.F.:*

Your Committee on Distribution beg to recommend that the subject matter in the Reports of the Grand Officers and Auxiliary Associations be referred to Committees as follows :—

COMMITTEE ON STATE OF THE ORDER—The Grand Master's Report : Page 1 to 16 inclusive (except Clause 7, page 4 ; Clause 16, page 13 ; Clause 22, page 14 ; and that part of pages 2 and 3 referring to Rebekah Degree Lodges) ; Grand Secretary's Report : Clauses 2, 7, 8.

LEGISLATION—Grand Secretary's Report : Clauses 1, 12, 13, 18.

JUDICIARY—Grand Master's Report : Pages 17, 18, 19, to Clause 29.

FINANCE—Grand Master's Report : latter part page 24, Clause 36 Grand Secretary's Report : Clauses 3, 4, and first part 14, and Clause 16, and all of the Grand Treasurer's Report, and the Auditors' Report.

PETITIONS AND CORRESPONDENCE—The Grand Master's Report : Clause 32, page 21, to the end of the Report (except latter part of Clause 36) ; Grand Secretary's Report : Clause 10.

APPEALS—Grand Master's Report : Page 19, Clause 30 ; Grand Secretary's Report : Clause 17.

MILEAGE AND PER DIEM—Grand Secretary's Report : Clause 5.

REBEKAH DEGREE LODGES—That part of Grand Master's Report, page 2 and 3, referring to said Lodges, also Clause 22, page 14 ; Grand Secretary's Report : Clause 19.

ODD FELLOWS' RELIEF ASSOCIATION—Grand Master's Report : Clause 7, page 4 ; Grand Secretary's Report : Clause 9, and all the Report of the Association.

INSURANCE—Grand Secretary's Report : Pages 10, 11, and first half of page 12.

Special Committees :—

No. 1—Grand Master's Report : Page 13, Clause 16.

No. 2—Grand Master's Report : Page 21, Clause 31.

No. 3—Grand Secretary's Report : Clause 6.

No. 4—Grand Secretary's Report : Latter part of Clause 14.

We would recommend a careful perusal of all the valuable tables in the Grand Secretary's Report, to every member of the Order.

Your Committee move the adoption of this report.

Fraternally submitted,

W. H. COLE,
S. H. GLASSFORD.

The following was read, and on motion Bro. Barnes was excused from attendance at the present session.

[Bro. Barnes was enabled to attend the last day's Session, his daughter having sufficiently recovered as to permit him to leave her.—Grand Sec.]

Toronto, August 8th, 1893.

*J. B. King, Esq., Grand Secretary I.O.O.F. :*

Dear Brother King,—After seeing you yesterday my little girl, 7 years old, was taken suddenly and dangerously ill, so I am detained here. Hope to be up sometime to-morrow, if she gets better. If I am not up please have me excused.

I am,

Yours truly and fraternally,

GEO. BARNES.

The Grand Lodge adjourned at 1:30 p.m.

# SECOND DAY.

## MORNING SESSION.

NIAGARA FALLS, August 10th, 1893.

The Grand Lodge assembled at 9 o'clock a m., Rev. T. W. Jolliffe, Grand Master, in the chair, and opened in regular form.

Prayer by the Grand Chaplain.

The following Grand Officers and a majority of the Representatives were present and answered the roll.

### OFFICERS:

| | |
|---|---|
| REV. T. W. JOLLIFFE, | Grand Master. |
| JOSEPH OLIVER, | Deputy Grand Master. |
| W. H. HOYLE, | Grand Warden. |
| J. B. KING, | Grand Secretary. |
| WM. BADENACH, | Grand Treasurer. |
| W. H. COLE, | Grand Representative. |
| HY. ROBERTSON, | Grand Representative. |
| O. E. FLEMING, | Grand Marshal. |
| ROBERT MEEK, | Grand Conductor. |
| A. MITCHELL, | Grand Guardian. |
| I. B. AULPH, | Grand Herald. |
| REV. WM. J. SANDERS, | Grand Chaplain. |
| P. E. FITZ-PATRICK, | Junior Past Grand Master. |

The minutes of yesterday's Session were read and confirmed.

The following, moved by Rep. M. L. Weber, seconded by Rep. G. J. Brill, was adopted :—

*Resolved,*—That the rate of mileage to be allowed for the present Session be five cents per mile one way, and the per diem two dollars, and that the Committee on Mileage and Per Diem be instructed to prepare their report accordingly.

**REPORT No. 3.**—Rep. John Donogh, P.G.M., from the Committee on Election Returns, made the following report, which was adopted :—

*To the Grand Lodge of Ontario :*

Your Committee on Election Returns beg leave to present the following report.

The canvass of the returns shows the following result :—

Total vote cast for Grand Master...... ... BRO. JOSEPH OLIVER...... 520
" " Deputy Grand Master.. " W. H. HOYLE........ 520
" " Grand Secretary....... " J. B. KING........... 523
" " Grand Treasurer....... " W. BADENACH........ 523

For Grand Warden, 1782 votes.   Necessary for choice, 892.

Bro. Thos. Woodyatt.................................. 720
" W. A. Miner................................... 82
" I. A. Young.................................. 215
" Hy. White..................................... 664
" A. B. Hurrell................................. 38
" S. K. Binkley................................ 63

There is therefore no election.

For Grand Representative 1778 votes.   Necessary for choice, 890.

Bro R. W. Bell, P.G.M.............................. 273
" P. E. Fitz-Patrick, P.G.M...................... 981
" W. H. Cole, P.G.M............................. 180
" J. B. McIntyre, P.G.M......................... 344

Bro. P. E. Fitz-Patrick has a majority of all votes cast.

The return from Cicerone Lodge, No. 195, did not contain the certificate of a visiting P.G. who voted in the Lodge, and this vote was not counted. The return from Glanworth Lodge, No. 289, was rejected, the number of votes cast not being filled in. The return from Manotick Lodge, No. 295, was rejected, number of votes not being filled in, no seal attached and no signature of Noble Grand.

No returns were received from the following Lodges :—

Mt. Zion, No. 46 ; Beaver, No. 82 ; Laurel, No. 110 ; Lucknow, No. 112; Naomi, No. 116; Concord, No. 142 ; Aurora, No. 148 ; Hayden, No. 152 ; Thamesville, No. 157 ; Oriental, No. 163 ; Hillsburg, No. 167 ; Montana, No. 177 ; Teeswater, No. 183 ; Egremont, No. 207 ; Mt. Brydges, No. 217 ; Merlin, No. 226; Hanover, No. 233 ; Acorn, No. 236 ; Fraternity, No 264 ; Morewood, No. 285 ; Chesterville, No. 288 ; Rodney, No. 291 ; Pontypool ; No. 296 ; Mayflower, No. 297.

Your Committee offer the following :

*Resolved,*—That the foregoing be adopted.

JOHN DONOGH,
H. M. BAUSLAUGH,
J. McCLURG, M.D.,
J. R. PECKHAM.

The Grand Master thereupon declared the following officers duly elected for the ensuing year :—

Bro. Joseph Oliver...........Toronto............Bro....Grand Master.
" W. H. Hoyle...........Cannington.........Deputy Grand Master.
" J. B. King..............Toronto.............Grand Secretary.
" Wm. Badenach..........Toronto.............Grand Treasurer.
" P. E. Fitz-Patrick.......Hamilton...........Grand Representative.

And, further, that there was no election of Grand Warden.

The Grand Master named the following scrutineers for the election :

Reps. John Donogh, P.G.M.; John Gibson, P.G.M.; H. M. Bauslaugh.

The ballot being taken, the scrutineers announced the following result of the first ballot :—

Whole vote cast, 334.   Necessary to a choice, 168.

Bro. S. K. Binkley.................................... 7
" Hy. White.................................... 139
" Thos Woodyatt.............................. 163
" J. A. Young.................................. 17
" —Bell........................................ 3
" W. A. Miner................................. 4
" A. B. Hurrell................................ 1

There being no Election a second ballot was ordered.

The scrutineers announced the second ballot as follows :—

Whole vote cast, 331.   Necessary to a choice, 166.

Bro. W. A. Miner................................. 2
" S. K. Binkley................................ 7
" Hy. White.................................... 143
" Thos. Woodyatt............................. 179

Whereupon the Grand Master declared Rep. Thos. Woodyatt duly elected Grand Warden for the ensuing year.

Rep. John Donogh, P.G.M., nominated Bro. Chas. Packert, of Avon Lodge, No. 41, as elective Auditor for the coming year. There being no further nominations Bro. Donogh, by request, cast the vote of the Grand Lodge for Bro. Packert.

The Grand Master declared Bro. Charles Packert duly elected Auditor

**REPORT No 4.**—Bro. Henry Robertson, P.G.M., from the Special Committee on Fraternal Relations, presented the following report, which was ordered to be spread upon the Journal:

*To the Grand Lodge of Ontario, I.O.O.F.:*

Your Committee on Fraternal Relations beg leave to present their third annual report.

All the proceedings of other Grand Lodges which have been received, have been carefully examined and perused by your Committee, with a view of extracting therefrom all items which might prove interesting or instructive to the Brethren of Ontario.

The selections have been made with care, so as not to have the report too long or tedious, and at the same time, it is hoped that from this report, our Brethren in Ontario will be enabled to have a somewhat clear idea of what is going on in the world of Oddfellowship around us.

The proceedings will be noticed and reviewed in the usual alphabetical order.

### ALABAMA.

Fifty-second annual session, Mobile, May 10, 1892.

The Order is progressing finely. Eleven new Lodges are reported, with an increase in membership of over seven hundred.

A proposition to have a paid Organizer or Lecturer was negatived.

### ARKANSAS.

Forty-third annual session, Eureka Springs, Oct. 25, 1892.

Every section of this jurisdiction is alive with activity, and the principles of Oddfellowship were never more closely adhered to. Fifteen new Lodges were organized, and two Rebekah Lodges. In the excellent report of Brother J. B. Friedheim, Grand Secretary, we find the following:—

" Effective work has been done in relieving and alleviating some of the ills which afflict the mind and body of man. The ministrations of the ' Relief Committee,' which are constant and inexhaustible, have been welcomed in the homes of nearly four hundred brothers for periods of divers length, aggregating 1,300 weeks, at an outlay of over seven thousand dollars; but this is only a tithe of the good that has been accomplished. Other influences, the value of which has no monetary comparison, has served to comfort and bless the weak and weary traveller as he nears the boundary of that bourne from which none return."

A series of resolutions were adopted in furtherance of the proposed Odd Fellows' Home and National Sanitarium at Hot Springs.

## BRITISH COLUMBIA.

Nineteenth annual session, New Westminster, Feb. 8, 1893.
Brothers W. L. Challoner and D. Barclay, of Ontario, were present as visitors.

On the state of the Order, the Grand Master says :—

" The increase to our membership has exceeded that of any previous year since our institution ; in fact, the increase is more than equal to the entire strength of the Order in this Province up to the year 1883 ; this in itself speaks very highly for the esteem and general popularity of the Order throughout the country.

"The membership in the Auxiliary Benefit Endowment Association has largely increased in numbers, which already shows the advantage of having a canvasser for this branch of the Order, but there is still room for improvement.

" I am pleased to observe that the ' Team Work ' has taken such a strong hold on most of the city Lodges, and when once introduced its vast superiority over the old style of work is so apparent that it requires no argument to convince any Lodge of this fact.

" No very serious questions have arisen during my term of office. My duties have been of a very pleasant character.

"I have visited quite a number of Lodges in the jurisdiction ; peace, harmony and general prosperity appears to dwell on every side. I am pleased to note that most of the Lodge rooms are well equipped with regalia and paraphernalia."

Five new Lodges were formed. One of these new Lodges, " Centennial," No. 20, at Nanaimo, and being the second Lodge in that place, reported a membership of 104 in a little more than six months after organization.

The first veteran jewel applied for in this jurisdiction was supplied to Brother George Norris, of Nanaimo.

The name of their Auxiliary Endowment Benefit Association was changed to the Odd Fellows' Relief Association of British Columbia. It is under the direct management of the Grand Lodge.

## CALIFORNIA.

Forty-first annual session, San Francisco, May 9, 1893.

The Grand Master reports eight new Lodges, and eleven new Rebekah Lodges. Prosperity prevails, and they have had a gratifying increase in membership.

A Board of Trustees was elected to devise ways and means to establish an Odd Fellows' Home. We copy part of the report of the Special Committee on this matter :—

" That we have made a diligent investigation of nearly all the I.O.O.F. Homes now in the United States, and find that in nearly every case the undertaking has met with such success that it has become the pride of the Order in the locality or State where the same has been located.

" We find that in every case the Homes were created by donations, not only from members of our Order, but from humanitarians not Odd Fellows.

Almost in every instance has the land for this purpose been donated, and in one case, that of Kansas, a man, not a member of the Order, donated 3,100 acres of land, with numerous buildings, including a house of sixty rooms, together with six hundred head of cattle, and $125,000 in cash, to establish an orphan's home.    A liberal offer was made in our own State a few years ago for this purpose.    We have no doubt, therefore, that when our Grand Lodge shall order the establishmeut of such a home in this jurisdiction, there will be for this purpose numerous and equally noble offers of donations. Already there are offers of donations before this committee, as well as petitions of several Lodges.

" We find from reports of the several Homes that the average assessment for the maintenance of such institutions does not exceed one cent per week *per capita* for each member of the Order within the jurisdiction.    This is generally payable quarterly with other dues.    The fund is generally known as the 'Odd Fellows' Home Fund.'    Your Committee would advise an Orphans' Home in connection with the Home for Aged and Indigent Odd Fellows, as we find that such have been maintained with success by nearly all the established Homes.

" Since nearly every Lodge in this jurisdiction has a Widow and Orphan's Fund which is seldom used, this could advantageously be converted into the Home Fund, either by loan or donation, in perfect harmony with the decision of the Sovereign Grand Lodge. (See page 12,664, Session of 1891.)

" The Home could be sustained partly by Subordinate Lodges or Encampments, or individual members thereof, or acceptable parties not Odd Fellows, purchasing life memberships, on paying from one to five thousand dollars, as the Grand Lodge may hereafter determine."

COLORADO.

Twenty-fifty annual session, Aspen, Oct. 18, 1892.

They have had a large increase in membership.  Five new Lodges are reported, with two more applications on hand. More interest is taken in the Rebekah Branch than ever before, ten Lodges having been instituted during the year.

The Entertainment Committee made a full report of their exertions on the occasion of the Triennial gathering of Masonic Knights Templars in Denver, in August, 1892.  They joined with the citizens in hospitable attentions to the visitors, and received numerous testimonials of their courtesy and fraternal co-operation.

There is a prospect that the Odd Fellows and Freemasons of Colorado will join together in establishing a Home for indigent Brethren.

A new constitution for Subordinate Lodges was adopted.

CONNECTICUT.

Annual session, Meriden, May 18, 1892.

On the condition of the Order, the Grand Master says :—

"Oddfellowship was never as flourishing in Connecticut as it is to-day. Substantial gains have been made during the year both in numbers and financial condition.    The net gain in membership for the year ending

December 31st, 1891, as you will see by the detailed statement of the Grand Secretary, is more than one thousand, while during the same period the Rebekah gain is over four hundred. It has been a year of unusual sickness, but I rejoice that the Lodges have all been equal to the strain, and that all legal benefits have been promptly paid. It has been a year of peace and harmony as is evidenced by the fact that there are no appeals for the consideration of the Grand Lodge."

They have several Lodges, and Rebekah Lodges working in German, and one Lodge working in Danish.

On the selection of District Deputies, Grand Master George H. Cowell has the following remarks, which are worthy of serious attention :—

" After careful investigation and mature deliberation on the subject I am of the opinion that the efficiency and potent influence of the District Deputies would be materially increased could they be selected from outside the Districts in which they officiate. The change would involve a little extra expense in travel, but in my judgment the greater benefit would amply compensate for that. The Deputy under this plan would be removed from all suspicion of local influence or prejudice. A live Odd Fellow, and no other should ever be appointed a Deputy, is constant and regular in attendance at his own Lodge, and as such is likely to take part in the discussion of topics in such Lodge with no thought that at a later day they may come before him for judicial consideration. Under these circumstances he is often hampered and handicapped by his action in his Subordinate Lodge.

" On the acknowledged principle that " a prophet is not without honor save in his own country," a Deputy from outside the District would be received with greater deference and his opinion and advice would have much greater weight.

" We may not be ready at this session to make so radical a change in our system of appointments, but the matter is worthy of thoughtful discussion and consideration.

" I would further say that the practice still indulged in by a few Lodges of nominating Deputies ought to be discouraged. The District Deputy is peculiarly the personal representative of the Grand Master, and he should be free and untrammelled in his selection.

" The recent action of the Executive Council in striking out from the report blanks sent to Subordinate Lodges the line heretofore printed for nominations to this office met my hearty approval."

Out of seventy-four Lodges, fifty-seven voted in favor of establishing an Odd Fellows' Home, and taxing themselves fifty cents per member each term, towards a fund for that purpose.

Brother John H. Barlow has an excellent report on Correspondence  Ontario receives a good notice. The author is an old friend of ours, for whom we entertain the warmest regards, and we are glad to fraternize with him again.

DELAWARE.

Fifty-ninth annual session, Wilmington, Nov. 16, 1892.

The Grand Master visited all the thirty-five Lodges in the State. Every Lodge except three has increased its membership.

One Lodge added one hundred to its roster. A new Lodge was opened at Stanton. The net gain was one hundred and forty.

### DISTRICT OF COLUMBIA.

Annual session, Washington, July 20, 1892.
On the subject of visitation, the Grand Master says :—

" Never in the history of the Order in this jurisdiction has there been more fraternal interest shown among the various Lodges than during the past term.  On January 4, Metropolis Lodge, No. 16, a Lodge noted for its progressiveness, started on a round of visitations to her sister Lodges.  It was my good pleasure to be present at this series of visitations, and I can testify to the cordial manner in which Metropolis was received, and the good that was thus accomplished in the interests of fraternity.

" In addition to the above social visits, I have, in company with the other officers of the Grand Lodge, paid the usual Semi-annual Visitation to the several Subordinate and Rebekah Degree Lodges.  In view of the very excellant manner in which the officers of the various Lodges are, to my personal knowledge, posted in the written and unwritten work of the Order (due to the thoroughness with which the various Grand Instructors have performed the duties assigned to them), I have, during this series of visitations, departed from the usual mode of procedure by oral examination, turning the visits into purely social, fraternal ones.  That the departure has been profitable, is shown by the increased attendance at the meetings, and also, in their very interesting character.  Many of these meetings have, by permission, been open ones, and have been the occasions of social visits from sister Lodges and outside friends of the Order ; and it is gratifying to report that the fraterna tie between the Subordinate and Rebekah Degree Lodges has thus been bound closer together.  The most interesting of these meetings were those where these two branches of our noble Order intermingled, demonstrating the correctness of the proverb, that, even in a Lodge of Odd Fellows, " it is not well that man should dwell alone."  Canton Potomac, Patriarchs Militant, under command of Captain J. A. Shackelford. has, upon these fraternal visitations, done faithful escort duty to the Grand Officers, the beautiful uniform, military tactics and kind words of the chevaliers adding much to the interest of the meetings."

They have 15 Lodges and 1,852 members.

### GEORGIA.

Fiftieth annual session, Brunswick, Aug. 15, 1892.
On the growth of the Order, the Grand Master says :—

" Soon after I assumed the duties of Grand Master I was confronted with the fact that there was a stringency in financial affairs all over the State, that would seriously interfere with the growth of the Order, and which threatened a decrease in the membership by suspensions.  For several months the effort to stimulate the brotherhood to activity was very laborious ; but, finally, with a fidelity rarely seen and never surpassed, the rank and file of the Order throughout the State rallied to the demands of the hour, and fully demonstrated the fact that the spirit of Oddfellowship in Georgia was active and aggressive.  The record shows that there have been resuscitated and instituted twelve Lodges and two Rebekah Degree Lodges, making a total of fourteen, and a net increase of about eight hundred members.

" A strong sentiment in favor of the Order has been manifested in Green-ville, Fort Gaines, Tallapoosa, Blue Ridge and Cedar Town, and, with a little effort, a good Lodge can be organized in each of these places this Fall."

Their Orphans' Home is to be located at Atlanta, that city having made the best offer, namely : Twenty-five acres of land and $10,000 in cash. The building will cost about $20,000, and the Committee have in sight $16,000.

The Grand Master appointed a State Organizer at a salary of $75 per month, and his work was so successful that the office was continued by the adoption of the following report :—

" We congratulate the Order on the exceptionally good work done dur-ing the last year by Grand Master Daniel and Brother Shea, in reorganizing defunct Lodges and instituting new ones. We congratulate the Order on the renewed spirit of Oddfellowship infused into it by these worthy brothers. We recommend that the office of State Organizer be continued, and that the sum of six hundred dollars ($600.00) be appropriated for this purpose, said sum to be paid out in such amounts and at such times as the Grand Master shall direct.

" We recommend that, to carry into effect a part of the Report of the Orphans' Home Committee, the State Organizer be made the agent of the Committee on Orphans' Home, and that he be instructed to visit all Lodges in the State, as far as practicable, and solicit from Lodges and individual brothers subscriptions to this most laudable of our charities.

We further recommend that the State Organizer make a specialty of visiting the weaker Lodges throughout the State, and endeavor to infuse new life into them and build them up, rather than to the establishment of new Lodges."

### IDAHO.

Tenth annual session, Pocatello, Oct 11, 1892.

The Order has made greater advancement than could be reasonably have been expected, considering the scarcity of money and the general depression in business throughout the State. Two new Lodges are reported, and four new Rebekah Lodges. The Grand Master visited twenty-seven out of the thirty-eight Lodges.

Their Odd Fellows' Home is in course of erection at Idaho Falls. The building is two stories and a basement, fifty feet by forty-six feet, and the contract price is $8,298.

The following resolution was adopted :—

" *Resolved,*—That all Lodges shall obtain from each of its members the names and addresses of two of his nearest relatives and that the Secretary re-cord same in a book provided for that purpose."

The time of meeting was changed from the first to the third Tuesday in October.

The Grand Representatives were instructed to vote for the eighteen-year-old amendment.

ILLINOIS.

Annual session, Springfield, Nov. 15, 1892.

The Grand Master congtatulates the Brotherhood upon the rapid and substantial growth of the Order during the year. Their net increase in membership is 3,867, the largest gain for one year in the history of the Order in the State. There were instituted during the year, thirty-eight Subordinate and twenty-six Rebekah Lodges.

The per capita tax is eighty cents per member.

INDIANA.

Fifty-sixth annual session, Indianapolis, Nov, 16, 1892.

From every part of the State comes the gratifying intelligence of great activity in the Lodges, and good fellowship among the members. The reports show five new Lodges, seven new Rebekah Lodges, and a net gain in membership of 2,206.

IOWA.

Forty-fifth annual session, Council Bluffs, Oct. 19, 1892.

Prosperity continues. They have a gain of twenty-seven Lodges and 2,959 members.

The following resolution was adopted :—

"*Resolved*, That in the future this Grand Lodge hold a three-days' session ; and a special committee of three be appointed by the in-coming Grand Master to prepare a mode of procedure for each day of the session, the report to be presented on the morning of the next session for adoption for the use of that and future sessions."

KANSAS.

Thirty-fifth annual session, Fort Scott, Oct. 11, 1892.

In the opening paragraphs of the report of the Grand Master, we find the following :—

"The duties of the office of Grand Master are in many respects exceedingly trying on his temper, but in most respects they tend to make the reflections of the past most pleasing. In this connection, however, there is one fact common to all who have filled the office for one year, and that is, they never ' hanker after ' the same position again.

" So far as my observation has extended, brotherly love and good-fellowship have prevailed throughout the jurisdiction, except among the members of three or four Lodges, and they, so far as I know, are now wheeled into line and are doing good work.

" The number of new Lodges and the increase in membership, the result of earnest endeavors on the part of nearly every Lodge in the State, have characterized this present Grand Lodge year as one of the most prosperous in the history of the Order. It is impossible, at this date, to make a complete showing of the number of members in good standing, owing to the delay on the part of the District Deputy Grand Masters in sending in their reports

Such a delay is inexplicable, because the Grand Master each year sends to the Lodges proper blanks, and requests the officer to immediately forward to the Grand Master the required report.  This report does not require but a few minutes of the time of the District Deputy Grand Master, and there is no reasonable excuse for so much delay.

"There have been 18 Subordinate and 41 Rebekah Lodges instituted up to this date, and one Rebekah Lodge resuscitated."

Our Brethren in Kansas are most fortunate in having received from Mr. E. V. Boissiere, who is not a member of the Order, a magnificent donation amounting in value to $100,000, for the purpose of establishing an Orphans' Home.  The gift is thus described by the Grand Master :—

" The most pleasing duty of my life is involved in the presentation of the following facts in connection with the welfare of our Order.  Through the wise efforts and untiring zeal of our beloved brother, L. C. Stine, Grand Treasurer, the Order has come in possession of a magnificent estate (as more fully described below), the gift of Mr. E. V. Boissiere, of his entire real and personal property, for the purpose of establishing and maintaining forever a home for the orphans of deceased Odd Fellows of Kansas.

" This munificent bequest is the largest ever given to any institution in this State, and is the most valuable endowment ever received by the Order in this or any other country, and it places the Order in Kansas in the front rank of all the States in the Union, by giving them a foundation for an orphans' home which is double in value to any other institution of this kind in the country.

" The following is a brief summary of the property given to this institution, which has been named by the donor, ' THE BOISSIERE ODD FELLOWS' ORPHANS' HOME AND INDUSTRIAL SCHOOL OF KANSAS,' and deeded to L. C. Stine, Geo. A. Huron, M. B. Ward, Geo. W. Jones, and C. L. Robbins, as trustees, namely : 3,156 acres of land, upon which there are nine stone buildings, one of them being a residence containing 60 rooms, that can be prepared for occupancy by the addition of heating apparatus, furnishings, and some general repairs.  There is an apple orchard containing 20 acres of the choicst varieties of apples ; there are 3 acres of highly-cultivated grapes ; a grove of mulberries containing 75 acres, and several acres of walnut trees. There are 400 acres in corn and other spring crops, 100 acres in tame grass. over 300 head of grade short-horned Durham cattle, 250 head of hogs, and about 40 head of horses.  There are 15 miles of stone-wall fence, which cost $12,500, and 25 miles of post-and-wire fence.  There are several large reservoirs which contain water the year round, when kept in proper repair.  There are blacksmith and carpenter shops equipped with tools, farm machinery of all kinds, including buggies, wagons, carts, etc.  There is a library containing over 2 000 volumes.

" The value of the entire property, at a conservative estimate, is $100,000.

" Mr. Boissiere, in making his deed of this property, made the following stipulations, which he insists shall be carried out to the letter :

" ' *First*.  This property is to be used to furnish a home for the orphans of deceased Odd Fellows of Kansas, and to educate them in such a way as to make them useful and honoured citizens.  He insists that this education shall be comprehensive and practical, covering all the lower branches, and a practical knowledge of chemistry, geometry, surveying, veterinary surgery, etc.  In short, the orphans shall be educated in such a way as to prepare them for domestic, agricultural and other useful spheres of life.

"'*Second.* The deed states in explicit terms that the Odd Fellows of Kansas must clothe and board the orphans in this Home ; that the income from the farm shall be used to beautify the grounds, build other buildings if necessary, keep up the general repairs and appearance of the Home, and pay the teachers and all the expense of education.

"'*Third.* The deed provides that separate accounts be kept between the Home and the farm, so that the farm products used shall be paid for by the Home, and the services done on the farm by way of labour on the part of the orphans, paid for by the farm at reasonable rates.'"

KENTUCKY.

Annual session, Covington, Oct. 11, 1892.

Grand Master Simpson delivered an excellent address, from which we make a few extracts :—

" Man is endowed with a social as well as a moral nature. His sense of duty springs from a knowledge of the relation he sustains to God and to his fellow-man, and if his moral obligation be commensurate with this khowledge, his social capacity must be of great importance. The most exalted attributes of his being are purely social. It is the development and exercise of these that assimilates him to his Maker, and invests him with sovereignty on earth. To the study and improvement of these attributes, philosophy has lent its loftiest energies, and to refine and exalt them, the holy influences of religion are directed. In the cultivation of his social being, is developed the highest principle of his moral constitution—benevolence—and without that principle which leads us to seek the improvement and happiness of others, friendship is hypocrisy and virtue but a name. The institution of Odd Fellowship en-larges the benevolence, improves the social condition, and invites men and sympathy and fraternal love. To the cultivation of these virtues, to the counseling one with the other as to the plans that will best subserve the interests and well-being of our brethren, to so legislate that the grand mission of Oddfellowship will be encouraged and strengthened and prospered in this jurisdiction are the objects of our meeting, and to you now assembled, my greeting is that the Lord has bountifully blessed the noble cause in which all our hearts are engaged, and to Him from whom cometh every good and perfect gift, our praises and thanks are due." . . .

" I am happy to inform the Grand Lodge that the condition of the Order is splendid. I know of no jars or factions, save in one or two Lodges ; the zeal and interest are good, while I have been disappointed as to the increase. Yet, we have every rea on to feel thankful for the health and prosperity of the Order, and that a kind Providence has spared us from any dire misfortunes from disease." . . .

" I have made some forty-five or fifty official visits, and have always, from every Lodge, received an Odd Fellows' welcome. I found the Lodges through-out the country better posted in the work than I had expected. Quite a number have degree staffs, and the work is beautifully placed on the floor. I had hoped to spend most of the months of August and September visiting Lodges, but on account of a severe illness of a month, from which I have just recovered, I could not make the visits."

" There is a growing desire all over this jurisdiction; in almost every Subordinate Lodge, for the establishing of an Odd Fellows' Orphans' Home. My brethren, the necessity of it can not, for one moment be doubted. We have a number of widows and little orphans over the state who need care and education that they can not receive from the various Lodges without bank-rupting them. I believe the entire Brotherhood are interested in the matter,

and I am satisfied that very substantial aid will be given outside of this Order.
At the last session of this Grand Body, a committee was appointed ; that committee has addressed a letter to each Subordinate Lodge, making the suggestions they thought necessary. I do most earnestly recommend that this Grand
Lodge take such action in the matter that ere another year the widows and
little orphans of our Brotherhood will have a place they can indeed call
' home, sweet home.' "

The death is recorded of their esteemed Grand Secretary,
William White, at the age of seventy-six. He had been Grand
Secretary for thirty-nine years.

Six new Lodges were instituted, and the net gain in membership was 477.

The following resolutions were adopted :—

" *Resolved*, Your Committee on Widows and Orphans' Home are of the
opinion that there seems to be a pronounced sentiment among the members
of the Order in this jurisdiction in favor of the establishing of a Home for
Widows and Orphans, or for Orphans and Indigent and Aged Members; and
recommend that a committee of five be appointed, to which shall be added
the Grand Master, and should it meet his approval to add three Sisters of
Rebekah Lodges, to report at the next session of this Grand Lodge :

1.   The amount that each Subordinate Lodge is willing to subscribe, and
the mode and manner of payment.

2.   The results of propositions for a site and location of such a Home."

" *Resolved*, That Subordinate Lodges in this jurisdiction are hereby
authorized and permitted to immediately re-take a ballot for a candidate for
membership where black balls appear, in order to verify the fact that black
balls may have not been cast by error."

LOUISIANA.

Fifty-ninth annual session, New Orleans, Mar. 1, 1892.

Their increase in membership during the year was 214, and
the Grand Master thinks that they have advanced wonderfully.
Their per capita tax is $1.25.   They have 26 Lodges, and 1,123
members.

LOWER PROVINCES.

Thirty-seventh annual session, Summerside, P.E.I., Aug.
10, 1892.

On the state of the Order, the Grand Master says :—

" The returns of the past year, which will be laid before you by the
Grand Secretary, show the state of the Order to be superior in every particular to what it was twelve months ago.   In Lodges, in membership, in disbursements for charitable purposes, for sick benefits and the relief of widows
and orphans, the figures of our Grand Secretary show a marked advance on
all former years : while the totals held as *trust* funds for the support of widows
and orphans, and the relief of suffering Brothers, show also a steady increase,
and testify to the zeal and good management which have prevailed generally
in our Lodges.

"As full details of our progress will be found in the Report of our Grand Secretary, it is not necessary for me to dwell minutely on the work of the year; but I cannot refrain from noting, briefly, a few of the more prominent points. Beginning with

NEW LODGES.

it will be found that *five* (5) have been added to the roll during the past year in promising localities and with exceptionally good charter members. The names of the new Lodges, and for which you are asked to grant charters, are :

> Orion No. 58, Port Maitland, Yarmouth Co., N. S.
> Rising Sun No. 59, Lunenburg, Lunenburg Co., N. S.
> La Have No. 60, Bridgewater, Lunenburg Co., N. S.
> Mayflower No. 61, Barrington, Shelburne Co., N. S.
> Vesta No. 62, North Sydney, Cape Breton.
> Also a Rebekah Lodge, Mizpah No. 5, Halifax, N. S."

The Odd Fellows' Relief Association received a renewal of the permit granted last year, to transact business in this jurisdiction.

The per capita tax is thirty-four cents. They have fifty-one Lodges, and 3,793 members. Increase, 923.

MAINE.

Forty-ninth anual session, Augusta, Oct. 18, 1892.

A constant improvement is being made throughout the jurisdiction, in the manner of conferring the degrees. Three Subordinate and five Rebekah Lodges were instituted during the term. We quote one of the recommendations of the Grand Master, and his reasons therefor, as worthy of our serious attention :—

"I recommend that a series of questions (like the following, or somewhat like them) be adopted and made a part of the report of the Investigating Committee :—

1.  Applicant's age?
2.  Applicant's residence?
3.  Married or single. If married does he live with his wife, if not, why not?
4.  Occupation?
5.  Is he physically qualified for admission?
6.  Is he addicted to intemperate use of liquor?
7.  Does he gamble?
8.  Is he habitually profane?
9.  Has he a good character among his neighbors?
10.  Does he possess sufficient education and intelligence to comprehend, and value the principles of Oddfellowship?
11.  Has he previously applied for membership in this or any lodge, if so, what lodge, and when?
12.  Is he a member of any beneficial fraternities or societies, if so what, and what benefits per week?

"Oddfellowship has been, is now, and I confidently hope and believe will be a very attractive Order to right-thinking men ; but at the same time, it is attractive to a class of men, of whom many are found in this, as in all States, who are undeserving and unworthy of ever entering its portals. There are too many cheap men already in the Order, and the same may be said with equal truthfulness of Masonry, Knights of Pythias and other Orders. There are too many, not yet affiliated with any Order, who believe, that in becoming Odd Fellows, they acquire standing and a badge of respectability, which is true. If all Investigating Committees did their duty, and actually *investigated*, the lodge might be comparatively safe from such invasions, but in too many instances these committees do *not* investigate, they do not even know, or attempt to know anything whatever of an applicant's character, standing, or his relations to other benefit paying organizations. The merest ' hearsay ' too often forms the only basis for a favorable report, and only the widest reputation for worthlessness seems to bring forward an unfavorable report.

" These questions, perhaps others might wisely be supplemented, or these advantageously changed, if printed into the report of the Investigating Committee for such committee to sign, as part and parcel of *their report*, would compel *them* to furnish *some facts* important to every member who desires to keep his lodge clean and clear of unworthy and improper persons, and would necessitate careful enquiry by such committee into *facts*, where now a report has nothing better than fancy, guess work or hearsay for a foundation.

" So long as benefit paying societies exist and multiply, and no laws exist excluding members of one from joining other societies of like nature, just so long each lodge of each Order is in danger of being victimized by some unworthy fellow, who joins all for the sake of the benefits. It seems to me that it is high time that investigation in this direction be made compulsory, so that our Lodges may know in advance the size of the risk they are taking."

In the report of the Grand Representatives we find the following graceful compliment to our Canadian Grand Sire :—

" For the first time in the history of American Oddfellowship, a brother, not a citizen of the United States, is elevated to the highest position in the gift of the Order. The eminent qualifications, sterling character, and great love for our noble Order, pointed out Bro. Campbell as a suitable person for this marked distinction, and the interests of our jurisdiction will not suffer at his hands."

MANITOBA.

Tenth annual session, Morden, Feb. 15, 1893.

The condition of the Order is one of continued growth. Most of the Lodges have increased their membership. Three new Lodges were formed. They have 26 Lodges and 1,850 members, a net gain of 190.

The worthy Grand Secretary, Brother R. H. Shanks, gives the following account of the visit of the Grand Sire :—

" It was with extreme pleasure we all heard, in September last, of the election of Bro. Dr. Cl. T. Campbell, of London, Ontario, to the highest office in the gift of the Order—the office of Grand Sire—and I at once wired him congratulations on behalf of Manitoba and invited him to pay us a visit on his return from Portland.

" He replied thanking me for the courtesy and asked me to arrange meetings at Winnipeg and Portage la Prairie. This was done and on Thursday, September 29th, he visited Minnehaha Lodge, No. 7, and witnessed an exemplification of the Third Degree. On Friday, September 30th, a reception was tendered him by Portage Lodge, No. 3, at Portage la Prairie, and on Saturday evening, October 1st, a public reception was tendered him in Oddfellows' Hall, Winnipeg, by Winnipeg Oddfellowship, but under the auspices of the two Grand bodies. At all these meetings, large numbers were present to testify their respect for our beloved Grand Sire, who by his quiet, unassuming manner and by his truly eloquent words of commendation and counsel, endeared himself to all.

"Our Grand Sire was accompanied in his visit by Bro. W. G. Dye, of Winona, Minn., Grand Marshal of the Sovereign Grand Lodge, who by his hearty manner and humorous speeches, made himself at home with his Canadian brethren.

"We also had the pleasure of welcoming Grand Representatives Moore, Cole and Macdonald of Ontario, and Ives of Minnesota—as well as Past Grand Rep. Welsh of Ontario."

The Odd Fellows' Relief Association, the Odd Fellows' Funeral Aid Association, of Manitoba, and the General Relief Board, of Winnipeg, were all recommended by the Grand Lodge.

### MASSACHUSETTS.

Annual session, Boston, Aug. 11, 1892.

There has been a steady, healthy growth, not only in members but in every element that tends to make a society strong and worthy of membership. There are 216 Lodges, and 44,809 members, a net gain of 2,581 during the year. On the important subject of dues and benefits, the Grand Master made some excellent observations, which are worthy of attention by all :—

" No subject more clearly affects the prosperity of our Order than the relation of dues and benefits. The payment of benefits is a cardinal principle of our Order  I do not hesitate to say that no important feature of oue institution is managed in such suicidal method as this. There is no system or the semblance of a system, about it. It constitutes the worst confusion of ideas that were ever engrafted into law. No consideration is given the wants, the needs, or the future necessities of the Order. No uniformity exists among the Lodges. While a few jurisdictions have given the subject considerable attention, and have drawn many valuable facts from their own experience, Massachusetts has gone on with a blind reliance upon chance and good fortune. This may well cause no great embarrassment while the Lodges are in their youth and while the average age of their membership is young ; but the time is coming, and that speedily, when we must rely upon close calculation and upon good financiering even to live. The tendency is all the time to increase the expense of maintaining the Lodge, and as the members grow older the liability of sickness and death increases rapidly. The most conclusive argument that can be made on this subject would be an examination of the financial returns submitted by the various Lodges each year of the Grand Lodge. A very large proportion of the Lodges over twenty-five years of age are spending for expenses and benefits more than their entire income ; and the number of such Lodges is increasing from year to year —the present reports showing sixty-four Lodges in this condition, while four of them are actually paying more for *benefits alone* than the total receipts of the Lodge from all sources. Is it not time for us to consider this subject in a reasonable light ?  These Lodges are capable of living only because in their younger days they were able to lay aside a fund for future use ; and yet we see Lodges, because they have accumulated a moderate fund, cutting down their receipts (but not expenses), to a point that must inevitably lead to ruin."

Their Odd Fellows' Home, with its outfit, has been completed at a cost of about $50,000, and they have no indebtedness.

### MICHIGAN.

Annual session, Detroit, Oct. 18, 1892.

The Grand Master thinks that our Order is governed by too much law, and that the great principles of our Order should control us in all our doings and sayings. The increase in membership was larger than was ever before reported in any given year. They have 403 Lodges, and 23,399 members, being a net gain of 2,101.

### MINNESOTA.

Fortieth annual session, Duluth, June 7, 1892.

The Grand Officers have been very conservative in granting charters for new Lodges, yet 17 applications were approved. Lodges, 187 ; members, 11,633 ; increase, 1,574. The Grand Secretary also says :—

" This increase has not been simply from a numerical standpoint. The stability of the Order has been fostered and promoted by the erection of buildings, leasing and furnishing of larger and more commodious halls, the purchase of new outfits of paraphernalia, adornment of the walls of lodge rooms, and last, but highly important, the cultivation of more intimate social relations, not only between lodges, but among brothers as well. In the practice of the latter, young members, and old ones, too, have found that there is a field in Oddfellowship which may be cultivated with benefit to the Order, but more especially with profit to themselves. Fraternity has been exemplified in a manner so conspicuous as to give enlightenment to members who for years have served at the altar without giving thanks.

" But this is not all. The grandest work performed is in the ministering to those of our brothers upon whom misfortune came with its always depressing weight ; the assuaging the anguish of burdened hearts, and in cheering the down-hearted. Could the recording angel's books be opened, what a galaxy of good deeds might be unfolded to our gaze. ' What's done we partly may compute, but know not what's prevented.' "

The following resolutions were adopted :—

" *Resolved,* That the incoming Grand Master be and is hereby authorized to convene the District Deputy Grand Masters whom he may appoint at such places and times as in his judgment will best serve their convenience, for the purpose of giving instructions in the laws, usages and unwritten work of the Order ; and

" *Resolved,* That the Grand Treasurer is hereby directed to pay deputies, who shall attend the session to which they may be called by the Grand Master, mileage at the rate of three cents a mile for each mile necessarily travelled in going to or returning therefrom ; it being understood that no deputy shall receive mileage for more than one such meeting, and that the one nearest his residence."      .      .      .

"*Resolved*, That this Grand Lodge recommend that each subordinate lodge in this jurisdiction give at least one entertainment, before the next session of the Grand Lodge, for the benefit of the Minnesota Odd Fellows' Home and Orphan Asylum."      .      .      .

"*Resolved*, That the Grand Master be directed to appoint a committee of three members of this Grand Lodge, who shall act as an advisory council to the Historian, and with whom he can consult on all questions in the performance of his duties.

"*Resolved*, That it is hereby made the duty of the Secretary of each subordinate lodge in this jurisdiction to furnish said Historian with statements and facts for the preparation of this history, such as he may desire or need, regarding such lodge.

"*Resolved*, That the Historian is hereby authorized to incur any requisite expense in the discharge of his duties, and that the Grand Secretary shall reimburse him for such expenditures by drawing warrants on the Grand Treasurer for the same,"

The per capita tax is fifty cents.

### MISSISSIPPI.

Fifty-fourth annual session, Holly Springs, May 3, 1892. The year's record is thus specified :—

" Looking over the field of our labors for the year ending December 31st 1891, we can truly say that it has been an eventful one for Oddfellowship in Mississippi.   The increase in membership for that period has been phenomenal, 259 above all losses.   We thought the previous year's gain of 120 was doing well.   The initiations during that time were 278, and the total members December 31st, 1891, 1,253, against 994 for the previous year. The number of Lodges was 35, against 28 at the end of 1890.   This is a net increase of 7 Lodges, besides the institution of three Rebekah Lodges, while we had none before."

A complete set of new constitutions was adopted for the Grand Lodge, Subordinate Lodges, and Rebekah Lodges.

### MONTANA.

Eighteenth annual session, Butte, Oct. 18, 1892. The Lodges have increased in numbers and in membership, and the outlook for the future is bright and promising.   Lodges, 42 ; members, 2,355 ; increase 330.

### NEVADA.

Twenty-sixth annual session, Virginia City, June 21, 1892. The reports show, one new Lodge, and two new Rebekah Lodges.   Lodges, 24 ; members, 1,570 ; increase, 48.

The following appeal appears to have been the principal one before the Grand Lodge :—

" The appeal is in reference to the Order of Business laid down in the Ritual, in regard to the use of the gavel by the N. G and V.G. after the Lodge had been regularly opened, and Brothers were then admitted to the Lodge-room.

" It appears that the V.G. of Elko Lodge, No. 18, I.O.O.F., entered the Lodge-room immediately after the Lodge was declared open by the R.S. of the N.G., and seated by the N.G., and took his seat as V.G.  The N.G. then sounded his gavel and directed the V.G. to answer the same.

" Under the head of Good of the Order, the legality of the instructions of the N.G. to the V.G. were called in question by W. W. Booher, P G.M., and the N.G. decided his action as according to law, hence the appeal."

The Committee on Appeals referred this appeal to the Grand Lodge without recommendation. A motion was made to re-commit the report to the Committee on Appeals. An amendment was carried to refer the appeal to the Grand Lodge, as a Committee of the Whole.  The Grand Lodge then solemnly went into Committee of the Whole, and after a lengthy discussion it was finally decided to dismiss the appeal.

## NEW HAMPSHIRE.

Forty-ninth annual session, Woodsville, Oct. 12, 1892.

From the report of the Grand Secretary, which appears first in the Journal, we make the following extract :—

" An increase of membership does not necessarily imply financial strength and permanency.  Along with the additions to numbers must be a corresponding increase in the means to be applied for the purposes of the organization.  Our returns for the year ending June 30 are of the most gratifying character.  The increase in membership was larger than the average for a period of more than thirty years.  It exceeded that of the previous year, which was regarded as a prosperous one.  But with this increase in members the increase in the number of weeks of sickness for which benefits were paid was correspondingly large, there being an excess over the previous year of 2,649 weeks  The increase also in the amount of benefits paid to the sick was $7,165.59—a sum nearly equal to the amount received for the initiation fees and the degrees conferred on the 407 candidates admitted to the Lodges.  From these statements we judge that the financial condition of the Order in the State is on the whole not materially different from what it was June 30, 1891."

The Grand Master gives some further information :—

" The condition of our Order in this jurisdiction has never been better. Numerically and financially the Order has shown a very gratifying increase. The number of Subordinate Lodges has increased by two, and there have been added to our list of Rebekah Lodges, seven.

" The number of members of Subordinate Lodges has increased 407, making a total of 11,597, the largest number enrolled under a society banner in this State by about 3,000.  The Rebekah Branch of the Order shows a still greater increase of 724, making a total of 6,729 in the State.

"The prevalence of 'la grippe' during the winter months gave our Order a very severe test, but I am pleased to report that nearly every Lodge in the State met the severe drains upon its finances without having recourse to invested funds. The same epidemic interfered very largely with the working forces of the Lodges, making it difficult to give the degree work as the Lodges were accustomed to render it, but I believe all the Lodges have recovered in the last six months what they lost in those preceding."

The remarks of the Grand Master on the minimum benefit law, display the true spirit of Oddfellowship. While deeming the law unjust to his own jurisdiction, Brother Frank M. Davis is thoroughly loyal to the majority in the Sovereign Grand Lodge :—

"The Sovereign Grand Lodge has, in its power if not in its wisdom, affirmed the minimum benefit law as passed at the session of 1891, with slight amendment. Onr Grand Representatives' report will soon show you the details of such action. While I believe that the Sovereign Grand Lodge has made a mistake, I do not anticipate any serious results to the Order, or to Subordinate Lodges, with very few exceptions. My own experience teaches me that Oddfellowship is not sought by people who wish an insurance only, but that it has commended itself to every thinking person by its steadiness of purpose in obeying the mandates expressed in the Grand Seal of our Order. That the difference in the ways of the East and the West is responsible for the passage of this law, and that while in New England there are no Lodges that do not care for their sick, there are in several other sections Lodges which cannot do so, and these are the Lodges for whose actions we are made to suffer. I believe, however, that attachment to the principles of our Order will show itself so deep-rooted that some way will be found out of the apparent difficulty by every Lodge, while still obeying the letter as well as the spirit of the law.

"During the year just past I have been asked in regard to the law, and have always maintained that the law was so plain that it could not be misunderstood by any one who would take the trouble to read it carefully. Notwithstanding the plain terms of the law, most Lodges of this jurisdiction have been satisfied to let the matter rest until the Sovereign Grand Lodge could again pass upon it. This the Sovereign Grand Lodge has done, and we as Odd Fellows should be willing to live up to the law, believing that whatever a majority think is wise will certainly not be of very great injury, and believing that Oddfellowship will yet stand the peer, if not the leader, of all fraternal organizations. I would recommend that a circular be issued to the Lodges of the State, calling attention to this law as it now exists."

The sum of $1,000 was donated to the Odd Fellows' Home at Concord.

NEW JERSEY.

Fifty-ninth annual session, Trenton, November 16, 1892.

Eight new lodges were instituted during the year. They have 234 lodges and 23,043 members, being a net gain of 680.

A special committee was appointed to protect Lodges in their real estate operations.

The following resolutions were adopted :

"*Resolved*, That the Representatives to the Sovereign Grand Lodge be directed to urge upon the Sovereign Grand Lodge the propriety of abolishing the present form of Visiting Cards, and in place of the same to issue an official receipt and a general term password uniform in their entire jurisdiction."

"*Resolved*, That the resolution of this Grand Lodge, session of 1890, directing the Grand Representatives to the Sovereign Grand Lodge to vote against the amendment to the Constitution admitting young men at the age of 18, be rescinded, and that the Grand Representatives to Sovereign Grand Lodge be instructed to vote in favor of said amendment admitting young men to our Order at age of 18."

NEW SOUTH WALES

Thirteenth annual session, Sydney, February 14, 1892.
The session lasted five days.
The Grand Master devoted his attention principally to the country districts. He travelled over 4,000 miles in making his official visitations. In the opening paragraph of his report he says :—

" New South Wales has been suffering from a commercial depression which has seriously affected the working classes, from which the great bulk of our members is derived. I am in hopes that the worst has passed, and that with an improvement in trade the Order will make more rapid strides. Several of our Subordinate Lodges have had serious difficulties to contend with in the suspension of so-called banks and the losing of their funds deposited with them, but the members of some of them have struggled manfully, and they may now be congratulated on being in a tolerably sound position. The finances of the Order, in view of the circumstances above referred to, are in a condition that should inspire us with feelings of pleasure, both Grand and Subordinate Lodge funds being in an exceedingly healthy condition.

"Several of our Subordinate Lodges have been heavily taxed through the increasing demand on their sick funds, and especially is this felt in depressed times, and considerably affects their progress. The death rate has also been under previous records, but we must expect in the natural order of things that as our Order increases in numbers and age so must we expect sickness and its incident liabilities."

Two new Lodges were formed. The Grand Secretary in his report has the following information :—

" For some time past the word 'depression' has become almost a stereotyped expression and has been prominently conspicuous in all references to this colony, but the year just closed has accentuated in a marked degree the expression referred to, and the year's record is one dark shadow from its advent to the close. Commercial depression, allied with industrial disorganization and financial disaster, are events so recent that extended dilation becomes unnecessary, but their influences upon the community where these elements exist must inevitably cause retrogression. I am pleased, however, to say that, although the presence of these influences have been severely felt, they have not to an appreciable extent trammelled our progress, and 'ever onward' continues to characterize the operations of the Order.

" The revenue returns for the past year are represented by the following figures : General Funeral Fund, £1,871 7s. 9d. ; Widow and Orphans' Fund, £265 6s. 3d. ; Incidental Fund, £706 17s. 7d. : the sum of £157 19s. 8d. was received for goods, the amount of £78 2s. was received on account of guarantee premiums, and the receipts from all sources under this head amounted to

£1,038 13s. 9d. ; total receipts, £3,285 7s. 9d., this amount being £75 9s. 1d. in excess of the previous year's record.

"The increase in funds is as under : Funeral Fund, £2,153 13s., £1,01. 5s. 3d. net being transferred from the hall account ; Widow and Orphans' Fund, £135 6s. 3d. The Incidental Fund has suffered a decline of £233 18s. 9d. The increase in funds, however, is most satisfactory, and cannot fail to secure your approval.

"The expenditure for the year is as follows: General Funeral Fund, £840 ; Widow and Orphans' Fund, £130. In addition to this expenditure the sums of £20 and £5 respectively should be added, as, although paid out of the incidental Fund, the disbursements were on account of deaths, and were voted as donation at the last session. The total amount disbursed under this heading would therefore be £995. The Incidental expenditure, which includes the amount above referred to, amounted to £1,272 12s. 6d., being £74 0s. 7d. in excess of that of the previous year.

"The operations of Subordinate Lodges for the past year are more favorable than that of the previous year, but the strain upon the Sick Fund has been very great. The fact that £3,831 13s. 3d. has been paid in sick benefits during the year will convey some idea of the extent of the benefits conferred. In addition to this the sum of £4,418 5s. 5d has been appropriated as surgeons' fees, while the sum of £1,185 11s. 5d. has been disbursed for dispensing medicine. The appropriation under the heading donation reached the sum of £160 13s. 3d. If we add the benefits under the previous headings we find the result to be as follows : Funeral Fund, £865 ; Widow and Orphans' Fund, £130 ; surgeons' fees, £4,418 5s. 5d. ; dispensing fees, £1,185 11s. 5d. ; sick benefits, £3,831 13s. 3d. ; donations, £160 13s. 3d.; total, £10,591 3s. 4d. The benefits thus conferred are too apparent to need any embellishment.

"Numerically our progress has been unequal to past experience, but the citcumstances were more favorable than were those of the past year. The following is the record under this heading : 655 were initiated during the year, while 23 were reinstated and 90 were received by clearance, the total being 768 ; against this 518 were written off by arrears ; 91 withdrew by clearance ; 34 ceesed membership by death ; 13 resigned and 1 was expelled ; total loss, 657, leaving a net increase on the year's operations of 111. The total membership has now reached 5,575 ; of this number 4,848 are financial, 627 being unfinancial."

NEW YORK.

Annual session, Buffalo, August 16, 1892.

These proceedings come to us in a bulky volume of over 750 pages and are full of interest commensurate with so large and important a jurisdiction.

A number of distinguished visitors were present during the session, among them being L. J. Retting, Grand Master of Vermont, C. L. Young, Past Grand Master of Ohio, H. Robertson, Grand Representative of Ontario, C. B. Ware, Grand Master of Connecticut, Cl. T. Campbell, Deputy Grand Sire, P. E. Fitz-Patrick, Past Grand Master, and Joseph Oliver, Deputy Grand Master of Ontario

From the very able address of the Grand Master, Bro. Jacob Stern, we make the following extracts :—

" In this jurisdiction this branch of the Order has been growing rapidly. The reported increase for the year 1891 was 23 Lodges and 3,802 members ;

and for the past six months the increase has been greater, as reference to the Grand Secretary's report will clearly show.

" The earnest and satisfactory work of the Lodges is entitled to hearty commendation.  Some troubles have arisen, but my appeal for harmony has generally proved successful.

" At present Pennsylvania only stands between the numerical place this jurisdiction *now* occupies and the place it *should* occupy, and I trust the day is not far distant when this great jurisdiction will take its place at the head of the column.  The adoption of a wise, broad, and liberal policy, the continuance of zealous and faithful work for the good of the Order, with unceasing energy, will accomplish the desired result."     .        .        .

" I have frequently  been called upon to grant permission to Lodges in this State to elect candidates living in other jurisdictions, and also permission for Lodges in adjacent jurisdictions to elect candidates living in this State.  In all cases I have adhered to the rule, and received the consent of the nearest Lodge in this State and of the Grand Master in other jurisdictions, as the case might be.

" After considerable correspondence and  personal consultation with the then Grand Master of Pennsylvania, we concluded to submit to our respective grand Lodges the adoption of the rule now in force in the State of Ohio, to wit : ' When an adjoining State jurisdiction shall have adopted a law granting equal privileges to Subordinate Lodges in this State, then a Subordinate Lodge of said adjoining jurisdiction may have the right to receive into membership persons whose residences are nearer to the Lodge applied to, than to the one in Ohio, without regard to the State.'  I understand that this rule has the sanction of the Grand Lodge, and its adoption by this Body would simplify matters.  Pennsylvania having at its last Grand Lodge session adopted this rule, I therefore recommend the adoption of the same by this jurisdiction."

One of his decisions was made to settle some doubts as to the rights of members to remain in the ante-room.

" The Outside Guardian is required to  invite all  brothers in the ante-rooms to enter the  Lodge-room proper at the time of the opening ; to take up the semi-annual password of such as  may refuse to enter ; to report to the Noble Grand the members who refuse to  enter, and  obtain his permission for their remaining—otherwise to clear the ante-room."

The Sovereign Grand Lodge has since decided that it is the duty of the Warden prior to the formal opening of the Lodge to collect the password from those  remaining in the ante room.

There are now 638 Lodges and 110 Rebekah Lodges in  the State.

The following resolutions were adopted :—

" *Resolved*,—When an adjoining State jurisdiction shall have adopted a law granting equal privileges to Subordinate Lodges in this State, then a Subordinate Lodge of said adjoining jurisdiction may have the right to receive into membership persons whose residences are nearer the Lodge applied to than the nearest Lodge in that jurisdiction.'

" *Resolved*,—That Subordinate Lodges under the jurisdiction of this Grand Lodge be authorized to set apart five per cent  of  their receipts from dues as a contingent fund, to be used for such expenditures as the Lodge may deem wise and proper."

" *Resolved*,—That a committee of three be appointed to review, and report any conflcts of law in, and to distinguish the decisions of the Grand Masters and of this Grand Lodge since the issue of the last Digest, and report the same to this Grand Lodge at its next session, to the end that this Grand Lodge may settle and determine its existing laws prior to the publishing of a new Digest."

" *Resolved*,—That we favor the establishment of Homes under the visitation and supervision of the Grand Lodge, and a proper system of districting the State for that purpose, and that a Special Committee of five be appointed by the incoming Grand Master to inquire into the whole subject and present a plan and rules for carrying out the objects above set forth, for presentation at the next session of this Grand Lodge."

A revision of the New York Digest was ordered, also the preparation of a uniform code of by-laws for Lodges.

### NORTH DAKOTA.

Second annual session, Devil's Lake, May 24, 1892.

The reports show seven new Subordinate and four Rebekah Lodges instituted during the year. They have 36 Lodges and 1,600 members, a gain of 173.

The following report was adopted.

" Your Committee to whom was referred the recommendations of the Grand Secretary that a Funeral Benefit Association be organized in this jurisdiction, recommend that the matter, together with all papers relating thereto, be referred to a special committee to report at the next session of this Grand Lodge, as the subject requires some consideration, which this Committee has not the time to give it, nor the statistics at hand necessary to assist us in rendering an intelligent report."

### OHIO.

Sixty-first annual session, Put-in-Bay, May 16, 1892.

The Grand Master instituted during the year four Subordinate Lodges and thirty-two Rebekah Lodges. He refused all request to permit foreign Lodges to initiate residents of Ohio. He mentions the death of their esteemed Grand Secretary, Wm. Chidsey, in his eightieth year. He was a member of the Grand Lodge since 1846. The net gain in membership was 2,064. On the nurse-hire system, he says :

" The members who have the opportunity to mingle with the Brotherhood in Ohio are led steadily and by degrees to the conclusion that there is something wrong about our nurse-hire system. While the hired nurse is in itself perhaps best for our sick Brothers, it nevertheless has a tendency to get us away from the imperative command ' to visit the sick.' When a nurse is hired and sent to the home of sickness, officers of Lodges, Relief Committees, and Brothers are liable to think that their whole duty has been done. I desire to heartily indorse the recommendation of my worthy predecessor, A. C. Cable, found on page 6174 of the Journal, as the proper solution of this question, to wit :

" That in addition to the hired nurse a detail be made, whose duty it shall be to call upon the sick Brother and his family daily, to ascertain what, if any, assistance can be rendered, imparting words of comfort and solace to them, thus letting the sick Brother, his family, and friends know and realize that they as Odd Fellows have an interest in them, and that we are Brothers, not only in name, but in truth and in fact ;  and that ' mutual assistance is a central link in the chain of Oddfellowship ; ' and that brotherly love is the ' bond of unity ; ' and that we as Odd Fellows ' tenderly raise up the stricken body and pour balm into the wounds of our Brothers in distress,' as did the Good Samaritan to the traveller whom He found ' bleeding and suffering by the wayside.' '

On the same subject the following report of the Judiciary Committee was adopted :—

" Your Committee on Judiciary, to whom was referred the report of the Committee on the State of the Order relating to nursing the sick, beg leave to report that we approve of the recommendation of the Grand Master, and we think Odd Fellows should live up to their profession of visiting the sick.   We therefore offer the following ammendment to Section 218, to wit :

" After the last word of said section shall be added, ' and when any Sub-ordinate Lodge shall have provided by its By-law for attendance upon the sick by the payment of a fixed sum for hiring nurses and watchers, such Lodge shall also provide for the daily visitation from its own members, of its sick and afflicted Brothers.' "

On the question of inter-State courtesies, the following report was adopted :

" Your Committee on the State of the Order, to whom was submitted the correspondence of Grand Master Witherup, of the Jurisdiction of Pennsylvania, to Grand Master Bowen, of Ohio, extending to the Jurisdiction of Ohio the privilege of admitting to membership in Ohio of an applicant from Pennsylvania, desiring to become an Odd Fellow, and whose place of residence is nearer a Lodge in Ohio than in Pennsylvania, and desiring that Ohio should extend to Pennsylvania the same courtesy, etc., would report as follows :

" *Resolved*, That our Representatives to the Sovereign Grand Lodge, at the next session thereof, confer with the Representatives of Pennsylvania, and endeavor to procure such legislation on said subject as shall be uniform in its character and general in its reach, so that a Lodge in a Sister State shall not bid for the increase of its membership from the citizens of a Sister State, by making the prices of admission less than those regulating the admission of such candidates in said Sister State, and that the Grand Secretary of Ohio notify the Grand Secretary of Pennsylvania of the action of this Grand Lodge in the premises."

It was decided not to entertain any appeal for aid when the same is to be used for the payment of real estate or for cancelling mortgages.

OREGON.

Thirty-seventh annual session, Astoria, May 18, 1892.
On the state of the Order the Grand Master says :

" Odd Fellowship in this jurisdiction has been favored by an increase of membership far beyond any reasonable hope and expectation.   While no

Subordinate Lodge has been eliminated from the list of 104 at the commencement of this Grand Lodge year, 11 new Lodges have been organized and are now in successful working condition, with a flattering prospect of acquiring an increased membership in the near future.

"Up to December 31, 1891, the reports from the various Lodges show an increase of membership within the jurisdiction of 575, making the total membership at that date 5,186.　The annual report of Subordinate Lodges for the last year show that $22,732.03 had been disbursed for relief of members, which is gratifying evidence that the Order is meeting all of its financial obligations.　Peace and harmony, to a marked degree, pervade the Lodges, and they all appear to be working in the true spirit of Fraternity."

The following resolution was adopted :

"*Resolved*,　That each Elective Officer of this Grand Lodge may at any time call together a sufficient number of duly qualified Past Grands to assist him in conferring the Grand Lodge Degree on any Past Grand who shall present a certificate from his Lodge showing that he is otherwise qualified, and the said Elective Officer shall report to the Grand Secretary all such degrees conferred."

It was decided that a Subordinate Lodge could not appropriate any of its funds to subsidize a railroad.


### PENNSYLVANIA.

From Pennsylvania we have as yet only the report of the the Grand Secretary, Brother J. B. Nicholson, Past Grand Sire. It is dated May 16, 1893, and was presented at the seventieth session of the Grand Lodge.　Every Brother in the land will rejoice to know that Brother Nicholson has almost completely recovered from the very serious attack of illness which prostrated him in December last.

Number of working Lodges, 1,063; increase, 21 ; number of members, 106,103 ; increase, 4,855.


### QUEBEC.

Thirteenth annual session, Farnham, August 16, 1892.
On the state of the Order the Grand Master says:

"The report of the Grand Secretary shows an increase of two Lodges, and the largest increase of membership yet recorded.

"Much of this encouraging state of affairs is due to my predecessor, D. J. Dickson, P.G.M.G.R., who established the Order in the Ancient Capital, near the close of his term of office.　There are excellent opportunities for the establishment of new Lodges in the Ottawa District, there being at the present time thirteen members resident in the city of Hull, and four members in the town of Buckingham, all of whom have been personally interviewed on the subject."

The following resolution was adopted :

"That all Past Grand Masters of this Grand Lodge be, and are hereby appointed a Special Committee with full power to act in conjunction with the

Grand Lodge of Ontario, in any steps that Grand Body may take to celebrate the Fiftieth Anniversary of the establishment of Oddfellowship in Canada, and that a sum not exceeding one hundred dollars be placed at the disposal of the Committee for any expense incurred by them in carrying out this resolution. Three to form a quorum of this Committee."

The Grand Representatives were instructed to support the eighteen-year-old amendment and the abolition of the system of Visiting Cards

Past Grand Masters are admitted to seats in the Grand Lodge with the power of making and debating motions, but without the right of voting.

The per capita tax was reduced to sixty cents.


### RHODE ISLAND.

Fiftieth annual session, Providence, February 7, 1893.

With a few exceptions the Lodges are in a prosperous condition. They have 50 Lodges and 6,373 members, a gain of 96· The average age of the membership is forty-one. We make the following extract from the report of the Committee on Laws of Subordinates, which shows that this jurisdiction is taking the right course in the matter of the relation of dues to benefits.

"In looking through the foregoing report what will be brought most forcibly to one's attention will be the tendency of the Lodges to curtail sick benefit expenditures and to increase the annual dues, and the payment of the same quarterly in advance. Thus it will be observed, that the laborious and carefully prepared work of the Special Committee on ' Dues and Benefits ' rendered six or eight years ago, is now being practically applied by many of our most active and representative Lodges, a positive assurance that work well done rarely goes unrewarded."


### SOUTH CAROLINA.

Fifty-third annual session, Orangeburg, May 10, 1893.
On the state of the Order the Grand Master says :

"Soon after I assumed the duties of Grand Master, I was confronted with the fact that there was a stringency in financial affairs all over the State that would seriously interfere with the growth of the Order, and which threatened a decrease in its membership by suspensions. For several months the effort to stimu ate the brotherhood to activity was very laborious, but finally, with a fidelity rarely seen and never surpassed, the rank and file of the Order throughout the State rallied to the demands of the hour, and fully demonstrated the fact that the spirit of Oddfellowship was alive and triumphant."

Two new Subordinate Lodges and one Rebekah Lodge were instituted during the year. They have 21 Lodges and 786 members ; increase, 82.

## SOUTH DAKOTA.

Seventeenth annual session, Madison, May 17, 1892.

While the growth in new Lodges has not been as large as in some previous years, still the increase in membership has been very satisfactory, as it is the result of renewed zeal and activity among all the Lodges. Three new Lodges were formed during the year and two Rebekah Lodges. They have 75 Lodges and 3,315 members. Increase, 193

The following resolutions were adopted :—

"*Resolved*,—That this Grand Lodge hereby express its opinion that a minimum amount of benefits should be fixed by the Sovereign Grand Lodge, below which no Subordinate Lodge shall be permitted to go, *provided*, that such amount pro rata shall not be less per week, for the first six months, than one-fourth the amount fixed by each individual Subordinate Lodge for annual dues."    .    .    .

"*Resolved*,—That this Grand Lodge create the office of Grand Instructor, and that his travelling expenses, not to exceed $300 be paid by this Grand Lodge. The duty of said Grand Instructor to be to visit the Lodges in the jurisdiction, and hold schools of instruction, whenever requested by the Lodges, and that each Subordinate Lodge pay for such services to the Grand Instructor the sum of $10."

## TENNESSEE.

Forty-second annual session, Jackson, October 19, 1892.

Brother William Austin Smith, Grand Master, deserves special mention. His record in official visitations is unsurpasssed. Although the Grand Lodge pays the Grand Master no salary and makes no provision for this purpose, Brother Smith during the year visited every organized body of Odd Fellows in Tennessee, including all the Subordinate Lodges, Rebekah Lodges, Encampments and Cantons. He travelled more than 5,800 miles by all sorts of conveyances, by night and day, without missing a single appointment, He delivered twenty public addresses on the beauties of the Order.

Seven new Lodges were formed. They have now 114 Lodges and 4,573 members, an increase of 296.

The following resolutions were adopted :—

"*Resolved*,—That authority is hereby conferred upon any Subordinate Lodge of the I.O.O.F., under the jurisdiction of the Grand Lodges of Virginia, Kentucky, Arkansas, Mississippi, Alabama, Georgia and North Carolina, to receive the application, initiate, and retain as a member any citizen of the State of Tennessee whose residence, at the time of said application, is nearer the Lodge to which application is made than to any Subordinate Lodge in the State of Tennessee."

"*Provided*, This shall only apply to such of the above named jurisdictions as shall adopt and continue in force a law granting equal privileges to Subordinate Lodges in this State ; and

"*Provided further*, That nothing in this resolution shall be construed to debar any person so initiated, who withdraws by card, from disposing same in a Lodge in Tennessee, located further from his residence.

2. *Resolved.*—That if, after the initiation of any person under the provision of the foregoing resolution, there shall be a Lodge organized under the jurisdiction of the Grand Lodge of the State of Tennessee nearer his residence than the one in which he was initiated, that the matter of changing his membership be left to his own personal preference."

## VERMONT.

Forty-sixth annual session, Montpelier, May 18, 1892.

The Grand Master reports four new Lodges and five new Rebekah Lodges. Harmony prevails. Brother Henry Clark reports on correspondence and gives Ontario a good notice.

They have 48 Lodges and 3,517 members.

## VIRGINIA.

Fifty-sixth annual session, Norfolk, April 11, 1893.

The Grand Master thus sets forth their progress :

" Notwithstanding this has been what is termed an ' off year,' it is with pleasure that I am able to state to you that our progress has been extremely gratifying and in every particular highly satisfactory ; conditions have been very unfavorable for this result—a very hot summer prevented many of the Lodges from doing much work during the warm months ; following this came the presidential election, with all the excitement and confusion which attend such an event ; added to this came the coldest winter that we have had for twenty years—the weather was such that many of the Lodges, especially in the rural districts, were unable to meet or to do any work, But now the conditions have changed ; the general election and excitement has subsided, the extreme cold weather has passed away, and we are just entering upon that season of the year when ' the soft zephyrs play among the branches '; we will bud forth again, and there will be ' life, beauty and joy ' throughout the Old Dominion."

They have 88 Lodges and 5,588 members, increase 417.

The " Lodge Deputy " system was found to be a signal failure and was abolished, and the former system of Districts, containing from two to ten Lodges in each, was re-adopted.

## WASHINGTON.

Fourteenth annual session, Walla Walla, May 10, 1892.

The Grand Master decided that the half-breed Indian wives of Brothers could not be admitted to a Rebekah Lodge.

In the report of the Grand Secretary we find the following on the Order :

" For never in the experience of this Grand Lodge has there been a year in which its increase has been so marked, and when we consider that the number of fraternal organizations is constantly increasing and that the competition for membership among them is very great, the gain to our membership is simply astonishing, and demonstrates beyond a doubt that the grand principles upon which our Order is founded are becoming more widely known and better understood by the world at large.

" The gain in the number of Subordinate Lodges since our last communication has been twenty-three, twelve of which have been instituted since January 1, 1892, the net gain in the number of Rebekah Lodges has been nine, twelve lodges having been instituted and three having surrendered their charters (Star Rebekah Lodge No. 7, Mizpah Rebekah Lodge No. 11 and Ruth Rebekah Lodge No. 17).

" The gain in the membership in the Subordinate Lodges during 1891 was 1,442, and the gain in membership in the Rebekah Lodges during the same time was 422, and the increase in financial ability to meet the calls upon the Lodges in fulfilling the requirements of the Order ' to visit the sick, relieve the distressed, bury the dead, protect and educate the orphan,' has more than kept pace with our numerical increase."

WISCONSIN.

Forty-sixth annual session, Janesville, June 7, 1892.

The Order continues prosperous.   The net gain in membership was 597.   Seven new Lodges were formed

The Grand Lodge voted $1,500 to the maintenance of their Odd Fellows' Home.

1893.

Forty-seventh annual session, Milwaukee, June 6, 1893.
On the state of the Order the Grand Secretary says :

" In presenting this my annual report of the transactions of this office for the past year, I desire to congratulate you upon the continued prosperity of the Order in all its branches, not alone in Wisconsin, but in every jurisdiction subordinate to the Sovereign Grand Lodge.   As will be seen from the returns there is a gain in the subordinate branch of five Lodges and 834 members, the largest gain since 1875, while the returns from the Rebekah Lodges show a gain of eight Lodges and 604 members.   Reports have been received from every Subordinate Lodge for the term ending December 31st, 1892, with a single exception, that of Spencer, No. 323, and this Lodge is considering the advisability of either surrendering its charter or consolidating with some other Lodge."

They have 317 Lodges and 16,894 members.

The Special Committee appointed to make a thorough inspection of their Odd Fellows' Home reported that everything was in a satisfactory condition.   The Home maintains an average of eighteen members ranging from five years to eighty years of age.   The expenditure for last year was $3,428.35, which would be an average cost of $3.65 per week for each inmate. $2,000 was voted by the Grand Lodge to the Home, and the following resolution was adopted.

" *Resolved*,—That on and after July 1, 1893, a per capita tax of twenty-five cents per member, to be known as the Odd Fellows' Home tax, be and the same is hereby levied on each member of a Subordinate Lodge, to be paid on or before Dec. 31st, in each year; provided that any Lodge may appropriate the gross amount from its treasury, or raise the same by subscriptions or entertainments; further

" *Resolved,*—That each Rebekah Lodge be requested, in such manner as it shall see fit, to contribute a like sum for the same purpose."

CONCLUSION.

At the date of closing our report, (August 1st,) the journals of the above named forty-one Grand Lodges have been received. The journals that have not been received are those of the following Grand Lodges, namely : Arizona, Florida, Maryland, Missouri, Nebraska, New Mexico, North Carolina, Pennsylvania, Texas, Utah, West Virginia and Wyoming. If any of these come to hand in time, they will be noticed in a supplementary report.

All of which is Fraternally submitted,

HENRY ROBERTSON,
*Chairman.*

COLLINGWOOD, August 1st, 1893.


The following was referred to the Committee on Legislation :—

Moved by Rep. A. H. Blackeby, seconded by Rep. J. Donogh, P.G.M., and

*Resolved,*—That no Subordinate Lodge in this jurisdiction shall employ as instructor in the new dramatized or floor work, any Brother (other than their own members) who has not first received the sanction of the Grand Master to act as such instructor. And any Brother acting as such instructor without having first obtained the permission of the Grand Master shall render himself liable to expulsion from the Order.


The following, on motion of Rep. A. H. Blackeby, seconded by Rep. G. J. Brill, was referred to the Committee on Legislation :—

Amend the Constitution so far as it refers to District Committees as follows :—

CLAUSE 98—Insert in 4th line, after the words " each year " the following :—

" Except in the case of newly instituted Lodges, which shall be entitled to elect, immediately after being instituted, one or more representatives, as their membership may warrant, in accordance with the provisions contained in clause 99."

CLAUSE 102—Change the wording of this clause so as to read as follows:—
" Such District Committee shall be convened by the District Deputy as soon as practicable after his appointment and shall be organized by the election of a secretary and the appointment by the D. D. G. M. of a warden, marshal, guardian, etc., etc.

The following were referred to the Judiciary Committee :—

By Rep. A. J. Johnston, Samaritan Lodge, No. 35.

When does a District Deputy cease to be District Deputy ?
When does a District Deputy's powers cease ?
(Would refer to White's Digest, 1889, clause 933, p. 228.)
See decision No. 1 of the G. M.

By Unity Lodge, No. 47.

CLAUSE 51 Con. Sub.—Latter part of clause reads, " The Lodge shall not be held to pay such benefit for any term of sickness shorter than one week, but after one week's sickness the Brother shall be entitled to benefits for each additional day or days that he may be ill."

Question—Is this portion of Clause 51 legal ?
See Journal S. G. L , 1892, p. 13,000. 13,057.

By Rep. F. A. Latshaw, Valley City Lodge, No. 117.

At an election for officers, after several ballots the vote stood 9, 7, 7, respectively. Clause 23, Constitution, directs that after each ballot the name of each candidate who may have received the smallest number of votes shall be withdrawn. It also declares that a majority of all legal votes cast shall be necessary to an election.

What is the proper course to pursue at the above election ?

By Rep. A. W. Cameron, Carleton Lodge, No. 240.

Can Lodges meeting outside the corporation limits of a city or town receive candidates for membership from said city or town without the consent of the Lodges therein ?

The following was referred to the Committee on Districts :—

By Pembroke Lodge, No. 203.

Moved by Bro. John Campbell, seconded by Bro. T. G. Hunt and

Resolved,—That owing to the distance of Pembroke Lodge, No. 203, I. O. O. F., from the nearest Lodge in District No. 41, being thirty-four miles, and from the farthest sixty-one miles, thereby causing much inconvenience to Pembroke Lodge and an unnecessary expense on the other Lodges in the District, we would therefore petition the Grand Lodge of the I. O. O. F. of Ontario, to strike Pembroke off District forty-one and place it as it was prior to eighteen hundred and ninety-one (1891).

11

**REPORT No. 4**—Bro. Hy. Robertson, P.G.M., from the Special Committee on " Insurance Act and Uniform Financial By-laws " made the following report, which was adopted :—

*To the Grand Lodge of Ontario, I.O.O.F. :*

Your Special Committee on the Insurance Act and Uniform Financial Clauses for Lodge By-laws, beg leave to report :—

1. That nothing has occurred during the past year with reference to " The Insurance Corporations Act," to call for the attention of your Committee.

2. With regard to the preparation of Uniform Financial Clauses for the By-laws of Lodges, your Committee are not agreed as to the advisability of the same, nor as to the form in which they should be presented, and they ask to be discharged from the further consideration of the subject.

3. As to Clause 20 of the Report of the Grand Secretary, your Committee desire to draw the attention of the Lodges to the valuable information contained therein, and they recommend that all Lodges not now incorporated, should be notified to procure incorporation as soon as possible.

All which is respectfully submitted.

HY. ROBERTSON,
W. H. COLE,
JOHN DONOGH,
W. H. HOYLE,
WM. BADENACH,
J. McLURG,
J. B. KING.

The following was referred to the Committee on State of the Order :—

A Lodge suspends or ignores its by-laws and takes members in at reduced rates.　What steps should other Lodges in the same city or town take to put a stop to such action ?

The Grand Master in a few very happy remarks, introduced Bro. Cl. T. Campbell, Grand Sire, who was most enthusiastically and cordially welcomed by the Grand Lodge.

The Grand Sire made a most feeling acknowledgment, appreciative of the very kind words of the Grand Master, and of his warm reception as Grand Sire, and the cordial greeting here extended to him.

Bro. P. E. Fitz-Patrick, P.G.M., presented the following request from the Rebekah Provincial Convention :—

NIAGARA FALLS, Aug. 9th, 1893.

*To the Grand Lodge of Ontario, I.O.O.F. :*

At a meeting of the Convention of the Daughters of Rebekah, the Finance Committee reported a deficit of $66.97, and recommended that this Convention ask for the sum of $100.00, to defray expenses of this meeting, and the following be the committee, viz:—Bros. P. E. Fitz-Patrick, ] A. Young, and R. Brockbank, to present the request at this session of Grand Lodge.

MAGGIE WADDELL,

*Secretary.*

The following, moved by P. E. Fitz-Patrick, seconded by Rep. R. Brockbank, was adopted :—

*Resolved,*—That the request of the Provincial Convention, Degree of Rebekah, be referred to the Committee on Finance, with instruction to recommend that an appropriation of $100 be made.

The following, moved by Bro. W. H. Cole, P.G M., was adopted :—

*Resolved,* That our Representative to the Sovereign Grand Lodge be instructed to procure such legislation that will permit of the Veteran Jewel being worn at all places, and on all occasions when it is legal to wear regalia, in lieu of regalia, by Brethren who own and are entitled to possess a Veteran Odd Fellow's Jewel.

No reports of committees being ready, the Grand Lodge, on motion to that effect, adjourned at 11:45 a.m. until 2 o'clock p.m.

---

## AFTERNOON SESSION.

---

NIAGARA FALLS, August 10, 1893.

The Grand Lodge re-assembled at two o'clock p.m., pursuant to adjournment, and opened in regular form. The minutes of the previous session were read and confirmed.

On motion, the calling of the roll was dispensed with.

**REPORT No. 5.**—Rep. S. M. Thompson, from Special Committee No. 1, made the following report, which was adopted :—

*To the Grand Lodge of Ontario, I.O.O.F. :*

Your Special Committee No. 1, to whom was referred Clause 16, page 13, Grand Master's Report *re* the Odd Fellows' Grand Demonstration, to be held at Chicago, on September 25th, beg leave to report :—

1. That this Grand Lodge should have an accredited Representative at that grand gathering of our Order, at the World's Fair.

2. That the Grand Master, Rev. Bro. T. W. Jolliffe, be such Representative.

3. That the Grand Lodge grant a sum not to exceed seventy-five dollars, for this purpose.

Your Committee therefore move the adoption of this report.

All of which is fraternally submitted.

S. M. THOMPSON.

**REPORT No. 6.**—Rep. J. H. Parnell, from Special Committee No. 4, made the following report, which on motion of Bro. W. H. Cole, P.G.M., was referred back to the Committee, with instructions to report in accordance with Clause 14 of the Grand Secretary's Report :—

(The Committee did not return this recommitted report, but submitted a new report agreeably to the motion of Bro. W. H. Cole.—GRAND SECY.)

**REPORT No. 7.**—Rep. Alf. Coyell, from the Special Committee on " Membership Souvenir," presented the following report, which was accompanied by a drawing, in colors, of the Souvenir, which was considered and adopted :—

*To the Grand Lodge of Ontario, I. O. O. F. :*

Your Committee on Membership Souvenir, appointed by the Grand Master, having fully considered the recommendation of the Grand Secretary and the report thereon by Special Committee No. 5, (Journal 1892, page 5337,) in which they are instructed to procure sample design and probable cost, have much pleasure in submitting for the approval of the Grand Lodge the accompanying design prepared by Messrs. Barclay, Clark & Co., the probable cost of which will be 10,000, $500.00 ; 20,000, $700.00 ; 25,000, $780.00; or 5 cents, $3\frac{1}{2}$ and $3\frac{3}{2}$ cents per copy.

Your Committee would strongly recommend that 25,000 copies of the same be procured by the Grand Lodge, the plate to be the property of the Grand Lodge for future use.

Your Committee would further recommend that each Lodge be required to furnish Grand Lodge, on a form to be supplied, a complete list of its members in good standing on the 30th June, 1893, with full particulars as to age, rank and standing, and further that the Grand Secretary be authorized on receipt of such completed list to send to each Lodge a filled up certificate for each member so reported, and that the certificate so filled be given to each member free of charge.

These elaborate certificates, procured in such quantities as would be required, will cost the Grand Body less than four cents per copy, and in giving to each Lodge the requisite number of certificates your Committee consider that the Body is but returning a portion of the funds contributed by itself.

Your Committee find that there is a growing desire among the members of the Order for some such Souvenir and which is supplied to their members by nearly all kindred organizations, and apparently very much appreciated by them, as they are to be seen neatly framed and hung in the homes of the members of the various orders which provide them.

Trusting that the Grand Lodge will see fit to adopt the foregoing recommendations, as your Committee deem it to be a matter of vital importance to the progress and propagation of our beloved Order, your Committee move the adoption of this report.

All of which is respectfully submitted.

ALFRED COYELL.

The roll of Lodges was now called when the following questions were submitted and referred to appropriate committees :—

## By Union Lodge, No. 16.

QUESTION—By resolution desires to know whether a Subordinate Lodge may reduce the amount of sick benefits at a less period than one year without conflicting with the laws of the Sovereign Grand Lodge providing clause 52 Constitution of Grand Lodge of Ontario was amended ?

Referred to the Judiciary Committee.

## By Rep. J. J. Craig, Fergus Lodge, No. 73.

QUESTION—Can a by-law be added to or explained by a simple motion on the books of the Lodge ?

Is custom or usage of any value in interpreting a by-law ?

Referred to the Judiciary Committee.

## By Rep. W. Hill, Peterborough Lodge, No. 111.

QUESTION—A Lodge which pays on the average over two dollars per week for sick benefits would it be lawful to adopt by-laws paying $4 00 per week for first six months, $2.00 per week for next six months and $1.00 per week thereafter ?

Referred to the Judiciary Committee.

The following by Rep. G. G. Henderson, Victoria Lodge, No. 64, was answered by the Chair in the affirmative, as to it being compulsory on Lodges to use the form of Medical Certificate provided by the Grand Lodge :—

QUESTION—Is it compulsory for Lodges to use the form of medical examination and certificate supplied by the Grand Lodge ; if so, how many Lodges in this jurisdiction are complying with the law ?

ANSWER—Yes.   See Clause 3, Con. of Subordinates ; a majority of Lodges are using the form, those Lodges not doing so should get a supply at once.

The following was referred to the Committee on Districts :—

*To the Grand Lodge of Ontario, I. O. O. F. :*

At the last regular meeting of Nipissing District, No. 29, the following resolution was carried :—

Sutton Lodge, No. 168, being unrepresented at each meeting, Dr. W. Robinson, seconded by Rep. Conway, moves, that it would be to the best interests of this district to disband the same and dispose of the Lodges in manner following, viz :—Place Naomi, No. 116, in Toronto District, No. 19 ; Nipissing, No. 79, and Sutton, No. 168, in Victoria District, No. 31 ; and Brougham, No. 155, in Ontario District, No. 30.   Above resolution met with the approval of all Lodges concerned, with the exception of Sutton, No. 168.

By Rep. F. J. Marshall, Grand Valley Lodge, No. 256:—

WHEREAS:—The forms issued by the Grand Lodge are the only forms that can be used by Subordinate Lodges as medical examination papers, and

WHEREAS:—Such forms are used and intended to procure a uniform examination of the candidates for admission into this Order, and

WHEREAS:—We believe it is necessary to further carry out the uniform admission to our Order,

We would submit the advisability of the Grand Lodge appointing a Medical Examiner to examine and pass all medical papers, same as regular life insurance companies before the applicant is admitted to the Initiatory Degree, and we would recommend that this be referred to a committee to consider the matter.

Referred to the Committee on Legislation.

**REPORT** No. 8.—Rep. J. T. Hornibrook P.G.M., from the Judiciary Committee, made the following report:—

*To the Grand Lodge of Ontario, I.O.O.F.* :

1. Your Committee on Judiciary, to whom was referred Secs. 27, 28, Grand Master's Report, recommend that decisions 1, 3, 4, 5, 6, 7, 8, 10, 13, 14, 17, 18, 20, 21, 22, 23, 24, be approved.

2. *Decision No. 2*—That all after the word claim be struck out.

3. *Decision No. 9*—Add "when the amount must be paid out of the Contingent Fund."

4. *Decision 11*—The Constitution and By-laws of the Lodge must govern in such cases.

5. *Decision 12*—Not approved, see Sec 359, 370, 371, 372.

6. *Decision 16*—Add after the word "theirs," "without the consent of said Lodge."

7. *Decision 15*—Not approved.

8. *Decision 19*—Approved. A Lodge has no right to compromise a claim for sick benefits.

9. Sec. 28—If Aylmer Lodge has paid all that their By-laws call for their contention in this matter is correct.

*Resolved.*—That the foregoing be adopted.

Fraternally submitted,

J. T. HORNIBROOK.

The report was on motion considered seriatim. Clauses 1, 2, 3, 4, 5, 6, 7, 8, were adopted.

The question being on the adoption of clause 9,

Rep. A. H. Blackeby moved that the consideration of clause 9, referring to Sec. xxviii of the Grand Master's Report *re* Aylmer and Ridgely Lodges be laid over until the Committee on

Appeals, to which the matter had been referred, should report, which was not agreed to.

The report as a whole was adopted.

It being now three o'clock, which hour had been set apart for the exemplification of the unwritten work, that order was proceeded with, when Grand Representatives W. H. Cole and Hy. Robertson, fully exemplified that work.

**REPORT No. 9.**—Rep. F. W. Armstrong, from the Committee on State of the Order, made the following report, which was adopted :—

*To the Grand Lodge of Ontario, I.O.O.F. :*

Your Committee on the State of the Order, to whom was referred clauses 17 and 18 of the Grand Master's Report, beg leave to report :—

That we heartily endorse the action of the Grand Master in acknowledging and congratulating our esteemed and worthy Bro. Dr. Cl. T. Campbell, on the honor conferred upon him by his elevation to the position of Grand Sire. We, as a Grand Body, highly appreciate this honor, and we trust that it may be an incentive to all Lodges in our jurisdiction to increased zeal and activity in the noble work.

May a kind and wise Providence so direct and order the steps of the Grand Sire, that he may fill the chair with credit to himself, with honor to his fellow-countrymen and with lasting benefit to our beloved Order throughout the world ; and when in due course of time he shall be called hence, may it be to a home where Friendship, Love and Truth are ever dominant; and where the links of Fraternity can never be broken.

*Resolved,*—that the foregoing be adopted.

All of which is respectfully submitted.

F. W. ARMSTRONG.

**REPORT No. 10.**—Rep A. W. Cameron, from the same Committee, made the following report, which was unanimously adopted, by a standing vote:—

*To the Grand Lodge of Ontario, I.O.O.F. :*

Your Committee on State of the Order to whom was referred section 9, Grand Master's Report, beg leave to report as follows :—

The Grand Master has during the past year paid some twenty-five visits to the Subordinate Lodges of Ontario.

It is gratifying to know that in all these visits our Grand Master was received " courteously and kindly." It is a pleasing duty for your Committee to be able to testify to the great good that has accrued to our Order as a direct result of these visits.

We would also bear willing testimony to the vigour and ability with which the principles of our Order have been vindicated by our Grand Master at public meetings and through the press when they were wantonly assailed ; this, with the ever increasing amount of correspondence and other duties appertaining to his office, all of which have been discharged with great fidelity, entitle him to the gratitude of the entire membership of this jurisdiction.

We therefore offer the following resolution :—

*Resolved.*—That the heartfelt thanks of this Grand Lodge are due and hereby tendered to our respected Grand Master, Rev. T. W. Jolliffe for his valued services during the past year.

Fraternally submitted,

A. W. CAMERON.

**REPORT No. 11.**—Rep. A. McFarlane, from the same Committee, made the following report, which was adopted :—

*To the Grand Lodge of Ontario, I.O.O.F. :*

Your Committee on the State of the Order, to whom was referred Clauses 3 and 12 of the Grand Master's Report, beg leave to report as follows :—

That having examined Clause 3, relative to Committees, approve of the same as appointed by said Grand Master, also approve of his action in the appointment of a D.D.G.M., as spoken of in Clause 12 of said report.

In regard to Clause 25, which was also submitted to said Committee would say, that while there is a difference of opinion among the members of the Committee, as regards the several plans suggested by the Committee of Representation, we think the thanks of this Grand Lodge are due to the members of said Committee for the pains they have taken in presenting their very carefully prepared report, and by the information attainable from aforesaid Clause, this Grand Lodge is in a position to discuss this very important matter and come to a decision as to the better method of representation.

We therefore submit for adoption the following :—

*Resolved,*—That this report be adopted.

All of which is respectfully submitted.

ALEX. McFARLANE.

**REPORT No. 12.**—Rep. J. B. Reid, from the Finance Committee, made the following report, which was adopted :—

*To the Grand Lodge of Ontario, I.O.O F. :*

Your Committee on Finance, to which was referred the request of Provincial Convention, Degree of Rebekah, asking for a grant of one hundred dollars, to help in defraying the expenses of their annual meeting of 1893, submit the following :—

Your Committee recommend that the request be granted, and that the sum of one hundred dollars be given to the Rebekah Convention.

Your Committee, however, at the same time, would express the hope, that the growth of the Rebekah branch of Oddfellowship in Ontario, will be rapid enough to prevent any further demands of this nature being made upon this Grand Lodge.

Your Committee move the adoption of this report.

Respectfully submitted.

J. B. REID.

**REPORT No. 13.**—Rep. A. A. Graham, from the Committee on the Rebekah Degree, made the following report, which was adopted :—

*To the Grand Lodge of Ontario, I.O.O.F., in session :*

Your Committee on Rebekah Degree report as follows :—

Clauses i. and ii. Grand Master's Report, your Committee recommend that Charters be granted to new Lodges which have been instituted.

Clause 22 Grand Master's Report, your Committee heartily endorse the remarks of the Grand Master.

Clause 19, Grand Secretary's Report, your Committee would suggest that the question of consideration of Constitution for Rebekah Lodges be left over until after the meeting of Sovereign Grand Lodge in September, that body having the same question under consideration by Special Committee.

Your Committee endorse that clause 19 of the Grand Secretary's Report *re* all Lodges of the Rebekah Degree being required to adopt, and have printed within three months after institution, a code of by-laws, rules of order, &c.

Your Committee recommend that this Grand Lodge give every assistance and the fullest encouragement and aid, in the furthering the spread of the Rebekah Degree in this Province, and would suggest that an efficient way to do so, would be by instructing the D.D.G. Masters of the various districts to use their influence when making official visits to aid the Degree of Rebekah, more especially in districts where no Lodges of the Rebekah Degree exists. But that any legislation affecting the definition of duties of Officers of Rebekah Convention, be laid over until after the meeting of Sovereign Grand Lodge in September, at which that matter will doubtless receive full consideration.

All of which is respectfully submitted.

*Resolved,*—That the foregoing be adopted

A. A. GRAHAM.

The following, on motion of Rep. Jno. Nott, seconded by Rep. S. H. Glassford, was adopted :—

*Resolved,*—That the thanks of this Grand Lodge be, and are hereby tendered to the Dominion Organ and Piano Company, of the town of Bowmanville, through the Grand Guardian, for their generous gift of a supply of fans for the use of the members of this Grand Lodge during this session.

On motion of Rep. J. A. Young, the Grand Master wired the following message of congratulation to the Grand Lodge of Massachusetts, now in session at Boston :—

*To James M. Price, Grand Master I.O.O.F., Boston, Mass. :*

Twenty-one thousand Odd Fellows of Ontario, Canada, in Grand Lodge assembled, and the Grand Sire, send their most cordial and fraternal greeting, to the Grand Lodge of Massachusetts, with best wishes for their continued prosperity.

T. W. JOLLIFFE,<br>
Grand Master.

Bro. Neil McEachren, P.G., of Buffalo, N.Y., was introduced to the Grand Lodge by Bro. W. H. Cole, P.G.M., and cordially welcomed by the Grand Master.

**REPORT No. 14**—Rep. R. W. Bell, P.G.M., from the Committee on Petitions and Correspondence, made the following report, which was adopted :—

*To the Grand Lodge of Ontario, I.O.O.F. :*

Your Committee on Petitions and Correspondence to whom was referred Clause xxxii. to the end of the Grand Master's Report, and Clause 10, Grand Secretary's Report, recommend as follows :—

That of Clause 32, the first and third paragraphs *re* employment of a paid organizer, and remuneration of the Grand Master be referred to Committee on State of the Order; that paragraph two *re* representation in this Grand Lodge, will be dealt with by the Special Committee on that subject; that regarding the fourth paragraph we cannot recommend the sale of supplies at actual cost, as such would necessitate an increase of Capitation Tax, which we feel is not in the interest of this Grand Lodge; that in regard to the recommendation from District No. 13, this Grand Lodge has no power to adopt such resolution.

In reference to Clause 33, we are heartily in accord with the views therein expressed and recommend the District Deputy Grand Masters to call the special attention of the Lodges in their Districts to the admonitions therein contained.

Regarding Clause xxxiv., Grand Master's Report, and Clause 10, Grand Secretary's Report, we are pleased to learn that the funds of Wellington Square Lodge have been restored to it, and trust with the Grand Master that prosperity may attend the brethren.

Referring to Clause 35 Grand Master's Report, we are pleased to note the courtesy and promptitude of the Grand Master in his correspondence during the past year, and can only reiterate the instructions of previous years that Lodges refer all matters coming under the jurisdiction of the D.D.G.M.'s to them, and so relieve the Grand Master of needless labour.

From Clause 36, Grand Master's Report, we are pleased to learn that the Grand Master has received such hearty co-operation from his D.D.G.M's, also from various Grand and Past Grand Officers, and trust the same courtesy and assistance may be extended to his successor.

All of which is respectfully submitted.

*Resolved,*—That the foregoing be adopted.

R. W. BELL.

**REPORT No. 15**—Rep. P. McCandlish, from the Committee on State of the Order, made the following report, which was adopted :—

*To the Grand Lodge of Ontario, I.O.O.F. ;*

Your Committee on State of the Order, beg leave to report as follows :—

Clause 1, Grand Master's Report, we confirm the action of the Grand Master and recommend that Charters be granted to the following new Lodges, viz :—

| | | | |
|---|---|---|---|
| Minnetonka | Lodge, | No. 292 | Keewatin. |
| Thomasburg | " | " 293 | Thomasburg. |
| Broadview | " | " 294 | Toronto. |
| Mannotick | " | " 295 | Mannotick. |
| Pontypool | " | " 296 | Pontypool. |
| Mayflower | " | " 297 | Parham. |
| Comber | " | " 294 | Comber |

and that the placing of these Lodges in the proper districts be left to the Committee on Districts.

Also Clause xi., Grand Master's Report,

Your Committee find that during the year two Lodges lost their effects from fire, one of whom has had its Charter destroyed, and is now working under a dispensation, they would therefore recommend that a Charter be granted said Lodge, viz :—Brougham, No. 155, Whitevale.

All of which is respectfully submitted.

P. McCANDLISH.

**REPORT No. 16**—Rep. A. B. Hurrell, from the Special Committee No. 3, made the following report, which was adopted :—

*To the Grand Lodge of Ontario, I.O O.F :*

Your Special Committee to which was referred Clause 6, of the Grand Secretary's Report, having reference to reduced rates on the several lines of railways and steamboats, beg to report :—

Your Committee are gratified to know that the growth of the Order is such that the most favorable terms of transportation for its officers and representatives have been arranged for.

Your Committee would recommend that the thanks of the Grand Lodge, be tendered to Mr. Maloney, the vising agent of the Transportation Companies for courtesies extended by him.

Your Committee move the adoption of this report.

All of which is respectfully submitted.

A. B. HURRELL.

**REPORT No. 17**—Rep. Jno. Donogh, P.G.M., from Committee on State of the Order, made the following report, which was adopted :—

*To the Grand Lodge of Ontario, I.O.O.F. :*

Your Committee on State of the Order, to whom was referred Clause—Grand Master's Report, beg leave to report the following :—

As to Tottenham Lodge, No. 255, your Committee recommend that the incoming Grand Master give special attention to the case of this Lodge, and if it be found impossible to revive it, that steps be taken for its amalgamation with some neighbouring Lodge, so that the members may be saved to the Order.

2. With reference to Fidelity Lodge No. 55, Seaforth, it is evident that if anything is done in the way of winding up the Lodge, it must be done through the agency of the members themselves and they should be incited to use every legitimate social influence to stir up interest and activity. We commend the suggestion made by Bro. Blackeby in his report to the Grand Master, and we believe this to be a case which calls for the supervision of the Grand Master.

3. The Clinton Lodge, No. 83, Clinton, is another Lodge which calls for the fostering care and sympathetic assistance of neighboring Lodges and we recommend that the Grand Master give special oversight to this case

*Resolved,*—That the foregoing be adopted.

JOHN DONOGH.

**REPORT No. 18**—Rep. M. L. Weber, from the Committee on Mileage and Per Diem, made the following report and table of Mileage and Per Diem, which was adopted :—

MILEAGE AND PER DIEM, SESSION 1893, AT NIAGARA FALLS.

| Officers. | No. | Location. | Miles Travelled. | Mileage | No. of Days. | Per Diem. | Total. |
|---|---|---|---|---|---|---|---|
| Rev. T. W. Jolliffe, Grand Master.... | ...... | Campbellford... | 220 | $11 00 | 3 | $6 00 | $17 00 |
| Joseph Oliver, Deputy Grand Master.. | ...... | Toronto ........ | 83 | 4 15 | 3 | 6 00 | 10 15 |
| W. H. Hoyle, Grand Warden.... .... | ...... | Cannington .... | 142 | 7 10 | 3 | 6 00 | 13 10 |
| J. B. King, Grand Secretary ......... | ..... | Toronto ....... | 83 | 4 15 | 5 | 10 00 | 14 15 |
| Wm. Badenach, Grand Treasurer...... | ...... | " ........ | 83 | 4 15 | 3 | 6 00 | 10 15 |
| W. H. Cole, Grand Representative... | ...... | Brockville...... | 294 | 14 70 | 3 | 6 00 | 20 70 |
| H'y. Robertson, " " | ...... | Collingwood ... | 170 | 8 50 | 3 | 6 00 | 14 50 |
| O. E. Fleming, Grand Marshal........ | ...... | Windsor ........ | 229 | 11 45 | 3 | 6 00 | 17 45 |
| Robt. Meek, Grand Conductor ........ | .... | Kingston ...... | 245 | 12 25 | 3 | 6 00 | 18 25 |
| A. Mitchell, Grand Guardian.......... | ...... | Bowmanville ... | 127 | 6 35 | 3 | 6 00 | 12 35 |
| I. B. Aulph, Grand Herald. ......... | ..... | Bracebridge .... | 205 | 10 25 | 3 | 6 00 | 16 25 |
| Rev. Wm. J. Saunders, Grand Chaplain. | .... | Lonsdale ....... | 210 | 10 50 | 3 | 6 00 | 16 50 |
| P. E. Fitz-Patrick, Junior P.G.M. ... | ...... | Hamilton ...... | 44 | 2 20 | 3 | 6 00 | 8 20 |
| | | | 2135 | 106 75 | 41 | 82 00 | 188 75 |

| Name of Lodge. | No. | Location. | Miles Travelled. | Mileage | No. of Days. | Per Diem. | Total. | Name of Representative. |
|---|---|---|---|---|---|---|---|---|
| Brock ......................... | 9 | Brockville...... | 294 | 14 70 | 3 | 6 00 | 20 70 | W. J. Simpson. |
| " ...................... | 9 | " ...... | 294 | 14 70 | 3 | 6 00 | 20 70 | A. Y. Kendall. |
| Cataraqui ... ................. | 10 | Kingston....... | 245 | 12 25 | 3 | 6 00 | 18 25 | F. R. Sargent. |
| " .................. | 10 | " .... | 245 | 12 25 | 3 | 6 00 | 18 25 | W. J. Moore. |
| " .................. | 10 | " ...... | 245 | 12 25 | 3 | 6 00 | 18 25 | J. S. R. McCann. |
| Otonabee .................... | 13 | Peterborough... | 166 | 8 30 | 2 | 6 00 | 14 30 | R. W. Bell, P.G.M. |
| " .................. | 13 | " | 166 | 8 30 | 3 | 6 00 | 14 30 | W. Mowey. |
| Union . .................... | 16 | St. Catherines.. | 12 | 60 | 3 | 6 00 | 6 60 | J. B. McIntyre, P.G.M. |
| " ................... | 16 | " | 12 | 60 | 3 | 6 00 | 6 60 | N. A. Lindsay. |
| " ................... | 16 | " | 12 | 60 | 3 | 6 00 | 6 60 | C. J. Moore. |
| Phœnix .................... | 22 | Oshawa ........ | 117 | 5 85 | 3 | 6 00 | 11 85 | R. McPherson. |
| Rose ..................... | 28 | Amherstburgh.. | 238 | 11 50 | 3 | 6 00 | 17 90 | H'y. Y. Pickering. |
| Chatham ................... | 29 | Chatham ...... | 184 | 9 20 | 3 | 6 00 | 15 20 | Jno. B. Kitchen. |
| " .................. | 29 | " ...... | 184 | 9 20 | 3 | 6 00 | 15 20 | W. L. G. Snell. |
| Eureka ................... | 30 | London ........ | 120 | 6 00 | 3 | 6 00 | 12 00 | Geo. Powell, Jr. |

| Lodge | No. | Place | | | | | | Representative |
|---|---|---|---|---|---|---|---|---|
| Eureka | 30 | London | 120 | 6 00 | 3 | 6 00 | 12 00 | Jno. Hunter. |
| Elgin | 32 | St. Thomas | 136 | 6 80 | 3 | 6 00 | 12 80 | Wm. Cross. |
| " | 32 | " | 136 | 6 80 | 3 | 6 00 | 12 80 | J. F. Brown. |
| " | 32 | " | 136 | 6 80 | 3 | 6 00 | 12 80 | W. E. Cox. |
| Erie | 33 | Port Burwell | 133 | 6 65 | 3 | 6 00 | 12 65 | J. H. Hoahal. |
| Gore | 34 | Brantford | 72 | 3 60 | 3 | 6 00 | 9 60 | Jas. Woodyatt, P.G.M. |
| " | 34 | " | 72 | 3 60 | 3 | 6 00 | 9 60 | Thos. Woodyatt. |
| " | 34 | " | 72 | 3 60 | 3 | 6 00 | 9 60 | Maxwell A. Craig. |
| Samaritan | 35 | Ingersoll | 101 | 5 05 | 3 | 6 00 | 11 05 | A. J. Johnston. |
| " | 35 | " | 101 | 5 05 | 3 | 6 00 | 11 05 | A. W. Bell. |
| St. Mary's | 36 | St. Mary's | 114 | 5 70 | 3 | 6 00 | 11 70 | Archie Baird. |
| " | 36 | " | 114 | 5 70 | 3 | 6 00 | 11 70 | Wm. Box. |
| Forest City | 38 | London | 120 | 6 00 | 3 | 6 00 | 12 00 | Wm. Maddiford. |
| " | 38 | " | 120 | 6 00 | 3 | 6 00 | 12 00 | R. J. C. Dawson. |
| Rondeau | 40 | Blenheim | 197 | 9 85 | 3 | 6 00 | 15 85 | W. H. Stephenson. |
| " | 40 | " | 197 | 9 85 | 3 | 6 00 | 15 85 | R. L. Gusnell. |
| Avon | 41 | Stratford | 103 | 5 15 | 3 | 6 00 | 11 15 | H'y. Baker. |
| " | 41 | " | 103 | 5 15 | 3 | 6 00 | 11 15 | Samuel Towner. |
| " | 41 | " | 103 | 5 15 | 3 | 6 00 | 11 15 | Samuel H. Weir. |
| Excelsior | 44 | Hamilton | 44 | 2 20 | 3 | 6 00 | 8 20 | Ernest Schultz. |
| " | 44 | " | 44 | 2 20 | 3 | 6 00 | 8 20 | A. C. Brunke. |
| Frontier | 45 | Windsor | 229 | 11 45 | 3 | 6 00 | 17 45 | F. C. Cassady. |
| " | 45 | " | 229 | 11 45 | 3 | 6 00 | 17 45 | J. R. Thomson. |
| Mount Zion | 46 | Newbury | 157 | 7 85 | 3 | 6 00 | 13 85 | C. Tucker. |
| Unity | 47 | Hamilton | 44 | 2 20 | 3 | 6 00 | 8 20 | T. B. S. Austin. |
| " | 47 | " | 44 | 2 20 | 3 | 6 00 | 8 20 | P. M. Candlish. |
| " | 47 | " | 44 | 2 20 | 3 | 6 00 | 8 20 | D. Moore. |
| Dominion | 48 | London | 120 | 6 00 | 3 | 6 00 | 12 00 | C. J. Wall. |
| " | 48 | " | 120 | 6 00 | 3 | 6 00 | 12 00 | W. F. Howell. |
| Canada | 49 | Toronto | 83 | 4 15 | 3 | 6 00 | 10 15 | F. Smith. |
| " | 49 | " | 83 | 4 15 | 3 | 6 00 | 10 15 | W. Menzies. |
| " | 49 | " | 83 | 4 15 | 3 | 6 00 | 10 15 | A. Coyell. |
| Otter | 50 | Tilsonburg | 104 | 5 20 | 3 | 6 00 | 11 20 | Geo. Geddes. |
| " | 50 | " | 104 | 5 20 | 3 | 6 00 | 11 20 | W. S. Buckborrough. |
| Bissell | 51 | Mitchell | 116 | 5 80 | 3 | 6 00 | 11 80 | Isaac Hord.　　[M. |
| Covenant | 52 | Toronto | 83 | 4 15 | 3 | 6 90 | 10 15 | J. T. Hornibrook, P.G. |
| " | 52 | " | 83 | 4 15 | 3 | 6 00 | 10 15 | H. Gilby. |
| Niagara Falls | 53 | Niagara Falls | | | 3 | 6 00 | 6 00 | J. R. Peckham. |
| " | 53 | " | | | 3 | 6 00 | 6 00 | Jno. Blair. |
| Collingwood | 54 | Collingwood | 170 | 8 50 | 3 | 6 00 | 14 50 | A. Chellen. |

MILEAGE AND PER DIEM, SESSION 1893, AT NIAGARA FALLS—*Continued.*

| Name of Lodge. | No. | Location. | Miles Travelled. | Mileage | No. of Days. | Per Diem. | Total. | Name of Representative. |
|---|---|---|---|---|---|---|---|---|
| Collingwood | 54 | Collingwood | 170 | $8 50 | 3 | $6 00 | $14 50 | A. McFadden. |
| Fidelity | 55 | Seaforth | 125 | 6 25 | 3 | 6 00 | 12 25 | Henry Town. |
| Queen City of Ontario | 56 | Toronto | 83 | 4 15 | 3 | 6 00 | 10 15 | John Donogh, P.G.M. |
| " | 56 | " | 83 | 4 15 | 3 | 6 00 | 10 15 | A. A. Graham. |
| Maple Leaf | 57 | Orangeville | 132 | 6 60 | 3 | 6 00 | 12 60 | D. B. Brown. |
| Howard | 58 | Strathroy | 142 | 7 10 | 3 | 6 00 | 13 10 | O. L. Berdan. |
| " | 58 | " | 142 | 7 10 | 3 | 6 00 | 13 10 | W. E. Todd. |
| Kingston | 59 | Kingston | 245 | 12 25 | 3 | 6 00 | 18 25 | Jno. Bullis. |
| " | 59 | " | 245 | 12 25 | 3 | 6 00 | 18 25 | G. W. Maxwell. |
| " | 59 | " | 245 | 12 25 | 3 | 6 00 | 18 25 | Geo. Lee. |
| Corinthian | 61 | Oshawa | 117 | 5 85 | 3 | 6 00 | 11 85 | Wm. Janes. |
| " | 61 | " | 117 | 5 85 | 3 | 6 00 | 11 85 | H. Jacobi. |
| " | 61 | " | 117 | 5 85 | 3 | 6 00 | 11 85 | C. Vanalstine. |
| Huron | 62 | Goderich | 148 | 7 40 | 3 | 6 00 | 13 40 | George Porter. |
| " | 62 | " | 148 | 7 40 | 3 | 6 00 | 13 40 | G. H. Nairn. |
| Barrie | 63 | Barrie | 139 | 6 95 | 3 | 6 00 | 12 95 | Alex. Brownlee. |
| " | 63 | " | 139 | 6 95 | 3 | 6 00 | 12 95 | Geo. Vickers, Sr. |
| Victoria | 64 | Hamilton | 44 | 2 20 | 3 | 6 00 | 8 20 | G. C. Henderson. |
| Friendship | 65 | Petrolia | 172 | 8 60 | 3 | 6 00 | 14 60 | J. J. Mathews. |
| " | 65 | " | 172 | 8 60 | 3 | 6 00 | 14 60 | Alex. Simpson. |
| Florence Nightingale | 66 | Bowmanville | 127 | 6 35 | 3 | 6 00 | 12 35 | Julius Roenigk. |
| " | 66 | " | 127 | 6 35 | 3 | 6 00 | 12 35 | Jno. McIntyre. |
| Exeter | 67 | Exeter | 151 | 7 55 | 3 | 6 00 | 13 55 | H'y. Lambrooke. |
| North Star | 68 | Stayner | 156 | 7 80 | 3 | 6 00 | 13 80 | J. W Shepherd. |
| Hope | 69 | Harrietsville | 119 | 5 95 | 3 | 6 00 | 11 95 | Wm. Barr. [M. |
| Lucan | 70 | Lucan | 129 | 6 45 | 3 | 6 00 | 12 45 | W. Macdiarmid, P.G. |
| The Toronto | 71 | Toronto | 83 | 4 15 | 3 | 6 00 | 10 15 | E. M. Clapp. |
| Eastern Star | 72 | Whitby | 115 | 5 75 | 3 | 6 00 | 11 75 | W. Robson. |
| " | 72 | " | 115 | 5 75 | 3 | 6 00 | 11 75 | J. E. Farewell. |
| Fergus | 73 | Fergus | 106 | 5 30 | 3 | 6 00 | 11 30 | J. J. Craig. |
| Bothwell | 74 | Bothwell | 162 | 8 10 | 3 | 6 00 | 14 10 | Geo. L. Taylor. |
| Warriner | 75 | Port Perry | 133 | 6 65 | 3 | 6 00 | 12 65 | John Nott. |

| Lodge | No. | Town | Members | | | | | Name |
|---|---|---|---|---|---|---|---|---|
| St. Thomas | 76 | St. Thomas | 136 | 6 80 | 3 | 6 00 | 12 80 | Fred. Doggett. |
| " | 76 | " | 136 | 6 80 | 3 | 6 00 | 12 80 | Jno. Waddell. |
| " | 76 | " | 136 | 6 80 | 3 | 6 00 | 12 80 | S. W. Down. |
| Oxford | 77 | Ingersoll | 101 | 5 05 | 3 | 6 00 | 11 05 | J. H. Ackert. |
| " | 77 | " | 101 | 5 05 | 3 | 6 00 | 11 05 | E. F. Waterhouse. |
| Durham | 78 | Port Hope | 147 | 7 35 | 3 | 6 00 | 13 35 | H'y. White. |
| " | 78 | " | 147 | 7 35 | 3 | 6 00 | 13 35 | J. H. Magill. |
| Nipissing | 79 | Uxbridge | 125 | 6 25 | 3 | 6 00 | 12 25 | J. H. Bustin. |
| Amity | 80 | Prescott | 304 | 15 20 | 3 | 6 00 | 21 20 | William Jacobs. |
| " | 80 | " | 304 | 15 20 | 3 | 6 00 | 21 20 | James Wilkin. |
| " | 80 | " | 304 | 15 20 | 3 | 6 00 | 21 20 | W. Rowe. |
| Belleville | 81 | Belleville | 196 | 9 80 | 3 | 6 00 | 15 80 | L. C. Pascoe. |
| " | 81 | " | 196 | 9 80 | 3 | 6 00 | 15 80 | Allan McFee. |
| " | 81 | " | 196 | 9 80 | 3 | 6 00 | 15 80 | J. A. Coon. |
| Beaver | 82 | Ruthven | 262 | 13 10 | 3 | 6 00 | 19 10 | C. C. Lypps. |
| Clinton | 83 | Clinton | 142 | 7 10 | 3 | 6 00 | 13 10 | S. S. Cooper. |
| Walkerton | 84 | Walkerton | 159 | 7 95 | 3 | 6 00 | 13 95 | Richard Lee. |
| Constellation | 85 | Burgessville | 102 | 5 10 | 3 | 6 00 | 11 10 | Henry Sneath. |
| Napanee | 86 | Napanee | 217 | 10 85 | 3 | 6 00 | 16 85 | G. B. Joy. |
| Empire | 87 | St. Catharines | 12 | 60 | 3 | 6 00 | 6 60 | W. H. Fletcher. |
| " | 87 | " | 12 | 60 | 3 | 6 00 | 6 60 | J. W. Grote. |
| Olive Branch | 88 | Woodstock | 92 | 4 60 | 3 | 6 00 | 10 60 | H. M. Bausbaugh. |
| " | 88 | " | 92 | 4 60 | 3 | 6 00 | 10 60 | John Mitchell. |
| Reliance | 89 | Guelph | 92 | 4 60 | 3 | 6 00 | 10 60 | John J. Cormie. |
| " | 89 | " | 92 | 4 60 | 3 | 6 00 | 10 60 | Roderick McLeod. |
| Ivy | 90 | Parkhill | 143 | 7 15 | 3 | 6 00 | 13 15 | Jno. Hamilton. |
| Grand River | 91 | Paris | 73 | 3 65 | 3 | 6 00 | 9 65 | John Flanagan. |
| " | 91 | " | 73 | 3 65 | 3 | 6 00 | 9 65 | Richard Brockbank. |
| Milton | 92 | Milton | 69 | 3 45 | 3 | 6 00 | 9 45 | Wm. McKenzie. |
| Western City | 93 | Chatham | 184 | 9 20 | 3 | 6 00 | 15 20 | A. M. Lafferty. |
| Aylmer | 94 | Aylmer | 126 | 6 30 | 3 | 6 00 | 12 30 | James McNally. |
| " | 94 | " | 126 | 6 00 | 3 | 6 00 | 12 30 | Wm. Warnock. |
| Nith | 96 | New Hamburg | 117 | 5 85 | 3 | 6 00 | 11 85 | Alex. Fraser. |
| Grand Union | 97 | Berlin | 104 | 5 20 | 3 | 6 00 | 11 20 | Jacob Baltz. |
| Minto | 98 | Harriston | 138 | 6 90 | 3 | 6 00 | 12 90 | J. L. Binns. |
| Lindsay | 100 | Lindsay | 153 | 7 65 | 3 | 6 00 | 13 65 | Geo. Lytle. |
| Golden Star | 101 | Brampton | 90 | 4 50 | 3 | 6 00 | 10 50 | J. J. Manning. |
| Deseronto | 102 | Deseronto | 217 | 10 85 | 3 | 6 00 | 16 85 | H. W. Solmes. |
| Cataract | 103 | Niagara Falls S. | .... | ...... | 3 | 6 00 | 6 00 | J. K. Herderson. |
| Crescent | 104 | Hamilton | 44 | 2 20 | 3 | 6 00 | 8 20 | W. R. Webb. |

## MILEAGE AND PER DIEM, SESSION 1893, AT NIAGARA FALLS—*Continued.*

| NAME OF LODGE. | No. | Location. | Miles Travelled. | Mileage | No. of Days. | Per Diem. | Total. | Name of Representative. |
|---|---|---|---|---|---|---|---|---|
| Crescent | 104 | Hamilton | 44 | $2 20 | 3 | $6 00 | $8 20 | W. C. Smith. |
| " | 104 | " | 44 | 2 20 | 3 | 6 00 | 8 20 | John Fotheringham. |
| Manilla | 105 | Manilla | 147 | 7 35 | 3 | 6 00 | 13 35 | Dr. A Gillespie. |
| St. Clair | 106 | Point Edward | 184 | 9 20 | 3 | 6 00 | 15 20 | C. Sanders. |
| Waterloo | 107 | Galt | 75 | 3 75 | 3 | 6 00 | 9 75 | C. L. McWilliams. |
| " | 107 | " | 75 | 3 75 | 3 | 6 00 | 9 75 | W. A. Dennis. |
| Royal Oak | 108 | Forest | 162 | 8 10 | 3 | 6 00 | 14 10 | Henry Barron. |
| Orion | 109 | Georgetown | 81 | 4 05 | 3 | 6 00 | 10 05 | W. A. Millar. |
| Laurel | 110 | Toronto | 83 | 4 15 | 3 | 6 00 | 10 15 | Chas. Collett. |
| Peterboro' | 111 | Pererborough | 166 | 8 30 | 3 | 6 00 | 14 30 | D. H. Moore. |
| " | 111 | " | 166 | 8 30 | 3 | 6 00 | 14 30 | W. Hill. |
| " | 111 | " | 166 | 8 30 | 3 | 6 00 | 14 30 | A. McIntosh. |
| Lucknow | 112 | Lucknow | 184 | 9 20 | 3 | 6 00 | 15 20 | D. Sheriff. |
| " | 112 | " | 184 | 9 20 | 3 | 6 00 | 15 20 | A. Ross. |
| Trenton | 113 | Trenton | 184 | 9 20 | 3 | 6 00 | 15 20 | Rev. W. F. Armstrong |
| Gananoque | 114 | Gananoque | 269 | 13 45 | 3 | 6 00 | 19 45 | John Ormiston. |
| " | 114 | " | 269 | 13 45 | 3 | 6 00 | 19 45 | T. O. Middleton. |
| " | 114 | " | 269 | 13 45 | 3 | 6 00 | 19 45 | Geo. Toner. |
| Harmony | 115 | Brantford | 72 | 3 60 | 3 | 6 00 | 9 60 | Robert Peirce. |
| " | 115 | " | 72 | 3 60 | 3 | 6 00 | 9 60 | S. M. Thomson. |
| Naomi | 116 | Markham | 105 | 5 25 | 3 | 6 00 | 11 25 | W. Robinson. |
| Valley City | 117 | Dundas | 51 | 2 55 | 3 | 6 00 | 8 55 | F. A. Latshaw. |
| " | 117 | " | 51 | 2 55 | 3 | 6 00 | 8 55 | W. Mitson. |
| Maitland | 119 | Wingham | 172 | 8 60 | 3 | 6 00 | 14 60 | Robert Allan. |
| Sydenham Valley | 120 | Wallaceburg | 208 | 10 40 | 3 | 6 00 | 16 40 | A. L. Shambleau. |
| " | 120 | " | 208 | 10 40 | 3 | 6 00 | 16 40 | D. Logan. |
| Saxon | 121 | Ailsa Craig | 137 | 6 85 | 3 | 6 00 | 12 85 | John D. Shipley. |
| Streetsville | 122 | Streetsville | 105 | 5 25 | 3 | 6 00 | 11 25 | Wm. McKeith. |
| Dresden | 124 | Dresden | 197 | 9 85 | 3 | 6 00 | 15 85 | W. H. Pollock. |
| " | 124 | " | 197 | 9 85 | 3 | 6 00 | 15 85 | Jas. King, Jr. |
| Stella | 125 | Carleton Place | 317 | 15 85 | 3 | 6 00 | 21 85 | W. H. Allen. |
| " | 125 | " | 317 | 15 85 | 3 | 6 00 | 21 85 | N. D. McCallum. |

| | | | | | | | | |
|---|---|---|---|---|---|---|---|---|
| Sarnia | 126 | Sarnia | 181 | 9 05 | 3 | 6 00 | 15 05 | E. P. Bately. |
| Mizpah | 127 | Belleville | 196 | 9 80 | 3 | 6 00 | 15 80 | F. M. Clarke. |
| " | 127 | " | 196 | 9 80 | 3 | 6 00 | 15 80 | John Cornelius. |
| Charity | 129 | Sunderland | 136 | 6 80 | 3 | 6 00 | 12 80 | N. McPhadden. |
| Livingstone | 130 | Thorold | 11 | 55 | 3 | 6 00 | 6 55 | Peter Steep. |
| Marion | 131 | Renfrew | 318 | 15 90 | 3 | 6 00 | 21 90 | A. W. Easton. |
| Oakville | 132 | Oakville | 62 | 3 10 | 3 | 6 00 | 9 10 | Robert Buzzard. |
| Glencoe | 133 | Glencoe | 150 | 7 50 | ...... | ......... | 13 50 | Jas. Harris. |
| Orient | 134 | Welland | 17 | 85 | 3 | 6 00 | 6 85 | Casper Ramey. |
| Peaceful Dove | 135 | Cannington | 142 | 7 10 | 3 | 6 00 | 13 10 | S. H. Glassford. |
| Cobourg | 136 | Cobourg | 152 | 7 60 | 3 | 6 00 | 13 60 | Wm. Russell. |
| St. Lawrence | 137 | Brockville | 302 | 15 10 | 3 | 6 00 | 21 10 | Chas. H. Frost. |
| " | 137 | " | 302 | 15 10 | 3 | 6 00 | 21 10 | D. Matheson. |
| Ancaster | 138 | Ancaster | 50 | 2 50 | 3 | 6 00 | 8 50 | A. Bradshaw. |
| Garnet | 139 | Mount Forest | 144 | 7 20 | 3 | 6 00 | 13 20 | Jno. Corley. |
| Leamington | 140 | Leamington | 273 | 13 65 | 3 | 6 00 | 19 65 | James Neil. |
| " | 140 | " | 273 | 13 65 | 3 | 6 00 | 19 65 | Jos. M. Henry. |
| Concord | 142 | Kingsville | 259 | 12 95 | 3 | 6 00 | 18 95 | M. G. Brethor. |
| Bay of Quinte | 143 | Picton | 217 | 10 85 | 3 | 6 00 | 16 85 | R. H. McKenna. |
| " | 143 | " | 217 | 10 85 | 3 | 6 00 | 16 85 | W. R. Powles. |
| Ridgetown | 144 | Ridgetown | 174 | 8 70 | 3 | 6 00 | 14 70 | S. J. Staples. |
| " | 144 | " | 174 | 8 70 | 3 | 6 00 | 14 70 | F. Eansor. |
| Vivian | 146 | Arnprior | 344 | 17 20 | 3 | 6 00 | 23 20 | Jno. S. Moir. |
| Model | 147 | Wyoming | 165 | 8 25 | 3 | 6 00 | 14 25 | Willi Hartley. |
| Aurora | 148 | Aurora | 114 | 5 70 | 3 | 6 00 | 11 70 | C. Collett. |
| Western Star | 149 | Brussels | 160 | 8 00 | 3 | 6 00 | 14 00 | Wm. Martin. |
| Sycamore | 151 | Arkona | 162 | 8 10 | 3 | 6 00 | 14 10 | Eli Detwiler. |
| Hayden | 152 | Norwich | 92 | 4 60 | 3 | 6 00 | 10 60 | J. M. McAllister. |
| Wildey | 153 | Granton | 174 | 8 70 | 3 | 6 00 | 14 70 | Jno. E. Murray. |
| Alpha | 154 | Almonte | 327 | 16 35 | 3 | 6 00 | 22 35 | Jos. Symington. |
| " | 154 | " | 327 | 16 35 | 3 | 6 00 | 22 35 | A. Fumerton. |
| Brougham | 155 | Whitevale | 112 | 5 60 | 3 | 6 00 | 11 60 | Samuel Pencock. |
| Pyramid | 156 | Newmarket | 118 | 5 90 | 3 | 6 00 | 11 90 | E. McCormick. |
| Thamesville | 157 | Thamesville | 170 | 8 50 | 3 | 6 00 | 14 50 | J. Davidson. |
| Progress | 158 | Guelph | 92 | 4 60 | 3 | 6 00 | 10 60 | R. A. Snider. |
| " | 158 | " | 92 | 4 60 | 3 | 6 00 | 10 60 | Geo. J. Brill. |
| Oak Leaf | 159 | Hamilton | 44 | 2 20 | 3 | 6 00 | 8 20 | W. K. Wilson. |
| Listowel | 160 | Listowell | 142 | 7 10 | 3 | 6 00 | 13 10 | J. E. Terhune. |
| Simcoe | 161 | Simcoe | 84 | 4 20 | 3 | 6 00 | 10 20 | H. Johnston. |
| Oriental | 163 | Cornwall | 350 | 17 50 | 3 | 6 00 | 23 50 | E. Oliver. |

12

MILEAGE AND PER DIEM, SESSION 1893, AT NIAGARA FALLS—*Continued.*

| Name of Lodge. | No. | Location. | Miles Travelled. | Mileage | No. of Days. | Per Diem. | Total. | Name of Representative. |
|---|---|---|---|---|---|---|---|---|
| Romeo | 164 | Stratford | 103 | $5 15 | 3 | $6 00 | $11 15 | Joseph Casson. |
| " | 164 | " | 103 | 5 15 | 3 | 6 00 | 11 15 | Peter McNab. |
| Beethoven | 165 | Brooklin | 120 | 6 00 | 3 | 6 00 | 12 00 | T. Wickett. |
| Hillsburgh | 167 | Hillsburg | 140 | 7 00 | 3 | 6 00 | 13 00 | Jas. Carmicheal. |
| Sutton | 168 | Sutton | 133 | 6 65 | 3 | 6 00 | 12 65 | Thos. B. Bentley |
| Grey | 169 | Durham | 162 | 8 10 | 3 | 6 00 | 14 10 | Wm. Laidlaw. |
| Denovo | 170 | Port Elgin | 187 | 9 35 | 3 | 6 00 | 15 35 | Geo. A. Henry. |
| Alliston | 171 | Alliston | 120 | 6 00 | 3 | 6 00 | 12 00 | W S. Ellis. |
| Penetangore | 172 | Kincardine | 212 | 10 60 | 3 | 6 00 | 16 60 | Alexander Kay. |
| " | 172 | " | 212 | 10 60 | 3 | 6 00 | 16 60 | W. T. Henry. |
| Emerald | 173 | Dunville | 57 | 2 85 | 3 | 6 00 | 8 85 | Jno. Steel. |
| Dolman | 174 | Ayr | 80 | 4 00 | 3 | 6 00 | 10 00 | Jas. G. Watson. |
| Dauncey | 176 | Thedford | 152 | 7 60 | 3 | 6 00 | 13 60 | J. H. Powell. |
| Montana | 177 | Wroxeter | 161 | 8 05 | 3 | 6 00 | 14 05 | A. E. Paulin. |
| Wellington Square | 178 | Burlington | 51 | 2 55 | 3 | 6 00 | 8 55 | V. H. Peart. |
| Madoc | 179 | Madoc | 227 | 11 35 | 3 | 6 00 | 17 35 | John R. Orr. |
| " | 179 | " | 227 | 11 35 | 3 | 6 00 | 17 35 | James White. |
| Owen Sound | 180 | Owen Sound | 205 | 10 25 | 3 | 6 00 | 16 25 | Geo. A. Ross. |
| Tecumseh | 102 | Otterville | 97 | 4 85 | 3 | 6 00 | 10 85 | Allen McFarlane |
| Teeswater | 183 | Teeswater | 164 | 8 20 | 3 | 6 00 | 14 20 | L. A. Brink. |
| Germania | 184 | Waterloo | 106 | 5 30 | 3 | 6 00 | 11 30 | Geo. Suggitt. |
| " | 184 | " | 106 | 5 30 | 3 | 6 00 | 11 30 | Chas. H. Froehlich. |
| Dufferin | 186 | Flesherton | 162 | 8 10 | 3 | 6 00 | 14 10 | David Clayton. |
| Cambridge | 188 | Preston | 79 | 3 95 | 3 | 6 00 | 9 95 | J. Maecker. |
| Parry Sound | 189 | Parry Sound | 238 | 11 90 | 3 | 6 00 | 17 90 | John Linton. |
| Chorazin | 190 | London E | 119 | 5 95 | 3 | 6 00 | 11 95 | Geo. Grant. |
| " | 190 | " | 119 | 5 95 | 3 | 6 00 | 11 95 | Wm. Reid. |
| Jarvis | 191 | Jarvis | 76 | 3 80 | 3 | 6 00 | 9 80 | J. B. McMicken. |
| Howick | 192 | Gorrie | 159 | 7 95 | 3 | 6 00 | 13 95 | Richard Ross. |
| Albert | 194 | Toronto | 83 | 4 15 | 3 | 6 09 | 10 15 | C. E. Holmes. |
| " | 194 | " | 83 | 4 15 | 3 | 6 00 | 10 15 | W. A. Smith |
| Cicerone | 195 | Woodville | 146 | 7 30 | 3 | 6 00 | 13 30 | Dan McMillan. |

| Florence | 196 | Florence | 170 | 8 50 | 3 | 6 00 | 14 50 | Isaac Unsworth. |
| Minerva | 197 | Hamilton | 44 | 2 20 | 3 | 6 00 | 8 20 | D. Robertson. |
| Weston | 200 | Weston | 92 | 4 60 | 3 | 6 00 | 10 60 | M. J. Cruickshank. |
| Beacon | 201 | Port Colborne | 29 | 1 45 | 3 | 6 00 | 7 45 | D. W. McKay. |
| Silver Star | 202 | Milverton | 121 | 6 05 | 3 | 6 00 | 12 05 | W. Acheson. |
| Pembroke | 203 | Pembroke | 395 | 19 75 | 3 | 6 00 | 25 75 | H. Chamberlain. |
| " | 203 | " | 395 | 19 75 | 3 | 6 00 | 25 75 | Jas. Duncan. |
| Acton | 204 | Acton | 105 | 5 25 | 3 | 6 00 | 11 25 | H. H. Worden. |
| Ahiram | 205 | Paisley | 175 | 8 75 | 3 | 6 00 | 14 75 | W. S. Given. |
| " | 205 | " | 175 | 8 75 | 3 | 6 00 | 14 75 | Adam McGill. |
| Silver City | 206 | Tiverton | 221 | 11 05 | 3 | 6 00 | 17 05 | Hugh H. McLean. |
| Egremont | 207 | Kerwood | 149 | 7 45 | 3 | 6 00 | 13 45 | A. H. Blackeby. |
| Millbank | 209 | Milbank | 124 | 6 20 | 3 | 6 00 | 12 20 | Geo. Thompson. |
| Brucefield | 210 | Brucefield | 145 | 7 25 | 3 | 6 00 | 13 25 | James Armstrong. |
| Lilly | 211 | Dorchester Sta | 112 | 5 60 | 3 | 6 00 | 11 60 | Frank Chittick. |
| Argyll | 212 | Napanee | 219 | 10 95 | 3 | 6 00 | 16 95 | Homer Miles. |
| Clifford | 214 | Clifford | 145 | 7 25 | 3 | 6 00 | 13 25 | Thos. Upton. |
| Freestone | 215 | Beamsville | 23 | 1 15 | 3 | 6 00 | 7 15 | F. S. Prodhomme. |
| Elmira | 216 | Elmira | 107 | 5 35 | 3 | 6 00 | 11 35 | M. L. Weber. |
| Mount Brydges | 217 | Mt. Brydges | 135 | 6 75 | 3 | 6 00 | 12 75 | James Weeks. |
| " | 217 | " | 135 | 6 75 | 3 | 6 00 | 12 75 | Robert Smith. |
| Enterprise | 218 | Essex Centre | 222 | 11 10 | 3 | 6 00 | 17 10 | Thos. Robinson. |
| " | 218 | " | 222 | 11 10 | 3 | 6 00 | 17 10 | Wallace May. |
| Georgian Bay | 219 | Waubaushene | 189 | 9 45 | 3 | 6 00 | 15 45 | Andrew Paterson. |
| Woodslee | 220 | S. Woodslee | 217 | 10 85 | 3 | 6 00 | 16 85 | J. A. Smith. |
| Chesley | 221 | Chesley | 169 | 8 45 | 3 | 6 00 | 14 45 | W. Halliday. |
| Hensall | 223 | Hensall | 159 | 7 95 | 3 | 6 00 | 13 95 | W. Colwell. |
| Ottawa | 224 | Ottawa | 344 | 17 20 | 3 | 6 00 | 23 20 | Wm. Prenter. |
| " | 224 | " | 344 | 17 20 | 3 | 6 00 | 23 20 | F. W. May. |
| Merlin | 226 | Merlin | 201 | 10 05 | 3 | 6 00 | 16 05 | David Walker. |
| Sauble | 227 | Tara | 187 | 9 35 | 3 | 6 00 | 15 35 | Jas. A. McDonald. |
| International | 228 | International B | 18 | 90 | 3 | 6 00 | 6 90 | A. B. Hurrell. |
| " | 228 | " | 18 | 00 | 3 | 6 00 | 6 90 | Frank Bowen. |
| Embro Star | 229 | Embro | 102 | 5 10 | 3 | 6 00 | 11 10 | Alex. McIntosh. |
| Prince of Wales | 230 | Toronto | 83 | 4 15 | 3 | 6 00 | 10 15 | Robt. Gray. |
| Elora | 231 | Eloro | 104 | 5 20 | 3 | 6 00 | 11 20 | Allan M. Bock. |
| Hanover | 233 | Hanover | 158 | 7 90 | 3 | 6 00 | 13 90 | Jno. Telford. |
| Ilderton | 234 | Ilderton | 132 | 6 60 | 3 | 6 00 | 12 60 | Jno. Clark. |
| Waterford | 235 | Waterford | 87 | 4 35 | 3 | 6 00 | 10 35 | Chas. Slaght. |
| " | 235 | " | 87 | 4 35 | 3 | 6 00 | 10 35 | Jas. E. Beemer. |

MILEAGE AND PER DIEM, SESSION 1893, AT NIAGARA FALLS—*Continued.*

| NAME OF LODGE. | No. | Location. | Miles Travelled. | Mileage | No. of Days. | Per Diem. | Total. | Name of Representative. |
|---|---|---|---|---|---|---|---|---|
| Acorn | 236 | Camlachie | 171 | $8 55 | 3 | $6 00 | $14 55 | H. West. |
| Farmersville | 237 | Athens | 306 | 15 30 | 3 | 6 00 | 21 30 | J. L. Gallagher. |
| Sterling | 239 | Stirling | 214 | 10 70 | 3 | 6 00 | 16 70 | W. R. Mathers. |
| " | 239 | " | 214 | 10 70 | 3 | 6 00 | 16 70 | W. H. Hubble. |
| Carleton | 240 | Ottawa | 344 | 17 20 | 3 | 6 00 | 23 20 | A. W. Cameron. |
| " | 240 | " | 344 | 17 20 | 3 | 6 00 | 23 20 | T. A. Hood. |
| Rideau | 241 | Smith's Falls | 300 | 15 00 | 3 | 6 00 | 21 00 | R. Hawkins. |
| " | 241 | " | 300 | 15 00 | 3 | 6 00 | 21 00 | A. Allan, Jr. |
| Wilton | 242 | Toronto | 83 | 4 15 | ? | 6 00 | 10 15 | Jno. B. Reid. |
| Port Arthur | 244 | Port Arthur | 941 | 47 05 | 3 | 6 00 | 53 05 | Joseph G. Ashforth. |
| Mallorytown | 245 | Mallorytown | 208 | 14 00 | 3 | 6 00 | 20 00 | V. Buell. |
| Orillia | 246 | Orillia | 169 | 8 45 | 3 | 6 00 | 14 45 | E. R. Robbins. |
| Gordon | 247 | Palmerston | 133 | 6 60 | 3 | 6 00 | 12 60 | J. Waldon. |
| Campbellford | 248 | Campbellford | 207 | 10 35 | 3 | 6 00 | 16 35 | J. B. Ferris. |
| " | 248 | " | 207 | 10 35 | 3 | 6 00 | 16 35 | E. T. Morton. |
| Beaverton | 249 | Beaverton | 156 | 7 80 | 3 | 6 00 | 13 80 | Jas. Birchard. |
| Ridgely | 250 | Oil Springs | 187 | 9 35 | 3 | 6 00 | 15 35 | J. W. Holme. |
| Bracebridge | 251 | Bracebridge | 197 | 9 85 | 3 | 6 00 | 15 85 | Moses Dickie. |
| Floral | 252 | Parkdale | 83 | 4 15 | 3 | 6 00 | 10 15 | A. F. Middleton. |
| Caledonia | 253 | Caledonia | 60 | 3 00 | 3 | 6 00 | 9 00 | R. E. Walker. |
| Alba | 254 | Pakenham | 329 | 16 45 | 3 | 6 00 | 22 45 | D. H. McIntosh. |
| Grand Valley | 256 | Grand Valley | 145 | 7 25 | 3 | 6 00 | 13 25 | F. J. Marshall. |
| Credit | 257 | Erin | 141 | 7 05 | 3 | 6 00 | 13 05 | J. S. Milloy. |
| Thamesford | 258 | Thamesford | 111 | 5 55 | 3 | 6 00 | 11 55 | J. A. Young. |
| " | 258 | " | 111 | 5 55 | 3 | 6 00 | 11 55 | Joel McLeod, Jr. |
| Lynden | 259 | Lynden | 59 | 2 95 | 3 | 6 00 | 8 95 | John Hagey. |
| Meaford | 260 | Meaford | 190 | 9 50 | 3 | 6 00 | 15 50 | S. D. Watt. |
| Gold Hill | 261 | Rat Portage | 1200 | 60 00 | 3 | 6 00 | 66 00 | George Barnes. |
| " | 261 | " | 1200 | 60 00 | 3 | 6 00 | 66 00 | A. J. Holmes. |
| Norwood | 262 | Norwood | 183 | 9 15 | 3 | 6 00 | 15 15 | E. Gear. |
| East Toronto | 263 | E. Toronto | 83 | 4 15 | 3 | 6 00 | 10 15 | F. Nettleton. |
| Fraternity | 264 | Perth | 287 | 14 35 | 3 | 6 00 | 20 35 | H. H. Neilson. |

| | No. | | | | | | | |
|---|---|---|---|---|---|---|---|---|
| Delta | 265 | Delta | 316 | 15 80 | 3 | 6 00 | 21 80 | Joel Barlow. |
| Missanabie | 266 | Chapleau | 559 | 27 95 | 3 | 6 00 | 33 95 | Wm. Jule. |
| Algoma | 267 | Fort William | 951 | 47 05 | 3 | 6 00 | 53 05 | J. T. Campbell. |
| Stanley | 268 | Lanark | 299 | 14 95 | 3 | 6 00 | 20 95 | James W. Campbell. |
| Woodstock | 269 | Woodstock | 92 | 4 60 | 3 | 6 00 | 10 60 | Jas. McLurg. |
| " | 269 | " | 92 | 4 60 | 3 | 6 00 | 10 60 | J. R. Armitage. |
| Lansdowne | 270 | Lansdowne | 270 | 13 50 | 3 | 6 00 | 19 50 | E. F. Johnstone. |
| North Bay | 271 | North Bay | 312 | 15 60 | 3 | 6 00 | 21 50 | E. W. Ross. |
| Lakeview | 272 | W. Toronto | 83 | 4 15 | 3 | 6 00 | 10 15 | Geo. R. Cumming. |
| Hastings | 273 | Hastings | 208 | 10 40 | 3 | 6 00 | 16 40 | B. F. Doxsee. |
| Midland | 274 | Midland | 202 | 10 10 | 3 | 6 00 | 16 10 | J. Porter. |
| Fairy | 275 | Huntsville | 228 | 11 40 | 3 | 6 00 | 17 40 | D. Wilkinson. |
| Sheard | 276 | New Dundee | 90 | 4 50 | 3 | 6 00 | 10 50 | A. B. McRae. |
| Lambton | 277 | Brigden | 193 | 9 65 | 3 | 6 60 | 15 65 | Thos. Hayne. |
| Rockliffe | 278 | Ottawa | 344 | 17 20 | 3 | 6 00 | 23 20 | J. K. Pearce. |
| Grenville | 289 | Kemptville | 319 | 15 95 | 3 | 6 00 | 21 95 | G. W. Griffith. |
| Balmoral | 280 | Merrickville | 308 | 15 40 | 3 | 6 00 | 21 40 | F. A. Tallman. |
| Arthur | 281 | Sault Ste. Marie | 685 | 34 25 | 3 | 6 00 | 40 25 | A. B. Cracknell. |
| Sudbury | 282 | Sudbury | 391 | 19 55 | 3 | 6 00 | 25 55 | A. W. Watson. |
| Earnscliffe | 283 | Janeville | 344 | 17 20 | 3 | 6 00 | 23 20 | B. Slimm. |
| Lyn | 284 | Lyn | 287 | 14 35 | 3 | 6 01 | 20 35 | W. Bowen. |
| Morewood | 285 | Morewood | 349 | 17 45 | 3 | 6 00 | 23 45 | A. W. Reveler. |
| Royal | 286 | Havelock | 189 | 9 45 | 3 | 6 00 | 15 45 | W. B. Burnett. |
| Ripley | 287 | Ripley | 187 | 9 35 | 3 | 6 00 | 15 45 | John Humberstone. |
| Chesterville | 288 | Chesterville | 342 | 17 10 | 3 | 6 00 | 23 10 | J. G. Gillespie. |
| Glanworth | 289 | Glanworth | 143 | 7 15 | 3 | 6 00 | 13 15 | S. A. Smith. |
| Tweed | 290 | Tweed | 220 | 11 00 | 3 | 6 00 | 17 00 | R. S. Richardson. |
| Rodney | 291 | Rodney | 165 | 8 25 | 3 | 6 00 | 14 25 | A. Humphrey. |
| Minnetonka | 292 | Keewatin | 1200 | 60 00 | 3 | 6 00 | 66 00 | T. A. Wilson. |
| Thomasburg | 293 | Thomasburg | 214 | 10 70 | 3 | 6 00 | 16 70 | Wilber Sherry. |
| Broadview | 294 | Toronto | 83 | 4 15 | 3 | 6 00 | 10 15 | G. E. Post. |
| Manotick | 295 | Manotick | 332 | 16 60 | 3 | 6 00 | 22 60 | Fred Gallagher. |
| Pontypool | 296 | Pontypool | 144 | 7 20 | 3 | 6 00 | 13 20 | R. J. Stuart. |
| Mayflower | 297 | Parham | 284 | 14 20 | 3 | 6 00 | 20 20 | A. F. Smith. |
| Total Mileage and Per Diem of Reps. | | | 58649 | 2932 45 | 1011 | 2022 00 | 4954 45 | |

## MILEAGE AND PER DIEM, SESSION 1893, AT NIAGARA FALLS—*Concluded.*

| | Location. | Miles Travelled. | Mileage | No. of Days. | Per Diem. | Total. |
|---|---|---|---|---|---|---|
| COMMITTEE ON LAWS OF SUBORDINATES. | | | | | | |
| W. A. Rawlings | St. Catharines | 12 | $ 60 | 3 | 86 00 | $6 60 |
| D. Robertson | " | 12 | 60 | 3 | 6 00 | 6 60 |
| J. A. Morton | Wingham | 172 | 8 60 | 3 | 6 00 | 14 60 |
| Total | | 196 | 9 80 | 9 | 18 00 | 27 80 |
| RECAPITULATION. | | | | | | |
| Officers | | 2135 | 106 75 | 41 | 82 00 | 188 75 |
| Representatives | | 58649 | 2932 45 | 1011 | 2022 00 | 4954 45 |
| Committee on Laws | | 196 | 9 80 | 9 | 18 00 | 27 80 |
| Total Miles | | 60980 | 3049 00 | 1061 | 2122 00 | 5171 00 |

At five o'clock the Grand Lodge, on motion, adjourned to meet at nine o'clock to-morrow morning.

# THIRD DAY.

## MORNING SESSION.

NIAGARA FALLS, August 11, 1893.

The Grand Lodge opened in regular form, Grand Master Rev. T. W. Jolliffe in the chair.

Prayer by the Grand Chaplain, Rev. W. J. Saunders,

Roll called, the following Grand Officers and a majority of the representatives were present :

### OFFICERS :

| | |
|---|---|
| REV. T. W. JOLLIFFE, | Grand Master. |
| JOSEPH OLIVER, | Deputy Grand Master. |
| W. H. HOYLE, | Grand Warden. |
| J. B. KING, | Grand Secretary. |
| WM. BADENACH, | Grand Treasurer. |
| W. H. COLE, | Grand Representative. |
| HY. ROBERTSON, | Grand Representative. |
| O. E. FLEMING, | Grand Marshal. |
| ROBERT MEEK, | Grand Conductor. |
| A. MITCHELL, | Grand Guardian. |
| I. B. AULPH, | Grand Herald. |
| REV. WM. J. SANDERS, | Grand Chaplain. |
| P. E. FITZ-PATRICK, | Junior Past Grand Master. |

The minutes of the last session were read and confirmed.

The following was adopted by a standing vote :—

*Resolved,*—That the thanks of this Grand Lodge are hereby tendered to Bro. S. K. Binkley, Mayor of Niagara Falls, for the many acts of courtesy shown to the members of this Grand Lodge during the present session, and for his reception of last evening.

Bro. S. K. Binkley acknowledged the resolution in a very felicitous speech.

Rep. John Donogh, P.G.M., moved the adoption of the report of the Special Committee on Reduction of Representatives (pages 5560-5569), which was made the first order of business after the opening of this morning's session.

Rep. J. T. Hornibrook, P.G.M., seconded by Rep. Hy. White, moved the following, which was adopted :—

*Resolved,*—·That the hearty thanks of this Grand Lodge are due and are hereby tendered to the Committee on Reduction of Representation, for their able, exhaustive, and interesting research and report, and that the further consideration of the report be indefinitely postponed.

**REPORT No. 19**—Rep. J. T. Hornibrook, from the Judiciary Committee, made the following report, which was adopted :—

*To the Grand Lodge of Ontario, I. O. O. F.:*

Your Committee on Judiciary, to whom was referred the question of Unity Lodge, No. 47, Hamilton, viz :—

Clause 51 Con. Sub.—Latter part of said clause. The Lodge shall not be held to pay such benefit for any term shorter than one week, but after one week's sickness the brother shall be entitled to benefits for such additional day or days that he may be ill.

QUESTION—Is this portion of Clause 51 legal ?

The Committee answers Yes.

The clause does not conflict with decision of S. G. L. 1892, p. 13, and 13,057.

*Resolved,*—That the foregoing be adopted.

　　　　　　　　　Fraternally submitted.

　　　　　　　　　　　　　J. S. R. McCANN.

**REPORT No. 20**—Rep. D. H. Moore, from the same Commit·tee made the following report :—

*To the Grand Lodge of Ontario, I. O. O. F.:*

Your Committee on Judiciary, to whom were referred the following questions, beg leave to submit the following report :—

Question by Rep. Johnston :—

1. When does a District Deputy cease to be District Deputy ?

2. When does a District Deputy's powers cease ?

ANSWER—The answer to both these questions is contained in decision No. 1 of the Grand Master, page 5476.

Question by Rep. F. A. Latshaw :—

At an election for officers, after several ballots the vote stood 9, 7, 7, respectively. Clause 23, Constitution, directs that after each ballot the name o each candidate who may have received the smallest number of votes shall be withdrawn. It also declares that a majority of all legal votes cast shall b necessary to an election.

What is the proper course to pursue at the above election ?

ANSWER—Cast the ballot of the Lodge between the candidates who may be ties, the name of the candidate who then receives the lowest number of votes to be withdrawn ; or continue the election till some candidate receives a minority vote.

Question by Rep. A. W. Cameron :—

A Lodge suspends or ignores its by-laws and takes members in at reduced rates ; what steps should other Lodges in the same city or town take to put a stop to such action ?

Answer—Your Committee consider that this question properly belongs to the Committee on the State of the Order and would recommend that it be so referred.

Question by Rep. A. W. Cameron :—

Can Lodges meeting outside the corporation limits of a city or town receive candidates for membership from said city or town without consent of the Lodges therein ?

Answer—Yes, if the candidates reside nearer the outside Lodges than to the city Lodges.

Question by Rep. J. J. Craig :—

Can a by-law be added to or explained by a simple motion on the books of the Lodge ?

Answer—No.

Is custom or usage of any value in interpreting a by-law ?

Answer—All by-laws should be interpreted according to the strict text of the same.

*Resolved,*—That the foregoing be adopted.

Fraternally submitted.

D. H. MOORE.

Rep. A. W. Cameron, seconded by Rep. F. Gallagher, moved the following :—

*Resolved,*—That the report be referred back to the Committee for further consideration.

Rep. ——— moved in amendment that the report be considered clause by clause.   The amendment prevailed.

The clauses were severally considered and adopted and the report as a whole was adopted.

**REPORT No. 21**—Rep. Wm. Menzies, from the same Committee, made the following report, which was considered and adopted :—

*To the Grand Lodge of Ontario, I.O.O.F. :*

Your Committee on Judiciary, to whom was referred the following questions, beg leave to report :—

Question—Union Lodge, No. 16, by resolution wishes to know whether a Subordinate Lodge may reduce the amount of sick benefits at a less period than one year without conflicting with the laws of the Sovereign Grand Lodge, providing Clause 52, Constitution of Grand Lodge of Ontario, were amended ?

ANSWER—Yes, by making provision in By-laws to that effect without amending Clause 52, Constitution of Grand Lodge of Ontario.

QUESTION—A Lodge which pays on the average, over two dollars per week, would it be lawful to adopt By-laws paying $4.00 per week for first six months, and $2.00 per week for next six months, and $1.00 per week afterwards?

ANSWER—Yes.

Your Committee move the following:—

*Resolved,*—That the foregoing be adopted.

W. MENZIES.

**REPORT No. 22**—Rep. W. Macdiarmid, from the Committee on Appeals, made the following report, which was adopted:—

*To the Grand Lodge of Ontario, I.O.O.F.:*

IN THE APPEAL OF RIDGELY LODGE, No. 250 )
     *vs.*          }
   AYLMER LODGE, No. 94.     )

The Committee on Appeals, to whom this matter was referred, report as follows:—

We have given this important matter very careful consideration, after hearing all that was alleged by both parties as well as the statements of Bro. Hayne, D.D.G.M., District No. 14, and perusing the by-laws of Aylmer Lodge and the correspondence that passed between the said Lodges in connection with this appeal.

Fortunately, all the facts necessary for the determination of the point at issue, are admitted by both parties; and nothing remains to be done except to apply the law to these admitted facts.

On 20th November, 1890, Rev. J. A. Ferguson, a member in good standing of Aylmer Lodge, was taken ill with typhoid fever at Oil Springs, where he was then residing, within the jurisdiction of Ridgely Lodge, and he was promptly taken under the care and attendance of Ridgely Lodge. The disease is considered contagious; and accordingly in such cases the services of a nurse were required. But before selecting the nurse, the Secretary of Ridgely Lodge notified Aylmer Lodge by telephone of the Brother's condition, and at the same time took the precaution of enquiring as to what weekly sum the by-laws of Aylmer Lodge allowed for nurse's compensation.

It now became the duty of Aylmer Lodge to state explicitly in answer to such a direct and important question, the sum allowed for such services by their laws. However, for some reason best known to the Secretary of Aylmer Lodge, no direct answer was given to the question. But Ridgely Lodge was directed by the Secretary of Aylmer Lodge to employ a nurse, and that "Aylmer Lodge would do what was right by them," (meaning Ridgely Lodge).

Relying on this direction and promise, and by the physician's instructions, Ridgely Lodge accordingly procured the services of a professional nurse from the City of London, whose terms were $10 a week and travelling expenses, and this is admitted by the parties to be a reasonable sum.

On the 26th Nov., a few days after the conversation by telephone aforementioned, Ridgely Lodge wrote Aylmer Lodge more fully concerning the sick Brother's condition and the employment of the nurse.

On the 2nd of December, the Secretary of Aylmer Lodge reported to his Lodge the conversation which he had with Ridgely Lodge concerning the sick Brother, and added also that they had agreed in getting a nurse to wait on the sick Brother.

On the 11th December, Ridgely Lodge wrote Aylmer, enquiring why the latter Lodge had not answered their letter of the 26th of November. It is important here to note that this letter was not answered, nor was any direct answer given by Aylmer Lodge as to the amount allowed by them for a nurse, until the 16th of December, when they wrote Ridgely Lodge that their by-laws allow only $6.00 a week. This was nearly three weeks after the nurse had been employed, and during a most critical stage of the patient's illness. Ridgely Lodge says, that to have discharged the nurse then would have been an inhuman act, and your Committee agree with them.

The nurse's services were continued by the physician's advice for a total period of ten weeks, at $10.00 a week and $5 00 for travelling expenses, making $105 00. Of this sum Aylmer has paid $60.00, being at the rate of $6.00 a week, and the balance claimed by Ridgely Lodge is $46.40, including notarial fees upon a draft for such balance which was dishonored by Aylmer Lodge.

The question now presents itself, Is Aylmer Lodge, under the above facts, liable for the said balance?

Your Committee have not overlooked the law as laid down in Digest, Secs. 119, 120, 121, 122, 123 and other sections, where it is held that the amount must be regulated by the sum allowed by the by-laws.

But in this case your Committee are unanimously of the opinion tha Aylmer Lodge would be liable for any reasonable sum expended by Ridgely Lodge for nursing even were it in excess of the amount allowed by their by-laws.

In this case it was the bounden duty of the Secretary of Aylmer Lodge to have promptly given a direct answer to the Secretary of Ridgely Lodge, enquiring at the outset of the illness. If he did not know what sum the by-laws allowed, it was his duty to have so informed Ridgely Lodge, and he should not have authorized the latter Lodge to employ a nurse under the promise that Aylmer Lodge would do what was right in the payment of that nurse. In any event, three weeks after they were in full possession of the facts, was a most unreasonably long time to take to look into their own by-laws and inform Ridgely Lodge as to the limit allowed for nurses. During this time, and relying on the Secretary's said promise, Ridgley Lodge had engaged the nurse, and the other Lodge had been notified of the terms of such engagement, and no dissent was expressed till the 16th of December.

Further, your Committee observe, in examining the by-laws of Aylmer Lodge, that no fixed sum is payable for nurses. The Visiting Committee are merely directed to employ a competent nurse to attend the sick Brother, to be paid from the funds of the Lodge, and your Committee consequently think that this part of the appeal, independent of the acts of Aylmer Lodge's Secretary in the premises, is governed by Sec. 120, White's Digest, and that Aylmer Lodge is liable for the sum claimed.

Your Committee now recommend that the appeal of Ridgely Lodge against the action of Aylmer Lodge be sustained and that the latter Lodge be, and they are hereby directed to pay forthwith to Ridgely Lodge, the sum of $46.40, being $45.00, the balance claimed for nurse's fees, and $1.40 for said notarial charges.

*Resolved,*—That the foregoing report be adopted.

W. MACDIARMID.

**REPORT No 23**—Rep. J. J. Manning, from the same Committee, made the following report, which was adopted :—

*To the Grand Lodge of Ontario, I.O.O.F. :*

> A. R. ROWLAND  
> *vs.*  
> EASTERN STAR LODGE, No. 72.

Your Committee on Appeals, to whom was referred the various Appeals of Rowland *vs.* Eastern Star Lodge, beg leave to report as follows :—

This appellant comes before this Grand Lodge, with no less than five appeals contained in over fifty pages of written matter, and containing references to as many more pages of Lodge minutes.

The duties of your Committee at the present session are so extensive in other matters laid before them that it will be impossible for the Committee to set out each of the many specifications laid in these complaints, and to deal with the same in this report. We must, therefore, ask this Grand Body to be content with a general statement of the charges laid and of this Committee's findings thereon :—

1. As to the appeal against the action of the Grand Master in refusing an arrest of judgment of said Lodge in expelling the appellant, your Committee find that by section 110 of the Grand Lodge Constitution, the granting or refusing of this arrest, is a matter wholly within the discretion of the Grand Master, and the Grand Master having exercised that discretion in this matter, his action therein is not a subject for review or appeal.

Your Committee, therefore, recommend that the appeal in this paragraph be dismissed.

2. As to the protest of the appellant, against the right of Representatives Robson and Wilson, to sit at this session of Grand Lodge, as Representatives of Eastern Star Lodge, your Committee find that on 4th April, 1893, the appellant was expelled from the said Lodge and was at the time of his making said protest, and still is an expelled member. Therefore, the appellant has no right to question the act of said Lodge in the premises.

As a matter of fact, said Bro. Wilson is not a Representative of said Lodge.

We therefore recommend that such protest be not sustained.

3. As to the appellant's appeal against the action of the District Committee, in refusing to give him a new trial or hear his appeal, it appears from the record that the appellant did not comply with the requirements of section 104, Grand Lodge Constitution, regarding " Petitions in Error," and no proof is adduced to the contrary by the appellant.

We therefore recommend that the appeal in this paragraph mentioned, together with all other appeals of the appellant to the said District Committee be dismissed.

4. As to the appeal of said appellant to this Grand Lodge, against the action and finding of Eastern Star Lodge, respecting a meeting held on 4th October, 1892, regarding a ballot had on the expulsion of a member and other matters, your Committee regard the charge as frivolous and recommend that it be not sustained

5. As to the appellant's complaint against Bro. D. Wilson, N.G., of Eastern Star Lodge, for permitting said Lodge to wear Lodge regalia at a funeral, your Committee agree that there was a violation of the law ; as a matter of fact the N. G. pleads guilty and attempts to justify the act on the following grounds :—1st, that the N. G. himself was at the time the subject of an undecided charge, and had been released by resolution of the Lodge

from the duties of his office, pending the decision thereof.   2nd, that the D. D.G.M., was also present at the funeral and made no objection to the wearing of such regalia ;  and that the Lodge had done the same on prior like occasions.

While we believe the N.G. was misled by these facts, your Committee desire to say that such a resolution was illegal, and did not relieve the N.G. from the functions of his office ;  neither did the previous wearing of the regalia in the presence of the D.D.G.M., justify their action in wearing Lodge regalia in the absence of the required dispensation.

Your Committee feel that no action is necessary in the matter, except the expression herein of their disapproval of the wearing of Lodge regalia at funerals.

6. As to the complaint of the appellant against the action of Eastern Star Lodge, on the charges preferred by appellant against Bro. Wm. Robson,

Your Committee are of the opinion that the reprimand administered to Bro. Robson in the report of the Trial Committee was under provocation sufficient punishment for his conduct, and accordingly we recommend that the appeal herein be dismissed.

All of which is respectfully submitted.

*Resolved,*—That the foregoing be adopted,

Representatives J. E. Farewell and Hy. White, members of this Committee, took no part in the above decisions.   Rep. Farewell being a member of Eastern Star Lodge, and Rep. White having been consulted professionally by the appellant respecting the matters in appeal.

Your Committee move the adoption of this report.

J. J. MANNING,

**REPORT No. 24**—Rep. J. H. Magill, from the same Committee, made the following report, which was adopted :—

*To the Grand Lodge of Ontario, I.O.O.F.:*

In *re* HASSARD, GARNET LODGE, No 139 }
       *vs.*
TEESWATER LODGE, No. 183.

Your Committee on Appeals beg to report after investigating the matter as far as possible, and after hearing the representatives of the above Lodges, that a reasonable time should be allowed the defendant Lodge to perfect their case, they apparently being at a disadvantage in this particular, and your Committee therefore recommend that the case be referred in the interests of all parties concerned to the District Committee of District No. 23 for adjudication and decision with instructions to said District Committee to investigate, hear and determine the matter within three months from this reference.

*Resolved,*—That the foregoing be adopted.

All of which is respectfully submitted.

J. H. MAGILL.

**REPORT No. 25**—Rep. Alf. Coyell, from the same Committee, made the following report :—

*To the Grand Lodge of Ontario, I.O.O.F. :*

IN *re* APPEAL, R. RONAN　　　　　⎱
　　　　　　*vs.*　　　　　　　　　　⎰
GRAND MASTER AND D.D.G.M. DISTRICT 39.

Your Committee on Appeals beg to report that :—

Whereas there is a material variance between the Constitution laid down for Degree Lodges and the By-Laws of Victoria Degree Lodge, No. 21, regulating elections of officers,

And whereas the election complained of herein was not carried out in conformity with the requirements of said Constitution,

Your Committee are of opinion that the election appealed against was illegal, and that the proceedings at the nomination and election of Degree Master in the above Lodge, in December, 1892, are void, and that a new election should be held.

*Resolved,*—That the foregoing be adopted.

All of which is respectfully submitted.

A. COYELL.

Rep. F. M. Clark, seconded by Rep. A. W. Cameron, moved that the report be recommitted to the Committee with instructions, which was not agreed to.

The report was adopted.

The following was adopted : On motion of Rep. Jno. Donogh, P.G.M., seconded by Rep. Ellis, they having voted in the majority when the report was adopted :—

*Resolved,*—That the report of the Committee on Districts, which was adopted at yesterday's session be now reconsidered, and that the said report be referred back to the Committee to reconsider.

**REPORT No 26**—Rep. J. A. Morton, from the Committee on Laws of Subordinates, made the following report, which, on motion of Rep. R. W. Bell, P.G.M., seconded by Rep. W. H. Cole, P.G.M., was recommitted to the Committee with instructions to reconsider their report so far as it relates to the By-laws of Otonabee Lodge, No. 13, viz : to strike out the reference to By-law No. 48, in said report.

*To the Grand Lodge of Ontario, I.O.O.F. :*

Your Committee on Laws of Subordinates appointed to examine the Constitution, By-laws and amendments thereto of Subordinate Lodges, submit the following report :—

During the past year a large number of By-laws and amendments have been submitted, all of which were carefully examined by the Chairman of this Committee, and a detailed report thereon with corrections (where required) sent to each Lodge through the Grand Secretary with as little delay as possible.

The authorities for such corrections will be found attached to this report.

During the present session your Committee have jointly gone over the work, done during the interim and would recommend that the By-laws as submitted, with the corrections as made by the Chairman of this Committee and further revised by the full Committee, and appended to this report, be adopted.

Your Committee would again call the attention of the Lodges to Clause 70 of the Constitution requiring all By-laws and amendments to be submitted in duplicate authenticated by the Seal of the Lodge and signatures of the Noble Grand and Secretary. Notwithstanding the fact that the attention of the Lodges has been repeatedly called by this Committee to their delinquency in this respect, many Lodges persist in noncompliance with the law, thus making it necessary for the Chairman to return all such By-laws and amendments, thereby entailing loss of time, expense and delays which would have been avoided by simply complying with the law.

Quite a number of intricate and obscurely worded By-laws have been submitted for approval which while not in themselves illegal, were susceptible of varied construction and liable to cause confusion. The Chaiman deeming it in the interest of the Lodges that amendments should be made in the verbiage, offered such variations as his experience suggested and it is a matter of gtatification to your Committee that the recommendations of the Chairman have invariably been thankfully acknowledged and cheerfully adopted.

Your Committee fully endorses the recommendation of the Grand Secretary in Clause 21 of his report, viz, that the Constitution of Subordinates be supplied to Lodges at the actual cost of printing the same.

This Committee further recommends that By-law 41 of this Grand Body be amended by striking out the word " five " and inserting in lieu thereof the word " three "—believing from experience that the work of this Committee can be as efficiently performed by three members as by five, and with a considerable saving of expense to Grand Lodge.

In 1890 that clause which assumed to confer on Subordinate Lodges the power to pass By-laws providing for the payment to a brother of a *Funeral Benefit* on the demise of his wife was eliminated from the Constitution of Subordinates. Through inadvertence a number of By-laws containing provision for payment of such a " Funeral Benefit " have been returned to the Lodges without comment thereon. We desire to call attention of our Lodges to this fact that such amendment may be made as will make the By-laws of each Subordinate Lodge conform to existing law.

*Resolved,*—That the foregoing be adopted.

WM. A. RAWLINGS.<br>
J. A. MORTON.<br>
D. ROBERTSON

### Cataraqui Lodge, No. 10.

Two copies of By-laws in proof sheet submitted.

55. Clause 22, strike out " $1.50 " and insert " $2.00."

55. Same Clause, strike out " 25 " and insert an amount equal to two dollars per week, also strike out "excepting Sunday." (See Constitution, Clause 51.)

Balance of By-laws approved.

#### *Second Report.*

Two copies of Constitution and By-laws submitted, amended as per previous report of this Committee and approved.

## OTONABEE LODGE, NO. 13.

Two copies of amendments to Clauses 39 and 48 of By-laws submitted.

Amendment to Clause 48 illegal, strike out " six " where it occurs the first time and insert " twelve " and strike out " two dollars per week for the second six months."

Amendment to Clause 39 approved.

*Second Report.*

Two copies of amendment to Clause 53 of By-laws submitted and approved.

## UNION LODGE, NO. 16.

Two copies of amendments to Clause 39 of By-laws in reference to funeral and sick benefits submitted and approved.

*Second Report.*

Two copies of amendments to By-laws in reference to gratuity to Widows submitted and approved.

## CHATHAM LODGE, NO. 20.

Two copies of new By-law, No. 65 *a*, in reference to providing a Contingent Fund submitted and approved.

## ST. MARY'S LODGE, NO. 36.

Two copies of amendments to Clauses 34, 35, 36, and 43 of By-laws submitted not properly certified.

2. Signature of Noble Grand omitted.

55. Amendment to Clause 43, strike out "one dollar" in 27th line and insert "two dollars" and after " week " in same line insert " for fifty two weeks of continuous disability."

Amendments to Clauses 34, 35, and 36 approved.

## OTTAWA DISTRICT, NO. 39.

One copy of By-lawo of Ottawa District Committee submitted.

According to the amendments adopted by the Grand Lodge at the last session the Secretary is appointed not elected.

Balance of By-laws approved.

## MOUNT ZION LODGE, NO. 46.

Two copies of Constitution and By-laws submitted.

Clause 42, strike out " 5.00 " and insert " 5.20."

Note for Lodge

If the amount payable to the orphan child or children as provided in Clause 62, is in addition to that paid the Widow the By-law is all right, but if it is the amount the Widow is to receive and in case of her death before the amount is paid, then to be paid for the benefit of the children, strike out all after children in 9th line, being a gratuity, the whole amount must be paid to her children or heirs.

## UNITY LODGE, NO. 47.

Two copies of amendments to Clauses 3, 4, and 5 of By-laws, in reference to admission fees and charges for Degrees, submitted and approved.

*Second Report.*

Two copies of By-laws in MSS. submitted.

43.   Clause 7, strike out " and  5 cents for the Special Expense Fund."

5.   Clause 12, after " done " insert " by a P. G. or N. G."

43.   Clause 39, strike out " 5  cents from  the quarterly  contributions of each brother, to which may be added."

42.   Clause 42, strike out " Lodge " where it occurs the  last time  and insert " Order."

55.   Clause 46, strike out " $1.00 " where it occurs the  first time  and  insert " $2.00."

55.   Same clause strike out " 25 cents " and insert " an amount  equal to $2.00 per  week."

41.   Clause 48, strike out " legal representatives " and insert " for the  benefit of."

After  " widows"  in last line  of next  paragraph  add " in  the  latter  case to be paid from the General  Fund."

That portion of Clause 46, which reads as follows " Provided also  that shou'd any brother receiving benefits for any sickness or disability be reported  recovered and able to attend to his usual occupation, have a relapse or  be taken  sick or disabled again within sixty days  of his reported recovery,  then  such brother shall only be entitled to receive such benefits  as  he would  have continued  to receive had he not been reported recovered, according to the rate of benefits  specified  by this By-law."

Not approved, Grand Master decides it illegal.

## DOMINION LODGE, NO. 48.

Two copies of new By-law No. 35, submitted and approved, not properly  certified, signature of Noble Grand omitted.

## OTTER LODGE, NO. 50.

Two copies of By-laws and two copies of amendments submitted.

42.   Clause 44, page 36, strike out " Lodge, except on first  mortgage on  real estate " and insert " Order."

15.   Clause 53, strike out " any cause other than."

52.   Clause 64, after " membership " insert " he having been first  notified of the action that would be  taken, a record of which must be  entered on  the minutes."

27.   Clause 69, after " members " insert " may wear " and strike out " Subordinate Lodge."

29 & 44.   Strike out the Form of Prayers.

41.   Amendment to Clause 58, add to this clause, " in  the  latter case  to  be paid from the General Fund," balance of amendments approved.

## COVENANT LODGE, NO. 52.

Two copies of amendment to By-laws submitted and approved.

## BARRIE LODGE, No. 63.

Two copies of amendments to Clauses 36 and 56 of By-laws submitted and approved.

## EXETER LODGE, No. 67.

Two copies of Constitution and By-laws submitted and approved.

13

*Second Report.*

Two copies of Constitution and By-laws submitted and approved.

## NORTH STAR LODGE, No. 68.

Two copies of amendments to Clause 50, of By-laws in reference to benefits to widows, also a new By-law, No. 52½ in reference to benefits on the decease of the wife of a brother, submitted and approved.

## BOTHWELL LODGE, No. 74.

Two copies of By-laws in MSS. submitted.
65.　Clause 12, strike out " $1.00 " and insert " $2.00."
42.　Clause 17, strike out " Lodge " and insert "Order."
50.　Clause 20, strike out all after " first " in 14th line to and including " months " where it occurs the second time and insert " fifty-two weeks of continuous sickness."
46.　Clause 26, strike out " or should his widow afterwards die," also strike out Clause 28.
47.　Clause 34, after "shall " in 3rd line insert " after due trial."

## AMITY LODGE, No. 80.

Two copies of Constitution and By-laws also two copies of amendment to Clause 37, submitted.
55.　Clause 60, strike out " $1.50 " on page 38 and insert $2.00."
50.　Also strike out " 75 cents " on page 39 and insert " $1.00."
52. Clause 81, after "membership" in 4th line insert " he having been first notified of the action that would be taken, a record of which must be entered on the minutes."
44.　Strike out the Form of Prayers.
Amendment to Clause 37, approved.

## BELLEVILLE LODGE, No. 81.

Two copies of By-laws with amendments submitted.
1.　Constitution incorrect.
11.　Clause 4, add to this clause " or conferring Degrees."
42.　Clause 44, page 38, strike out " Lodge " on 5th line and insert " Order."
55.　Clause 47, strike out " $1.00 " wherever it occurs and insert " $2.00."
Also add to this clause :
45.　" A member admitted on an unexpired Withdrawal Card shall be entitled to benefits immediately upon admission to membership."
44.　Strike out Form of Prayers.

*Second Report.*

Two copies of Constitution and By-laws submitted.
1.　Constitution incorrect.
By-laws as amended approved.

## CONSTELLATION LODGE, No. 85.

Two copies of By-laws in proof sheet submitted.
7.　Clause 18, after " Lodge " in 22nd line insert " except the vote be by ballot."
6.　Clause 20, strike out "report the same " and insert " announce the condition of the vote."
Clause 45, strike out " pink and royal blue " and insert "first and second," also strike out " scarlet " and after " Degree " insert "of Truth."

55.  Clause 59, strike out "scarlet" and after "Degree" insert "of Truth;" strike out "royal blue" and after "Degree" insert "of brotherly love;" also strike out "$1.00" and insert "$2.00;" also add to Clause 59, the following :

45.  "A member admitted on an unexpired Withdrawal Card shall be entitled to benefits immediately upon admission to membership."

Clause 61, strike out "scarlet" and after "Degree" insert "of Truth;" also strike out "royal blue" and after "Degree" insert "of brotherly love."

Clause 67, strike out "scarlet" and after "Degree" insert "of Truth."

45.  Clause 70, add to this clause "except members admitted by card."

15.  Clause 72, after "suspended" insert "for non-payment of dues."

52.  Clause 77, after "membership" insert "he having been first notified of the action that would be taken, a record of which must be entered on the minutes."

47.  Clause 79, after "shall" in 11th line insert "after due trial."

47.  Clause 81, after "shall" in 3rd line insert "after due trial."

48.  Clause 83, after "Lodge" in 2nd line insert "on the form provided by the Grand Lodge."

Clause 88, strike out "scarlet" and after "Degree" insert "of Truth."

### IVY LODGE, No. 90.

Two copies of By-laws in proof sheet submitted.

11.  Clause 5, add to this clause "or conferring Degrees."

12.  Clause 45, strike out entire clause.

46.  Clause 54, strike out "or should his widow afterwards die."

46.  Clause 56, strike out entire clause.

52.  Clause 63, after "membership" insert "he having been first notified of the action that would be taken, a record of which must be entered on the minutes."

27.  Clause 68, after "members" insert "may wear" and strike out "Subordinate Lodge."

22.  Clause 69, after "Degrees" in 1st line, insert "and ballotting thereon" and strike out all after "Truth" in 2nd line.

35.  New Clause 38, strike out "and Widows' and Orphans' Fund."

### GRAND RIVER LODGE, No. 91.

Two copies of amendment to Clause 29 of By-laws, submitted and approved.

### GRAND UNION LODGE, No. 97.

Two copies of amendment to Clause 37 of By-laws in reference to dues, submitted and approved.

### CATARACT LODGE, No. 103.

Two copies of amendments to Clauses 46, 53 and 55 of By-laws submitted not properly certified, signature of Noble Grand and Secretary omitted; amendments approved.

### WATERLOO LODGE, No. 107.

Two copies of new By-law No. 7, in reference to calling special meetings, submitted and approved.

### STREETSVILLE LODGE, No. 122.

2.  Two copies of the Constitution and By-laws of Grand River Lodge No. 91, adopted by this Lodge with certain changes, also one copy of amendments submitted, not certified.

55.  Amendment to Clause 44, strike out "$1.00" and insert "$2.00." Balance of By-laws and amendments approved.

## DRESDEN LODGE, NO. 124.

Two copies of Constitution and By-laws submitted.

48. By-laws Clause 5, after "certificate" insert "on the form provided by the Grand Lodge."

55. Clause 44, strike out "$1.50, also $1.00 ;" and insert "$2.00 ; " also add to this clause the following :—

45. "A member admitted on an unexpired Withdrawal Card shall be entitled to benefits immediately upon admission to membership."

13. Clause 47, after "him" in 2nd line insert "pertaining to his rights to benefits."

46. Clause 51, strike out "or should his widow afterwards die ;" also strike out all after "fourth" in 11th line to "and" in 15th line.

52. Clause 66, after "membership" insert "he having been first notified of the action that would be taken, a record of which must be entered on the minutes."

Amendment to Clause 14 approved.

## MIZPAH LODGE, NO. 127.

Two copies of By-laws in MSS. submitted.

33. Clause 45, strike out the words "Sundays not to be counted in computing sick benefits," also add to this clause the following:

45. "A member admitted on an unexpired Withdrawal Card shall be entitled to benefits immediately upon admission to membership."

Balance of By-laws approved.

## PEACEFUL DOVE LODGE, NO. 135.

Two copies of amendments to Clauses 38, 46, and 54 of By-laws submitted and approved.

### Second Report.

Two copies of amendments to Clauses 43, 55, 61, and 66 of By-laws submitted and approved.

## ST. LAWRENCE LODGE, NO. 137.

Two copies of amendment to Clause 17 of By-laws submitted and approved.

## LISTOWEL LODGE, NO. 160.

Two copies of By-laws and amendments submitted.

48. Clause 5, after "certificate" insert "on the form provided by the Grand Lodge."

32. Clause 7, strike out "and to act as outside conductor."

Clause 30, amend this clause so that the dues shall not be less than ten cents per week (Constitution, Clause 47).

42. Amendment to Clause 35, strike out "Lodge" in last line and insert "Order."

15. New Clause 38 on page 3 of amendments, strike out "or any other cause."

44. Strike out Form of Prayers.

1. Constitution incorrect.

### Second Report.

Two copies of amendments to By-laws, with corrections as previously ordered by this Committee, submitted and approved.

## SIMCOE LODGE, NO. 161.

Two copies of amendments to Clauses 35, 36, 37, and 38 of By-laws submitted and approved.

*Second Report.*

Two copies of Constitution and By-laws, also two copies of amendments, submitted.

1. Constitution incorrect.

42. By-laws, Clause 42, strike out " Lodge " in 8th line and insert " Order."

55. Clause 45, strike out " one dollar " and insert " two dollars."

52. Clause 63, after " membership " insert " he having been first notified of the action that would be taken, a record of which must be entered on the minutes."

47. Clause 67, after " shall " in 3rd line insert " after due trial."

Amendment to Clause 66, not approved (see clauses 66, 67, and 68 of Constitution).

Other amendments approved.

### ORIENTAL LODGE, No. 163.

Two copies of Constitution and By-laws submitted.

52. Clause 57, after " membership " insert " he having been first notified of the action that would be taken, a record of which must be entered on the minutes."

27. Clause 63, after " members " insert " may wear " and strike out " Subordinate Lodge."

### GREY LODGE, No. 169.

Two copies of By-laws in MSS. submitted.

48. Clause 2, after " examination " insert " in accordance with the form provided by the Grand Lodge."

55. Clause 44, strike out " $1.00 also $1.50 " and inssrt " $2.00 " and add to the same clause the following :

45. " A member admitted on an unexpired Withdrawal Card shall be entitled to benefits immediately upon admission to membership."

52. Clause 58, after " membership " insert " he having been first notified of the action that would be taken, a record of which must be entered on the minutes "

22. Clause 65, after " Degrees " in first line insert " and balloting thereon," and strike out all after " Truth."

Balance of By-laws approved.

### PENETANGORE LODGE, No. 172.

Two copies of By-laws, also two copies of amendments submitted.

42. Clause 55, strike out " Lodge " in 9th line and insert " Order."

45. Clause 58, add to this Clause, " a member admitted on an unexpired Withdrawal Card shall be entitled to benefits immediately upon his admission to membership."

45. Clause 91, add to this Clause " except members admitted by card

Amendments approved.

### DOLMAN LODGE, No. 174.

Two copies of Constitution and By-laws, also two copies of amendments to Clauses 36, 51, 53, and 54 submitted.

1. Constitution incorrect.

11. By-laws, Clause 5, add " or conferring degrees."

42. Clause 41, strike out " Lodge " in eighth line and insert " Order."

55. Clause 44, strike out " $1.50 " and insert " $2.00."

46. Clause 54, strike out all after " be " in fourth line to end of clause.

46. Clause 56, strike out entire clause.

52. Clause 63, after " membership " insert " he having been first notified of the action that would be taken, a record of which must be entered on the minutes."

27. Clause 68, after " members " insert " may wear " and strike out " Subordinate Lodge."

Clause 69, strike out all after " application " in third line and insert " and on presentation of a certificate from the P.S. he shall be balloted for " (see Constitution, Clause 14).

29 and 44. Strike out Form of Prayers.

Amendments approved.

## OWEN SOUND LODGE, No. 180.

Two copies of new By-law 41, in reference to sick benefits, submitted and approved.

## ALBERT LODGE, No. 194.

Two copies of Constitution and By-laws, also two copies of amendments to Clauses 22, 23, and 24 submitted. Amendments approved.

55. By-laws, Clause 49, strike out " one dollar " and insert " two dollars," also add to this clause :

45. " A member admitted on an unexpired Withdrawal Card shall be entitled to benefits immediately upon admission to membership."

52. Clause 66, after " membership " insert " he having been first notified of the action that would be taken, a record of which must be entered on the minutes."

29 and 44. Strike out the Form of Prayers.

## MINERVA LODGE, No. 197.

Two copies of amendments to Clauses 11, 40, 41, 60, 63, and 78 submitted and approved.

## MILLBANK LODGE, No. 209.

Two copies of amendments to Clause 37 of By-laws submitted and approved.

## BRUCEFIELD LODGE, No. 210.

Two copies of Constitution and By-laws with amendments submitted.

42. Clause 40, strike out " Lodge " in 8th line and insert " Order."

52. Clause 57, after " membership " insert " he having been first notified of the action that would be taken, a record of which must be entered on the minutes."

55. Amendment to Clause 43, strike out " one dollar " and insert " two dollars;" also add to this clause :

45. " A member admitted on an unexpired Withdrawal Card shall be entitled to benefits immediately upon admission to membership."

## ELMIRA LODGE, No. 216.

Two copies of Constitution and By-laws of Waterloo Lodge, adopted by Elmira Lodge, with certain amendments submitted.

55. Clause 44, strike out " $1.25 " also " $1.00, " and insert " $2.00 " in each case.

52. Clause 58, after " membership " insert " he having been first notified of the action that would be taken, a record of which must be entered on the minutes."

48. Clause 19, after " examination " insert " on the form provided by the Grand Lodge."

Balance of By-laws and amendments approved.

## PRINCE OF WALES LODGE, No. 230.

Two copies of By-laws in MSS. submitted.

11. Clause 5, add to this clause " or conferring Degrees."

25. Clause 17, strike out " the election for this office shall be annually, in July."

42. Clause 45, strike out " Lodge " in 8th line and insert " Order."

55. Clause 48, strike out " one dollar " and insert " two dollars."

12. Clause 51, strike out entire clause.

52. Clause 61, after "membership" insert "he having been first notified of the action that would be taken, a record of which shall be entered on the minutes."

27. Clause 69, after "members" insert "may wear" and strike out "Subordinate Lodge."

## ELORA LODGE, No. 231.

Two copies of By-laws in MSS. submitted.

47. Clause 2, add to this clause the following : "after due trial in accordance with the Constitution."

45. Clause 69, add to this clause the following : "A member admitted on an unexpired Withdrawal Card shall be entitled to benefits immediately upon admission to membership."

45. Clause 82, add to this clause, "except members admitted on an unexpired Withdrawal Card."

15. Clause 85, strike out "or suspended for other cause."

## FARMERSVILLE LODGE, No. 237.

Two copies of Constitution and By-laws submitted.

1. Constitution incorrect.

48. By-laws, Clause 2, after "certificate" insert "on the form provided by the Grand Lodge."

42. Clause 37, strike out "Lodge " in 7th line and insert "Order."

55. Clause 42, strike out all after "week " in 2nd line on page 34 and insert "if he shall not have attained the Degree of Truth $2.00 per week," also add to this clause :

45. "A member admitted on an unexpired Withdrawal Card shall be entitled to benefits immediately upon admission to membership."

13. Clause 49, after "matter" insert "pertaining to his rights to benefits."

37. Clause 54, strike out "per annum "

52. Clause 62, add to this clause the following : "he having been first notified of the action that would be taken, a record of which must be entered on the minutes."

39. Clause 63, strike out "except the latter."

18. Clause 66, after "Degrees" in 1st line insert "and balloting thereon ;" strike out all after "lodge " in 2nd line and insert "while open in the Degree of Truth."

44. Strike out the Form of Prayers.

Amendment to Clause 59 approved.

## CARLETON LODGE, No. 240.

Two copies of By-laws in MSS. submitted.

48. Clause 1, after "certificate " insert "on the form provided by the Grand Lodge."

38. Clause 5, strike out all after "following " to end of clause.

42. Clause 41, strike out "Lodge " in 9th line and insert "Order."

12. Clause 48, strike out entire clause.

52. Clause 61, after "membership " insert "he having been first notified of the action that would be taken, a record of which must be entered on the minutes."

Balance of By-laws approved.

## WILTON LODGE, No. 242.

Two copies of Constitution and By-laws submitted.

48. Clause 5, after "certificate " insert "on the form provided by the Grand Lodge."

42. Clause 60, strike out "Lodge " in last line and insert "Order "

Amendments to Clauses 42, 48 and 64 approved.

41. Amendment to Clause 71, add to this clause " if paid to the widows or orphans from the Widows' and Orphans' Fund until exhausted, if paid to dependant relatives from the General Fund."

Balance of By-laws approved.

*Second Report.*

Two copies of Constitution on By-laws submitted and approved.

## Gold Hill Lodge, No. 261.

2. Two copies of Constitution and By-laws, also one copy of amendment to Clause 37, submitted not properly certified.

48. Clause 2, after "examination" insert "as per form provided by the Grand Lodge."

30. Clause 37, after " brother " in 6th line insert "except unpaid benefits for a previous sickness."

55. Clause 44, after "usual" insert "or other attainable ;" also strike out "10 cents " and insert " $2.00 " and add to this clause the following :—

45. " A member admitted on an unexpired Withdrawal Card shall be entitled to benefits immediately upon admission to membership."

12. Clause 47, strike out entire clause.

52. Clause 61, after "membership" insert "he having been first notified of the action that would be taken, a record of which must be entered on the minutes."

27. Clause 65, after "members" insert "may wear "and strike out " Subordinate Lodge."

Amendment approved.

*Second Report.*

Two copies of amendment to Clause 37 of By-laws submitted.

After "brother" in 6th line insert " except unpaid benefits for a previous sickness."

## Norwood Lodge, No. 262.

2. One copy of By-laws and two copies of amendments to Clause 8 submitted.

48. By-laws, Clause 4, after "certificate" insert "on the form provided by the Grand Lodge"

Clause 38, strike out "$5.00 " and insert "$5.20."

42. Clause 43, strike out " Lodge " in 8th line and insert "Order."

55. Clause 46, strike out "$1.00 " and insert "$2.00."

52. Clause 59, after "membership" insert "he having been first notified of the action that would be taken, a record of which must be entered on the minutes."

44. Strike out the Form of Prayers.

1. Constitution incorrect.

Amendment approved.

*Second Report.*

Two copies of Constitution and By-laws also two copies of amendment to Clause 8 of By-laws submitted.

1. Constitution incorrect.

48. By-laws, Clause 4, after "certificate" insert " on the form provided by the Grand Lodge."

57. Amend Clause 38, so that the dues shall not be less than ten cents per week.

42. Clause 43, strike out " Lodge " in 8th line and insert " Order."

55. Clause 46, strike out " $1.00 " and insert " $2.00," also add to this clause the following :—

45. "A member admitted on an unexpired Withdrawal Card shall be entitled to benefits immediately upon his admission to membership."

52. Clause 59, after "membership" insert "he having been first notified of the action that would be taken, a record of which must be entered on the minutes."

44. Strike out the Form of Prayers.

Amendment to Clause 8, changing the evenings of meeting, approved.

## ALGOMA LODGE, No. 267.

2. One copy of By-laws and two copies of amendments to Clauses 18, 38 and 40 submitted.

48. Clause 3, after "certificate" insert " on the form provided by the Grand Lodge."

42. Clause 43, strike out "Lodge" in 8th line and insert "Order."

46. Clause 54, strike out entire clause.

52. Clause 62, after " membership " insert the following : " He having been first notified of the action that would be taken, a record of which must be entered on the minutes."

30. Amendment to Clause 38, after "brother," where it occurs the fourth time, insert " except unpaid benefits for a previous sickness."

45. Amendment to Clause 46, add the following :  " A member admitted on an unexpired Withdrawal Card shall be entitled to benefits immediately upon admission to membership."

44. Strike out Form of Prayers.

*Second Report.*

Two copies of amendments to By-laws in MSS. submitted and approved.

## NORTH BAY LODGE, No. 271.

Two copies of amendments to Clauses 63, 72, 74, 76, also new Clause 74 a, submitted and approved.

## HASTINGS LODGE, No. 273.

Two copies of Constitution and By-laws, also two copies of amendments, submitted.

48. Clause 6, after " certificate " insert " on the form provided by the Grand Lodge ."

55. Clause 46, strike out " $1.50 " and insert " $2.00, " also add to Clause 46 the following :—

45. " A member admitted on an unexpired Withdrawal Card shall be entitled to benefits immediately upon admission to membership."

52. Clause 63, after " membership " insert " he having been first notified of the action that would be taken, a record of which must be entered on the minutes."

29 & 44. Strike out Form of Prayers.

Amendment to Clause 48, and new Clauses 30½ and 48½ approved.

50. Amendment to Clause 46, not approved.

## FAIRY LODGE, No. 275.

Two copies of amendment to Clause 44 of By-laws submitted and approved.

## LYN LODGE, No. 284.

2. Two copies of Constitution and By-laws submitted, not certified ; Seal of Lodge and signatures of N. G. and Secretary omitted ; By-laws approved except Clauses 48, 49 and 50 which are incomplete, and would advise the Lodge to fill in the amounts payable in each case in Clauses 48 and 49 ; also state the amount of

gratuity and how payable in Clause 50, if it is the intention of the Lodge to have such a By-law and forward to this Committee properly certified in duplicate for approval.

### *Second Report.*

Two copies of amendments to Clauses 48 and 49 submitted and approved.

### RIPLEY LODGE, No 287

Two copies of Constitution and By-laws submitted.
55.   Clause 35, strike out " twenty-six " and insert " fifty-two ;" also strike out " $1.50 " and insert " $2.00."

### THOMASBURG LODGE, No. 293.

2.   Two copies of By-laws in MSS. submitted not certified.
48.  Clause 3, after "Physician" insert "selected by the Lodge;" after " form " insert " provided by the Grand Lodge," and strike out all after " Lodge " in the 8th line.
11.   Clause 5, add to this clause " or conferring Degrees."
52.   Clause 62, after " membership " insert " he having been first notified of the action that would be taken, a record of which shall be entered on the minutes."
27.  Clause 67, after " members " insert " may wear " and strike out " Subordinate Lodge."
Clause 69, after " Degrees " insert " and balloting thereon " and strike out remainder of clause.
Balance of By-laws approved.

### *Second Report*

Two copies of amendment to Clause 35 submitted and approved.

### MANOTICK LODGE, No. 295.

2.   Two copies of Constitution and By-laws submitted, only one copy properly certified.
38.   Clause 7, after " when " insert " by resolution passed at the preceding regular meeting the Lodge may omit such meeting."
42.   Clause 40, strike out " Lodge " in 8th line and insert " Order."
Clause 43, add to this clause the following :—
45.   "A member admitted on an unexpired Withdrawal Card shall be entitled to benefits immediately upon admission to membership."
52.   Clause 58, after " membership " insert " he having been first notified of the action that would be taken, a record of which must be entered on the minutes."
45.   Clause 65, add to this clause " except members admitted by card."

### MAY QUEEN, No. 5.
#### *Degree of Rebekah.*

Two copies of By-laws in proof sheet submitted.
Clause 2 does not embrace all who are eligible for membership.
Clause 4, strike out " Chaplain and Organist " (they are not officers of the Lodge).
Clause 6, after " made " insert " only " and strike out " and on."
Clause 18, after " votes " in fifth line insert " except the vote be by ballot."

### NAOMI LODGE, No. 6.
#### *Degree of Rebekah.*

Two copies of By-laws and amendments submitted
Clause 2, does not embrace all who are eligible for membership.

Clause 21, after "the " in second line where it occurs the first time insert " two meetings " and strike out " and at the time of election."

Amendment changing meetings from "alternate " to every Tuesday, approved.

## EDNA LODGE, No. 14.

### *Degree of Rebekah.*

Two copies of new By-law in reference to the duties of the Visiting Committee, submitted and approved.

## OLIVE BRANCH LODGE, No. 16.

### *Degree of Rebekah.*

Two copies of amendments to Clauses 7 and 8 of By-laws submitted and approved.

## FLORAL LODGE, No. 20.

### *Degree of Rebekah.*

One copy of By-laws in MS. submitted.

Clause 38, after " shall " in third line insert " after due trial."

## DONALDA LODGE, No. 20.

### *Degree of Rebekah.*

One copy of By-laws in MS. submitted not certified.

Clause 3, strike out " five " in both places and insert " three."

Clause 15, after " the" where it occurs the first time insert " two " and strike out " and at the time of election."

Clause 16, strike out all after " V.G." in second line to end of clause.

## INGLEWOOD LODGE, No. 23.

### *Degree of Rebekah.*

Two copies of By-laws submitted.

29.   Strike out Form of Prayers and Odes.

By-laws approved.

---

## AUTHORITIES FOR CORRECTIONS.

### ARRANGED BY COMMITTEE ON LAWS OF SUBORDINATES, 1892-93.

1.   Lodges having Constitution, Rules of Order, or Rules of Procedure on Trials incorrect, are referred to revised Const. Jour., 1890, Appendix, and Journal of Grand Lodge Ont., 1892, page 5331.

2.   Duplicate copies of By-laws, authenticated by the Seal of Lodge and signature of N. G. and Secretary must be submitted.—Const. Sub., Clause 70.

3.   Membership cannot be restricted to persons not over a certain age.— Digest, S.G.I., 1883, 605 ; 1889, 492.

4.   Blank votes must be counted.—Digest 1889, S.G.L., 1009.

5.   P.G.'s charge can only be given by a P.G., or N.G.—Digest 1889, S.G.I., 676.

6.   The V.G. may assist at the examination of a ballot and announce the condition of the vote, but the N.G. alone declares the result.—Digest 1889, S.G.L., 660.

7.   N.G. can vote same as other members at an election by ballot (for a candidate or an officer) but has no casting vote ; when the vote is an open one he

has only a casting vote in cases of tie.—Book of Laws, page 33, Note 105 ; also Jour. 1880, page 1924.

8.   In the absence of the N.G. the V.G. takes the chair.—Digest 1889, S.G.L. 1054.

9.   Subordinates cannot alter Rules of Order.—Rule XXI.

10.   Junior P.G. cannot be fined as an officer.—Digest 1889, S.G.L., 1061.

11.   No one can enter or retire from lodge-room during initiation or confering degrees.—Book of Laws, page 28—Notes 69, 70.   Jour. S.G.L., 1884, pages 9736, 9802.

12.   A Lodge cannot refuse benefits to a Brother leaving its jurisdiction while sick.—Digest 1889, S.G.L., 73.

13.   A member under charges retains all his rights except those specified in Digest 1889, S.G.L., 779.

14.   N.G. can only fill vacancies in committees originally appointed by him.—Jour. G.L. of Ontario, page 1245.

15.   A member suspended for cause (other than non-payment of dues) returns to the full enjoyment of his position in the Lodge at the expiration of his term of suspension.—Digest 1889, S.G.L., 779.

16.   Cannot refuse a widow or orphans benefits because she or they may be inmates of some charitable institution.—Jour. of Ontario, 1875, page 1407.

17.   By-laws cannot be suspended on motion.—Digest 1889, S.G.L., 155.

18.   Degrees must be applied for and balloted for when the Lodge is open in the Degree of Truth.—Digest 1889, S.G.L., 307.—Const. Clause 14.

19.   Lodge cannot make a by-law dispensing with payment of benefits.—Digest 1889, S.G.L., 8.

20.   The sitting Past Grand should not be fined because the Returns to the G.L. have not been made out and forwarded.—Book of Laws, page 36.

21.   Terms of office commence in January, if annual.—Const. Subordinates, Clause 38.

22.   All the business of the Subordinate Lodge must be transacted in the Degree of Truth.—Digest 1889, S.G.L., 1458.

23.   A member in arrears may visit his own Lodge until suspended, but is not entitled to vote.—Digest 1889, S.G.L., 1701.

24.   N.G. alone can call special meetings or V.G. in the absence (from town) of the N.G.—Const. Subordinates, Clause 38.

25.   All officers must be elected each term.—Const. Subordinates, Clause 22.

26.   Lodges cannot make a By-law refusing a sick Brother benefits who may be out of his house after certain hours in the evening.—Jour. of Ontario, 1878, page 92.

27.   Encampment regalia may be worn in Subordinate Lodges by Encampment members.—Jour. S.G.L., 1882. pages 8993, 9095.

28.   During a ballot members may be admitted (Book of Laws, page 32, note 92), and at any t me except during opening, initiations and conferring Degrees.—Book of Laws, page 33, note 106.

29.   The S.G.L. prohibits Lodges and individuals printing its forms.—Digest 1889, S.G.L., 1744-1745.

30.   No claim can be allowed as an offset for dues, except benefits for a previous sickness which have not been paid.—Jour. of Ontario, 1880, pages 1924, 1979.

31.   The proposition fee of a rejected candidate should be returned him.—Book of Laws, page 28, note 68.

32.   It is a prerogative of the N.G. to appoint the V.G. or a P.G. to act a Outside Conductor.—Book of Laws, page 33, note 109.

33.   Continuous stipulated weekly benefits must be paid.—Digest 1889 S.G.L., 10.

34.   Degrees must be paid for in full before a ballot can be taken.—Const. Subordinates, Clause 14.

35.   Widows' and Orphans' Fund cannot be diverted from the purpose for which it was created.—Digest 1889, 410-411.

36.   A Lodge cannot refuse benefits to a Brother otherwise beneficial because he is an inmate of some public institution.—Digest 1889, 68.

37.   Lodges cannot pay Widows' and Orphans' Benefits by annuities.—Journal of Ontario, 1888, page 4412.   Confirmed 1890, Jour., page 4871.

38.   A Lodge cannot by vote at a previous meeting change the regular meeting on account of a holiday falling on the same night.—Jour. of Ontario, 1891, page 2119, but may by resolution omit such meeting.—Const. Subordinates, Clause 35.

39.   Where a Brother has been found guilty of crime and sentenced to imprisonment by a court of law, the Lodge should cause a charge to be preferred and proceed with the trial.—Digest 1889, S.G.L. 1305, also Jour. of Ontario, 1888, page 4288.

40.   Constitution of Subordinates, Clause, 16, re Non-beneficial Degrees repealed.—Jour., 1889, page 4603.

41.   Benefits cannot be paid to the dependent relatives of a deceased Brother from the W. and O. Fund.—Jour. S.G.L., 1886, pages 10528-10661.

42.   Lodges are strictly prohibited from loaning their funds to members of the Order—Jour. of Ontario, 1888, page 4363, also 1889, page 4505—or investing in private enterprise.—Const., Clause 49.

43.   Lodges cannot set apart a portion of the dues to form a Contingent Fund. —Jour. S.G.L., 1888, pages 11372-11398.—Const. Subordinates, Clause 45.

44.   Lodges opening and closing with prayer must use the new form adopted by the Sovereign Grand Lodge—Jour. S.G.L., pages 11773-11811.

45.   A member admitted on an unexpired Withdrawal Card shall be entitled to benefits immediately upon his admission to membership.—Cons. Subordinates, Clause 56.

46.   A gratuity to a widow must be paid in full ; marriage or death does not release the Lodge from liability for any unpaid portion.—Jour. Ontario, 1890, page 4719.

47.   A Lodge cannot suspend or expel a member (unless for non-payment of dues) until he has first received a fair trial in accordance with the Constitution.—Const. Subordinates, Clause 58.

48.   A physician's certificate, on application for membership, must be on the form provided by the Grand Lodge.—Const. Subordinates, Clause 3.

49.   One ballot shall be taken for all the Degrees for which a member may apply.—Const. Subordinates, Clause 14.

50.   Weekly sick benefits cannot be reduced until a member has been in receipt of benefits continuously for twelve months.—Const., Clause 52, and then to not less than one dollar per week.—Jour. Ontario, 1891, page 5173.

51.   A gratuity to a widow must be paid to the widow, unless she was guilty of unbecoming conduct, or not capable of caring for her children.—Jour. 1890, pages 4820-4910.

52.   A member cannot be suspended for non-payment of dues until he has been first notified of the action that would be taken, a record of which must be entered on the minutes.—Digest S.G.L., 1889, Section 707.

53.   Funeral benefits must be paid, but only to dependent relatives.—Digest S.G.L., 1889, Section 99.

54.   A Lodge cannot charge more than one dollar for a Dismissal Certificate. —Digest S.G.L., 1889, Section 235.

55   Weekly sick benefits must not be less than two dollars to every member for the first fifty-two weeks of continuous sickness or disability.—Journal Ontario, 1891, page 5173.

56. The fees for Degrees must not be less than two dollars each.—Const. Sub., Clause 46.

57. Weekly dues must not be less than ten cents per week.—Const. Sub. Clause 47.

**REPORT No. 27**—Rep. J. A. Morton, from the Committee on Laws of Subordinates, made the following amended report, which was adopted :—

*To the Grand Lodge of Ontario, I.O.O.F.:*

Your Committee on Laws of Subordinates, in accordance with the instructions of your Grand Body, amend that portion of their report relating to Otonabee Lodge, No 13, by striking out all reference to Clause 48 of its By-laws.

W. A. RAWLINGS.<br>J. H MORTON.<br>D. ROBERTSON.

**REPORT No. 28**—Rep. J. H. Parnell, from Special Committee No. 4, made the following report, amended as directed by the Grand Lodge (Report No. 6 p. 5606) :—

*To the Grand Lodge of Ontario, I.O.O.F.:*

Your Special Committee, to whom was referred the latter part of clause 14 of the Grand Secretary's Report, beg leave to submit the following :—
Brother Ormiston having for many years been a zealous and valuable member of this Grand Lodge, your Committee heartily endorse the suggestions of the Grand Secretary, and would respectfully recommend that our Representatives in the Sovereign Grand Lodge be directed to request that this Grand Lodge be authorized to recognize his services, and that the title of Past Grand Master be given to Bro. Ormiston—no such title having been given for the year in which he served as Grand Master.

Your Committee move the adoption of the report.

All of which is respectfully submittted.

J. H. PARNELL,<br>*Chairman.*

**REPORT No. 29**—Rep. J. McLurg, from the Committee on Legislation, made the following report, which was adopted :—

*To the Grand Lodge of Ontario, I.O.O.F.:*

Your Committee on Legislation to whom was referred the amendments proposed to Clauses 98 and 102 of the Grand Lodge By-Laws, beg to report and recommend the following :

Amend Clause 98 by adding to the fourth line after the words "each year," the following :—

Except in the case of newly instituted Lodges, which shall be entitled to elect such representatives as their membership may warrant, from their own

Past Grands, or failing such, any Past Grand, in accordance with the provisions contained in Clause 99.

Amend Clause 102 by striking out the word appointment in the third line and substitute therefor the word election.

*Resolved,*—That the foregoing be adopted.

All of which is respectfully submitted.

J. McLURG.

**REPORT No. 30**—Rep. T. Hayne, from Special Committee No. 2, made the following report, which was adopted :—

*To the Grand Lodge of Ontario, I.O.O.F.:*

We, your Special Committee No. 2, to whom was referred clause No. 31, of the Grand Master's Report, beg to submit the following :—

That we, your Committee, heartily endorse the sentiments therein contained, and would call special attention to that portion of the Clause 31 which reminds us that in view of the shortness of life, it is necessary that we should do all we can now to alleviate the sufferings of others. Your Committee would also recommend that memorial notices of the death of Bro. G. P. Dickson, P.G., and that of Bro. H. McAfee, P.G.M., be entered in the Journal of this Grand Lodge in the usual form.

All of which is respectfully submitted.

T. HAYNE.

**REPORT No. 31**—Rep. J. McLurg, from the Committee on Legislation, made the following report, which was adopted :—

*To the Grand Lodge of Ontario, I.O.O.F.:*

Your Committee on Legislation, to whom was referred Clause 18 of the Grand Secretary's Report, would submit the form annexed hereto as a proper and safe report and claim for sick benefits by non-resident members.

*Resolved,*—That the foregoing be adopted.

All of which is respectfully submitted.

J. McLURG,

## SICK BENEFIT CLAIM.

To........Lodge....,I.O.O.F.,.............,Ont.

I,.................................of......................

**State cause and nature of illness.** hereby declare that I am a member in good standing of........ Lodge, No....I.O.O.F.,.............,Ont.

That on the........day of............A. D , 18....,I was taken ill from...........................................

, ...............................................................

**Duration of illness.** that I remained continuously ill till the......day of A. D., 18.. and that during the time of such illness or disability, I was unable to, and did not attend to any work, trade, employment or business.

**Attending Physician.** That during the said period I was attended by Dr......... of...........whose certificate is annexed hereto.

**State time and name of Lodge to which notice was given.** That on the....day of........A. D., 18.... I caused notice of illness to be given to......Lodge, No..., I.O.O.F., of........ The certificate of said Lodge also being annexed hereto.

And I declare the above statements to be true, upon my honor as an Oddfellow.

Yours in F., L. and T.,

....................... Beneficiary.

...................Address.

## PHYSICIAN'S CERTIFICATE.

**Physician is requested to give full particulars of disease or injury.** 1.—This is to certify that Bro.............being a member in good standing in......Lodge, No. .., .. .........., was unable to follow any trade, employment or business, as set forth above by him, being afflicted with............................

**State whether discharged from further attendance, or still under medical attendance, or still able to follow any trade, employment or business.** The cause of said illness or disability was as follows :—........

................................................................

................................................................

................................................................

................................................................

That I was notified of his illness and began attendance upon him on the....day of..........A D., 18... That I continued in attendance from that date to the.....day of..........A.D., at which date...........................................

...................Physician.

## LODGE'S CERTIFICATE.

We the undersigned Noble Grand and Recording Secretary of.......... Lodge, No......I.O.O.F., of..............certify that Bro..........duly notified this Lodge of his illness on the.....day of...............18..... and that the Sick Committee visited the said Brother from time to time during such illness. We also certify that we have examined the declaration of the said Brother, and the certificate of the attending Physician, and declare the same to be true to the best of our knowledge and belief, and that the said

Brother was unable to follow any trade, employment or business during such period as stated in his declaration.

LODGE SEAL..

.....................................
Noble Grand.

.....................................
Rec. Secretary.

NOTE.—If the Brother be not near a Lodge, he will get the above Certificate signed by a Justice of Peace or Clergyman, or, if under the care of an Odd Fellows' Relief Board, he will have it certified by the proper officers of the Board, striking out the words which do not apply.

## COPY OF BY-LAW.

If a Brother be a non-resident, it shall be necessary that a statement or statements of his case, setting forth the nature of his sickness or disability, the time of its commencement and duration, be transmitted to the N. G. of this Lodge, certified by the Lodge nearest to the place where he may be for the time residing or detained, and under the seal of such Lodge; or if he be not near any Lodge by a Justice of the Peace, or a Clergyman, or duly licensed Physician; such statement or statements shall be in accordance with the forms appended to these By-Laws; such Brother shall receive the benefits provided by the By-Laws 18 and 34, provided always, that no benefits shall be paid, unless such statement or statements shall have been presented to the Lodge within 60 days from the date of the commencement of such sickness or disability, or such By-law as the Lodge may have on this subject.

14

## SICK BENEFIT CLAIM

OF

.....................................

.....................................

TO

..................LODGE.

No. ....., I.O.O.F.,

.............. ...,   —   —   ONT.

Notice of illness received.........................

Claim received.....................................

Cheque No...........issued.........................

for $................

**REPORT No. 32**—Rep. M. L. Weber, from the Committee on Mileage and Per Diem, made the following report, which was adopted :—

*To the Grand Lodge of Ontario, I.O.O.F. :*

Your Committee on Mileage and Per Diem beg to submit their final report and certify that they have carefully revised the mileage sheets prepared by the Grand Secretary, and have made such corrections as have been brought to their notice.

Your Committee would recommend the payment to the Officers and Representatives, the amounts as shown on the book returned to the Treasurer, and recommend that the Grand Master issue his order on the Grand Treasurer for the sum of five thousand one hnndred and seventy-one dollars ($5,171.00), to pay said mileage and per diem.

All of which is respectfully submitted.

*Resolved,*—That the foregoing be adopted.

M. L. WEBER.

**REPORT No. 33**—Rep. A. M. Lafferty, from the Committee on Legislation, made the following report, which was adopted :—

*To the Grand Lodge of Ontario, I.O.O.F. :*

Your Committee on Legislation, to whom was referred the question of " The advisability of the Grand Lodge appointing a Medical Examiner to examine and pass all medical papers, same as life insurance companies, before the applicant is admitted to the Initiatory Degree," beg to report, that they deem any legislation on the matter inexpedient, and ask to be discharged from further consideration of the question.

*Resolved,*—That this report be adopted.

ALFRED M. LAFFERTY.

**REPORT No. 34**—Rep. A. H. Blackeby, from the Committee on Finance, made the following report, which was considered seriatim :—

*To the Grand Lodge of Ontario, I.O.O.F. :*

Your Committee on Finance beg leave to report that the following accounts be paid :

| | |
|---|---:|
| Morgan, Puhl & Morris, badges | $ 47 75 |
| Dominion Odd Fellow, printing reports | 123 00 |
| Bro. Chas. Packert, auditor | 25 50 |
| "　A. C. Stewart,　" | 26 70 |

2. We recommend that the sessional officers be paid as follows :

| | |
|---|---:|
| J. A. Young, Assistant Secretary, per diem | $ 2 00 |
| A. Scott, official reporter........ " | 5 00 |
| Janitor | 10 00 |

3. As a slight appreciation of the services during the year of Bro. W. A Rawlings, we recommend a payment of $50.

4. Having ascertained from Bro. Geo. Ross' Report that the affairs of Mystic Lodge have been finally wound up and that there remains to the credit of that Lodge the sum of $75.70, we recommend the payment of $50 of this amount to the widow of the late Bro. Stock, in accordance with the wishes of the Brothers of the defunct Lodge ; and also the payment of $1.25, expenses incurred by Bro. Ross in closing up the affairs of the Lodge.

5. That the salaries of the Grand Lodge Officers for the coming year be as follows :

Grand Secretary........................................... $1,500
Grand Treasurer........................................      200

6. There arise many occasions during the year when it would be exceedingly advantageous to the Order to have some person in authority in a position to do outside work.  Weak Lodges might be strengthened by such a visit.  Lodges that have got astray in the secret work could be set aright. Difficulties which an endless amount of correspondence might fail to straighten out could be surmounted by a few hours' interview.  In all these cases no better qualified or more acceptable man could be chosen than our Grand Secretary, by whom our work in its most minute details has been thoroughly mastered and who is a recognized authority on the secret work.  To enable our Secretary to perform these services to the Order it would be necessary that he secure competent assistance and for that purpose we recommend that $300 be appropriated.

7. We recommend that the bonds of the Grand Officers and the Insurance of the effects of the Grand Lodge be continued.

8. Your Committee have had before them Bro. John Ormiston and heard his statement as to the amount expended by him during the six months he occupied the position of Grand Master, and we recommend that the sum of $50 be voted that Brother for necessary expenses incurred by him during that period.

9. We recommend that one thousand copies of the Journal of Proceedings of this Session be printed and distributed in same manner as last year.

10. The work of the Grand Secretary and Grand Treasurer has been performed in an efficient manner and the expenses of the office of the Grand Secretary have been kept as low as is consistent with a due regard to prompt and creditable service.

11. We recommend that the Committee on Laws of Subordinates and all Special Committees appointed during the year be paid mileage and per diem at same rates as are paid Representatives at this Grand Lodge Session.

12. We recommend that the Grand Master be authorized to draw upon the Grand Treasurer during the year for such sums as he may deem advisable—not in the aggregate to exceed $500.

All of which is respectfully submitted.

*Resolved*,—That the foregoing be adopted.

A. H. BLACKEBY.

Clauses 1 to 5 adopted.

On the motion to adopt Clause 6, Rep. Jno. Ormiston, seconded by Rep. W. F. Howell, moved that "$300" in the last line of Clause 6 be struck out and $100 be inserted.—Amendment carried.

The Report as so amended was adopted.

**REPORT No. 35**—Rep. W. A. Dennis, from the same Committee, made the following report, which was adopted :—

*To the Grand Lodge of Ontario, I.O.O.F. :*

Having reference to paragraph 3 in the Auditor's Report, we are gratified to learn that the Brethren of Egremont Lodge No. 207, Kerwood, are again actively at work after about a year had elapsed without a meeting being held and notwithstanding their having been discouraged by many adverse circumstances. As a slight token of sympathy and encouragement from this Grand Lodge, we recommend that the account standing against the Lodge for per cap. tax and the fine imposed for delay in making returns while the Lodge was practically dormant, be remitted.

We also recommend that the fines imposed upon Hanover and Sycamore Lodges be remitted and that the Grand Secretary be empowered to straighten out the disputed account between the Hanover Lodge and Grand Lodge.

We therefore move the adoption of this report.

All of which is respectfully submitted.

W. A. DENNIS.

**REPORT No. 36**—Rep. N. S. Given, from the same Committee, made the following report, which was adopted :—

*To the Grand Lodge of Ontario, I.O.O.F.:*

We, your Finance Committee, to whom was referred the item of expenditure of $50 for report of Committee on Fraternal Relations, beg leave to report that the amount be paid, but inasmuch as there is an additional expenditure of $51 for printing the report, making a total of $101, your Committee would recommend that in the future it be discontinued, as we do not think it of sufficient value to the jurisdiction,

We therefore move the adoption of this report.

Respectfully submitted.

N. S. GIVEN.

**REPORT No. 37**—Rep. D. Robertson, from the Committee on Legislation, made the following report, which was adopted :—

*To the Grand Lodge of Ontario, I.O.O.F.:*

Your Committee on Legislation, to whom was referred Clause 1 of the Grand Secretary's Report, beg leave to submit the following :

That the subject matter of the Clause may be best dealt with by the Subordinate Lodges.

*Resolved,*—That the report be adopted.

D. ROBERTSON.

**REPORT No. 38**—Rep. J. J. Craig, from the Committee on State of the Order, made the following report, which was adopted :—

*To the Grand Lodge of Ontario, I.O.O.F.:*

We, your Committee on the State of the Order, having considered Clause 15 of the Grand Master's Report relating to appeals for aid, beg leave to report as follows :—

Your Committee fully approve of the course pursued by the Grand Master in withholding his sanction from applications for leave to canvass Subordinate Lodges in this jurisdiction for funds to aid various enterprises. While some of these schemes are no doubt worthy, we believe it would be exceedingly difficult to discriminate, and for this and the reasons assigned by the Grand Master, we agree that the safe plan to follow was that adopted by him.

In regard to Clause 20, of the same report, referring to The Dominion Odd Fellow, your Committee fully recognize the importance of having a reliable official organ and appreciate the successful efforts of the editor of the Odd Fellow in supplying an interesting and instructive journal.

We furthermore admit the desirability of having a copy of this publication in the hands of every brother, and we believe this result would be largely attained if the publishers could see their way clear to make an appreciable reduction in the annual subscription.

We recommend that Subordinate Lodges undertake to secure a fair percentage of their membership as subscribers.

*Resolved,*—That the foregoing be adopted.

Respectfully submitted.

J. J. CRAIG.

**REPORT No. 39**—Rep. Jno. Ormiston, from the same Committee, made the following report, which was not adopted :—

*To the Grand Lodge of Ontario, I.O.O.F.:*

Your Committe on State of the Order, to whom was referred Clauses 14 and 32 of Grand Master's Report *re* " Grand Instructor," beg to say that while they are in full sympathy with the Grand Master, and that there is great need of the services of some competent brother, who can assist the Grand Master, or rather perform the multifarious duties to which he cannot possibly attend, being as the Clause sets forth unable to respond " to a tithe of the calls that come to him."

Your Committee feel that they cannot advise at the present session the creation of a new office, but they would recommend that the Grand Master utilize the services of some available brother to the end that weak lodges may be visited, stimulated and instructed, and that steps may be taken towards the organization of new lodges where there is an expressed desire for them.

For this purpose your Committee favour the appropriation of a sum not to exceed $500 to be used at the discretion of the Grand Master, the results of which may be reported at the next meeting of Grand Lodge.

They would therefore recommend that the Finance Committee be instructed to set apart the said sum to be used by the Grand Master for the objects set forth in this report.

All of which is respectfully submitted.

*Resolved,*—That the foregoing be adopted.

JNO. ORMISTON.

**REPORT No. 40**—Rep. Thos. Woodyatt, from the Committee on Legislation, made the following report, which was adopted :—

*To the Grand Lodge of Ontario, I.O.O.F.:*

Your Committee on Legislation, to whom was referred the following resolution, viz : " That no subordinate lodge in this jurisdiction shall employ an instructor in the new dramatized or floor work any brother other than their own members, who has not first received the sanction of the Grand Master to act as such instructor, and any brother acting as such instructor without having first obtained the permission of the Grand Master shall render himself liable to expulsion from the Order," we beg to report—

That we deem such resolution inexpedient.

*Resolved,*—That this report be adopted.

Fraternally submitted. THOS. WOODYATT.

**REPORT No. 41**—Rep. J. McLurg, from the same Committee, made the following report, which was adopted :—

*To the Grand Lodge of Ontario, I.O.O.F.:*

Your Committee on Legislation, to whom was referred Clause 13 of the Grand Secretary's Report, beg leave to report, that we deem it inexpedient to make any change, but to leave the matter to local legislation.

All of which is respectfully submitted.

*Resolved,*—That this Report be adopted.

J. McLURG.

**REPORT No. 42**—Rep. J. E. Terhune, from the same Committee, made the following report, which was adopted :—

*To the Grand Lodge of Ontario, I.O.O.F.:*

Your Committee on Legislation, to whom was referred Clause 12 of the Grand Secretary's Report, would recommend, that Grand Lodge By-law No. 97 be amended by adding thereto the following :

" Save for the purpose of defraying the expenses of the Rebekah Provincial Convention and that a per capita tax of twenty cents be imposed on all Rebekah Degree Lodges for the purpose of defraying such expenses, to be collected emi-annually."

All which is respectfully submitted.

We therefore move that this report be adopted.

J. E. TERHUNE.

Rep. R. Meek presented the following :—

THE MAYOR'S OFFICE, KINGSTON, ONT., August 8, 1893.

MY DEAR SIR,—The high position attained by your Order among the fraternal societies in this city has naturally developed among all classes of citizens considerable interest in its work. This interest has been largely increased through the enterprise displayed by members of the Order in erecting a magnificent block of buildings, made necessary by its growth and consequent increasing requirements which speaks well for the intrinsic merit of the Order as well as for the zeal and character of its membership here. On all hands I hear a desire expressed that the Grand Lodge shou'd honor this city by selecting it as the place of its annual meeting in 1894. It is perhaps needless for me to mention the many advantages possessed by Kingston for such meetings. Its beautiful situation at the head of the Thousand Islands, the beauties of which can be so easily enjoyed by visiting members, ought in itself to prove sufficiently attractive, but in addition to this, we can promise a temperature so agreeable as to remove one of the greatest discomforts of summer meetings held elsewhere. I may also add that our hotel accommodation will be found equal to any requirement likely to arise. I have, therefore, much pleasure, on behalf of the citizens of Kingston, in inviting the Grand Lodge to hold its next meeting in this city, feeling assured, should it decide to come, that the visit will prove pleasant to members of the Grand Lodge, their Brethren in this district and to the citizens generally.

I am, Sir,

Yours very truly,

NEIL C. POLSON,
*Mayor.*

*Rev. T. W. Jolliffe, Grand Master I.O.O.F.,*
*Ontario, and the Officers and Representa-*
*tives Grand Lodge.*

Rep. F. R. Sargent moved, seconded by Rep. Jno. Bullis, the following :—

*Resolved,*—That when this Grand Lodge adjourns, it does so to meet in Kingston on the second Wednesday in August, 1894, on the invitations of the Kingston Lodges and the Mayor of the city.

Rep. Jno. Hunter, seconded by Rep. G. Powell, moved in amendment, that " Kingston " be struck out and " London " inserted.

Rep. P. McCandlish moved in amendment to the amendment, that " Kingston " be struck out and " Hamilton " inserted.

The question being on the amendment of Rep. P. McCandlish, it was not agreed to.

The question then being on the amendment of Rep. Hunter, it was declared in the negative.

The question recurring on the motion of Rep. F. R. Sargent, it was adopted.

The following, moved by Rep. Thos. Woodyatt, seconded by Rep. J. McLurg, was adopted :—

*Resolved,*—That the incoming Grand Master, Joseph Oliver, be an accredited representative from this jurisdiction to the gathering of our Order at Chicago on September 25th next, in conjunction with Grand Master Jolliffe, this not involving any additional expense on the Grand Lodge.

The following, moved by Rep. R. W. Bell, P.G.M., seconded by Rep. Jno. Donogh, P.G.M., was adopted :—

*Resolved,*—That the most cordial thanks of this Grand Lodge be and are hereby tendered to Grand Master Jolliffe for the exceedingly able and efficient manner in which he has presided over the jurisdiction during the past year and over the present meeting.

The following, moved by Rep. R. W. Bell, P.G.M., seconded by Rep. Jno. Donogh, P.G.M., was adopted :—

*Resolved,*—That this Grand Lodge extend its hearty thanks to Mr Moloney, the representative of the railways, for his courteous attention in vising the tickets of our members.

**REPORT No. 43**—Rep. W. J. Henry, from the Committee on Districts, made the following report, amended as directed by the Grand Lodge, which was adopted :—

*To the Grand Lodge of Ontario, I. O. O. F.:*

Your Committee on Districts, to whom was referred the petitions of Naomi Lodge District, No. 29; and Pembroke Lodge, of District No. 41, after re-considering their former report, recommend as follows, viz. : That Naomi Lodge being represented as being in such a condition as to be almost extinct, be transferred from District No. 29, to District No. 19, in the hopes that this arrangement will revive it, and that no further change be made at present in District 29.

2. That your committee would not advise any change in District No. 41.

Your Committee would move the adoption of this report.

All of which is respectfully submitted,

W. J. HENRY.

**REPORT No. 44**—Bro. W. F. Mountain, from the Committee on General Purposes, made the following report, which was adopted :—

*To the Grand Lodge of Ontario, I. O. O. F.:*

Your Committee on General Purposes beg to report that they have had several meetings during the year, at which Tenders for Supplies were considered and contracts awarded, and the welfare of the Order and interests of the Grand Lodge carefully guarded.

Though no particular instructions had been received to provide badges for this session, yet acting on the resolution of last year, which it was considered covered this year also, your Committee accepted the tender of Messrs. Morgan, Puhl & Morris for badges for this year's meeting. The Committee ordered the badges similar to those of the two previous years, though by getting a plainer ribbon and having them printed instead of embossed, they could be procured at a much less expense; the cost of the present badges is 12½c. each.

As directed by the Grand Lodge, the Committee authorized the Grand Secretary to have the Journal of Proceedings of 1892 bound in cloth, and had the portrait of the Grand Master inserted. The cost was just as had been tendered and the work done by The Dominion Odd Fellow Printing Co. in a most satisfactory manner. Owing to the flattering letters of appreciation received by your Committee in regard to the improved appearance of the Journal, your Committee deem that the extra expense was fully justified and would recommend that the Journal of 1893 be printed and bound in a similar form to that of 1892, the work to be done by the same company, if they will print and bind the Journal at the same price or lower than last year.

Your Committee received from the chairman of the Special Committee on Reduction of Representation, Bro. Jno. Donogh, P.G.M., the report of that Committee, and had it printed and distributed as directed by the Grand Lodge (Journal 1892, page 5341).

Your Committee authorized the Grand Secretary to issue the annual statistical statement to the Lodges ; believing it to be a wise policy to keep the Lodges well posted on the progress of the Order.

The circulars required during the year have been printed and issued with a due regard to economy and the necessity of their issue.

Fraternally submitted.

W. F. MOUNTAIN,
W. BADENACH,
J. B. KING.


Rep. H. M. Bauslaugh, of Olive Branch Lodge No. 88, presented the following obituary on the death of the late Bro. James Hay :—

The late Bro. James Hay, P.G. of Olive Branch Lodge No. 88, Wood-stock, Ontario, was a native of Fala, Scotland. Coming to America in his youth he first settled in the Sunny South, in the neighborhood of New Orleans. Some few years afterward he came north and settled at Woodstock, C.W., where he founded what has since become one of the largest furniture factories in the country and to this medium the town of Woodstock owes largely its present standing as a town. Bro. Hay was an active worker in the cause of education and for many, many years he was on the school trustee board, a position which he held at the time of his death.

Bro. Hay was one of the first members initiated into Olive Branch Lodge No. 88, I.O.O.F. (his eldest son, the present mayor, being one of the charter members), and for many years he was an active and faithful member. Often have we heard him relate the circumstance that brought Oddfellowship to his notice.

Sailing up the Mississippi River in a steamboat, he noticed a man who was unable to do anything for himself through sickness carefully cared for by two or three men, one of whom was constantly by his side. By some means or other he found out that these men were not relatives of the sick one, so he began to enquire why it was that they were so attentive to him. He was informed that they were members of the Independent Order of Odd Fellows. Bro. Hay made up his mind then that the first opportunity he had he would become an Odd Fellow, which he did, and for over twenty years he was enabled to practice the principles of the Order.

When Maple Leaf Encampment No 55 was instituted he at once became a Patriarch and in due time a Past Chief

Bro. Hay was possessed of a strong and robust nature, but three or four ago he fell from a platform at the factory and sustained injuries from which he never fully recovered, his health failed slowly, and although he took the best of care of himself it was plainly seen that he was approaching the end. For ten or twelve weeks before his death he was confined to the house where he was visited by members of the Lodge and Encampment regularly. Later on paralysis seized him and on the 4th of April, 1893, he passed away, being in his 70th year, leaving a widow, four sons and two daughters. He was buried by the Order, to which he was greatly attached.

Rep. J. B. Kitchen, of Chatham Lodge No. 29, presented the following obituary, on the death of the late Bro. Jno. Schneider, P.G. :—

In the death of John Schneider, P.G. and P.C.P., which occurred June 16th, 1893, Chatham Lodge No. 29, suffered an irreparable loss. Bro. Schneider was born in the City of Ulm, Germany, ——— 1822, was initiated in Chatham Lodge No. 29, Sept. 5th, 1854, charter member Chatham Encampment No. 10, Nov. 9th, 1871.

He was a noble man and true Odd Fellow—of a modest and retiring disposition, yet firm and unhesitating in the maintenance of truth and right. He was noted for strict honesty and integrity, and was for over quarter of a century treasurer of his Lodge, giving freely of his time to the work and best interests of the Order, ever prompt and faithful in the discharge of duty. He loved Oddfellowship for the good he found in it, and maintained an unbroken membership for nearly thirty-nine years. He gave honor to his Lodge and his example is worthy of emulation.

Under Grand Lodge By-law 15, nominations for Grand Officers were now called for.

GRAND MASTER.

Rep. A. H. Blackeby nominated Bro. W. H. Hoyle, Cannington.

DEPUTY GRAND MASTER.

Rep. J. Donogh, P.G.M., nominated Rep. Thos. Woodyatt, Brantford.

Rep. W. F. Howell nominated Bro. Leonard Ferguson, St. Thomas.

GRAND WARDEN.

Rep. W. J. Henry nominated Bro. J. R. Peckham, Niagara Falls.

Rep. A. A. Graham nominated Bro. O. E. Fleming, Windsor.

Rep. Harry Gilby nominated Bro. Alf. Coyell, Toronto.

Rep. J. T. Hornibrook, P.G.M., nominated J. A. Young, Thamesford.

Rep. R. Brockbank nominated Bro. Hy. White, Port Hope.

Rep. S M. Thomson nominated Bro. S. K. Binkley, Niagara Falls.

Rep. A. Jacobi nominated Bro. J. W. Grote, St. Catharines.

Rep. J. D. McDermid nominated Bro. Wm. Warnock, Aylmer.

Rep. Goslan nominated Bro. Jno. Gibson, Blenheim.

Rep. R. J. Stewart nominated Bro. J. B. Ferris, Campbellford.

Rep. Shambleau nominated Bro. G. Mitchell, Wallaceburgh.

Rep. C. J. Wall nominated Bro. E. O. Berdan, Strathroy.

Rep P. Brown nominated Bro. W. A. Miner, St. Thomas.

Rep. S. K. Marshall nominated Bro. Rev. W. Saunders, Lonsdale.

### GRAND SECRETARY.

Rep. Jos. Oliver nominated Bro. J. B. King, Toronto.

### GRAND TREASURER.

Bro. J. T. Hornibrook, P.G.M., nominated Bro. Wm. Badenach, Toronto.

### GRAND REPRESENTATIVE.

Bro. W. H. Cole, P.G.M., nominated Bro. Hy. Robertson, P.G.M., Collingwood.

Rep. W. A. Dennis nominated Bro. Jno. Donogh, P.G.M., Toronto.

Rep. F. Gallagher nominated Bro. J. B. McIntyre, P.G.M., St. Catharines.

Rep. H. M. Bauslaugh nominated Bro. R. W. Bell, P.G.M., Peterborough.

Rep. —— nominated Rev. Bro. T. W. Jolliffe, Campbell-ford.

The Installation of Officers was now proceeded with.

Bros. J. T. Hornibrook, P.G.M., and Jno. Donogh, P.G.M., at the request of the Chair, introduced Bro. Jos. Oliver, Grand Master elect, who was duly obligated and installed Grand

Master for the coming year by the Grand Master, Rev. Bro. T. W. Jolliffe, whereupon Bro. Jolliffe took his Chair as Junior Past Grand Master.

Bro. Jos. Oliver, Grand Master, then proceeded to instal the other Grand Officers elect, as follows :—

Bros. R. W. Bell, P.G.M., and P. E. Fitz-Patrick, P.G.M., by request, introduced Bro. W. H. Hoyle, Deputy Grand Master elect, who was duly installed as Deputy Grand Master for the ensuing year.

By request of the Chair, Bro. S. M. Thomson and Rev. Bro· W. J. Saunders introduced Bro Thomas Woodyatt, Grand Warden elect, who was duly installed Grand Warden for the incoming year.

By request of the Chair, Bros. R. W. Bell, P.G.M., and P. E. Fitz-Patrick, P.G.M., introduced Bro. J. B. King, Grand Secretary elect, who was duly installed Grand Secretary for the 28th time.

Rev. Bro. T. W. Jolliffe, P.G.M., and Bro. R. Brockbank, at the request of the Grand Master, introduced Bro. Wm. Badenach, Grand Treasurer elect, who was for the 18th time installed Grand Treasurer.

The Grand Master made the following appointments ; the several Brothers were regularly introduced and installed into their respective offices :—

Bro. Dr. J. McLurg, Woodstock, Grand Marshal.
Bro. L. C. Pascon, Belleville, Grand Conductor.
Bro. M. L. Weber, Elmira. Grand Guardian.
Bro. Andrew Patterson, Waubaushene, Grand Herald.
Rev. Bro. F. W. Armstrong, Trenton, Grand Chaplain.

The Grand Master named the following to be District Deputy Grand Masters for the coming year :—

## LIST OF DISTRICTS.

| DISTRICTS. | LODGES, | No. | LOCATION. | NAME AND P.O. ADDRESS OF D.D.G.M. |
|---|---|---|---|---|
| Essex, No. 1. | Rose | 28 | Amherstburg | W. H. Ryall, Leamington. |
|  | Frontier | 45 | Windsor |  |
|  | Beaver | 82 | Ruthven |  |
|  | Leamington | 140 | Leamington |  |
|  | Concord | 142 | Kingsville |  |
|  | Enterprise | 218 | Essex Centre |  |
|  | Woodslee | 220 | South Woodslee |  |
|  | Comber | 298 | Comber |  |
| Kent, No. 2. | Chatham | 29 | Chatham | O. F. Bennett, Merlin. |
|  | Rondeau | 40 | Blenheim |  |
|  | Western City | 98 | Chatham |  |
|  | Sydenham Valley | 120 | Wallaceburg |  |
|  | Dresden | 124 | Dresden |  |
|  | Merlin | 226 | Merlin |  |
| Bothwell, No. 3. | Mt. Zion | 46 | Newbury | W. G. Rogers, Glencoe. |
|  | Bothwell | 74 | Bothwell |  |
|  | Glencoe | 133 | Glencoe |  |
|  | Ridgetown | 144 | Ridgetown |  |
|  | Thamesville | 157 | Thamesville |  |
|  | Florence | 196 | Florence |  |
|  | Rodney | 291 | Rodney |  |
| Elgin, No. 4. | Elgin | 32 | St. Thomas | James Smith, Harrietsville. |
|  | Erie | 33 | Pt. Burwell |  |
|  | Hope | 69 | Harrietsville |  |
|  | St. Thomas | 76 | St. Thomas |  |
|  | Aylmer | 94 | Aylmer |  |
|  | Glanworth | 289 | Glanworth |  |
| Otter, No. 5. | Otter | 50 | Tilsonburg | Peter Geddes, Tilsonburg. |
|  | Constellation | 85 | Burgessville |  |
|  | Hayden | 152 | Norwich |  |
|  | Tecumseh | 182 | Otterville |  |
| Long Point, No. 6. | Simcoe | 161 | Simcoe | John W. Horton, Simcoe. |
|  | Jarvis | 191 | Jarvis |  |
|  | Equity | 232 | Hagersville |  |
|  | Waterford | 235 | Waterford |  |
|  | Caledonia | 253 | Caledonia |  |
| Welland, No. 7. | Orient | 134 | Welland | A. B. Hurrell, Internat'l Bridge. |
|  | Emerald | 173 | Dunnville |  |
|  | Beacon | 201 | Pt. Colborne |  |
|  | International | 228 | Internat'l Bridge |  |
| Niagara, No. 8. | Union | 16 | St. Catharines | J. B. McIntyre, P.G.M., St. Catharines. |
|  | Niagara Falls | 53 | Niagara Falls |  |
|  | Empire | 87 | St. Catharines |  |
|  | Cataract | 103 | Niagara Falls South |  |
|  | Livingstone | 130 | Thorold |  |
|  | Freestone | 215 | Beamsville |  |

LIST OF DISTRICTS—*Continued.*

| DISTRICTS. | LODGES. | No. | LOCATION. | NAME AND P.O. ADDRESS OF D.D.G.M. |
|---|---|---|---|---|
| Hamilton, No. 9. | Excelsior | 44 | Hamilton | J. Anderson, M.D., Hamilton. |
| | Unity | 47 | Hamilton | |
| | Victoria | 64 | Hamilton | |
| | Crescent | 104 | Hamilton | |
| | Valley City | 117 | Dundas | |
| | Ancaster | 138 | Ancaster | |
| | Oak Leaf | 159 | Hamilton | |
| | Wellington Sq're. | 178 | Burlington | |
| | Minerva. | 197 | Hamilton | |
| Brant, No. 10. | Gore | 34 | Brantford | Henry Gmelin, Ayr. |
| | Grand River | 91 | Paris | |
| | Harmony | 115 | Brantford | |
| | Dolman | 174 | Ayr | |
| | Lynden | 259 | Lynden | |
| | Sheard | 276 | New Dundee | |
| Oxford, No. 11. | Samaritan | 35 | Ingersoll | James McLurg, M.D., Woodstock. |
| | Oxford | 77 | Ingersoll | |
| | Olive Branch | 88 | Woodstock | |
| | Lily | 211 | Dorchester | |
| | Embro Star | 229 | Embro | |
| | Thamesford | 258 | Thamesford | |
| | Woodstock | 269 | Woodstock | |
| London, No. 12. | Eureka | 30 | London | J. M. Symonds, London. |
| | Forest City | 38 | London | |
| | Dominion | 48 | London | |
| | Howard | 58 | Strathroy | |
| | Chorazin | 190 | London East | |
| | Egremont | 207 | Kerwood | |
| | Mt. Bridges | 217 | Mt. Bridges | |
| | Ilderton | 234 | Ilderton | |
| North Middlesex, No. 13. | Lucan | 70 | Lucan | Alex. Thoman, Arkona. |
| | Ivy | 90 | Parkhill | |
| | Royal Oak | 108 | Forest | |
| | Saxon | 121 | Ailsa Craig | |
| | Sycamore | 151 | Arkona | |
| | Wildey | 153 | Granton | |
| | Dauncey | 176 | Camlachie | |
| | Acorn | 236 | Thedford | |
| St. Clair, No. 14. | Friendship | 65 | Petrolea | Alex. Simpson, Petrolea. |
| | St. Clair | 106 | Point Edward | |
| | Sarnia | 126 | Sarnia | |
| | Model | 147 | Wyoming | |
| | Ridgely | 250 | Oil Springs | |
| | Lambton | 277 | Brigden | |

LIST OF DISTRICTS—*Continued.*

| DISTRICTS. | LODGES. | No. | LOCATION. | NAME AND P.O. ADDRESS OF D.D.G.M. |
|---|---|---|---|---|
| Huron, No. 15. | Fidelity | 55 | Seaforth | |
| | Huron | 62 | Goderich | |
| | Exeter | 67 | Exeter | Samuel Alexander Popplestone, Exeter. |
| | Clinton | 83 | Clinton | |
| | Brucefield | 210 | Brucefield | |
| | Hensall | 223 | Hensall | |
| Perth, No. 16. | St. Mary's | 36 | St. Mary's | |
| | Avon | 41 | Stratford | |
| | Bissell | 51 | Mitchell | |
| | Nith | 96 | New Hamburg | Weir Acheson, Milverton. |
| | Romeo | 164 | Stratford | |
| | Silver Star | 202 | Milverton | |
| | Millbank | 209 | Millbank | |
| Royal City, No. 17. | Fergus | 73 | Fergus | |
| | Reliance | 89 | Guelph | |
| | Grand Union | 97 | Berlin | |
| | Waterloo | 107 | Galt | |
| | Progress | 158 | Guelph | S. Law, Guelph. |
| | Germania | 184 | Waterloo | |
| | Cambridge | 188 | Preston | |
| | Elmira | 216 | Elmira | |
| | Elora | 231 | Elora | |
| Credit, No. 18. | Milton | 92 | Milton | |
| | Golden Star | 101 | Brampton | |
| | Orion | 109 | Georgetown | G. Hillmer, Oakville. |
| | Streetsville | 122 | Streetsville | |
| | Oakville | 132 | Oakville | |
| | Acton | 204 | Acton | |
| Toronto, No. 19. | Canada | 49 | Toronto | |
| | Covenant | 52 | Toronto | |
| | QueenCity of Ont. | 56 | Toronto | |
| | The Toronto | 71 | Toronto | |
| | Laurel | 110 | Toronto | |
| | Naomi | 116 | Markham | |
| | Albert | 194 | Toronto | W. J. Cruickshank Weston. |
| | Weston | 200 | Weston | |
| | Prince of Wales | 230 | Toronto | |
| | Wilton | 242 | Toronto | |
| | Floral | 252 | Parkdale | |
| | East Toronto | 263 | Toronto | |
| | Lake View | 272 | West Toronto Junc. | |
| | Broadview | 294 | Toronto | |
| North York, No. 20. | Aurora | 148 | Aurora | Fred Saxton, Newmarket. |
| | Pyramid | 156 | Newmarket | |
| Dufferin, No. 21. | Maple Leaf | 57 | Orangeville | |
| | Hillsburg | 167 | Hillsburg | R. Hughes, Orangeville. |
| | Grand Valley | 256 | Grand Valley | |
| | Credit | 257 | Erin | |

LIST OF DISTRICTS—*Continued.*

| DISTRICTS. | LODGES. | No. | LOCATION. | NAME AND P.O. ADDRESS OF D.D.G.M. |
|---|---|---|---|---|
| Harriston, No. 22. | Minto | 98 | Harriston | |
| | Garnet | 139 | Mount Forest | |
| | Listowel | 160 | Listowel | John Waldon, |
| | Grey | 169 | Durham | Palmerston. |
| | Clifford | 214 | Clifford | |
| | Gordon | 247 | Palmerston | |
| Wingham, No. 23. | Maitland | 119 | Wingham | |
| | Western Star | 149 | Brussels | |
| | Montana | 177 | Wroxeter | Lemuel Hearts, |
| | Teeswater | 183 | Teeswater | Teeswater. |
| | Howick | 192 | Gorrie | |
| Lucknow, No. 24. | Lucknow | 112 | Lucknow | |
| | Penetangore | 172 | Kincardine | David Sheriff, |
| | Silver City | 206 | Tiverton | Lucknow. |
| | Ripley | 287 | Ripley | |
| Walkerton, No. 25. | Walkerton | 84 | Walkerton | |
| | Denovo | 170 | Port Elgin | |
| | Ahiram | 205 | Paisley | F. Biette, |
| | Chesley | 221 | Chesley | Paisley. |
| | Sauble | 227 | Tara | |
| | Hanover | 233 | Hanover | |
| Georgian Bay, No. 26. | Collingwood | 54 | Collingwood | |
| | North Star | 68 | Stayner | |
| | Owen Sound | 180 | Owen Sound | |
| | Dufferin | 186 | Flesherton | |
| | Thornbury | 243 | Thornbury | Alex. Brownlee, |
| | Meaford | 260 | Meaford | Barrie. |
| | Barrie | 63 | Barrie | |
| | Alliston | 171 | Alliston | |
| | Tottenham | 255 | Tottenham | |
| Orillia, No. 27. | Georgian Bay | 219 | Waubaushene | J. Hugh Hammond |
| | Orillia | 246 | Orillia | Orillia. |
| | Midland | 274 | Midland | |
| Parry Sound No. 28. | Parry Sound | 189 | Parry Sound | Thos. A. Clark, Parry Sound. |
| Uxbridge, No. 29. | Nipissing | 79 | Uxbridge | Thomas Brigham |
| | Brougham | 155 | Whitevale | Bentley, |
| | Sutton | 168 | Sutton | Sutton West. |

LIST OF DISTRICTS—*Continued.*

| DISTRICTS. | LODGES. | No. | LOCATION. | NAME AND P.O. ADDRESS OF D.D.G.M. |
|---|---|---|---|---|
| Ontario, No. 30. | Phœnix | 22 | Oshawa | Chas. H. Giles, Oshawa. |
|  | Corinthian | 61 | Oshawa |  |
|  | Flo. Nightingale. | 66 | Bowmanville |  |
|  | Eastern Star | 72 | Whitby |  |
|  | Warriner | 75 | Port Perry |  |
|  | Beethoven | 165 | Brooklyn |  |
| Victoria, No. 31. | Lindsay | 100 | Lindsay | S. H. Glassford, Cannington. |
|  | Manilla | 105 | Manilla |  |
|  | Charity | 129 | Sunderland |  |
|  | Peaceful Dove | 135 | Cannington |  |
|  | Cicerone | 195 | Woodville |  |
|  | Beaverton | 249 | Beaverton |  |
| Durham, No. 32. | Durham | 78 | Port Hope | Stanley Barr, Cobourg. |
|  | Cobourg | 136 | Cobourg |  |
| Peterboro', No. 33. | Otonabee | 13 | Peterboro' | W. B. Burnett, Havelock. |
|  | Peterboro' | 111 | Peterboro' |  |
|  | Norwood | 262 | Norwood |  |
|  | Havelock | 286 | Havelock |  |
|  | Thomasburg | 293 | Thomasburg |  |
|  | Pontypool | 296 | Pontypool |  |
| Midland, No. 34. | Madoc | 179 | Madoc | E. W. Gaudrie, Campbellford. |
|  | Sterling | 239 | Sterling |  |
|  | Campbellford | 248 | Campbellford |  |
|  | Hastings | 273 | Hastings |  |
| Bay of Quinte, No. 35. | Belleville | 81 | Belleville | Rev. F. W. Armstrong, Trenton. |
|  | Napanee | 86 | Napanee |  |
|  | Desoronto | 102 | Deseronto |  |
|  | Trenton | 113 | Trenton |  |
|  | Mizpah | 127 | Belleville |  |
|  | Bay of Quinte | 143 | Picton |  |
|  | Argyle | 212 | Napanee |  |
| Kingston, No. 36. | Cataraqui | 10 | Kingston | Robert Meek, Kingston. |
|  | Kingston | 59 | Kingston |  |
|  | Gananoque | 114 | Gananoque |  |
|  | Lansdowne | 270 | Lansdowne |  |
|  | Tweed | 290 | Tweed |  |
|  | Mayflower | 297 | Parham |  |
|  | Cornucopia | 299 | McLaren's Depot |  |

15

LIST OF DISTRICTS—*Continued.*

| DISTRICTS. | LODGES. | No. | LOCATION. | NAME AND P.O. ADDRESS OF D.D.G.M. |
|---|---|---|---|---|
| St. Lawrence, No. 37. | Brock | 9 | Brockville | G. B. Magee, Merrickville. |
| | St. Lawrence | 137 | Brockville | |
| | Farmersville | 237 | Athens | |
| | Rideau | 242 | Smith's Falls | |
| | Mallorytown | 245 | Mallorytown | |
| | Delta | 265 | Delta | |
| | Balmoral | 280 | Merrickville | |
| | Lyn | 284 | Lyn | |
| Eastern, No. 38. | Oriental | 163 | Cornwall | M. Meyers, Cornwall. |
| Ottawa, No. 39. | Ottawa | 224 | Ottawa | J. A. Jones, M.D. Kemptville. |
| | Carleton | 240 | Ottawa | |
| | Rockliffe | 278 | Ottawa | |
| | Grenville | 279 | Kemptville | |
| | Earnscliffe | 283 | Janeville | |
| | Morewood | 285 | Morewood | |
| | Chesterville | 287 | Chesterville | |
| | Manotick | 295 | Manotick | |
| Lanark, No. 40. | Stella | 125 | Carleton Place | N. D. McCallum, Carleton Place. |
| | Alpha | 154 | Almonte | |
| | Fraternity | 264 | Perth | |
| | Stanley | 268 | Lanark | |
| Renfrew, No. 41. | Marion | 131 | Renfrew | M. D. Graham, Renfrew. |
| | Vivian | 146 | Arnprior | |
| | Pembroke | 203 | Pembroke | |
| | Alba | 254 | Pakenham | |
| Muskoka, No. 42. | Bracebridge | 251 | Bracebridge | D. Wilkinson, Huntsville. |
| | Fairy | 275 | Huntsville | |
| North Bay, No. 43. | North Bay | 271 | North Bay | E. W. Ross, North Bay. |
| Sudbury, No. 44. | Sudbury | 282 | Sudbury | Alex. Hay Beath, Sudbury. |
| Sault Ste. Marie, No. 45. | Arthur | 281 | Sault Ste. Marie | George Hunter, Sault Ste. Marie |
| Chapleau, No. 46. | Missanabie | 266 | Cheapleau | Walter Hepburn, Chapleau. |
| Thunder Bay, No. 47. | Porth Arthur | 244 | Port Arthur | Caleb H. Shera, Port Arthur. |
| | Algoma | 267 | Fort William | |
| Rainy River No. 48. | Gold Hill | 261 | Rat Portage | A. J. Holmes, Keewatin. |
| | Minnetonka | 292 | Keewatin | |

## DISTRICT DEPUTIES FOR REBEKAH LODGES.

| NAME. | LODGE. | No. | LOCATION. |
| --- | --- | --- | --- |
| Sister Mrs. Laura Childs.. { | Victoria ......... | 1 | London. |
|  | May Queen ..... | 5 |  |
| "　　" Electa Jacobi .. | Oshawa ......... | 3 | Oshawa. |
| "　　" Esther Fraser . | Naomi ........ | 6 | Windsor. |
| "　　" Elisabeth Lee { | Louise .......... | 10 | Kingston. |
|  | Aberdeen ....... | 30 |  |
| "　　" Maggie Little .. | Beatrice...... ... | 12 | Guelph. |
| "　　" Mary Moore.... | Jubilee.......... | 13 | Chatham. |
| "　　" Barbara Scott .. | Edna .... ... | 14 | St. Thomas. |
| "　　" Agnes Peach.... | Harmony ....... | 15 | Gananoque. |
| "　　" Laura E. Ryan { | Olive Branch.... | 16 | Toronto. |
|  | Hebron ......... | 31 |  |
| "　　" PenelopeSavage { | Myrtle .......... | 17 | Elora. |
|  | Ivy ........ ... | 26 |  |
| "　　" Emily L. Pattison | Excelsior ....... | 16 | International Bridge. |
| Bro. D. Wilson ............. | Mizpah .......... | 19 | Collingwood. |
| Sister Mrs. J. H. Hughes.... | Donalda.......... | 20 | North Bay. |
| "　　" Sarah Cracknell. | Flora............ | 21 | Sault Ste. Marie. |
| Bro. W. H. Smith.......... | Lucknow ....... | 22 | Lucknow. |
| " Charles Slaght ........ | Inglewood ..... | 23 | Waterford. |
| " Wm. Glover .......... | Prudence........ | 24 | Brantford. |
| " R. D. Hall............ | Alberta ......... | 25 | Kincardine. |
| " J. R. Peckham ........ | Esther .... ... | 27 | Niagara Falls. |
| " Jno. Gibson, P.G.M. .. | Colfax ... ..... | 28 | Sarnia. |
| " Peter McCallum ...... | Athewell ....... | 29 | Almonte. |

The business of the Session being concluded, the Grand Chaplain offered prayer.

At 12:50 p.m. the Deputy Grand Master, by direction of the Chair, declared the Thirty-ninth Session of the Grand Lodge of Ontario adjourned *sine die*.

# APPENDIX.

ABSTRACT FROM SEMI-ANNUAL RETURNS.

## MEMBERSHIP.

| No. of Lodge. | NAME OF LODGE. | Initiated. | Reinstated. | Admitt'd by card | Suspended for Cause. | Susp'nded N.P.D | Withdrawn. | Expelled. | Died. | Members per last Report. | Present Membership. | Number of Brothers Sick. |
|---|---|---|---|---|---|---|---|---|---|---|---|---|
| 9 | Brock | 8 | | | | | | | | 105 | 113 | 9 |
| 10 | Cataraqui | 28 | 1 | | | 6 | 2 | | | 223 | 244 | 24 |
| 13 | Otonabee | 15 | | | | 9 | | | | 129 | 135 | 17 |
| 16 | Union | 10 | | | | | | | 1 | 223 | 232 | 26 |
| 22 | Phœnix | | | | | 4 | 1 | | 1 | 82 | 76 | 10 |
| 28 | Rose | 5 | | | | | 2 | | | 97 | 100 | 1 |
| 29 | Chatham | 2 | | | | 5 | | | 1 | 160 | 156 | 25 |
| 30 | Eureka | 4 | | | | 7 | | | 1 | 112 | 108 | 19 |
| 32 | Elgin | 12 | 1 | | | 4 | 2 | | 1 | 223 | 229 | 18 |
| 33 | Erie | | | | | | | | | 18 | 18 | 3 |
| 34 | Gore | 13 | | | | 3 | 1 | | 3 | 209 | 215 | 29 |
| 35 | Samaritan | 6 | | 1 | 1 | | | | | 160 | 166 | 24 |
| 36 | St. Mary's | 4 | | | | | 2 | | 2 | 140 | 140 | 14 |
| 38 | Forest City | 2 | | | | 5 | | | 1 | 125 | 121 | 26 |
| 40 | Rondeau | 7 | | | | | 1 | 1 | | 105 | 110 | 8 |
| 41 | Avon | 6 | | | | 5 | 1 | 1 | 1 | 211 | 209 | 33 |
| 44 | Excelsior | 5 | | | | 3 | | | 1 | 139 | 140 | 15 |
| 45 | Frontier | 4 | 2 | | | 8 | | | 2 | 257 | 253 | 21 |
| 46 | Mount Zion | | | | | | | | | 26 | 26 | 1 |
| 47 | Unity | 6 | 1 | 1 | | 9 | 1 | | 3 | 287 | 282 | 44 |
| 48 | Dominion | 4 | | | | 8 | 3 | | | 161 | 154 | 20 |
| 49 | Canada | 4 | 1 | | | 8 | 2 | | | 208 | 203 | 12 |
| 50 | Otter | 12 | | | | 6 | 1 | | | 110 | 115 | 13 |
| 51 | Bissell | | 7 | | | 5 | | | | 28 | 24 | 3 |
| 52 | Covenant | 2 | | 3 | | 2 | 1 | | 2 | 184 | 184 | 19 |
| 53 | Niagara | 3 | | 1 | | 11 | | | | 126 | 119 | 12 |
| 54 | Collingwood | 3 | | | | 8 | 2 | | 1 | 149 | 141 | 18 |
| 55 | Fidelity | | | | | | | | | 17 | 17 | 6 |
| 56 | Queen City of Ontario | 3 | | | | 4 | 3 | | 1 | 170 | 165 | 22 |
| 57 | Maple Leaf | 7 | | 1 | | 5 | | | | 44 | 47 | 4 |
| 58 | Howard | 9 | 2 | 3 | | 3 | 3 | | 1 | 94 | 101 | 9 |
| 59 | Kingston | 17 | 1 | | | | 5 | | | 239 | 252 | 31 |
| 61 | Corinthian | 3 | 1 | | | | 1 | | 1 | 199 | 201 | 22 |
| 62 | Huron | 3 | | | | | 2 | | | 120 | 121 | 20 |
| 63 | Barrie | 4 | | 1 | | 1 | 3 | | 1 | 115 | 115 | 12 |
| 64 | Victoria | 4 | 1 | | | 1 | 2 | | | 65 | 67 | 11 |
| 65 | Friendship | 7 | 2 | | | | 1 | | | 173 | 181 | 10 |
| 66 | Florence Nightingale | 2 | | | | 5 | 1 | | 1 | 151 | 146 | 10 |
| 67 | Exeter | 7 | 1 | 1 | | | | | | 35 | 44 | 3 |
| 68 | North Star | | | | | | | | | 49 | 49 | 5 |
| 69 | Hope | 11 | | 1 | | | 6 | | | 57 | 63 | 9 |
| 70 | Lucan | | 1 | | | | | | | 23 | 24 | 3 |
| 71 | The Toronto | 2 | 1 | | | | | | | 57 | 60 | 9 |
| 72 | Eastern Star | 5 | 1 | | | | 1 | 1 | 2 | 99 | 101 | 7 |
| 73 | Fergus | 7 | 1 | | | 2 | | | | 61 | 67 | 6 |
| 74 | Bothwell | 1 | | | | | | | 1 | 48 | 48 | 5 |
| 75 | Warriner | 2 | | 1 | | 4 | | | | 80 | 79 | 13 |
| 76 | St. Thomas | 8 | 1 | | | 5 | 1 | | 1 | 344 | 346 | 51 |
| 77 | Oxford | 3 | | | | 2 | | | 1 | 109 | 109 | 12 |
| 78 | Durham | 8 | | | | | 1 | | | 116 | 123 | 6 |
| 79 | Nipissing | 8 | | | | 1 | 1 | | | 57 | 63 | 7 |
| 80 | Amity | 10 | | | | 5 | | | | 172 | 177 | 28 |
| 81 | Belleville | 1 | 1 | 1 | | 5 | 3 | | 1 | 197 | 191 | 19 |
| 82 | Beaver | 1 | | | | 2 | | | | 57 | 56 | 6 |
| 83 | Clinton | | | | | | | | | 24 | 24 | 5 |
| 84 | Walkerton | 5 | | 1 | | 1 | | 3 | | 60 | 62 | 9 |
| 85 | Constellation | 15 | 6 | | | 2 | 1 | | | 30 | 48 | 2 |
| 86 | Napanee | 3 | 1 | | | | 2 | | | 58 | 60 | 7 |
| 87 | Empire | | | | | | | | 1 | 124 | 123 | 11 |
| 88 | Olive Branch | 3 | 2 | | | 1 | | | 1 | 131 | 134 | 11 |
| 89 | Reliance | 3 | | 1 | | 3 | | | 7 | 156 | 156 | 22 |

## Term Ending 30th June, 1892.

### SICK BENEFITS AND RELIEFS.

| Number of Weeks' Sickness. | Amount paid for Sick Benefits. | Amount paid for Burying Deceased Bros. | No. of Brothers' Wives Died. | Amount paid for Burying Bros' Wives. | No. of Widows. | Amount paid for Relief of Widows. | No. of Orphans. | Amount paid for Educating Orphans. | Paid to Lodge Surgeon. | Paid for Nursing Sick Brothers. | Paid for Special Relief & Charity. | Total Relief | No. of Lodge. |
|---|---|---|---|---|---|---|---|---|---|---|---|---|---|
| | $ c | $ c | | $ c | | $ c | | $ c | $ c | $ c | $ c | $ c | |
| 22 | 66 50 | | | | | | | | | | | 66 50 | 9 |
| 86-4 | 260 00 | | 2 | 30 00 | 1 | 15 00 | | | 50 00 | 20 50 | | 375 50 | 10 |
| 75 | 301 12 | | | | | | | | 14 50 | | | 315 62 | 13 |
| 209 | 609 00 | 250 00 | | | | 255 00 | | | | | | 1114 00 | 16 |
| 25 | 75 00 | 40 00 | 1 | 15 00 | | | | | 24 00 | | 20 00 | 174 00 | 22 |
| 17 | 49 00 | | | | | | | | | | | 49 00 | 28 |
| 93 | 267 00 | 25 00 | | | 8 | 160 00 | 4 | 80 00 | 94 13 | | 24 50 | 650 63 | 29 |
| 135 | 179 10 | 40 00 | | | | | | | 41 00 | | | 260 10 | 30 |
| 148 | 496 57 | | | | 4 | 55 00 | | | 83 00 | 2 00 | 20 00 | 656 57 | 32 |
| 21 | 63 00 | | | | | | | | | | | 63 00 | 33 |
| 140 | 666 10 | 80 00 | 2 | 400 00 | | | | | | 94 00 | | 1240 10 | 34 |
| 111 | 366 00 | | | | 5 | 100 00 | | | | | | 466 00 | 35 |
| 66 | 174 00 | 40 00 | | | 2 | 190 00 | | | | | 20 00 | 424 00 | 36 |
| 134 | 391 50 | 120 00 | 3 | 60 00 | | | | | | | | 571 50 | 38 |
| 19-5 | 78 64 | | 1 | 20 00 | 1 | 18 00 | | | | 75 00 | | 191 64 | 40 |
| 136-6 | 547 02 | 100 00 | 1 | 25 00 | | | | | | 15 00 | | 687 02 | 41 |
| 145 | 406 75 | 50 00 | | | 3 | 320 00 | | | 50 00 | | | 826 75 | 44 |
| 221-6 | 700 68 | 100 00 | | | 14 | 15 00 | | | | | 184 60 | 1000 28 | 45 |
| 1 | 1 00 | | | | | | | | | | | 1 00 | 46 |
| 301 | 848 00 | 225 00 | 2 | 50 00 | 13 | 231 68 | 3 | 26 67 | 109 00 | 83 87 | 8 70 | 1582 92 | 47 |
| 123 | 367 00 | | | | | 26 00 | | | | | | 393 00 | 48 |
| 58-6 | 206 00 | | | | 3 | 130 00 | | | 104 00 | | 16 64 | 456 64 | 49 |
| 72 | 180 00 | | | | | | | | 3 00 | 35 00 | | 218 00 | 50 |
| 7 | 21 00 | | | | | | | | | | | 21 00 | 51 |
| 63-5 | 242 35 | 40 00 | | | 1 | 300 00 | | | 96 50 | 4 00 | 39 72 | 722 57 | 52 |
| 55-5 | 206 03 | | | | | | | | 44 50 | | 10 00 | 260 53 | 53 |
| 65-3 | 196 00 | 80 00 | | | 3 | 45 00 | | | 75 00 | | | 396 00 | 54 |
| 24 | 72 00 | 16 00 | | | | 60 00 | | | | | | 148 00 | 55 |
| 83-3 | 330 07 | 40 00 | 1 | 20 00 | 5 | 172 00 | | | 77 50 | | | 639 57 | 56 |
| 20-4 | 61 50 | | 1 | 15 00 | | | | | | | | 76 50 | 57 |
| 37-3 | 86 60 | 30 00 | | | 1 | 76 50 | | | | | | 193 10 | 58 |
| 126-5 | 381 00 | 100 00 | | | 8 | 112 50 | | | 52 50 | | 20 00 | 676 00 | 59 |
| 93-5 | 275 22 | 44 00 | | | 1 | 125 00 | | | 78 00 | 21 25 | | 543 47 | 60 |
| 49 | 148 35 | | | | 8 | 112 50 | | | | | | 260 85 | 61 |
| 60-3 | 189 00 | | | | 3 | 65 00 | 4 | 25 00 | | | | 279 00 | 62 |
| 63 | 147 00 | | | | 3 | 40 00 | | | 25 50 | | | 212 50 | 63 |
| 44 | 105 90 | | | | 5 | 75 00 | | | | 1 60 | | 182 50 | 64 |
| 37-2 | 149 10 | 50 00 | | | 2 | 325 00 | | | 52 50 | 6 75 | 30 00 | 613 35 | 65 |
| 6 | 18 00 | | | | | | | | | | 6 00 | 24 00 | 66 |
| 13 | 30 00 | | 1 | 15 00 | | | | | | | | 54 00 | 67 |
| 41-6 | 124 80 | | | | | | | | | | | 124 80 | 68 |
| 13 | 39 00 | | | | | | | | | | | 39 00 | 69 |
| 17-3 | 68 97 | 20 00 | | | | | | | | | 4 56 | 93 53 | 70 |
| 34-5 | 110 42 | 41 50 | | | 4 | 82 50 | | | 41 53 | | | 275 95 | 71 |
| 26 | 78 50 | | | | | | | | 22 87 | | 10 00 | 111 37 | 72 |
| 29-4 | 78 50 | 30 00 | | | 1 | 15 00 | | | 2 00 | | | 125 50 | 73 |
| 72-3 | 217 47 | | | | | | | | 23 50 | | | 240 97 | 74 |
| 316 | 955 85 | 50 00 | 2 | 50 00 | 7 | 50 00 | | | | 64 00 | 87 00 | 1256 85 | 75 |
| 49 | 157 00 | 30 00 | | | | | | | 3 00 | | | 190 00 | 76 |
| 40-5 | 122 15 | | | | | | | | 44 62 | 30 00 | 20 00 | 216 77 | 77 |
| 9-5 | 30 00 | | | | | | | | 62 75 | | 38 00 | 130 75 | 78 |
| 97 | 235 50 | | | | | | | | 28 00 | | | 263 50 | 79 |
| 89 | 267 00 | 50 00 | | | 2 | 180 00 | | | 50 00 | | | 547 00 | 80 |
| 21 | 50 40 | | | | 2 | 22 50 | | | | | | 72 90 | 81 |
| 14 | 42 00 | | | | | | | | | | | 42 00 | 82 |
| 29 | 85 00 | | | | | | | | | | | 85 00 | 83 |
| 3 | 9 00 | | | | | | | | | | | 9 00 | 84 |
| 16 | 48 00 | | | | 1 | 12 50 | | 25 00 | | | | 85 50 | 85 |
| 67 | 168 00 | | | | 1 | 25 00 | 3 | 7 50 | | | | 200 50 | 86 |
| 40-1 | 97 32 | 30 00 | | | 1 | 100 00 | | | | 45 00 | 22 00 | 294 32 | 87 |
| 88-4 | 304 63 | 40 00 | 1 | 20 00 | 1 | 231 25 | | | 2 00 | 6 00 | | 603 88 | 88 |

## ABSTRACT FROM SEMI-ANNUAL RETURNS.

### MEMBERSHIP.

| No. of Lodge. | NAME OF LODGE. | Initiated. | Reinstated. | Admitt'd by card. | Suspended for Cause. | Susp'ded N.P.D | Withdrawn. | Expelled. | Died. | Members per last Report. | Present Membership. | Number of Brothers Sick |
|---|---|---|---|---|---|---|---|---|---|---|---|---|
| 90 | Ivy | 2 | | | | 4 | 1 | | | 69 | 66 | 18 |
| 91 | Grand River | 17 | | | | | | | 1 | 90 | 106 | 13 |
| 92 | Milton | 2 | 1 | | | | | | | 31 | 34 | 2 |
| 93 | Western City | 3 | | | | | | | | 67 | 70 | 9 |
| 94 | Aylmer | 4 | | 1 | | | 1 | | | 121 | 125 | 6 |
| 96 | Nith | 1 | | | | 1 | | | 1 | 70 | 69 | 12 |
| 97 | Grand Union | 5 | 3 | | | 2 | | | | 64 | 70 | 6 |
| 98 | Minto | 1 | | | | | | 1 | | 42 | 42 | 4 |
| 00 | Lindsay | 6 | | 1 | | | | | 1 | 75 | 81 | 6 |
| 101 | Golden Star | 1 | 1 | | | | 1 | | | 54 | 55 | 5 |
| 102 | Deseronto | 2 | | | | 2 | | | 2 | 88 | 86 | 5 |
| 103 | Cataract | 2 | | | 3 | | | | | 52 | 51 | 9 |
| 104 | Crescent | 8 | | 2 | | 10 | 1 | | 1 | 232 | 230 | 20 |
| 105 | Manilla | 1 | 1 | | | | | | | 24 | 26 | 6 |
| 106 | St. Clair | 1 | | | | | 2 | | | 98 | 97 | 10 |
| 107 | Waterloo | 11 | | | | | 1 | | 1 | 120 | 129 | 23 |
| 108 | Royal Oak | 4 | | | | 4 | | | | 83 | 83 | 7 |
| 109 | Orion | 2 | 1 | | | 5 | | | | 53 | 51 | 7 |
| 110 | Laurel | | | | | | | | | 27 | 27 | |
| 111 | Peterboro' | 26 | | 1 | | | 2 | | 2 | 212 | 235 | 14 |
| 112 | Lucknow | 4 | | 1 | | 1 | 1 | | 1 | 75 | 77 | 5 |
| 113 | Trenton | 1 | 1 | | | | | | | 68 | 70 | 7 |
| 114 | Gananoque | 16 | | 1 | | 10 | | 1 | | 236 | 242 | 23 |
| 115 | Harmony | 21 | 1 | | | 7 | 1 | | | 131 | 145 | 9 |
| 116 | Naomi | | | | | | | | | 9 | 9 | |
| 117 | Valley City | 4 | | | | | 1 | | 1 | 103 | 105 | 8 |
| 119 | Maitland | 3 | | | | | 3 | 3 | | 59 | 56 | 11 |
| 120 | Sydenham Valley | 10 | | | | | 1 | | 1 | 160 | 168 | 15 |
| 121 | Saxon | | | | | | 1 | | | 29 | 28 | 1 |
| 122 | Streetsville | | 1 | | | 9 | 2 | | | 58 | 48 | |
| 124 | Dresden | 13 | 1 | | | 11 | 4 | | 1 | 112 | 110 | 9 |
| 125 | Stella | 19 | | | | | | | 1 | 108 | 126 | 12 |
| 126 | Sarnia | 11 | | | | | | | | 65 | 76 | 10 |
| 127 | Mizpah | 7 | | | | | | | | 105 | 112 | 6 |
| 128 | Mystic | | | | | 8 | | | 1 | 9 | | |
| 129 | Charity | | 1 | | | | | | | 26 | 27 | |
| 130 | Livingstone | 1 | | | | | | | | 44 | 45 | 2 |
| 131 | Marion | 6 | 2 | | | | 2 | | | 60 | 66 | 5 |
| 132 | Oakville | 7 | | | | 5 | 1 | | | 52 | 53 | 3 |
| 133 | Glencoe | 5 | | | | | | | | 50 | 55 | 4 |
| 134 | Orient | | 1 | | | 1 | 2 | | | 23 | 21 | 2 |
| 135 | Peaceful Dove | | | | | | | | | 30 | 39 | 7 |
| 136 | Cobourg | 4 | | | | | | | | 82 | 86 | 9 |
| 137 | St. Lawrence | 9 | | 1 | | | 1 | | | 96 | 105 | 12 |
| 138 | Ancaster | 5 | 1 | | | | | | 1 | 49 | 54 | 10 |
| 139 | Garnet | 5 | | | | | | | | 60 | 65 | 4 |
| 140 | Leamington | 4 | | 2 | | 5 | 1 | | | 133 | 133 | 8 |
| 142 | Concord | 3 | 1 | | | 6 | | | | 68 | 66 | 6 |
| 143 | Bay of Quinte | 3 | | | | | 2 | | 1 | 101 | 101 | 3 |
| 144 | Ridgetown | 6 | 2 | 4 | | 3 | 4 | | | 99 | 104 | 8 |
| 146 | Vivian | 1 | | | | | 1 | | 3 | 71 | 68 | 6 |
| 147 | Model | 5 | | | | | | | 1 | 35 | 39 | 3 |
| 148 | Aurora | | 2 | | | 2 | | | 1 | 86 | 85 | 16 |
| 149 | Western Star | 1 | | | | | 1 | | | 30 | 30 | 6 |
| 151 | Sycamore | | | | | | | | 1 | 40 | 39 | 5 |
| 152 | Hayden | 13 | 2 | 1 | | | 1 | | | 63 | 78 | 9 |
| 153 | Wildey | 2 | 1 | | | 1 | | | | 32 | 34 | 8 |
| 154 | Alpha | 3 | | | | 1 | | | | 131 | 133 | 20 |
| 155 | Brougham | 1 | 1 | | | | 1 | | | 15 | 16 | 1 |
| 156 | Pyramid | | 1 | | | | 2 | | | 46 | 45 | 1 |
| 157 | Thamesville | 2 | | 1 | | | | | 1 | 50 | 52 | 2 |

TERM ENDING 30TH JUNE, 1892.—*Continued.*

## SICK BENEFITS AND RELIEFS.

| Number of Weeks' Sickness. | Amount paid for Sick Benefits. | Amount paid for Burying Deceased Bros. | No. of Brothers' Wives Died. | Amount paid for Burying Bros.' Wives. | No. of Widows. | Amount paid for Relief of Widows. | No. of Orphans. | Amount paid for Educating Orphans. | Paid to Lodge Surgeon. | Paid for Nursing Sick Brothers. | Paid for Special Relief & Charity. | TOTAL RELIEF. | No. of Lodge. |
|---|---|---|---|---|---|---|---|---|---|---|---|---|---|
| | $ c | $ c | | $ c | | $ c | | $ c | $ c | $ c | $ c | $ c | |
| 58 | 179 00 | | | | 1 | 30 00 | | | | 3 00 | | 212 00 | 90 |
| 48 | 191 00 | 150 00 | | | | | | | 18 00 | | | 359 00 | 91 |
| 3-1 | 12 57 | | | | | | | | | | | 12 57 | 92 |
| 28 | 84 00 | | | | 1 | 30 00 | 4 | 79 69 | 17 50 | | 5 00 | 216 19 | 93 |
| 12 | 42 00 | | | | | | | | 6 00 | | 12 75 | 60 75 | 94 |
| 46-4 | 139 50 | 80 00 | | | | 150 00 | | | | | | 369 50 | 96 |
| 32-2 | 58 72 | | | | | | | | | | | 58 72 | 97 |
| 8 | 32 00 | | 1 | 15 00 | | | | | | | | 47 00 | 98 |
| 18 | 36 30 | 30 00 | | | | | | | | | | 66 30 | 100 |
| 21 | 63 00 | | | | 3 | 40 00 | | | 17 75 | 2 50 | | 123 25 | 101 |
| 13-1 | 39 60 | 80 00 | | | 2 | 75 00 | | | | | | 194 60 | 102 |
| 63-4 | 244 00 | 40 00 | | | 1 | 90 00 | | | 28 99 | 50 00 | 8 00 | 460 99 | 103 |
| 157 | 541 00 | | | | 1 | 20 00 | | | 92 25 | | 1 25 | 654 50 | 104 |
| 17 | 51 00 | | 1 | 15 00 | | | | | | | 8 80 | 74 80 | 105 |
| 40-6 | 124 54 | | | | | | | | | 29 50 | | 154 04 | 106 |
| 46 | 138 00 | | | | | | | | 19 00 | | 55 55 | 212 55 | 107 |
| 58½ | 175 00 | | | | | | | | | | | 175 00 | 108 |
| 37 | 106 00 | | | | | | | | | | 21 30 | 127 30 | 109 |
| | | | | | | | | | | | | | 110 |
| 62-4 | 363 30 | 80 00 | | | | | | | 106 00 | | | 549 30 | 111 |
| 16 | 48 00 | 30 00 | | | 1 | 100 00 | | | | 70 00 | 10 00 | 258 00 | 112 |
| 14-4 | 43 50 | | | | | | | | | | | 43 50 | 113 |
| 54-2 | 159 79 | | | | | | | | | 41 50 | | 201 29 | 114 |
| 52-6 | 185 00 | | | | 1 | 15 00 | | | | 180 15 | 3 73 | 383 88 | 115 |
| | | | | | | | | | | | | | 116 |
| 29-3 | 117 69 | 50 00 | | | | | | | 43 25 | | 37 50 | 248 44 | 117 |
| 26 | 78 00 | | | | | | | | | | 20 00 | 98 00 | 119 |
| 88 | 264 00 | 30 00 | | | | | | | | | 25 00 | 319 00 | 120 |
| 2 | 6 00 | | | | | | | | | | | 6 00 | 121 |
| | | | | | | | | | | | | | 122 |
| 29 | 67 00 | 30 00 | | | 3 | 100 00 | | | | | | 197 00 | 124 |
| 30-5 | 92 50 | 30 00 | | | 4 | 45 00 | | | | | | 167 50 | 125 |
| 66 | 198 00 | | | | | | | | | 35 00 | | 233 00 | 126 |
| 11-4 | 36 50 | | | | | | 1 | 15 00 | 37 50 | | 20 00 | 109 00 | 127 |
| | | | | | | | | | | | | | 128 |
| | | | | | | | | | | | | | 129 |
| 3 | 4 50 | | | | | | | | | | | 4 50 | 130 |
| 14 | 49 00 | | 1 | 15 00 | 1 | | 6 | | | | | 64 00 | 131 |
| 6-1 | 18 00 | | | | | | | | | | | 18 00 | 132 |
| 13 | 31 00 | | | | | | | | 8 00 | | | 39 00 | 133 |
| 17 | 51 00 | | | | | | | | 4 00 | | | 55 00 | 134 |
| 24 | 72 00 | | | | | | | | | | 5 00 | 77 00 | 135 |
| 37 | 111 00 | | | | | | | | | | | 111 00 | 136 |
| 36-2 | 109 00 | | 1 | 15 00 | | | | | | | | 124 00 | 137 |
| 29-5 | 88 77 | 40 00 | | | 1 | 30 00 | | | 20 50 | | | 179 27 | 138 |
| 7 | 21 00 | | | | 1 | 30 00 | 2 | 30 00 | | | | 81 00 | 139 |
| 41 | 107 00 | | | | | | | | | | 30 00 | 137 00 | 140 |
| 32 | 68 40 | | | | | | | | | | 2 25 | 70 65 | 142 |
| 8-4 | 20 60 | 35 00 | | | 1 | 50 50 | | | | | 5 00 | 110 60 | 143 |
| 28 | 68 00 | | | | | | | | | | | 68 00 | 144 |
| 40-4 | 121 71 | 60 50 | 1 | 15 00 | 3 | 157 50 | 24 | 12 50 | | | | 367 21 | 146 |
| 13 | 39 00 | 30 00 | | | 1 | 100 00 | | | | | | 169 00 | 147 |
| 51 | 127 07 | 40 00 | | | 1 | 20 00 | | | | 16 25 | | 203 32 | 148 |
| 27 | 82 50 | | | | | | | | | | | 82 50 | 149 |
| 9 | 27 00 | 30 00 | | | 3 | 45 00 | 10 | 63 00 | | | 2 00 | 167 00 | 151 |
| 45-1 | 135 47 | | | | | | | | | | | 135 47 | 152 |
| 12 | 36 00 | | | | | | | | 2 00 | | | 38 00 | 153 |
| 66-2 | 232 00 | 30 00 | 1 | 15 00 | | 120 00 | | | 6 00 | | | 403 00 | 154 |
| | 8 50 | | 1 | 20 00 | | | | | 3 50 | | 5 00 | 37 00 | 155 |
| 20 | 30 00 | | 1 | 20 00 | | | | | | | | 50 00 | 156 |
| 6 | 18 00 | 73 66 | | | 5 | 45 00 | | | | 18 00 | | 154 66 | 157 |

ABSTRACT FROM SEMI-ANNUAL RETURNS.

MEMBERSHIP.

| No. of Lodge. | NAME OF LODGE. | Initiated. | Reinstated. | Admitt'd by card. | Suspended for Cause. | Susp'nded N.P.D. | Withdrawn. | Expelled. | Died. | Members per last Report. | Present Membership. | Number of Brothers Sick. |
|---|---|---|---|---|---|---|---|---|---|---|---|---|
| 158 | Progress | 6 | 1 | 1 | | | 1 | | 1 | 104 | 110 | 14 |
| 159 | Oak Leaf | 1 | | | | 2 | | | | 41 | 40 | 3 |
| 160 | Listowel | 3 | | | | | | | 2 | 85 | 86 | 6 |
| 161 | Simcoe | 1 | 2 | | | 2 | 2 | | | 73 | 72 | 7 |
| 163 | Oriental | | | 1 | | | 1 | | | 39 | 39 | 2 |
| 164 | Romeo | 5 | 1 | | | 8 | | 1 | | 129 | 126 | 19 |
| 165 | Beethoven | | | | | | | | | 41 | 41 | 3 |
| 167 | Hillsburg | 2 | | | | | | | | 39 | 41 | 1 |
| 168 | Sutton | 2 | | | | 2 | 1 | | 1 | 38 | 36 | 6 |
| 169 | Grey | | | | | 11 | | | | 40 | 29 | 1 |
| 170 | Denovo | 6 | 1 | | | 2 | 1 | | 1 | 44 | 47 | 6 |
| 171 | Alliston | 1 | | 1 | | 4 | | | | 37 | 35 | 3 |
| 172 | Penetangore | 6 | | 1 | | 4 | 4 | | 2 | 112 | 109 | 15 |
| 173 | Emerald | 2 | | | | 1 | 3 | | | 27 | 25 | 2 |
| 174 | Dolman | 4 | | | | 3 | | | 2 | 51 | 50 | 6 |
| 177 | Montana | 3 | | | | | | | | 21 | 24 | 2 |
| 176 | Dauncey | 3 | | | | | | | | 21 | 24 | |
| 178 | Wellington Square | 5 | | | | | | | | 24 | 29 | 3 |
| 179 | Madoc | 32 | 1 | | | | 5 | | | 83 | 111 | 8 |
| 180 | Owen Sound | 4 | | | | 3 | 1 | | | 58 | 58 | 5 |
| 182 | Tecumseh | 3 | 3 | | | | | | | 51 | 57 | 9 |
| 183 | Teeswater | | | | | 10 | | | 1 | 47 | 36 | |
| 184 | Germania | 12 | | | | 1 | | | | 66 | 77 | 8 |
| 186 | Dufferin | 6 | | | | | 1 | | | 21 | 26 | 1 |
| 188 | Cambridge | 3 | | | | 1 | | | | 49 | 51 | 3 |
| 189 | Parry Sound | 2 | | | | 1 | | | | 51 | 52 | 6 |
| 190 | Chorazin | 1 | 1 | | | 6 | | | | 126 | 122 | 17 |
| 191 | Jarvis | | 1 | | | 1 | | | | 24 | 24 | 4 |
| 192 | Howick | | | | | 4 | | | | 17 | 13 | 1 |
| 194 | Albert | 5 | 1 | 3 | | 4 | 1 | | | 156 | 160 | 16 |
| 195 | Cicerone | 1 | | | | | 1 | | | 21 | 21 | 2 |
| 196 | Florence | 2 | | | | | | | | 83 | 85 | 6 |
| 197 | Minerva | 2 | | 1 | | | | | | 81 | 84 | 6 |
| 200 | Weston | 1 | | | | | | | | 38 | 39 | 2 |
| 201 | Beacon | 4 | | | | | | | | 33 | 37 | 2 |
| 202 | Silver Star | 9 | | | | | | | 2 | 43 | 50 | 4 |
| 203 | Pembroke | 4 | | | | 6 | 2 | | 1 | 107 | 102 | 9 |
| 204 | Acton | 1 | | | | 4 | | | | 18 | 15 | 1 |
| 205 | Ahiram | 15 | | | | 1 | | | | 88 | 102 | 7 |
| 206 | Silver City | | 1 | 1 | | | | | | 66 | 68 | 3 |
| 207 | Egremont | | 2 | | | | | | | 6 | 8 | |
| 209 | Millbank | 1 | | 1 | | | 1 | | | 13 | 14 | 2 |
| 210 | Brucefield | 1 | | | | | 1 | | | 25 | 25 | 6 |
| 211 | Lilly | 1 | | | | 5 | | | | 42 | 38 | 4 |
| 212 | Argyll | 4 | 1 | | | | 3 | | 1 | 79 | 81 | 7 |
| 214 | Freestone | 1 | 1 | | | | | | | 72 | 74 | 13 |
| 215 | Clifford | 4 | | | | | | | | 29 | 33 | 8 |
| 216 | Elmira | 5 | 1 | | | 3 | | | | 37 | 40 | 2 |
| 217 | Mount Brydges | 16 | 1 | | | 1 | | | 1 | 77 | 92 | 10 |
| 218 | Enterprise | 11 | 2 | 1 | | 1 | 1 | | | 108 | 120 | 12 |
| 219 | Georgian Bay | 8 | | | | 3 | 2 | | | 71 | 74 | 4 |
| 220 | Woodslee | | 2 | | | | 1 | | | 13 | 14 | 1 |
| 221 | Chesley | 2 | | | | | | | | 27 | 29 | 3 |
| 223 | Hensall | 4 | | | | 1 | 1 | | | 51 | 53 | 9 |
| 224 | Ottawa | 7 | | 1 | | | 2 | | 1 | 140 | 145 | 19 |
| 226 | Merlin | | 3 | | | 5 | 1 | | | 34 | 31 | 2 |
| 227 | Sauble | | | | | | | | | 17 | 17 | 1 |
| 228 | International | 5 | | | | 4 | | | 1 | 144 | 144 | 13 |
| 229 | Embro Star | 5 | | | | | 1 | | | 48 | 52 | 2 |
| 230 | Prince of Wales | 2 | | | | | | | 1 | 47 | 48 | 4 |
| 231 | Elora | 1 | | | | | 1 | | | 64 | 64 | 13 |

## Term Ending 30th June, 1892.—*Continued.*

### SICK BENEFITS AND RELIEFS.

| Number of Weeks' Sickness. | Amount paid for Sick Benefits. $ c | Amount paid for Burying Deceased Bros. $ c | No. of Brothers' Wives Died. | Amount paid for Burying Bros' Wives. $ c | No. of Widows. | Amount paid for Relief of Widows. $ c | No. of Orphans. | Amount paid for Educating Orphans. $ c | Paid to Lodge Surgeon. $ c | Paid for Nursing Sick Brothers. $ c | Paid for Special Relief & Charity. $ c | Total Relief. $ c | No. of Lodge. |
|---|---|---|---|---|---|---|---|---|---|---|---|---|---|
| 64–5 | 188 15 | | | | 1 | 30 00 | | | 2 00 | | | 220 15 | 158 |
| 4–6 | 21 26 | | | | 2 | 70 00 | | | 14 50 | | | 105 76 | 159 |
| 21 | 55 00 | 80 00 | 1 | | 1 | 76 07 | | | | | | 211 07 | 160 |
| 25 | 64 00 | | | | .. | | | | | | | 64 00 | 161 |
| 2 | 6 00 | | | | 1 | 15 00 | | | | | | 21 00 | 163 |
| 109–4 | 368 25 | | 1 | 25 00 | | | | | | | | 393 25 | 164 |
| 21 | 55 00 | | | | | | | | 20 50 | | | 75 50 | 165 |
| 2 | 6 00 | | | | | | | | | | 5 00 | 11 00 | 167 |
| 20–5 | 72 50 | 40 00 | | | | | | | 2 00 | | | 114 50 | 168 |
| 5 | 15 00 | | | | | | | | | | | 15 00 | 169 |
| 16–3 | 49 08 | 30 00 | 1 | 15 00 | 1 | 200 00 | | | 11 00 | 12 32 | | 317 40 | 170 |
| 8 | 16 00 | | | | | | | | | | | 16 00 | 171 |
| 50 | 176 00 | 70 00 | 1 | 20 00 | 2 | 400 00 | | | | 5 50 | 2 00 | 673 50 | 172 |
| 7 | 21 00 | | | | | | | | | | 13 00 | 34 00 | 173 |
| 37 | 113 50 | 80 00 | | | 2 | 250 00 | | | | | | 443 50 | 174 |
| 6 | 17 00 | | | | | | | | | | | 17 00 | 177 |
| | | | | | | | | | | | | | 176 |
| 1 | 9 00 | | | | 1 | 15 00 | | | | | | 24 00 | 178 |
| 31–5 | 111 25 | | | | 1 | 15 00 | | | | | | 126 25 | 179 |
| 28 | 126 00 | | | | | | | | 8 00 | | | 134 00 | 180 |
| 25–5 | 74 69 | | | | | | | | | | | 74 69 | 182 |
| | | 35 00 | | | | | | | | | | 35 00 | 183 |
| 32 | 96 00 | | 1 | 15 00 | | | | | | | | 111 00 | 184 |
| 26 | 13 00 | | | | | | | | | | | 13 00 | 186 |
| 4 | 12 00 | | | | | | | | | | | 12 00 | 188 |
| 8 | 24 00 | | | | | | | | | | 2 00 | 26 00 | 189 |
| 35–2 | 141 50 | | | | 1 | 12 50 | | | 52 75 | | | 206 75 | 190 |
| 7 | 21 00 | | | | | | | | | | 30 00 | 51 00 | 191 |
| 2 | 6 00 | | | | | | | | | | | 6 00 | 192 |
| 54–2 | 217 16 | | 1 | 20 00 | 1 | 20 00 | 2 | 40 00 | 96 50 | | 22 48 | 418 14 | 194 |
| 18 | 54 00 | | | | | | | | | | 29 50 | 83 50 | 195 |
| 30 | 78 00 | | | | | | | | | | 5 00 | 83 00 | 196 |
| 15 | 60 00 | | | | 1 | 100 00 | | | 52 00 | | | 212 00 | 197 |
| 10 | 40 00 | | | | | | | | | | 61 30 | 101 30 | 200 |
| 4 | 12 00 | | | | | | | | | | | 12 00 | 201 |
| 18 | 54 00 | 193 35 | | | | | | 10 00 | | | | 257 35 | 202 |
| 12–1 | 37 00 | | 2 | 40 00 | | | | | | | 5 00 | 82 00 | 203 |
| 1 | 5 00 | | | | | | | | | | | 5 00 | 204 |
| 17–6 | 57 00 | | | | | | | | | | | 57 00 | 205 |
| 41 | 123 00 | | | | 1 | 100 00 | | | 33 00 | | | 256 00 | 206 |
| | | | | | | | | | | | | | 207 |
| 8 | 32 00 | | 1 | 15 00 | | | | | | | 5 00 | 52 00 | 209 |
| 16 | 32 00 | | | | | | | | | | | 32 00 | 210 |
| 7–2 | 26 14 | | | | | | | | | | | 26 14 | 211 |
| 33 | 99 00 | 30 00 | | | 2 | 80 00 | | | | | 3 50 | 212 50 | 212 |
| 47–5 | 230 57 | | | | | | | | | | | 230 57 | 214 |
| 24 | 72 00 | | | | | | | | | | | 72 00 | 215 |
| 3 | 9 00 | | | | | | | | | | | 9 00 | 216 |
| 19 | 56 00 | | | | 1 | 15 00 | | | | | | 71 00 | 217 |
| 20 | 87 00 | | | | | | | | | | 6 06 | 93 06 | 218 |
| 10 | 30 00 | | | | | | | | | | | 30 00 | 219 |
| 5 | 16 00 | | 1 | 20 00 | | | | | | | | 36 00 | 220 |
| 5 | 15 00 | | | | | | | | | | | 15 00 | 221 |
| 22–2 | 66 40 | | | | | | | | | | | 66 40 | 223 |
| 72–3 | 216 50 | | 1 | 20 00 | | | | | | | | 236 50 | 224 |
| 3 | 9 00 | | | | | | | | | | | 9 00 | 226 |
| 2 | 6 00 | | | | | | | | | | | 6 00 | 227 |
| 43–1 | 157 50 | 45 00 | | | 4 | 52 50 | | | 3 50 | | 64 00 | 322 50 | 228 |
| 23–4 | 71 00 | | | | | 75 00 | | | | | | 146 00 | 229 |
| 24 | 72 00 | 40 00 | | | 1 | 48 00 | | | 38 50 | 23 38 | 2 00 | 223 88 | 230 |
| 50–1 | 151 00 | | | | | | | | 48 75 | | | 199 75 | 231 |

ABSTRACT FROM SEMI-ANNUAL RETURNS.

MEMBERSHIP.

| No. of Lodge. | NAME OF LODGE. | Initiated. | Reinstated. | Admitt'd by card. | Suspended for Cause. | Susp'nded N.P.D | Withdrawn. | Expelled. | Died. | Members per last Report. | Present Membership. | Number of Brothers sick. |
|---|---|---|---|---|---|---|---|---|---|---|---|---|
| 232 | Equity | | 1 | | | 1 | | | | 27 | 27 | |
| 233 | Hanover | | | | | | | | | 18 | 18 | |
| 234 | Ilderton | 1 | | | | 2 | | | | 34 | 33 | 1 |
| 235 | Waterford | 10 | | | | 3 | 2 | | 1 | 102 | 106 | 16 |
| 236 | Acorn | 2 | 1 | | | | 1 | | | 21 | 23 | 1 |
| 237 | Farmersville | | | | | | | | | 43 | 43 | 7 |
| 239 | Stirling | 7 | | | | | 2 | | | 121 | 126 | 12 |
| 240 | Carleton | 8 | | | | 5 | | | | 117 | 120 | 9 |
| 241 | Rideau | 3 | 1 | 1 | | | 2 | | | 110 | 113 | 3 |
| 242 | Wilton | 1 | | 1 | | 2 | 1 | | 1 | 91 | 89 | 12 |
| 243 | Thornbury | 2 | 2 | | | | | | 1 | 31 | 34 | 3 |
| 244 | Port Arthur | 7 | | 2 | | | | | | 66 | 75 | 2 |
| 245 | Mallorytown | 1 | 1 | | | | | | | 45 | 47 | 3 |
| 246 | Orillia | | 1 | | 4 | 1 | | | | 45 | 41 | 5 |
| 247 | Gordon | 5 | | | | | | | | 39 | 44 | 2 |
| 248 | Campbellford | 3 | | | | | 1 | | 1 | 101 | 102 | 6 |
| 249 | Beaverton | 5 | | 1 | | 1 | | | | 43 | 4· | 7 |
| 250 | Ridgley | 18 | | | | 11 | 2 | | | 82 | 87 | 6 |
| 251 | Bracebridge | 4 | 1 | | | | | | | 61 | 66 | 6 |
| 252 | Floral | | | | | 5 | | | | 43 | 38 | 1 |
| 253 | Caledonia | 2 | | | | | | | | 13 | 15 | 2 |
| 254 | Alba | 3 | 1 | | | 2 | 1 | | | 45 | 46 | 3 |
| 255 | Tottenham | | | | | 3 | 1 | | | 14 | 10 | |
| 256 | Grand Valley | 2 | | | | | | | | 33 | 35 | |
| 257 | Credit | 1 | | | | | | | | 39 | 40 | 2 |
| 258 | Thamesford | 7 | | | | 1 | 1 | | 1 | 103 | 107 | 13 |
| 259 | Lynden | 1 | | | | 1 | | | | 26 | 26 | 2 |
| 260 | Meaford | 4 | | 1 | | | | | | 38 | 43 | 1 |
| 261 | Gold Hill | 7 | 2 | | | | | | 1 | 130 | 138 | 6 |
| 262 | Norwood | | | 1 | | 4 | | | 1 | 45 | 41 | 6 |
| 263 | East Toronto | | | | | | | | | 54 | 54 | 5 |
| 264 | Fraternity | 8 | | | | | | | 1 | 50 | 57 | 5 |
| 265 | Delta | 4 | | | | | 1 | | | 42 | 45 | 5 |
| 266 | Missanabie | 10 | | | | | 1 | | | 73 | 82 | 10 |
| 267 | Algoma | 2 | | | | | | | | 55 | 57 | 4 |
| 268 | Stanley | 3 | | | | | | | | 34 | 37 | 6 |
| 269 | Woodstock | 8 | | | | 4 | 1 | | | 59 | 62 | 9 |
| 270 | Lansdowne | 1 | | | | | 2 | | | 64 | 63 | 4 |
| 271 | North Bay | 11 | | 2 | | | | | | 58 | 71 | 3 |
| 272 | Lakeview | 3 | | | | | | | | 73 | 76 | 3 |
| 273 | Hastings | 1 | | | | 2 | 1 | | | 40 | 38 | 3 |
| 274 | Midland | 7 | | | 1 | | | | | 44 | 50 | 6 |
| 275 | Fairy | 3 | | | | | | | | 41 | 44 | 5 |
| 276 | Sheard | 3 | | | | | 1 | | | 29 | 31 | 2 |
| 277 | Lambton | 4 | | | | | | | | 51 | 55 | 1 |
| 278 | Rockliffe | 14 | | | | 3 | | | | 42 | 53 | 4 |
| 279 | Grenville | 4 | | | | 2 | 1 | 1 | | 76 | 76 | 6 |
| 280 | Balmoral | 1 | | | | | 1 | | | 42 | 42 | 9 |
| 281 | Arthur | 8 | | | | 1 | 1 | | | 47 | 53 | 1 |
| 282 | Sudbury | 10 | | | | | 3 | | | 37 | 44 | |
| 283 | Karnscliffe | 3 | | | | | | | 2 | 44 | 45 | 2 |
| 284 | Lyn | 3 | | | | | 1 | | | 25 | 27 | 3 |
| 285 | Morewood | 1 | | | | | | | | 17 | 18 | |
| 286 | Royal | 14 | | 1 | | | | | | 22 | 37 | 3 |
| 287 | Ripley | 25 | | 10 | | | 1 | | | | 34 | |
| 288 | Chesterville | 29 | | 2 | | | | | | | 31 | |
| 289 | Glanworth | 40 | | 6 | | | | | | | 46 | |
| 290 | Tweed | 46 | | 5 | | | | | | | 51 | |
| 291 | Rodney | 22 | | 14 | | | | | | | 36 | |
| | | 1248 | 93 | 92 | 9 | 424 | 168 | 13 | 87 | 18390 | 19122 | 1934 |

### Term Ending 30th June, 1892.—*Continued.*

## SICK BENEFITS AND RELIEFS.

| Number of Weeks' Sickness. | Amount paid for Sick Benefits. | Amount paid for Burying Deceased Bros. | No. of Brothers' Wives Died. | Amount paid for Burying Bros'. Wives. | No. of Widows. | Amount paid for Relief of Widows. | No. of Orphans. | Amount paid for Educating Orphans. | Paid to Lodge Surgeon. | Paid for Nursing Sick Brothers. | Paid for Special Relief & Charity. | Total Relief. | No. of Lodges. |
|---|---|---|---|---|---|---|---|---|---|---|---|---|---|
| | $ c | $ c | | $ c | | $ c | | $ c | $ c | $ c | $ c | $ c | |
| | | | | | | | | | | | | | 232 |
| | | | | | | | | | | | | | 233 |
| 6 | 18 00 | | 1 | 15 00 | | | | | | | | 33 00 | 234 |
| 47 | 141 02 | 30 00 | | | 1 | 30 00 | | | | 12 00 | | 213 02 | 235 |
| 17 | 51 00 | | | | | | | | | | | 51 00 | 236 |
| 30 | 90 00 | | | | | | | | | | | 90 00 | 237 |
| 25-2 | 75 65 | | | | | | | | | | | 75 65 | 239 |
| 24 | 72 00 | | | 20 00 | | | | | | | | 92 00 | 240 |
| 12-3 | 31 50 | | | | | | | | | | | 31 50 | 241 |
| 46 | 184 01 | 27 05 | | | | | | | 45 50 | | 7 28 | 263 84 | 242 |
| 8 | 24 00 | | | | | | | | 15 50 | | | 39 50 | 243 |
| 10-4 | 34 48 | | | | | | | | | | | 31 48 | 244 |
| 5 | 15 00 | | | | | | | | | | | 15 00 | 245 |
| 18 | 54 00 | | 1 | 25 00 | | | | | | | | 79 00 | 246 |
| 16 | 42 00 | | 1 | 20 00 | | | | | 19 50 | | 80 | 82 30 | 247 |
| 15 | 45 00 | 40 00 | | | | | | | 9 00 | | | 94 00 | 248 |
| 23-2 | 70 35 | | | | | | | | | | 10 00 | 80 35 | 249 |
| 40 | 120 00 | | | | | | | | | | | 120 00 | 250 |
| 27 | 80 26 | | | | | | | | 16 00 | | | 96 26 | 251 |
| 2 | 6 00 | | | | | | | | 19 00 | | | 25 00 | 252 |
| 3 | 9 00 | | | | | | | | | | 3 00 | 12 00 | 253 |
| 10-1 | 30 50 | | | | | | | | | | | 30 50 | 254 |
| | | | | | | | | | | | | | 255 |
| | | | | | | | | | 9 45 | | | 9 45 | 256 |
| 2-4 | 7 50 | | | | | | | | | | | 7 50 | 257 |
| 31-3 | 94 50 | | | | | | | | 49 50 | | | 144 00 | 258 |
| 24-2 | 68 85 | | | | | | | | | | | 68 85 | 259 |
| 6-4 | 19 50 | | | | | | | | | | | 19 50 | 260 |
| 40-3 | 107 05 | | | | 1 | 10 00 | | | | 61 00 | | 178 05 | 261 |
| 29 | 87 00 | 30 00 | | | | | | | 20 00 | | 5 00 | 142 00 | 262 |
| 39-3 | 119 00 | | | | | | | | 27 00 | | 20 00 | 166 00 | 263 |
| 12-5 | 38 13 | 30 00 | | | | | | | | 5 00 | | 73 13 | 264 |
| 12 | 36 00 | | | | | | | | | | | 36 00 | 265 |
| 35-3 | 141 60 | | | | | | | | | | | 141 60 | 266 |
| 16-5 | 51 25 | | | | | | | | | | 5 00 | 56 25 | 267 |
| 20-3 | 61 50 | | | | | | | | | | | 61 50 | 268 |
| 32-6 | 102 88 | | | | | | | | 41 25 | | | 144 13 | 269 |
| 8 | 24 00 | | 1 | 15 00 | | | | | | | | 39 00 | 270 |
| 13 | 52 00 | | | | | | | | | | | 52 00 | 271 |
| 6-3 | 22 50 | | | | | | | | 17 50 | | | 40 00 | 272 |
| 4-5 | 18 75 | | | | | | | | | | | 18 75 | 273 |
| 29-2 | 86 95 | | | | | | | | 30 00 | | | 116 95 | 274 |
| 6-4 | 18 72 | | | | | | | | 29 90 | | | 48 62 | 275 |
| 3-3 | 10 28 | | | | | | | | 15 50 | | 5 00 | 30 78 | 276 |
| 2-2 | 6 53 | | | | | | | | | | | 6 53 | 277 |
| 12-5 | 38 50 | | 1 | 30 00 | | | | | | | | 68 50 | 278 |
| 15 | 45 00 | | 1 | 30 00 | | | | | | | | 75 00 | 279 |
| 31-5 | 79 55 | | | | | | | | | | | 79 55 | 280 |
| 2 | 8 00 | | | | | | | | | | | 8 00 | 281 |
| | | | | | | | | | | | | | 282 |
| 6 | 18 00 | 53 50 | | | | | | | | 6 00 | | 77 50 | 283 |
| 6 | 15 00 | | | | | | | | | 20 00 | | 35 00 | 284 |
| | | | | | | | | | | | | | 285 |
| 9 | 27 00 | | | | | | | | | | | 27 00 | 286 |
| | | | | | | | | | | | | | 287 |
| | | | | | | | | | | | | | 288 |
| | | | | | | | | | | | | | 289 |
| | | | | | | | | | | | | | 290 |
| | | | | | | | | | | | | | 291 |
| 8188-1 | 25518 40 | 3584 56 | 42 | 1195 00 | 175 | 6649 50 | 63 | 414 36 | 2544 71 | 1095 07 | 1171 77 | 42173 40 | |

ABSTRACT FROM SEMI-ANNUAL RETURNS.

| No. of Lodge. | NAME OF LODGE. | No. of Degrees Conferred. | No. of Past Grands in Good Standing. | RECEIPTS OF LODGES. | | | Current Expenses. |
|---|---|---|---|---|---|---|---|
| | | | | Initiations, Admission by Card, and Degrees. | Dues and Reinstatements. | All other Sources. | |
| | | | | $  c | $  c | $  c | $  c |
| 9 | Brock | 28 | 32 | 106 90 | 231 55 | 86 83 | 212 04 |
| 10 | Cataraqui | 84 | 25 | 378 90 | 694 80 | 347 48 | 450 90 |
| 13 | Otonabee | 50 | 14 | 288 40 | 412 74 | | 267 25 |
| 16 | Union | 20 | 41 | 139 90 | 645 75 | 413 75 | 318 70 |
| 22 | Phœnix | 2 | 15 | 7 75 | 280 39 | 58 80 | 107 93 |
| 28 | Rose | 17 | 14 | 76 20 | 251 00 | 45 00 | 204 51 |
| 29 | Chatham | 8 | 34 | 51 00 | 627 04 | 373 00 | 180 91 |
| 30 | Eureka | 12 | 36 | 46 05 | 424 45 | 17 00 | 194 02 |
| 32 | Elgin | 18 | 22 | 155 00 | 755 25 | 246 96 | 299 81 |
| 33 | Erie | | 12 | 30 | 25 00 | 16 00 | 10 50 |
| 34 | Gore | 43 | 43 | 219 90 | 842 59 | 373 00 | 404 43 |
| 35 | Samaritan | 15 | 36 | 87 70 | 426 65 | 360 03 | 347 81 |
| 36 | St. Mary's | 7 | | 47 25 | 335 75 | 554 50 | 496 63 |
| 38 | Forest City | | 24 | 12 10 | 487 20 | 118 20 | 166 15 |
| 40 | Rondeau | 12 | 14 | 127 97 | 306 97 | 346 10 | 515 28 |
| 41 | Avon | 18 | 47 | 73 80 | 720 81 | 751 26 | 686 21 |
| 44 | Excelsior | 12 | 29 | 50 80 | 467 45 | 27 98 | 546 23 |
| 45 | Frontier | 12 | 24 | 93 95 | 681 21 | 643 06 | 35 80 |
| 46 | Mount Zion | | 8 | | 74 75 | 15 45 | 59 02 |
| 47 | Unity | 12 | 35 | 111 80 | 996 57 | 736 73 | 381 26 |
| 48 | Dominion | 12 | 33 | 31 05 | 442 26 | 54 28 | 152 33 |
| 49 | Canada | | 26 | 89 00 | 648 15 | 13 70 | 262 90 |
| 50 | Otter | 35 | 22 | 149 00 | 286 82 | 22 50 | 222 90 |
| 51 | Bissell | | 7 | 30 | 67 00 | 3 00 | 28 73 |
| 52 | Covenant | | | 92 00 | 646 54 | 36 00 | 331 50 |
| 53 | Niagara | 19 | 25 | 66 60 | 408 59 | 135 35 | 164 59 |
| 54 | Collingwood | 9 | 21 | 70 30 | 451 60 | 207 12 | 327 66 |
| 55 | Fidelity | | 9 | 30 | 31 50 | 225 00 | 171 25 |
| 56 | Queen City of Ontario | 7 | 26 | 47 10 | 574 81 | 12 00 | 287 46 |
| 57 | Maple Leaf | 17 | 12 | 89 00 | 158 50 | | 136 11 |
| 58 | Howard | 31 | 27 | 184 80 | 261 45 | 194 00 | 56 75 |
| 59 | Kingston | 44 | 38 | 216 75 | 638 40 | 207 60 | 563 98 |
| 61 | Corinthian | 6 | 33 | 43 50 | 599 03 | 55 00 | 152 25 |
| 62 | Huron | 7 | 26 | 31 20 | 339 77 | 211 75 | 122 82 |
| 63 | Barrie | 12 | 12 | 39 80 | 352 93 | 489 00 | 308 71 |
| 64 | Victoria | 19 | 18 | 29 30 | 8 00 | | 110 05 |
| 65 | Friendship | 16 | 26 | 91 20 | 421 29 | 393 21 | 706 94 |
| 66 | Florence Nightingale | 7 | 37 | 56 25 | 423 75 | 213 18 | 154 60 |
| 67 | Exeter | 25 | 18 | 104 90 | 136 71 | 63 88 | 173 37 |
| 68 | North Star | 1 | 12 | 4 50 | 85 00 | | 42 00 |
| 69 | Hope | 31 | 14 | 141 50 | 183 88 | 83 40 | 89 36 |
| 70 | Lucan | | 10 | 1 00 | 79 84 | 43 82 | 83 13 |
| 71 | The Toronto | 5 | 18 | 36 23 | 206 20 | 108 50 | 257 40 |
| 72 | Eastern Star | 3 | 24 | 46 50 | 326 50 | | 99 40 |
| 73 | Fergus | 24 | 19 | 78 50 | 208 62 | 167 60 | 142 87 |
| 74 | Bothwell | | | 13 15 | 91 20 | 146 80 | 38 96 |
| 75 | Warriner | 1 | 24 | 23 50 | 247 25 | 70 00 | 148 21 |
| 76 | St. Thomas | 27 | 46 | 190 50 | 1057 45 | 396 05 | 325 81 |
| 77 | Oxford | 4 | 22 | 25 60 | 265 00 | | 89 00 |
| 78 | Durham | 21 | 19 | 139 20 | 391 38 | 55 00 | 412 08 |
| 79 | Nippissing | 12 | 23 | 88 60 | 201 85 | 28 00 | 130 50 |
| 80 | Amity | 37 | 31 | 245 90 | 530 65 | 53 75 | 622 70 |
| 81 | Belleville | 5 | 26 | 37 25 | 634 75 | 223 24 | 516 32 |
| 82 | Beaver | 5 | 13 | 25 60 | 88 00 | 25 00 | 49 23 |
| 83 | Clinton | | 10 | 1 90 | 77 50 | | 62 80 |
| 84 | Walkerton | | 18 | 52 50 | 153 13 | 106 75 | 134 33 |
| 85 | Constellation | 32 | 13 | 189 30 | 105 00 | 83 15 | 118 33 |
| 86 | Napanee | 9 | 16 | 57 00 | 180 50 | | 123 43 |
| 87 | Empire | 3 | 16 | 25 90 | 234 50 | 176 65 | 180 89 |
| 88 | Olive Branch | 12 | 27 | 58 40 | 402 62 | 255 00 | 382 47 |
| 89 | Reliance | 6 | 24 | 60 80 | 498 81 | 250 00 | 315 64 |

## TERM ENDING 30TH JUNE, 1892.

| ASSETS—HOW INVESTED. | | | | FUNDS. | | | | |
| Cash in Bank or in Treasurer's hands. | Invested in Mortgages and Securities. | Invested in Buildings and Lands. | Invested in Furniture and Regalia. | General Benefit Fund. | W. and O. Fund. | Contingent Fund. | Total Funds. | No. of Lodge. |
|---|---|---|---|---|---|---|---|---|
| $ c | $ c | $ c | $ c | $ c | $ c | $ c | $ c | |
| 1084 85 | 4000 00 | | 1000 00 | 4432 64 | 1652 21 | | 6084 85 | 9 |
| 4433 99 | | | 1866 63 | 5094 06 | 1157 50 | 49 06 | 6300 62 | 10 |
| 931 43 | | | 2200 00 | 3131 43 | | | 3131 43 | 13 |
| 369 00 | 7150 00 | 12000 00 | 1717 35 | 14036 85 | 7145 00 | 54 50 | 21236 35 | 16 |
| 805 78 | | | 750 00 | 1555 78 | | | 1555 78 | 22 |
| 331 08 | | 2879 50 | 1089 60 | 4153 67 | 133 50 | 13 01 | 4300 18 | 28 |
| 1299 18 | | 10400 00 | 1126 14 | 12825 32 | | | 12825 32 | 29 |
| 529 17 | | 6816 65 | 1000 00 | 7254 21 | 158 79 | 932 82 | 8335 82 | 30 |
| 614 68 | 4125 78 | | 1035 54 | 4846 10 | 904 40 | 24 50 | 5775 00 | 32 |
| 317 80 | | 800 00 | 250 00 | 1067 80 | 300 00 | | 1367 80 | 33 |
| 504 83 | 13500 00 | | 796 06 | 11276 32 | 3281 04 | 243 53 | 14800 89 | 34 |
| 1807 93 | 7 50 | 6458 15 | 2275 00 | 8186 02 | 2362 56 | | 10548 58 | 35 |
| 127 48 | | 15000 00 | 450 00 | 15577 48 | | | 15577 48 | 36 |
| 193 02 | 3020 00 | 8473 13 | 1000 00 | 12686 77 | | 15 00 | 12701 77 | 38 |
| 1100 31 | | | 1238 50 | 2320 36 | | 18 45 | 2338 81 | 40 |
| 600 40 | | 11888 05 | 1988 77 | 14344 01 | | 133 21 | 14477 22 | 41 |
| 1092 89 | | | 462 57 | 1328 03 | 819 25 | 8 18 | 2155 46 | 44 |
| | | 9181 01 | 2147 49 | 11274 39 | | 54 11 | 11328 50 | 45 |
| 150 44 | | 1100 00 | 150 00 | 1400 44 | | | 1400 44 | 46 |
| 1082 04 | 3440 00 | 6870 00 | 865 00 | 5384 08 | 6583 63 | 196 87 | 12164 58 | 47 |
| 1175 15 | 750 00 | 7187 75 | 1090 26 | 6272 55 | 3030 61 | | 10203 16 | 48 |
| 190 68 | | 6200 00 | 550 00 | 5324 76 | 1386 46 | 229 46 | 6940 68 | 49 |
| 492 67 | | 6500 00 | 600 00 | 6592 67 | | | 6592 67 | 50 |
| 143 44 | | | | 143 44 | | | 143 44 | 51 |
| 277 55 | 723 00 | 10844 51 | 200 00 | 9130 95 | 2741 14 | 172 92 | 12045 01 | 52 |
| 1251 00 | 1000 00 | 44 00 | 1000 00 | 3295 00 | | | 3295 00 | 53 |
| 250 02 | 1600 00 | 3231 24 | 2261 95 | 7342 97 | | 24 | 7343 21 | 54 |
| 232 47 | | 4750 47 | 350 00 | 4388 82 | 944 12 | | 5332 94 | 55 |
| 779 52 | 185 94 | 4000 00 | 421 25 | 2982 44 | 2372 34 | 31 93 | 5386 71 | 56 |
| 356 78 | 1200 00 | | 750 00 | 1699 50 | 609 28 | | 2306 78 | 57 |
| 208 75 | 4500 00 | 2500 00 | 900 00 | 8108 75 | | 23 50 | 8132 25 | 58 |
| 250 33 | | 5850 00 | 1250 00 | 7228 41 | 99 87 | 22 05 | 7350 33 | 59 |
| 2531 87 | 2518 62 | 290 00 | 1567 00 | 6906 49 | | | 6906 49 | 61 |
| 1293 39 | 4213 08 | | 741 62 | 3079 74 | 3167 00 | 1 35 | 8248 00 | 62 |
| 443 12 | 1500 00 | | 900 00 | 2843 12 | | | 2843 12 | 63 |
| 2145 00 | | | 789 30 | 1088 16 | 1904 20 | 41 94 | 2934 30 | 64 |
| 224 93 | | 14152 51 | 2000 00 | 16377 44 | | | 16377 44 | 65 |
| 673 78 | 1350 00 | 4585 92 | 1300 00 | 7883 20 | | 26 50 | 7909 70 | 66 |
| 651 32 | | 2750 00 | 150 00 | 2295 41 | 1255 83 | 80 | 3552 04 | 67 |
| 459 70 | | | 757 19 | 1216 89 | | | 1286 89 | 68 |
| 1583 00 | | 800 00 | 250 00 | 1987 79 | 626 76 | 18 51 | 2633 06 | 69 |
| 84 36 | | | 550 00 | 9.3 41 | 1155 03 | 84 36 | 2232 80 | 70 |
| 484 26 | | 550 00 | 423 35 | 637 42 | 464 60 | 305 59 | 1407 61 | 71 |
| 66 95 | | | 1000 00 | 1066 95 | | | 1066 95 | 72 |
| 864 05 | 3496 13 | | 558 19 | 4918 37 | | | 4918 37 | 73 |
| 208 44 | 575 00 | | 600 00 | 1270 41 | 113 03 | | 1383 44 | 74 |
| 874 01 | 1369 91 | | 900 00 | 2977 95 | | 166 00 | 3143 95 | 75 |
| 128 79 | 10314 77 | 324 00 | 1300 00 | 9203 46 | 2800 00 | 64 10 | 12067 56 | 76 |
| 351 60 | | | 1425 00 | 1776 00 | | 16 00 | 1792 00 | 77 |
| 3076 26 | 1500 00 | | 2000 00 | 4999 81 | 1500 00 | 76 45 | 6576 26 | 78 |
| 1598 09 | | | 700 00 | 2288 09 | | | 2288 09 | 79 |
| 2540 60 | 1000 00 | | 2020 90 | 4087 18 | 1451 17 | 23 15 | 5561 50 | 80 |
| 4507 94 | | | 4013 00 | 5910 64 | 2547 00 | 63 30 | 8520 94 | 81 |
| 248 28 | 300 00 | 1100 00 | 500 00 | 2148 28 | | | 2148 28 | 82 |
| 138 85 | | | 650 00 | 788 85 | | | 788 85 | 83 |
| 452 65 | 1063 30 | | 550 00 | 2060 69 | | 5 26 | 2065 95 | 84 |
| 1513 36 | 300 00 | | 400 00 | 2213 36 | | | 2213 36 | 85 |
| 73 99 | 2000 00 | | 1372 88 | 2299 63 | 877 11 | 270 13 | 3446 87 | 86 |
| 1736 24 | 3000 00 | | 1696 14 | 5063 69 | 1368 70 | | 6432 38 | 87 |
| 29 66 | 1609 36 | 1602 92 | 750 00 | 2627 47 | 1361 55 | 2 92 | 3991 94 | 88 |
| 761 98 | 4100 00 | | 1600 00 | 5076 87 | 1363 75 | 21 36 | 6461 98 | 89 |

### ABSTRACT FROM SEMI-ANNUAL RETURNS.

| No. of Lodge. | NAME OF LODGE. | No. of Degrees Conferred. | No. of Past Grands in Good Standing. | Initiations, Admission by Card, and Degrees. | | Dues and Reinstatements. | | All other Sources. | | Current Expenses. | |
|---|---|---|---|---|---|---|---|---|---|---|---|
| | | | | $ | c | $ | c | $ | c | $ | c |
| 90 | Ivy | 3 | 14 | 27 | 00 | 216 | 43 | 130 | 50 | 46 | 53 |
| 91 | Grand River | 33 | 27 | 198 | 00 | 310 | 30 | 122 | C0 | 85 | 56 |
| 92 | Milton | | | 21 | 00 | 95 | 38 | 66 | 53 | 113 | 38 |
| 93 | Western City | 5 | 23 | 38 | 90 | 234 | 43 | 10 | 00 | 65 | 99 |
| 94 | Aylmer | 12 | 29 | 94 | 50 | 318 | 75 | 290 | 37 | 116 | 86 |
| 96 | Nith | | 24 | 6 | 30 | 206 | 50 | 105 | 50 | 72 | 67 |
| 97 | Grand Union | 29 | 18 | 115 | 30 | 288 | 84 | 107 | 50 | 611 | 86 |
| 98 | Minto | | | 20 | 60 | 112 | 47 | 95 | 67 | 100 | 54 |
| 100 | Lindsay | 15 | 27 | 161 | 75 | 277 | 20 | | | 74 | 30 |
| 101 | Golden Star | | | 18 | 40 | 159 | 50 | 603 | 45 | 97 | 28 |
| 102 | Desoronto | | 17 | 22 | 30 | 280 | 00 | 2 | 35 | 68 | 31 |
| 103 | Cataract | | | 26 | 00 | 142 | 50 | 68 | 75 | 126 | 93 |
| 104 | Crescent | 29 | 32 | 124 | 90 | 765 | 85 | 105 | 29 | 65 | 50 |
| 105 | Manilla | 8 | 16 | 28 | 30 | 85 | 50 | 10 | 00 | 49 | 34 |
| 106 | St. Clair | 3 | | 16 | 30 | 376 | 50 | 149 | 05 | 166 | 98 |
| 107 | Waterloo | 30 | 23 | 191 | 80 | 371 | 55 | 273 | 50 | 414 | 11 |
| 108 | Royal Oak | 7 | 22 | 48 | 90 | 227 | 00 | 14 | 00 | 155 | 70 |
| 109 | Orion | 11 | 18 | 43 | 90 | 187 | 38 | 86 | 75 | 55 | 69 |
| 111 | Peterboro' | 48 | 22 | 544 | 40 | 690 | 24 | 277 | 12 | 827 | 35 |
| 112 | Lucknow | 13 | 23 | 62 | 56 | 205 | 05 | 278 | 12 | 163 | 64 |
| 113 | Trenton | | 8 | 11 | 50 | 174 | 00 | 35 | 07 | 102 | 67 |
| 114 | Gananoque | 42 | 20 | 243 | 50 | 602 | 78 | 140 | 18 | 338 | 91 |
| 115 | Harmony | 55 | 27 | 343 | 60 | 551 | 85 | 174 | 00 | 413 | 16 |
| 116 | Naomi | | 8 | | | 32 | 00 | | | 8 | 00 |
| 117 | Valley City | 13 | 30 | 49 | 30 | 363 | 50 | 164 | 50 | 167 | 86 |
| 119 | Maitland | 8 | 13 | 40 | 00 | 130 | 50 | 42 | 90 | 135 | 30 |
| 120 | Sydenham Valley | 17 | 30 | 135 | 55 | 448 | 45 | 97 | 00 | 253 | 27 |
| 121 | Saxon | | 17 | 1 | 00 | 92 | 20 | 85 | 49 | 39 | 10 |
| 122 | Streetsville | | 15 | 2 | 00 | 164 | 50 | 53 | 00 | 276 | 59 |
| 124 | Dresden | 32 | 20 | 247 | 00 | 348 | 69 | 329 | 78 | 472 | 07 |
| 125 | Stella | 40 | 17 | 261 | 70 | 320 | 20 | 133 | 80 | 205 | 49 |
| 126 | Sarnia | 16 | 23 | 144 | 00 | 184 | 55 | 155 | 22 | 272 | 35 |
| 127 | Mizpah | 9 | 22 | 111 | 50 | 316 | 50 | 73 | 37 | 228 | 83 |
| 129 | Charity | | 8 | | | 97 | 50 | 9 | 50 | 45 | 45 |
| 130 | Livingston | 1 | 19 | 10 | 60 | 95 | 10 | 103 | 56 | 133 | 66 |
| 131 | Marion | 18 | 11 | 87 | 50 | 211 | 10 | 81 | 00 | 99 | 70 |
| 132 | Oakville | 15 | 7 | 92 | 00 | 146 | 50 | 40 | 00 | 243 | 32 |
| 133 | Glencoe | 11 | 16 | 66 | 80 | 198 | 71 | 18 | 90 | 175 | 09 |
| 134 | Orient | 8 | 9 | 26 | 20 | 51 | 85 | | | 72 | 59 |
| 135 | Peaceful Dove | | 21 | | 30 | 133 | 50 | | | 65 | 68 |
| 136 | Cobourg | 7 | 23 | 54 | 60 | | | | | 118 | 83 |
| 137 | St. Lawrence | 23 | 22 | 107 | 80 | 330 | 25 | 31 | 67 | 149 | 14 |
| 138 | Ancaster | 9 | 13 | 50 | 30 | 122 | 50 | | | 70 | 23 |
| 139 | Garnet | 15 | 17 | 80 | 30 | 121 | 06 | 86 | 90 | 150 | 62 |
| 140 | Leamington | 8 | 12 | 57 | 75 | 329 | 28 | 23 | 32 | 137 | 25 |
| 142 | Concord | | 11 | 64 | 40 | 151 | 20 | 41 | 80 | 145 | 43 |
| 143 | Bay of Quinte | 7 | 27 | 57 | 20 | 305 | 19 | 1 | 10 | 109 | 34 |
| 144 | Ridgetown | 20 | 20 | 127 | 00 | 298 | 96 | 455 | 97 | 711 | 98 |
| 146 | Vivian | 5 | 13 | 26 | 35 | 134 | 70 | 107 | 00 | 94 | 18 |
| 147 | Model | 8 | 11 | 61 | 20 | 92 | 50 | 35 | 50 | 87 | 17 |
| 148 | Aurora | 6 | 24 | 19 | 20 | 247 | 00 | 171 | 00 | 178 | 08 |
| 149 | Western Star | 1 | 19 | 3 | 00 | 106 | 24 | 57 | 50 | 123 | 16 |
| 151 | Sycamore | | | | 30 | 101 | 00 | 27 | 17 | 92 | 57 |
| 152 | Hayden | 36 | 18 | 171 | 90 | 274 | 40 | 62 | 43 | 190 | 60 |
| 153 | Wildey | 6 | 17 | 27 | 10 | 138 | 50 | 97 | 50 | 144 | 00 |
| 154 | Alpha | 13 | 18 | 76 | 90 | 369 | 70 | 167 | 87 | 304 | 06 |
| 155 | Brougham | 6 | 10 | 43 | 80 | 67 | 00 | 51 | 30 | 23 | 10 |
| 156 | Pyramid | | 18 | 2 | 60 | 81 | 60 | | | 39 | 66 |
| 157 | Thamesville | 8 | 11 | 42 | 90 | 134 | 00 | 27 | 50 | 60 | 00 |

TERM ENDING 30TH JUNE, 1892.—*Continued.*

| ASSETS—HOW INVESTED. | | | | FUNDS. | | | | |
| Cash in Bank or in Treasurer's hands. | Invested in Mortgages and Securities. | Invested in Buildings and Lands. | Invested in Furniture and Regalia. | General Benefit Fund. | W. and O. Fund. | Contingent Fund. | Total Fund. | No. of Lodge. |
|---|---|---|---|---|---|---|---|---|
| $ c | $ c | $ c | $ c | $ c | $ c | $ c | $ c | |
| 1441 36 | 1985 00 | | 326 00 | 2821 28 | 921 08 | | 5752 36 | 90 |
| 688 43 | 3832 30 | | 800 00 | 2314 01 | 2966 39 | 40 33 | 5320 73 | 91 |
| 255 41 | 687 00 | | 600 00 | 1287 00 | | 255 41 | 1542 41 | 92 |
| 191 85 | 1200 00 | | 391 98 | 1783 83 | | | 1783 83 | 93 |
| 2810 38 | 1700 00 | | 700 00 | 4756 36 | 454 02 | | 5210 38 | 94 |
| 387 51 | 3550 00 | | 634 00 | 4571 51 | | | 4571 51 | 96 |
| 154 17 | 1750 00 | | 832 00 | 1979 66 | 150 00 | 606 51 | 2736 17 | 97 |
| 869 95 | | 2200 00 | 500 00 | 3389 90 | 180 05 | | 3569 95 | 98 |
| 1075 70 | 1100 00 | | 1000 00 | 3175 70 | | | 3175 70 | 100 |
| 1798 60 | 1030 00 | | 495 26 | 2314 38 | 993 38 | 16 10 | 3323 86 | 101 |
| 2415 34 | | | 675 00 | 2508 54 | 377 43 | 204 37 | 3090 34 | 102 |
| 842 01 | 400 00 | | 500 00 | 1742 01 | | | 1742 01 | 103 |
| 673 94 | | 6870 00 | 845 80 | 6069 91 | 2310 50 | 10 33 | 8359 74 | 104 |
| 452 40 | 361 12 | | 400 00 | 1213 52 | | | 1213 52 | 105 |
| 1866 76 | | 5330 00 | 588 81 | 7785 57 | | | 7785 57 | 106 |
| 930 73 | 2350 00 | 3400 00 | 625 00 | 5967 93 | 1308 95 | 28 85 | 7305 73 | 107 |
| 1297 00 | 9 50 | | | 2947 00 | | | 2947 00 | 108 |
| 553 93 | 1900 00 | | 600 00 | 3038 40 | | 15 53 | 3053 93 | 109 |
| 5754 93 | | 25 00 | 1474 89 | 5009 35 | 1515 00 | 130 47 | 7254 82 | 111 |
| 240 67 | 3729 00 | | 669 35 | 3865 31 | 773 71 | | 4639 02 | 112 |
| 1062 84 | | | 684 00 | 1746 84 | | | 1746 84 | 113 |
| 3250 63 | 1110 00 | | 1975 00 | 5260 01 | 1063 97 | 41 65 | 6365 63 | 114 |
| 137 30 | 6200 00 | | 1302 06 | 5543 70 | 2025 39 | 137 90 | 7706 99 | 115 |
| 194 17 | | 612 00 | 200 00 | 1006 17 | | | 1006 17 | 116 |
| 592 76 | 3800 00 | 500 00 | 1574 03 | 3636 79 | 2766 10 | 63 87 | 6466 76 | 117 |
| 1908 33 | | 750 00 | 338 50 | 2496 47 | 500 36 | | 2996 83 | 119 |
| 287 44 | | 5718 24 | 1650 00 | 7655 68 | | | 7655 68 | 120 |
| 643 64 | 1200 00 | | 750 00 | 1793 96 | 794 18 | 5 50 | 2593 64 | 121 |
| 44 02 | | 4500 00 | 700 00 | 5244 02 | | | 5244 02 | 122 |
| 1315 79 | 500 00 | 4414 08 | 163 43 | 5862 70 | 526 28 | 4 32 | 6393 30 | 124 |
| 1924 40 | | | 1018 00 | 2331 02 | 610 00 | 1 38 | 2942 40 | 125 |
| 760 13 | | | 1200 00 | 1960 13 | | | 1900 13 | 126 |
| 1689 67 | | | 1220 29 | 2886 08 | | 23 88 | 2909 96 | 127 |
| 269 45 | 130 00 | | 180 00 | 579 45 | | | 579 45 | 129 |
| 1031 88 | | | 1000 00 | 2031 88 | | | 2031 88 | 130 |
| 607 90 | 2000 00 | | 600 00 | 2670 44 | 354 89 | 182 59 | 3207 90 | 131 |
| 31 32 | | 3302 55 | 600 00 | 2948 74 | 844 10 | 141 03 | 3933 87 | 132 |
| 201 90 | 1150 00 | | 691 20 | 1225 01 | 762 89 | 55 17 | 2043 07 | 133 |
| 426 32 | | | 600 00 | 600 00 | 425 21 | 1 11 | 1026 32 | 134 |
| 872 63 | 1000 00 | | 600 00 | 1727 63 | 745 00 | | 2472 63 | 135 |
| 1099 48 | | | 2242 50 | 3333 88 | 2 10 | 6 00 | 3341 98 | 136 |
| 1729 41 | | | 761 00 | 1430 08 | 1060 33 | | 2490 41 | 137 |
| 1107 36 | | | 250 00 | 906 50 | 416 86 | 34 00 | 1357 36 | 138 |
| 1360 70 | | | 566 90 | 1927 60 | | | 1927 60 | 139 |
| 396 12 | | | 1306 09 | 1702 21 | | | 1702 21 | 140 |
| 108 57 | | 3000 00 | 400 00 | 3508 57 | | | 3508 57 | 142 |
| 2121 47 | | 3550 75 | 1267 89 | 5735 80 | 1204 31 | | 6940 11 | 143 |
| 1044 20 | 450 00 | | 1600 00 | 2650 20 | 444 00 | | 3094 20 | 144 |
| 9 18 | 1900 00 | | 865 00 | 2774 18 | | | 2774 18 | 146 |
| 768 68 | | | 300 00 | 576 22 | 483 36 | 9 10 | 1068 68 | 147 |
| 61 70 | | 3098 02 | 394 06 | 3384 28 | 1060 80 | | 4444 78 | 148 |
| 156 14 | 17 00 | | 1043 00 | 951 99 | 264 15 | | 1216 14 | 149 |
| 235 55 | 563 00 | 1300 00 | 300 00 | 2398 50 | | | 2398 50 | 151 |
| 387 36 | 1000 00 | | 360 00 | 1747 36 | | | 1747 36 | 152 |
| 933 57 | | 1575 00 | 200 00 | 2708 57 | | | 2708 57 | 153 |
| 15 11 | 2620 00 | | 1500 00 | 2515 72 | 1169 33 | 450 00 | 4135 11 | 154 |
| 983 91 | | | 150 00 | 935 21 | 198 70 | | 1133 91 | 155 |
| 183 55 | 700 00 | | 600 00 | 1483 55 | | | 1483 55 | 156 |
| 654 84 | | | 375 00 | 1029 84 | | | 1029 84 | 157 |

## ABSTRACT FROM SEMI-ANNUAL RETURNS.

| No. of Lodge. | NAME OF LODGE. | No. of Degrees Conferred. | No. of Past Grands in Good Standing. | Initiations, Admission by Card, and Degrees. $ c | Dues and Reinstatements. $ c | All other Sources. $ c | Current Expenses. $ c |
|---|---|---|---|---|---|---|---|
| 158 | Progress | 18 | 25 | 133 90 | 357 10 | 116 05 | 263 48 |
| 159 | Oak Leaf | 5 | 15 | 18 60 | 134 00 | 30 02 | 79 68 |
| 160 | Listowel | | | 77 50 | 195 00 | 11 35 | 143 63 |
| 161 | Simcoe | | 18 | 10 00 | 208 60 | 25 00 | 191 86 |
| 163 | Oriental | 2 | 10 | 9 75 | 100 50 | 23 75 | 125 79 |
| 164 | Romeo | 15 | 23 | 58 00 | 456 99 | 75 00 | 168 70 |
| 165 | Beethoven | | 16 | | 84 50 | 30 00 | 61 14 |
| 167 | Hillsburg | 6 | 13 | 32 60 | 70 50 | 1 25 | 6 00 |
| 168 | Sutton | 9 | 11 | 35 40 | 101 20 | 56 00 | 9 27 |
| 169 | Grey | 6 | 5 | 18 00 | 63 50 | 7 50 | 43 17 |
| 170 | Denovo | 18 | 13 | 78 41 | 152 20 | 78 80 | 88 15 |
| 171 | Alliston | 6 | 11 | 27 10 | 76 90 | | 488 85 |
| 172 | Penetangore | | | 101 90 | 343 65 | 214 75 | 306 22 |
| 173 | Emerald | 6 | 14 | 40 00 | 64 50 | 96 00 | 75 50 |
| 174 | Dolman | 12 | 16 | 63 10 | 136 00 | 10 00 | 65 15 |
| 176 | Dauncey | 9 | 1 | 45 00 | 66 00 | | 182 75 |
| 177 | Montana | 9 | 2 | 27 00 | 42 45 | 32 35 | 64 59 |
| 178 | Wellington Squaie | 1! | 6 | 84 30 | 61 50 | | 150 10 |
| 179 | Madoc | 95 | 15 | 535 90 | 311 80 | 80 31 | 213 04 |
| 180 | Owen Sound | 9 | 16 | 73 80 | 143 29 | 58 83 | 213 80 |
| 182 | Tecumseh | 10 | 14 | 28 20 | 107 70 | 37 25 | 52 98 |
| 183 | Teeswater | | 12 | | 1.0 53 | 42 90 | 60 08 |
| 184 | Germania | 36 | 23 | 132 53 | 222 97 | 76 40 | 200 89 |
| 186 | Dufferin | 20 | 9 | 93 70 | 76 20 | | 67 05 |
| 188 | Cambridge | 6 | 13 | 47 30 | 147 45 | 21 75 | 65 23 |
| 189 | Parry Sound | 7 | 15 | 50 00 | 134 63 | 91 80 | 44 22 |
| 190 | Chorazin | 8 | 28 | 26 50 | 517 21 | 107 92 | 190 62 |
| 191 | Jarvis | | 11 | | 62 40 | 64 57 | 121 20 |
| 192 | Howick | 3 | | 9 00 | 44 97 | | 32 78 |
| 194 | Albert | 14 | 33 | 121 96 | 520 64 | 219 00 | 254 97 |
| 195 | Cicerone | 1 | 9 | 8 00 | 50 00 | | 23 85 |
| 196 | Florence | 8 | 27 | 38 05 | 221 00 | 83 00 | 70 45 |
| 197 | Minerva | 3 | 12 | 35 50 | 187 75 | 88 56 | 123 49 |
| 200 | Weston | | | 24 50 | 131 25 | 118 05 | 169 70 |
| 201 | Beacon | 14 | 10 | 71 00 | 68 58 | 55 85 | 224 55 |
| 202 | Silver Star | 20 | 13 | 91 00 | 177 41 | | 5 00 |
| 203 | Pembroke | 12 | 19 | 66 50 | 283 30 | 90 55 | 121 14 |
| 204 | Acton | 1 | 4 | 6 00 | 52 50 | 20 00 | 67 23 |
| 205 | Ahiram | 49 | 19 | 282 80 | 290 83 | 167 40 | 70 88 |
| 206 | Silver City | 1 | 17 | 7 50 | 9 24 | 120 71 | 117 77 |
| 209 | Millbank | 3 | 10 | 17 00 | 45 00 | 25 00 | 5 70 |
| 210 | Brucefield | 3 | 14 | 16 90 | 90 15 | 26 00 | 43 01 |
| 211 | Lilly | 6 | 8 | 23 22 | 126 60 | 16 75 | 111 80 |
| 212 | Argyll | 12 | 17 | 69 60 | 164 20 | 185 34 | 103 32 |
| 214 | Freestone | 7 | 17 | 29 00 | 243 30 | 121 65 | 254 00 |
| 215 | Clifford | 12 | 14 | 92 30 | 80 75 | 27 00 | 68 48 |
| 216 | Elmira | 6 | 10 | 56 75 | 116 88 | 2 00 | 172 57 |
| 217 | Mount Brydges | 20 | 18 | 186 45 | 284 35 | 1527 94 | 1592 25 |
| 218 | Enterprise | 28 | 10 | 203 10 | 343 50 | 89 55 | 241 27 |
| 219 | Georgian Bay | 9 | 18 | 107 40 | 174 00 | 83 00 | 153 79 |
| 220 | Woodslee | 2 | 3 | 8 00 | 39 00 | 3 00 | 11 27 |
| 221 | Chesley | | 10 | 12 00 | 60 37 | | 79 17 |
| 223 | Hensall | 12 | 21 | 56 70 | 166 10 | 104 50 | 62 67 |
| 224 | Ottawa | 18 | 19 | 108 90 | 416 21 | 50 00 | 244 52 |
| 226 | Merlin | 3 | 9 | 50 | 90 50 | | 20 39 |
| 227 | Sauble | | 7 | | 36 50 | 12 50 | |
| 228 | International | 9 | 23 | 48 60 | 488 20 | 414 36 | 457 68 |
| 229 | Embro Star | 12 | 11 | 33 40 | 133 00 | | 15 00 |
| 230 | Prince of Wales | 3 | 9 | 28 05 | 110 52 | 170 55 | 247 50 |
| 231 | Elora | 3 | 13 | 18 60 | 189 78 | 31 14 | 75 65 |

TERM ENDING 30TH JUNE, 1892.—*Continued.*

| ASSETS—HOW INVESTED. | | | | FUNDS. | | | | |
|---|---|---|---|---|---|---|---|---|
| Cash in Bank or in Treasurer's hands. | Invested in Mortgages and Securities. | Invested in Buildings and Lands. | Invested in Furniture and Regalia. | General Benefit Fund. | W. and O. Fund. | Contingent Fund. | Total Funds. | No. of Lodge. |
| $ c | $ c | $ c | $ c | $ c | $ c | $ c | $ c | |
|  | 5174 61 |  | 900 00 | 3714 75 | 2359 86 |  | 6074 61 | 158 |
| 589 56 |  | 45 00 | 350 00 | 984 56 |  |  | 984 56 | 159 |
| 1221 90 |  |  | 908 85 | 1875 75 | 255 00 |  | 2130 75 | 160 |
| 280 80 | 100 00 | 2000 00 | 650 00 | 3030 80 |  | 1 79 | 3032 59 | 161 |
| 324 06 |  |  | 800 00 | 1124 06 |  |  | 1124 06 | 163 |
| 671 15 | 2900 00 |  | 223 46 | 3688 15 |  | 107 16 | 3795 25 | 164 |
| 2142 72 |  |  | 400 00 | 1389 67 | 1154 05 |  | 2543 72 | 165 |
| 204 16 |  | 850 00 | 70 00 | 1121 26 |  |  | 1124 26 | 167 |
| 96 97 |  | 4140 20 | 338 00 | 4575 17 |  |  | 4575 17 | 168 |
| 182 95 | 200 00 | 346 06 | 300 00 | 673 75 | 355 26 |  | 1029 01 | 169 |
| 48 38 | 1150 00 |  | 200 00 | 1388 38 |  | 10 00 | 1398 38 | 170 |
| 81 89 | 333 28 |  | 745 00 | 1158 17 |  | 2 00 | 1160 17 | 171 |
| 457 92 | 2867 50 |  | 1488 96 | 4441 64 | 372 72 |  | 4814 36 | 172 |
| 416 76 | 278 00 | 1600 00 | 600 00 | 2894 76 |  |  | 2894 76 | 173 |
| 44 98 | 760 00 |  | 310 00 | 1114 98 |  |  | 1114 98 | 174 |
|  |  |  | 84 50 | 84 50 |  |  | 84 50 | 176 |
| 716 81 |  |  | 150 00 | 575 68 | 285 36 | 5 77 | 866 81 | 177 |
| 141 16 |  |  |  | 141 16 |  |  | 141 16 | 178 |
| 1243 32 | 40 00 |  | 1312 86 | 2575 38 |  | 20 80 | 2596 18 | 179 |
|  |  |  |  | 1515 63 | 1430 05 | 116 53 | 3062 21 | 180 |
| 527 29 | 490 75 |  | 124 80 | 1142 84 |  |  | 1142 84 | 182 |
| 900 00 | 225 46 |  | 240 00 | 746 26 | 619 20 |  | 1365 46 | 183 |
| 1245 53 | 300 00 |  | 234 56 | 1545 53 | 184 75 | 49 81 | 1780 09 | 184 |
| 401 85 |  |  | 485 00 | 378 43 | 485 00 | 23 42 | 886 85 | 186 |
| 484 85 |  | 850 00 | 350 00 | 1684 00 |  |  | 1684 00 | 188 |
| 1140 00 | 225 00 | 2000 00 | 1085 00 | 3166 76 | 1284 11 |  | 4450 87 | 189 |
| 805 31 | 1450 50 | 2300 00 | 530 00 | 3640 93 | 1345 34 | 119 04 | 5105 31 | 190 |
| 1347 77 | 208 00 |  | 736 00 | 1617 24 | 674 53 |  | 2291 77 | 191 |
| 601 51 | 222 50 |  | 191 15 | 910 16 | 105 00 |  | 1015 16 | 192 |
| 667 60 | 2000 00 |  | 1063 18 | 1838 65 | 1974 66 | 817 47 | 4630 78 | 194 |
| 406 00 |  |  | 100 00 | 339 44 | 100 00 | 66 56 | 506 00 | 195 |
| 1094 30 | 1900 00 |  | 303 00 | 2994 30 | 303 00 |  | 3297 30 | 196 |
| 1690 96 |  |  | 281 65 | 1095 77 | 857 23 | 19 61 | 1972 61 | 197 |
| 43 12 |  | 2346 74 | 300 00 | 2193 46 | 405 64 | 76 | 2689 86 | 200 |
| 849 84 |  |  | 536 95 | 943 12 | 443 67 |  | 1386 79 | 201 |
| 910 29 | 450 00 |  | 300 00 | 1406 57 | 253 72 |  | 1660 29 | 202 |
| 2070 92 |  |  | 1542 42 | 1967 28 | 1597 03 | 49 03 | 3613 34 | 203 |
| 21 63 | 296 25 |  | 150 00 | 467 88 |  |  | 467 88 | 204 |
| 190 80 |  | 3717 38 | 507 22 | 4415 40 |  |  | 4415 40 | 205 |
| 66 36 | 1433 92 |  | 500 00 | 2000 28 |  |  | 2000 28 | 206 |
| 774 22 | 250 00 |  | 150 00 | 1174 22 |  |  | 1174 22 | 209 |
| 296 89 | 756 00 |  |  | 1052 89 |  |  | 1052 89 | 210 |
|  |  | 675 00 | 200 00 | 875 00 |  |  | 875 00 | 211 |
| 1271 06 | 1500 00 |  | 1645 32 | 3501 30 | 915 08 |  | 4416 38 | 212 |
| 245 62 | 2600 00 |  | 214 74 | 2845 62 | 214 74 |  | 3060 36 | 214 |
| 916 97 | 1200 00 |  | 500 00 | 1412 55 | 704 42 | 500 00 | 2616 97 | 215 |
| 1075 63 | 221 00 |  | 255 00 | 1615 63 |  |  | 1615 63 | 216 |
| 546 56 |  | 3308 26 | 609 88 | 3735 70 | 711 00 | 18 00 | 4464 70 | 217 |
| 1223 25 | 189 12 |  | 500 00 | 1912 37 |  |  | 1912 37 | 218 |
| 755 98 |  | 1479 35 | 400 00 | 1970 30 | 574 10 | 90 93 | 2635 33 | 219 |
| 404 43 | 100 00 | 65 00 | 200 00 | 769 43 |  |  | 769 43 | 220 |
| 276 00 | 700 00 |  | 200 00 | 1176 00 |  |  | 1176 00 | 221 |
| 98 48 |  | 1400 00 | 210 00 | 1708 48 |  |  | 1708 48 | 223 |
| 2521 40 |  |  | 700 00 | 1999 38 | 1217 42 | 4 60 | 3221 40 | 224 |
| 119 90 |  | 1500 00 | 144 51 | 1764 41 |  |  | 1764 41 | 226 |
|  |  |  | 245 00 | 245 00 |  |  | 245 00 | 227 |
| 914 31 |  | 3937 58 | 1395 22 | 4762 63 | 1415 35 | 33 13 | 6211 11 | 228 |
| 612 60 |  |  | 455 32 | 1067 92 |  |  | 1067 92 | 229 |
| 361 66 |  |  | 411 00 | 360 93 | 411 00 | 93 | 772 86 | 230 |
| 612 29 |  |  | 840 00 | 1452 29 |  |  | 1452 29 | 231 |

## ABSTRACT FROM SEMI-ANNUAL RETURNS.

| No. of Lodge. | NAME OF LODGE. | No. of Degrees Conferred. | No. of Past Grands in Good Standing. | Initiations, Admission by Card, and Degrees. | Dues and Reinstatements. | All other Sources. | Current Expenses. |
|---|---|---|---|---|---|---|---|
| | | | | $ c | $ c | $ c | $ c |
| 232 | Equity | | | | 45 00 | | 1 50 |
| 233 | Hanover | 4 | | | 30 00 | 35 00 | 45 00 |
| 234 | Ilderton | 3 | 10 | 15 80 | 120 40 | 84 17 | 81 62 |
| 235 | Waterford | | 14 | 74 80 | 285 00 | 6 29 | 153 54 |
| 236 | Acorn | 8 | 10 | 42 80 | 56 00 | 56 70 | 53 05 |
| 237 | Farmersville | 3 | 14 | | | | |
| 239 | Stirling | 21 | 13 | 106 50 | 299 00 | 198 00 | 116 69 |
| 240 | Carleton | 22 | 21 | 112 50 | 434 50 | 219 75 | 562 65 |
| 241 | Rideau | | | 51 30 | 315 10 | 38 50 | 175 27 |
| 242 | Wilton | 1 | 10 | 28 60 | 258 93 | 16 38 | 212 44 |
| 243 | Thornbury | | | 27 00 | 93 50 | 78 00 | 109 51 |
| 244 | Port Arthur | 19 | 10 | 155 40 | 267 20 | 46 14 | 326 22 |
| 245 | Mallorytown | 3 | 11 | 11 00 | 117 00 | 30 00 | 30 10 |
| 246 | Orillia | 5 | 6 | 9 40 | 118 71 | 8 75 | 67 15 |
| 247 | Gordon | 7 | 12 | 51 00 | 164 34 | | 09 56 |
| 248 | Campbellford | 6 | 9 | 43 50 | 214 36 | 162 76 | 308 74 |
| 249 | Beaverton | 6 | 13 | 64 90 | 136 50 | 15 00 | 59 80 |
| 250 | Ridgely | 33 | 11 | 246 70 | 259 25 | 207 50 | 208 00 |
| 251 | Bracebridge | 7 | 11 | 63 30 | 236 40 | | 221 99 |
| 252 | Floral | | 11 | 80 | 114 00 | | 107 20 |
| 253 | Caledonia | 9 | 2 | 32 00 | 16 50 | | |
| 254 | Alba | 9 | 8 | 37 95 | 141 50 | 74 28 | 105 60 |
| 255 | Tottenham | | 4 | | 37 13 | 22 00 | 41 20 |
| 256 | Grand Valley | 3 | 9 | 28 30 | 107 50 | 54 25 | 66 10 |
| 257 | Credit | 4 | 5 | 19 50 | 90 75 | | 19 45 |
| 258 | Thamesford | 19 | 8 | 109 50 | 279 75 | 90 50 | 61 82 |
| 259 | Lynden | 1 | 26 | 9 60 | 78 00 | | 24 37 |
| 260 | Meaford | | | 61 00 | 90 98 | 5 97 | 129 55 |
| 261 | Gold Hill | 28 | 8 | 143 40 | 367 10 | 7 10 | 157 46 |
| 262 | Norwood | | 7 | 5 00 | 149 20 | 34 50 | |
| 263 | East Toronto | | 10 | 30 | 169 20 | 12 00 | 70 77 |
| 264 | Fraternity | 25 | 6 | 127 15 | 154 75 | | 108 73 |
| 265 | Delta | | | 61 60 | 102 54 | | |
| 266 | Missanabie | 18 | 7 | 180 30 | 302 00 | | 165 56 |
| 267 | Algoma | | | 32 10 | 189 00 | 12 00 | 203 40 |
| 268 | Stanley | 11 | 3 | 67 25 | 105 50 | 13 00 | 78 21 |
| 269 | Woodstock | 20 | 6 | 112 50 | 230 20 | 36 75 | 114 05 |
| 270 | Lansdowne | 3 | 6 | 12 00 | 148 50 | 22 32 | 85 00 |
| 271 | North Bay | 33 | 6 | 229 90 | 228 75 | 82 00 | 532 71 |
| 272 | Lakeview | 3 | 5 | 33 36 | 140 00 | | 53 00 |
| 273 | Hastings | 3 | 4 | 16 60 | 111 11 | 20 93 | 60 82 |
| 274 | Midland | | | 89 80 | 113 50 | | 112 73 |
| 275 | Fairy | 7 | 3 | 52 60 | 116 75 | 15 45 | 53 70 |
| 276 | Sheard | 9 | 2 | 46 55 | 93 50 | 4 00 | 86 83 |
| 277 | Lambton | 15 | 8 | 78 00 | 154 53 | | 80 32 |
| 278 | Rockliffe | | 6 | 171 20 | 154 75 | 60 50 | 278 02 |
| 279 | Grenville | 19 | 2 | 72 00 | 218 22 | 71 26 | 95 63 |
| 280 | Balmoral | 1 | 2 | 9 90 | 109 00 | | 141 08 |
| 281 | Arthur | 21 | 2 | 101 40 | 87 50 | | 66 90 |
| 282 | Sudbury | | | 258 50 | 129 65 | | 116 00 |
| 283 | Earnscliffe | 4 | 3 | 47 80 | 145 40 | | 101 13 |
| 284 | Lyn | 7 | 2 | 33 00 | 81 00 | | 27 25 |
| 285 | Morewood | 3 | | 11 00 | 31 45 | 18 00 | 09 64 |
| 286 | Royal | | | 172 00 | 85 00 | 41 00 | 304 80 |
| 287 | Ripley | 75 | | 442 05 | 92 50 | | 255 82 |
| 288 | Chesterville | 85 | 1 | 321 00 | 75 00 | | 107 15 |
| 289 | Glanworth | 3 | | 240 00 | 69 00 | | 261 27 |
| 290 | Tweed | 138 | | 245 00 | | | 73 07 |
| 291 | Rodney | 74 | 2 | 250 00 | 70 55 | | 195 72 |
| | | 3004 | 3440 | 18603 49 | 55048 64 | 23444 00 | 41313 71 |

## TERM ENDING 30TH JUNE, 1892.—*Continued.*

| ASSETS—HOW INVESTED. | | | | FUNDS. | | | | |
| Cash in Bank or in Treasurer's hands. | Invested in Mortgages and Securities. | Invested in Buildings and Lands. | Invested in Furniture and Regalia. | General Benefit Fund. | W. and O. Fund. | Contingent Fund. | Total Funds. | No. of Lodge. |
|---|---|---|---|---|---|---|---|---|
| $ c | $ c | $ c | $ c | $ c | $ c | $ c | $ c | |
| 530 55 | | | 450 00 | 980 55 | | | 980 55 | 232 |
| 100 00 | | | 100 00 | 200 00 | 80 00 | | 280 00 | 233 |
| 7 29 | | 1748 51 | 225 00 | 1828 54 | 141 56 | 10 70 | 1980 80 | 234 |
| 935 50 | | | 1100 00 | 2035 50 | | | 2035 50 | 235 |
| 617 29 | | | 140 00 | 757 29 | | | 757 29 | 236 |
| | | | | | | | | 237 |
| 216 16 | 1600 00 | | 1093 68 | 2907 05 | | 47 79 | 2954 84 | 239 |
| 622 46 | 12 00 | | 2100 00 | 2715 26 | | 19 20 | 2734 46 | 240 |
| 1448 99 | | | 1600 95 | 2376 64 | 673 31 | | 3049 95 | 241 |
| 860 17 | | | 283 51 | 122 84 | 1017 51 | 3 33 | 1143 68 | 242 |
| 167 10 | | 300 00 | 196 67 | 286 76 | 292 73 | 84 24 | 663 77 | 243 |
| 963 56 | 250 00 | | 1300 00 | 1979 64 | 529 94 | 3 94 | 2513 54 | 244 |
| 117 49 | 510 00 | 500 00 | 542 85 | 1016 30 | 592 01 | 62 03 | 1670 34 | 245 |
| 20 94 | | | 500 00 | 520 94 | | | 520 94 | 246 |
| 503 30 | | | | 333 21 | 166 39 | 3 70 | 503 30 | 247 |
| 1233 12 | | | 1070 43 | 1798 25 | 195 61 | 209 69 | 2203 55 | 248 |
| 2 77 | 1070 00 | | 175 00 | 638 93 | 558 53 | 50 31 | 1247 77 | 249 |
| 411 62 | | 1650 50 | 292 50 | 2354 62 | | | 2354 62 | 250 |
| 256 07 | 300 00 | | 693 00 | 732 45 | 476 62 | | 1209 07 | 251 |
| 292 44 | | | 525 00 | 817 44 | | | 817 44 | 252 |
| 265 20 | | | 20 00 | 285 70 | | | 285 70 | 253 |
| 884 84 | | | 200 00 | 1051 97 | | 32 87 | 1084 84 | 254 |
| | | | | | | | | 255 |
| 231 34 | | | 214 00 | 210 14 | 235 20 | | 445 34 | 256 |
| 569 93 | | | 223 19 | 793 12 | | | 793 12 | 257 |
| 377 16 | 1500 00 | | 362 26 | 1846 98 | 383 61 | 8 83 | 2239 42 | 258 |
| 547 57 | | | 165 91 | 713 48 | | | 713 48 | 259 |
| 339 71 | | | 275 00 | 599 13 | | 15 58 | 614 71 | 260 |
| 466 50 | 75 00 | 1050 00 | 900 00 | 2482 47 | 4 50 | 4 53 | 2491 50 | 261 |
| 429 88 | | | 360 00 | 789 88 | | | 789 88 | 262 |
| 321 59 | | | 125 00 | 166 22 | 268 92 | 11 45 | 446 59 | 263 |
| 752 54 | | | 213 61 | 754 19 | 211 25 | 71 | 966 15 | 264 |
| 334 79 | | | 235 00 | 473 42 | 96 37 | | 569 79 | 265 |
| 607 41 | 400 00 | | 931 32 | 1988 73 | | | 1988 73 | 266 |
| 611 76 | | | 400 00 | 1041 76 | | | 1041 76 | 267 |
| 465 83 | | | 327 46 | 640 71 | 113 65 | 38 93 | 793 29 | 268 |
| 669 06 | | | 245 00 | 914 66 | | | 914 66 | 269 |
| 324 79 | | | 570 00 | 740 63 | 154 16 | | 894 79 | 270 |
| 80 24 | 425 00 | | 900 00 | 1405 24 | | | 1405 24 | 271 |
| 500 48 | | 122 00 | 134 66 | 776 56 | 40 58 | | 817 14 | 272 |
| 521 64 | | | 345 75 | 863 31 | | 4 08 | 867 39 | 273 |
| 200 87 | | | 600 00 | 800 87 | | | 800 87 | 274 |
| 347 55 | | | 270 23 | 441 25 | 161 08 | 15 45 | 617 78 | 275 |
| 238 75 | | | 179 38 | 401 91 | | 16 22 | 418 13 | 276 |
| 171 23 | 400 00 | | 250 73 | 808 46 | | 13 50 | 821 96 | 277 |
| 52 80 | | | 550 00 | 602 80 | | | 602 80 | 278 |
| 226 79 | | 200 00 | 316 21 | 674 40 | | 68 60 | 743 00 | 279 |
| 171 98 | | | 155 60 | 265 57 | 62 01 | | 327 58 | 280 |
| 393 66 | | | 250 00 | 638 66 | 5 00 | | 643 66 | 281 |
| | | | | | | | | 282 |
| 149 15 | | | 290 00 | 439 15 | | | 439 15 | 283 |
| | | 200 00 | 100 00 | 275 00 | 2 00 | 23 00 | 300 00 | 284 |
| 26 81 | | | 158 25 | 185 06 | | | 185 06 | 285 |
| 111 20 | | | | 111 20 | | | 111 20 | 286 |
| 278 73 | | | 117 69 | 396 42 | | | 396 42 | 287 |
| 109 48 | | | 181 37 | 275 85 | 15 00 | | 290 85 | 288 |
| 79 73 | | 75 00 | 100 00 | 254 73 | | | 254 73 | 289 |
| 171 93 | | | | 171 93 | | | 171 93 | 290 |
| 130 83 | | | 82 04 | 212 87 | | | 212 87 | 291 |
| **164875** 01 | 174030 70 | 262857 03 | **159482** 09 | 637795 16 | 116485 77 | 8682 50 | 762963 43 | |

## ABSTRACT FROM SEMI-ANNUAL RETURNS.

### MEMBERSHIP.

| No. of Lodge | NAME OF LODGE | Initiated | Reinstated | Admitt'd by card | Suspended for Cause | Susp'nded N.P.D. | Withdrawn | Expelled | Died | Members per last Report | Present Membership | Number of Brothers Sick |
|---|---|---|---|---|---|---|---|---|---|---|---|---|
| 9 | Brock | 2 | | | | | 1 | | 2 | 113 | 112 | 6 |
| 10 | Cataraqui | 10 | | 1 | | 7 | 1 | | 2 | 244 | 245 | 21 |
| 13 | Otonabee | 11 | | | | 12 | 2 | | 1 | 135 | 131 | 8 |
| 16 | Union | | | 1 | | 15 | 1 | | 1 | 232 | 216 | 21 |
| 22 | Phœnix | 1 | | | | | | | 1 | 76 | 76 | 1 |
| 28 | Rose | | | | | | | | | 100 | 100 | 5 |
| 29 | Chatham | 5 | | 2 | | 5 | | | | 156 | 158 | 12 |
| 30 | Eureka | | | | | 1 | | | 3 | 108 | 104 | 16 |
| 32 | Elgin | 9 | | | | 3 | 1 | | | 229 | 234 | 14 |
| 33 | Erie | 1 | 1 | | | 1 | 1 | | | 18 | 18 | |
| 34 | Gore | 12 | 1 | 1 | | | 1 | | 3 | 215 | 225 | 22 |
| 35 | Samaritan | 1 | | 2 | | 11 | | | 2 | 166 | 155 | 10 |
| 36 | St. Mary's | 1 | | | | | 3 | | 1 | 140 | 137 | 8 |
| 38 | Forest City | 2 | | | | | 1 | | | 121 | 122 | 15 |
| 40 | Rond Eau | 3 | | | | 10 | | | | 110 | 103 | 11 |
| 41 | Avon | 6 | 1 | | | | | | 2 | 209 | 214 | 14 |
| 44 | Excelsior | 3 | | | | 1 | | | 2 | 140 | 140 | 11 |
| 45 | Frontier | 7 | | 3 | | 8 | 2 | | 4 | 253 | 249 | 22 |
| 46 | Mount Zion | 2 | | | | 3 | | | | 26 | 25 | |
| 47 | Unity | 3 | | | | 7 | | | 1 | 282 | 277 | 21 |
| 48 | Dominion | 5 | | | | 4 | | | 1 | 154 | 154 | 9 |
| 49 | Canada | 5 | | | | 1 | 2 | | | 203 | 205 | 8 |
| 50 | Otter | 14 | 2 | 1 | | | | | | 115 | 132 | 6 |
| 51 | Bissell | | | | | | 1 | | | 24 | 23 | 2 |
| 52 | Covenant | 2 | | 1 | | | 2 | | 1 | 184 | 184 | 11 |
| 53 | Niagara Falls | 4 | | | | 1 | | | | 119 | 122 | 5 |
| 54 | Collingwood | 6 | 1 | 1 | | | 3 | | 1 | 141 | 145 | 1 |
| 55 | Fidelity | | | | | | | | | 17 | 17 | 1 |
| 56 | Queen City of Ontario | 2 | | | | 3 | | | | 165 | 164 | 8 |
| 57 | Maple Leaf | 1 | | | | 1 | | | | 47 | 47 | 1 |
| 58 | Howard | 7 | 1 | | | | 1 | | 1 | 101 | 107 | 4 |
| 59 | Kingston | 14 | 1 | | | 10 | 1 | | | 252 | 256 | 18 |
| 61 | Corinthian | 3 | 1 | | | | 4 | | | 201 | 201 | 17 |
| 62 | Huron | 2 | 1 | | | 9 | | | | 121 | 115 | 9 |
| 63 | Barrie | 2 | | | | 3 | | | 1 | 115 | 113 | 7 |
| 64 | Victor a | 1 | | 1 | | | 2 | | | 67 | 67 | 3 |
| 65 | Friendship | 3 | | | | 7 | | | | 181 | 177 | 5 |
| 66 | Florence Nightingale | 1 | | | | 5 | 1 | | | 146 | 141 | 9 |
| 67 | Exeter | 3 | | | | | | | | 44 | 47 | 3 |
| 68 | North Star | 1 | | | | 6 | | | | 49 | 44 | 1 |
| 69 | Hope | 7 | | | | | | | | 63 | 70 | 7 |
| 70 | Lucan | | | | | | | | | 24 | 24 | 2 |
| 71 | The Toronto | 7 | | | | 1 | | | | 60 | 66 | 2 |
| 72 | Eastern Star | 4 | | | | | | | 3 | 101 | 102 | 8 |
| 73 | Fergus | 9 | 1 | | | | | | | 67 | 77 | 1 |
| 74 | Bothwell | 2 | | | | 6 | | | | 48 | 44 | 3 |
| 75 | Warriner | | | | | 7 | 2 | | | 79 | 70 | 6 |
| 76 | St. Thomas | 3 | 1 | | | 2 | | | 2 | 346 | 346 | 3 |
| 77 | Oxford | 1 | | 1 | | 7 | 1 | | | 109 | 103 | 5 |
| 78 | Durham | 2 | | | | 10 | 2 | | 1 | 123 | 112 | 4 |
| 79 | Nipissing | | | | | | | | | 63 | 63 | 4 |
| 80 | Amity | 15 | 1 | | | | | | | 177 | 193 | 16 |
| 81 | Belleville | 3 | | | | 3 | 3 | | 1 | 191 | 187 | 9 |
| 82 | Beaver | 2 | 1 | | | 6 | | | | 56 | 53 | 1 |
| 83 | Clinton | | | | | | | | | 24 | 24 | 3 |
| 84 | Walkerton | | 1 | | | 2 | | | | 62 | 61 | 4 |
| 85 | Constellation | 6 | 1 | | | | | | | 48 | 55 | |
| 86 | Napanee | 1 | | | | | | | | 60 | 61 | 2 |
| 87 | Empire | 2 | | | | 17 | | | | 123 | 108 | 6 |
| 88 | Olive Branch | | | | | 11 | | | 1 | 134 | 122 | 8 |
| 89 | Reliance | 3 | | | | 5 | | | | 156 | 154 | 8 |
| 90 | Ivy | 4 | | | | 1 | | | | 66 | 69 | 8 |

## Term Ending 31st December, 1892.

### SICK BENEFITS AND RELIEFS.

| Number of Weeks' Sickness. | Amount paid for Sick Benefits. | Amount paid for Burying Deceased Bros. | No of Wives of Bros. Dead. | Amount paid for Burying Bros.' Wives. | No. of Widows. | Amount paid for Relief of Widows. | No. of Orphans. | Amount paid for Educating Orphans. | Paid to Lodge Surgeon. | Paid for Nursing Sick Brothers. | Paid for Special Relief & Charity. | Total Relief. | No. of Lodge. |
|---|---|---|---|---|---|---|---|---|---|---|---|---|---|
| | $ c | $ c | | $ c | | $ c | | $ c | $ c | $ c | $ c | $ c | |
| 25 | 73 00 | 60 00 | 1 | 15 00 | 2 | 206 00 | | | | | 24 80 | 378 80 | 9 |
| 102-1 | 306 50 | 60 00 | 1 | 15 00 | 3 | 215 00 | | | 50 00 | | 21 40 | 667 00 | 10 |
| 52-3 | 209 71 | | | | | | | | 67 50 | | 10 00 | 287 21 | 13 |
| 176 | 531 50 | 50 00 | | | | 230 00 | | | | | | 811 50 | 16 |
| 4 | 12 00 | | 1 | 15 00 | | | | | 23 00 | | 50 00 | 100 00 | 22 |
| 68 | 201 00 | | | | | | | | | | | 201 00 | 28 |
| 67 | 201 00 | | | | 7 | 115 00 | 8 | 80 00 | 90 75 | 8 75 | | 495 50 | 29 |
| 173 | 402 00 | 225 00 | | | | | | | | | 26 00 | 653 00 | 30 |
| | 317 99 | | 1 | 20 00 | 4 | 55 00 | | 43 00 | 87 00 | | | 522 99 | 32 |
| | | | | | | | | | | | | | 33 |
| 81 | 386 86 | 160 00 | | | | 800 00 | | | | 113 08 | | 1459 94 | 34 |
| 102 | 347 00 | 100 00 | | | 7 | 309 00 | | | | 5 00 | | 761 00 | 35 |
| 56 | 155 00 | 60 00 | | | 2 | 200 00 | | | | | 20 00 | 455 00 | 36 |
| 136 | 389 50 | | 1 | 20 00 | | | | | 37 50 | | 50 25 | 506 25 | 38 |
| 49-3 | 192 83 | | | | 1 | 12 00 | | | | 15 50 | | 220 33 | 40 |
| 60-2 | 236 50 | 50 00 | 2 | 50 00 | 1 | 150 00 | | | | 27 00 | 10 00 | 523 50 | 41 |
| 57 | 204 00 | 50 00 | | | 2 | 170 00 | | | 50 50 | | 7 00 | 481 50 | 44 |
| 136-1 | 342 97 | 100 00 | | | 17 | 15 00 | | | 14 00 | | 139 00 | 610 97 | 45 |
| | | | | | | | | | | | | | 46 |
| 181 | 414 00 | 75 00 | 5 | 75 00 | 14 | 265 00 | 3 | 20 00 | 106 25 | | 20 00 | 1005 25 | 47 |
| 41 | 118 00 | 150 00 | | | 2 | 25 00 | | | | | 28 17 | 322 17 | 48 |
| 62-5 | 219 50 | | | | 2 | 60 00 | 3 | 40 00 | 101 50 | | 16 24 | 437 24 | 49 |
| 37-4 | 102 72 | | | | | | | | 6 00 | 8 00 | 10 00 | 126 72 | 50 |
| 3 | 9 00 | | | | | | | | | | 2 00 | 11 00 | 51 |
| 34 | 135 76 | 80 00 | | | 2 | 300 00 | | | 92 00 | | 54 72 | 662 48 | 52 |
| 28 | 102 00 | | | | | | | | 20 50 | | | 122 50 | 53 |
| -4 | 2 00 | 22 00 | | | 3 | 45 00 | | | 145 50 | | | 214 50 | 54 |
| 6 | 18 00 | | | | | | | | | | | 18 00 | 55 |
| 56-6 | 227 40 | | | | 4 | 72 00 | | | 74 00 | | | 373 40 | 56 |
| 1 | 3 00 | | | | | | | | | | | 3 00 | 57 |
| 15 | 33 50 | 30 00 | | | | | | | 16 00 | 32 00 | | 111 50 | 58 |
| 88-5 | 321 95 | | | | 7 | 105 00 | | | 62 50 | | | 489 45 | 59 |
| 83-3 | 244 27 | | | | | | | | 78 00 | | | 322 27 | 61 |
| 76 | 198 00 | | | | 9 | 120 00 | | | | 68 00 | 10 00 | 396 00 | 62 |
| 53 | 166 00 | | | | 3 | 65 00 | 4 | 25 00 | 15 00 | | | 271 00 | 63 |
| 34 | 72 00 | | | | 3 | 40 00 | | | 25 00 | | 25 00 | 162 00 | 64 |
| 42 | 61 40 | | | | 4 | 60 00 | | | | | | 121 40 | 65 |
| 50 | 190 98 | | | | 1 | 20 00 | | | 42 00 | | 14 50 | 276 48 | 66 |
| 8 | 24 00 | | | | | | | | | | | 24 00 | 67 |
| 1 | 3 00 | | | | | | | | | | | 3 00 | 68 |
| 47-6 | 143 58 | | | | | | | | | | 5 00 | 148 58 | 69 |
| 6 | 18 00 | | | | | | | | | | | 18 00 | 70 |
| 2-5 | 10 85 | | | | | | | | | | 4 80 | 15 65 | 71 |
| 20-3 | 88 30 | 70 00 | | | 6 | 111 50 | | | 42 50 | | | 312 30 | 72 |
| 5-3 | 16 50 | | | | | | | | 25 12 | | 20 00 | 61 62 | 73 |
| 16 | 38 00 | | | | 2 | 30 00 | | 30 00 | | | | 98 00 | 74 |
| 18-4 | 55 72 | | | | | | | | 19 00 | | | 74 72 | 75 |
| 193 | 466 00 | 100 00 | | | 9 | 100 00 | | | | | 81 00 | 767 00 | 76 |
| 24 | 72 00 | | 1 | 15 00 | | | | | 6 00 | | | 93 00 | 77 |
| 26 | 78 00 | 30 00 | | | | | | | 48 74 | 32 00 | | 188 74 | 78 |
| 7-4 | 20 75 | | 1 | 20 00 | | | | | 8 00 | | 37 00 | 85 75 | 79 |
| 111 | 277 50 | | | | | | | | | | 20 00 | 297 50 | 80 |
| 79-2 | 238 00 | 50 00 | | | 1 | 150 00 | | | 50 00 | 82 00 | 78 00 | 645 00 | 81 |
| 13 | 31 20 | | | | 2 | 30 00 | | | | | | 61 20 | 82 |
| 26 | 70 00 | | | | | | | | | | | 79 00 | 83 |
| 23-4 | 60 00 | | | | | | | | | | | 60 00 | 84 |
| | | | | | | | | | | | | | 85 |
| 7 | 21 00 | | 1 | 12 50 | 1 | 25 00 | | | | | | 58 50 | 86 |
| 43 | 99 00 | 50 00 | | | 1 | 25 00 | 3 | 23 00 | | | | 197 00 | 87 |
| 18-3 | 46 57 | 40 00 | | | | | | | | 5 00 | 117 50 | 209 07 | 88 |
| 50 | 187 95 | | | | | | | | | | 3 00 | 190 95 | 89 |
| 54 | 162 00 | | | | | | | | | | | 162 00 | 90 |

### ABSTRACT FROM SEMI-ANNUAL RETURNS.

#### MEMBERSHIP.

| No. of Lodge. | NAME OF LODGE | Initiated. | Reinstated. | Admitt'd by card. | Suspended for Cause. | Susp'nded N.P.D. | Withdrawn. | Expelled. | Died. | Members per last Report. | Present Membership. | Number of Brothers Sick. |
|---|---|---|---|---|---|---|---|---|---|---|---|---|
| 91 | Grand River | 7 | | | | 2 | | | | 106 | 111 | 8 |
| 92 | Milton | 1 | | | | | | | | 34 | 35 | 2 |
| 93 | Western City | 3 | | | | | | | | 70 | 73 | 3 |
| 94 | Aylmer | 5 | | | | | | | | 125 | 130 | 8 |
| 96 | Nith | | | | | 2 | 1 | | | 69 | 66 | 1 |
| 97 | Grand Union | 12 | | 1 | | | | | | 70 | 83 | 9 |
| 98 | Minto | 1 | | | | | | | | 42 | 43 | 2 |
| 100 | Lindsay | 6 | | | | | | | | 81 | 87 | 3 |
| 101 | Golden Star | | | | | 12 | | | | 55 | 43 | 2 |
| 102 | Deseronto | 2 | | | | 1 | | | | 86 | 87 | 4 |
| 103 | Cataract | 2 | | 1 | | | | | | 51 | 54 | 6 |
| 104 | Crescent | 7 | | | | | | | | 230 | 237 | 16 |
| 105 | Manilla | | | | | | | | | 26 | 26 | 1 |
| 106 | St. Clair | | | | | 3 | | | | 97 | 94 | 4 |
| 107 | Waterloo | 7 | | 1 | | 3 | | | | 129 | 134 | 7 |
| 108 | Royal Oak | 3 | 1 | | | | | | 2 | 83 | 85 | 6 |
| 109 | Orion | | | 1 | | | 1 | | | 51 | 51 | 5 |
| 110 | Laurel | | | | | | | | | 27 | 27 | |
| 111 | Peterboro' | 9 | | | | | | | | 235 | 244 | 17 |
| 112 | Lucknow | 10 | | | | | 1 | | 1 | 77 | 85 | 6 |
| 113 | Trenton | 2 | | | | 6 | 1 | | | 70 | 65 | 5 |
| 114 | Gananoque | 8 | 1 | | | 6 | 4 | | | 242 | 241 | 22 |
| 115 | Harmony | 10 | 2 | 2 | | | | | | 145 | 150 | 9 |
| 116 | Naomi | | | | | | | | | 9 | 9 | |
| 117 | Valley City | | | | | | 1 | | | 105 | 105 | 4 |
| 119 | Maitland | 3 | | | | | 1 | | 1 | 56 | 57 | 1 |
| 120 | Sydenham Valley | 4 | | | | 15 | | | 3 | 168 | 154 | 10 |
| 121 | Saxon | 1 | | | | | | | | 28 | 29 | |
| 122 | Streetsville | | | | | | 1 | | | 48 | 47 | |
| 124 | Dresden | 10 | | | | | | | | 110 | 120 | 4 |
| 125 | Stella | 2 | | 1 | | 2 | 3 | | 1 | 126 | 123 | 4 |
| 126 | Sarnia | 5 | | 1 | | | | | | 76 | 83 | 4 |
| 127 | Mizpah | 7 | 1 | | | 4 | 1 | | | 112 | 115 | 4 |
| 129 | Charity | 1 | | | | | 1 | | | 27 | 27 | 1 |
| 130 | Livingstone | 1 | 1 | | | 3 | | | | 45 | 44 | 2 |
| 131 | Marion | 4 | | | | 3 | | | | 66 | 67 | 4 |
| 132 | Oakville | 1 | | | | | | | | 53 | 54 | 3 |
| 133 | Glencoe | 2 | 1 | | | 4 | | | | 55 | 54 | 2 |
| 134 | Orient | | | | | | | | | 21 | 21 | 1 |
| 135 | Peaceful Dove | 1 | | | | | | | | 39 | 40 | 1 |
| 136 | Cobourg | 7 | 1 | | | | | | 2 | 86 | 92 | 4 |
| 137 | St. Lawrence | 4 | | | | 5 | 1 | | | 105 | 103 | 5 |
| 138 | Ancaster | 10 | 1 | | | | 1 | | | 54 | 64 | 3 |
| 139 | Garnet | | | | | 1 | | | | 65 | 64 | 5 |
| 140 | Leamington | 9 | | 2 | | | 4 | | 1 | 133 | 139 | 6 |
| 142 | Concord | 3 | 1 | | | 3 | 1 | | | 66 | 66 | 5 |
| 143 | Bay of Quinte | 1 | | 1 | | 4 | | | | 101 | 99 | 4 |
| 144 | Ridgetown | 5 | | | | 3 | | | | 104 | 106 | 7 |
| 146 | Vivian | 1 | | | | | | | | 68 | 69 | 1 |
| 147 | Model | 1 | | | | | | | | 39 | 40 | 1 |
| 148 | Aurora | | | | | 5 | 1 | | | 85 | 79 | 6 |
| 149 | Western Star | | | | | 5 | 1 | | | 30 | 24 | |
| 151 | Sycamore | 1 | | | | 2 | | | | 39 | 38 | |
| 152 | Hayden | 6 | 2 | 1 | | | 1 | | | 78 | 86 | 8 |
| 153 | Wildey | 3 | 2 | | | | | | | 34 | 39 | 3 |
| 154 | Alpha | 3 | 1 | 1 | | 8 | 3 | | | 133 | 127 | 8 |
| 155 | Brougham | | | | | | | | | 16 | 16 | 3 |
| 156 | Pyramid | | | | | 4 | 1 | | | 45 | 40 | 2 |
| 157 | Thamesville | 4 | | | | 7 | | | | 52 | 49 | 1 |
| 158 | Progress | 2 | | | | | 1 | | | 110 | 111 | 3 |
| 159 | Oak Leaf | 1 | 2 | | | 1 | | | | 40 | 42 | 2 |

## Term Ending 31st December, 1892.—*Continued.*

### SICK BENEFITS AND RELIEFS.

| Number of Weeks' Sickness. | Amount paid for Sick Benefits. | Amount paid for Burying Deceased Bros. | No. of Wives of Bros. Died. | Amount paid for Burying Bros.' Wives. | No. of Widows. | Amount paid for Relief of Widows. | No. of Orphans. | Amount paid for Educating Orphans. | Paid to Lodge Surgeon. | Paid for Nursing Sick Brothers. | Paid for Special Relief & Charity. | Total Relief. | No. of Lodge. |
|---|---|---|---|---|---|---|---|---|---|---|---|---|---|
| | $ c | $ c | | $ c | | $ c | | $ c | $ c | $ c | $ c | $ c | |
| 38 | 152 00 | | | | | 12 00 | | | 6 00 | | 35 00 | 205 00 | 91 |
| 3 | 12 00 | | | | | | | | | | | 12 00 | 92 |
| 6 | 18 00 | | | | 1 | 10 00 | 4 | 10 00 | 35 50 | | | 73 50 | 93 |
| 71 | 126 00 | | | 15 00 | | | | | 6 00 | | | 147 00 | 94 |
| 12 | 36 00 | | | | 1 | 150 00 | | | | 34 00 | | 220 00 | 96 |
| 50-3 | 110 53 | | | | | | | | | | | 110 53 | 97 |
| 11 | 44 00 | | | | | | | | | | | 44 00 | 98 |
| 17 | 42 15 | | | | | | | | | | | 42 15 | 100 |
| 7 | 21 00 | | 1 | 15 00 | 3 | 40 00 | | | 12 50 | | 10 00 | 98 50 | 101 |
| 28-5 | 86 10 | | | | | | | | | 27 65 | | 113 75 | 102 |
| 54 | 211 00 | | 1 | 15 00 | | | | | 40 50 | 54 75 | | 321 25 | 103 |
| 114 | 423 00 | 50 00 | 1 | 25 00 | 1 | 120 00 | | | 92 00 | | 15 00 | 725 00 | 104 |
| | 27 00 | | | | | | | | | | | 27 00 | 105 |
| 12 | 47 45 | | 1 | 20 00 | | | | | | | | 67 45 | 106 |
| 24 | 72 00 | | | | | | | | 33 75 | | 31 75 | 137 50 | 107 |
| 60-4 | 182 00 | 400 00 | | 20 00 | | | | | | 2 50 | | 604 50 | 108 |
| 35 | 88 00 | | | | | | | | | | 2 25 | 90 25 | 109 |
| | | | | | | | | | 45 00 | | | 45 00 | 110 |
| 83-5 | 334 80 | | | | | | | | | | | 334 80 | 111 |
| 22 | 66 00 | | | | | | | | | | 15 80 | 81 80 | 112 |
| 14-4 | 43 75 | | | | | | | | | | | 43 75 | 113 |
| 60-3 | 179 42 | | | | | | | | | 15 18 | | 194 60 | 114 |
| 91-6 | 315 56 | | | | 1 | 15 00 | | | | 106 16 | 65 00 | 501 72 | 115 |
| | | | | | | | | | | | | | 116 |
| 8-4 | 34 27 | | | | | | | | 42 50 | | 5 00 | 81 77 | 117 |
| 1 | 3 00 | | | | | | | | | | 35 00 | 38 00 | 119 |
| 69-4 | 202 72 | 130 00 | | | 9 | 354 00 | | | 12 00 | 4 00 | 40 00 | 742 72 | 120 |
| | | | | | | | | | | | | | 121 |
| | | | 1 | 15 00 | | | | | | | | 15 00 | 122 |
| 20 | 52 00 | | | | 3 | 50 00 | | | 50 00 | | 16 00 | 168 00 | 124 |
| 6-2 | 18 50 | | | | | | | | | | | 18 50 | 125 |
| 17-3 | 53 00 | | | | | | | | | | | 53 00 | 126 |
| 12-4 | 38 00 | | | | | | | | 56 25 | | | 94 25 | 127 |
| 2 | 6 00 | | | | | | | | | | | 6 00 | 129 |
| 21 | 67 50 | | | | | | | | | | 17 00 | 84 50 | 130 |
| 18 | 63 00 | | 1 | 15 00 | | | | | | 6 00 | | 84 00 | 131 |
| 14 | 42 00 | | | | | | | | | | | 42 00 | 132 |
| 7 | 17 00 | | | | | | 1 | 30 00 | | | | 47 00 | 133 |
| 3 | 9 00 | | | | | | | | | | | 9 00 | 134 |
| 3 | 9 00 | | | | | | | | | | 5 00 | 14 00 | 135 |
| 26 | 78 00 | 80 00 | 1 | 15 00 | 2 | 13 00 | | | | 41 50 | | 357 50 | 136 |
| 44-2 | 133 00 | | | | | | | | | | 12 00 | 145 00 | 137 |
| 7 | 21 25 | | | | 1 | 10 00 | | | 24 00 | | | 55 25 | 138 |
| 15-2 | 46 08 | | | | 1 | 15 00 | 2 | 15 00 | | 40 45 | 10 00 | 126 53 | 139 |
| 35-3 | 64 50 | 45 00 | | | | | | | | 119 00 | 10 00 | 238 50 | 140 |
| 16 | 31 40 | | | | | | | | | 42 00 | | 73 40 | 142 |
| 8-3 | 19 28 | | | | | | | | | | 15 00 | 34 28 | 143 |
| 31 | 91 00 | | | | | | | | | | 10 00 | 101 00 | 144 |
| 14 | 12 00 | 30 00 | | | 5 | 50 00 | 24 | 160 10 | | | | 252 10 | 146 |
| 4 | 12 00 | | | | | | | | | | 5 00 | 17 00 | 147 |
| 36-1 | 107 11 | | | | 2 | 40 00 | | | | | 10 00 | 157 11 | 148 |
| | | | | | | | | | | | | | 149 |
| | | | | | 4 | 67 50 | 9 | 54 00 | | | | 121 50 | 151 |
| 38-4 | 139 43 | | | | | | | | | | | 139 43 | 152 |
| 3 | 9 00 | | | | | | | | | | | 9 00 | 153 |
| 51-5 | 159 50 | | | | | | | | | | | 159 50 | 154 |
| 4 | 51 00 | | | | | | | | 5 75 | | | 56 75 | 155 |
| 1 | 1 50 | | | | | | | | | | | 1 50 | 156 |
| 1 | 3 00 | | | | 3 | 45 00 | | | | | 10 00 | 58 00 | 157 |
| 36 | 108 00 | 40 00 | | | 2 | 300 00 | | | | | | 448 00 | 158 |
| 6-3 | 26 00 | | 1 | 20 00 | 2 | 70 00 | | | 13 50 | | 2 00 | 131 50 | 159 |

## ABSTRACT FROM SEMI-ANNUAL RETURNS.

### MEMBERSHIP.

| No. of Lodge. | NAME OF LODGE. | Initiated. | Reinstated. | Admitt'd by card. | Suspended for Cause. | Susp'nded N.P.D. | Withdrawn. | Expelled. | Died. | Members per last Report. | Present Membership. | Number of Brothers Sick. |
|---|---|---|---|---|---|---|---|---|---|---|---|---|
| 160 | Listowel | 4 | | | | | 1 | | | 86 | 89 | 4 |
| 161 | Simcoe | 2 | | | | 2 | | | | 72 | 72 | 5 |
| 163 | Oriental | 2 | 2 | | | | 1 | | | 39 | 42 | 3 |
| 164 | Romeo | 2 | | | | 1 | | | | 126 | 127 | 9 |
| 165 | Beethoven | | | | | 3 | 2 | | | 41 | 36 | 3 |
| 167 | Hillsburg | 2 | | | | 1 | | | | 41 | 42 | 3 |
| 168 | Sutton | | | | | | | | | 36 | 36 | 1 |
| 169 | Grey | | | | | | | | | 29 | 29 | |
| 170 | Denovo | | 1 | | | | 1 | | | 47 | 47 | |
| 171 | Alliston | 1 | | | | 2 | 2 | | | 35 | 32 | 1 |
| 172 | Penetangore | 5 | 1 | | | | 1 | | 1 | 109 | 113 | 8 |
| 173 | Emerald | 1 | | | | 3 | | | | 25 | 23 | |
| 174 | Dolman | | | | | | | | 1 | 50 | 49 | 1 |
| 176 | Dauncey | 2 | | | | | | | | 24 | 26 | 2 |
| 177 | Montaua | 1 | | | | 2 | | | | 24 | 23 | 1 |
| 178 | Wellington Square | 4 | | 1 | | | | | | 29 | 34 | 2 |
| 179 | Madoc | 11 | | | | | 3 | | | 111 | 119 | 7 |
| 180 | Owen Sound | 2 | | 1 | | | | | | 58 | 61 | 4 |
| 182 | Tecumseh | 5 | | | | | | | | 57 | 62 | 7 |
| 183 | Teeswater | | 1 | | | 4 | | | 1 | 36 | 32 | 2 |
| 184 | Germania | 18 | 1 | | | | | | | 77 | 96 | 3 |
| 186 | Dufferin | | | | | | | | | 26 | 26 | 8 |
| 188 | Cambridge | 1 | | | | 1 | | | | 51 | 51 | 8 |
| 189 | Parry Sound | 6 | | | | 4 | | | | 52 | 54 | 4 |
| 190 | Chorazin | 3 | | | | | | | 1 | 122 | 124 | 11 |
| 191 | Jarvis | | | | | 1 | | | | 24 | 23 | 2 |
| 192 | Howick | | | | | 1 | | | | 13 | 12 | |
| 194 | Albert | 4 | | 1 | | 1 | | | 1 | 160 | 163 | 8 |
| 195 | Cicerone | 1 | | | | | | | | 21 | 22 | |
| 196 | Florence | 3 | | | | 3 | | | 1 | 85 | 84 | 3 |
| 197 | Minerva | 1 | | | | 9 | | | | 84 | 76 | 4 |
| 200 | Weston | 3 | | | | | 1 | | | 39 | 41 | |
| 201 | Beacon | 1 | | | | 3 | | | | 37 | 35 | 2 |
| 202 | Silver Star | 4 | | | | 4 | | | 1 | 50 | 49 | 1 |
| 203 | Pembroke | 9 | | | | 3 | 1 | | | 102 | 107 | 5 |
| 204 | Acton | | | | | | | | | 15 | 15 | 1 |
| 205 | Ahiram | 8 | | | | 4 | 2 | | | 102 | 104 | 2 |
| 206 | Silver City | 3 | | | | | | | | 68 | 71 | 4 |
| 207 | Egremont | 6 | | | | | | | | 8 | 14 | |
| 209 | Millbank | 2 | 1 | | | | 1 | | | 14 | 16 | 2 |
| 210 | Brucefield | 1 | | | | | | | | 25 | 26 | 2 |
| 211 | Lilly | | | | | 1 | 1 | | | 38 | 36 | 6 |
| 212 | Argyll | 4 | | | | | | | | 81 | 85 | 8 |
| 214 | Clifford | 1 | | | | | | | | 74 | 75 | 7 |
| 215 | Freestone | | | | | | | | 1 | 33 | 32 | 2 |
| 216 | Elmira | 1 | 2 | | | | 1 | | | 40 | 42 | 2 |
| 217 | Mount Brydges | 11 | | | | 1 | | | 1 | 92 | 101 | 4 |
| 218 | Enterprise | 6 | 2 | | | 8 | | | | 120 | 120 | 11 |
| 219 | Georgian Bay | 4 | | | | | | | | 74 | 78 | |
| 220 | Woodslee | 2 | | | | 1 | | | | 14 | 15 | 2 |
| 221 | Chesley | 1 | | | | | 1 | | | 29 | 29 | |
| 223 | Hensall | 2 | | | | | | | | 53 | 55 | 1 |
| 224 | Ottawa | 4 | | | | 4 | 3 | | 1 | 145 | 141 | 9 |
| 226 | Merlin | 1 | | | | | | | | 31 | 32 | 3 |
| 227 | Sauble | | | | | | | | | 17 | 17 | |
| 228 | International | 5 | | | | 3 | | | | 144 | 146 | 12 |
| 229 | Embro Star | 2 | 1 | | | | | | 1 | 52 | 54 | 2 |
| 230 | Prince of Wales | 4 | | | | 2 | 2 | | 1 | 46 | 46 | 2 |
| 231 | Flora | 2 | | | | 2 | | | | 64 | 64 | 4 |
| 232 | Equity | | | | | | 1 | | | 27 | 26 | 1 |
| 233 | Hanover | | | | | | | | | 16 | 18 | |
| 234 | Ilderton | | | | | | | | | 33 | 33 | |

## TERM ENDING 31st DECEMBER, 1892—*Continued*.

### SICK BENEFITS AND RELIEFS.

| Number of Weeks' Sickness | Amount paid for Sick Benefits. | Amount paid for Burying Deceased Bros. | No. of Wives of Bros. Died. | Amount paid for Burying Bros. Wives. | No. of Widows. | Amount paid for Relief of Widows. | No. of Orphans. | Amount paid for Educating Orphans. | Paid to Lodge Surgeon. | Paid for Nursing Sick Brothers. | Paid for Special Relief & Charity. | Total Relief | No. of Lodge. |
|---|---|---|---|---|---|---|---|---|---|---|---|---|---|
| | $ c | $ c | | $ c | | $ c | | $ c | $ c | $ c | $ c | $ c | |
| 31 | 101 00 | | | | | | | | | | 5 00 | 106 00 | 160 |
| 19 | 49 00 | | | | | | | | | | | 49 00 | 161 |
| 6 | 18 00 | | | | 1 | 15 00 | | | | | | 33 00 | 163 |
| 43-4 | 148 26 | | | | | | | | | | | 148 26 | 164 |
| 67 | 73 00 | | | | | | | | 20 50 | | | 93 50 | 165 |
| 6 | 19 71 | | | | | | | | | | 25 00 | 44 71 | 167 |
| 19-5 | 69 00 | | | | | | 1 | 100 00 | | | 5 00 | 174 00 | 168 |
| | | | | | | | | | | | | | 169 |
| | | | | | | | | | | | 2 00 | 2 00 | 170 |
| 1 | 3 00 | | | | | | | | | | | 3 00 | 171 |
| 38 | 114 00 | 35 00 | | | 1 | 200 00 | | | | 10 00 | 4 00 | 363 00 | 172 |
| | | | | | | | | | | | 5 00 | 5 00 | 173 |
| 16 | 48 00 | 40 00 | | | 1 | 125 00 | | | 9 95 | | | 222 95 | 174 |
| 2 | 6 00 | | | | | | | | | | | 6 00 | 176 |
| 3 | 6 00 | | | | | | | | | | | 6 00 | 177 |
| 12 | 36 00 | | | | 1 | 15 00 | | | | | | 51 00 | 178 |
| 27-3 | 69 50 | | | | 1 | 15 00 | | | | | | 84 50 | 179 |
| 37-5 | 165 75 | | | | | | | | 4 00 | | | 169 75 | 180 |
| 50-2 | 150 90 | | | | | | | | | | 5 00 | 155 90 | 182 |
| 7 | 21 00 | 30 00 | | | | | | | | | 48 00 | 99 00 | 183 |
| 3 | 9 00 | | 1 | 15 00 | | | | | | | 5 00 | 29 00 | 184 |
| 30 | 25 00 | | | | | | | | | | | 25 00 | 186 |
| 14 | 42 00 | | | | | | | | | | 10 19 | 52 19 | 188 |
| 9 | 27 00 | | | | | | | | | | | 27 00 | 189 |
| 48 | 192 00 | 50 00 | | | 2 | 25 00 | 5 | | 50 50 | 12 00 | 20 00 | 349 50 | 190 |
| 4-1 | 12 43 | | | | | | | | | | | 12 43 | 191 |
| | | | | | | | | | | | | | 192 |
| 40-1 | 160 60 | 40 00 | 1 | 20 00 | 2 | 20 00 | 2 | 40 00 | 68 00 | | 61 80 | 410 40 | 194 |
| | | | | | | | | | | | | | 195 |
| 13 | 33 00 | 30 00 | | | | | | | | | | 63 00 | 196 |
| 19 | 68 00 | | | | | | | | | | 25 40 | 93 40 | 197 |
| | | | | | | | | | | | | | 200 |
| 12 | 36 00 | | | | | | | | | | | 36 00 | 201 |
| | | 32 00 | 1 | 15 00 | | | 9 | 125 00 | | | | 172 00 | 202 |
| 18-2 | 55 00 | 40 00 | | | | | | | | 1 50 | | 96 50 | 203 |
| 3 | 9 50 | | | | | | | | | | | 9 50 | 204 |
| 2-4 | 7 50 | | | | | | | | | | | 7 50 | 205 |
| 34 | 102 00 | | | | | | | | 34 00 | 10 00 | 25 00 | 171 00 | 206 |
| | | | | | | | | | | | | | 207 |
| 2 | 8 00 | | | | | | | | | | | 8 00 | 209 |
| 6 | 12 00 | | | | | | | | | | | 12 00 | 210 |
| 10 | 40 00 | | 1 | 15 00 | | | | | | | | 55 00 | 211 |
| 37-5 | 113 50 | | | | 1 | 60 00 | | | | | | 173 50 | 212 |
| 32-1 | 160 71 | | | | | | | | | | | 160 71 | 214 |
| 5 | 15 00 | | | | | | | | | | | 15 00 | 215 |
| 11 | 33 00 | | | | | | | | | | | 33 00 | 216 |
| 8 | 24 00 | 30 00 | | | 2 | 121 50 | | | | | | 175 50 | 217 |
| 28 | 84 00 | | | 15 00 | | | | | 1 00 | 5 00 | 10 00 | 115 00 | 218 |
| | | | | | | | 1 | 25 00 | | | 25 00 | 50 00 | 219 |
| 7 | 21 00 | | | | 1 | 86 00 | | | | | | 107 00 | 220 |
| | | | | | 2 | 100 00 | | | | | | 100 00 | 221 |
| 2 | 6 00 | | | | | | | | | | | 6 00 | 223 |
| 55-2 | 166 28 | 65 00 | 1 | 20 00 | 1 | 31 00 | | | | | | 282 28 | 224 |
| 8 | 24 00 | | | | | | | | | | | 24 00 | 226 |
| | | | | | | | | | | | | | 227 |
| 39-5 | 119 04 | | 1 | 20 00 | 4 | 195 00 | | | | | 15 00 | 349 04 | 228 |
| 5 | 15 00 | 50 00 | | | | | | | | | | 65 00 | 229 |
| 4 | 12 00 | 40 00 | | | | | | | 24 50 | | | 76 60 | 230 |
| 7-4 | 22 50 | | | | | | | | 48 00 | | | 70 50 | 231 |
| 6 | 18 00 | | | | | | | | | | | 18 00 | 232 |
| | | | | | | | | | | | | | 233 |
| | | | | | | | | | | | 5 00 | 5 00 | 234 |

## ABSTRACT FROM SEMI-ANNUAL RETURNS.

### MEMBERSHIP.

| No. of Lodge. | NAME OF LODGE. | Initiated. | Reinstated. | Admitt'd by card. | Suspended for Cause. | Susp'nded N.P.D. | Withdrawn. | Expelled. | Died. | Members per last Report. | Present Membership. | Number of Brothers Sick. |
|---|---|---|---|---|---|---|---|---|---|---|---|---|
| 235 | Waterford | 4 | | | | 4 | 2 | | 1 | 106 | 103 | 7 |
| 236 | Acorn | 2 | | | 1 | 1 | | | | 23 | 23 | 4 |
| 237 | Farmersville | 1 | | | | 6 | | | 1 | 43 | 37 | 3 |
| 239 | Stirling | 7 | | | | | 1 | | | 126 | 132 | 7 |
| 240 | Carleton | 7 | | | | 1 | 1 | 1 | | 120 | 124 | 6 |
| 241 | Rideau | 2 | | | | | 1 | | | 113 | 114 | 3 |
| 242 | Wilton | 3 | | 1 | | 7 | 2 | | | 89 | 84 | 4 |
| 243 | Thornbury | | | | | | | | | 34 | 34 | |
| 244 | Port Arthur | 4 | | | | 5 | 2 | | | 75 | 72 | 1 |
| 245 | Malloryton | | | | | 5 | | | | 47 | 42 | 1 |
| 246 | Orillia | | | | | 7 | | | | 41 | 34 | |
| 247 | Gordon | | | | | | | | | 44 | 44 | 3 |
| 248 | Campbellford | 1 | | | | | | | | 102 | 103 | 2 |
| 249 | Beaverton | 1 | | | | | | | | 48 | 49 | 1 |
| 250 | Ridgely | 4 | | | | 6 | 1 | | | 87 | 84 | 3 |
| 251 | Bracebridge | 1 | | | | | 1 | | | 66 | 66 | |
| 252 | Floral | 1 | | | | | | | | 38 | 39 | |
| 253 | Caledonia | | | 1 | | | | | | 15 | 16 | 1 |
| 254 | Alba | 1 | | | | | | | | 46 | 47 | 1 |
| 255 | Tottenham | | | | | | | | | 10 | 10 | |
| 256 | Grand Valley | 2 | | | | 3 | | | 1 | 35 | 33 | 1 |
| 257 | Credit | 1 | | | | 3 | | | | 40 | 38 | 6 |
| 258 | Thamesford | 4 | | | | | | | | 107 | 111 | 8 |
| 259 | Lynden | | | | | 1 | 1 | | | 26 | 24 | 3 |
| 260 | Meaford | 5 | | | | | | | | 43 | 48 | 1 |
| 261 | Gold Hill | 12 | | 3 | | 12 | 14 | | | 138 | 127 | 4 |
| 262 | Norwood | | | | | 3 | 1 | | 1 | 40 | 35 | 2 |
| 263 | East Toronto | 5 | | | | | | | | 54 | 59 | 3 |
| 264 | Fraternity | 6 | | 2 | | | 2 | | | 57 | 63 | 2 |
| 265 | Delta | 1 | | | | | 2 | | 1 | 45 | 43 | 2 |
| 266 | Missanabie | 3 | | | | | | | | 82 | 85 | 7 |
| 267 | Algoma | 3 | | | | 2 | | | | 57 | 58 | 3 |
| 268 | Stanley | 2 | | | | 4 | 1 | | | 37 | 34 | 3 |
| 269 | Woodstock | 20 | 1 | 1 | | 2 | 1 | | | 62 | 61 | 4 |
| 270 | Lansdowne | 9 | 1 | 1 | | 1 | | | | 63 | 73 | 8 |
| 271 | North Bay | 2 | | | | | | | | 71 | 73 | |
| 272 | Lakeview | 1 | | | | | | | | 76 | 77 | 4 |
| 273 | Hastings | | | 1 | | | | | | 38 | 39 | 6 |
| 274 | Midland | | | | 1 | | | | | 50 | 49 | 4 |
| 275 | Fairy | 2 | | | | 4 | | | | 44 | 42 | 2 |
| 276 | Sheard | 4 | | | | 2 | 2 | | | 31 | 31 | 3 |
| 277 | Lambton | 5 | | | | 2 | | | | 55 | 58 | |
| 278 | Rockcliffe | 4 | | | | | 1 | | 2 | 53 | 54 | 4 |
| 279 | Grenville | 5 | 1 | | | 5 | 2 | | | 76 | 75 | 4 |
| 280 | Balmoral | 3 | | | | 2 | | | | 42 | 43 | 1 |
| 281 | Arthur | 10 | | | | 3 | 1 | | | 53 | 59 | 4 |
| 282 | Sudbury | 8 | | | | | | | | 44 | 52 | |
| 283 | Earnscliffe | 8 | | | | | | | | 45 | 53 | 2 |
| 284 | Lyn | 2 | | | | | 1 | | | 27 | 28 | |
| 285 | Morewood | 2 | | | | | | | | 18 | 20 | 2 |
| 286 | Royal | 2 | | | | | | | | 37 | 39 | 4 |
| 287 | Ripley | 5 | | | | | | | | 34 | 39 | |
| 288 | Chesterville | 3 | | | | | | | | 31 | 34 | 2 |
| 289 | Glanworth | 1 | | | | | 1 | | 1 | 46 | 45 | |
| 290 | Tweed | 5 | | | | | | | 1 | 51 | 55 | 1 |
| 291 | Rodney | 11 | | 1 | | | | | | 36 | 48 | |
| 292 | Minnetonka | 32 | | 16 | | | | | | | 48 | 2 |
| 293 | Thomasburg | 54 | | 8 | | | | | | | 62 | 3 |
| 294 | Broadview | 33 | | 10 | | | | | | | 43 | |
| | 31st Dec., 1892 | 906 | 49 | 75 | 2 | 491 | 137 | 1 | 70 | | 19450 | 1099 |
| | 30th June, 1892 | 1248 | 93 | 92 | 9 | 424 | 168 | 13 | 81 | 18390 | | 1934 |
| | Year 31st Dec., 1892 | 2154 | 142 | 167 | 11 | 915 | 305 | 14 | 151 | 18390 | 19450 | 3033 |

## Term Ending 31st December, 1892—*Continued.*

### SICK BENEFITS AND RELIEFS.

| Number of Weeks' Sickness | Amount paid for Sick Benefits | Amount paid for Burying Deceased Bros. | No. of Wives of Bros. Died | Amount paid for Burying Bros.' Wives | No. of Widows | Amount paid for Relief of Widows | No. of Orphans | Amount paid for Educating Orphans | Paid to Lodge Surgeon | Paid for Nursing Sick Brothers | Paid for Special Relief & Charity | Total Relief | No. of Lodge |
|---|---|---|---|---|---|---|---|---|---|---|---|---|---|
|  | $ c | $ c |  | $ c |  | $ c |  | $ o | $ c | $ c | $ c | $ c |  |
| 22-1 | 66 45 | 30 00 |  |  |  |  |  |  | 38 00 |  |  | 134 45 | 235 |
| 16 | 48 00 |  |  |  |  |  |  |  |  |  |  | 48 00 | 236 |
| 22-3 | 67 50 | 30 00 |  |  | 1 | 10 00 |  |  |  |  |  | 107 50 | 237 |
| 42-1 | 126 20 |  |  |  |  |  |  |  |  |  |  | 126 20 | 239 |
| 48-4 | 146 00 |  |  |  |  |  |  |  |  |  |  | 146 00 | 240 |
| 5 | 11 00 |  |  |  |  |  |  |  |  |  | 5 00 | 16 00 | 241 |
| 7-6 | 31 43 |  |  |  |  |  |  |  | 44 50 |  |  | 75 93 | 242 |
|  |  |  |  |  |  |  |  |  |  |  |  |  | 243 |
| 15-6 | 59 53 |  |  |  |  |  |  |  |  |  |  | 59 53 | 244 |
| 3 | 9 00 |  | 1 | 15 00 |  |  |  |  |  |  |  | 24 00 | 245 |
|  |  |  |  |  |  |  |  |  |  |  |  |  | 246 |
| 7 | 21 00 |  |  |  |  |  |  |  | 22 00 |  |  | 43 00 | 247 |
| 6 | 18 00 |  |  |  | 1 |  | 7 |  |  |  | 10 00 | 28 00 | 248 |
| 5-4 | 16 50 |  |  |  |  |  |  |  |  |  |  | 16 50 | 249 |
| 9 | 27 00 |  |  |  |  |  |  |  |  |  | 5 00 | 32 00 | 250 |
|  |  |  |  |  |  |  |  |  |  |  |  |  | 251 |
|  |  |  |  |  |  |  |  |  | 19 50 |  |  | 19 50 | 252 |
| 2 | 6 00 |  |  |  |  |  |  |  |  |  |  | 6 00 | 253 |
| 1-1 | 3 50 |  | 1 | 15 00 |  |  |  |  |  |  |  | 18 50 | 254 |
|  |  |  |  |  |  |  |  |  |  |  |  |  | 255 |
| 22-2 | 67 00 |  |  |  |  |  |  |  | 40 30 |  |  | 107 30 | 256 |
| 29-4 | 120 50 |  |  |  |  |  |  |  |  |  | 8 00 | 128 50 | 257 |
| 27 | 81 00 | 40 00 |  |  |  |  |  |  | 50 25 | 32 00 | 10 00 | 213 25 | 258 |
| 15-3 | 40 50 |  |  |  |  |  |  |  |  | 7 50 |  | 48 00 | 259 |
| 5 | 15 00 |  |  |  |  |  |  |  |  |  |  | 15 00 | 260 |
| 28-2 | 73 65 |  |  |  |  |  |  |  |  | 10 00 | 20 00 | 103 65 | 261 |
| 16 | 48 00 | 30 00 |  |  |  |  |  |  | 17 50 |  |  | 95 50 | 262 |
| 7-2 | 22 00 |  |  |  |  |  |  |  | 28 75 |  | 5 00 | 55 75 | 263 |
| 4 | 12 00 |  |  |  |  |  |  |  |  |  |  | 12 00 | 264 |
| 4 |  | 30 00 |  |  |  |  |  |  |  | 15 00 |  | 45 00 | 265 |
| 33-4 | 135 75 |  |  |  |  |  |  |  |  |  |  | 135 75 | 266 |
| 13-2 | 41 45 |  |  |  |  |  |  |  |  |  |  | 41 45 | 267 |
| 28-2 | 85 00 |  |  |  |  |  |  |  |  |  |  | 85 00 | 268 |
| 6-1 | 18 43 |  |  |  |  |  |  |  | 59 75 |  |  | 78 18 | 269 |
| 17 | 51 00 |  |  |  | 1 | 20 00 |  |  |  |  |  | 71 00 | 270 |
|  |  |  |  |  |  |  |  |  |  |  |  |  | 271 |
| 6-2 | 73 50 |  |  |  |  |  |  |  | 37 00 |  |  | 110 50 | 272 |
| 22 | 107 71 |  |  |  |  |  |  |  |  |  | 5 00 | 112 71 | 273 |
| 8-1 | 24 40 |  |  |  |  |  |  |  | 20 00 |  |  | 44 40 | 274 |
| 2-3 | 7 30 |  |  |  |  |  |  |  | 30 05 |  |  | 37 35 | 275 |
| 8-4 | 25 50 |  |  |  |  |  |  |  | 16 00 |  |  | 41 50 | 276 |
|  |  |  |  |  |  |  |  |  |  |  |  |  | 277 |
| 7 | 21 00 | 25 00 |  |  |  |  |  |  |  |  |  | 46 00 | 278 |
| 20 | 60 00 |  | 1 | 20 00 |  |  |  |  |  | 12 50 | 3 00 | 95 50 | 279 |
|  | 26 14 |  |  |  |  |  |  |  |  |  |  | 26 14 | 280 |
| 13-3 | 54 00 |  |  |  |  |  |  |  |  | 35 00 |  | 89 00 | 281 |
|  |  |  |  |  |  |  |  |  |  |  |  |  | 282 |
| 4-4 | 13 50 | 43 00 |  |  |  |  |  |  |  |  |  | 56 50 | 283 |
|  |  |  |  |  |  |  |  |  |  |  |  |  | 284 |
| 2 | 6 00 |  |  |  |  |  |  |  |  |  |  | 6 00 | 285 |
| 21-3 | 64 50 |  |  |  |  |  |  |  |  |  |  | 64 50 | 286 |
|  |  |  |  |  |  |  |  |  |  |  |  |  | 287 |
| 3 | 9 00 |  | 1 | 20 00 |  |  |  |  |  |  |  | 29 00 | 288 |
|  |  |  |  |  |  |  |  |  |  |  |  |  | 289 |
| 1 | 3 00 |  |  |  |  |  |  |  |  |  |  | 3 00 | 290 |
|  |  |  |  |  |  |  |  |  |  |  |  |  | 291 |
| 6 | 18 00 |  |  |  |  |  |  |  |  |  |  | 18 00 | 292 |
| 1 | 3 00 |  |  |  |  |  |  |  |  |  |  | 3 00 | 293 |
|  |  |  |  |  |  |  |  |  |  |  |  |  | 294 |
| 5846-5 | 18566 68 | 3117 | 31 | 62250 | 186 | 665650 | 86 | 82010 | 256316 | 104002 | 166357 | 3504953 |  |
| 8188-1 | 2551840 | 358456 | 42 | 1195 | 175 | 664950 | 63 | 41436 | 254471 | 109507 | 117177 | 4217340 |  |
| 14034-6 | 44085 08 | 3615 73 | 73 | 63445 | 361 | 133060 | 149 | 123446 | 5107 87 | 2135 09 | 2835 34 | 77222 93 |  |

## ABSTRACT FROM SEMI-ANNUAL RETURNS.

| No. of Lodge. | NAME OF LODGE | No. of Degrees Conferred. | No. of Past Grands in Good Standing. | RECEIPTS OF LODGES. | | | Current Expenses. |
|---|---|---|---|---|---|---|---|
| | | | | Initiations, Admission by Card, and Degrees. $ c | Dues and Reinstatements. $ c | All other Sources. $ c | $ c |
| 9 | Brock | 6 | 32 | 20 50 | 274 75 | 233 06 | 183 20 |
| 10 | Cataraqui | 37 | 26 | 162 90 | 647 30 | 350 72 | 480 05 |
| 12 | Otonabee | 35 | 15 | 209 10 | 308 50 | 132 95 | 340 95 |
| 16 | Union | 3 | 49 | 20 20 | 631 50 | 182 50 | 304 46 |
| 22 | Phœnix | | 16 | 5 00 | 257 65 | 68 77 | 177 50 |
| 28 | Rose | 2 | 20 | 9 40 | 246 20 | 107 50 | 196 42 |
| 29 | Chatham | 12 | 35 | 95 60 | 421 10 | 449 50 | 329 87 |
| 30 | Eureka | 2 | 37 | 4 70 | 366 03 | 56 00 | 118 78 |
| 32 | Elgin | 14 | 23 | 115 50 | 716 30 | 178 25 | 287 82 |
| 33 | Erie | 2 | 12 | 11 60 | 32 90 | 10 50 | 40 00 |
| 34 | Gore | 43 | 43 | 214 90 | 814 79 | 315 95 | 218 67 |
| 35 | Samartan | 1 | 37 | 25 50 | 425 00 | 368 75 | 445 01 |
| 36 | St. Mary's | 2 | | 14 75 | 369 35 | 273 38 | 496 63 |
| 38 | Forest City | 9 | 34 | 29 35 | 451 90 | 108 20 | 121 38 |
| 40 | Rond Eau | 9 | 14 | 87 90 | 273 22 | 15 41 | 166 17 |
| 41 | Avon | 18 | 47 | 77 00 | 683 16 | 732 00 | 947 18 |
| 44 | Excelsior | 7 | 30 | 31 80 | 464 60 | 23 51 | 181 88 |
| 45 | Frontier | 13 | 25 | 277 75 | 660 89 | 771 64 | 812 39 |
| 46 | Mount Zion | 4 | 9 | 25 00 | 43 50 | 16 00 | 73 03 |
| 47 | Unity | 2 | 35 | 45 50 | 940 50 | 213 49 | 295 59 |
| 48 | Dominion | | | 31 40 | 519 95 | 3 00 | 131 10 |
| 49 | Canada | 9 | 27 | 67 70 | 517 79 | 101 49 | 194 55 |
| 50 | Otter | 24 | 23 | 142 00 | 405 50 | 46 50 | 356 00 |
| 51 | Bissell | | 6 | 30 | 39 00 | | 13 00 |
| 52 | Covenant | | | 26 70 | 618 03 | 29 67 | 281 28 |
| 53 | Niagara Falls | 9 | 26 | 54 50 | 304 98 | 147 50 | 343 16 |
| 54 | Collingwood | 16 | 22 | 129 10 | 489 70 | 15 00 | 180 18 |
| 55 | Fidelity | | 9 | 30 | 50 50 | | 127 13 |
| 56 | Queen City of Ontario | 13 | 27 | 55 20 | 440 52 | 74 40 | 193 15 |
| 57 | Maple Leaf | 2 | 13 | 12 00 | 84 50 | 3 88 | 37 70 |
| 58 | Howard | 27 | 28 | 137 60 | 310 15 | 5 05 | 264 37 |
| 59 | Kingston | 41 | 40 | 194 55 | 679 45 | 85 38 | 291 47 |
| 61 | Corinthian | 10 | 34 | 48 50 | 616 33 | 109 57 | 175 55 |
| 62 | Huron | 8 | 26 | 32 50 | 398 08 | 14 90 | 108 05 |
| 63 | Barrie | 3 | 12 | 14 00 | 330 37 | | 177 43 |
| 64 | Victoria | 6 | 19 | 35 20 | 220 50 | | 99 72 |
| 65 | Friendship | 7 | 27 | 39 30 | 589 42 | 306 34 | 810 24 |
| 66 | Florence Nightingale | 2 | 38 | 18 60 | 437 25 | 193 68 | 170 34 |
| 67 | Exter | 9 | 19 | 39 30 | 148 43 | 195 07 | 384 60 |
| 68 | North Star | 3 | 12 | 16 30 | 79 50 | | 136 81 |
| 69 | Hope | 21 | 15 | 85 50 | 249 75 | 6 00 | 78 69 |
| 70 | Lucan | | 10 | | 74 57 | 44 46 | 62 93 |
| 71 | The Toronto | 22 | 19 | 110 03 | 175 10 | 103 12 | 126 44 |
| 72 | Eastern Star | 13 | 24 | 65 25 | 276 80 | 2 02 | 56 12 |
| 73 | Fergus | 14 | 19 | 77 75 | 163 20 | 217 86 | 48 70 |
| 74 | Bothwell | 3 | 14 | 20 70 | 126 50 | 20 75 | 90 24 |
| 75 | Warriner | | 24 | | 158 00 | 38 00 | 162 33 |
| 76 | St. Thomas | 17 | 47 | 102 00 | 952 50 | 419 72 | 338 13 |
| 77 | Oxford | 6 | 21 | 21 20 | 186 00 | | 90 50 |
| 78 | Durham | 11 | 18 | 49 60 | 382 95 | 225 75 | 150 74 |
| 79 | Nipissing | | 24 | | 150 01 | 17 00 | 36 35 |
| 80 | Amity | 48 | 32 | 299 70 | 499 75 | 62 00 | 663 11 |
| 81 | Belleville | 12 | 24 | 76 50 | 487 15 | 102 00 | 314 71 |
| 82 | Beaver | 6 | 12 | 33 40 | 135 00 | 25 50 | 10 04 |
| 83 | Clinton | | 10 | 60 | 44 90 | 12 50 | 43 70 |
| 84 | Walkerton | 5 | 18 | 17 50 | 201 25 | 592 96 | 256 88 |
| 85 | Constellation | 22 | 14 | 108 55 | 114 50 | 98 25 | 189 73 |
| 86 | Napanee | 3 | 15 | 18 50 | 163 25 | 130 90 | 233 18 |
| 87 | Empire | 3 | 18 | 40 15 | 233 50 | 28 10 | 148 93 |
| 88 | Olive Branch | 3 | 27 | 8 20 | 307 47 | 196 35 | 305 20 |
| 89 | Reliance | 9 | 24 | 70 40 | 478 74 | 257 13 | 107 93 |
| 90 | Ivy | | | 84 50 | 205 17 | 34 12 | 92 35 |

TERM ENDING 31ST DECEMBER, 1892.—*Continued.*

| ASSETS—HOW INVESTED. | | | | FUNDS. | | | | |
| Cash in Bank or in Treasurer's hands. | Invested in Mortgages and Securities. | Invested in Buildings and Lands. | Invested in Furniture and Regalia. | General Benefit Fund. | W. and O. Fund. | Contingent Fund. | Total Funds. | No. of Lodge. |
|---|---|---|---|---|---|---|---|---|
| 1057 16 | 4000 00 | …… | 1000 00 | 4610 95 | 1446 21 | …… | 6057 16 | 9 |
| 4459 53 | …… | …… | 1842 88 | 5223 95 | 942 50 | 135 96 | 6302 41 | 10 |
| 1043 82 | …… | …… | 2200 00 | 3243 82 | …… | …… | 3243 82 | 13 |
| 234 54 | 7100 00 | 12000 00 | 1717 35 | 20052 59 | 99 30 | …… | 21051 89 | 16 |
| 859 70 | …… | …… | 740 00 | 1599 70 | …… | …… | 1599 70 | 22 |
| 196 76 | …… | 2879 50 | 1089 60 | 4019 35 | 133 50 | 13 01 | 4165 86 | 28 |
| 1453 01 | …… | 10400 00 | 1286 87 | 12248 65 | 669 66 | 221 57 | 13139 88 | 29 |
| 184 12 | …… | 8942 17 | 1000 00 | 10126 29 | …… | …… | 10126 29 | 30 |
| 392 11 | 4349 83 | 54 00 | 980 54 | 4897 08 | 849 40 | 30 00 | 5776 48 | 32 |
| 293 00 | …… | 800 00 | 250 00 | 1093 00 | 250 00 | …… | 1343 00 | 33 |
| 224 43 | 13500 00 | …… | 716 46 | 11615 38 | 2586 36 | 239 15 | 14440 89 | 34 |
| 1416 69 | 7 00 | 6458 15 | 2414 55 | 8242 83 | 2053 56 | …… | 10296 39 | 35 |
| …… | …… | 15000 00 | 450 00 | 15450 00 | …… | …… | 15450 00 | 36 |
| 171 85 | 500 00 | 10993 15 | 1000 00 | 12649 67 | …… | 15 33 | 12665 00 | 38 |
| 1090 84 | …… | …… | 1251 45 | 2288 16 | 54 13 | …… | 2342 29 | 40 |
| 577 33 | …… | 11520 55 | 2386 27 | 14365 49 | …… | 118 66 | 14484 15 | 41 |
| 1599 92 | …… | …… | 439 45 | 1265 79 | 765 40 | 8 18 | 2039 37 | 44 |
| 32 83 | …… | 8751 27 | 2147 49 | 10931 59 | …… | …… | 10931 59 | 45 |
| 161 91 | …… | 1100 00 | 175 00 | 1436 91 | …… | …… | 1436 91 | 46 |
| 951 74 | 3440 00 | 6825 00 | 910 00 | 5282 11 | 6624 21 | 220 42 | 12126 74 | 47 |
| 1190 00 | 750 00 | 7187 75 | 1090 00 | 6317 75 | …… | 3900 00 | 10217 75 | 48 |
| 245 87 | …… | 6152 00 | …… | 4869 45 | 1300 46 | 227 96 | 6397 87 | 49 |
| 741 11 | …… | 6500 00 | 600 00 | 7841 11 | …… | …… | 7841 11 | 50 |
| 158 74 | …… | …… | …… | 158 74 | …… | …… | 158 74 | 51 |
| 108 19 | 623 00 | 11033 16 | 200 00 | 9361 82 | 2462 78 | 139 75 | 11964 35 | 52 |
| 1804 94 | 1000 00 | 44 00 | 1000 00 | 3848 94 | …… | …… | 3848 94 | 53 |
| 469 14 | 1600 00 | 3231 24 | 2261 95 | 7567 09 | …… | 15 24 | 7582 33 | 54 |
| 102 34 | …… | 4750 00 | 200 00 | 5052 34 | …… | …… | 5052 34 | 55 |
| 829 29 | 138 41 | 4000 00 | 421 25 | 2972 63 | 2358 54 | 57 78 | 5388 95 | 56 |
| 258 21 | 1200 00 | …… | 750 00 | 1586 58 | 621 63 | …… | 2208 21 | 57 |
| 553 40 | 4500 00 | 2500 00 | 1100 00 | 8633 80 | …… | 19 60 | 8653 40 | 58 |
| 581 06 | …… | 5950 00 | 1250 00 | 7674 82 | 104 67 | 1 57 | 7781 06 | 59 |
| 1105 56 | 4500 00 | …… | 1525 00 | 6690 75 | …… | 439 81 | 7130 56 | 61 |
| 1134 19 | 3100 00 | 1137 71 | 741 62 | 2971 76 | 3140 41 | 1 35 | 6113 52 | 62 |
| 339 06 | 1500 00 | …… | 900 00 | 2739 06 | …… | …… | 2739 06 | 63 |
| 2138 98 | …… | …… | 769 30 | 1691 47 | 1208 30 | 28 51 | 2928 28 | 64 |
| 209 19 | …… | 14152 52 | 1900 00 | 16261 71 | …… | …… | 16261 71 | 65 |
| 376 49 | 6435 92 | …… | 1300 00 | 8083 31 | …… | 29 10 | 8112 41 | 66 |
| 123 42 | …… | 2750 00 | 300 00 | 3172 62 | …… | 80 | 3173 42 | 67 |
| 415 69 | …… | …… | 757 19 | 1172 88 | …… | …… | 1172 88 | 68 |
| 1678 14 | …… | 800 00 | 250 00 | 2091 77 | 626 76 | 9 61 | 2729 14 | 69 |
| 57 31 | 1558 67 | …… | 550 00 | 930 51 | 1178 13 | 57 34 | 2165 98 | 70 |
| 730 42 | …… | 651 10 | 245 03 | 907 08 | 464 60 | 254 90 | 1626 55 | 71 |
| 42 60 | …… | …… | 1000 00 | 1042 60 | …… | …… | 1042 60 | 72 |
| 712 54 | 3906 13 | …… | 544 16 | 5252 83 | …… | …… | 5252 83 | 73 |
| 188 15 | 575 00 | …… | 600 00 | 1235 86 | 127 29 | …… | 1363 15 | 74 |
| 1051 17 | 1133 34 | …… | 900 00 | 2934 51 | …… | 150 00 | 3084 51 | 75 |
| 433 71 | 10378 94 | 324 00 | 1300 00 | 9550 75 | 2800 00 | 85 90 | 12436 65 | 76 |
| 416 00 | …… | …… | 1425 00 | 1825 00 | …… | 16 00 | 1841 00 | 77 |
| 649 02 | 4255 00 | …… | 2000 00 | 5295 77 | 1500 00 | 108 25 | 6904 02 | 78 |
| 1382 90 | …… | …… | 700 00 | 2082 90 | …… | …… | 2082 90 | 79 |
| 2668 12 | 1000 00 | …… | 2220 90 | 4310 15 | 1549 22 | 29 65 | 5889 02 | 80 |
| 4423 53 | …… | …… | 4013 00 | 5946 21 | 2436 16 | 54 16 | 8436 53 | 81 |
| 370 94 | 300 00 | 1100 00 | 500 00 | 2270 94 | …… | …… | 2270 94 | 82 |
| 100 00 | …… | …… | 650 00 | 750 00 | …… | …… | 750 00 | 83 |
| 128 80 | 1380 55 | …… | 600 00 | 2109 35 | …… | …… | 2109 35 | 84 |
| 1646 89 | 400 00 | …… | 400 00 | 1837 41 | 609 48 | …… | 2446 89 | 85 |
| 89 71 | 2000 00 | …… | 1372 88 | 2320 20 | 872 26 | 270 13 | 3462 59 | 86 |
| 1092 06 | 3000 00 | …… | 1696 14 | 5000 65 | 1387 55 | …… | 6388 20 | 87 |
| 491 91 | 1029 55 | 2202 92 | 700 00 | 3059 91 | 1361 55 | 2 92 | 4424 38 | 88 |
| 969 37 | 4400 00 | …… | 1600 00 | 5584 32 | 1382 69 | 2 36 | 6969 37 | 89 |
| 1610 80 | 1985 00 | …… | 326 00 | 3921 80 | …… | …… | 3921 80 | 90 |

ABSTRACT FROM SEMI-ANNUAL RETURNS.

| No. of Lodge. | NAME OF LODGE. | No. of Degrees Conferred. | No. of Past Grands in Good Standing. | RECEIPTS OF LODGES. | | | Current Expenses. |
| --- | --- | --- | --- | --- | --- | --- | --- |
| | | | | Initiations, Admission by Card and Degrees. | Dues and Reinstatements. | All other Sources. | |
| | | | | $ c | $ c | $ c | $ c |
| 91 | Grand River | 13 | 27 | 74 70 | 309 30 | 114 00 | 101 52 |
| 92 | Milton | | | 6 00 | 56 54 | 40 40 | 73 24 |
| 93 | Western City | | | 58 90 | 239 75 | | 65 50 |
| 94 | Alymer | | | 105 75 | 426 75 | 91 86 | 382 82 |
| 96 | Nith | | 22 | 30 | 201 30 | 10 00 | 47 21 |
| 97 | Grand Union | 38 | 18 | 179 90 | 281 81 | 168 75 | 414 42 |
| 98 | Minto | | | 12 00 | 120 06 | 101 10 | 129 66 |
| 100 | Lindsay | 26 | 28 | 165 20 | 161 50 | 2 60 | 71 09 |
| 101 | Golden Star | | | | 102 50 | 58 60 | 77 50 |
| 102 | Deseronto | 12 | 18 | 60 60 | 227 50 | 121 00 | 107 87 |
| 103 | Cataract | 6 | 15 | 36 55 | 171 70 | 239 50 | 112 35 |
| 104 | Crescent | 17 | 33 | 86 60 | 763 70 | 101 60 | 274 35 |
| 105 | Manilla | | 16 | | 74 50 | 41 20 | 80 63 |
| 106 | St. Clair | | 16 | | 316 50 | 114 25 | 189 40 |
| 107 | Waterloo | 18 | 25 | 123 90 | 380 85 | 342 37 | 213 66 |
| 108 | Royal Oak | | | 37 30 | 210 00 | 45 20 | 113 73 |
| 109 | Orion | 1 | 18 | 8 50 | 151 47 | 81 43 | 83 07 |
| 110 | Laurel | | | | 34 06 | | 80 26 |
| 111 | Peterboro' | 46 | 23 | 220 30 | 619 76 | 160 92 | 393 63 |
| 112 | Lucknow | 30 | 13 | 169 84 | 187 67 | 238 50 | 122 42 |
| 113 | Trenton | 3 | 9 | 22 00 | 172 50 | 25 00 | 101 92 |
| 114 | Gananoque | 20 | 19 | 109 25 | 549 77 | 132 60 | 376 00 |
| 115 | Harmony | 44 | 27 | 216 80 | 468 40 | 179 73 | 271 53 |
| 116 | Naomi | | | | | | |
| 117 | Valley City | 2 | 31 | 6 10 | 319 49 | 190 25 | 165 84 |
| 119 | Maitland | 7 | 14 | 34 50 | 169 75 | 52 00 | 171 25 |
| 120 | Sydenham Valley | | 30 | 80 50 | 404 75 | 272 80 | 233 75 |
| 121 | Saxton | | | 6 30 | 57 85 | 45 39 | 56 47 |
| 122 | Streetsville | | 12 | 50 | 87 50 | 115 50 | 78 50 |
| 124 | Dresden | 18 | 21 | 200 15 | 308 71 | 183 33 | 893 41 |
| 125 | Stella | 14 | 18 | 63 90 | 339 45 | 59 55 | 247 98 |
| 126 | Sarnia | 9 | 23 | 68 00 | 177 00 | 68 25 | 112 03 |
| 127 | Mizpah | 23 | 22 | 164 00 | 239 00 | 26 18 | 290 44 |
| 129 | Charity | 3 | 9 | 13 80 | 58 55 | 3 14 | 53 15 |
| 130 | Livingstone | 5 | 18 | 25 60 | 94 25 | 60 99 | 96 62 |
| 131 | Marion | 12 | 12 | 61 00 | 203 75 | 79 60 | 71 48 |
| 132 | Oakville | 9 | 6 | 37 50 | 66 75 | 166 00 | 82 93 |
| 133 | Glencoe | 3 | 11 | 21 35 | 100 56 | | 72 75 |
| 134 | Orient | | 0 | 60 | 32 80 | | 10 25 |
| 135 | Peaceful Dove | 2 | 21 | 11 30 | 95 30 | 60 00 | 62 45 |
| 136 | Cobourg | 8 | 23 | 83 00 | 214 81 | 27 50 | 173 66 |
| 137 | St. Lawrence | 20 | 22 | 73 00 | 230 50 | 38 00 | 127 44 |
| 138 | Ancaster | 30 | 11 | 178 40 | 169 50 | 13 55 | 80 35 |
| 139 | Garnet | 3 | 18 | | 181 86 | | 83 50 |
| 140 | Leamington | 31 | 13 | 159 75 | 255 12 | 10 54 | 171 53 |
| 142 | Concord | | 6 | 44 20 | 123 20 | | 126 48 |
| 143 | Bay of Quinte | 6 | 28 | 36 90 | 289 02 | 145 61 | 110 20 |
| 144 | Ridgetown | 6 | 21 | 53 00 | 169 25 | 46 50 | 217 15 |
| 146 | Vivian | 4 | 14 | 16 00 | 97 25 | 28 30 | 132 11 |
| 147 | Model | 4 | | 20 30 | 103 58 | 46 25 | 61 29 |
| 148 | Aurora | 7 | 19 | 21 80 | 179 00 | 295 45 | 403 22 |
| 149 | Western Star | | 18 | 30 | 39 00 | 18 75 | 158 09 |
| 151 | Sycamore | 3 | | 11 60 | 91 50 | 135 35 | 145 94 |
| 152 | Hayden | 16 | 19 | 62 80 | 216 50 | 135 00 | 161 55 |
| 153 | Wildey | 6 | 18 | 32 00 | 103 50 | 65 00 | 66 49 |
| 154 | Alpha | | | 72 60 | 317 50 | 205 00 | 211 90 |
| 155 | Brougham | | 10 | 60 | 53 90 | | 2 00 |
| 156 | Pyramid | | 18 | 50 | 76 75 | 68 35 | 58 50 |
| 157 | Thamesville | 4 | 10 | 38 30 | 100 75 | 25 00 | 110 90 |
| 158 | Progress | 3 | 26 | 35 20 | 258 65 | 114 57 | 167 70 |
| 159 | Oak Leaf | 3 | 15 | 9 00 | 140 00 | | 67 35 |

## Term Ending 31st December, 1892.—*Continued.*

| Assets—How Invested. | | | | Funds. | | | | |
|---|---|---|---|---|---|---|---|---|
| Cash in Bank or in Treasurer's hands. | Invested in Mortgages and Securities. | Invested in Buildings and Lands. | Invested in Furniture and Regalia. | General Benefit Fund. | W. and O. Fund. | Contingent Fund. | Total Funds. | No. of Lodge. |
| $ c | $ c | $ c | $ c | $ c | $ c | $ c | $ c | |
| 840 43 | 3862 00 | 20 00 | 800 00 | 2378 45 | 3082 05 | 61 93 | 5522 43 | 91 |
| 273 11 | 697 00 | | 600 00 | 1297 00 | | 273 11 | 1570 11 | 92 |
| 96 69 | 1500 00 | | 372 38 | 1969 07 | | | 1969 07 | 93 |
| 2925 92 | 1700 00 | | 850 00 | 5021 90 | 454 02 | | 5475 92 | 94 |
| 116 85 | 3550 00 | 203 00 | 634 00 | 4503 85 | | | 4503 85 | 96 |
| 262 37 | 1750 00 | | 950 00 | 2281 37 | 150 00 | 531 00 | 2962 37 | 97 |
| 930 30 | | 2200 00 | 500 00 | 3630 30 | | | 3630 30 | 98 |
| 1135 15 | 1100 00 | | 1175 00 | 3410 15 | | | 3410 15 | 100 |
| 1783 70 | 1060 00 | | 485 26 | 2324 33 | 988 53 | 16 10 | 3328 96 | 101 |
| 2601 83 | | | 675 00 | 2693 30 | 397 75 | 186 78 | 3277 83 | 102 |
| 638 00 | 400 00 | | 500 00 | 911 54 | 626 46 | | 1538 00 | 103 |
| 600 60 | | 6870 00 | 846 28 | 6005 45 | 2300 50 | 10 33 | 8316 28 | 104 |
| 460 47 | 361 12 | | 400 00 | 1221 59 | | | 1221 59 | 105 |
| 2066 13 | | 5330 00 | 588 81 | 7984 94 | | | 7984 94 | 106 |
| 486 96 | 3350 00 | 3400 00 | 600 00 | 6497 16 | 1308 95 | 30 85 | 7836 96 | 107 |
| 848 23 | 950 00 | | 700 00 | 2498 23 | | | 2498 23 | 108 |
| 621 41 | 1900 00 | | 600 00 | 3121 41 | | | 3121 41 | 109 |
| 46 74 | 100 00 | | 200 00 | 344 74 | | 2 00 | 346 74 | 110 |
| 5936 43 | 25 00 | | 1474 89 | 5760 65 | 1545 30 | 130 37 | 7436 32 | 111 |
| 627 34 | 3710 00 | | 669 35 | 4332 98 | 673 71 | | 5006 69 | 112 |
| 1136 67 | 100 00 | | 684 00 | 1770 67 | 150 00 | | 1920 67 | 113 |
| 450 60 | 4160 60 | | 2000 00 | 5380 29 | 1164 43 | 66 48 | 6611 20 | 114 |
| | 6560 09 | | 1310 63 | 5506 48 | 2208 09 | 156 15 | 7870 72 | 115 |
| | | | | | | | | 116 |
| 859 73 | 3800 00 | 500 00 | 1574 00 | 3744 15 | 2931 61 | 57 97 | 6733 73 | 117 |
| 1994 84 | | 750 00 | 350 00 | 2584 48 | 510 36 | | 3094 84 | 119 |
| 69 02 | 3414 00 | 1883 15 | 1610 00 | 6926 15 | | 50 02 | 6976 17 | 120 |
| 696 71 | 1200 00 | | 750 00 | 1882 77 | 807 44 | 6 50 | 2646 71 | 121 |
| 154 02 | | 4500 00 | 700 00 | 5354 02 | | | 5354 02 | 122 |
| 544 76 | 500 00 | 5137 51 | 797 44 | 6437 37 | 538 02 | 4 32 | 6979 71 | 124 |
| 2080 07 | | | 1000 00 | 2455 69 | 622 00 | 2 38 | 3080 07 | 125 |
| 508 70 | | | 1200 00 | 1798 70 | | | 1798 70 | 126 |
| 1740 16 | | | 1220 29 | 2936 57 | | 23 88 | 2960 45 | 127 |
| 269 45 | 230 00 | | 170 00 | 669 45 | | | 669 45 | 129 |
| 1031 60 | | | 1000 00 | 1031 60 | | 1000 00 | 2031 60 | 130 |
| 780 27 | 2000 00 | | 600 00 | 2842 81 | 354 89 | 182 57 | 3380 27 | 131 |
| 123 16 | | 3302 55 | 600 00 | 3040 58 | 844 10 | 141 03 | 4025 71 | 132 |
| 363 06 | 1050 00 | | 656 64 | 1222 30 | 776 20 | 71 20 | 2069 70 | 133 |
| 435 22 | | | 600 00 | 600 00 | 434 11 | 1 11 | 1035 22 | 134 |
| 962 78 | 1000 00 | | 600 00 | 1817 78 | 745 00 | | 2562 78 | 135 |
| 1132 68 | | | 2245 00 | 3369 58 | 2 10 | 6 00 | 3377 68 | 136 |
| 1798 47 | | | 742 00 | 1414 04 | 1126 43 | | 2540 47 | 137 |
| 1327 31 | | | 250 00 | 1090 30 | 458 91 | 18 10 | 1577 31 | 138 |
| 1360 70 | | | 541 00 | 1901 70 | | | 1901 70 | 139 |
| 411 50 | | | 1306 09 | 1713 39 | | 4 20 | 1717 59 | 140 |
| 75 99 | | 3000 00 | 400 00 | 3475 99 | | | 3475 99 | 142 |
| 2569 55 | | 3550 75 | 1267 89 | 6143 06 | 1229 07 | 16 06 | 7388 19 | 143 |
| 994 80 | 450 00 | | 1700 00 | 2700 80 | 444 00 | | 3144 80 | 144 |
| 164 52 | 1500 00 | | 865 00 | 2529 52 | | | 2529 52 | 146 |
| 903 58 | | | 300 00 | 682 40 | 504 08 | 17 10 | 1203 58 | 147 |
| 44 85 | | 4198 02 | 384 06 | 3606 40 | 1620 53 | | 4626 93 | 148 |
| 56 10 | 17 00 | | 1043 00 | 851 95 | 264 15 | | 1116 10 | 149 |
| 206 56 | 593 00 | 1300 00 | 300 00 | 2399 56 | | | 2399 56 | 151 |
| 506 18 | 1000 00 | | 380 00 | 1886 18 | | | 1886 18 | 152 |
| 1052 98 | | 1575 00 | 200 00 | 2827 98 | | | 2827 98 | 153 |
| 138 81 | 2720 00 | | 1500 00 | 2691 87 | 1231 63 | 435 31 | 4358 81 | 154 |
| 998 18 | | | 150 00 | 948 34 | 199 84 | | 1148 18 | 155 |
| 202 20 | 700 00 | | 600 00 | 1502 20 | | | 1502 20 | 156 |
| 677 82 | | | 375 00 | 638 67 | 414 15 | | 1052 82 | 157 |
| 5055 46 | | | 900 00 | 3797 62 | 2157 84 | | 5955 46 | 158 |
| 539 71 | | 45 00 | 350 00 | 934 71 | | | 934 71 | 159 |

17

### ABSTRACT FROM SEMI-ANNUAL RETURNS.

| No. of Lodge. | NAME OF LODGE. | No. of Degrees Conferred. | No. of Past Grands in Good Standing. | Initiations, Admission by Card, and Degrees. | | Dues and Rein-statements. | | All other Sources. | | Current Expenses. | |
|---|---|---|---|---|---|---|---|---|---|---|---|
| | | | | $ | c | $ | c | $ | c | $ | c |
| 160 | Listowel | 3 | 15 | 50 | 00 | 254 | 64 | 40 | 99 | 127 | 63 |
| 161 | Simcoe | 10 | 19 | 52 | 40 | 206 | 95 | 45 | 00 | 107 | 54 |
| 163 | Oriental | | | 21 | 75 | 104 | 00 | 25 | 00 | 101 | 20 |
| 164 | Romeo | 6 | 24 | 29 | 00 | 393 | 66 | 63 | 60 | 138 | 70 |
| 165 | Beethoven | | 16 | 1 | 60 | 137 | 00 | 30 | 00 | 146 | 09 |
| 167 | Hillsburg | 3 | 13 | 22 | 30 | | | | | 56 | 00 |
| 168 | Sutton | | 12 | | 35 | 80 | 50 | 155 | 50 | 126 | 34 |
| 169 | Grey | 2 | 5 | 6 | 00 | 25 | 50 | 4 | 00 | 13 | 50 |
| 170 | Denovo | | 13 | 3 | 20 | 108 | 95 | | 17 | 137 | 24 |
| 171 | Alliston | 8 | 10 | 19 | 30 | 87 | 50 | 37 | 28 | 57 | 48 |
| 172 | Pentangore | 20 | 13 | 78 | 10 | 337 | 45 | 47 | 35 | 130 | 70 |
| 173 | Emerald | | 14 | 14 | 00 | 55 | 09 | 8 | 17 | 53 | 03 |
| 174 | Dolman | | 15 | 1 | 40 | 104 | 00 | 65 | 52 | 55 | 03 |
| 176 | Dauncey | 6 | 1 | 32 | 30 | 60 | 00 | 26 | 20 | 28 | 16 |
| 177 | Montana | | | 10 | 00 | 43 | 25 | 18 | 00 | 67 | 60 |
| 178 | Wellington Square | 12 | 6 | 88 | 00 | 83 | 00 | | | 80 | 33 |
| 179 | Madoc | 37 | 15 | 139 | 50 | 316 | 95 | 25 | 13 | 370 | 99 |
| 180 | Owen Sound | 2 | 17 | 32 | 38 | 155 | 98 | 351 | 10 | 462 | 93 |
| 182 | Tecumseh | 11 | 15 | 54 | 00 | 143 | 00 | 77 | 21 | 129 | 35 |
| 183 | Teeswater | | 11 | | 30 | 93 | 75 | | | 53 | 40 |
| 184 | Germania | 33 | 24 | 157 | 75 | 201 | 05 | 62 | 65 | 208 | 03 |
| 186 | Dufferin | | 10 | | 30 | 57 | 00 | | | 72 | 59 |
| 188 | Cambridge | 3 | 12 | 17 | 30 | 140 | 11 | 18 | 75 | 75 | 93 |
| 189 | Parry Sound | 15 | 16 | 124 | 60 | 177 | 70 | 77 | 04 | 155 | 97 |
| 190 | Chorazin | 3 | 29 | 25 | 30 | 381 | 55 | 122 | 76 | 347 | 04 |
| 191 | Jarvis | | 11 | 2 | 10 | 56 | 40 | 42 | 48 | 80 | 86 |
| 192 | Howick | | | 1 | 30 | 44 | 25 | | | 12 | 40 |
| 194 | Albert | 12 | 34 | 100 | 78 | 501 | 32 | 416 | 55 | 441 | 42 |
| 195 | Cicerone | 2 | 9 | 12 | 00 | 32 | 00 | | | 31 | 60 |
| 196 | Florence | 9 | 27 | 47 | 80 | 164 | 87 | 60 | 50 | 47 | 67 |
| 197 | Minerva | 9 | 12 | 40 | 00 | 207 | 49 | 39 | 45 | 99 | 15 |
| 200 | Weston | 3 | 11 | 36 | 80 | 75 | 50 | 28 | 50 | 165 | 43 |
| 201 | Beacon | 1 | 11 | 11 | 25 | 84 | 68 | 69 | 95 | 93 | 83 |
| 202 | Silver Star | | | 56 | 00 | | | 151 | 07 | 60 | 00 |
| 203 | Pembroke | 24 | 20 | 157 | 50 | 286 | 47 | | 75 | 143 | 49 |
| 204 | Acton | | | 2 | 00 | 25 | 50 | 19 | 50 | 53 | 25 |
| 205 | Abiram | 21 | 19 | 136 | 00 | 293 | 62 | 158 | 50 | 108 | 51 |
| 206 | Silver City | 9 | 18 | 37 | 08 | 213 | 77 | 66 | 00 | 30 | 30 |
| 207 | Egremont | 12 | 3 | 54 | 00 | 27 | 43 | | | 20 | 56 |
| 209 | Millbank | 3 | 10 | 18 | 00 | 55 | 25 | 13 | 60 | 40 | 00 |
| 210 | Brucefield | | 14 | 7 | 50 | 69 | 00 | | | 37 | 00 |
| 211 | Lilly | | 10 | | 40 | 70 | 00 | | | 13 | 83 |
| 212 | Argyll | 7 | 18 | 62 | 92 | 172 | 35 | 69 | 25 | 136 | 77 |
| 214 | Clifford | | 18 | 7 | 00 | 150 | 00 | 45 | 00 | 54 | 25 |
| 215 | Freestone | | 14 | 1 | 50 | 103 | 50 | 24 | 01 | 60 | 34 |
| 216 | Elmira | | | 16 | 25 | 111 | 50 | 37 | 75 | 20 | 60 |
| 217 | Mount Brydges | 40 | 19 | 229 | 25 | 286 | 46 | 21 | 65 | 300 | 98 |
| 218 | Enterprise | 9 | 11 | 83 | 35 | 367 | 15 | 214 | 95 | 220 | 68 |
| 219 | Georgian Bay | 27 | 19 | 112 | 40 | 210 | 75 | 145 | 00 | 293 | 75 |
| 220 | Woodslee | 6 | 3 | 45 | 80 | 46 | 00 | | | 50 | 11 |
| 221 | Chesley | 9 | 10 | 33 | 00 | 56 | 65 | 50 | 10 | 332 | 15 |
| 223 | Hensall | 6 | 23 | 28 | 60 | 142 | 00 | | | 42 | 42 |
| 224 | Ottawa | 6 | 19 | 62 | 85 | 236 | 60 | 33 | 50 | 203 | 21 |
| 226 | Merlin | 3 | 13 | 20 | 00 | 45 | 50 | 15 | 25 | 33 | 36 |
| 227 | Sauble | | 7 | | | 12 | 00 | 10 | 00 | | |
| 228 | International | 14 | 23 | 60 | 60 | 490 | 55 | 240 | 57 | 285 | 93 |
| 229 | Embro Star | 6 | 10 | 32 | 40 | 143 | 75 | | | 64 | 50 |
| 230 | Prince of Wales | 8 | 8 | 63 | 85 | 114 | 50 | 199 | 80 | 214 | 11 |
| 231 | Elora | 4 | 14 | 33 | 80 | 165 | 92 | 27 | 25 | 79 | 08 |
| 232 | Equity | | 7 | | | 55 | 50 | | | | |
| 233 | Hanover | | 4 | | | 15 | 00 | 35 | 00 | 45 | 00 |
| 234 | Ilderton | | 10 | | 30 | 89 | 27 | 98 | 90 | 48 | 80 |

**TERM ENDING 31ST DECEMBER, 1892.—*Continued*.**

| Cash in Bank or in Treasurer's hands. | Invested in Mortgages and Securities. | Invested in Buildings and Lands. | Invested in Furniture and Regalia. | General Benefit Fund. | W. and O. Fund. | Contingent Fund. | Total Funds. | No. of Lodge. |
|---|---|---|---|---|---|---|---|---|
| $ c | $ c | $ c | $ c | $ c | $ c | $ c | $ c | |
| 1333 90 | | | 1000 00 | 2078 90 | 255 00 | | 2333 90 | 160 |
| 230 40 | 100 00 | 2200 00 | 650 00 | 3178 61 | | 1 79 | 3180 40 | 161 |
| 344 61 | | | 800 00 | 1144 61 | | | 1144 61 | 163 |
| 285 03 | 2900 00 | 536 74 | 210 60 | 3930 45 | | 1 92 | 3932 37 | 164 |
| 2072 73 | | | 300 00 | 1211 18 | 1154 05 | 7 50 | 2372 73 | 165 |
| | | 850 00 | 60 00 | 910 00 | | | 910 00 | 167 |
| 14 83 | | 4140 20 | 333 00 | 4488 03 | | | 4488 03 | 168 |
| 204 48 | 200 00 | 346 06 | 300 00 | 1050 54 | | | 1050 54 | 169 |
| 21 46 | 1150 00 | | 200 00 | 1361 46 | | 10 00 | 1371 46 | 170 |
| 398 77 | 110 00 | | 745 00 | 1253 77 | | | 1253 77 | 171 |
| 577 12 | 2717 50 | | 1468 96 | 4545 57 | 238 01 | | 4783 58 | 172 |
| 443 33 | 294 17 | 1600 00 | 500 00 | 2837 50 | | | 2837 50 | 173 |
| 37 92 | 650 00 | | 300 00 | 953 90 | | 44 02 | 997 92 | 174 |
| | | | 95 00 | 95 00 | | | 95 00 | 176 |
| 714 76 | | | 150 00 | 571 35 | 293 41 | | 864 76 | 177 |
| 180 83 | | | | 180 83 | | | 180 83 | 178 |
| 1433 41 | 40 50 | | 1312 86 | 2770 97 | | 15 80 | 2786 77 | 179 |
| 1921 21 | | | 800 00 | 1174 63 | 1430 05 | 116 53 | 2721 21 | 180 |
| 516 25 | 490 75 | | 150 32 | 1157 32 | | | 1157 32 | 182 |
| | 837 67 | 225 44 | 240 00 | 665 16 | 637 95 | | 1303 11 | 183 |
| 1669 76 | 200 00 | | 211 11 | 2032 76 | | 48 11 | 2080 87 | 184 |
| 338 14 | | | 545 00 | 869 52 | | 13 62 | 883 14 | 186 |
| 608 33 | | 850 00 | 350 00 | 1808 33 | | | 1808 33 | 188 |
| 1202 44 | 375 00 | 2000 00 | 1085 00 | 3319 10 | 1343 34 | | 4662 44 | 189 |
| 662 38 | 1150 00 | 2300 00 | 575 00 | 3536 48 | 1347 24 | 103 66 | 4987 38 | 190 |
| 1385 07 | 208 00 | | 736 00 | 1644 41 | 684 66 | | 2329 07 | 191 |
| 60 86 | 222 50 | 600 00 | 191 15 | 960 39 | 114 12 | | 1074 51 | 192 |
| 324 43 | 177 50 | 3400 00 | 957 93 | 1966 37 | 2041 92 | 851 57 | 4859 86 | 194 |
| 418 40 | | | 100 00 | 100 00 | 339 44 | 78 96 | 518 40 | 195 |
| 1360 61 | 1900 00 | | 303 00 | 3563 61 | | | 3563 61 | 196 |
| 1785 25 | | | 281 65 | 1110 94 | 935 31 | 20 65 | 2066 90 | 197 |
| 1924 00 | | 2346 00 | 300 00 | 2147 73 | 510 75 | 6 76 | 2665 24 | 200 |
| 885 89 | | | 536 95 | 979 16 | 443 68 | | 1422 84 | 201 |
| 676 57 | 450 00 | | 300 00 | 1497 86 | 128 71 | | 1626 57 | 202 |
| 2259 65 | | | 1540 17 | 2065 31 | 1692 48 | 42 03 | 3799 82 | 203 |
| 6 33 | 296 25 | | 150 00 | 452 58 | | | 452 58 | 204 |
| 117 84 | | 3500 00 | 500 00 | 4117 84 | | | 4117 84 | 205 |
| 152 51 | 1379 99 | | 450 00 | 1592 75 | 389 75 | | 1982 50 | 206 |
| 91 95 | | 425 00 | 100 00 | 616 95 | | | 616 95 | 207 |
| 800 00 | 250 00 | | 150 00 | | 1200 00 | | 1200 00 | 209 |
| 336 39 | 756 00 | | | 1092 39 | | | 1092 39 | 210 |
| 342 00 | | 675 00 | 200 00 | 1217 00 | | | 1217 00 | 211 |
| 1271 06 | 1500 00 | | 1645 25 | 3516 82 | 899 49 | | 4416 31 | 212 |
| 232 66 | 2600 00 | | 214 74 | 3047 40 | | | 3047 40 | 214 |
| 969 64 | 1200 00 | | 500 00 | 1939 92 | 729 72 | | 2669 64 | 215 |
| 676 53 | 800 00 | | 255 00 | 1731 53 | | | 1731 53 | 216 |
| 607 33 | | 3408 26 | 609 88 | 4625 47 | | | 4625 47 | 217 |
| 1553 02 | 96 62 | | 500 00 | 2149 64 | | | 2149 64 | 218 |
| 1045 96 | | 1479 35 | 426 22 | 2301 50 | 559 10 | 90 93 | 2951 53 | 219 |
| 346 23 | 100 00 | 65 00 | 200 00 | 711 23 | | | 711 23 | 220 |
| | 700 00 | | 500 00 | 1200 00 | | | 1200 00 | 221 |
| 220 66 | | 1400 00 | 210 00 | 1830 66 | | | 1830 66 | 223 |
| 2293 82 | | | 700 00 | 1763 72 | 1225 50 | 4 60 | 2993 82 | 224 |
| 143 29 | | 1500 00 | 144 50 | 1753 28 | | 34 51 | 1787 79 | 226 |
| | | | 245 00 | 245 00 | | | 245 00 | 227 |
| 945 07 | | 4087 58 | 1395 22 | 5010 42 | 1379 07 | 38 98 | 6428 47 | 228 |
| 537 87 | | | 500 00 | 1037 87 | | | 1037 87 | 229 |
| 449 20 | | | 400 00 | 849 01 | | 19 | 849 20 | 230 |
| 673 68 | | | 840 00 | 1513 68 | | | 1513 68 | 231 |
| 568 05 | | | 450 00 | 1018 05 | | | 1018 05 | 232 |
| 100 00 | | | 200 00 | 200 00 | 100 00 | | 300 00 | 233 |
| 159 59 | | 1748 51 | 225 00 | 1973 51 | 148 89 | 10 70 | 2133 10 | 234 |

### Abstract from Semi-Annual Returns.

| No. of Lodge. | NAME OF LODGE. | No. of Degrees Conferred. | No. of Past Grands in Good Standing. | Initiations, Admission by Card, and Degrees. | Dues and Reinstatements. | All other Sources. | Current Expenses. |
|---|---|---|---|---|---|---|---|
| | | | | $ c | $ c | $ c | $ c |
| 235 | Waterford | 18 | 14 | 59 40 | 358 18 | | 151 33 |
| 236 | Acorn | 6 | 10 | 34 00 | 62 58 | 40 08 | 50 73 |
| 237 | Farmersville | 3 | 15 | | 99 50 | | 92 00 |
| 239 | Stirling | 21 | 14 | 110 00 | 287 45 | | 180 22 |
| 240 | Carleton | 18 | 23 | 102 65 | 365 70 | 197 50 | 559 20 |
| 241 | Rideau | 3 | 15 | 22 80 | 310 20 | 230 58 | 204 96 |
| 242 | Wilton | | | 58 35 | 238 87 | 57 89 | 125 24 |
| 243 | Thornbury | | | | | | |
| 244 | Port Arthur | 12 | 9 | 82 90 | 198 25 | 126 31 | 191 35 |
| 245 | Mallorytown | | 12 | 30 | 153 50 | 27 00 | 105 25 |
| 246 | Orillia | | 6 | 65 | 89 44 | 47 45 | 97 68 |
| 247 | Gordon | 8 | 13 | 9 30 | 129 35 | | 39 30 |
| 248 | Campbellford | 5 | 9 | 20 50 | 196 93 | | 123 81 |
| 249 | Beaverton | 8 | 13 | 30 00 | 81 08 | 161 83 | 83 40 |
| 250 | Ridgely | | | 56 55 | 135 50 | 230 50 | 473 60 |
| 251 | Bracebridge | | | 36 90 | 170 20 | | 73 52 |
| 252 | Floral | 3 | 12 | 16 60 | 64 50 | | 38 17 |
| 253 | Caledonia | | | 4 00 | 18 00 | | 38 85 |
| 254 | Alba | 3 | 9 | 12 35 | 135 00 | 28 25 | 47 32 |
| 255 | Tottenham | | | | | | |
| 256 | Grand Valley | 7 | 10 | 46 30 | 70 00 | 78 85 | 49 92 |
| 257 | Credit | | 5 | 6 00 | 97 50 | 24 32 | 64 69 |
| 258 | Thamesford | 16 | 9 | 84 20 | 321 25 | 7 41 | 36 49 |
| 259 | Lynden | 2 | 4 | 6 80 | 66 00 | 27 01 | 26 69 |
| 260 | Meaford | 8 | 8 | 43 50 | 136 26 | 2 00 | 49 61 |
| 261 | Gold Hill | 28 | 6 | 211 15 | 282 15 | 24 70 | 157 64 |
| 262 | Norwood | | 5 | | 83 43 | 12 00 | |
| 263 | East Toronto | 6 | 11 | 55 50 | 151 85 | 2 25 | 82 18 |
| 264 | Fraternity | 14 | 7 | 92 60 | 170 30 | | 335 82 |
| 265 | Delta | 1 | 6 | 7 60 | 113 85 | | 36 00 |
| 266 | Missanabie | 12 | 8 | 70 90 | 238 45 | 51 00 | 144 05 |
| 267 | Algoma | | | 46 60 | 185 70 | 28 00 | 216 55 |
| 268 | Stanley | 4 | 4 | 32 80 | 74 50 | | 25 43 |
| 269 | Woodstock | 26 | 7 | 203 75 | 246 64 | 5 55 | 497 44 |
| 270 | Lansdowne | 23 | 7 | 106 00 | 222 00 | | 172 13 |
| 271 | North Bay | 6 | 7 | 41 20 | 174 50 | 220 30 | 308 46 |
| 272 | Lakeview | | | 11 50 | 189 60 | | 73 26 |
| 273 | Hastings | | 5 | | 141 01 | 21 68 | 38 85 |
| 274 | Midland | 1 | 5 | 3 00 | 128 75 | | 99 66 |
| 275 | Fairy | 11 | 4 | 60 30 | 121 11 | | 65 99 |
| 276 | Sheard | 11 | 3 | 51 25 | 72 00 | 25 85 | 16 33 |
| 277 | Lambton | 15 | 9 | 94 80 | 159 35 | 18 55 | 121 51 |
| 278 | Rockcliffe | | 7 | 41 90 | 129 75 | 46 25 | 210 68 |
| 279 | Grenville | 10 | 2 | 55 95 | 206 20 | | 131 34 |
| 280 | Balmoral | 3 | 3 | 39 15 | 97 75 | | 143 50 |
| 281 | Arthur | 21 | 4 | 108 00 | 126 00 | 25 00 | 117 60 |
| 282 | Sudbury | 22 | 4 | 164 50 | 101 00 | | 218 30 |
| 283 | Earnscliffe | 24 | 4 | 88 60 | 119 00 | 46 50 | 260 72 |
| 284 | Lyn | 2 | 2 | 14 00 | 84 00 | | 70 39 |
| 285 | Morewood | | | 22 00 | 63 54 | | 86 85 |
| 286 | Royal | | 1 | 31 05 | 91 50 | 31 14 | 57 84 |
| 287 | Ripley | 15 | 1 | 60 00 | 88 97 | | 25 00 |
| 288 | Chesterville | 5 | 2 | 25 60 | 100 50 | | 52 91 |
| 289 | Glanworth | 3 | 1 | 12 00 | 135 00 | | |
| 290 | Tweed | 15 | 1 | 55 00 | 196 75 | | 125 30 |
| 291 | Rodney | 21 | 2 | 127 50 | 78 10 | 9 88 | 157 62 |
| 292 | Minnetonka | 96 | | 465 20 | 108 00 | | 380 39 |
| 293 | Thomasburg | 147 | 1 | 654 80 | 81 60 | | 80 67 |
| 294 | Broadview | 73 | 1 | 368 00 | | | 85 85 |
| | 31st Dec., 1892 | 2325 | 3383 | 14121 23 | 51017 93 | 19180 00 | 38589 38 |
| | 30th June, 1892 | 3004 | 3440 | 18603 49 | 55048 64 | 23444 09 | 41313 71 |
| | Year 31st Dec., 1892 | 5329 | 6823 | 32724 27 | 106066 57 | 42624 09 | 79903 09 |

## Term Ending 31st December, 1892.—Continued.

| Assets—How Invested. | | | | Funds. | | | | |
|---|---|---|---|---|---|---|---|---|
| Cash in Bank or in Treasurer's hands. | Invested in Mortgages and Securities. | Invested in Buildings and Lands. | Invested in Furniture and Regalia. | General Benefit Fund. | W. and O. Fund. | Contingent Fund. | Total Funds. | No. of Lodge. |
| $ c | $ c | $ c | $ c | $ c | $ c | $ c | $ c | |
| 1067 36 | | | 1100 00 | 2167 36 | | | 2167 36 | 235 |
| 679 34 | | | 140 00 | 819 34 | | | 819 34 | 236 |
| 883 17 | | | 350 00 | 811 45 | 421 72 | | 1233 17 | 237 |
| 394 59 | 1600 00 | | 1173 68 | 3107 38 | | 60 89 | 3168 27 | 239 |
| 595 11 | | | 2100 00 | 2695 11 | | | 2695 11 | 240 |
| 1808 69 | | | 1602 28 | 2528 87 | 756 56 | 125 54 | 3410 97 | 241 |
| 1014 11 | | | 283 51 | 246 43 | 1017 51 | 33 68 | 1297 62 | 242 |
| | | | | | | | | 243 |
| 1120 14 | 250 00 | | 1300 00 | 2086 11 | 578 09 | 5 94 | 2670 14 | 244 |
| 60 04 | 610 00 | 500 00 | 542 85 | 992 93 | 656 67 | 63 29 | 1712 89 | 245 |
| 520 94 | | | | 520 94 | | | 520 94 | 246 |
| 559 65 | | | | 389 56 | 166 39 | 3 70 | 559 65 | 247 |
| 1671 66 | | | 1073 83 | 2489 36 | 195 61 | 60 52 | 2745 49 | 248 |
| 175 78 | 1070 00 | | 175 00 | 662 34 | 580 75 | 177 39 | 1420 78 | 249 |
| 317 57 | 143 00 | 1650 50 | 292 50 | 2381 90 | | 21 67 | 2403 57 | 250 |
| 255 53 | 400 00 | | 693 00 | 815 17 | 533 36 | | 1348 53 | 251 |
| 311 35 | | | 525 00 | 836 35 | | | 836 35 | 252 |
| 242 85 | | | | 242 85 | | | 242 85 | 253 |
| 994 62 | | | 180 00 | 1114 25 | | 60 37 | 1174 62 | 254 |
| | | | | | | | | 255 |
| 269 27 | | | 214 00 | 234 07 | 249 20 | | 483 27 | 256 |
| 504 56 | | | 223 19 | 727 75 | | | 727 75 | 257 |
| 373 85 | 1600 00 | | 382 61 | 1942 45 | 383 61 | 10 40 | 2336 46 | 258 |
| 572 69 | | | 165 91 | 738 60 | | | 738 60 | 259 |
| 496 46 | | | 275 00 | 742 26 | | 29 20 | 771 46 | 260 |
| 704 81 | 75 00 | 1050 00 | 900 00 | 2712 86 | 6 50 | 10 45 | 2729 81 | 261 |
| 350 00 | | | 335 00 | 685 00 | | | 685 00 | 262 |
| 394 23 | | | 110 00 | 189 04 | 304 89 | 10 30 | 504 23 | 263 |
| 697 87 | | | 483 24 | 911 38 | 269 02 | 71 | 1181 11 | 264 |
| 251 48 | | | | 132 34 | 119 14 | | 251 48 | 265 |
| 175 55 | 700 00 | | 996 00 | 1871 55 | | | 1871 55 | 266 |
| 644 06 | | | 450 00 | 1094 06 | | | 1094 06 | 267 |
| 462 70 | | | 327 46 | 622 68 | 128 55 | 38 93 | 790 16 | 268 |
| 531 21 | | | 598 23 | 1129 43 | | | 1129 43 | 269 |
| 355 66 | | | 700 00 | 884 48 | 171 18 | | 1055 66 | 270 |
| 207 78 | 262 60 | | 1000 00 | 1470 38 | | | 1470 38 | 271 |
| 462 41 | | 137 50 | 184 93 | 755 68 | | 29 16 | 784 84 | 272 |
| 532 77 | | | 345 75 | 870 85 | | 7 67 | 878 52 | 273 |
| 188 56 | | | 600 00 | 788 56 | | | 788 56 | 274 |
| 425 63 | | | 270 23 | 487 41 | 201 45 | 7 00 | 695 86 | 275 |
| 300 00 | | | 179 38 | 460 45 | | 18 93 | 479 38 | 276 |
| 308 37 | 400 00 | | 250 00 | 939 82 | | 18 55 | 958 37 | 277 |
| 14 02 | | | 550 00 | 564 02 | | | 564 02 | 278 |
| 223 62 | | 200 00 | 366 04 | 789 66 | | | 789 66 | 279 |
| 139 24 | | | 228 60 | 286 28 | 81 56 | | 367 84 | 280 |
| 585 51 | | | 375 00 | 955 51 | 5 00 | | 960 51 | 281 |
| 139 56 | | | 450 00 | 589 56 | | | 589 56 | 282 |
| 185 18 | | | 330 00 | 471 68 | | 46 50 | 518 18 | 283 |
| | | 200 00 | 100 00 | 290 75 | 2 00 | 7 25 | 300 00 | 284 |
| 19 50 | | | 158 25 | 177 75 | | | 177 75 | 285 |
| 140 80 | | | 123 70 | 223 50 | 1 00 | | 264 50 | 286 |
| 294 92 | | | 154 69 | 449 61 | | | 449 61 | 287 |
| 160 67 | | | 200 00 | 325 57 | 35 10 | | 360 67 | 288 |
| 155 92 | | 75 00 | 100 00 | 330 92 | | | 330 92 | 289 |
| 341 78 | | | 50 00 | 383 43 | | 8 35 | 391 78 | 290 |
| 188 69 | | | 200 60 | 389 29 | | | 389 29 | 291 |
| 174 81 | | | 275 00 | 449 81 | | | 449 81 | 292 |
| 233 60 | | | 419 13 | 652 73 | | | 652 73 | 293 |
| 160 65 | | | 121 50 | 282 15 | | | 282 15 | 294 |
| 175026 83 | 183920 20 | 261451 31 | 165584 93 | 669406 77 | 103769 46 | 12807 04 | 785083 27 | |
| 164875 01 | 174030 70 | 262857 03 | 159482 00 | | | | | |
| 177183 30 | 184220 20 | 261451 31 | 165681 60 | 669527 15 | 104031 79 | 12898 47 | 786557 41 | |

# Minutes of the Third Annual Provincial Convention

OF THE

# DEGREE OF REBEKAH, I.O.O.F., ONTARIO,

HELD AT NIAGARA FALLS, AUG. 8, 1893.

NIAGARA FALLS, August 8, 1893.

The Third Annual Session of the Provincial Convention of the Degree of Rebekah, convened in the Odd Fellows' Hall, Niagara Falls, Ont , this day, at 10 o'clock a.m., the President, Sister Mrs. Prudence King, in the chair. The Convention opened by the singing of the Ode, followed by prayer by the Chaplain, Sister Penelope Savage.

The President then appointed the following Committee on Credentials : Sisters P. Savage, A. Edwards and Bro. P. McCallum.

The report of the Committee on Credentials was then read, as follows :—

We, your Committee, to whom was referred the credentials of Delegates, beg leave to submit the following list of delegates entitled to seats from the Degree of Rebekah Lodges of Ontario :—

| Victoria, No. 1 | SISTER E. A. PARKHOUSE. |
|---|---|
| Oshawa, No. 3 | " MARY E. DICKIE. |
| May Queen, No. 5 | " THOMPSON SHOWLER. |
| Naomi, No. 6 | " JANE DOUGLAS. |
| "   " | " ESTHER FRAZER. |
| Louise, No. 10 | " ELIZABETH LEE. |
| "   " | " ELLEN PERRY. |
| Beatrice, No. 12 | " RACHAEL MAHONEY. |
| Jubilee, No. 13 | " MARY MOORE. |
| Edna, No. 14 | " BARBARA SCOTT. |
| Harmony, No. 15 | " MINNIE WEBSTER. |
| "   " | " AGGIE EDWARDS. |
| Olive Branch, No. 16 | " M. A. PIERCE. |
| "   " | " L. E. RYAN. |
| "   " | " EMMA SEELS. |
| Myrtle, No. 17 | " PENELOPE SAVAGE. |
| Excelsior, No. 18 | " E. PATTISON. |
| Mizpah, No. 19 | " IDA CLELLAND. |
| Donalda, No. 20 | " J. H. HUGHES. |
| Flora, No. 21 | " S. J. CRACKNELL. |

Lucknow, No, 22................Brother W. H. Smith.
Inglewood, No. 23...............    ''      Lewis Masecar.
Prudence, No. 24 .... ...........    ''      Thos. L. Wood.
Alberta, No. 25......... .......Sister Sadie Schade.
Ivy, No. 26 ...................    ''      Minnie S. Bascom.
Esther, No. 27.................. Brother S. D. Warren.
Colfax, No. 28................ .....Sister Jane Luscombe.
At the Well, No. 29......... .....Brother Peter McCallum.

Respectfully submitted,

P. McCALLUM,
A. EDWARDS,
P. SAVAGE.

The roll was then called, with all Officers present, as follows :—

President............Sister Prudence King.
Vice-President ......    ''      Elizabeth Reid.
Secretary ............    ''      Maggie Waddell.
Treasurer ............    ''      Hester Shiels.
Warden ............    ''      Elizabeth Seaton.
Inside Guardian.......    ''      Nellie Smith.
Chaplain ............    ''      Penelope Savage.

All delegates answered to their names except Sisters Mary E. Dickie, Emma Seels, Ida Clelland, and Brother T. L. Wood.

---

Sister Mrs. Prudence King, President, presented the following report, which was on motion referred to a Special Committee on Distribution :—

Niagara Falls, Ont., August 8, 1893.

*To the Rebekah Convention, I. O. O. F. :*

Sisters and Brothers.—The ceaseless flight of time has again brought us together in Annual Session in this historic town and within sound of Niagara's thundering cataract, and we are reminded that a year has passed since we parted with joyous hopes for a year of success and happiness to individual and to Lodge. I need hardly assure you that I greatly appreciate the honor you then conferred on me in selecting me to preside over the body, and though the duties have been by no means arduous, I have, in every way that I have been able, endeavoured to uphold the honor of the Rebekahs and advance their interests, and in doing so, advance the noble cause of Odd-fellowship.

I am pleased indeed, to meet those whose friendship I have before made, as well as those we meet for the first time, and I welcome you to this Convention with the hope that its deliberations will be fraught with much good to the cause we all hold so dear.

I am pleased to report that the year has been a most prosperous one, old Lodges seem to have awakened, and new ones started up to help carry along our banner.

Ten new Lodges have been instituted, as follows:—

| | | | | | | |
|---|---|---|---|---|---|---|
| Nov. | 2, 1892 | Flora Rebekah Lodge, | No. 21 | ...... | Sault Ste. Marie. |
| Dec. | 9, " | Lucknow Rebekah Lodge, | " 22 | ...... | Lucknow. |
| " | 27, " | Inglewood " | " | " 23 | ...... | Waterford. |
| Feb. | 24, 1893 | Prudence " | " | " 24 | ...... | Brantford. |
| April | 17, " | Alberta " | " | " 25 | .... | Kincardine. |
| " | 28, " | Ivy " | " | " 26 | ... | Galt. |
| May | 18, " | Esther " | " | " 27 | ...... | Niagara Falls. |
| " | 29, " | Colfax " | " | " 28 | ...... | Sarnia. |
| June | 20, " | At the Well " | " | " 29 | ..... | Almonte. |
| July | 6, " | Aberdeen " | " | " 30 | ...... | Deseronto. |

and a petition, I understand, has been received for a Lodge at East Toronto.

A petition was granted by the Grand Master for a Lodge at Wingham, but as yet the Lodge has not been instituted ; the reason I am unable to say.

The membership on June 30th, as reported to the Grand Secretary, was 1,446, being an increase of 445 since we last met, a result which must fill each sister's and brother's heart with gratitude.

There are quite a number of Rebekah Lodges in Ontario, which I think, with a reasonable effort might be revived, and their co-operation again secured. I refer to "Our Sister Lodge" at Point Edward, Hope Lodge at Hamilton, Ruth Lodge at Napanee, Bethuel Lodge at Barrie, Picton Lodge at Picton ; these Lodges were once active but are now dormant. I would be pleased indeed to learn a year hence that each of these Lodges has been restored to active life and usefulness.

We have in the Rebekah Degree an opportunity by which we ladies, who are privileged to become members, may add greatly to our usefulness, and aid greatly in the great philanthropic work Oddfellowship is engaged in. Our Lodge work gives us, who regularly attend to its duties, an insight into general business, which will not only enlarge our ideas and be a benefit to us in the every-day duties of life, but will also bring us into contact with that portion of Oddfellowship in which woman is

so well fitted to take even more than her share.  To be as useful as we desire to be in this sphere, our work and conduct of
Lodge business must be most carefully guarded—no personal
feelings should be allowed to sway judgment when considering
matters of interest to our Lodges, or when selecting officers
upon whom for a season the welfare not only of the Lodge, but
the good of the whole Order, so largely depends.  The general
good should be paramount.  We all are apt at times to be
warped in judgment by personsl feelings.  If we would keep
our Lodges in a state of prosperity and usefulness, every member must be most guarded and circumspect in all matters relating to our own Lodge work, and in no case say, in the absence
of a sister or brother, that which we would not say in their
presence.  By carefully guarding our acts in this respect and by
faithfully attending to all the duties which for the time our
Lodges place upon us, we may make the Rebekah branch of
Odd Fellows one whose influence will be felt all over our fair
land, and bring upon it showers of blessing.

On April 12th, I wired to Sister King, President of the
Rebekah Convention of Ohio, a message of congratulation, believing that such exchange of courtesies is both beneficial and
pleasant, and I ask approval of my act.  The reply received
from Sister King, which is herewith submitted, will show the
appreciation of our Sister Convention, and will, I trust, justify
my action.

The beautiful floor work has done much to make the
Rebekah Degree popular, and deservedly so.  The movements
required in the work can be done by none so gracefully and perfectly as by ladies, but to do so in a satisfactory manner the
greatest of care must be exercised, and perfection in this, as in
everything else in life, is only attained by sacrifice of time and
thorough devotion to the work in hand.

The operations of the Rebekah Lodges have, I believe, been
seriously impeded for want of a constitution for Subordinates.
I would suggest that the Grand Lodge be requested to provide
a Constitution and to supply each Lodge with a number of
copies, and that this Convention pass a law requiring every
Lodge to adopt a code of By-laws as promptly as possible.

In November last, I received from the Grand Sire, Bro. Dr.
Campbell, a circular in regard to the National Rebekah Convention, to assemble in Chicago in September next.  As each
jurisdiction will have to bear the expense of the delegates it may
elect, it will be for this Assembly to decide if it will be represented on that occasion.  The circular is appended hereto.

I do not consider that the duties of the officers of the

Rebekah Convention are sufficiently defined at present, and it is difficult to know just what duties those officers are required to perform. Under the laws of the order, the Lodges are requested to report directly to the Grand Secretary, and no provision is made for reports to this Convention. It will be for you to consider what, if any, changes in the law should be recommended to the Grand Lodge.

I would suggest that it would be made a part of the duty of each D. D. G. M. of a Rebekah Lodge to report half-yearly to the President as well as to the Grand Master, in order that officers may have a knowledge of how the several Lodges are working. At present, as I understand the law, this Convention has no supervision whatever over Subordinates. It is difficult to know what, if any, powers it has other than a supervision over its own annual meetings. I believe some action should be made by this meeting to bring the Convention, the Lodges and the Grand Lodge into closer touch with each other for the welfare of each.

I am pleased to report that the Grand Master has deputized two Sisters (D. D. G. M.) to institute Rebekah Lodges, and I am satisfied that these Sisters did their work well. It was my pleasant privilege to be present and assist at one of these—I refer to Ivy, No. 26, at Galt—Sister Brill, accompanied by the excellent staff of Beatrice Lodge, of Guelph, did the work most creditably. I have to thank both Beatrice and Ivy Lodges for kindness received. I was also privileged to be present and assist the D. D. G. M., Brother R. Brocklank, in the institution of Prudence Lodge, in my old home, Brantford. There, also, I was the recipient of courtesies I will not soon forget and for which I am deeply grateful.

I am pleased to bear testimony to the zeal of our Secretary, Sister Waddell, with whom my relations during the year have been pleasant and agreeable.

In June I issued a circular to the Lodges, urging each to be alive to the duty of the hour, and to show the Order the wisdom of having women as an auxiliary to its great mission. I believe good results have followed it.

In closing my report, I desire to express again my appreciation of the honor I have received at your hands, and I earnestly hope our deliberations of this year will be pleasant and profitable, and redound to the benefit of the Rebekahs and of the Order we all so much love and respect, and that the friendships here formed may be such as will leave but pleasant memories during our future lives.

Respectfully submitted

MRS. PRUDENCE KING,
*President.*

The Secretary, Sister Mrs. Maggie Waddell, then presented the following report, which was on motion referred to the Committee on Distribution :—

*To the Officers and Members of the Provincial Convention of the Degree of Rebekah, I.O.O F., of Ontario:*

Third Annual Assembly, Niagara Falls, Ont., 1893.

Another year has flown, and we, the Officers and Representatives of noble sentiment and trustworthy aims have assembled from all parts of Ontario for mutual counsel and advice and for the best interest of our beloved Order, subject to the approval of the Grand Lodge.

It gives me great pleasure to welcome you, my Sisters and Brothers, to the Third Annual Convention. I am glad to see among your number many who have attended both of the previous Sessions and that have been instrumental in its organization ; such members challenge our sincere admiration, for, without their persistent efforts, we might still be groping in the dark, wholly depending on another branch of the Order.

To the new members allow me to say, we are doubly glad to welcome you in our ranks, for, without your assistance and encouragement, we would be little better off than we were a year ago, for whatever fails to advance in prosperity has a tendency to retrograde, and what is true in individual cases is equally true in Associations.

The new enthusiastic members in an Order are sometimes the shining lights, like the brilliant stars in the Heavens, snedding their light over the more somber hues of those who have been longer in the work, thereby rekindling the drowsy interest to a new and more intense activity.

When, two years ago, you conferred on me the honor of electing me your Secretary, I little dreamed of the responsibility, and as the time goes on I find the work increasing ; had I known or suspected at that time that there would have been so much work I would have hesitated seriously before accepting the trust,but by coustant study I have been able to keep up the work. It is certainly very gratifying to report that we have added ten new Lodges to our number—Donalda, No. 20, North Bay ; Flora Lodge, No. 21, Sault Ste Marie ; Lucknow Lodge, No. 22, Lucknow ; Inglewood Lodge, No. 23, Waterford ; Prudence Lodge, No. 24, Brantford ; Alberta Lodge, No. 25, Kincardine ; Ivy Lodge, No. 26, Galt ; Esther Lodge, No. 27, Niagara Falls ; Colfax Lodge, No. 28, Sarnia ; At the Well Lodge, No 29, Almont, making a total of twenty-three Lodges in Ontario.

As promptly as possible the minutes of 1892 were compiled and printed as ordered by Grand Lodge Journal, also a number in pamphlet form which I distributed to the Secreraries of the different State Assemblies. I have received a number in return.

The past year has been a fruitful one in the history of our Order in Ontario and it gives me great pleasure to say that our particular branch thereof has been fully abreast of the progressive spirit of the times in advancement. While the number representing our present membership does not seem to indicate as large a percentage of gain as has actually been the case, yet a great deal of decaying and useless timber has been turned away by careful guardians of the interest of our Rebekah Lodges. That judicious pruning adds to the growth of plant life has been demonstrated by the best horticulturists. That it will prove beneficial to the interest of our beloved Order, years to come will demonstrate.

The increase in membership has not been of the fungus or mushroom growth, but more the natural steady advancement made by the vine when properly cultivated by capable gardeners and whose progress is smiled upon by a beneficent Creator who is pleased with the philanthropist's efforts to ameliorate the condition of his fellow men and make plain and smooth the rough and rugged places in life's journey.

I have written and sent out about 425 letters, cards and circulars.

EXPENSES FOR THIS YEAR.

| | | | |
|---|---|---|---:|
| Aug. | 10. | Mileage and per diem | $208 44 |
| " | 10. | Check | 50 |
| " | 10. | Cashing check | 25 |
| " | 10. | Postage, Treas | 12 |
| " | 15. | 1 quire foolscalp | 20 |
| " | 15. | 1 ledger, Treas | 75 |
| " | 21. | 100 letter-heads Pres | 1 00 |
| " | 21. | 50 envelopes, Pres | 50 |
| " | 21. | 100 receipts | 1 25 |
| " | 21. | 100 envelopes, large | 75 |
| " | 21. | Copying book. | 1 50 |
| " | 21. | Copying ink | 25 |
| " | 21. | Letterheads, Sec | 1 50 |
| Sept. | 14. | Pens and blotting paper | 50 |
| Oct. | 14. | 50 letterheads, Treas | 75 |
| " | 25. | 25 envelopes, Treas | 50 |
| Dec. | 17. | 50 envelopes, small | 50 |
| Jan. | 23. | 100 envelopes, Sec | 75 |
| June | 2. | 50 envelopes, Sec | 50 |
| " | 25. | 50 envelopes, Sec | 50 |
| " | 25. | 75 certificates | 1 00 |
| July | 6. | 100 envelopes, Sec | 75 |
| " | 11. | 1 quire foolscalp. | 20 |
| " | 22. | 1 letter-file | 2 00 |
| " | 29. | To letter-heads | 50 |
| " | 15. | To badges for Convention | 6 00 |

| | | | |
|---|---|---|---|
| July | 15. Express on same...... | 8 | 25 |
| " | 27. Express on programmes...... | | 35 |
| Dec. | 13, 1892. Expense visiting Victoria Lodge No. 1...... | 1 | 00 |
| Aug. | 14, 1892. Drayage on books at Windsor...... | 1 | 00 |
| " | 8, 1893. To postage...... | 9 | 32 |
| " | 8. Expenses of President...... | 8 | 40 |
| " | 8. Expenses of Treasurer...... | $251 | 78 |

|  | | |
|---|---|---|
| Received from J. B. King, Capitation Tax, April 20...... | $112 | 50 |
| "    "    "    "    " Aug. 5...... | 144 | 60 |
| Which has been handed over to our Treasurer. | $257 | 10 |

Victoria Lodge, No 1, London, had at last report 2 Brothers,
10 Sisters. Total, 12 Members assets of $44.64. Present
membership is 2 Brothers and 10 Sisters. Total, 12. Assets,
$45.92 ; relief, $10.00

Oshawa Lodge, No. 3, Oshawa, had at last report 7 Brothers,
26 Sisters. Total number of members, 33 Assets, $237 21.
Present membership is 8 Brothers, 17 Sisters. Total, 25.
Assets, $214 36.

May Queen Lodge, No. 5, London, had at last report 24
Brothers, 63 Sisters. Total, 87. Members with assets, $48.85.
Present membership is 18 Brothers, 34 Sisters. Total, 52.
Assets, $137.49; relief, $18.00.

Naomi Lodge, No. 6, Windsor, had at last report 23 Brothers, 53 Sisters Total, 76. With assets, $810.22. Present
membership is 72 Brothers and 59 Sisters. Total, 131. Assets,
$789.78 ; relief, $13.00

Louise Lodge, No 10, Kingston, had at last report 27 Brothers, 52 Sisters. Total, 79. With assets, $161.30. Membership
at present, 48 Brothers, 52 Sisters. Total, 100. Assets, $275 26.

Beatrice Lodge, No. 12, Guelph, had at last report 47 Brothers, 40 Sisters. Total, 87. With assets, $104.81. Present
membership is 40 Brothers, 43 Sisters. Total, 83. Assets,
$151 76.

Jubilee Lodge, No 13, Chatham, had at last report 5 Brothers, 26 Sisters. Total, 31. With assets, $65.85. Present
membership is 7 Brothers and 27 Sisters. Total, 34. Assets,
$54.91.

Edna Lodge, No. 14, St. Thomas, had at last report 39
Brothers, 47 Sisters. Total, 86. With assets, $215.23. Present
membership is 36 Brothers, 46 Sisters. Total, 82. Assets,
$168.35 ; relief, $291.85.

Harmony Lodge, No. 15, Gananoque, had at last report 94 Brothers, 99 Sisters. Total, 193. With assets, $377 89. Present membership, 77 Brothers and 96 Sisters. Total, 173. Assets, $395.35.

Olive Branch Lodge, No. 16, Toronto, had at last report 114 Brothers, 89 Sisters. Total, 203. With assets, $420.61. Present membership is 120 Brothers, 87 Sisters. Total, 207. Assets, $490 14 ; relief, $5.00.

Myrtle Lodge, No. 17, Elora, had at last report 14 Brothers, 17 Sisters. Total, 31. With assets, $20.53. Present membership, 18 Brothers, 17 Sisters. Total, 35. Assets, $23.02.

Excelsior Lodge, No. 18, International Bridge, had at last report 18 Brothers, 28 Sisters. Total, 46. With assets, $65.00 Present membership 21 Brothers, 32 Sisters. Total, 53. Assets, $37.79.

Mizpah Lodge, Collingwood, had at last report 25 Brothers, 13 Sisters. Total, 38. With assets, $13.31. Present membership, 30 Brothers, 34 Sisters. Total, 64 Assets, $15 79.

LODGES THAT HAVE BEEN INSTITUTED SINCE JULY 1ST, 1892.

Donalda Lodge, No. 20, North Bay, instituted July, 1892, by our worthy Brother, Past Master P. E. Fitzpatrick. Present membership is 22.

Flora Lodge, No. 21, Sault Ste. Marie, instituted October, 1892, by our worthy Brother, A. B. Cracknell. Present membership, 16 Brothers, 10 Sisters. Total, 26. Assets, none.

Lucknow Lodge, No. 22, Lucknow, instituted November. 1892, by our esteemed Grand Secretary, Bro J. B. King. Present membership, 39 Brothers, 27 Sisters. Total, 66. Assets, $28.73 ; relief, $2.00.

Inglewood Lodge, No. 23, Waterford, instituted by our worthy Brother, John Waddell, December 27th, 1892. Present membership, 14 Brothers, 13 Sisters. Total, 27. Assets, $2.53.

Prudence Lodge, No. 24, Brantford, instituted Feb. 24th, 1893, by our worthy Brother, R. Brockbank, assisted by our very worthy President, Sister King. Present membership, 30 Brothers, 35 Sisters. Total, 65. Assets, $6.95.

Alberta Lodge, No. 25, Kincardine, instituted April 17, 1893, by our worthy Grand Secretary, Bro. J. B. King. Present membership, 25 Brothers, 22 Sisters. Total, 47. Assets, $12.00.

Ivy Lodge, No. 26, Galt, instituted by our worthy and much esteemed Sister, Alma Brill, of Guelph, April 29th, 1893. Present membership, 33 Brothers, 30 Sisters. Total, 63. Assets, $27.10.

Esther Lodge, No. 27, Niagara Falls, instituted May 18th, 1893, by our worthy and much esteemed Sister, Esther Fraser, of Windsor. Present membership, 20 Brothers, 12 Sisters. Total, 32. Assets, $18.55.

Colfax Lodge, No. 28, Sarnia, instituted May 29th, 1893, by Past Grand Master John Gibson. Present membership, 7 Brothers, 7 Sisters. Total, 14. Assets, none.

Atthewell Lodge, No. 29, Almont, instituted June 20th, 1893, by our worthy Brother, Peter McCallum. Present membership, 11 Brothers, 22 Sisters. Total, 33. Assets, $4.95.

Number of Lodges last report, 13. Instituted during the year, 10. Total, 23.

Membership last report, 440 Brothers, 561 Sisters. Total, 1,001.

Admitted during the year, 435 Brothers, 375 Sisters. Total, 810.

Died, 6 Brothers, 6 Sisters. Total, 12.

Withdrawn and suspended, 173 Brothers, 180 Sisters Total, 353.

Total present membership, June 30, 1893, 705 Brothers, 741 Sisters. Total, 1,446.

I often wonder if our immortal and noble-minded Schuyler Colfax, realized when he instituted the Degree in 1857 what the growth and outcome would be. Knowing as he did the many attempts that have been made to establish a Degree for women, but without success, owing in part to the deep-seated prejudices and narrow-mindedness of our Brother-man at that time, who, like Paul, thought if women learn anything, let them ask their husbands at home.

The establishment of the Degree, like all other experiments, had to abide its time and grow slowly but surely into favour, and our Brothers became more enlightened and liberal-minded, and it began to dawn on their beclouded brain the extent and power of woman's intelligence and capabilities that the old foggy notions vanished like the mist of the morning, and with the growth of civilization these ideas have almost become extinct, and we Sisters who have waited so long for our God-given rights and as the laws limiting the membership of this Degree to grow stronger and wider each year, are rejoicing that we are enabled to stand on a firm foundation in the front ranks, recognized as capable of occupying the highest station of the Order.

We are co-workers in the great cause, a universal Brotherhood, as it were, linked together with the bonds of Friendship, Love and Truth, whose aims are to alleviate the helpless and distressed and to minister to the needy members of our fraternal family, as it were, and, if I mistake not, members of the oldest women's society now in existence.

For more than fifteen years after the establishment of this Degree the Sisters were not eligible to hold office, and not until the year 1867, were we permitted to hold anything but minor offices, but as time rolled on and our Brothers became more lenient we were allowed to occupy all the offices. Yet, with this advancement, we are aware our Order is but yet in its infancy, but, with the nourishing food it receives yearly, it is rapidly growing out of its swaddling clothes and in a few more years it will have grown to maturity, and with its growth our power of doing good will increase and the fruits of our labor become more apparent, as some of the work pertaining to Oddfellowship is especially adapted to us.

Then, Sisters, in view of all this, let us not be discouraged, but profit by the failures and successes and grasp the idea of our Grand Sire, Cl. T. Campbell, that the salt of Oddfellowship is to be found in the Degree of Rebekah, that the Rebekah has come to stay.

And, while it behoves us as zealous workers to labor for the good of our Order and for our fellow women, we should not allow our zeal to overcome our discretion, but try to carry out the principles that we espouse.

We have assembled here to day at Niagara Falls, in the very midst of nature's choicest and most beautiful bounties and within view of the grandest exhibition of the Creator's handiwork, from all over Ontario, to review the work of the past year; to devise the best and most practical method for promoting the growth and welfare of our cherished Order ; to become more thoroughly conversant with its laws and usages.

I sincerely hope all selfishness, small differences of opinion and petty jealousies will be cast aside, remembering ever it is for the good of the Order. We are here for labor, and we have work to do which no other branch of the Order can do and whatever is worth doing is worth doing well.

It is gratifying to see so many new Lodges represented, and my earnest desire is that we may legislate wisely and for the advancement of the Rebekah Degree. The outlook for this Degree in this jurisdiction has never been so promising as at the present time. We should then labor with renewed vigor and diligence.

I feel I should be wanting in not giving proper expression of sincere gratitude to our most worthy President, Sister King, to Grand Master, Rev. T. W. Jolliffe, for their kindness to me during my term, and I especially thank Grand Secretary J. B. King for his wise consel and the prompt manner he has responded to all my enquiries.

Thanking you, one and all, I surrender to the disposition of your will the important trust that has been in my official keeping for the past year, and I trust that the events of this Session will be productive to the good of the Order and pleasant and profitable to those in attendance.

All of which is respectfully submitted in Friendship, Love and Truth.

MISS MAGGIE WADDELL,<br>
Secretary.

Sister Mrs. Hester Shields, Treasurer, read the following report, which was on motion referred to tne financial committee.

*To the President, Officers and Members of the Provincial Convention, Degree of Rebekah, I O O F :*

| 1892. | | Dr. | |
|---|---|---:|---:|
| June 8th, Mrs. Waddell, credit by cash | | $199 | 10 |
| " " " " " | | 100 | 60 |
| Total | | $299 | 70 |
| Aug. 10th, Mrs. Waddell, to cash for expenses | $ 38 20 | | |
| " " Mileage, per diem | 208 44 | | |
| " " Cheque | 50 | | |
| " " Cashing cheque | 25 | | |
| " " Postage | 12 | | |
| " " Mrs. Waddell, for expenses | 50 00 | | |
| Total | | $297 | 51 |
| Balance to date | | 2 | 19 |
| 1893, April 28th, Received from Secretary | $112 50 | | |
| Aug. 8th, " " " | 144 60 | | |
| | | $257 | 10 |
| Total cash on hand | | $259 | 29 |

This being the close of my official term as your Treasurer, I now take this opportunity to express my thanks to the officers and delegates of this convention for their many favours and acts of kindness.

Respectfully submitted,

HESTER SHIELDS,<br>
Treasurer.

18

The President appointed the following committees :—

SPECIAL COMMITTEE ON DISTRIBUTION—Sister Savage, Sister Bascom and Brother Warren.

COMMITTEE ON LEGISLATION—Bro. Mascar, Sisters Pierce and Cracknell.

COMMITTEE ON THE STATE OF THE ORDER—Sisters Ryan, Douglas, Schade, Scott and Edwards.

COMMITTEE ON FINANCE—Bro. Smith, Sisters Dickie, Perry, Fraser and Bro. McCallum.

COMMITTEE ON CORRESPONDENCE—Sisters Lee, Mahoney and Moore.

At this stage of proceedings Grand Secretary J. B. King addressed the convention and advised them not to ask for any new legislation, as the Sovereign Grand Lodge had appointed a Committee at its last session to revise the whole Rebekah Degree, and that no doubt that at the next session of that body a new constitution will be adopted and distributed to all Rebekah Lodges.

Moved by Bro. McCallum, seconded by Sister Pattison,—

That we adjourn until 2 p. m. Carried.


TUESDAY, Aug. 8th, 2 o'clock p. m.

Convention met pursuant to adjournment, with the President, Sister Prudence King, in the chair. All officers and delegates present except Sister Seels and Bro. Wood, neither of whom attended convention on account of sickness in their families.

The report of Special Committee on Distribution of the President's, Secretary's and Treasurer's reports was then read by Bro. S. D. Warren and the subjects referred to the various Committees, as follows :—

STATE OF THE ORDER, President's Report—Clauses 1, 2, 3, 4, 5, 6, 7, 12, 13 and 14.

Secretary's Report—Clauses 1, 2, 4, 5.

COMMITTEE ON LEGISLATION, President's Report— Clauses 8, 10, 11.

COMMITTEE ON FINANCE, President's Report—Clause 9.

Secretary's Report—Clause 3, and the whole of the Treasurer's report.

Clause 13, Secretary's Report—Report of Special Committee.

*Resolved,*—That the foregoing be adopted.

All of which is respectfully submitted.

S. D. WARREN.
PENELOPE SAVAGE.
WINNIE L. BASCOM.

The following reports of the work of the several Lodges were then submitted :—

*To the Provincial Convention Degree of Rebekah :*

Ivy Lodge, No. 26, Galt, Ont.—Instituted April 28th, 1893, by Sister Brill, D.D., being the first Sister authorized to do such work, assisted by Sister King, President of the Rebekah Convention, and also Bro. Blackeby. The Degree Staff, from Guelph, exemplified the floor work as recommended by the Grand Lodge in such an encouraging manner that we selected our captain, picked our staff of officers, intend to "beg, borrow or steal" the money to purchase our paraphernalia and expect to be able to put through all the material we can find to work on in the next year. We think our officers are filling their positions in an able manner for young members. We think our Lodge in a prosperous condition, having started with a membership of fifty-six and still on the increase.

WINNIE L. BASCOM, N.G.,

*Representative.*

*To the Grand Convention of the Degree of Rebekah, I.O.O.F.:*

SISTERS AND BRETHREN,—On behalf of Mizpah Degree Lodge, No. 19, Collingwood, I beg to report that our lodge is in a very flourishing condition and is rapidly growing in favour among the members of the Subordinate Lodge, and that we are adding to our members at nearly every meeting. When the last Grand Convention met we were a young institution, having only been in existence for a month and a-half and having forty-two members, twenty-six brothers and sixteen sisters. I am pleased to be able to report that during the year we have nearly doubled our numbers, having initiated four brothers and nineteen sisters, making a total of sixty-five members. It is also a pleasure to me to report that since our institution we have not had to suspend a member for any cause whatever. The meetings are well attended and all take an interest in the welfare of the lodge. On the 24th of May last, Mizpah Lodge was visited by the degree team of Olive Branch Lodge, Toronto, who exhibited to our members the dramatized work. This visit, it is needless to say, was a great event in the history of our lodge and will be remembered with pleasure. Its effects will also present themselves in the near future, as a degree team will soon be at work. In closing I may say that there is no doubt of the future success of Mizpah Lodge.

IDA G. CLELAND.

COLLINGWOOD, Aug. 8, 1893.

I take great pleasure in reporting the continued prosperity of Myrtle Lodge, No. 17, Elora.

A very successful year has been passed, not so much in the addition of great numbers, but in the continued and, I may say, increased interest taken by the members in the Order.

During the winter months the attendance was fairly good and the evenings were spent in profitable social intercourse and amusements, after the ordinary work had been accomplished. On two occasions the members united with the members of the Odd Fellows' Lodge in giving public entertainments in the Odd Fellows' Hall. At both friends were invited, and a sufficient number accepted to fill to its utmost capacity the room, a most enjoyable and pleasant programme being supplied by the conjoined committees.

During the year the Sisters made themselves a set of beautiful regalia, of which they are justly proud. They had to bear the loss of one of their number by death, and one who from the inception of the lodge took a leading and very active part in the work. The members will long remember with sacred pleasure the smiling face and general loving manner of Sister Bock.

The finances have been fairly well attended to, very few allowing themselves to get into arrears. The work of the lodge was well conducted, the officers taking a pride in doing it well.

There is no doubt but the success of Myrtle Lodge in the immediate future is assured, and though it cannot become large in numbers it will certainly do a good work and be the source of much profit and pleasure to its members.

PENELOPE SAVAGE, PAST GRAND,

AUG. 5th, 1893.                              Myrtle Lodge, No. 17, Elora.

*To the Third Annual Provincial Convention of the Degree of Rebekah, at Niagara Falls, August 8th, 1893:*

WORTHY PRESIDENT AND REPRESENTATIVES,—On behalf of Harmony Lodge, No. 15, D. of R., Gananoque, we beg leave to present this report and are also desirous of conveying to you greeting for a prosperous session, trusting that every judicious effort put forth may be crowned with success for the advancement of the Order we love so well.

Although we are the most easterly of the D. of R. Lodges in Ontario, yet we are strong in sympathy with every move in the good work in which you are engaged.

May the good accomplished at this time radiate and enthuse to increased activity every member of our Order.

During the past year we are indeed pleased to report progress. Not in membership, but in a clearer and more perfect knowledge of the great principles symbolized by the triple chain. At the close of the term, ending June 30th, 1893, our membership stood :—Brothers 80 and Sisters 93, making a total of 173. This is a slight decrease in the total as reported June 30th, 1892, and is owing to causes over which we had no control. However, we are looking forward to a marked increase during the present term.

Our financial standing, although not great, is quite satisfactory. We are well equipped with pharaphernalia for degree, staff officers' regalia, badges, etc. We have no benefits in connection with the lodge, as it has been deemed advisable not to take this step.

In January of this year we adopted the Grand Lodge floor work, whereas formerly we were using the California Beautified Work. The change was decidedly better, and proves very interesting and beneficial in vivifying and impressing the beautiful lessons of our Ritual.

With our efficient staff of officers for the present term, we anticipate still greater advantages, to enable us to perform faithfully the ennobling duties of Odd Fellowship.

Again we trust that divine wisdom and strength may be granted this assembly during this session.

MRS. MINNIE WEBSTER,<br>AGGIE EDWARDS,

GANANOQUE, Aug. 8th, 1893.                              *Representatives.*

*To the Provincial Convention, Degree of Rebekah, I.O.O.F.*

WORTHY PRESIDENT :—On behalf of Excelsior Lodge, No. 18, I am pleased to report that we are in good working order.

You will perhaps remember that at the last Grand Convention we reported a membership of 46. During the past year we have initiated six ladies and four gentlemen, have granted one withdrawal card, and suspended one for non-payment of dues, leaving us with 54 members at the present time. We have had twelve of our members on the sick list who have needed attendance during the year, all of whom, I am happy to say, are entirely recovered.

We have had one open meeting, which, in my opinion, was productive of some good.

We have, as a lodge, paid one visit each to Colfax and Vesta Lodges of Buffalo, and have received return visits from them.

We have increased our available assets during the past twelve months to the value of $200. This we have done partly from dues and partly by holding one social, one picnic, and one ball.

On May the 7th we accepted an invitation from the Subordinate Lodge, No. 228, to attend with them Divine worship in commemoration of the 76th anniversary of the Order.

We have almost completed our purchase of paraphernalia for conferring the Degree in the beautified form, as recommended by the Sovereign Grand Lodge.

I might add, we have appointed our Recording Secretary as lodge correspondent to the *National Odd Fellow*, by doing which we have helped to keep our lodge prominently before the Odd Fellows and Rebekahs of Buffalo and the western part of New York State.

E. PATTISON,<br>
Representative.

*To the Officers and Representatives of the Third Annual Convention of the Rebekah Degree, Ontario, I.O.O.F.:*

Beatrice Lodge, No. 12, Guelph, has at present forty brothers and forty-three sisters. Total, eighty-three. Receipts, $82.05. Assets, $200.19. Funeral benefits, $10.

We have four *Past Grands* in good standing. Although we have lost members by removal from the city and otherwise, we cannot but feel that our lodge is in a flourishing condition. We have every prospect of increasing our membership during the present term. Our Degree work is taken up with enthusiasm, and each one feels her personal responsibility in making our initiatory ceremony impressive and effective. We have had the honor, assisted by our worthy President, Sister King, of instituting Ivy Lodge, No. 26, of Galt, with a membership of 56. That our Order may prosper and extend its field of usefulness is the sincere wish of Beatrice Lodge, No. 12, Guelph, Ont.

I also wish to make mention of our late Bro. Thomas Hayes, who was one of the first to join the Order in Guelph, died on June 21st, '93, after a lingering illness of over one year. During this painful period we have had opportunity of attempting at last to carry out the principles of Odd Fellowship. That we have not failed in this particular is evidenced by the deep gratitude of our afflicted sister and worthy Vice Grand, Mrs Thomas Hayes.

Yours fraternally,<br>
RACHAEL MAHONEY.

*To the Officers and Members of the Rebekah Convention:*

As representative of Louise Lodge, No. 10, Kingston, I beg leave to report that for the past half year the lodge has increased in membership, also in finances, to that extent which assures us of the prosperity of the lodge in future. The business has been done in a harmonious and business-like way and each and every member has striven with each other to do all they can to promote the welfare of this Degree in this city. Since the last meeting of the Convention, assisted by the members of Louise Lodge, I had the pleasure of instituting a Lodge of Rebecca Degree in the town of Deseronto, starting with a membership of 37. Judging from the appearances of the members the prosperity of that lodge is assured.

Respectfully submitted.     Yours in F.L.T.,

ELIZABETH LEE,<br>
Representative.

Considerable discussion took place on the unwritten work, when it was decided to lay it over until to-morrow, when the Grand Sire, Cl. T. Campbell, would be present.

The Election of Officers was then proceeded with.  The President appointed Brothers Fitz-Patrick, Dickie and Brockbank scrutineers.

Nominations for President were as follows :  Sisters Reid, Seaton and Brill.

First Ballot—Sister Reid, 20 ;  Seaton, 4 ;  Brill, 7.

Sister Reid was declared elected President for the ensuing year.

Nominations for Vice-President were as follows :  Sisters Brill, Seaton, Ryan, Edwards and Lee.

First ballot—Sister Brill, 5 ;  Seaton, 8 ;  Ryan, 9 ;  Edwards, 3 ;  Lee, 7.

Second ballot—Sister Brill, 4 ;  Seaton, 8 ;  Ryan, 13 ;  Lee, 6.

Third ballot—Sister Seaton, 10 ;  Ryan, 12 ;  Lee, 9.

Fourth ballot—Sister Seaton, 19 ;  Ryan, 13.

Sister Seaton was declared elected for the ensuing year.

Nominations for Secretary:  Sister Waddell was declared elected by acclamation for the ensuing year.

Nominations for Treasurer were as follows :  Sisters Smith, Shields and Pierce.

First ballot—Sister Smith, 12 ;  Shields, 11 ;  Pierce, 7.

Second ballot—Sister Smith, 20 ;  Shields, 12.

Sister Smith was then declared elected for the ensuing year.

Moved by Sister Moore, seconded by Sister Douglas,—

That a vote of thanks be tendered the scrutineers.

Carried.

A circular was then read from the Sovereign Grand Lodge asking this Convention to send delegates to the National Convention.

Referred to Financial Committee.

Moved by Sister Seaton, seconded by Sister Fraser,—

That we adjourn to meet at 9 a. m., August 9th, 1893.

Carried.

## SECOND DAY.

NIAGARA FALLS, August 9th, 1893.

The Convention met pursuant to adjournment, with the President, Sister Prudence King, in the Chair, all Officers and Delegates present.

The Committee on Correspondence reported as follows :—

*To the Provincial Convention Degree of Rebekah, I.O.O.F. :*

We your Committee on Petitions and Correspondence beg leave to report that we have examined the voluminious correspondence of the President and Secretary, and also been assured by them that the work has been done with promptness and despatch. The thanks of this Convention is due, and is hereby tendered to the President and Secretary for their very efficient work during their term of office.

*Resolved,* That the foregoing be adopted.

All of which is respectfully submitted.

ELIZABETH LEE,
MARY E. MOORE,
RACHAEL MAHONEY.

Moved by Sister Savage, seconded by Sister Pattison,—

That the report of the Committee on Correspondence be adopted.

Carried.

### REPORT OF COMMITTEE ON FINANCE.

*To the Provincial Convention Degree of Rebekah, I.O.O.F. :*

We your Committee on Finance beg leave to report that we have examined the reports and books of the Secretary and Treasurer, and find them correct.

We find that the actual amount of tickets and per diem will amount to $281.60. We also recommend that $50.00 be placed in the hands of the Secretary to defray current expenses, making a total of $331.60.

The total amount of cash in hands of the Treasurer, $264.63, leaving a deficit of $66.97. We will also recommend that this Convention ask for the sum of $100.00 from the Grand Lodge to defray expenses of this meeting, and that the following Committee, Brothers J. B. King, Fitz-Patrick and Young be requested to bring this matter before the Grand Lodge. We also beg leave to report that Clause 3 of the Secretary's report be referred to the Committee on the State of the Order. Your Committee, to whom Clause 9 of President's report was referred, would recommend that, owing to the low state of the finances of the Convention, that no expenses be paid delegates to Chicago.

Respectfully submitted,

W. H. SMITH.

Moved by Sister Fraser, seconded by Sister Perry,—

That the foregoing report be adopted.

Carried.

Moved by Sister Maggie Waddell, seconded by Sister Pattison,—

That the Grand Lodge be asked to donate to the Provincial Convention Degree of Rebekah, the net proceeds of all charters issued and supplies sold to Rebekah Degree Lodges.

Moved by Sister Lee, seconded by Sister Pierce,—

That this motion be referred to the Committee on Legislation.

Carried.

### REPORT OF COMMITTEE ON LEGISLATION.

*To the Provincial Convention Degree of Rebekah, I.O.O.F. :*

The Committee on Legislation beg leave to report that we think it inexpedient to act on the motion of Sister Waddell asking the Grand Lodge to give this Convention the net proceeds of charters issued and supplies sold.

> BRO. L. MASCAR,
> SISTER CRACKNELL,
> SISTER PIERCE.

Moved by Sister Savage, seconded by Bro. McCallum,—

That the report be adopted.

Carried.

The Committee on State of the Order reported as follows :—

*To the Officers and Members of the Provincial Convention Degree of Rebekah, I.O.O.F. :*

Your Committee, to whom was referred the State of the Order, have examined the clauses of the President's and Secretary's reports, as referred to them, and also the reports of the representatives of the different Lodges.

We are pleased to note progress throughout the jurisdiction of Ontario, with very few exceptions, and to note particularly the increase in the number of Lodges, as well as membership.

We think with the Worthy President that the dormant lodges mentioned might with a reasonable effort be revived to active life and usefulness, feeling as we do that the many privileges granted us and in the every-day duties of life, giving us an insight into general business, and that time is not far distant when the influence will be felt all over our fair land and bring upon it showers of blessing.

We find that the Lodges using the Beautified Floor Work are in a more flourishing condition, both financially and numerically.

We are pleased to see that the Sisters appointed to institute Rebekah Lodges, have performed their duties so satisfactorily.

We feel that much of the progress of our Order during the past year is due to the untiring zeal of our worthy Secretary, M. Waddell, who has performed her work faithfully and well.

We approve greatly of the circular issued by the Worthy President and feel confident that in time good results will follow.

The verbal and written reports brought in by the delegates show a marked advancement in every line of our work. Many judicious efforts have been put forth to carry out the great principles of Friendship, Love and Truth.

It gives us great pleasure to meet with the Sisters and Brothers of the Third Annual Convention, and to see among the numbers so many that have attended both Conventions, and we are indeed glad to welcome the new members among our ranks.

May we each carry away with us new ideas and increased enthusiasm which will enable us to co-operate more fully in the grand work of Oddfellowship.

Respectfully submitted.

LAURA E. RYAN,
BARBARA SCOTT,
SAIDEE SCHADE,
JANE DOUGLAS,
AGGIE EDWARDS.

Moved by Sister Savage, seconded by Sister Webster,—

That the foregoing report be adopted.

Carried.

Moved by Bro. Smith, seconded by Sister Pierce,—

That Bro. Brockbank be placed on Finance Committee, *vice* Bro. King, who had to attend to his Grand Lodge duties.

Carried.

Quite a discussion took place as to the advisability of sending delegates to the National Convention, which resulted in the adoption of the following :—

Moved by Sister Ryan, seconded by Sister Douglas,—

*Resolved,*—That the nominations be opened for Representatives to the National Convention, to be held in Chicago.

The following Sisters were nominated and declared elected by acclamation as delegates to the National Convention at Chicago :—

Sisters Reid, Waddell, Brill and Savage.

The report of the Committee on Legislation was then read as follows :—

*To the Provincial Convention Degree of Rebekah, I.O.O.F. :*

We, your Committee on Legislation, to whom was referred Clauses 8, 10 and 11 of the President's Report, beg leave to report that we deem it inexpedient to ask for legislation, for the reason that we find at last session of the Sovereign Grand Lodge (Journal, page 13142 and 13192), that a committee of five were appointed to revise and collate the laws pertaining to the Rebekah Degree, omitting such as have become obsolete, and suggesting such new provisions as will make said laws complete and just and may prove to the advantage of Rebekah Lodges ; said Committee to report at the next annual session.

Resolved, that the foregoing be adopted.

All of which is respectfully submitted.

L. MASCAR,
M. A. PIERCE,      } Committee.
S. J. CRACKNELL,

Moved by Sister Savage, seconded by Sister Douglas,—

That the report of the Committee be adopted.

Carried.

Moved by Sister Fraser, seconded by Sister Perry,—

That we adjourn to meet at 8 p.m.

Carried.

### EVENING SESSION.

The Convention met, pursuant to adjournment, with the President, Sister P. King, in the chair.

Moved by Brother Mascar, seconded by Sister Shields,—

That we adjourn to attend Esther Lodge No. 27, and to witness the exemplification of the beautified work to be given by Edna Lodge, No. 14, of St. Thomas.

Carried.

## THIRD DAY.

NIAGARA FALLS, August 10, 1893.

The Convention met, pursuant to adjournment, with the President, Sister Prudence King, in the chair.

Roll call ; all officers and delegates present.

The Inside Guardian announced that the Grand Sire, Cl. T. Campbell, and Grand Master, Jos. Oliver, were in waiting to install the officers of this Convention. They were then admitted and received with honors. The Grand Sire, assisted by the Grand Master, then proceeded to install the following officers :— Sister Elizabeth Reid, as President ; Sister Elizabeth Seaton, as Vice President ; Sister Maggie Waddell, as Secretary ; Sister Nellie Smith, as Treasurer ; Sister Elizabeth Lee, as Warden ;

Sister Sarah Jane Cracknell, as Inside Guardian; Sister Rachael Mahoney, as Chaplain.

The Grand Master then declared the officers of Rebekah Convention of the Province of Ontario duly installed for the ensuing year.

The Grand Sire then addressed the Convention at some length, stating that when he instituted the Rebekah Convention at Stratford that he hoped that it would be a success, but his hopes have been more than realized with the efficient staff of officers that have been in charge of this branch. It has grown very rapidly, not only in numbers but also in usefullness, and it is to-day one of the best branches of Oddfellowship, and hoped that the Rebekahs would continue to prosper in the future as they had done in the past.

The Grand Sire then exemplified the unwritten work, which was much appreciated by all the delegates.

Moved by Sister Ryan, seconded by Sister Cracknell,—

That a vote of thanks be tendered the retiring officers.

Carried.

Sister Prudence King, on retiring from the chair of President, addressed the Convention, thanking them for the honor they had conferred on her, and expressed the hope that the great prosperity would attend the Rebekahs, that they might aid on in any possible way the great cause of Oddfellowship.

Sister Hester Shields then addressed the Convention, thanking them for the honor conferred on her, having held the office of Treasurer for two years past.

Moved by Sister Ryan, seconded by Sister Fraser,—

That all communications be sent direct to the Secretary of the Convention with the seal of the Lodge attached.

Carried.

Moved by Sister Pattison, seconded by Sister Webster,—

That a vote of thanks be tendered Edna Lodge, No. 14, St. Thomas, for the able manner in which their staff exemplified the beautified work.

Carried.

Moved by Sister Lee, seconded by Sister Scott,—

That a hearty vote of thanks be tendered to the Odd Fellows of Niagara Falls for the able manner in which we have been entertained and for their untiring efforts to make us welcome to their city.

Carried.

The business of the Convention being concluded, the closing Ode was sung and prayer offered by the Chaplain.

The President, Sister Ried, then declared the Convention adjourned, to meet at Kingston the Tuesday before the meeting of Grand Lodge of Ontario.

MAGGIE WADDELL,
*Secretary.*

## REPORT OF THE REPRESENTATIVES

### OF THE

# SOVEREIGN GRAND LODGE, I.O.O F.

### SESSION OF 1893.

### HELD AT MILWAUKEE, WISCONSIN.

*To the Grand Master of the Grand Lodge of Ontario, I.O.O.F. :*

The Representatives to the Sovereign Grand Lodge beg leave to submit the following report :—

The sixty-ninth annual communication of the Sovereign Grand Lodge was held at the City of Milwaukee, Wisconsin, commencing on the 18th day of September, 1893, and closing on the 23rd. There were 180 Representatives in attendance, all the jurisdictions being represented except New Mexico

Grand Sire Cl T. Campbell, of Ontario, proved to be a most efficient and admirable presiding officer, and the thanks of the Sovereign Grand Lodge were unanimously tendered to him for the courteous and able manner in which he presided over the deliberations.

The Ontario Representatives served on the following committees : Robertson, on Appeals, Patriarchs Militant Law and on Memorial Day Service ; Fitz-Patrick, on Returns ; Moore, on Patriarchal Branch and Doggett on Patri-archs Militant. P.G. Rep. John Welsh, of Stratford, was also present and acted as Grand Messenger.

. The address of the Grand Sire is a very able and interesting document. From it we make the following extracts :—

" REPRESENTATIVES—I welcome you to the Sixty-ninth Annual Session of the Sovereign Grand Lodge, in this beautiful city by the inland seas of America. After a year of labor in your own jurisdictions, you have re-assembled for mutual counsel to review the work of the Order ; to overlook its situation ; to regulate its operations ; to meet the requirements of its future.

Never before have you met under happier auspices ; never before have you been greeted by brighter prospects. Only a short distance from this city the nations of the earth are engaged in friendly rivalry, as they display the choicest products of their energy and enterprise. The labor of the husbandman ; the skill of the artisan ; the genius of the artist ; the patient industry of the student, have combined to show the highest mental and manual development of the human race. With less ostentatious parade you are here uncovering to public gaze a grander exhibition of man's moral and social development through the educative influence and practical operations of Oddfellowship. As the representative parliament of this great Order your annual assembling emphasizes the vast extent and beneficent power of this Association, organized for mutual helpfulness and for the cultivation of those virtues that alone can raise humanity out of barbarism and lift it nearer to its most holy Pattern. And, while the magnificent exposition in Chicago reveals the intellectual capabilities of our race, the work of the Order whose destinies you direct illustrates the grand possibilities that lay dormant in the human heart until the Spirit of Altruism breathed into it the breath of a diviner life and awakened its sublimest aspirations. Humanity may well be proud of the revelations of the fairy palaces of the White City on the Lake ; but no less cause for pride have they whose labours have erected the stately temple of Oddfellowship, wherein the noblest works of Friendship, Love and Truth stand radiant with beauty and with blessing.

The reports of your officers presented to-day, with their accompanying statistics, show that

THE STATE OF THE ORDER

is eminently satisfactory. A net increase in our members during 1892 of over 50,000—unprecedented in our history—has given a membership at the close of that year, in the jurisdictions reporting directly to you, of 747,295 ; making, with the estimated number under the independent Grand Lodges of 26,136 and the 96,312 Sisters in the Rebekah branch, a grand total of 869,743. So far as can be learned, the increase this year is still greater than in 1892 ; but even at the same rate, our total membership to-day, male and female, will be over 900,000. An Association that has attained such vast proportions ; with an annual revenue of eight and one-half million dollars ; increasing rapidly each year in wealth and numbers, may well be proud—not of the rank and position these elements of strength may bring— but of the opportunities that are thus brought within its reach of accomplishing the great objects of its existence—the relief of human suffering and the advancement of the human race. Scarcely can the magnitude of its work be estimated. To say that the Subordinate Branches of our Order expended last year nearly three and one-half millions of dollars for the assistance of those in need ; to point to the many towns on this continent where comfortable homes are maintained as refuges for the young and for the old who might else be homeless ; to enumerate all the educational and charitable institutions conducted under our auspices might give some tangible evidence of the beneficent work of Oddfellowship. But a still greater work remains untabulated in the silent and unobtrusive influence exerted on society through the operations of our 15,000 Subordinate Branches, wherein, week after week through all the year, are taught those lessons of morality, charity and fraternity which our members carry into practical effect in their intercourse with each other and the world at large.

While Oddfellowship has become so widespread, carrying on its operations in Europe, Asia and America under the flags of not less than fifteen nations and almost encircling the civilized world with its chain of Lodges, it is in the United States and Canada that it has attained its greatest power and has became a recognized factor in the development of civilization. Exceeding all other secular societies on this continent in numbers, so far as can be ascertained, it acknowledges no superior among them all in the vast extent of its benevolence. Yet, though its prosperous condition in North America is more familiar to us, and its career more noticeable, the fact must not be overlooked that

IN FOREIGN LANDS

its work is no less satisfactory, when surrounding circumstances are considered. While its growth may not be as marked as with us, yet it has been sufficient to be encouraging. In Australasia, depression in trade and financial disturbances may affect our Order, as it does all other organizations, but there is no reason to be alarmed for the future of Oddfellowship, which is too firmly planted in those distant lands and well able to battle successfully with adverse circumstances.

From the continent of Europe we have most cheering reports through our Special Deputy, Grand Representative Block. (Off. Doc. C.) The appointment of our esteemed Brother to the position he now occupies was the outcome of a wise policy, as is evidenced not only by the steady progress the Order has been making in the jurisdictions which he has been visiting, but also in the letters I have received from leading Odd Fellows in Europe, who all speak in the highest terms of our Deputy, and gratefully acknowledge the valuable assistance they have received from him. At first, some doubt was felt in Germany lest the appointment of a Special Deputy for Europe might have been prompted by a fear on our part that irregularities existed in that jurisdiction in the management of Oddfellowship, which required correction. Of course, this was a mistaken idea. The appointment was not intended as a reflection on the zealous and enthusiastic brethren who have been so successful in carrying on the work of the Order in Germany for the past twenty years. But, with a number of jurisdictions in Europe, it would have been an invidious distinction to have selected some as the special objects of our Deputy's attention and to have excluded others. And, while some parts of the continent might have needed a supervision from which others could have been relieved, yet all would be benefited by having near at hand an experienced Brother with whom they might take counsel and who would serve as a vital connecting link between the S. G. L. and the various bodies to whom we have given a *quasi* independence. I have reason to believe, however, that our Brethren now thoroughly understand the situation, as the cordial reception they have tendered Bro. Block amply testifies.

In contrast to the position we hold in Europe is the state of the Order in the Spanish-American countries, from all of which come reports by no means encouraging. This is especially true of South America, the Order in Peru and Chili being decidedly moribund. If there is any possibility of preserving life in the Lodges there, they might be relieved from the payment of per capita tax, while those that are dead beyond resurrection should have their charters recalled.

During the year the desire was expressed by some residents of Rome to have Oddfellowship introduced into Italy, and our Special Deputy submitted the matter for my consideration. As he purposed visiting that city, I authorized him to make a careful investigation as to the laws of Italy and their bearing on organizations like ours ; as to the character of the people, and their ability to appreciate the spirit of our Order and especially as to the number and social position of those who are making inquiries and who might be expected to seek admission. Our experience in foreign countries, peopled by other than Teutonic and allied races, has not been so satisfactory as to justify hasty action ; and I deemed it proper that no decisive steps should be taken towards introducing the Order into Italy until the most convincing evidence should be produced that its establishment would be successful. In this conservative view I had the hearty concurrence of Bro. Block and, on careful examination of the field, we concluded that while there were no intrinsic hindrances to the growth of the Order in Italy, yet nothing should be done at present beyond supplying all applicants with needed information and then waiting until a sufficient number should become so educated in the principles of Oddfellowship that they would be competent to operate it effectually.

### THE REBEKAH DEPARTMENT.

No branch of the Order has made more gratifying progress than this. The enthusiasm which woman has shown and the energy she has brought to bear on her work have made her department an unqualified success, and justifies her claim to the fullest recognition as an essential element in Oddfellowship.

### OUR RELATIONS WITH THE CATHOLIC CHURCH.

During the year I was informed that the authorities of the Roman Catholic Church had appointed a committee of Bishops to inquire into the character of benevolent and other organizations, with a view to deciding whether Catholics

might be allowed to apply for admission therein.   And a letter was written by one
of the committee in which he asked permission to examine our books and Rituals.
The letter and my reply are submitted. (Off. Doc. E.)   While advising that all
possible information be given the committee, I, of course, declined to allow them a
perusal of our Rituals—a privilege belonging solely to those who have taken the
obligations of the Order.

I have heard nothing further on this subject, and have made no inquiry.
The matter is one which does not materially concern us.   Our doors are open to
Catholics as well as Protestants, if they are properly qualified   With disputed
questions of creed we have nothing to do.   If the authorities of the Catholic
Church forbid their adherents seeking admission to our Order, the loss is theirs.
The position Oddfellowship occupies renders it unnecessary for us to seek the
recognition of any particular sect or party, though we will be pleased, at all times,
to have the support of all good men, of whatever race or creed, who reverence God
and seek the advancement of humanity.

## INSURANCE LEGISLATION.

Under the authority of the resolutions adopted last year, certificates were prepared for organizations doing an insurance business among Odd Fellows, and have
been granted to some thirteen applicants. (Off. Docs. F. and G.)   I am of the
opinion that this does not comprise the full number of insurance companies using
the name of the Order.   By reference to my decisions, it will be seen that certain
questions have required my consideration, probably not anticipated in the legislation of 1892.   These embrace the rights of Grand Bodies in the matter of organ-
izing endowment associations ; the privilege of societies using the name of the
Order to extend their operations outside our membership, and, in general, the
class of associations coming within the purview of your legislation on this subject.

Under the laws of 1877, 1878 and 1879, the S. G. L. gave Subordinate Grand
Bodies the power to organize and operate endowment associations, confined to the
membership of their own jurisdictions.   But experience showed that private
companies were springing up, of a purely business character, unauthorized by any
Body in Oddfellowship, yet using the name of the Order and operating among its
members.   It was to meet this condition, primarily, that you took up the consideration of the question of insurance in 1887, on the recommendation of Grand Sire
White, and the investigations of special committees during the ensuing years
have eventuated in the legislation enacted at your last session.

There can be no doubt that the object of this legislation was the protection of
Odd Fellows in their dealings with private business corporations operating under
the name of the Order.   It could scarcely have been intended, for example, that
where the members of a Lodge formed a little benefit club, confined to their own
locality and operated by unsalaried officials, that they should be required to pay
$20 to the S. G. L. and to their State Grand Lodge for the privilege of helping
each other by trifling assessments.   Further, in the matter of Grand Lodge
Endowment Associations, organized under the law of 1878, there is nothing in the
legislation of last year repealing that authority.   And as the object sought in the
aforesaid legislation is abundantly secured when Grand Lodges themselves operate
and control these associations, it does not appear that there is any necessity for so
rigid an interpretation of the laws as would require a Grand Lodge to secure a
license from this Body, and then from itself, to do something the general law has
recognized as a part of its legitimate work.   On the other hand, where associations
of a purely private character take into membership people of all classes, there is
no reason why they should either call themselves Odd Fellows' companies, or
obtain a license from this Body to do business. * * *

The work incident to

## THE OFFICE OF THE GRAND SIRE

has been extensive and varied, covering much that does not call for a report to this
Body.   The correspondence connected with the supervision of an Association of
nearly 900,000 men and women necessarily involves much time and labor, but I
have endeavored to answer all communications with such promptness as the due
consideration of the matters submitted would permit.   Many questions on which

my decisions were asked were plainly answerable under existing law, but such as seem to call for your action are appended. (Off. Doc. A.)

All work of the office which has had to receive the cognizance of the Grand Secretary, such as the issuing of Commissions and Warrants, the approval of laws, etc., will be reported by that officer.

During the year I have received many invitations to visit different sections of the United States and Canada, and have to regret that the claims of my own profession have in most cases prevented my acceptance. I visited the Brethren in North Dakota, Manitoba and Minnesota on my return from the Portland session. The Anniversary of the Order was spent with the Order in Grand Rapids, Michigan. In January I dedicated the hall of the new temple in Toronto, Ontario, and on the 18th of July I assisted in laying the corner-stone of what will be, when completed, the most magnificent edifice ever devoted to the service of the Fraternity. These, with sundry visits in my own province, cover my work in this department. I regret that I have not been able to do more, not only on account of the personal pleasure it would give to meet with the membership, but because I am satisfied that a visit from the principal officer of the Order would often be of material service. I can only hope that future Grand Sires may have opportunity for this work, which circumstances do not allow me. * * *

### THE GRAND SIRE'S DECISIONS.

1. In any conflict between the " Floor Work " and Ritual, or law, the latter must govern.

2. The obligation to a candidate must be administered by a V.G. or P.V.G. Where the instructions in " Floor Work " say that " positions on a staff are to be governed by the questions of fitness," it means fitness within the limitations of law.

4. A P.G. should wear a P.G.'s collar in Lodge (if obtainable), and should neither enter, leave nor remain in a Lodge when open without it.

5. It is optional with a P.G.M. when visiting a Lodge to announce himself as P.G.M. or P.G.

6. During the absence of a N.G. the V.G. should perform all the duties devolving upon the N.G. which require to be performed at that time. The immediate filling of a vacancy in an appointed office during a temporary absence of the N.G. might not be necessary, and would not, therefore, devolve upon the V.G. unless the Lodge so instructed him.

7. When the officers of a Lodge or Encampment under the S. G. L., being duly elected and properly qualified, are installed by the D. D. G. Sire, or other person authorized by the Grand Sire, and have taken the obligations of office, such installation is valid, although there may have been certain irregularities connected with it.

8. A member of a Lodge acting as counsel for a Brother under trial has the same right to vote on the penalty that he would have were he not counsel.

9. When charges against a Brother have been referred to the Committee on Trial, the committee cannot allow the accuser to amend the charges by introducing new specifications not contained in the original charge. Supplemental charges might be preferred in the Lodge and referred to the committee.

10. The Minimum Benefit Law of 1892, being practically a repeal of the law of 1891, revives the powers of Grand Bodies, which were abrogated by the latter. On and after January 1st, 1893, the powers that were withdrawn from Subordinates in the matter of benefits by the legislation of 1891 may be exercised by them to the same extent as prior to January, 1892, except in so far as they may conflict with the requirements of the Minimum Benefit Law—that is to say, the payment of not less than $2 per week for the first year of continuous sickness, and not less than $1 per week during the further continuance of the same sickness.

11. The requirement of the Minimum Benefit Law that not less than one year's benefits shall be paid before the amount can be reduced below $2 per week, is substantially fulfilled by the payment of benefits for fifty-two consecutive weeks.

19

12. If a Lodge does not pay benefits for the first week of sickness, the reduction in the amount of weekly benefits does not take place at the end of a year's disability, but only after a year's benefits have been paid.

13. When a Lodge has been paying a sick member continuous benefits for several years, it will now be required to pay him not less than $1 per week, commencing with the 1st of January, 1892.

14. Whether or not a Lodge may provide by its By-Laws for the payment of a larger weekly benefit to sick Brothers who are confined to the house than it does to those not so confined, is a matter for local Legislation, provided the same has been authorized by legislation of the Subordinate Grand Lodge and that under no circumstances it pays less than the minimum benefit required by general law.

15. Where a Lodge provides for " night watchers " for sick members, this is to be considered as a form of " attentive benefits," and any expense incurred in payment of such watchers is altogether apart from the sick benefits due under the general or local law.

16. It is not legal for a Lodge, with or without the consent of its Grand Lodge, to have a by-law providing for the initiation of persons over 55 years of age, as "non-beneficial members; " or changing the status of one already a member of such Lodge from a beneficial to a non-beneficial member on reaching a certain age. Members in good standing are entitled to benefits irrespective of age—the only exception permitted by general law being in the case of aged Odd Fellows re-admitted to membership.

17. A Lodge having knowingly admitted a non-resident member to membership in violation of its Constitution, and having received his fees and dues, cannot, when he becomes ill, refuse him benefits and declare his membership void on account of its illegality. The Lodge cannot take advantage of its own violation of law to escape payment of its debts.

18. A lady elected to membership in a Rebekah Lodge, but marrying a person not an Odd Fellow before she has received the Degree, is not entitled to admission and ceased to be eligible on the date of her marriage.

19. In a jurisdiction where Rebekah Lodges have yearly terms, the T.P.W. may be for the year, or there may be a P.W. for each half year, at the option of the Grand Lodge.

20. A Brother who has received the Rebekah Degree in a Grand Lodge or in a Rebekah Lodge, is eligible to be an applicant for a Charter for a Rebekah Lodge, or to be admitted to membership in such Lodge after its institution, on a favorable ballot, provided he is in good standing in his Subordinate Lodge, and is not a suspended or expelled member of a Rebekah Lodge.

21. A State or Provincial Rebekah Convention has no power to impose a tax on the Rebekah Lodges of the jurisdiction for any purpose. But the Grand Lodge of the jurisdiction may impose a tax on its Rebekah Lodges, collect the same, and day the amount over to the Rebekah Convention, for its maintenance.

22. When a Grand Master, in the exercise of his supervisory powers, suspends a Lodge for violation of law, he has power to restore it without waiting for action by his Grand Lodge, unless the Constitution and instructions of the Grand Lodge limit his authority in this respect.

23. A Grand Master has the right to appoint a P.G., who is also a P.G. in good standing in a Rebekah Lodge, as his Deputy, to institute a Rebekah Lodge.

24. The interpretation of the Constitution of a Grand Body during its recess, is vested in its principal officer, subject to a review by such Grand Body at its session following; and it is the duty of such officer to administer the local law according to his conscientious interpretation thereof. He may seek the Grand Sire's opinion thereon; but such opinion, if given, is not necessarily mandatory. The responsibility of interpreting and executing the local law rests on the Grand Master and Grand Patriarch.

25. Subordinates have a right to make By-Laws for their internal government. A Grand Body cannot make By-Laws for its Subordinates, but has the right of supervision, and may approve or disapprove. It may frame a model code of By-

Laws, and recommend the same to its Subordinates, but cannot compel its adoption. It can, however, enact a uniform Constitution, and may therein regulate the matter of benefits so far as the general law allows ; and the By-Laws of Subordinates must conform to such Constitution.

26. A committee of a Grand Body appointed to supervise the By-Laws of its Subordinates has no right to make new laws for them, or to disapprove By-Laws which are not in conflict with law ; and it can only amend a by-law in so far as may be necessary to make it conform to the general or local law.

29. The only qualification necessary for a P.G. to be a candidate for election as Representative of his Lodge in its Grand Lodge, is that he should be a member of his Lodge in good standing.

30. Executive officers of Grand Lodges have no option, but must grant licenses to Odd Fellows' Insurance Associations making application therefor, who have complied with the requirements of law, except in a jurisdiction where the Grand Lodge has decided not to license such bodies.

31. An insurance organization, to be permitted to use the name of the Order, or to receive the certificate of the S.G.L. must be one that confines its operations to Odd Fellows exclusively.

32. The right of a State Grand Body to organize and operate through its officers an endowment association has not been withdrawn, and such an association does not require any certificate from the S.G.L., or other license, so long as it does not go out of its own jurisdiction.

33. Voluntary associations of members of the Order in a town or city for purposes of mutual aid, whose operations are confined to their own locality, having no paid canvassers and not doing a general business, do not require to take out an insurance certificate."

The above decisions are as they were finally approved by the Sovereign Grand Lodge.

The Report of the Grand Treasurer shows the financial condition of the Sovereign Grand Lodge for the fiscal year ending August 19th, 1893. The Receipts for the past year were $71,186.60 and the Disbursements $86,005.60. The excess of disbursements over receipts, $6,819, was caused mainly by the large amount paid for mileage at the Session held at Portland, Oregon, in 1892. The report shows the available assets of the Sovereign Grand Lodge to be $79,076.72.

The following statistics are taken from the report of the Grand Secretary :—

RETURNS FOR THE YEARS 1891 AND 1892.

|  | Dec. 31st, 1891. | Dec. 31st, 1892. | Increase. |
|---|---|---|---|
| Grand Lodges | 53 | 55 | 2 |
| Grand Encampments | 49 | 50 | 1 |
| Subordinate Lodges | 9,524 | 9,936 | 412 |
| Subordinate Encampments | 2,346 | 2,483 | 137 |
| Rebekah Degree Lodges | 2,564 | 2,905 | 341 |
| Lodge initiations | 80,119 | 85,509 | 5,390 |

RETURNS FOR THE YEARS 1891 AND 1892—*Continued.*

|                                | Dec. 31st, 1891. | Dec. 31st, 1892. | Increase.     |
| ------------------------------ | ---------------: | ---------------: | ------------: |
| Encampment initiations         |           15,640 |           16,732 |         1,090 |
| Lodge members                  |         *696,189 |          747,295 |        51,106 |
| Encampment members             |          124,076 |          132,542 |         8,466 |
| Rebekah Lodge members          |         †154,851 |          180,869 |        26,018 |
| Relief by Lodges               |    $2,775,630 73 |    $3,015,979 93 |   $260,349 20 |
| Relief by Encampments          |       274,839 89 |       301,801 88 |     26,961 99 |
| Relief by Rebekah Lodges       |        34,250 18 |        32,675 03 |     ‡1,575 15 |
| Total relief                   |     3,064,720 80 |     3,350,456 84 |    285,736 04 |
| Revenue of Lodges              |     6,882,697 94 |     7,594,828 58 |    712,130 64 |
| Revenue of Encampments         |       656,373 84 |       657,781 99 |      1,408 15 |
| Revenue of Rebekah Lodges      |       229,822 24 |       356,520 36 |    126,698 12 |
| Total revenue                  |     7,768,894 02 |     8,609,130 93 |    840,236 91 |

* Excluding Denmark and Switzerland, independent.      † Excluding Switzerland, independent.      ‡ Decrease.

STATISTICS OF THE ORDER FROM 1830 TO DECEMBER 31ST, 1892,

INCLUDING AUSTRALASIA, GERMANY, DENMARK AND SWITZERLAND.

| | |
| --- | ---: |
| Initiations in Subordinate Lodges | 1,872,869 |
| Members relieved | 1,716,945 |
| Widowed families relieved | 203,341 |
| Members deceased | 167,547 |
| Total relief | $60,921,287 05 |
| Total receipts | 159,197,674 43 |

CONDITION OF THE ORDER DECEMBER 31ST, 1892.

| | |
| --- | ---: |
| Sovereign Grand Lodge | 1 |
| Independent Grand Lodges (German Empire, Australasia, Denmark and Switzerland) | 4 |
| Subordinate Grand Encampments | 53 |
| Subordinate Grand Lodges | 65 |
| Subordinate Encampments | 2,503 |
| Subordinate Lodges | 10,274 |
| Encampment members | 133,349 |
| Lodge members | 773,431 |
| Rebekah Lodges | 2,916 |
| Sisters members of Rebekah Lodges | 96,312 |
| Brothers members of Rebekah Lodges | 84,721 |
| Cantons of Patriarchs Militant (estimated) | 630 |
| Chevaliers, rank and file (estimated) | 26,400 |

During the recess charters were issued for the organization of 18 new bodies, as follows :—Grand Lodges in Indian Territory and Oklahoma ; a Grand Encampment in Oklahoma ; Subordinate Lodges at Innisfail, in Alberta ; Estevan, Maple Creek and Regina, in Assiniboia; Claremore, in Indian Territory, and Eslof in Sweden ; a Rebekah Lodge at El Reno, in

Oklahoma, and Subordinate Encampments at Tucson, in Arizona ; Purcell and Ardmore, in Indian Territory ; Gallup, in New Mexico ; Kingfisher and Hennessey, in Oklahoma, and Farnham and St John's, in Quebec.

There were 26 appeal cases considered and determined. The appeal of Unity Lodge, No. 47, of Hamilton, from the action of the Grand Lodge of Ontario was dismissed by the adoption of the following report, which was presented by Rep. Bruton of North Carolina :—

" *To the Sovereign Grand Lodge, I. O. O. F.* :

Your Committee on Appeals, to whom was referred the appeal of Unity Lodge, No. 47, of Hamilton, Ont., from the action of the Grand Lodge of Ontario, beg leave to report as follows :—

At the last session of the Grand Lodge of Ontario, Unity Lodge, No. 47, submitted the following question :—

*Clause 51, Con. Sub., latter part of said clause.*—'The Lodge shall not be held to pay such benefit for any term of sickness shorter than one week, but after one week's sickness the Brother shall be entitled to benefits for such additional day or days that he may be ill. Is this portion of clause 51 legal ?'

This question was submitted to the Judiciary Committee, who reported as follows :—' Yes. The clause does not conflict with the decision of Sovereign Grand Lodge, 1892, pp. 13000—13057.'

The report was adopted by the Grand Lodge, and from this decision Unity Lodge appealed, as it does not consider it in conformity with the sixth clause of Report No. 12, Journal S. G. L., 1892, page 13000, which reads as follows :— ' Now, it is a fundamental principle of the Order that dues accrue from week to week, and benefits are payable weekly ; fractions of a week are not considered in either case, etc.'

*Facts.*—Unity Lodge pays benefits as follows :—1st week, $2.00 ; 2nd week, $3.00 ; next 52 weeks, $4.00 ; next 26 weeks, $3.00 ; next 26 weeks, $2.00 ; further, $1.00.

DECISION.

The payment of a sick benefit is one of the fundamental principles of the Order, and no other rule is recognized than that ' benefits are payable weekly. That is, every member entitled to benefits is entitled to the same at the end of each Lodge week, and not at the end of a month or quarter ; and where a local legislation provides for the payment of benefits for fractions of a week after the first week, as in this case, the right to enjoy the benefits accrues at the end of the week of which the fraction is a part. The amount due the beneficiary is limited by the amount which the Lodge has agreed to pay for that week for which the fraction is a part. The fact that a Brother recovers from a spell of sickness four days prior to the end of a Lodge week does not warrant him in demanding immediately upon the date of his recovery the amount due him for the fractional part of the week he was ill, to wit : three-sevenths.

To this extent only ' fractional parts of a week are not considered ' in the payment of benefits.

Your Committee would therefore recommend the following :—

*Resolved,*—That the appeal of Unity Lodge, No. 47, of Hamilton, Ont., be dismissed, and the decision of the Grand Lodge of Ontario be sustained."

The resolution presented by Rep. Robertson as to the rank of Bro John Ormiston, was referred to the Committee on the State of the Order, and their report on the same was adopted as under :—

" *To the Sovereign Grand Lodge, I. O. O. F.* :

Your Committee on the State of the Order, to whom was referred the resolution of Rep. Robertson, of Ontario, as follows :—

'*Resolved*,—That the Grand Lodge of Ontario be permitted to confer the rank of Past Grand Master upon Brother Ormiston, who was elected Grand Master of that jurisdiction and served a part of a year as such, but was compelled through illness to resign his office during his term.'

Would most respectfully report that in our opinion the honors of the Grand Master or the privilege of being classed among the Past Grand Masters of Ontario, which we understand to be the meaning of the words ' Being permitted to confer the rank of Past Grand Master on the Brother,' can only be done as a reward for faithful service rendered. All the precedents established by the S. G. L. point to the conclusion, and, in fact, Sections 278, 284, 289 and other Sections of the Digest declare the honors *can only* be conferred as a reward for service in the office for which the honors are sought.

The facts connected with the application from Ontario appear to be as follows :—

Brother Ormiston was duly elected and installed Grand Master of the Grand Lodge of Ontario and occupied the office over one-half of the year for which he was elected, when he tendered his resignation on account of sickness that rendered him incapable of performing the duties of the office. The resignation was not formally accepted, neither was the Deputy Grand Master (who served out the balance of the term) elected to or installed into the office, nor was he entitled to under the law, or awarded the honors of the office for such service. thus leaving a blank in the list of Past Grand Masters for that year, and the Grand Lodge of Ontario now seeks to fill that vacancy by placing therein the name of Brother Ormiston.

It appears to your Committee that if the above recital of the facts are correct, and the Grand Lodge of Ontario can easily ascertain if they are so (we do not question them), that the Brother did not voluntarily withdraw from the performance of the duties of the office and is therefore entitled to the honors of Past Grand Master. We therefore recommend the adoption of the following resolution :—

*Resolved*,—That the subject-matter contained in the resolution of Brother Robertson be referred back to the Grand Lodge of Ontario, to further investigate and make such a disposition of it as will be right and just between the claims of Brother Ormiston and the well established laws and usages of the Order."

The first and second clauses of the Insurance Resolutions of 1892, (Journal, page 13,081,) were amended to read as follows :—

" *Resolved, First*,—That every association doing a life or accident, or life and accident business, and using the name of the Order or claiming to be an Odd Fellows' Insurance Company, or the membership of which is limited by its charter, articles of association, fundamental law, by-laws, resolutions or practice, to members of this Order, shall, on or before the first of June next, file with the Grand Secretary of the Sovereign Grand Lodge, and of the Grand Lodge of every Jurisdiction in which it proposes to transact business, a copy of its charter, articles of incorporation, fundamental law, by-laws and all amendments thereto, and of all resolutions and action had by the company or association affecting the liability or status of persons insured therein, verified by affidavits of its President, Secretary and Treasurer, and signed by said officers and the directors or managers of such company or association, and if hereafter the charter, articles of association, or fundamental law of any such company or association shall be annulled or altered, or the by-laws thereof be changed or amended, or any resolution passed affecting the liability or status of persons insured therein, a copy shall forthwith be filed with the Sovereign Grand Lodge, and with the Grand Lodge of each Jurisdiction in which such company or association is doing business, *provided, however*, that any such company or association which has already filed such statements as required by this resolution shall not again be required to file them.

*Second.* — That on or before the first day in June of each year hereafter, every such company or association shall file with the Secretary of the Sovereign Grand Lodge, and of the Grand Lodge of every Jurisdiction in which it proposes to transact business, upon blanks furnished by the Secretary of the Sovereign Grand Lodge, a report similarly verified, for the year ending on the 31st December, or prior thereto, setting forth :—

1st. Full name of corporation and principal place of business.

2nd. Date of incorporation and commencement of business.

3rd. Character of business.

4th. Names and residences of President, Secretary, Treasurer and Directors or Managers.

5th. Number of policies in force on December 31st of previous year.

6th. Number of new policies issued during the year.

7th. Number of policies lapsed during the year.

8th. Number of policies in force on December 31st of the year covered by the report.

9th. A list of all losses paid during the preceding year, giving name of the assured, his residence, amount paid and the cause of death.

10th. Amount of entrance fee.

11th. Amount of periodical dues.

12th. Maximum amount of risk on any one life.

13th. Whether policies issued for a specified amount to be paid, or amount dependent upon assessment.

14th. What portion of premium (if any) is set apart for mortuary purposes, and what for expenses ?

15th. How is mortuary fund invested ?

16th. Whether the association issues endowment certificates ?

17th. Are assessments graded on any table of mortality ?  How are they graded ?

18th. How, and when, are officers and directors elected ?

19th. What medical examinations are required before issuing policies ?

20th. What amount of money will an ordinary assessment for the payment of a single assessment yield ?

21st. Has the association an emergency or reserve fund ?

22nd. What is the amount ?

23rd. How is it invested ?

24th. For what purposes is it used ?

25th. A list of all the assessments during the year, their purpose in detail, date of assessment and amount realized on each.


STATEMENT OF ASSETS.

26th. Cost value of real estate, its character, and how and when acquired

27th. Description of encumbrances thereon and for what purpose created ?

28th. Loans and how secured ?   Details.

29th. Bonds, stocks, etc., owned absolutely.

30th. Agents' ledger balances.

31st. Cash in office.

32nd. Cash in banks and what banks ?

33rd. All other assets in detail.

34th. Are any of your funds loaned to any officer or director of your company, or are they or any of them interested in such loans, directly or indirectly, or in any way responsible therefor ?

### STATEMENT OF LIABILITIES.

35th. Losses due or unpaid.
36th. Taxes due and unpaid.
37th. Salaries, rents and officers' expenses due and unpaid.
38th. Borrowed money.
39th. Advanced assessments.
40th. All other liabilities, indicating their character."

And a new clause was added, fixing a penalty for the violation of these Resolutions, which reads as follows :—

" *Thirteenth,*—Any wilful violation of, or omission to perform and comply with the provisions of these resolutions by any officer, director or manager of such company or association shall constitute an offence against the laws of the Order and shall be punished by suspension or expulsion from the Order."

A Special Committee was appointed to revise and collate all the laws pertaining to the Rebekah Degree, and to report at next session, and subsequently the following resolution was passed :—

" *Resolved,*—That all Laws, Rules and Regulations of this Sovereign Grand Lodge now in force, or that may hereafter be adopted for the government of Subordinate Grand Jurisdictions, or in any way affect the rights of individual members, shall be made to apply, where applicable, in all their force to State and Territorial Grand Jurisdiction of the Degree of Rebekah, and in so applying them, when necessary, where the male gender is referred to in said laws, the same shall be construed to mean the female gender.

That this resolution shall be in full force and effect until a code of laws shall have been adopted by this Sovereign Grand Lodge for the government of the Degree of Rebekah."

By the adoption of the following amendment to Section 91 of White's Digest, the word " Orphans " is restricted to mean those only who are under the age of twenty-one years :—

" That Section 91 of White's Digest (1889) be and the same is hereby amended so as to read as follows :—

*Resolved,*—That the only persons who are the beneficiaries of a funeral benefit are the widow, orphans under the age of twenty-one years, or dependent relatives of the deceased, or relatives upon whom the deceased was dependent at the time of death.   Dependent relatives are relatives who were members of the family of the deceased and were dependent upon the deceased for support at the time of death."

The following resolutions were passed, creating a new Jewel for those members who have been in continuous membership for fifty consecutive years or more :—

" *Resolved,*—That the Committee on Printing and Supplies be, and they are hereby authorized and directed to design, or cause to be designed, a suitable jewel to be worn by such members, and which shall be known as ' The Honorable Veteran Jewel, I. O. O. F.'

*Resolved,*—That ' The Honorable Veteran Jewel, I. O. O. F.,' shall be furnished and sold to members in good standing, who have held continuous membership in the Order for fifty consecutive years or more, and in the same manner and on the same terms as ' The Veteran Jewel, I. O. O. F.,' is now sold and distributed."

In addition to the particulars heretofore required, the annual returns to be made by State Grand Bodies are hereafter to contain the following details :—The number of weeks sick benefits paid, the amount paid for relief of orphans, the amount paid for the working or current expenses of Subordinates, the amount paid for expenses of the Grand Body, receipts from dues, receipts from admissions and degrees, and receipts from rents and invested funds.

Power was given to the Grand Sire to organize a Grand Lodge in Sweden.

The Sovereign Grand Lodge authorized the purchase of the building now occupied by the Grand Secretary in Baltimore, Maryland, at the price of $25,000.   It is a new building, 30 x 90, having two fronts, four stories high, and a basement, with good vaults, centrally located (23 and 25 North Liberty Street), and it is stated to be most suitable and satisfactory for the headquarters of the Order.

A Special Committee, consisting of Reps. Thomas of Utah, Robertson of Ontario, and Fessenden of Maine, was appointed to formulate a uniform plan of procedure to be followed by all Subordinate Lodges in the celebration of Memorial Day.

All the proposed constitutional amendments were rejected. The only division that was taken was on the amendment to admit members at the age of 18, which was rejected by a vote of 81 yeas to 96 nays.   The vote in 1892 was 83 yeas to 78 nays. It was again proposed for next session, and there is also another proposal to make the age nineteen.

The proposal to abolish the Visiting Card was again defeated.

The Special Committee on Dues and Benefits, through their Chairman, Rep. Carlin, of Illinois, presented a lengthy and exhaustive report, which forms a most valuable contribution to the literature of this important subject.  A large amount of information is given, together with numerous tables as to membership, sickness, deaths, averages and experiences.  Among these tables are two which were compiled by our Grand Secretary, Bro. J. B. King, which the Committee say they esteem so valuable that they insert them in full.  The document is too long to be copied in this report, but we would call the especial attention of our members to it and invite its careful perusal as it will appear in the Revised Journal.  The following are the conclusions arrived at by the Committee :—

"1st. That as a man grows older, his yearly average of sickness increases ; and as a lodge grows older, its proportion of old men increases and its payment for benefits increase.

2nd. That the average expectation of sickness and mortality must form the basis of any estimate of the proper relation of dues to benefits.

3rd. That a Lodge should calculate what it is likely to be called on to pay in benefits when it has attained to full maturity, say the age of thirty-five, and not what it is paying during the early years of its existence.

4th. That a system of dues and benefits, to be perfectly fair and equitable, must recognize the comparative liability on account of the different ages of its members, and must charge them dues according to age when admitted.

5th. That no other form of benefit except sick and funeral should be provided without a proportionate increase in dues, and that all additional aid to members should take the form of special relief to an extent dependent upon the circumstances of the case and the ability of the Lodge."

The same Committee also presented the following resolutions :—

"3rd *Resolved*,—That Subordinate Grand Lodges be, and they are hereby directed, to so legislate as to provide a minimum of ten cents per week dues, or $5.20 per annum, from all members.

4th. *Resolved*,—That Subordinate Grand Lodges be, and they are hereby directed, to so legislate as to provide that not more than one-half year's dues shall be allowed for one week's sick benefits, and that a funeral benefit shall not exceed five times one year's dues.

*Provided*,—However, That Grand Lodges may make such provision as they deem expedient for considering as dues, receipts of Lodges from safe, permanent investments."

After considerable discussion, it was finally determined to postpone the further consideration of these resolutions until the next Session, and the Representatives were requested to bring them before their respective Grand Lodges and to get an expression of opinion thereon from the various Jurisdictions, to be submitted to the Sovereign Grand Lodge when the matter shall come up for determination.

Subsequently, the following report from the same Committee was adopted, under which it will be necessary that the Grand Lodge should take action :—

*" To the Sovereign Grand Lodge, I.O.O.F. :*

Your Special Committee on Dues and Benefits, believing that the membership generally of the Order, should have information regarding sickness, deaths, expense of management, receipts from all sources, and all expenditures by Subordinates, to the end that necessary legislation may be ultimately enacted, either by Subordinate Grand Lodges, or by this Grand Lodge, so regulating dues and benefits as to secure the permanency of the fundamental principle, that substantial benefits must be paid, we submit the following, and recommend its adoption :

1st. *Resolved,*—That all Grand Lodges be, and they are hereby requested, to select a committee of three members, whose duty it shall be to consider the subject of dues and benefits in their respective jurisdictions, and, for the purpose of securing uniformity in the information to be collected and disseminated, we recommend that said committees examine the returns from Subordinate Lodges for the past ten years, and report to their several Grand Lodges the following, for each of said years :

1st.  Members

2nd.  Number sick.

3rd.  Weeks benefits paid.

4th.  Deaths.

5th.  Amount paid for sick benefits.

6th.  Amount paid for funeral benefits and funeral expenses.

7th.  Amount paid for widowed families.

8th.  Amount paid for relief and education of orphans.

9th.  Amount paid for special relief.

10th.  Amount paid for total relief.

11th.  Average sickness per member.

12th.  Average cost per member for total relief.

13th.  Average cost per member for current or working expenses of Lodges.

14th.  Current or working expenses of Lodges.

15th.  Total cost per member for all Lodge expenditures.

16th.  Receipts from dues.

17th.  Receipts from initiations and degrees.

18th.  Receipts from rent of property, and other investments.

19th.  Total receipts of Lodges.

20th. Net increase or decrease in value of real estate, at fair cash value, and of good securities and cash.

2nd. *Resolved,*—That Grand Lodges be further requested to maintain such Committee on Dues and Benefits, and to the facts suggested to be collated for the past ten years, said committee likewise tabulate like facts for succeeding years.

3rd. *Resolved,*—That Representatives report this action to their several Grand Lodges."

The resolution offered by Rep. Robertson to allow the Veteran Jewel to be worn in lieu of regalia was reported against by the Committee on Legislation and their report was adopted. A number of propositions in regard to the regalia of the Order and in the line of simplification received the same treatment, but the whole matter will come up again next year on a series of resolutions from the Representatives from Washington, proposing Badges in lieu of the Collars now in use, which resolutions were postponed till next Session. In the preamble to these resolutions we find the following very sensible and appropriate remarks :—

"Our Order has come to be encumbered with a system of regalia which has grown until at times it seems to be of greater importance than our principles and to hide and overshadow the objects of Oddfellowship. To provide our Order with a senseless, useless, and childish combination of tinsel, velvet, and gew-gaws, we have authorized and encouraged investments of hundreds of thousands of dollars in what we call regalia. No person yet has been found who can offer an excuse for its existence. No Odd Fellow can tell why he is called upon to array himself in such toggery before he can be admitted to the Sessions of our Order, from the Initiatory Degree to the meetings of the Sovereign Grand Lodge. No Lodge can understand why they have to invest from one hundred to one thousand or more dollars in regalia before they can be permitted to proceed in humanity's name to the accomplishment of those ends within the scope of Oddfellowship. We have allowed the investments to be industriously worked and farmed until the problem which sometimes seems sought is, who's shall be the most gorgeous display, instead of the exemplification and execution of the principles we endeavor to teach. We have encouraged a childish vanity in the regalia authorized, and diverted our energies and resources from the real into superficial channels. Exclusive of team paraphernalia our Order has locked up in authorized' regalia over three million dollars. Contemplate the dead investment. Does not the condition call for such changes as will stop the increase of these useless investments and give the Order a regalia sensible and expressive, and which can be provided any Lodge, if desired, as a work of love from the skillful hands of the mothers, wives and sisters ?

With this end in view we herewith offer an amendment to the By-laws of the Sovereign Grand Lodge, in the preparation of which we beg to acknowledge the valuable assistance given us by the report of the Special Committee on Regalia, appointed in 1890, reported by Representative J. B. Goodwin, of Georgia, in 1891, and to emphasize their conclusion and firm conviction 'that legislation is needed.'"

Your Representatives would like to receive the instructions of the Grand Lodge on this subject.

Another matter upon which your Representatives were requested to ask instructions is that of fixing a minimum rate of fees for the Degrees. The proposal is, that not less than $20 shall be charged for conferring the Initiatory, First, Second and Third Degrees, and that Grand Lodges shall be directed to so legislate. As this is a radical departure from the rule now existing, by which all matters of this kind are left to local legislation, it is desirable that the Grand Lodge should give an expression of opinion as to its advisability.

An illustration of the conservative tendencies of the Sovereign Grand Lodge is found in the fact that no less than 44 propositions for new regulations or amendments were rejected. About one-half that number were accepted or accepted in a modified form. Among the "slaughtered innocents" were the following, besides those already mentioned :—Proposals to repeal the legislation allowing Grand Lodges to donate surplus funds to Odd Fellows' Homes ; to repeal the law prohibiting Grand

Lodges from conferring the Grand Lodge Degree for pecuniary consideration ; to allow Grand Lodges to provide for a fund for benefits to aged Odd Fellows who have lost membership through surrender of charters ; to make dues commence from the time the Brother attains the Third Degree ; to compel the payment of benefits for the first week's sickness ; to prepare a funeral ceremony for the Patriarchal Branch and to prepare a new Digest.   .

The next Session of the Sovereign Grand Lodge will be held at Chattanooga, Tennessee, on the third Monday in September, 1894.

All which is fraternally submitted.

HY. ROBERTSON,
P. E. FITZ-PATRICK,
*Grand Representatives.*

COLLINGWOOD, October 11, 1893.

# ODD FELLOWS' RELIEF ASSOCIATION OF CANADA.

## OFFICIAL MINUTES

### OF THE

# NINETEENTH ANNUAL MEETING

### HELD AT KINGSTON, ONTARIO.

KINGSTON, July 19, 1893.

The Odd Fellows' Relief Association of Canada convened in the new Odd Fellows' Hall at 3 o'clock.

The following. among others, were present :   Rev. Bro. T. W. Jolliffe, Grand Master, Campbellford ; Bro. Joseph Oliver, Toronto, Deputy Grand Master, and Bro. J. B. King, Toronto, Grand Secretary, Grand Lodge of Ontario ; John Donogh, P.G. M., Toronto, and L. C. Pascoe, Belleville, members of the Advisory Committee of the Association in the Grand Lodge of Ontario ; L. Ferguson, St. Thomas ; Rev. James Kines, P.G.M., Carleton Place ; J. H. Magill, Port Hope ; J. R. Boothby, Stratford ; J. R. Beal, Pembroke ; F. W. Martin, Picton; C. R.Cotton, Gananoque ;  R. W. Haydon, Almonte ;  A. McFee and P. Acton, Belleville ; J. H. Walford, Renfrew ; W. H. Wallis, Lansdowne ; A. H. Blackeby, Galt ; John Robinson, Prescott ; and J. A. Young, Thamesford.

Dr. Fowler, President, took the chair and called the meeting to order. The afternoon Session was, he said, for business purposes, and he therefore proceeded to call for the minutes of the last meeting, which, being printed, were taken as read.

Moved by Rev. Bro. D. C. Sanderson, seconded by Bro.

Harris, that the following be the Committee to strike the Sessional Committees and to distribute the work :

Bros. J. A. Young, Thamesford, chairman ; J. R. Beal, Pembroke ; C. R. Cotton. Gananoque ; John Robinson, Prescott, and J. S. R. McCann, Kingston. Carried.

The following reports were then presented :

The Directors', by Bro. T. Donnely.

The Secretary's, by Bro. R. Meek.

The Superintendent of Agencies', by Bro. A. H. Blackeby.

The Treasurer's, by Bro. J. B. McIver.

The Auditors', by Bro. A. T. Smith and Bro. John Nicolle.

These were received, commented on briefly, and the contents of them referred to the appropriate committees.

Bro. Young, from the Special Committee, submitted his report, appointing the following committees :

FINANCE—Bros. John Donogh, P.G.M., Toronto, chairman ; J. B. King, G. S., Toronto ; J. H. Magill, Port Hope ; J. S. R. McCann and G. W. Maxwell, Kingston.

ROUTINE AND CORRESPONDENCE—Bros. J. H. Magill, Port Hope, chairman ; A. McFee, Belleville ; D. C. Sanderson, Kingston.

MEMBERSHIP AND GRAND LODGE RELATIONS—Bros. L. C. Pascoe, Belleville, chairman ; J. R. Boothby, Stratford ; W. H. Wallis, Lansdowne ; John Harris and A. T. Smith, Kingston.

AGENCIES AND EXTENSION OF THE WORK—Bros. L. Ferguson, St. Thomas, chairman ; C. R Cotton, Gananoque ; J. Robinson, Prescott ; George Lee, Kingston ; A. H. Blackeby, Galt.

SPECIAL QUESTIONS—Bros. Rev. James Kines, P.G.M, Carleton Place, chairman ; J. R. Beal, Pembroke ; and J. H. Walford, Renfrew.

ASSESSMENT, RATINGS, ETC.—Bros. J. A. Young, Thamesford, chairman ; R. W. Haydon, Almonte ; F. W. Martin, Picton.

LAWS AND AMENDMENTS—Bros. John Ormiston, Gananoque, chairman ; J. H. Walford, Renfrew ; P. Acton, Belleville ; John Ilett.

The Committee recommended the following distribution of work :

To Finance—Paragraphs marked " 2 " in the Directors' Report, the reports of the Treasurer and Auditors.

To Routine and Correspondence—The paragraphs marked " 3 " in the reports of the Directors and Secretary.

To Membership and Grand Lodge Relations—The paragraphs marked " 4 " in the reports of the Directors and Secretary.

To Agencies and Extension of the Work—The paragraphs marked " 5 " in the reports of the Directors, Secretary and Superintendent of Agents and the correspondence referred to the Association by the Directors.

To Special Questions—Correspondence in the hands of the Secretary.

To Assessments, Ratings, Etc.—Paragraphs marked " 7 " in the Secretary's Report.

To Laws and Amendments—Paragraphs marked " 8 " in the Secretary's Report.

The reports were adopted.

After references by the Grand Master, the Deputy Grand Master, the Grand Secretary and others on the work of the Association, the meeting adjourned, on motion of Bro. Kines, until 8 o'clock, for the benefit of committees.

---

## THE DIRECTORS' REPORT.

---

*To the Members of the Odd Fellows' Relief Association of Canada :*

Brethren,—Your Directors have much pleasure in submitting to you their Nineteenth Annual Report, evidencing as it does that the Association has had a year of great prosperity, in the steady growth of its membership, in a favorable death rate, and in a large accession to its reserve fund.

The prevalent dull times, affecting this country as all other countries, have touched us but slightly. The lapses and withdrawals show a slight increase, but so do the applications for increase of benefits, and while the applications for membership are somewhat fewer than last year, we are pleased to be able to state that the falling off occurred in the earlier part of the fiscal year, while the latter part witnessed renewed life among the applications and a large increase in their number, so that we enter on a new year of existence confidently anticipating a year of great prosperity in the extension of our business.

The new members enrolled during the past year have been chiefly young men, as shown by the average age, under 29.  It is gratifying to note that the Association has inspired in so desirable a class of insurers confidence in its solidity and permanency.

The average age of the whole membership has also been reduced, so that now it is only 36.48, an extremely favourable circumstance when we consider that we have passed our nineteenth year.

Another cause for congratulation lies in the low death rate, 5.36, which is the lowest in the history of the Association since the year 1879, when, however, we had been but a few years in existence and had a membership under 1,000.

A tangible and material evidence of our prosperity during the past year is found in the handsome addition we have been able to make to the reserve fund, to the credit of which we have placed the sum of $16,467.07, the largest amount by far that has ever been added thereto since the Association began.

We wish to draw attention to the desirability of improving our facilities for the extension of the work in the outlying Provinces of the Dominion.  The ground to be covered is so vast that it is impossible for one man to attend to it so as to produce the best results.  We think it would pay the Association to employ in such distant Provinces general agents, who would always be on hand there to forward the interests of the Association.  We recommend this to your serious consideration.

The changing of beneficiaries seems to be a stumbling block in the way of many of the members.  They often attempt what cannot legally be effected, and it is well that a word of caution should be given in this connection.  It is advisable in all cases that the beneficiary should be definitely settled, that the name should be given in full, and the relationship ; and in making changes regard must be had for the law of the land, as well as that of the Association, for a member cannot divert the benefits outside of a certain limit or relationship once he has by his certificate created a trust that must remain.  We refer to the Widows' and Childrens' Act and the new Ontario Insurance Law for further evidence upon this point.

20

We regret to have to record the death, since our last annual meeting, of Dr. W. H. Henderson, one of our esteemed colleagues on the Board. Cut off in the prime of life, his death was a great loss to the profession, of which he was a distinguished member, and to this Association, where his wisdom and sagacity made him a valued colleague. Bro. Wm. Mundell was elected by the Directors to fill the unexpired term.

Owing to legislation governing such Associations as ours, changes in the Constitution and working of the O.F.R.A. have become imperative, and as a result additional expense has been entailed and more work has been thrown upon the officers of the Association. But certainly this will be attended with corresponding advantages by the stamp of the Government's approval of such Associations as can comply with the law , and the exclusion from the Province of those which have not been doing business upon a sound financial basis.

The books, accounts and securities of the Association have been examined by the Auditors quarterly, according to the terms of Sec. 2 of Article XI. of the Constitution. The Auditors have also examined the statements made up and transmitted to the Sovereign Grand Lodge, and the several Grand Lodges, as required by the Law of the Order, 1892, and they have also certified to the correctness of the exhibits sent to the Government in compliance with the Insurance Corporations' Act of 1892.

As a copy of the Sovereign Grand Lodge statement has to be mailed to each member before June 1 (and was this year issued in March), in addition to the annual report herewith presented, the members of the Odd Fellows' Relief Association have reason to feel that they are being furnished with ample information in respect to the finances, and that the former practice of sending out a quarterly printed balance sheet can very well be dispensed with.

Matters of importance will come before the Annual Meeting, but it is not necessary to recapitulate them. They are dealt with in detail by the reports of our officers.

Three of the Directors, F. Fowler, M.D., S. Oberndorffer, and J. B. McIver, who were elected in January, 1891, for three years, and could, therefore, hold office until January, 1894, desire to resign, so that an election may occur, and that the term of the Board may, in time, begin and end with the fiscal year of the Association.

Yours fraternally,

FIFE FOWLER,

Kingston, July 14, 1893. *President.*

## REPORT OF THE SECRETARY.

*To the Odd Fellows' Relief Association of Canada :*

BRETHREN,—I have to report very satisfactory results in connection with the business of this Association for the fiscal year ending on June 30th.

The second half of 1892 was quiet, and afforded evidence of how vitally the general depression in trade was affecting the Benevolent and Fraternal Associations, but with the advent of 1893 new life was put into their business, and the O. F. R. A.'s record has been one of marked interest and improvement.

The accompanying financial and statistical statement speaks for themselves. They show that the Association is growing steadily in membership and favour and usefulness, that its stability is clearly indicated, and that its future is most promising.

### FIXED ASSESSMENTS.

In June, by circular, the attention of the Association was called to the advisability of having its assessments fall due on fixed dates. The importance of the matter became the more apparent by the study of the following Section (40) of the Insurance Corporations' Act of 1892 :—

" No forfeiture or suspension shall be incurred by any member of a friendly society, or person insured therein, by reason of any default in paying any contribution or assessment, except such as are payable at fixed dates, until after notice to the member stating the amount due by him, and apprising him that in case of default of payment by him within a reasonable time, not being less than thirty days, and at a place, to be specified in such notice, his interest or benefit will be forfeited or suspended, and until after default has been made by him in paying his contribution or assessment in accordance with such notice."

The directors gave the subject their careful consideration. They were impressed with the fact that fixed dates for the payments of assessments would be an advantage, and so decided to recommend them for these reasons : (1) That they would save the Association a great deal of embarrassment consequent upon enforced delays in the suspension of defaulting members ; (2) that they would facilitate collections, no longer dependant upon uncertain notices ; (3) that they would equalize the labours of officers and agents ; and (4) that they would economize in postage, the account for which is growing with the business of the Association.

## BI MONTHLY ASSESSMENTS.

It had on several occasions been suggested to the directors that they reduce the number of assessments to six per annum, and the question was discussed in connection with the propositions to have calls fall due upon fixed dates. The idea was not to collect a larger sum yearly from the members, but to have this sum collected bi-monthly. The directors deemed it expedient to remit the issue to the Association, with explanations and voting slips, so that they might express a preferance, and that this preference might be accepted in legislating upon the subject. Two plans were prepared. They were described in the circulars to members in this way :

"Plan No. 1. To keep the ratings as they now are, and to make seven Mortuary Assessments and the Annual Call in each year payable at the following dates : Jan. 15, Mar. 1, April 15, June 1 (Annual Call), July 15, Sept. 1, Oct. 15 and Dec. 1.

"Plan No. 2. To take the same number of assessments as proposed in plan No. 1, but to divide the yearly product by six and so make the Calls payable bi-monthly on the first days of February, April, June, August, October and December, or on the succeeding dates if the first day of the month were a Sunday.

"Thus a member insured for $1,000, at the age of 25, under the present rating, will be called upon to pay $9 annually, divided into bi-monthly assessments of $1.50 each ; a member now insured for $1,500, at the age of 35, would pay $14.65 per year, divided into six parts of $2.44 each, and a member insured for $2,000, at the age of 45, would have to pay $23.40 per year, or $3.90 each alternate month.

"For those who joined under the old ratings it would be in exactly the same proportion, viz., multiply the present Mortuary Assessment by seven, add the Annual Call and divide the result by six. This gives the bi-monthly assessment.

"Example : A member joined Class A, paying $1.10 ; he afterwards joined Class B, paying $1.30 ; his present rating on the $1,500 would be $1.75 per call. Seven times $1.75 is $12.25 ; add the Annual Call and the total is $13.25, which make his bi-monthly assessment $2.21."

## RESULT OF THE VOTING.

To each member a voting slip was sent, either directly or through the agent, with the request that the questions upon it be answered, and that it be returned to me not later than July 1. The returns have not been complete. A great many members have not voted, some because they were not sufficiently interested in the matter, some because they were satisfied with the management in any case and with any departure it might make, and some without assigning any cause for their silence. The vote is as follows :

|  | YEAS. | NAYS. |
|---|---|---|
| 1. Are you in favour of having assessments become due on fixed dates, according to Plan No. 1? | 662 | 983 |
| 2. Are you in favour of bi-monthly assessments, and consequently of a new rating, the amount thus collected to be equal to the product of seven Mortuary Calls and the Annual Call according to the present rating? | 1105 | 724 |

### STANDING OF BRAKEMEN.

At different times the law in regard to the standing of those who become brakemen after joining the Association has been criticized, and in my report of a year ago I intimated that several members had questioned the equity of this law.  At the Annual Meeting on July 20, 1892, the difficulty was dealt with by the Committee on Laws and Amendments, which recommended the following :

"That brakemen are not eligible for membership, and those who become brakemen after joining the Association shall have no claim for injury received while serving permanently or temporarily in that capacity, but so soon as they are changed to the list of ordinary class from the extra-hazardous class, and so report themselves, their membership shall be restored."

An amendment to the report was carried laying the subject over until this year, but with the understanding that the Secretary should ascertain the feelings of the members upon it.

In the meantime three members who became brakemen, all temporarily, I believe, appealed to the Directors for protection. One of them had been identified with the Association for many years, and claimed that it would be a positive hardship to cancel his certificate.  The solicitor of the Association was asked for an opinion.  He held that brakemen were bound by any alteration or amendment of the law of a reasonable character, made subsequently to his becoming a member ; that paragraph XI., of the conditions of membership, was reasonable, that it was legally binding, and that the one that violated it forfeited his claims upon the funds of the Association.  But pending a disposition of the question of brakemen's privileges by the Association, those making a reference of their cases to the Directors were informed that their assessments would be accepted until the Annual Meeting, to be refunded in the event of the law as it stands being confirmed by the members.  I had the questions addressed to the members, and their answers as thus expressed by their votes:

|  | YEAS. | NAYS. |
|---|---|---|
| 3. Are you in favour of permitting men who are not brakemen when they join the Association, to remain in good standing if they become brakemen afterwards, and to rate them in the extra-hazardous class?.............................. | 1,326 | 439 |

A point made by one member, and with the desire that it should be emphasized at the Annual Meeting, was that the occupation of a yardman was as dangerous as that of a brakeman, and that they should be placed in the same category.  The Association has before it at present the claim of one who was the beneficiary of a member falling into arrears on going into the railway service, and who was killed while acting as a yard-man.

### RATING OF ENGINEERS AND FIREMEN.

At the Annual Meeting of the Association in January, 1892, Bro. L. C. Pascoe, of Belleville, gave notice that at the next meeting he would introduce a motion with the object in view of reducing the rating of engineers and firemen to that of ordinary members.

At the meeting on July 20, 1892, the matter was brought up and disposed of in this way :

" Bro. L. C. Pascoe moved, seconded by Bro. L. Ferguson,

"That the motion of which notice was given at the Annual Meeting in January be substituted for that clause of the conditions referring to engineers and firemen, namely, that the words engineer and firemen on railways in the fourth line of Paragraph 12, Article XIII., and embracing the conditions of membership, be struck out, and that Section 3 of Article XIV. be amended by removing engineers and firemen on railway trains from the extra-hazardous class."

" After considerable debate, it was moved in amendment to the amendment by Bro. Rev. W. B. Carey,

"That the rating of engineers and firemen as in the ordinary class be laid over until the next Annual Meeting, the Secretary meanwhile to ascertain, by correspondence, the opinion of the members in regard to the same."

" Bro. Pascoe accepted this amendment and withdrew his motion.

" Bro. Carey's amendment was then put to a vote and carried."

The only method open to me to secure the opinion of members upon the question was to refer it to them on the voting slips, and from the returns I submit this result :

|  | YEAS. | NAYS. |
|---|---|---|
| 4. Are you in favour of rating engineers and firemen as ordinary members and so removing them from the extra-hazardous class ? | 360 | 1376 |

The amendment in the laws affecting brakemen (and yardmen if they are listed as extra-hazardous occupations) can be carried into effect at once, but I would respectfully suggest that the change in the manner of making assessments to the bi-monthly system (if ordered) be deferred until the beginning of 1894. The present register will then be full, and there will have to be a transfer of the accounts to a new book, and it would be expedient to make the change in rating at the same time.

### ONTARIO'S INSURANCE LAW.

The Association has complied with all the requirements of the Ontario Insurance Department, has filed its statements, by.

laws, and literature with the Registrar of Friendly Societies, has applied for and been granted a renewal of its Certificate. This Certificate reads as follows:

## DEPARTMENT OF INSURANCE.

### CERTIFICATE OF REGISTRY AS A FRIENDLY SOCIETY.

Whereas, by the application of the Odd Fellows' Relief Association of Canada, made pursuant to The Insurance Corporations' Act, 1892, it has been made to appear to the undersigned, the Registrar of Friendly Societies for the Province of Ontario, that the said applicant is entitled to registry as a Friendly Society ; now, therefore,

This is to certify that the said Friendly Society is accordingly registered for the transaction of insurance against death and disability, in the Province of Ontario, for the term beginning 1st July, 1893, and ending on the 30th June, 1894, subject to the provisions of the aforesaid act.

J. HOWARD HUNTER.

*Registrar of Friendly Societies.*

Entered in the Friendly Societies'
Register, No. 72, Folio 8.

WILL J. VALE,
*Entry Clerk.*

## SOVEREIGN GRAND LODGE LAW.

The Sovereign Grand Lodge, at its session in the city of Portland, Oregon, in 1892, passed a law in regard to Fraternal Insurance Associations. It provides that the O. F. R. A. shall, in common with all similar organizations, file before the first of June, in each year, with the Grand Secretaries of the Sovereign Grand Lodge and several Grand Lodges, a copy of its Charter, Articles of Incorporation, etc., and a report setting forth the facts of its business; that it shall also file with each Lodge a certificate from the Insurance Department, stating that it has complied with the law of the land ; that it shall forward $10 with its statement to each Lodge, and receive from each a Certificate to the effect that it has fulfilled all the requirements of the law. The Association undertakes to send each member, each year, before June 1st, a copy of its return to the Sovereign Grand Lodge and Grand Lodges, and to attach to all outgoing policies copies of the certificates granted it by the Grand Lodges and the Insurance Department, also of its charter, by-laws, etc.

The Certificates of the Sovereign Grand Lodge came to hand as follows :

*Insurance Certificate as authorized by the Grand Lodge Session of 1892, Journal, pages 13,077, 13,157.*

## SOVEREIGN GRAND LODGE OF THE INDEPENDENT ORDER OF ODD FELLOWS.

*To Whom It May Concern* :

This certifies that the Odd Fellows' Relief Association of Canada, Kingston, Ontario, having complied with the laws of the I. O. O. F. relative to organizations, for the transacting Life, or Accident, or Life and Accident Insurance, is hereby entitled to transact such business for the period of one year from the date of this Certificate, within the territorial limits of such Grand Lodge, or Grand Lodges, as through its or their Executive Officers shall grant permission for that purpose under the laws of the order, and also within the limits of such States, Territories, Provinces or Countries as may be under the immediate jurisdiction of this Sovereign Grand Lodge, and in which no subordinate Grand Lodge exists.

Provided always, that neither this Sovereign Grand Lodge, nor any State, Territorial or Provincial Grand Lodge, nor any Subordinate Body in Oddfellowship whatsoever, shall be held responsible for the engagements or contracts of the Association herein named, nor shall this Certificate be considered or assumed to be an endorsement or recommendation of said Association, nor a guarantee of its solvency or responsibility.

In Witness Whereof we have signed this Certificate, and caused the seal of the Sovereign Grand Lodge to be affixed, in the City of Baltimore, State of Maryland, in the United States of America, on this Twenty-second day of March, in the year one thousand eight hundred and ninety-three, and of our Order of the Seventy-Fourth year.

CL. T. CAMPBELL,
*Grand Sire.*

THEO. A. ROSS,
*Grand Secretary.*

### THE GRAND LODGE CERTIFICATES.

Certificates similar in wording to that of the Sovereign Grand Lodge have been received by the Odd Fellows' Relief Association of Canada from the Grand Lodges of Manitoba, Ontario, Quebec and the Maritime Provinces, dating from and running for the same time. These are on file in the office of the Secretary at Kingston, Ontario.

The British Columbia Grand Lodge has been communicated with in regard to its Certificate, but action is not expected until the February meeting of the Lodge, when application upon the subject will be renewed.

### THE PROPOSED AMENDMENTS.

The proposed amendments have been referred to the members direct, or through the agencies, and therefore have been fairly well understood by them.   They are as follows:

#### ARTICLE VI.—(CONSTITUTION.)

I. In Section 1, change 50 to 45.

II. Add new section, the following :—The following shall be the fees chargeable for admission to the Association, except in the case provided for by Section 5 of this article :

| From 21 to 29 years, $ | 500 | ...................................$ 1 00 |
| " " " " | 1,000 | ............................... 2 00 |
| " " " " | 1,500 | ............................... 3 00 |
| " " " " | 2,000 | ............................... 4 00 |
| From 30 to 34 years, | 500 | ............................... 1 50 |
| " " " " | 1,000 | ............................... 3 00 |
| " " " " | 1,500 | ............................... 4 50 |
| " " " " | 2,000 | ............................... 6 00 |
| From 35 to 39 years, | 500 | ............................... 2 50 |
| " " " " | 1,000 | ............................... 5 00 |
| " " " " | 1,500 | ............................... 7 50 |
| " " " " | 2,000 | ............................... 10 00 |
| From 40 to 44 years, | 500 | ............................... 3 00 |
| " " " " | 1,000 | ............................... 6 00 |
| " " " " | 1,500 | ............................... 9 00 |
| " " " " | 2,000 | ............................... 12 00 |

III. In Section 4, after "examination," insert before "to be" "shall be $1.00."

#### ARTICLE VII.

I. Omit the portions of columns under 44 and its ratings.

II. Add new section as follows :—A member desiring to increase his benefits to any higher amount payable by this Association shall surrender his certificate, and forward the same to the Secretary, together with a written application for such increase, and a fee of 50 cents   The application shall also be accompanied by a medical certificate, as on an original application for membership, except when made within thirty days from becoming a member of the Association.  Upon receipt of such application, the above requirements being complied with to the satisfaction of the Directors, the Secretary shall enter the required changes in the register, and shall forthwith forward to the member a new certificate for the increased amount granted, and such increased benefit shall date from the time of the issuing of such new certificate.   The member shall thereafter pay on such new certificate the rate provided for his actual age at the date of making application for such increase, and his first payment thereon shall be the assessment falling due next after the issuing of such new certificate.

III. Add new section :—If a member desires to reduce his benefit to any lower amount payable by the Association, he shall surrender his certificate to the Association and give written notice to the Secretary to change to the lower amount designated, accompanying the same with a fee of 50 cents ; whereupon the Secretary shall issue a new certificate for the amount required, and such change shall date from the issuing of such certificate.  Such member shall pay full rates on all assessments due on or before said change.

### ARTICLE IX.

I. Substitute for Section 1 :—There shall be six assessments in each year upon the members of the Association, which assessments shall be due and payable on the first days of February, April, June, August, October and December, or on the next following day, not being a Sunday or statutory holiday, if such first day of the month shall fall on a statutory holiday or Sunday. Each member shall pay his assessments to the Secretary of the Association according to the rating at which he became a member or the rating applicable to any increase or decrease of benefits procured by him.

II. Substitute for Section 2 :—Upon the admitted disability of a member, as hereinbefore provided, satisfactory proofs having been previously furnished, each member of the Association shall, if the available funds shall not be sufficient to meet the current claims on the Association, be assessed by the Secretary, and shall then pay to him a sum according to one half of the regular schedule of rates on $1,000.

III. Substitute for Section 3 :—To provide for the payment of the general expenses of the Association, there shall, on the 30th day of June in each year, be appropriated out of the yearly assessment income of the Association, a sum equal to one dollar per head of the membership on said date.

### ARTICLE XV.

I. Change of beneficiary, substitute for Section 2 :—A member in good standing may at any time change his beneficiary or beneficiaries, subject to the conditions of the preceding section, and to the provisions of any law in force in Ontario with regard to securing to wives and children, or other relatives, the benefit of life assurance. For that purpose, he shall, by a writing, signed by him and attested by a witness, and either endorsed or attached to, or identifying his certificate by its number or otherwise, direct the payment of the benefit under said certificate to any person or persons whom he may name. Such writing, together with the certificate, shall be forwarded to the Secretary, whereupon a new certificate shall be issued payable to such beneficiaries as he shall have named.

II. Add new section :—If the beneficiary or beneficiaries under a certifidate be the wife and children of the member, or some one of them, the certificate is deemed a trust in their favor, and so long as any object of the trust remains the member cannot divert it away from such object, except so far as he may transfer or vary it within such class. If the beneficiary be the mother of the member the certificate is also a trust for her and is no longer under the member's control.

III. Add new section :—No certificate shall be assigned to others as collatera security for debt, nor shall the beneficiary or beneficaries be changed except in the manner provided for in this Constitution.

IV. Add new section :—In case a certificate shall have been issued but not received by a member prior to his death, or in case proceedings for a change of beneficiary as herein provided have not been completed, the Association shall pay the benefit to the beneficiary named in the application for membership originally made by the deceased brother, provided such member has complied with the laws of the Association.

### ARTICLE XVI.

I. Add as Section 2, page 9 :—If death or injury be directly or indirectly caused by or due to any unlawful or foolhardy undertaking, in which a member shall engage or participate, or to any immoral conduct or intemperance of which he shall be guilty, no benefit whatever shall be paid by the Association therefor.

### ARTICLE III.   (BY-LAWS.)

I. Amend Section 1 as follows :—The Secretary shall send by mail to the post office address of each member, before each assessment is due, a notice giving the names of the deceased members, the name and number of the lodge to which each belonged, and the amount due by each member to whom said notice shall be sent, or the Secretary may employ a suitable person, an Odd-Fellow and a member of the Association, in each town or city where the members reside, who shall act for the Secretary in serving such notices, either personally or by mail, but the giving of such notice shall not be construed as a condition precedent to the payment of any of the ordinary assessments, nor shall it be obligatory on the Association to give such notice, but the same shall be intended as a reminder to the members, who shall, however, whether in receipt of such notice or not, pay their assessments on the dates prescribed in the Constitution ; and any member failing to pay such assessment shall forfeit his membership in the Association and all benefits therefrom.  Provided that any member may deposit with the Secretary any amount he may deem proper, which amount shall be placed to his credit to meet future assessments.

II. Substitute for Section 2, page 13, the following :—A member of the Association who has forfeited his standing therein, and wishes to be reinstated, shall make application in writing in the following form :

To the Directors of the Odd Fellows' Relief Association of Canada :

" I, the undersigned, formerly a member of this Association, having forfeited my membership by non-payment of assessments, hereby make application for reinstatement, in accordance with the laws of the Association.  I hereby bind myself and my beneficiaries to the terms of the agreement made in my original application."

...............................................
Applicant's Signature.

He shall also pay the full amount of his arrears on all assessments made before the date of forfeiture, together with the amount of all assessments due since said date, said amounts to accompany his application for reinstatement, and shall furnish a physician's certificate on the form prescribed for persons on original application for membership as to his health and fitness, which certificate must be approved by the Medical Referee, the same as upon original application.  If such applicant shall have passed the age of fifty-five years, and three months elapsed since forfeiture, he cannot be reinstated unless his application be approved by the Board of Directors or a majority of them.

III. Substitute for Section 3 :—The first assessment payable by any member of the Association shall be that falling due next after such member shall have been registered on the books of the Association.

IV. Add as Clause 3 :—If a member dies before the date on which an assessment is due, such assessment shall nevertheless be payable upon his certificate, and payment thereof must in all cases be made before the Association shall proceed to a settlement of the death claim.

V. Add as Clause 4 :—Whenever there are no available funds to pay the benefits due by the Association the Directors shall order a special assessment to be made by the Secretary, which shall be paid by each member to the Secretary within thirty days from the date of the call.  Such extra assessment shall be refunded to the members paying the same as soon as the funds of the Association will permit, by the Directors remitting their ordinary assessments until the extra sums paid by them are fully repaid.

### ARTICLE IV.

I. Add new section as follows :—A member may withdraw from the Association at any time by giving notice to the Secretary and paying all assessments to date, and such notice of withdrawal shall be a bar to any action which may be taken subsequently in respect to the certificate or any claim arising in connection therewith.

### ARTICLE VI.

I. Omit last clause, Section 1, and add :—But the standing of the holder thereof shall not be affected by the existence or non-existence of such certificate, or by the failure of the member to produce the same when required. The books of the Association, with entries therein, and the application for the certificate bearing the applicant's signature, shall be sufficient evidence of his membership, and of the issue of his certificate.

II. Add **new section, page 13** :—If a member, whose certificate has **been** cancelled for **any cause, desires again** to become a member of the Association, **he** shall surrender his former certificate, or furnish a statutory declaration **as to its** loss, and make application for a new certificate in the manner and form **prescribed** in this Constitution.

III. Add new **section, page 13** :—If it shall appear that a member has made a mistake in giving **his age at the time of** admission he shall make a written statement of the facts to **the Association.** The Directors, if satisfied that no fraud was intended, may **recommend that the** age and assessment of the member be corrected. The written **statement of the** member shall be retained by the Secretary, who shall make the **correction in** accordance with the facts. The member shall be assessed at his **correct** age from and after the date of receipt by the Secretary of his notice of error, provided he shall not have been ineligible on account of **age at** the time of admission ; and, if at the time of admission he reported his age **as less** than it actually was, he shall pay the difference between what he has paid **and the** amount that would have been payable by him from the time of admission **up to** the date of making correction, if he had been assessed **at** his correct **age.**

### COMMENTS ON THE CHANGES.

Some of the amendments have been suggested by the experience of the last year, and it is proposed to make the law more workable, more practicable and more in harmony with the law of the land. There are a few points, however, which require explanation.

Section 1, of Article VI. of the Constitution limits the age of applicants to 45 years. The rating of members over that is very low, and it is thought to be better that there should be a limit in the age than an alteration in the assessments, especially so as this is a departure upon which other orders have recently decided.

Article VII. is not vitally changed. The idea is simply to make clear the procedure of members in increasing or decreasing their benefits.

Article IX. provides for the payment of assessments on fixed dates, in accordance with the recent vote of the members.

Article XIII. is a change similarly authorized by the vote of the Association.

Article XV. makes more definite the regulations of the Association touching the change of a beneficiary, the assignment of a trust, and the loss of a certificate.

Article XVI. makes a provision which is considered wise and in harmony with the law of other benevolent orders on this point.

Article III. of the By-laws is amended so as to be in unison with Article IX. of the Constitution in its altered form. It also gives a more concise direction concerning arrearages and reinstatements, and suggests a protection in the event of epidemics, provided by other societies, and not resorted to as a rule.

Article IV. of the By-laws guards the Association against claims on behalf of former members who have withdrawn from membership.

Article VI. of the By-laws has been remodelled to meet exigencies such as have arisen in the past experience of the Association.

The form of certificate, in blank, should be embodied in the Constitution as Article XIX.

### CHANGE OF RATING.

If the change of bi-monthly assessments be decided upon the rating of present members will be based upon the amounts they have paid annually during the last three years, namely, the product of seven Mortuary Calls and the Annual Call, divided by six. The bi-monthly rating of new members will be :—

| Age. | $500. | $1,000. | $1,500. | $2,000. | Age. | $500. | $1,000. | $1,500. | $2,000. |
|---|---|---|---|---|---|---|---|---|---|
| 21 | $ 73 | $1 45 | $2 09 | $2 73 | 36 | $ 85 | $1 71 | $2 48 | $3 25 |
| 22 | 73 | 1 46 | 2 10 | 2 75 | 37 | 86 | 1 73 | 2 51 | 3 29 |
| 23 | 74 | 1 47 | 2 12 | 2 78 | 38 | 87 | 1 75 | 2 55 | 3 34 |
| 24 | 74 | 1 49 | 2 15 | 2 80 | 39 | 89 | 1 78 | 2 59 | 3 39 |
| 25 | 75 | 1 50 | 2 16 | 2 82 | 40 | 91 | 1 82 | 2 65 | 3 47 |
| 26 | 75 | 1 51 | 2 18 | 2 85 | 41 | 92 | 1 85 | 2 69 | 3 53 |
| 27 | 76 | 1 52 | 2 20 | 2 87 | 42 | 94 | 1 88 | 2 74 | 3 60 |
| 28 | 76 | 1 53 | 2 21 | 2 90 | 43 | 96 | 1 92 | 2 80 | 3 67 |
| 29 | 77 | 1 55 | 2 23 | 2 92 | 44 | 99 | 1 98 | 2 88 | 3 79 |
| 30 | 78 | 1 57 | 2 27 | 2 97 | 45 | 1 02 | 2 03 | 2 97 | 3 90 |
| 31 | 79 | 1 59 | 2 30 | 3 01 | 46 | 1 05 | 2 10 | 3 07 | 4 04 |
| 32 | 80 | 1 61 | 2 33 | 3 06 | 47 | 1 10 | 2 20 | 3 21 | 4 22 |
| 33 | 82 | 1 64 | 2 37 | 3 11 | 48 | 1 15 | 2 31 | 3 39 | 4 46 |
| 34 | 83 | 1 66 | 2 40 | 3 15 | 49 | 1 23 | 2 46 | 3 61 | 4 76 |
| 35 | 84 | 1 68 | 2 44 | 3 19 | | | | | |

### WORK OF THE AGENTS.

The Association has reason to congratulate its agents upon the excellence of their work. Most of them are active and energetic men, and in pursuance of the instructions given to them have been bringing a large number of the initiates of the order into our membership.

In the oversight of the agencies, the Superintendent, Bro. A. H. Blackeby, has done good service, and his labours in the past year are a further evidence of the necessity of such an official. He has been available when new Lodges have been organized, and has thus been instrumental in leading many members into this auxiliary. In addition, he has visited the Lodges where agencies have not been, and established them, and visited other Lodges and put new life into the work which has been conducted in our behalf. His report shows the extent of his travels, and yet it does not emphasize the value of his services to the Association. Active as he is, however, he cannot cover the territory which the Association assumes to occupy, and therefore I have urged the Directors to take into consideration the question of giving him assistance so far as the outlying provinces are concerned.

THE SETTLEMENT OF CLAIMS.

All claims against the Association are paid as soon as they mature if the papers are complete. The beneficiaries, or those acting in their behalf, are put to as little trouble as possible, and, as a rule, there has been no delay in settling the details. The instructions to agents are quite concise, and when they are followed correctly the claim is settled very often at once, the record coming in by the one mail and the draft in payment of the benefit going out by the next.

On June 28th Bro. W. Hault of Ingersoll died, but the fact was not reported to me until July 4th, when the statistical record of 1892-93 had been closed. It does not, therefore, appear in the financial calculations, nor does it particularly affect the same. The incident, it is to be hoped, will stimulate the agents to notify the head office promptly of every circumstance which affects the business of the Association. The members desire the officers to be prompt in all they undertake, and they in turn are dependant upon the members and agents for the removal of all hindrances to progressive service.

REVISING THE RECORDS.

During the last year new books have been procured, and the clerical work of several years has been revised and consolidated for statistical and financial purposes. The new insurance law has added to the labour of the staff, the Government fiscal year closing on Dec. 31st, while that of the Association ends on June 30th. But the statistical records are now complete, and the reference of the Auditors thereto is quite gratifying.

THE MAILING DEPARTMENT.

An accurate register is kept of all the matter mailed from the office. The summary below will not be understood without this explanation—that the postals embrace the receipts and single assessments ; the letters, the assessments to agents, notices of arrears, certificates to members and correspondence ; the supplies, the parcels, lithographs and circulars to agents :

|  | Post Cards, Receipts. | Letters, Certificates, &c. | Circulars, Lithos, and Packages. |
|---|---|---|---|
| July | 565 | 348 | 707 |
| August | 638 | 473 | 44 |
| September | 920 | 609 | 434 |
| October | 1,140 | 522 | 108 |
| November | 294 | 456 | 114 |
| December | 861 | 735 | 146 |
| January | 640 | 421 | 114 |
| February | 765 | 562 | 124 |
| March | 1,028 | 498 | 293 |
| April | 946 | 905 | 366 |
| May | 731 | 439 | 42 |
| June | 1,055 | 779 | 1,255 |
| Total | 9,587 | 6,747 | 3,747 |

CONCLUSION.

My intercourse with the directors, the agents and members of the Association has been of the pleasantest character. The business has been well organized, and having now the support and encouragement of the Order its future is promising of increased prosperity.

Very Fraternally,

R. MEEK.

KINGSTON, July 11, 1893.

# STATISTICS FOR THE YEAR ENDING 30TH JUNE, 1893

MEMBERSHIP.

| | | |
|---|---|---|
| Membership on 30th June, 1892 | | 5,603 |
| Less Applications for Increases not previously deducted | | 27 |
| | | 5,576 |
| Applications received during the year | | 1,225 |

*Less.*

| | | |
|---|---|---|
| Applications rejected | 54 | |
| Dead | 35 | |
| Lapsed | 178 | |
| Withdrawn | 19 | |
| Applications for Increases (not affecting membership) | 32 | 318 |
| Net increase | | 907 |
| Total Membership, 30th June, 1893 | | 6,483 |

### INSURANCE.

Insurance in force 30th June, 1892, as revised per Gov't Returns.....$7,681,000 00
    Amount for which new Certificates issued..........$1,483,000 00
    Amount of increases during year..... .............    17,500 00

                                         $1,500,500 00

*Less.*

Death Claims Matured. .. .......... $ 45,000 00
Lapsed and Withdrawn............... 261,500 00
                                 306,500 00

    Net increase during the year.... ...... ........... 1,194,000 00

Total Insurance in force on 30th June, 1893... .....................$8,875,000 00

### ASSESSMENT.

Amount of Assessment 30th June, 1892........... ..... .....$9,383 46
    Increase, per call ..................... .............. ...... 1,487 76

    Net amount of Assessment 30th June, 1893.............    $10,871 22

### GENERAL SUMMARY.

| Date. | Membership. | Insurance. | Assessment. | Average Age. |
|---|---|---|---|---|
| June 30, 1892. ..... | 5,576 | $7,681,000 00 | $ 9,383 46 | 37.5 |
| Increase for year.... | 907 | 1,194,000 00 | 1,487 76 | 28.67 |
| Total, July 1, 1893.. | 6,483 | $8,875,000 00 | $10,871 22 | 36.48 |

### FACTS FOR THE BENEFICIARIES.

In connection with the deaths during the year these figures will prove interesting :
    Average age of deceased members, 44.5 years.
    Insurance on the same, $15,000.00.
    Death rate for year, 5.37 per 1,000.

### MEMBERSHIP AND DEATHS SINCE ORGANIZATION.

| Fiscal Period. | Gross Membership | Deaths. | Net Membership | Death Rate per 1,000 per annum each period. | Average Death Rate per 1,000 per annum each period. |
|---|---|---|---|---|---|
| 12 mos. ending June 30, '75 | 364 | | 364 | | |
| "     "     "     " '76 | 813 | 3 | 810 | 3.69 | 2.55 |
| "     "     "     " '77 | 885 | 7 | 878 | 7.91 | 4.85 |
| "     "     "     " '78 | 854 | 5 | 849 | 5.85 | 5.14 |
| "     "     "     " '79 | 832 | 4 | 828 | 4.81 | 5.07 |
| 18 mos.  "   Dec. 31, '80 | 984 | 10 | 974 | 6.78 | 6.13 |
| 12 mos.  "     "     " '81 | 1,040 | 6 | 1,034 | 5.77 | 6.06 |
| "     "     "     " '82 | 1,193 | 11 | 1,182 | 9.22 | 6.60 |
| "     "     "     " '83 | 1,494 | 7 | 1,487 | 4.68 | 6.27 |
| "     "     "     " '84 | 1,875 | 7 | 1,869 | 3.73 | 5.81 |
| "     "     "     " '85 | 2,203 | 16 | 2,187 | 7.26 | 6.06 |
| "     "     "     " '86 | 2,418 | 10 | 2,408 | 4.14 | 5.75 |
| "     "     "     " '87 | 2,641 | 18 | 2,623 | 6.82 | 5.91 |
| "     "     "     " '88 | 2,848 | 19 | 2,829 | 6.07 | 6.02 |
| "     "     "     " '89 | 3,099 | 25 | 3,074 | 8.07 | 6.29 |
| "     "     "     " '90 | 4 036 | 27 | 4,009 | 6.69 | 6.35 |
| "     "     "     " '91 | 5,135 | 33 | 5,102 | 6.43 | 6.36 |
| 6 mos.  "   June 30, '92 | 5,625 | 22 | 5,603 | *3.91 | 6.00 |
| 12 mos.  "     "     " '93 | 6,518 | 35 | 6,483 | 5.37 | 5.97 |

                                            *For 6 mos.

| Name. | Address. | Date of Certificate. | Date of Death. | Cause of Death. | Age. | Amount paid into Assoc'n. | Benefits. | Beneficiaries. |
|---|---|---|---|---|---|---|---|---|
| W. N. Hardy | Tweed | May 28, '92 | July 21, '92 | Railway Accident | 21 | ........ | $1,000 00 | Mother. |
| W. H. Henderson | Kingston | Nov. 29, '84 | Aug. 13, '92 | Bright's Disease | 36 | 8 88 85 | 1,500 00 | Mother. |
| D. Ross | New Glasgow | Oct. 24, '84 | Sep. 8, '92 | Dropsy of Lungs | 55 | 162 80 | 1,500 00 | Wife. |
| J. T. Fletcher | Waterville | Dec. 24, '84 | Sep. 9, '92 | Kicked by a Horse | 53 | 106 55 | 1,500 00 | Wife. |
| C. N. Ridley | Belleville | Nov. 8, '82 | Sep. 12, '92 | Hæmaturia | 67 | 111 25 | 1,500 00 | Daughter. |
| D. McKenzie | Hamilton | Aug. 26, '76 | Oct. 2, '92 | Paralysis and Dropsy | 60 | 232 50 | 1,000 00 | Wife. |
| W. Sudworth | Ingersoll | Jan. 7, '80 | Oct. 3, '92 | Blood Poisoning | 65 | 136 75 | 1,100 00 | Wife.* |
| G. E. Taylor | Halifax | Oct. 16, '91 | Oct. 13, '92 | Typhoid Fever | 22 | 6 00 | 1,000 00 | Wife. |
| W. J. Thompson | Whitby | May 16, '83 | Oct. 15, '92 | Typhoid Fever | 41 | 74 05 | 1,000 00 | Wife & Children |
| G. Waterman | Ayr | Jan. 21, '90 | Oct. 20, '92 | Tuberculosis of Lungs | 30 | 19 00 | 1,000 00 | Wife. |
| J. F. Sutherland | Mount Brydges | Mar. 30, '80 | Oct. 26, '92 | Railway Accident | 45 | 130 00 | 2,000 00 | Wife. |
| J. Humphrey | Byron | Sep. 23, '90 | Oct. 27, '92 | Acute Nephritis | 51 | 110 15 | 1,000 00 | Wife. |
| J. Hopperton | St. Thomas | Mar. 30, '80 | Oct. 30, '92 | Railway Accident | 33 | 96 90 | 2,000 00 | Wife. |
| W. Anderson | Sydenham Valley | Oct. 18, '85 | Nov. 5, '92 | Heart Disease | 51 | 18 75 | 1,500 00 | Wife. |
| W. W Disher | St. Thomas | Ap'l. 6, '81 | Dec. 29, '92 | Apoplexy | 54 | 138 50 | 1,500 00 | Wife. |
| E. Brown | Fredericton | Jan. 12, '85 | Jan. 2, '93 | Carcinoma of Stomach | 57 | 83 75 | 1,000 00 | Wife. |
| O. Hewat | Stirling | Jan. 27, '91 | Jan. 3, '93 | Catarrh of Stomach | 35 | 18 60 | 1,000 00 | Heirs. |
| C. S. Male | Oshawa | May 4, '75 | Jan. 18, '93 | Pneumonia | 77 | 183 00 | 1,000 00 | Heirs. |
| J. A. M'Kerracher | Lanark | Feb. 14, '90 | Feb. 9, '93 | Abdominal Tumor | 42 | 32 65 | 1,000 00 | Wife. |
| A. Murphy | Chatham | Nov. 3, '84 | Feb. 9, '93 | Pneumonia | 44 | 75 60 | 1,000 00 | Executors. |
| G. L. Edgett | Moncton | Nov. 15, '87 | Feb. 23, '93 | Railway Accident | 42 | 53 05 | 1,000 00 | Father. |
| G. S. Caldback | Toronto | Dec. 20, '89 | Feb. 28, '93 | Cerebral Apoplexy | 37 | 32 95 | 1,000 00 | Wife. |
| A. M. Wilson | Granton | Jan. 12, '91 | Feb. 28, '93 | Typhoid Fever | 32 | 6 50 | 1,000 00 | Mother |
| W. J. Wilson | Kingston | May 18, '92 | Mar. 2, '93 | Typhoid Fever | 35 | 18 00 | 1,000 00 | Heirs. |
| J. Cumming | Minnedosa | May 25, '92 | Ap'l. 6, '93 | Pneumonia | 45 | 12 75 | 1,000 00 | Wife. |
| T. Y. Greet | Kingston | Feb. 6, '89 | Ap'l. 17, '93 | Stricture of Œsophagus | 46 | 46 00 | 1,000 00 | Wife. |
| A. McL. Shaver | Blenheim | Dec. 14, '89 | May 4, '93 | Heart Failure | 34 | 43 80 | 1,500 00 | Wife. |
| H. Meyer | Preston | Ap'l. 21, '80 | May 13, '93 | Pulmonary Phthisis | 57 | 112 75 | 1,000 00 | Wife. |
| T. Fleming | Trenton | May 8, '91 | May 18, '93 | Tubercular Phthisis | 46 | 44 90 | 2,000 00 | Wife. |
| J. Hutcheson | Brantford | June 19, '83 | May 26, '93 | Blood Poisoning | 51 | 132 00 | 1,500 00 | Wife. |
| A. Stockford | Kingsville | Feb. 24, '92 | June 3, '93 | Lobar Pneumonitis | 23 | 19 26 | 2,000 00 | Mother. |
| A. D. White | Charlottetown | Sep. 24, '84 | June 13, '93 | Tubercular Laryngitis | 44 | 113 40 | 1,500 00 | Wife. |
| J. Schneider | Chatham | Feb. 2, '76 | June 16, '93 | Heart Disease | 70 | 224 10 | 1,500 00 | Wife. |
| T. Hayes | Guelph | Oct. 21, '75 | June 21, '93 | Rheumatoid Arthritis | 55 | 137 25 | 1,000 00 | Wife. |
| W. Hault | Ingersoll | Feb. 27, '78 | June 29, '93 | Heart Failure | 61 | 163 45 | 1,500 00 | Wife. |

*Disability Claim of **$400** previously paid.

## REPORT OF THE GENERAL AGENT.

*To the Board of Directors of the O. F. R. A. of Canada :*

BRETHREN,—My last Annual Report was written at Virden, Man. I was then on my way east after visiting most of the Lodges in Manitoba and the N. W. T. Since then these places have been visited by me in the order named :—Portage la Prairie, Rat Portage, Port Arthur, Fort William, Hillsburg, Port Burwell, Kerwood, Farnham, Montreal, Huntingdon, Wakefield, Ottawa, Owen Sound, Sault Ste. Marie, Sudbury, North Bay, Huntsville, Thomasburg, Guelph, St. Mary's, Thedford, Kincardine, Tiverton, Ripley, Exeter, Paris, London, Lucknow, Ancaster, Strathroy, Ridgetown, Rodney, Windsor, Amherstburg, Ruthven, Leamington, Merlin, Welland, Port Colborne, International Bridge, Waterloo, Berlin, Fergus, Preston, Guelph, Oshawa, Toronto, Morwood, Chesterville, Listowel, Millbank, Milverton, Hanover, Woodstock, Lucan, Granton, Ilderton, Beaverton, West Toronto, Paisley, Clifford, Georgetown, Alliston, Tottenham, Bothwell, Thamesville, Newbury, Oakville, Ottawa, Manotick, Lindsay, Cobourg, Manilla, Uxbridge, London East, Parham, Pontypool, Ancaster, Hamilton, Aurora, Stayner, Parry Sound, Orangeville, Chesley, Brantford, Wingham, Brucefield, Camlachie, Thedford, Sarnia, Wallaceburg, Dresden, Petrolia, Oil Springs, Ailsa Craig, Paris, Ingersoll, Hamburg, Sutton, Whitevale, Durham, Seaforth and Goderich.

I was also present at the meetings of the Grand Lodges of Ontario and Quebec and the Grand Encampment of Ontario.

Thirty-one new agents were appointed and changes were made in twelve of the old agencies.

In a few of the places visited in Ontario the Lodges were not using the medical examination forms provided by the Grand Lodge. In each case the attention of the members was drawn to the fact that this was a violation of the Constitution, and usually the Secretary was at once instructed to write for a supply.

There are but few Lodges now in Ontario in which the Association has not secured a foothold. In a portion of these few it will be necessary to infuse new life into the Lodge before the Association can hope to do anything. They are, for the most part, Lodges located in small country places and are slowly retrograding. There are, in these villages, more societies than can find material to work upon, and the very fact that the Odd

Fellows' Lodges have not taken up the insurance branch mili-
tates against their success.  Other Lodges, in places no larger,
are alive and prosperous because their members are insured in
our Association, and they use our economical form of insurance
as an inducement to candidates to become members of the I.O.
O.F.

In the case of all the new Lodges started during the year a
very considerable proportion of the members have taken out
certificates of insurance in our Association.

The local agents have been very watchful in looking after
the interests of the Association in nearly all cases.  In the few
instances where it was found they were not doing so new agents
were appointed.

At some points the agents pointed out to me that the five-
cent registration fee was a continual source of annoyance to
them.  In revising the ratings, in case a revision is made, it
would perhaps be as well to include this fee in the assessment
and pay the agents a small additional commission in lieu thereof.

As usual, my relations with the various Grand Bodies and
Grand Officers with which and with whom I have been brought
into contact during the year have been of the most agreeable
and fraternal character.

Trusting that the year into which we have now entered may
be for the Association even more prosperous than the one
through which we have just passed,

I am, Yours Fraternally,

A. H. BLACKEBY.

GALT, July 3rd, 1893.

## TREASURER'S STATEMENT OF RECEIPTS AND DISBURSEMENTS FOR YEAR ENDING 30TH JUNE, 1893.

### RECEIPTS.

FRONTENAC LOAN AND INVESTMENT SOCIETY :
  Balance of Current Account on 30th June, 1892.....................  $153 86

ADMISSION FEES :
  Gross receipts during year ending 30th June, 1893.......$ 2,715 50
    Deduct Commission to Agents............. .. ....... 1,497 36
                                                                1,218 14

ANNUAL CALL :
  Gross receipts on account thereof, including balance on
    30th June, 1892...............................$ 5,785 10
    Deduct Commission to Agents ...................... 316 34
                                                                5,468 76

ASSESSMENTS :
   Gross receipts on account thereof, including balance on
          30th June, 1892 ..... ............ .... ... ...$67,364 84
        Deduct Commission to Agents...................... 3,742 05

                                               63,622 79
FEES :
   Amount received for Changed Certificates .... .... .... . .... .      52 00

INTEREST FROM ALL SOURCES, VIZ. :
     Debentures.......... .... .....................$ 1,029 57
     Special Deposits.   .  .... ... ...... ....      300 11
     Current Bank Account ..... ..... ...............    125 03

                                           1,454 71
TORONTO GENERAL TRUSTS Co.
   Received in the matter of Southwell Estate......................    500 00

FREEHOLD LOAN AND SAVINGS Co. :
   Received amount of Debentures matured........................  15,000 00

                                         $87,470 26

## DISBURSEMENTS.

BENEFICIARIES, VIZ. :
  Claims which were unadjusted on 30th June, 1892 :
    Hattie Hipkiss, Toronto............................... 2,000 00
    Annie C. McNab, St. Thomas..... .............. 2,000 00
    Margaret Jane Williams, Lindsay...................,... .. 1,500 00
    Estate of T. Price, Arnprior........................... 1,000 00
    Estate of G. R. Reid, Petrolia.  ...................... 1,000 00

                                         7,500 00

  Adjusted Claims pertaining to year ending 30th June, 1893 :
    Mary Hardy, Tweed............................ 1,000 00
    Ella Rosamond Henderson. Kingston..  ... ............ 1,500 00
    Lydia G. Fletcher, Waterville, N.B.............. .... 1,500 00
    Executor of Estate of C. N. Ridley, Belleville.......... 1,500 00
    Eliza J. Sudworth, Ingersoll............................ 1,100 00
    Mary Ann Taylor, Halifax, N.S.................... 1,000 00
    Mary Ann Waterman, Ayr...................... 1,000 00
    Annie Sutherland, Mount Brydges...................... 2,000 00
    Elizabeth Ann Ross, New Glasgow, N.S............. 1,500 00
    Rachel Hopperton, St. Thomas................... 2,000 00
    Almira J. McKenzie, Hamilton ...................... 1,000 00
    Ann Humphrey, Stratford.................................. 1,000 00
    Janet Anderson, Wallaceburg........................ 1,500 00
    Eliza J. Thompson, Whitby............................ 1,000 00
    Amelia A. Disher, St. Thomas..  ..... ........... 1,500 00
    Jane Brown, Fredericton, N.B............  ............. 1,000 00
    C. Matilda McKerracher, Lanark.................... 1,000 00
    Executors of Alexender Murphy, Chatham.............. 1,000 00
    Hiram Edgett, Moncton, N.B........................ 1,000 00
    Elizabeth A. Caldbeck, Toronto..... ............... 1,000 00
    Guardians of Estate of O. Hewat, Stirling.............. 1,000 00
    Executors of A. M. Wilson, Fish Creek................ 1,000 00
    Administrators of C. S. Male, Oshawa................ . 1,000 00
    Executors of W. J. Wilson, Kingston.............. 1,000 00
    Caroline Shaver, Blenheim........................... 1,500 00
    Helena E. Greet, Kingston............................ 1,000 00
    Annie Fleming, Trenton........  ..............  .... 2,000 00
    Sarah Jane Hutchinson, Brantford..... ............. 1,500 00
    Emily Cumming, Minnedosa, Man................... 1,000 00
    Ellen Stockford, Harrow, Ont........................ ... 2,000 00

                                         38,100 00

DISABILITY CLAIMS :

| | | |
|---|---:|---:|
| Abednego Bardwell, Guelph | $500 00 | |
| James M. Gordon, Beaverton | 500 00 | |
| | | 1,000 00 |

EXPENSES :

| | | |
|---|---:|---:|
| Directors | 80 00 | |
| Office rent | 132 88 | |
| Fuel for office | 39 00 | |
| Printing and Advertising | 503 10 | |
| Books, Stationary and Binding | 115 06 | |
| Auditors, six months ending 30th June, 1892 | 40 00 | |
| Travelling expenses, Superintendent of Agencies | 800 00 | |
| North-West Agency, expenses | 26 40 | |
| Quebec Agency, expenses | 4 00 | |
| Ontario Agency, expenses | 4 75 | |
| Postage Exchange, Telegrams, &c | 469 34 | |
| Annual Meeting, expenses | 88 20 | |
| Medical Examinations of Applications | 171 75 | |
| Law Expenses | 38 82 | |
| Fraternal Association, membership fee | 30 00 | |
| "        "        delegate's expenses | 11 50 | |
| Registration under Insurance Law | 25 00 | |
| Duplicate of Insurance Registration | 5 00 | |
| Extra work in Secretary's office | 60 00 | |
| Caretaker of office | 36 00 | |
| Fitting up office | 92 48 | |
| Post Office Box Rent | 6 00 | |
| Premium on Bonds | 25 00 | |
| Telephone Rent | 25 00 | |
| Water and Gas for Office | 11 70 | |
| City Directory | 2 00 | |
| Insurance of Office Furniture | 3 00 | |
| Rubber Stamp | 1 25 | |
| Provincial Grand Lodges, Registration | 40 00 | |
| Sovereign Grand Lodges, Registration and Duplicate | 14 00 | |
| Incidentals | 12 00 | |
| | | 2,913 23 |

SALARIES :

| | | |
|---|---:|---:|
| R. Meek, Secretary | 1,200 00 | |
| F. R. Sargent, Registrar | 553 50 | |
| D. F. Lloyd, retired, balance of salary | 146 50 | |
| K. Abraham, Clerk | 250 00 | |
| D. Callaghan, Treasurer | 200 00 | |
| A. H. Blackeby, Superintendent of Agencies | 900 00 | |
| | | 3,250 00 |

OFFICE FURNITURE :

| | | |
|---|---:|---:|
| Desk for Secretary's Office | | 35 00 |

INVESTMENTS MADE DURING THE YEAR :

| | | |
|---|---:|---:|
| Freehold Loan and Savings Company | 1,000 00 | |
| Western Canada Loan and Savings Company | 11,000 00 | |
| London and Canadian Loan and Agency Company | 1,000 00 | |
| Huron and Erie Loan and Savings Company | 5,000 00 | |
| Imperial Loan and Investment Company | 4,000 00 | |
| British Canadian Loan and Investment Company | 3,000 00 | |
| Bank of Montreal | 4,000 00 | |
| Merchants' Bank of Canada | 1,000 00 | |
| | | 30,000 00 |

| | |
|---|---:|
| Balance, Current account, Frontenac Loan and Investment Society | 4,672 03 |
| | $87,470 26 |

Certified correct.

A. T. SMITH, } Auditors.
JOHN NICOLLE, }

KINGSTON, July 10th, 1893.

## TREASURER'S STATEMENT OF ASSETS AND LIABILITIES FOR YEAR ENDING 30th JUNE, 1893.

### ASSETS.

| | | |
|---|---|---|
| ANNUAL CALL | | $    492 95 |
| ASSESSMENTS | | 10,090 45 |
| OFFICE FURNITURE | | 326 80 |
| FRONTENAC LOAN AND INVESTMENT SOCIETY, current account | | 4,672 03 |

INVESTMENTS, VIZ.:

Debentures :

| | | |
|---|---|---|
| Freehold Loan and Savings Co., Toronto | $ 1,000 00 | |
| Western Canada Loan and Savings Co., Toronto | 11,000 00 | |
| London and Canadian Loan and Agency Co., Toronto | 1,000 00 | |
| Huron and Erie Loan and Savings Co., London | 5,000 00 | |
| Imperial Loan and Investment Co., Toronto | 4,000 00 | |
| British Canadian Loan and Investment Co., Toronto | 3,000 00 | |
| | | 25,000 00 |

SPECIAL DEPOSITS :

| | | |
|---|---|---|
| Bank of Montreal | 10,000 00 | |
| Merchants' Bank of Canada | 5,000 00 | |
| | | 15,000 00 |
| | | $55,582 23 |

### LIABILITIES.

LIABILITIES TO THE ASSOCIATION.

PERMANENT FUND :

| | | |
|---|---|---|
| Amount on 30th June, 1892 | 2,233 30 | |
| Surplus from Revenue and Expenditure | 23,348 93 | |
| | 25,582 23 | |
| Transferred to Reserve Fund | 16,467 07 | |
| | | 9,115 16 |

RESERVE FUND :

| | | |
|---|---|---|
| Amount on 30th June, 1892 | 25,000 00 | |
| Transfer from Permanent Fund | 16,467 07 | |
| | | 41,467 07 |

LIABILITIES TO BENEFICIARIES.

UNADJUSTED CLAIMS, ADMITTED, BUT AWAITING

PROOFS OF DEATH, VIZ :

| | | |
|---|---|---|
| H. Meyer, Preston, died 13th May, 1893 | 1,000 00 | |
| A. D. White, Charlottetown, P.E.I., died 13th June 1893 | 1,500 00 | |
| J. Schneider, Chatham, died 16th June, 1893 | 1,500 00 | |
| T. Hayes, Guelph, died 21st June, 1893 | 1,000 00 | |
| | | 5,000 00 |
| | | $55,582 23 |

Certified correct.

A. T. SMITH, } Auditors.
JOHN NICOLLE, }

July 10th, 1893.

## TREASURER'S STATEMENT OF REVENUE AND EXPENDITURE FOR YEAR ENDING 30TH JUNE, 1893.

### REVENUE.

| | | |
|---|---:|---:|
| ADMISSION FEES | | $ 2,715 50 |
| ANNUAL CALL, gross receipts | $ 5,785 10 | |
| Deduct amount belonging to last year | 81 27 | |
| | | 5,703 83 |
| ANNUAL CALL, unpaid but collectible | 524 40 | |
| Deduct estimated commission | 31 45 | |
| | | 492 95 |
| ASSESSMENTS, gross receipts | 67,364 84 | |
| Deduct amount belonging to last year | 8,706 37 | |
| | | 58,658 47 |
| ASSESSMENTS, unpaid but collectible | 10,696 87 | |
| Deduct estimated commission | 606 42 | |
| | | 10,090 45 |
| FEES | | 52 00 |
| INTEREST | | 1,454 71 |
| | | $79,167 91 |

### EXPENDITURE.

| | |
|---|---:|
| EXPENSES | $ 2,913 23 |
| SALARIES | 3,250 00 |
| COMMISSION TO AGENTS | 5,555 75 |
| DISABILITY CLAIMS | 1,000 00 |
| DEATH CLAIMS, pertaining to year ending 30th June, 1893, adjusted and paid | 38,100 00 |
| UNADJUSTED CLAIMS | 5,000 00 |
| SURPLUS OVER EXPENDITURE, for year ending 30th June, 1893 | 23,348 93 |
| | $79,167 91 |

D. CALLAGHAN,
*Treasurer.*

Certified correct.

A. T. SMITH, } Auditors.
JOHN NICOLLE, }

July 10th, 1893.

## THE AUDITOR'S REPORT.

*To the President, Directors and Members of the Odd Fellows' Relief Association of Canada :*

BRETHREN,—We beg to report that we have completed the audit of the Association's books for the year ending June 30th, 1893.

We have made a careful examination of all vouchers for moneys received by your Secretary from all sources, and have compared the same with the original entries in his books and find them correct.

The changed certificates, releases of claims, &c., have also been carefully examined, and we take pleasure in certifying to their correctness in every particular.

We have also examined the various books kept for statistical purposes, and we consider that it would be difficult to devise a more complete record of the work done by the Association.

We have also examined the books of account of your Treasurer, and find them to correspond with those of your Secretary. All moneys received by the Treasurer have been promptly deposited in the Bank to the credit of the Association. Vouchers were presented for our inspection for all payments made and found correct. The balance of cash on deposit, as shown by the books and statements of the Treasurer, corresponds with the certificate of the Manager of the Frontenac Loan and Investment Society, appended hereto.

The statements submitted herewith are correct abstracts from the books of the Treasurer.

We have carefully examined the securities for all permanent investments made by the Association of its Reserve Fund, and found them perfectly correct.

We congratulate the Association on the favourable terms which have been secured, and the substantial additions to the Reserve Fund which have been made during the year, and beg to express our admiration of the methodical and efficient system of book-keeping, and to congratulate the Association upon having secured such an efficient staff of officers.

All of which is respecefully submitted.

A. T. SMITH,    } Auditors.
JOHN NICOLLE, }

KINGSTON, July 11th, 1893.

---

FRONTENAC LOAN AND INVESTMENT SOCIETY,

KINGSTON, July 11th, 1893.

I hereby certify that the balance on deposit at the credit of the Odd Fellows' Relief Association at the close of 30th June, 1893, was $4,672.03, as shown by the books of the Frontenac Loan and Investment Society on that date.

THOMAS BRIGGS, Manager.

## REPORT ON THE SECURITIES.

KINGSTON, July 10th, 1893.

The following are the Securities for investments in the name of the Odd-Fellows' Relief Association :—

WESTERN CANADA LOAN AND SAVINGS Co.

| | | | | | |
|---|---|---|---|---|--:|
| Debenture No. 1364, expires July, | 1894 | | $1,000 00 | |
| " No. 1365, " " | 1894 | | 1,000 00 | |
| " No. 1366, " " | 1895 | | 1,000 00 | |
| " No. 1367, ", " | 1895 | | 1,000 00 | |
| " No. 1368, " " | 1896 | | 1,000 00 | |
| " No. 1369, " " | 1896 | | 1,000 00 | |
| " No. 1370, " " | 1897 | | 1,000 00 | |
| " No. 1371, " " | 1897 | | 1,000 00 | |
| " No. 1375, " Jan. 1, | 1898 | | 1,000 00 | |
| " No. 1381, " July, | 1898 | | 1,000 00 | |
| " No. 1382, " " | 1898 | | 1,000 00 | $11,000 00 |

IMPERIAL LOAN AND INVESTMENT Co. OF CANADA.

| | | | |
|---|---|--:|--:|
| Debenture No. 117, expires Jan., | 1898 | $1,000 00 | |
| " No. 118, " " | 1898 | 1,000 00 | |
| " No. 119, " " | 1898 | 1,000 00 | |
| " No. 120, " " | 1898 | 1,000 00 | 4,000 00 |

HURON AND ERIE LOAN AND SAVINGS Co.

| | | | |
|---|---|--:|--:|
| Debenture No. 6361, expires Jan., | 1898 | $1,000 00 | |
| " No. 6362, " " | 1898 | 1,000 00 | |
| " No. 6363, " " | 1898 | 1,000 00 | |
| " No. 6364, " " | 1898 | 1,000 00 | |
| " No. 6365, " " | 1898 | 1,000 00 | 5,000 00 |

BRITISH CANADIAN LOAN AND INVESTMENT Co.

| | | | |
|---|---|--:|--:|
| Debenture No. C 124, expires Jan., | 1898 | $1,000 00 | |
| " No. C 125, " " | 1898 | 1,000 00 | |
| " No. C 126, " " | 1898 | 1,000 00 | 3,000 00 |

LONDON AND CANADIAN LOAN AND AGENCY Co.

| | | | |
|---|---|--:|--:|
| Debenture No. 0319, expires Jan., | 1898 | $1,000 00 | 1,000 00 |

FREEHOLD LOAN AND SAVINGS Co.

| | | | |
|---|---|--:|--:|
| Debenture No. 769, expires Jan., | 1898 | $1,000 00 | 1,000 00 |

BANK OF MONTREAL DEPOSIT RECEIPTS.

| | | |
|---|--:|--:|
| No. 91425, 3½ per cent | $1,000 00 | |
| No. 91426, 3½ " | 1,000 00 | |
| No. 91427, 3½ " | 1,000 00 | |
| No. 91428, 3½ " | 2,000 00 | |
| No. 91429, 3½ " | 5,000 00 | 10,000 00 |

MERCHANTS' BANK OF CANADA DEPOSIT RECEIPTS.

| | | |
|---|--:|--:|
| No. 00856, 3½ per cent | $1,000 00 | |
| No. 00857, 3½ " | 1,000 00 | |
| No. 00858, 3½ " | 1,000 00 | |
| No. 00859, 3½ " | 1,000 00 | |
| No. 00860, 3½ " | 1,000 00 | 5,000 00 |

| | |
|---|--:|
| | $40,000 00 |

A. T. SMITH,  
JOHN NICOLLE, } Auditors.

## EVENING SESSION.

At 8 o'clock in the evening the Association resumed business, and with a large attendance of members.

Dr. Fowler, on taking the chair and calling the meeting to order, said : —

It affords me abundant satisfaction and a great deal of pleasure to preside here, more especially when I contrast the small beginning of the Association, nearly twenty years ago, with the magnificent showing which we have to-day. Then a few earnest, courageous Odd Fellows in Kingston founded the institution, and their confidence in it has been justified by the great increase in its membership. Then its membership was almost entirely confined to the Odd Fellows resident in Kingston and its vicinity, and they were counted by tens ; now the members are to be counted by thousands, and they are to be found in every province of the Dominion, and in far distant lands. We find, too, in regard to other considerations, that the confidence of the originators of the Association has been fully sustained in its successful operations. This is exemplified in its finances. Formerly there was not a reserve fund, and as the claims upon its funds were presented the calls or assessments were made. Now there is a good reserve, which is rapidly being increased, and the presence of it is a guarantee of stability and of protection against the burdens an epidemic and a sudden increase of mortality among the members might entail. Then the confidence of the Order in the Association is made manifest by the attendance of members here this evening, and of the presence of the Grand Master, the Deputy Grand Master, the Grand Secretary of Ontario, and other leading Odd Fellows. These show their sympathy with the work of the Association, their unbounded confidence in it, and their satisfaction with the progress it has made. We have here to-day many keen business men, whose examination into the financial affairs of the Association assures them and us that it is in a sound condition, that its business is conducted upon correct principles. It is not necessary for me to detain you by making further remarks. I thank you for your presence, and trust that your interest in the Association, in its work, growth and usefulness, will be increased by the reports and discussions that will follow. (Applause.)

Bro. S. Oberndorffer followed with a reference to the devotion of Dr. Fowler to the business of the Association. He had been very watchful of it from its inception, and a great deal of its success was due to him.

### REPORT OF THE FINANCE COMMITTEE.

Bro. J. Donogh, from the Committee on Finance, presented the following report :—

*To the Odd Fellows' Relief Association of Canada :*

Your Committee on Finance beg leave to report as follows on the various matters submitted to them for consideration :

We have carefully examined and checked over the various debentures and deposit receipts, which represented the amount invested at the credit of the Reserve Fund, and find the same correct, and we also approve of the character of the securities in which the investments have been made.

We have also examined the original certificate of the Manager of the Frontenac Loan and Investment Society, showing that the balance on deposit at the credit of the O. F. Relief Association at the close of June 30th, 1893, was $4,672.03. which corresponds with the cash account of the Secretary and Treasurer.

We have also been shown the original certificate of the Auditors and compared the same with the published copy.

We also find that the unpaid claims shown in the Treasurer's Statement under the title " Liabilities to Beneficiaries," and amounting to $5,000.00, have since the first of July been fully paid off.

We have carefully and critically examined the books of account and the various forms employed in both the Secretary's and the Treasurer's offices, and we take pleasure in testifying to the neatness and painstaking accuracy which characterize the work, and we desire to say further that, viewed from an accountant's standpoint, we consider that the state of perfection of systems employed for the registration of members. the record of accounts, and the handling and care of the moneys received and disbursed, leaves so little room for improvement that we have no suggestions to offer on this line.

We believe it to be justly the due of the Directors and Officers to call the attention of the members to the wise caution with which the business of the Association has been conducted, and to the fidelity and strict economy with which the financial affairs have been managed.

An examination of the books has shown us the commendable promptness with which all claims have been settled.  Although not compelled to make payments in a shorter time than sixty days the Association has in every case paid a claim on the very day on which proofs were completed.  Unquestionably this extra punctuality should enhance the value of a certificate to every holder.

The Financial Report is gratifying in the extreme, and every member of the Association should have his attention called to the facts presented.  The available assets of the Association were reported on June 30th, 1892, as being $27,233.30, while on June 30th, 1893, they amounted to $35,582.23, an increase of more than double in one year.

The surplus of revenue over expenditure for the past year amounted to $23,348.93, and the Reserve Fund has, with rapid strides, reached $41,467.07.

We would ask the Association to commend in the strongest terms the action of the Directors in transferring to the credit of the Reserve Fund $16,467.07. Having entered upon this policy it should be continued until this Fund shall have reached such an amount as will place the Association beyond the danger of attack from either a natural or unexpected increase in the death rate.

The death rate during the past year has been almost abnormally low, and the increase in the issue of new certificates has been very large, and it is during these prosperous years that a fund should be accumulated which shall give to every certificate-holder a guarantee that carries on its face the stamp of stability.

The returns called for by the Ontario Government and the Sovereign Grand Lodge have very largely increased the duties of the employees of the Association, and we learn that during the past year the Secretary has paid out for extra assistance the small advance in salary made to him by the Directors.

We recommend that the Secretary be reimbursed for the amount expended by him for such clerical assistance.

We believe that services faithfully rendered by the officers and employees should be recognized by the payment of salaries commensurate with the duties required, and we recommend that this meeting convey to the Directors an assurance of hearty support in any action which they may take in the direction of suitably remunerating the various officers and employees.

Attention has been called to the fact that the reports of the proceedings of this Association are only to be found in complete form in one file in the hands of the Treasurer. As every year will render more valuable these early records, and increase the danger of their loss, we believe it to be necessary that steps be taken to obtain a reprint of the entire records up to date.

We recommend that an appropriation, not to exceed $200, be made for the pur-pose of publishing 150 copies of these reports in bound form, and they be sold at cost to such members as may desire them.

All of which is respectfully submitted.

> JOHN DONOGH, *Chairman.*
> J. B. KING.
> J. S. R. McCANN.
> J. H. MAGILL.

Bro. Donogh moved the adoption of the report, and the Grand Secretary seconded it. The motion was carried.

## MEMBERSHIP AND GRAND LODGE RELATIONS.

Bro. A. T. Smith, from the Committee on Membership and Grand Lodge Relations, presented the following report, and on his motion, seconded by Rev. Bro. Kines, it was adopted :—

*To the Odd Fellows' Relief Association of Canada* :

Your Committee congratulate the Association on the large percentage of young men that have been admitted during the year showing such a low average age.

We feel that this satisfactory state of affairs is owing largely to the friendly relations which exist between this Association and the several Grand Lodges, and to the faithful, energetic work of the Agents. We earnestly hope that the pres-ent relations may be carefully fostered, and that the Agents will be encouraged to secure young members as soon as they are initiated into the Order.

We congratulate the Association for the splendid increase in membership dur-ing the year, and we feel assured that as the benefits of membership become better known amongst the brethren the increase from year to year will be greater. The operations of the Association are very apparent in the large amount of insurance in force.

We regret that owing to the injudicious conduct of some Associations that have been foisted on the various Grand Lodges, the Sovereign Grand Lodge has, in its wisdom, passed very stringent laws in connection with the same. We feel that it is somewhat of a hardship for an Association such as ours to be put to the expense of extra clerical work, still we feel that in the end all Associations doing a legitimate business will benefit by the legislation referred to.

While we deeply regret that so many of our brethren throughout the country have been called away during the year just closed, it is a subject for congratulation that the Association has in every case promptly paid all claims, and we feel that it is nobly performing the work for which it was instituted.

We congratulate the Association on the low death rate, showing conclusively that careful judgment has been exercised in the selection of desirable risks.

All of which is respectfully submitted.

> L. C. PASCOE, *Chairman.*
> J. R. BOOTHBY.
> W. H. WALLIS.
> JNO. HARRIS.
> A. T. SMITH.

### AGENCIES AND EXTENSION OF THE WORK.

Bro. L. Ferguson, from the Committee on Agencies, etc., presented the following report :—

*To the Odd Fellows' Relief Association of Canada :*

Your Committee beg leave to submit as follows :—

1. With reference to the paragraph in the report of the Directors, and also that in the report of the Secretary, dealing with the subject of affording increased assistance for facilitating the work in the outlying provinces, we would recommend that the Directors consider the advisability of appointing two special agents, one in the Maritime Provinces and one in the Province of Manitoba. These Special Agents to be remunerated by a fixed amount, based on what would be the cost of their travelling expenses, and further by a small fee on each accepted application received from their respective territories.

2. In taking up the report of the Superintendent of Agencies we do not see how the recommendation of Bro. Blackeby, relating to the registration fee, can be carried out in view of the fact that the table of figures sent to members by the Secretary was based upon the result of seven mortuary assessments and the annual call. But in dealing with this matter we recommend that in future on all mounts received in payment of assessments from the territory covered by any particular agent, the usual six per cent. be allowed such agent.

3. With regard to the letters submitted we have no remarks to offer. Most of them deal with applications for positions as agents, and the Directors are in a better position to deal with such offers than this committee. On the correspondence with the Grand Secretary of British Columbia we commend the action of our Secretary and trust that continued efforts will be made to secure the sanction of the Grand Lodge of British Columbia to the workings of our Association until the desired result is obtained and our Association is recognized as the insurance auxiliary of the order in every province of the Dominion.

4. It affords us a good deal of pleasure to be able to testify to the valuable and efficient work performed during the year by the Superintendent of Agencies. His zeal and activity in promoting the interests of the Association are well known, and the Association is to be congratulated on having such an active worker as Bro. Blackeby enlisted in its service.

Respectfully and fraternally submitted.

L. FERGUSON, *Chairman.*
JOHN ROBINSON.
C. R. COTTON.
GEORGE LEE.

Bro. Ferguson, seconded by Bro. J. A. Young, moved the reading of the report clause by clause.—Carried.

Bro. T. Donnelly, seconded by Bro. Godwin, moved the amendment of the first clause by the erasure of the last sentence, referring to the manner in which the Special Agents should be remunerated. This matter to be dealt with by the Directors.

The amendment, after some discussion, was carried.

The remaining clauses were passed, and the report as amended was adopted on motion of Bro. Ferguson.

### THE QUACKENBUSH CASE.

Rev. Bro. James Kines, from the Committee on Special Questions, presented the following report :—

*To the Odd Fellows' Relief Association of Canada :*

Your Committee on Special Questions beg leave to report as follows :—

There was referred to us the case of Bro. George Quackenbush, of Carleton Place, Ont., who was injured in the discharge of his duties while employed in the yard of the C. P. R. as yardman, and from which injuries he subsequently died.

Believing that his employment as yardman might forfeit his claim on the Association he hesitated to send in his last call, and while hesitating the accident occurred.

We learn that the day before he died his name was stricken from the roll as a lapsed member, and this, according to our law, destroys his legal claim on this Association.

Yet in view of the following facts, that up to this time he had been a faithful member of the Association, paying promptly all calls, that having from extreme conscientiousness believed his present occupation nullified his claim, that inasmuch as his work was not that of a brakeman but yardman and so did not forfeit said claim, and, further, that his brethren in Carleton Place believe that this Association would be justified in granting at least a gratuity to the widow of the deceased, your Committee recommend that the sum of $800 be granted to the widow, for which consideration she relinquishes all claims, fancied or real, on the said Association.

All of which is respectfully submitted.

> JAMES KINES, *Chairman.*
> J. R. BEAL.
> J. H. WALFORD.

Rev. Bro. Kines moved the adoption of the report, seconded by Bro. Haydon.

Moved by J. B. King, seconded by J Oliver, and resolved,— That the report of the Committee on Special Questions be referred to the Directors, with instructions that they take legal advice on the matter, and, if the Association can legally do so, effect a compromise with the widow.

The amendment, after considerable discussion, was carried.

### ROUTINE AND CORRESPONDENCE.

Bro. J. H. Magill, from the Committee on Routine and Correspondence, submitted the following report :—

*To the Odd Fellows' Relief Association of Canada :*

We beg leave to report as follows :—

Relative to changes in the names of Beneficiaries we would recommend that the name be definitely stated on taking out the certificate ; that the name be given in full, and the relationship of the beneficiary to the insured stated ; and that in the absence of definite instructions a will be made stating to whom the insured desires the benefits to be payable.

We are glad to learn that the necessary conditions for carrying on the work of the Association in harmony with the laws of the land and Order have been fully complied with, as is evidenced by the certificates from the Ontario Government and the different Grand Lodges now on view in the Secretary's office.

Inasmuch as the President of the Association is also the medical referee, and has been paid by fees, we recommend that the Directors give him an honorarium of $300 per annum, in recognition of the most valuable services as President and Medical Examiner of Applications.

Whereas ample information of the state of the finances of the Association, through the Sovereign Grand Lodge Statement and the annual statement of this Association, reaches the members of this Association, we recommend that the quarterly statement hitherto printed be dispensed with.

All of which is respectfully submitted in F. L. and T.

> J. H. MAGILL, *Chairman.*
> A. McFEE.
> D. C. SANDERSON.

The report was considered clause by clause, somewhat amended, and, on motion of Bro. Magill, seconded by Bro. Sanderson, adopted as above.

### ASSESSMENTS AND RATINGS.

Bro. J. A. Young, from the Committee on Assessments and Ratings, submitted the following report :—

*To the Odd Fellows' Relief Association of Canada :*

We, your Committee on Assessments and Ratings, beg to submit the following amendments to the Constitution :—

Strike out Sec. 1, and insert :   "Applicants for membership shall from the date of their acceptance pay assessments according to the following schedule of rates and ages :"   [As printed in the Secretary's report.]

There shall be six assessments in each year upon the members of the Association, which assessments shall be due and payable on the 15th day of the following months, viz., January, March, May, July, September and November, or on the next following day not being a Sunday or statutory holiday, if such 15th day fall upon a Sunday or statutory holiday.   Each member shall pay his assessments to the Secretary of the Association, according to the rating at which he became a member, or the rating applicable to any increase or decrease of benefits procured by him.

Amend Art. XIII, Clause XI, to read :   "Brakemen or yardmen shall not be eligible for membership, but members of the Association on becoming brakemen or yardmen shall be transferred to the extra-hazardous class and pay the extra-hazardous rate, but on ceasing to be so employed shall, if otherwise qualified, be replaced in the ordinary class."

Amend Clause XII, of the same Article, by striking out the words on fourth line, "or as engineers and firemen on railways."

Add new clause, Number 13 :   "Engineers and firemen on railways shall be rated in the ordinary class."

We recommend that the making of assessments on the bi-monthly plan be deferred until the beginning of 1894.

All of which is respectfully submitted.

*Resolved,*—That the foregoing be adopted.

> J. A. YOUNG, *Chairman.*
> R. W. HAYDON.
> F. W. MARTIN.

The first three paragraphs of the report were, on motion of Bro. Young, adopted as they were read.

Bro. Kines moved, seconded by Bro. Elliott, that the clause relating to engineers and firemen be struck out, and that engineers and firemen remain in the hazardous class.

Bro. Young, seconded by Bro. Pascoe, moved the adoption of that clause of the report dealing with engineers and firemen.

Bro. Kines' amendment was lost, and the report, as a whole, adopted on motion of Bro. Young.

## LAWS AND AMENDMENTS.

Bro. J. H. Walford, from the Committee on Laws and Amendments, presented the following report :—

*To the Odd Fellows' Relief Association of Canada :*

Your Committee, to whom was referred the question of the proposed amendments to the Constitution and By-laws of the Association, beg leave to report :—

That they approve of the amendments submitted to them, with the exception of those numbered I of Article VI and I of Article VII.

They do not think it in the interest of the Association to lower the age of applicants for membership as proposed, but would recommend that, instead, the assessments for the ages proposed to be struck out be increased to amounts more in proportion to the risk of carrying the insurance for such ages.

They also recommend that in place of Sec. 2, Art. IX of the Constitution, and Sec. 5, Art. III of the By-laws, as in the proposed amendments, the following be substituted :

" Whenever, in the opinion of the Board of Directors, the interests of the Association shall require that an extra assessment be made, the Board shall order the same to be made by the Secretary, and such assessment shall be payable by each member within thirty days from the date of the call. Such extra assessment shall be refunded to the members paying the same as soon as in the opinion of the Directors the funds of the Association will permit by remitting their ordinary assessments until the extra sums paid by them are fully repaid."

They further recommend that clause 2 of Sec. 6 in the proposed amendments to the Constitution be adopted with the addition of the following rates :

| | | | | |
|---|---|---|---|---|
| From 48 to 49 years.... .... ............ | $ 500 00 | $ 5 00 |
| " " | .......... .. ............. | 1,000 00 | 10 00 |
| " " | .. .................. . | 1,500 00 | 15 00 |
| " " | .......... ............. | 2,000 00 | 20 00 |

All of which is respectfully submitted.

J. H. WALFORD.
P. ACTON.

On motion of Bro. Donogh, seconded by Bro. Oliver, the consideration of Clause II of the report was deferred until the next annual meeting.—Carried.

The report, as amended, was adopted, on motion of Bro. Walford.

### ELECTION OF DIRECTORS.

On motion of Rev. Bro. Kines, the Secretary was directed to cast a ballot in favour of Dr. F. Fowler, J. B. McIver and S. Oberndorffer, and they were declared re-elected as Directors for the ensuing three years.

On motion of Bro Godwin, the Secretary was directed to cast a ballot in favour of Bros. A. T. Smith and John Nicolle, and they were declared re-elected as Auditors of the Association for the ensuing year.

Moved by Rev. Bro. D. C. Sanderson, seconded by Bro. J. H. Magill, that the sum of $225 be placed to the credit of the Directors as payment for the services of said Directors for the ensuing year.—Carried.

### REVISING THE BY-LAWS.

On motion of Bro. W. Mundell, seconded by Bro. J. B. McIver, the following revision in the By-Laws was authorized:—

#### AMENDMENTS TO THE CONSTITUTION.

Art. I, Sec. 2.—Amend last three lines so as to read " at said office or at such other place in said City as shall be selected by the Directors."

Art. II, Sec. 1.—In third line substitute " to make " for " for the purpose of making."

Art. III, Sec. 1.—In second line substitute " who shall " for " to." In third line strike out " who." In fourth line substitute " shall have been " for " are," and insert " shall have " before " qualified."

Art. IV, Sec. 1.—In second line strike out second " who." Sec. 2, amend first four lines to read as follows : " Three Directors shall retire each year and three shall be elected at each annual meeting in their stead. Such Directors shall serve for a term of three years, or until their successors shall have been elected and shall have qualified." Amend last Clause by striking out " Provided that," changing " may " to " shall," inserting " or " before " subsequent," and numbering in Sec. 3. Sec. 3, to be numbered Sec. 4. Secs. 4, 5 and 6, to be numbered 5, 6 and 7, and last mentioned Sec. 5 to be amended by changing " officers, offices and proxies," to the singular, interesting " shall " before " during," and substituting " his " for " their respective."

Art. V, Number it VII and put as Art. V present Art. XI.

Art. VI, Number it VIII and put as Art. VI present Art. XII. Put as Sec. 3 of new Art. VIII the Sec. numbered 2, Art. VI, in proposed amendments with the addition stated in Report of Committee on Laws and Amendments and changing " 5 " to " 6 " in the beginning thereof. Sec. 3, Number this 6. Sec. 4, in third line, insert " shall be $1.00 and shall " in place of " to." Sec. 5, strike out " of the Association " after " referee."

Art. VII, expunge and replace by present Art. XIII, to be numbered IX, and amended as to Clause 2 by this meeting, by striking out of Clause 12 " or as engineers or firemen on railways " and replacing last seven words by " along with the

22

call due on May 15th."   Add as Sec. XIII new Sec. as to engineers and firemen passed at this meeting.

Art. VIII, Number this X, and put as Sec. 1.  "The limit of benefits payable by this Association shall be $500, $1,000, $1,500 and $2,000," continuing with Sec. in Clause 2, Art. VII, proposed amendments.  As Sec. 2, put Sec. in Clause 3, Art. VII, proposed amendments.  As Secs. 3 to 7, put present Secs. 1 to 5.  As Sec. 8, put Sec. 1 of Art. XVI.  As Sec. 9, put Sec. in Clause 1 of Art. XVI, proposed amendments.

Art. IX, Number XII, and amend as follows :  Substitute for Sec. 1 Sec. in Clause 1, Art. IX, proposed amendments, as amended at this meeting.  Expunge Secs. 2 and 3, and put as Sec. 2 the Sec. containing schedule of rates as passed at this meeting, and as Sec. 3, Sec. in Clause 3, Art. VI, By-Laws, of proposed amendments.  Add as Sec. 4, Sec. in Clause 3, Art. IX, proposed amendments.  Add as Sec. 5 new section relating to special assessment contained in Report of Committee on Laws and amendments.

Art. X, Number this XIII.

Art. XIV amend (1) by striking out last seven words of Sec. 3 and substituting "and members becoming brakemen or yardmen after joining the Association ;" (2) by inserting "and yardmen " after "trains" in Sec. 4.

Art. XV, Number XI, and amend as follows :  Substitute for Sec. 2 Sec. contained in Clause 1, Art. XV, of proposed amendments.  Transfer Sec. 3 to Art. IV, By-Laws, as Sec. 3, and replace by Sec. in Clause 2, Art. XV, proposed amendments.  Add as Sec. 3, Clause 3 following above, and as Sec. 5, Clause 4, thereafter.  Present Sec. 4 number Sec. 6.

Art. XVII, transfer to By-Laws as Sec. 2, Art. III.

Art. XVIII, Number Art. VII.

AMENDMENTS TO THE BY-LAWS.

Art. III of By-Laws, Number this IV, and substitute for Sec. 1 the Sec. in Clause 1, Art. III, proposed amendments.  Substitute for Sec. 2, the Sec. in Clause 2, Art. III, proposed amendments, and transfer it so as to be Sec. 4 of new Art. V.  Put as Sec. 2, Art. XVII, Sec. 1, Constitution.  Substitute for Sec. 3 the Sec. in Clause 3, Art. III, proposed amendments.  Add as Sec. 4 the Sec. next following above in proposed amendments.

Art. IV of By-Laws, Number this V. and put as Sec. 2, Sec. 1 of Art. VI, amended as per Art. VI, Clause 1, proposed amendments.  As Sec. 3, put Sec. 3, Art. XV, of Constitution.  As Sec. 5, put new Sec. as in Art. IV, proposed amendments.  As Sec. 6, put Sec. in Clause 2, Art. 6, proposed amendments.

Art. V, Number this Art. III.

Art. VII, Number this VI.

Art. VIII, Number this VII.

NON-RESIDENT DIRECTORS.

On motion of Bro. Blackeby, seconded by Bro. A. T. Smith, the following were elected the Non-Resident Directors :

Ontario—John Donogh, Toronto ; John Ormiston, Gananoque ; L. Ferguson, St. Thomas.

Quebec—W. Marriage, Montreal ; C. G. Gymer, Richmond ; Charles Griffith, Montreal.

Maritime Provinces—J. H. Sutherland, Halifax, N.S. ; B. Bremner, Charlottetown, P.E.I. ; J. L. Stewart, Chatham, N.B.

Manitoba and North-West Territories—R H. Shanks, Winnipeg ; Dr. Riddell, Crystal City ; J. K. Drinnon, Medicine Hat.

The usual votes were made for the expenses of the hall, etc., for the meeting.

### RESOLUTION OF THANKS.

Bro. Joseph Oliver, of Toronto, Deputy Grand Master, moved that the thanks of the Association be tendered to the President, the directors and the officers, and all who were associated with them in the business of the Association. In doing so he desired to say that for several years he had watched closely the manner in which the affairs of the institution had been directed. He had felt chary in regard to assessment associations of this kind, but prior to joining the O.F.R.A. he had taken notice of its course, and now he was assured that there was no similar association that was on a firmer and sounder basis. (Applause.) He was not saying this because he was at the meeting. He had endeavoured, so far as he could, to impress this thought upon the Order, and to show that it had within it all the advantages which could be got in any other organization, that it was more profitable to pay dues into one organization giving all possible benefits than into three or four for the same results. He hoped the Association would be as prosperous in the future as in the past. He certainly would do all in his power to present the claims of the Association upon the Order as opportunity offered. He had great pleasure in moving the resolution of thanks to the management of the Association. (Applause.)

Bro. John Donogh seconded the motion. He appeared in a double capacity, as a member of the Grand Lodge Advisory Committee, and as a member of the Association. The progress of the institution was very gratifying, and it gave him great pleasure, therefore, to endorse the sentiments of the Deputy Grand Master. He would be glad to say to the Grand Lodge that a very careful examination had been made of the affairs of the Association, and he found the management capable and worthy of the trusts committed to them. He found an efficient clerical staff, an excellent system of accounts, a zealous staff of agents, indeed everything which could conduce to a full appreciation of the Association by the Order. He was satisfied that were the merits of the Association better understood the membership would not be 5,000 or 6,000 but 20,000. He would take pleasure in doing all he could to advance the interests of the Association. (Applause.) He had looked over the records and seen that his lodge (Queen City of Toronto) had sent in sixteen applications in the last six months, and the only fault he had to find was that if the medical referee erred at all it was on the side of safety and caution. All things considered he felt that the O.F.R.A. was second to no association of the kind in Canada. (Applause.)

The President, in replying, said he appreciated very highly the sentiments of men so high in the Order and so keen in business as the Deputy Grand Master and Bro. Donogh. He was very glad that the Association deserved the good words that had been spoken of it.

Bro. T. Donnelly moved that the thanks of the Association be tendered to those who had come to the meeting from a distance and had given their valuable assistance at the meeting. The work of the Committees had been well done, the Finance Committee especially presenting a statement at once lucid, interesting and satisfying.

Bro. McIver seconded the motion, and it was carried amid applause.

At 11 p.m. the meeting adjourned.

----

MEETING OF THE DIRECTORS.

At a meeting of the Directors, held in the Association's office on Friday, July 21, the various officers were re-elected for the ensuing year.

# LIST OF PAST GRAND MASTERS.

THOMAS REYNOLDS[1] ................. Brockville......1856 to 1859
CHAUNCEY YALE[2]..................... St. Catharines .........1859
S. G. DOLSON ........................        "         .........1860
WILLIAM BISSELL[3] .................. London ..............1861
H. C. BINGHAM ...................... Brantford .............1862
JAMES WOODYATT...................... "           .............1863
JAMES SMITH[4] ..................... London ..............1864
JAMES D. TAIT ...................... St. Catharines ......  1865
RICHARD WIGMORE[5] ............. .. London..............1866
HENRY McAFEE[6]...................... Windsor .............1867
JOHN BARR[7] ....................... Hamilton .............1868
THOMAS PARTRIDGE ................ London..............1869
WILLIAM N. FORD...................... St. Mary's ...........1870
JOHN GIBSON........................ Stratford ...........1871
JOHN MURRAY......................... Niagara Falls .........1872
GEORGE WRIGHT ..................... Toronto  ............1873
WM. FITZSIMMONS ...... .......... Brockville  ...........1874
H. E. BUTTERY[8].. .................. London..............1875
J. HAM PERRY ...................... Whitby  ............1876
CL. T. CAMPBELL..................... London..............1877
J T. HORNIBROOK..................... Toronto  ............1878
FIFE FOWLER ....................... Kingston .........  1879
W. H. COLE ........................ Brockville ............1880
J. B. McINTYRE ..................... St. Catharines ...... ..1881
HENRY ROBERTSON.................... Collingwood ...........1882
WM. MACDIARMID..................... Lucan..............1883
A. L. MORDEN ...................... Napanee ....... ...1884
N. H. MARTIN ...................... Chatham .............1885
JOHN ORMSBY DONOGH .............. Toronto  ............1886
JOHN R. REID...................... Brockville ............1887
E. R. ROBINSON.................... London..............1888
R. W. BELL ........................ Peterboro' ...........1889
.............................................................1890
P. E. FITZ-PATRICK ................. Hamilton............ 1891
REV. T. W. JOLLIFFE ............... Campbellford .........1892

1. Died 14th September, 1859.   2. Died 15th April, 1866.   3. Died 4th November, 1878.
4. Died 26th November, 1890.   5. Died 1st March, 1890.   6. Died October 23rd, 1892.
7 Died 25th January, 1883.   8. Died 26th November, 1876.

## LIST OF LODGES.

| LODGE. | No. | LOCATION. | NIGHT OF MEETING. |
|---|---|---|---|
| Brock | 9 | Brockville | Tuesday |
| Cataraqui | 10 | Kingston | Tuesday. |
| Otonabee | 13 | Peterborough | Monday. |
| Union | 16 | St. Catharines | Monday. |
| Phœnix | 22 | Oshawa | Tuesday. |
| Rose | 28 | Amherstburg | Wednesday. |
| Chatham | 29 | Chatham | Tuesday. |
| Eureka | 30 | London | Tuesday. |
| Elgin | 32 | St. Thomas | Friday. |
| Erie | 33 | Port Burwell | Thursday. |
| Gore | 34 | Brantford | Monday |
| Samaritan | 35 | Ingersoll | Thursday. |
| St. Mary's | 36 | St. Mary's | Tuesday |
| Forest City | 38 | London | Monday |
| Rondeau | 40 | Blenheim | Friday. |
| Avon | 41 | Stratford | Wednesday. |
| Excelsior | 44 | Hamilton | Thursday. |
| Frontier | 45 | Windsor | Wednesday. |
| Mount Zion | 46 | Newbury | Thursday |
| Unity | 47 | Hamilton | Wednesday. |
| Dominion | 48 | London | Wednesday. |
| Canada | 49 | Toronto | Friday. |
| Otter | 50 | Tilsonburg | Monday |
| Bissell | 51 | Mitchell | Monday. |
| Covenant | 52 | Toronto | Tuesday |
| Niagara Falls | 53 | Niagara Falls | Tuesday. |
| Collingwood | 54 | Collingwood | Thursday |
| Fidelity | 55 | Seaforth | Wednesday. |
| Queen City of Ontario | 56 | Toronto | Monday. |
| Maple Leaf | 57 | Orangeville | Thursday. |
| Howard | 58 | Strathroy | Wednesday. |
| Kingston | 59 | Kingston | Friday. |
| Corinthian | 61 | Oshawa | Thursday. |
| Huron | 62 | Goderich | Thursday. |
| Barrie | 63 | Barrie | Monday. |
| Victoria | 64 | Hamilton | Alternate Tuesdays. |
| Friendship | 65 | Petrolia | Friday |
| Florence Nightingale | 66 | Bowmanville | Wednesday. |
| Exeter | 67 | Exeter | Tuesday. |
| North Star | 68 | Stayner | Thursday. |
| Hope | 69 | Harrietsville | Saturday. |
| Lucan | 70 | Lucan | Tuesday. |
| The Toronto | 71 | Toronto | Monday. |
| Eastern Star | 72 | Whitby | Tuesday. |
| Fergus | 73 | Fergus | Tuesday. |
| Bothwell | 74 | Bothwell | Tuesday. |
| Warriner | 75 | Port Perry | Monday. |
| St. Thomas | 76 | St. Thomas | Thursday. |
| Oxford | 77 | Ingersoll | Monday. |
| Durham | 78 | Port Hope | Tuesday. |
| Nipissing | 79 | Uxbridge | Thursday. |
| Amity | 80 | Prescott | Thursday. |
| Belleville | 81 | Belleville | Thursday. |
| Beaver | 82 | Ruthven | Tuesday. |
| Clinton | 83 | Clinton | Tuesday. |
| Walkerton | 84 | Walkerton | Friday. |
| Constellation | 85 | Burgessville | Tuesday, |
| Napanee | 86 | Napanee | Tuesday. |
| Empire | 87 | St. Catharines | Thursday. |
| Olive Branch | 88 | Woodstock | Monday. |
| Reliance | 89 | Guelph | Monday. |
| Ivy | 90 | Parkhill | Thursday. |
| Grand River | 91 | Paris | Friday. |

## LIST OF LODGES—*Continued.*

| LODGE. | No. | LOCATION. | NIGHT OF MEETING. |
| --- | --- | --- | --- |
| Milton | 92 | Milton | Tuesday. |
| Western City | 93 | Chatham | Monday. |
| Aylmer | 94 | Aylmer | Tuesday. |
| Nith | 96 | New Hamburg | Thursday |
| Grand Union | 97 | Berlin | Friday. |
| Minto | 98 | Harriston | Friday. |
| Lindsay | 100 | Lindsay | Monday. |
| Golden Star | 101 | Brampton | Thursday. |
| Deseronto | 102 | Deseronto | Wednesday. |
| Cataract | 103 | Niagara Falls South | Thursday. |
| Crescent | 104 | Hamilton | Friday. |
| Manilla | 105 | Manilla | Monday. |
| St. Clair | 106 | Point Edward | Thursday. |
| Waterloo | 107 | Galt | Monday. |
| Royal Oak | 108 | Forest | Monday. |
| Orion | 109 | Georgetown | Monday. |
| Laurel | 110 | Toronto | Alternate Mondays. |
| Peterborough | 111 | Peterborough | Thursday. |
| Lucknow | 112 | Lucknow | Friday. |
| Trenton | 113 | Trenton | Wednesday. |
| Gananoque | 114 | Gananoque | Monday. |
| Harmony | 115 | Brantford | Tuesday. |
| Naomi | 116 | Markham | Monday. |
| Valley City | 117 | Dundas | Wednesday. |
| Maitland | 119 | Wingham | Thursday. |
| Sydenham Valley | 120 | Wallaceburg | Friday. |
| Saxon | 121 | Ailsa Craig | Wednesday. |
| Streetsville | 122 | Streetsville | Friday. |
| Dresden | 124 | Dresden | Monday. |
| Stella | 125 | Carleton Place | Friday. |
| Sarnia | 126 | Sarnia | Tuesday. |
| Mizpah | 127 | Belleville | Monday. |
| Charity | 129 | Sunderland | Monday. |
| Livingstone | 130 | Thorold | Tuesday. |
| Marion | 131 | Renfrew | Monday. |
| Oakville | 132 | Oakville | Monday. |
| Glencoe | 133 | Glencoe | Tuesday. |
| Orient | 134 | Welland | 1st and 3rd Tuesday. |
| Peaceful Dove | 135 | Cannington | Thursday. |
| Cobourg | 136 | Cobourg | Wednesday. |
| St. Lawrence | 137 | Brockville | Thursday. |
| Ancaster | 138 | Ancaster | Monday. |
| Garnet | 139 | Mount Forest | Tuesday. |
| Leamington | 140 | Leamington | Thursday. |
| Concord | 142 | Kingsville | Friday. |
| Bay of Quinte | 143 | Picton | Wednesday. |
| Ridgetown | 144 | Ridgetown | Wednesday. |
| Vivian | 146 | Arnprior | Tuesday. |
| Model | 147 | Wyoming | Monday. |
| Aurora | 148 | Aurora | Tuesday. |
| Western Star | 149 | Brussels | Thursday. |
| Sycamore | 151 | Arkona | Tuesday. |
| Hayden | 152 | Norwich | Friday. |
| Wildey | 153 | Granton | Wednesday. |
| Alpha | 154 | Almonte | Monday. |
| Brougham | 155 | Whitevale | Thursday. |
| Pyramid | 156 | Newmarket | Tuesday. |
| Thamesville | 157 | Thamesville | Thursday. |
| Progress | 158 | Guelph | Thursday. |
| Oak Leaf | 159 | Hamilton | Alternate Tuesdays. |
| Listowel | 160 | Listowel | Tuesday. |
| Simcoe | 161 | Simcoe | Friday. |
| Oriental | 163 | Cornwall | Monday. |
| Romeo | 164 | Stratford | Tuesday. |
| Beethoven | 165 | Brooklin | Friday. |

## LIST OF LODGES—*Continued.*

| LODGE. | No. | LOCATION. | NIGHT OF MEETING. |
| --- | --- | --- | --- |
| Hillsburg | 167 | Hillsburg | Friday. |
| Sutton | 168 | Sutton | Monday. |
| Grey | 169 | Durham | Monday. |
| Denovo | 170 | Port Elgin | Monday. |
| Alliston | 171 | Alliston | Monday. |
| Penetangore | 172 | Kincardine | Tuesday |
| Emerald | 173 | Dunnville | Tuesday. |
| Dolman | 174 | Ayr | Tuesday. |
| Dauncey | 176 | Thedford | Tuesday. |
| Montana | 177 | Wroxeter | Wednesday. |
| Wellington Square | 178 | Burlington | Alternate Mondays. |
| Madoc | 179 | Madoc | Monday. |
| Owen Sound | 180 | Owen Sound | Thursday. |
| Tecumseh | 182 | Otterville | Monday. |
| Teeswater | 183 | Teeswater | Wednesday. |
| Germania | 184 | Waterloo | Thursday. |
| Dufferin | 186 | Flesherton | Tuesday. |
| Cambridge | 188 | Preston | Wednesday. |
| Parry Sound | 189 | Parry Sound | Monday. |
| Chorazin | 190 | London East | Monday. |
| Jarvis | 191 | Jarvis | Monday. |
| Howick | 192 | Gorrie | Tuesday. |
| Albert | 194 | Toronto | Friday. |
| Cicerone | 195 | Woodville | Tuesday. |
| Florence | 196 | Florence | Monday. |
| Minerva | 197 | Hamilton | Alt. Wednesdays. |
| Weston | 200 | Weston | Tuesday. |
| Beacon | 201 | Port Colborne | Wednesday. |
| Silver Star | 202 | Milverton | Friday. |
| Pembroke | 203 | Pembroke | Tuesday. |
| Acton | 204 | Acton | Wednesday. |
| Ahiram | 205 | Paisley | Tuesday. |
| Silver City | 206 | Tiverton | Friday. |
| Egremont | 207 | Kerwood | Friday. |
| Millbank | 209 | Millbank | 1st and 3rd Wednesdays. |
| Brucefield | 210 | Brucefield | 2nd and 4th Fridays. |
| Lilly | 211 | Dorchester Station | Monday. |
| Argyle | 212 | Napanee | Thursday. |
| Clifford | 214 | Clifford | Friday. |
| Freestone | 215 | Beamsville | Monday. |
| Elmira | 216 | Elmira | Friday. |
| Mount Brydges | 217 | Mount Brydges | Friday. |
| Enterprise | 218 | Essex Centre | Thursday. |
| Georgian Bay | 219 | Waubaushene | Thursday. |
| Woodslee | 220 | South Woodslee | Wednesday. |
| Chesley | 221 | Chesley | 2nd and 4th Tuesday. |
| Hensall | 223 | Hensall | Friday. |
| Ottawa | 224 | Ottawa | Monday. |
| Merlin | 226 | Merlin | Thursday. |
| Sauble | 227 | Tara | Friday. |
| International | 228 | International Bridge | Thursday. |
| Embro Star | 229 | Embro | Tuesday. |
| Prince of Wales | 230 | Toronto | Tuesday. |
| Elora | 231 | Elora | Thursday. |
| Equity | 232 | Hagarsville | Wednesday. |
| Hanover | 233 | Hanover | Wednesday. |
| Ilderton | 234 | Ilderton | 1st and 3rd Thursdays. |
| Waterford | 235 | Waterford | Thursday. |
| Acorn | 236 | Camlachie | Tuesday. |
| Farmersville | 237 | Farmersville | Wednesday. |
| Stirling | 239 | Stirling | Wednesday. |
| Carleton | 240 | Ottawa | Thursday. |
| Rideau | 241 | Smith's Falls | Monday. |
| Wilton | 242 | Toronto | Tuesday. |
| Thornbury | 243 | Thornbury | Friday. |

## LIST OF LODGES—*Continued.*

| LODGE. | No. | LOCATION. | NIGHT OF MEETING. |
|---|---|---|---|
| Port Arthur | 244 | Port Arthur | Wednesday. |
| Mallorytown | 245 | Mallorytown | Wednesday. |
| Orillia | 246 | Orillia | Monday. |
| Gordon | 247 | Palmerston | Thursday. |
| Campbellford | 248 | Campbellford | Tuesday. |
| Beaverton | 249 | Beaverton | Monday. |
| Ridgely | 250 | Oil Springs | Monday. |
| Bracebridge | 251 | Bracebridge | Monday. |
| Floral | 252 | Toronto | Monday. |
| Caledonia | 253 | Caledonia | 1st and 3rd Fridays. |
| Alba | 254 | Pakenham | Thursday. |
| Tottenham | 255 | Tottenham | Wednesday. |
| Grand Valley | 256 | Grand Valley | Friday. |
| Credit | 257 | Erin | Tuesday. |
| Thamesford | 258 | Thamesford | Thursday. |
| Lynden | 259 | Lynden | Wednesday. |
| Meaford | 260 | Meaford | Monday. |
| Gold Hill | 261 | Rat Portage | Thursday. |
| Norwood | 262 | Norwood | 1st and 3rd Tuesdays. |
| East Toronto | 263 | East Toronto | Tuesday. |
| Fraternity | 264 | Perth | Monday. |
| Delta | 265 | Delta | Tuesday. |
| Missanabie | 266 | Chapleau | Tuesday. |
| Algoma | 267 | Fort William West | Thursday. |
| Stanley | 268 | Lanark | Thursday. |
| Woodstock | 269 | Woodstock | Friday. |
| Lansdowne | 270 | Lansdowne | Tuesday. |
| North Bay | 271 | North Bay | Tuesday. |
| Lakeview | 272 | Toronto Junction | Friday. |
| Hastings | 273 | Hastings | Monday. |
| Midland | 274 | Midland | Friday. |
| Fairy | 275 | Huntsville | Monday. |
| Sheard | 276 | New Dundee | Wednesday. |
| Lambton | 277 | Brigden | Tuesday. |
| Rockliffe | 278 | Ottawa | Tuesday. |
| Grenville | 279 | Kemptville | Monday. |
| Balmoral | 280 | Merrickville | Monday. |
| Arthur | 281 | Sault Ste. Marie | Thursday. |
| Sudbury | 282 | Sudbury | Alternate Wednesdays. |
| Earnscliffe | 283 | Janeville | Wednesday. |
| Lyn | 284 | Lyn | Wednesday. |
| Morewood | 285 | Morewood | 1st and 3rd Wednesdays. |
| Royal | 286 | Havelock | Thursday |
| Ripley | 287 | Ripley | Monday. |
| Chesterville | 288 | Chesterville | Friday. |
| Glanworth | 289 | Glanworth | Tuesday. |
| Tweed | 290 | Tweed | Tuesday. |
| Rodney | 291 | Rodney | Friday. |
| Minnetonka | 292 | Keewatin | Wednesday |
| Thomasburg | 293 | Thomasburg | Friday. |
| Broadview | 294 | Toronto | Monday. |
| Manotick | 295 | Manotick | Friday. |
| Pontypool | 296 | Pontypool | Friday. |
| Mayflower | 297 | Parham | Wednesday. |
| Comber | 298 | Comber | |

## REBEKAH DEGREE LODGES.

| LODGE. | No. | LOCATION. | — |
|---|---|---|---|
| Victoria | 1 | London | |
| Oshawa | 4 | Oshawa | |
| May Queen | 5 | London East | |
| Naomi | 6 | Windsor | |
| Louise | 10 | Kingston | |
| Beatrice | 12 | Guelph | |
| Jubilee | 13 | Chatham | |
| Edna | 14 | St. Thomas | |
| Harmony | 15 | Gananoque | |
| Olive Branch | 16 | Toronto | |
| Myrtle | 17 | Elora | |
| Excelsior | 18 | International Bridge | |
| Mizpah | 19 | Collingwood | |
| Donalda | 20 | North Bay | |
| Flora | 21 | Sault Ste. Marie | |
| Lucknow | 22 | Lucknow | |
| Inglewood | 23 | Waterford | |
| Prudence | 24 | Brantford | |
| Alberta | 25 | Kincardine | |
| Ivy | 26 | Galt | |
| Esther | 27 | Niagara Falls | |
| Colfax | 28 | Sarnia | |
| At-the-Well | 29 | Almonte | |
| Aberdeen | 30 | Deseronto | |
| Hebron | 31 | York | |

## DEGREE LODGES.

| Metropolitan | 2 | Toronto | |
|---|---|---|---|
| Victoria | 21 | Ottawa | |
| Leamington | 22 | Leamington | |

# Memories.

> " His memory is the shrine
> Of pleasant thoughts, soft as the scent of flowers ;
>   Calm as on windless eve the sun's decline ;
> Sweet as the song of birds among the flowers ;
>   Rich as a rainbow with its hues of light ;
> Pure as the moonbeams of an Autumn night—
>       Weep not for him ! "

> " We'll not forget thee, we who stay
>   To work a little longer here ;
> Thy name, thy faith, thy love shall lie
>   On memory's page all bright and clear.
> And when o'erwearied by the toil
>   Of life our heavy limbs shall be,
> We'll come, and one by one lie down
>   Upon dear mother earth with thee."

# In Memoriam

# HENRY McAFEE

PAST GRAND MASTER

PAST GRAND PATRIARCH

Frontier Lodge, No. 45.

Frontier Encampment, No. 2.

Died at Windsor, Ontario.

OCTOBER 23RD, 1892

AGED 76 YEARS, 10 MONTHS.

———

" A pioneer of Oddfellowship in Ontario, he continued active in its work, as a faithful earnest worker, until failing health compelled his retirement ; even then, his zeal for the cause of Oddfellowship never abated, but remained warm and strong to the end."

$In Memoriam$

# GEORGE P. DICKSON, P.G.

### DIED AT TORONTO, MAY 13th, 1893.

### AGED 82 YEARS.

———

A pioneer of Oddfellowship in Canada, indeed.  He died, leaving behind a noble record of good deeds.  The memory of his early work for Oddfellowship will be co-existent with the Order itself.

" There is no death.  An angel form
Walks o'er the earth with silent tread
And bears our best beloved friends away,
And then we call them—dead."

# In Memoriam

## JOHN SCHNEIDER

**PAST GRAND**

of Chatham Lodge, No. 29.

**PAST CHIEF PATRIARCH**

of Chatham Encampment, No. 10, Chatham.

**DIED JUNE 16TH, 1893**

**AGED 71 YEARS.**

---

" He was a noble man and a true Odd Fellow. He loved Oddfellowship for the good he found in it, and maintained an unbroken member ship for nearly thirty nine years. He gave honor to his Lodge and his example is worthy of emulation."

---

## JAMES HAY

**PAST GRAND**

Olive Branch Lodge, No. 88.

**PAST CHIEF PATRIARCH**

Maple Leaf Encampment, No. 55, Woodstock.

**DIED APRIL 4TH, 1893.**

**AGED 70 YEARS.**

" An Oddfellow true and good,
Sincere in friendship, ready in relief,
Discreet in trusts, faithful in brotherhood,
Tender in sympathy and kind in grief."

PAGE.

-----

## ERRATUM.

In Report No. 17, page 5613, second line of clause 2, read " building " for " winding."